THEIRS

THE VERONIA COLLECTION

SERENA AKEROYD

Copyright © 2018 by Gemma Mazurke

All rights reserved.

No part of this book may be reproduced in any form or by any electronic or mechanical means, including information storage and retrieval systems, without written permission from the author, except for the use of brief quotations in a book review.

Created with Vellum

Serena Akeroyd

PREPARE TO LOVE THE WEIRD

PERRY & HER PRINCES

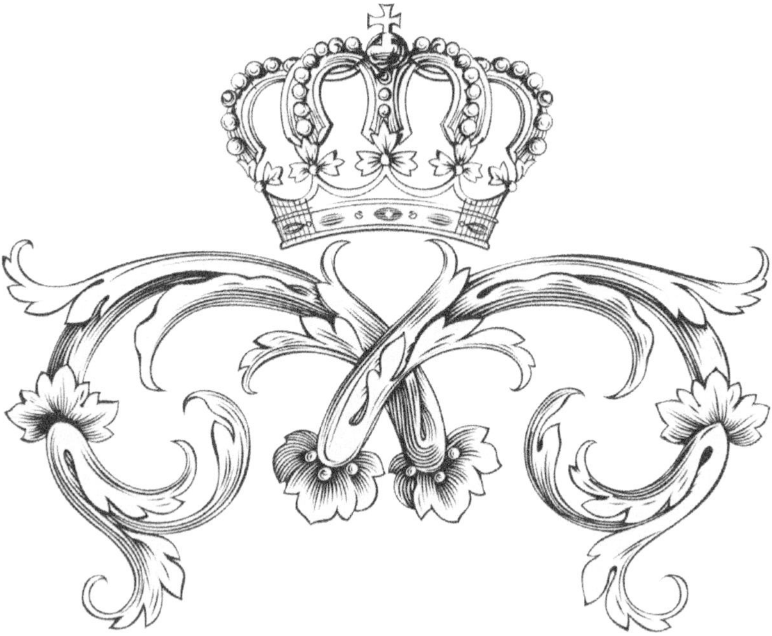

CHAPTER ONE

"WHAT'S WRONG?"

Tilting her head away from the view outside the limo's window, Perry stared under her lashes at George DeSauvier, who looked totally at home in the swank car whereas Perry was still goggle-eyed over it.

But then, this was his world.

The guy she'd met and known since college was, bizarre though it may be, a prince.

An honest to God prince.

And she regularly shot the shit with him, because royal or not, he was actually a cool guy and the best friend she'd ever had.

"Nothing's wrong," she immediately denied, still looking at him in his rather royal get-up.

She wasn't used to *this* George. She was used to the one who wore jeans and tee shirts. Sure, they had fancy labels on them, but they were still regular. Even his work clothes didn't look this special, and in his three-piece suit, he suddenly seemed very, very regal. As well as gorgeous.

Panty-melting gorgeous.

She'd never seen tailoring like the suit he was wearing. The teeny-tiny stitches were a dead giveaway that every piece of clothing was custom made by hand, and toss in the sheen of luxurious silk, the suit all but screamed money. But Jesus, the man came from Veronia. Where they literally crapped gold before breakfast.

Okay, maybe not literally. Still, they were loaded. And George crapped gold at least twice a day.

On top of that, he was delicious. Where did it say in royal decrees that princes had to be handsome? She wasn't sure. But he was. Very much so.

Enough that, many times in their friendship, she'd often wished they were more than just friends. Still, he'd come to mean a lot to her, and she'd never wanted to screw things up by taking things to another level. It probably wasn't even allowed. Some law written in the annals of his country's rule book undoubtedly said royal blood and common folk couldn't marry.

Not that that stopped her from loving him, of course.

As a friend. Or so she tried to tell herself, and putting that in jeopardy wasn't worth it—that was a fact.

Even if he did look like sin with his glossy black hair glinting in the Veronian sunlight, showing off chestnut and mahogany highlights that any woman would kidnap her stylist for. His stormy blue eyes could flash from gray to blue in an instant—depending on his mood. He had a beak of a nose, Roman and unashamed, topped by strong dark brows that reminded her of wings. His forehead was demarcated by a widow's peak, his jaw strong and stubborn.

He wasn't pretty-boy-handsome. He looked like the man he was. One hundred percent.

But in his suit? With his hair slicked back instead of tousled? He was more man than she could handle.

Though her ability to handle him, or not, was not her current issue.

"There's definitely something wrong," he countered, and reached for her hand. Bridging their fingers, he settled the union on his lap—exactly where she didn't need to be caged.

Moments before, when they'd climbed into the limo, she'd thought about perching on that lap and riding him until the cows came home.

Hell, the buffalo and woolly mammoth too.

Sucking in a breath as she tried to dispel those images, she murmured, "I'm just nervous."

"I'd never have guessed," he said wryly, and she elbowed him in the side.

"Shut up," she chided, but her own lips were twitching at the sight of the mischievous grin curving that beautiful mouth. "And forgive me for sounding very *Prince & Me*—" She'd loved that movie back in college, when binge-watching TV hadn't really been a thing yet. "—but it's the first time this Tennessee girl gets to meet the royal family of a country half a world away. You tell me how I can be anything other than freaked out?"

His eyes were twinkling when he turned to look at her—the gray-blue gleaming almost cerulean when he was happy or amused. "You meet with a royal four to five times a week, Perry. It should be nothing to you now."

She grunted but knew she couldn't argue. Not really. They did meet up four to five times a week. For coffee or dinner, to watch a movie, or to hang out and work on their own particular shit in his or her apartment. Still...

"You're not like a normal royal person though, are you?"

"A royal person?" he snickered. "Wait until I tell Edward that one."

She glowered at him. "Don't you dare." Edward was George's elder brother.

While George was second in line, Edward was the Crown Prince of Veronia. She'd only seen him on the TV and in the tabloids. Even that was pretty rare, thanks to the nation's privacy laws where the press was concerned.

This was the first time she'd be meeting any of George's family, and describing herself as nervous was the biggest understatement of the year.

They were never going to be like George.

He'd been educated in England and then had gone to college for his MBA in the States. He'd had to have more bodyguards than the President on campus at first, but he'd led a relatively normal student life when the brouhaha had calmed down. And since his graduation, he'd stayed in Boston. Had worked there.

George was an Americanized Veronian.

He drank pickle juice from the jar and yelled at her for throwing out the crumbs—basically pure sugar—from the bottom of cereal packets.

They drank beer together in front of Red Sox games, yelled at the TV as they dove into pizza, and had gorged on funnel cakes at the fair.

The rest of his family?

They were going to have sticks up their asses, Perry just knew it. Knew it and was dreading it, because she was about to meet them, and decorum wasn't exactly her middle name. She barely kept it together at faculty meetings, never mind at receptions with monarchs!

"You're you. They're not." It was as simple and as terrifying as that.

His lips twitched at her weak reasoning. "Royal or not, they could never be me. I'm one of a kind."

"Your ego certainly is," she retorted with a huff, tugging her hand from his and folding her arms under her boobs.

As usual, they bounced.

Jesus, breasts were annoying.

She was saving up for a breast reduction, but every time she found another first edition, the surgery was thrown on the backburner.

Her obsession with books was almost up there with her obsession on the man at her side and shrimp cocktail-flavored chips.

It was a problem—of the twelve-steps variety.

Glaring down at her boobs, which were always so, so *there*, she moved her arms and tugged at her jacket.

They'd changed on the plane ride over here—private jet, of course. Only the best for royalty.

She'd spent the first four hours of the nine-hour journey gawking at everything.

Having only ever flown in the cattle section, this kind of luxury was beyond anything her plebian mind could have dreamed up. When they'd landed, the limo hadn't been something to sniff at either.

"Do I look okay?"

He sighed. "Yes. You look fine. I picked the damn outfit, didn't I?"

Though it had been mortifying giving him her sizes, she'd passed this task onto him. She was a scientist, dammit. Not some fashion blogger.

She went to work in black pants and a smart-ish white blouse. She basically dressed like a nerdy waitress. In fact, waitresses had more style than she did, and there was no way in hell she was going to meet a royal freakin' family in clothes that would put their staff to shame.

A neat skirt suit had been his selection. Tucked in at the waist, the jacket was navy blue, which set off her skin tone well and matched his suit—although she wasn't certain if that was intentional or not. She was pale by nature, too pale, but the color made her look a little less pallid. Seemed to bring out the faint rose in her cheeks as well.

The tailoring cut into her waist, augmenting what little shape there was, and made her hips look trimmer. It didn't button, but hung loosely, revealing the almost golden shirt he'd picked for her. It wasn't shiny gold, like lamé, but it was a shocking enough shade of yellow that she'd never have picked it in a million years. Yet somehow, it suited her.

Made her hair, hair almost as dark as his, seem to have more tones than it did. Hers was just dark brown. His was like a freaking advertisement for hair dye.

The skirt was tighter than she'd have gone for herself. It clung to her ass and thighs in a way that had made her groan with mortification in the private bathroom on the jet. Still, she'd given him free dibs to do what he had to do, and boy, had he.

She was also, for the first time in her life, wearing heels.

Honest to God heels.

"You do know you're going to have to be my crutch, don't you?" she grumbled again as she rocked her feet in the clunky things on her feet.

How did women wear these things?

"I'll be your crutch any day of the week," he teased. "Just stick close to me, and we'll make sure you don't fall on your butt and flash everyone."

Before her cheeks could burn with heat, she snapped, "Like I could flash anyone in this skirt. The damn thing's so tight, I can barely breathe."

He snorted. "Just because it fits, doesn't mean it's constricting."

"My clothes fit."

"No. They don't. They're all four sizes too big. There's a difference."

She huffed. "I hope the other clothes you bought me don't cut off blood supply to my legs too."

He just stared her down, unapologetic as hell. "You shouldn't have given me free reign."

She grumbled, "I see that now." Perry prodded him in the side, and grunted back at him when he grabbed it and firmly held her hand in his.

He'd always been touchy feely, and she'd always liked it, but at the moment, she was too on edge to be held down.

Still, when she tried to tug her fingers from his grasp, he clung tight.

So tightly in fact, that she turned to look at him to read his expression.

He wasn't glowering down at her in outrage, if anything, he was looking out of the window. Seemingly ignoring her as he took in his homeland.

One thing she'd noticed in her short time here, was how special Veronia was.

Beautiful? Sure, but different too. Unique. Bridging cultures in a way that charmed her American soul down to the ground.

On the coast between Monaco and Italy, they were currently riding down a boulevard that had the glorious Mediterranean Ocean sparkling beside them. She had that side because she'd never seen the Med—as he called it—before, but he was looking out onto the towns they passed from the airport to the royal palace in Madela, the capital city.

Whenever people saw the limo with its little flags flying on the fender, they stopped, stared, and then started waving at the vehicle.

It was sweet to behold, and she realized that the royal family was beloved here. Nice to see in these dark times.

She was here for George, not the country. He'd said Veronia needed her, so here she was.

But it was nice to see she wasn't helping a douchebag leader, but a royal family the people loved, and who cared for their nation. Now she thought about it, whenever people started waving, he tensed at her side.

"When was the last time you were back here?" she asked out of curiosity.

Now she thought about it, it had to be a long time. Like four years? That couldn't be right, could it?

But they'd stayed together for the last four Christmases... that was when folk usually went home, right? Well, apart from her, she thought guiltily. In this, they were both as bad as each other.

He cleared his throat. "Five years ago."

She stared at him. "How did I not figure that out sooner?"

He shot her a look, which combined with his wry smile, almost had her blushing. "Because you're worse with dates than a two-year-old?"

She huffed. "I'm not that bad."

"You're chronologically challenged," he argued. "And we both know it. If calendars with reminders didn't exist, we both know you'd be lost."

She blew him a raspberry, uncaring that the gesture made her seem the two-year-old he'd just labeled her as. "That's not fair. When it comes to the important stuff, I know my shit."

"It's totally fair. You're a scientist, Perry. It's kind of disturbing that you can't remember stuff for toffee." He just cocked a brow when she flipped him the bird, but the faint amusement curving his lips disappeared as he murmured, "I've not considered this home for a long time."

She blinked. "Why not?" He'd spoken of Veronia before. Often. But it had always been with love and a warmth that spoke of a place that was home.

He cut her another glance. "Never you mind, nosy."

She elbowed him in the side. "That's no answer."

She was relentless with him because he was with her. Such a cop-out would only have had him peppering her with more questions.

However, fate was on his side as he pointed out of the window. "That's Masonbrook Palace."

Her mouth dropped open, all thoughts of his weird mood fading into dust at the sight of the building she'd seen a thousand times in photos where the Royal Family waved to their public on wedding days and christenings.

The portico was pillared, and cars swept through its tunnel to alight onto the entrance of the castle. But the portico's roof was used as the terrace. She'd seen it so many times on a TV screen and in a magazine that she couldn't deal with seeing it in the flesh.

As they neared the palace, she gulped at the sight of the armed guards in traditional dress. She'd seen the kilt-like uniforms before, but in person, it had her eyes widening. Tens of armed and kilted men guarded the grand gates that soared twenty feet into the air and were decorated with the royal rearing unicorn-stamped crests of the reigning royal family.

The DeSauviers had ruled Veronia for four hundred years, and their family had helped forge the country into the rich and proud nation it was today.

Either side of the neatly graveled drive, there were endless lawns. She could imagine gardeners cutting the damn thing with nail scissors and winced at the notion of how much water was wasted on maintaining the grounds which, though wasteful, were astonishing in their beauty.

Huge flowerbeds with roses the size of her head decorated the manicured lawns, and at the head of the drive, where the car had to turn into the portico, there was a kind of ornamental roundabout that had a fountain spouting water a hundred feet into the air.

She gaped at it all, even as her conservationist heart died a death at the sight.

As the car pulled into the portico, armed guards appeared out of nowhere to line up against the two openings and ensure the prince's safety as he alighted from the vehicle.

Her door was opened at the same time as George's, and a white gloved hand appeared in front of her for her to use as aid in leaving the car.

Aid she was relieved to have, if she was being honest. These heels weren't wise on flat floors. Never mind graveled ones.

She smiled at the attendant who was dressed in a smart black suit and white shirt, and gripped his arm tightly as he helped her around the car.

When she could, she dove back to George's side, clutching at him to stand tall and upright.

He chuckled as they headed onto the wide bottom step that led to the palace entrance, then he ironed his face of all emotion in the blink of an eye between making sure she was standing straight and turning on his heel to face his men.

George snapped a salute to the left. The armed guard replicated the sharp movement within a handful of seconds and with such precision, a clapping sound echoed through the air. George turned to the right and gave another crisp salute.

He turned back to her and gripped her arm, then helped her up the stairs. They walked arm-in-arm through a grand front door the size of the giant in the Jack and the Beanstalk stories, and in to a carpeted entranceway.

She gulped at the sheer mass of riches surrounding her.

Wherever she looked, there was a painting or a statue or something that was a reminder of the family's wealth.

This was so much more than money though.

This was... *heritage*. Culture. Class. So many things merging into one that she couldn't quite catch her breath.

A huge chandelier hung overhead. The rounded teardrop crystals were pendulous with their weight as they helped illuminate the vast space. The staircase before her was long, and she cringed at having to ascend them in heels.

More staff of the household variety, in suits for the men and black skirts and white blouses for the women, were lined up in the hall. They wore something similar to her usual get up, so she was inordinately relieved she'd left her wardrobe in George's hands.

George, in prince mode, smiled at them all as they passed them, and he paused to clap one man on the shoulder.

"Henri, it's good to be home."

"Your Highness, the staff are delighted to see you once again in the palace," came Henri's more stilted response, but from the warmth in his eye, on an otherwise stoic, expressionless face, Perry figured Henri actually liked George.

Even though it was hard to discern much from his rigid features.

Jesus, these guys made the Brit's stiff upper lip look positively flaccid.

Her nose twitched with the desire to laugh, but she managed to contain it, just in time to hear Henri continue, "Your parents are in the Limoges Reception Room."

"Lead on, MacDuff," George said with a smile, and Henri bowed in response, then stepped ahead of them and began to lead them down a hallway to the left of the staircase.

"Oh, thank God," she whispered under her breath. "I don't have to climb the stairs."

George laughed, and his amusement spilled into the grand vestibule.

Henri jumped and shot a look back at George in surprise, one that had her wincing.

This place was so somber. Elegant and beautiful, but like a funeral home.

George didn't stop chuckling at Henri's startled glance, just snickered. "I think I like you weak, helpless, and dependent on me."

She snorted. "The shoes aren't permanently attached, bud. They can come off at will. My will."

He pouted at her. "Shame."

She rolled her eyes, then felt her throat clog as they passed a piece of work that could only be a Michelangelo. It was huge, the size of a car, and depicted a Dante-esque version of heaven and hell.

More works of exquisite art were rammed down her throat as they walked down the long corridor. Her heels stuck in the rich blue carpet with every step, and she was cringing, totally unfocused on the beauty around her by the time they reached a set of white, grand doors. Doors that came complete with the royal crest emblazoned upon them.

At the sight of them, she nearly jumped for joy.

Well, she would have done, were it not for the torture devices known as high heels on her feet.

Henri tapped once on the door with his knuckles, and with a swoosh, they opened. Two men dressed in the kilt uniform, with black shirts and heavily embroidered waistcoats, guarded the doors.

They remained saluting as she and George passed through them and dropped the salute only when they'd headed deeper into another astonishing room.

An honest to God throne sat bang in the center of an atrium the size of a tennis court.

This was the *small* reception room? God, she didn't even want to imagine the electricity bill for this place.

But then, did royal families worry about switching off lights to save energy?

She doubted it. They would though. If she had her way.

They had to lead by example. If they wanted their public to be more environmentally aware, they'd have to make changes too. And considering the country was heading for an ecological disaster, change had to be imminent.

George's father sat on the throne and standing to either side of him were a woman she knew from pictures to be George's mother, and then, his brother, Edward.

God, he was more handsome in real life than the magazine gave him credit. He was like an older George. In fact, they were spookily alike. But he had light brown hair that shined blond thanks to his natural highlights, and his eyes were green.

As she glanced over his beautiful mother and handsome father, she realized George took after Marianne DeSauvier's coloring, and Edward Philippe's—but when it came to looks, they were their father to the bone. Blood will out, didn't they say? Well, it certainly had in the DeSauvier sons.

She swallowed when they stepped in front of the thrones and felt her legs tremble with the need to curtsey.

Only trouble was, in these heels, she wasn't sure if her center of balance was up to curtseying.

"The reception room? Really, Father, was that necessary?"

A gleam appeared in Philippe's eye, but he got to his feet like he wasn't sitting on a throne, but a Barcalounger, and strode toward his son.

She squeaked when he wrapped his arms around George and squeezed tight. The move knocked her hand off his arm, and she had to fight for balance as George, laughing, squeezed his father back.

Philippe clapped his shoulder. "It's good to see you, son."

"You too, Papa," came the light-hearted response.

At his words, Marianne rushed forward, Edward too.

Perry stood awkwardly to the side as the family welcomed their wayward son home.

As Edward hugged his brother, he chided, "You've been gone too long, but I understand why now."

George cleared his throat, cut her a glance. "This is Perry." He smiled at her, gripped her hand in his and tucked it through his arm. "Perry, this is my family."

She gulped as all the attention was aimed at her. "Hi?"

She almost died at the trite greeting that spilled from her slack lips, but because that wasn't possible, instead of dying, she whacked George on the arm when he burst out laughing.

He grabbed hold of her and hooked his battered arm over her shoulder. In almost a headlock, she had no choice but to grip him tightly from the side. It was grip him or fall over.

Fun.

She glowered down at her heels. "Be grateful for the shoes, bud, or I'd tackle you faster than Gronk on a good day," she told him grimly, then realized she'd just threatened and committed an act of violence against a prince, in a foreign land, with armed guards at her back, and a king and queen watching on.

Okay, so now she wanted to DIE. With capital letters.

When the ground didn't open and swallow her up, even though she asked kindly, she shot a limpid smile at the people staring at her like she was a shark in a koi pond.

"It's a pleasure to meet you," she managed to get out after clearing her throat. Twice.

"Perry, this is Marianne, Philippe, and Edward. We don't stand on ceremony when those doors are closed."

She held out her hand to the king and was relieved to see it wasn't trembling. "That's good to know."

Philippe—as handsome as his sons and with a back so straight, he'd do a soldier proud—grabbed her hand, twisted it slightly, and stunned the shit out of her by raising her knuckles to his mouth.

"It's a pleasure, Perry. If I may call you that?"

She half-smiled half-gaped. "Of course, sir. I mean, Your Highness."

She knew not to call him sir! She knew he was a 'Highness.' What the hell was wrong with her?

George snorted. "Perry is a true American. She has no idea outside of what Netflix has informed her about royal protocol."

"That's because somebody didn't think to tell me how it worked in the real world," she snapped. "And I can't just call him Philippe. He's a king!"

Marianne laughed, making Perry jolt. When the older woman clapped her hands, Perry wasn't sure whether it was for good or ill. Until the statuesque blonde declared, "She's good for you, child." She then proceeded to clap those same hands on George's cheeks and popped him a kiss on the nose.

George just chuckled. "She's something."

There was a weird vibe floating around here, and Perry wasn't entirely sure what it was, just that the way they were looking at her was enough to make her cheeks glow crimson.

Permanently.

"Is there somewhere we can sit?" she blurted out. "I'm really sorry, but George insisted I wear these stupid shoes."

"For the cameras, dear," Marianne told her calmly, but in a move that would confound Kung Fu masters, managed to maneuver them so she had a hold of Perry and was half-dragging half-guiding her across the reception room to another doorway.

"The cameras?" Perry asked weakly, wishing the doorway was one step away instead of ten.

Was everywhere in this goddamn place so big?

Before Marianne could answer, she jerked the queen to a halt, and protocol be damned, declared, "That's it. I can't take it anymore." She kicked her leg back, grabbed the heel, and let her toes sink into the plush carpet underfoot. When she did the same with the other leg, she let out a sigh of relief so deep it totally overwhelmed any mortification she might have felt at behaving thusly in front of royalty.

George should never have put her in the damn things when he knew she always, always wore flats.

Goddamn his hide.

Silence fell at her behavior, then snickers started at her back. Knowing it was George, she shot him a glare over her shoulder. Edward and he were chuckling at her antics, while Philippe had that whole 'shark in a koi pond' look about him again.

"I'm really sorry," she aimed at Marianne, who Perry could tell, didn't know where to look. "But it's your son's fault."

"Like I said, dear, the cameras," came Marianne's faint and stunned response.

"Don't worry, Mother. You'll get used to Perry's ways."

Perry scoffed. Like the royal family would have time to 'get used to her.'

She was only going to be here for two weeks. And that was if she didn't accidentally do something that was akin to treason.

Was triggering a heart attack an act of treason?

She wasn't sure.

Philippe sure looked pasty at her behavior.

With her shoes in hand, she turned to Marianne. "I promise I'm perfectly polite and decent and respectful. But if I had to take another step, I'd have either started sobbing or would have fallen."

Marianne's lips twitched. "I appreciate that, dear, however you'll have to get used to them. We have a certain image to uphold."

Perry frowned.

Royal protocol dictated their staff wear heels?

She hadn't noticed on the female members of the line up at the front entrance. Had just taken note of their black skirts and white shirts.

Heels?

Since when was that uniform standard?

Before she could ask, Marianne murmured, "We're in private here, so it's okay. I'll have one of the staff bring a pair of flats for you to wear when we head through into the reception."

"There's a reception?" George asked, and she realized he'd approached and was at her side.

"Yes, George," Marianne informed him kindly. "This is your first time back in almost six years. The press want to see you, and by see, I mean more than a glimpse of you and Perry getting out of the car!"

He groaned, managing to sound like an angry teen who didn't want to get out of bed yet. "On our first day?"

"You know it's best to feed the beasts a tidbit to stop them from starving and turning rabid, son," Philippe said quietly as he stepped ahead and opened the door onto a small sitting room. "We only invited fifty journalists. It won't take long."

Perry's eyes widened. *Only* fifty?

What the hell had she let herself in for?

CHAPTER TWO

EDWARD WATCHED the stunning brunette slip from his mother's arm into the high-backed Louis Quinze sofa.

She had about as much decorum as Oliver Twist but there was a charm about her he could sense enchanted his brother.

If he was being honest, it enchanted him, too.

She wasn't utterly naïve, a total, disastrous ingenue, but she was close to it. For their world, she was at any rate.

There was no avariciousness as she peered around the small lounge. No jealousy or envy as she looked over the glittering silver tea service from which his mother served them all.

She was wide-eyed and beautiful with it. Her interest genuine.

When his cock stirred, he shot George a look. The small smile on his brother's face told Edward he understood.

George had always been a strange one. Edward had hoped his years abroad would have changed him, but it would seem not.

In Veronian, and under his breath, he murmured, "Why have you brought her here?"

"To introduce you, of course."

Veronia was suffering with the worst drought since their records began. George had recommended bringing Perry home to consult, as she was one of the United States' most renowned specialists in water conservation techniques.

Edward, however, knew bullshit when he heard it. For whatever reason, George had decided it was time. But they were too old for these games.

Gone were the days when they could get away with being playboy princes.

Edward was widowed, but he'd have to remarry soon. The country needed an heir that wasn't his brother or his cousin, Xavier.

They needed young blood to secure the royal seat for the next generation.

Sharing his brother's girlfriend wasn't something that could be on the agenda anymore. Regardless of the impetuous desire.

He took a seat in an armchair and used the delicate teacup his mother handed him to hide his erection.

Chatter went on around him, laughter too, as Perry's artless replies had his brother chuckling in a way Edward hadn't heard since they were children. She even managed to make his parents laugh.

The amusing thing was, Perry didn't know why. He could sense it frustrated her, but she was also relieved.

This was no pampered socialite accustomed to court protocol.

When she'd taken off her heels and had stood barefoot in the small throne room, they'd all been frozen in place at her remarkable lack of decorum. George had been the first to thaw, though. Mostly, Edward assumed, because he was used to her ways.

He'd elbowed Edward in the side even before he'd started laughing. "I wondered how long she'd last," he'd mumbled under his breath in their native tongue.

The sight of her small feet, with shell pink-lacquered toes curling into the thick royal blue carpet shouldn't have his erection thickening at the memory, but it did.

There was something about her...

Something that made him understand why George had brought her here. He knew she would be like kindling to Edward's barely there fire. He gritted his jaw angrily. Hating how well his brother knew him.

Perry was not his type in the least. She was short and brunette. Rounded and curvy. He liked tall blondes, damn it. Slender with long legs.

Perry was none of those things.

Why the hell was she like catnip to him then? It had been a long time since he'd fought an erection in public, yet this crazy brunette with her madcap chatter stirred him to life in a way his wife never had.

Rubbing his jaw, he saw George cut him a glance. "What?" he asked, aware his parents' attention was on Perry.

They were both cognizant of the fact this visit had more layers to it than a Napoleon.

Though Perry was here on business, they'd heard enough about her to know that George was interested in the American woman.

In more ways than just water conservation.

But if the looks George was shooting his way were anything to go by, his plans were completely different to what Edward and their parents had assumed.

"Nothing," came his brother's innocent response.

"You know we can't do this," he said in a low voice, recognizing the laissez-faire tone and distrusting it.

"Who says we can't?"

Edward gritted his teeth, leaned forward, and placed the teacup on the table. Getting to his feet, he was careful to shield his lower half from the others in the room as he swung behind the sofa to the bay windows that overlooked the garden.

This was his mother's favorite sitting room. It was small and delicate. Prissy and very female. Her writing desk was here, and she often received visitors in this room too.

He liked it because it looked out on to the fountain, which was a feat of engineering miracles.

An ancestor had diverted a stream from the mountain behind the palace, and using water pressure created from clever plumbing, produced the magnificent stream that powered the water a hundred feet into the air.

It was a reminder of what his family had achieved in the past, when such a fountain was inconceivable. It was a simple reminder, granted. Especially considering his family's touch was visible in every aspect of everyday life in the capital, but it touched him more than anything else.

Rubbing his chin as he watched the mist from the powerful stream, he wondered how long it would be before Perry put the engineering marvel on her hit list. He guessed it made sense. They were drastically short of water, and they were shooting it into the air because of tradition... Hardly smart, but a lot of royal traditions were dumb.

Perry, if she tried that argument with him, would find he'd agree with her totally. Still, it was one of his mother's favorite monuments—so, for as much as it was possible to avoid the hundred-foot water spout, he'd try to divert Perry's attention away from it.

Pondering how many 007 moves he'd have to pull to achieve that, or George would have to pull more specifically, a movement to his side had him shifting his gaze when he saw his prodigal brother had appeared to his left.

"Why have you done this?"

George sighed. "There's no reason we can't."

"There's every reason, dammit. You know I can't..."

"Why not?" his brother snapped. "We've sacrificed a lot for our country. Why do we have to sacrifice our happiness in this too?"

"Because it's not normal, you fool. We live in the public eye!"

"We can hide it. There's no reason for anyone to ever know."

"How can we? We can barely take a leak in a public restaurant without someone trying to photo it."

"You marry her," George said softly, so quietly that Edward had to strain to hear the madness spilling from his brother's lips. "You make it respectable. No one needs to know about my part in your marriage."

Jesus.

This was no fanciful notion. George had been thinking about this, planning it.

Lifting a shaky hand, Edward ran it through his hair. "You can't be serious."

"I am. Deadly. You were miserable with Arabella, Edward. You know it, and I do too. I'm sorry she died, and it was unfair for her to die so young—she didn't deserve that. But it would have ended with a divorce. She could never have given you what you wanted. What you need."

"This whole conversation is ludicrous."

"Is it?" George eyed him. "Or is it ludicrous that I have the answer to our prayers, and you're trying to back away from it?"

Edward's nostrils flared. "How is she that? Have you spoken to her about this? Is she aware of your plans?"

George snorted. "If you think that, you're a bigger fool than you seem. Do you think she'd have taken her damn shoes off, if she'd thought she was here as my girlfriend?"

Edward scowled at him. "You do realize that's one of the reasons why she could never be crown princess? Or, God help her, queen one day?" Hell, were they seriously having this conversation?

George shook his head. "The public would eat the whole 'prince and a commoner' thing up. You know it. I know it. They didn't exactly love Arabella, did they? Not that she did anything to endear herself to them. But they'd love Perry. How couldn't they?"

Edward turned back to look at Perry, who was engaged in a rousing conversation with his parents about... Edward blinked, sure his ears deceived him. She really couldn't be talking about how a dead body would nourish a tree through the coldest of winters with his mother and father, could she?

His very conservative, very serious parents. Parents who had taken three months to speak without formality to his fiancée.

George smiled when he saw where his attention was focused. "See? If she can do that to Mother and Father, what could she do to the rest of the country? She's fresh blood, Edward. She'll bring life to this stuffy place."

He heaved in a breath. "Does she know how you feel about her?"

"No."

Edward had figured as much. There was a distance on her part that spoke of two people who were very close, but not close enough to be physically intimate. "Why not?"

"We were friends first. Then, when I realized she'd be perfect for us, I was hesitant to ruin things."

Edward narrowed his eyes as he realized there was plenty his brother wasn't telling him when George's voice trailed off.

"You're being presumptuous in the extreme. She might not want us."

"She wants me," George said softly. "I know she does. She just doesn't act on it."

"Why not?"

"For one of the reasons I haven't. Fear."

"Fear of what?"

"Losing our friendship."

"But you're willing to risk it on this?"

"For *our* happiness, Edward?" George met his glance and held it. "Yes. Yours, mine, and hers."

Edward shook his head. "You're crazy."

He shrugged. "Maybe. Don't rule anything out, okay? Just keep an open mind."

How could he do anything else?

George clapped him on the back before returning to the seating area and taking part in whatever his parents and Perry were discussing.

He watched them, shaking his head a little at his brother's plan.

It couldn't work. Surely?

He gnawed at the inside of his cheek, trying to deny the visceral attraction he felt for the small woman on the sofa.

He didn't know where it had come from, considering she wasn't his type. And he didn't even know if it was reciprocated, because when he'd shaken her hand, she'd been distracted—by her heels, apparently.

His lips twitched at the thought.

A man whose handsomeness had been described in too many news journals to count, hadn't been gorgeous enough to distract a woman from the pain her shoes caused her.

A full blown grin had him turning back to smirk out at the fountain.

How could he not be attracted to such a woman? One who didn't fawn or fuss. Didn't flutter her lashes up at him or touch him inappropriately with the hope of bedding a man who would one day be king.

She was... a breath of fresh air.

George was right about that.
He clenched his hands into fists.
This was madness.
His brother was mad. This had just made it official.

CHAPTER THREE

XAVIER DESAUVIER, Duke of Ansian and Lorrena, prowled around the ballroom with ease. His ease also spoke of a familiar boredom in being at the reception.

Such functions were too common and too bland for him to do anything more than attend.

Actually taking part required far too much energy.

Of course, when his uncle the king caught sight of him in the crowd, Xavier was the recipient of many displeased looks. But Uncle Philippe often did that.

He'd always just shrug as if to say, 'I'm here, aren't I?'

His mother's brother would always grit his teeth and then return his attention to whichever boring official he was talking to.

He supposed it was rather ill-behaved of him to refuse to speak to the attendees, but the truth was, he didn't have a clue why he was here. Just knew that when his Aunt Marianne sent him an invitation in a blue envelope, his attendance was required.

As such, he gave it to his social secretary, a perennially underworked member of his household, who knew to mark the important dates in his diary.

He had to admit, the grand ballroom looked particularly marvelous tonight.

The parquet floor gleamed underfoot, but he groaned at the damage the women's stupid heels caused to the antique wood. Overhead, a fresco of cherubs dancing and frolicking amid a cloudy sky was a beautiful sight to behold, and the walls were paneled with various artworks that predated the Renaissance.

Mock candles flickered authentically, giving the air a rather romantic and antique feel, and with the women dressed in ball gowns and men in official dress—tuxedos—he'd admit, it looked like something from a movie.

Dining tables for diplomats lined the large atrium, leaving the center open for dancing. The orchestra had yet to strike up though, as now was the time for conversation before the lighthearted side of the night could occur—a thought that had him rolling his eyes.

Lighthearted and ballroom dancing did not go together in his opinion. But then, little of this life did to the family's black sheep.

It was a painful cosmic joke that he was third in line to a throne he didn't even truly believe in. Not that he didn't recognize how fair a king Philippe was, but such power should not be doled out because of a family's DNA.

Still, Philippe would have to pop his clogs, then Edward, and then George, before Xavier would ever set one butt cheek on the throne.

Hallelujah.

On his journey around the room's perimeter, a journey that had him avoiding anyone of any import as people huddled in the center desperately trying to speak to their monarchs, he saw a small brunette huddled in a chair. As he neared, he realized she wasn't huddled, she was crouching, then he saw the screen.

She was on her phone.

At an event.

His lips curved into a grin. That was his kind of woman.

Relieved he wasn't the only one bored out of his skull, he approached her. When he appeared in her line of sight, she tilted her face to stare at him, and he was surprised by the delicate beauty before him.

She was small, that he'd already seen. Round in all the right places, but her face was what caught him. It was stunning. Cat's eyes stared up at him from within their almond-shaped cast, and her cheekbones could splinter ice, they were so high and sharp.

She had pouty lips and a button nose. A widow's peak framed her brow, which was covered with wispy bangs from a blanket of unrelieved black hair.

She had to have some Asian influence. The hair and eye shape alone were a clue, but they were faint enough to tell him they were traits from a great grandparent. Barely there, yet prominent enough to make her delicate beauty astonishing.

"Excuse me?"

The woman's voice grated a little as was the way with the American accent.

Germans, Americans, and British people... They all brayed rather than spoke, he found.

Of course, his native tongue was of the Romance linguistic tree. His language was seduction in verbal form. Who could compete with that?

"I'm afraid I can't excuse you." He grinned. "Are you playing games at a royal event?"

Her eyes widened, but without looking at her hands, she shielded her phone. "I beg your pardon?"

"You heard what I said," he said teasingly. "I wish I'd thought of playing games sooner, but I'd prefer to read."

She frowned. "You would?"

He nodded, raised his champagne flute to his lips. "Indeed. I'm a reader not a player."

That had her laughing, and his own lips twitched at the tinkling sound. "I'd have to agree. I'm the same, but I can't concentrate when it's so loud." She grimaced. "That's why I downloaded that game."

This was loud? This boring event—with barely there background music from a six-piece orchestra, and inconsequential chatter that could make or break the country—was loud?

Better and better.

Beauty and brains on the same wavelength as his own.

"Would you like to go out to the gardens?"

She bit her lip, peered around him. "Are we okay to do that?"

He shrugged. "Usually, no. But I know the king. He'll let me get away with it."

"How do you know him?" she asked with a scowl.

"I'm his nephew," Xavier murmured, curious as to her reaction. Usually, making such a statement would have most women panting.

The woman before him didn't pant. She frowned in disgruntled surprise. "You are?"

He nodded, amused at her suspicious query. "That's why I can move freely about the palace." He cocked a brow at her. "Do you wish to leave the noise and go to the gardens?"

He could tell she was cautious, but he could also sense that she was eager to leave the party. He himself wanted to huff at such a notion. This wasn't his idea of a damn party.

She gnawed at her bottom lip. "Do you think anyone would mind if we did slip away?"

He shook his head. "I doubt it."

Philippe would mind, but his uncle would just lecture him tomorrow over the phone.

He usually did anyway.

She slipped to her feet, and when she barely came to his throat, he had to admit he was surprised by how small she was.

Surprised and, bizarrely enough, turned on.

She was like a fairy, he realized with no small amusement. All graceful limbs and light steps.

"I'm Xavier," he introduced himself as he held out a hand, indicating she could start walking.

Her lips curved in a shy smile. "I'm Perry."

"Perry? Isn't that a boy's name?" He tried to remember the last time he'd visited America and failed.

They had bizarre ways of naming their children.

Coming from a British background—he and his cousins, Edward and George, had all attended British boarding schools—to him, randy meant horny. For a child to be named thus would cause raised brows in Veronia.

Naming a girl with a boy's name would also cause a stink.

Her nose wrinkled. "Perry can be a girl's name."

It could? *Huh*. What did he know?

Shrugging, he murmured, "You see that door to the right of the suit of armor?" When she nodded, he said, "That's where we're going."

Once she knew their direction, her pace picked up, giving him the chance to study her from behind.

She wore, he realized, flats. A notion that had him hiding an outright grin. She was small and wore no heels—could the woman be more unusual if she tried?

Even the women approaching six feet wore heels, ones that had them appearing more statuesque and Amazonian, uncaring if they were taller than any man attending.

Yet this small, beautiful creature wore flats.

Intrigued, he watched as she turned her head over her shoulder to make sure he was still following. He shot her a smile he hoped was encouraging and received a warm curve of her lips in response.

She opened the door, and he escaped with her, closing it behind him.

The silence after the gala was almost deafening, and Xavier lifted a hand to rub at the back of his neck in relief.

"You really didn't like it in there, did you?" Perry asked quietly as they stepped down the darkened corridor. It was only vaguely lighted with strip lights on the perimeter of the floor, which made the glossy tiles seem like a runway.

"No. I really didn't like it in there," he confessed. "I hate those events."

"I can't blame you. That was my first, and I was very bored. If that was your…"

"Let me see, at a rough estimate, hundred and twentieth?" God help him, it could have been more.

There'd been a time when he'd been terrified of Aunt Marianne and had gone to two or more of these damn events a week.

"Ouch," she said, cringing. "I feel bad for you."

"Yes, we royals have it tough."

She shot him a sharp look, but whether she saw his wink in the faint light, he didn't know.

"I wouldn't say it's all bad," she replied ruefully after a few minutes of silence. "This isn't terrible, after all."

Her words went in tandem with the magnificent view that appeared at the end of the corridor.

Two ornate glass doors overlooked a raised terrace, which in turn, overlooked the gardens. In the distance, the Ansian mountain range, which were a part of his ducal lands, were looming presences, only visible thanks to the twinkling lights of the houses and amenities on the craggy plains.

In front of the rises, there was the city of Madela. A glorious metropolis that gleamed like a treasure trove. The Arc, their national monument, soared higher into the air than even the Eiffel Tower. Older than that infamous statue, it was a feat of technological engineering that had stunned Europe at the time.

With a similar infrastructure to that of the *Tour Eiffel*, designed with ore from Veronian mines, the piece soared into the air in a straight line but as it approached the summit, it began to curve until it was almost overhanging.

He'd seen the plans. Had studied them as a child. Architecturally, it made sense. The overhang was more illusion than reality. But from a distance, and from below, it seemed like a half-done arch that could topple over at any minute.

Veronians were, after all, known for their sense of humor.

Regardless, the monument was very impressive considering the time period, as well as its size. At night, it was lit up like a Christmas tree, and the sight never failed to remind him of home.

"It's so beautiful," she murmured softly when he opened the door for her, letting her pass through first.

"That it is. Veronia may have its flaws, but its natural beauty and the touches man has made to it never cease to astonish me."

"What flaws does it have?"

"I shouldn't tell a foreigner," he teased as they stepped out onto the raised terrace. There were steps that led down into the gardens, but he shepherded her to the side where there was a better view and a small seating area.

The night was balmy and temperate, warm enough—even though autumn was approaching—to sit outside without her needing a wrap to cover her shoulders.

In her floor-length ball gown, the only thing uncovered was her chest and shoulders.

And what that lack of covering revealed had his cock hardening in response.

Creamy pearl skin was taut with defined muscles in her arms, but the roundness of her hips spoke of a woman who wasn't ashamed of her curves.

She had large breasts, enough to make a man's hands sweat with the need to cup them. And in the sapphire blue gown, with its sweetheart neckline, the round globes were plumped and straining.

As he took a seat, he tried not to peer down said neckline.

Proud of his restraint, he watched her ruffle her skirts as she settled back in the seat.

It amused him further when she didn't sit with a ramrod straight spine as most of the court would have done. She leaned back against the filigree metalwork of the garden chair and sighed as she looked at the ornate flowerbeds before her.

When she didn't tease him for more information, he prompted, "You wanted to know about Veronia's flaws?"

She jerked a shoulder. "Not if you're not willing to tell me them."

His eyes widened. She was taking him at his word? Not pumping him for gossip? Not avariciously seeking news she could sell to the tabloids?

Was it a ploy?

His suspicious thoughts filled him with guilt, but he ran a sharp eye over her, trying to ascertain her game.

Everyone wanted to know more about Veronia. Everyone. They were a ridiculously wealthy country, but had intense privacy laws which made gossip like a powder keg at times.

And if any information came from a source such as he?

That would be like gold to the press.

"We're struggling to cope with the demands of our population," he said smoothly, watching as she gently turned her head to look at him.

There was no eager zealousness in her gaze as she stared at him. And with the terrace illuminated, he could see her as well as he would in day light.

She stared at him, those almond eyes seeing more than he felt sure he was imparting.

"In what way?"

"It's well known we're overpopulated."

She pursed her lips. Her disapproval amusingly evident. "As is most of the planet."

He nodded. "Indeed. Veronia comes after Japan with its head per capita. We're not the largest nation in the world, but we attract a lot of émigrés seeking..."

"A tax-free haven?" She cocked a brow at him, daring him to deny it.

He shot her a swift grin. "That, as well as its other charms. Three hundred and twenty days a year of sunshine? Beautiful coastlines. Culture, history. Monuments? It's a fascinating country."

"Have you lived here all your life?" she asked, her eyes seeming to soften at his passionate words.

"No. Unfortunately not." When her head tilted to the side in question, he explained, "I attended a boarding school in England. I also studied at university there."

She sat up, her interest evident. "What did you study?"

"Botany and horticulture."

"Really?" Perry's eyes widened. "How fascinating!"

It was his turn for his to widen. Nobody had ever called his degrees fascinating.

If anything, if he dared mention anything green, people's eyes would glaze over, and he'd change the topic onto boring politics or something that would make it seem like he was interested in maintaining a conversation. It was why he preferred to avoid these events like the plague!

"Do you work in the field?"

He shook his head. "I can't." He grimaced. "I'd love to, but my estates require too much of my time. I've been implementing changes into the way the farms work on my land. Making sure we're not abusing the soil, developing ways to irrigate the crops without wasting water, that kind of thing."

"Now that *is* fascinating," she murmured, leaning forward. "Did previous generations not leave enough fields to lie fallow?"

Surprised that she knew enough to understand what 'fallow' even meant, he murmured, "That, but also, we used to have a too-large head of cattle that fed from the land. The numbers were impossible to maintain. These last few years, I've been working to breed a variation that's less hard on our resources."

For some reason, the more questions she asked, and the more he answered, well aware he was talking to someone with a brain filled with something other than just gossip and court intrigue, he found her more and more attractive.

Her beauty had stunned him from the start.

But her intelligence?

It floored him.

She was genuinely interested in his work. More than that, she was curious and eager to learn and understand. Had even made suggestions that made damn sense, when it came to his recent experimentation with effective and non-chemical pesticides.

After close to an hour of speaking on various matters, as well as his pet project—an organic fruit farm he was cultivating not far from here—he saw her yawn.

Disappointed, his tone was a little stiff as he murmured, "I'm sorry. I must be boring you."

She scowled. "No! Not at all. Yours is the first decent conversation I've had all evening. I'm just..." She sighed. "I arrived this morning. So the jet lag's fatal."

His eyes flashed with regret. "I'm so sorry. Here I am, keeping you awake."

"No, please, don't apologize. I've really enjoyed it." She smiled at him, and the smile lit her green eyes in a way that turned them into glinting amber.

Arousal sluggishly pulsed through his veins at her visceral response. Even innocent, it affected him like nothing else.

He got to his feet before he said or *did* something rash. "Let me escort you home."

She shook her head. "That's not necessary." Her smile lessened the rejection as she took his hand and got to her feet. "I'm staying here."

His back stiffened at her words. "You are?"

"I am."

He frowned. "Why?"

"I'm here to work on Veronia's environmental problems. I'm going to be spending the next month here, trying to ascertain the root causes of why the drought has hit the country so hard when rain levels haven't dropped."

"Poor infrastructure," Xavier immediately retorted. "I've told the king's advisors several times that the dams were not only poorly located but badly maintained. They leak more than they hold."

Her eyes flashed with anger. "Really?" She gritted her teeth. "Well, don't you worry." Perry patted his hand. "I'll make sure the king is aware of *that*."

His lips twitched at the sudden appearance of the tigress before him. Quite certain Uncle Philippe was about to have an ear lashing, he murmured, "If you only arrived this morning, then you can't know the palace well. Where are your quarters?"

She grimaced. "I don't know. It's called the Tulip Room. The maid told me to remember that, and everyone on staff would be able to guide me back."

His brows rose. She was in the private wing of the palace. Philippe must really be rolling out the red carpet for her...

He wondered why he hadn't known of an environmental scientist making an appearance in their nation.

If anyone would be interested in that, it was him. Had his uncle kept it from him?

Xavier grimaced as he guided her off the terrace; it was far more likely he'd not been paying attention.

Politics bored him. To death.

"I know where your room is," he advised her kindly, leading her through the palace's many corridors and up several grand staircases to reach the private area of the palace. "I know this place like the back of my hand," he told her.

"You do? It's like a maze to me." She shrugged. "But then, I'm used to a two-bedroom apartment." Her snicker had him chuckling. "My lab back in Boston is big though, but it's still smaller than this place."

"I can believe it. I spent many nights here as a child though. Played in most of the rooms, even when I wasn't supposed to."

Her green eyes sparkled with merriment. "Really? It's hard to imagine you as a child, Xavier."

He laughed. "It is? Why?"

"I don't know," she said calmly, turning to look at a magnificent marble statue of Aphrodite flowing to shore on a clamshell. Á la Botticelli's masterpiece. "You're very serious. Somber, almost. It's just hard to picture you as lighthearted as a child."

He shrugged. "My responsibilities are numerous now. I don't have it as easy as I did then."

"True." She smiled up at him. "We spend our teen years praying to be twenty-one, then we hit it, and wish all we had to worry about was homework and not getting detention."

"I can't imagine you were a troublemaker," he chided as he guided her into the opulent, gilded hallway that put St. Catharine's Palace in St. Petersburg to shame.

With its voluptuous molding and dreamy blue walls, it was the epitome of eighteenth-century splendor.

"No, I was a good girl," she admitted with a wrinkle of her nose. "Boring."

"That I also doubt," he teased as they approached her bedroom door. With a gallant waft of his hand, he murmured, "Your quarters, milady."

She laughed. "I'm no lady."

Her words hit him with their rawness. He reached for her chin, held her in place as he stared straight into her eyes and murmured, "You are a true lady."

She licked her lips in astonishment. "T-Thank you. That's kind."

He meant it.

He'd known ladies of the court all his life. This American commoner had more charm and class than those protocol-peddling jackals.

"You're welcome. It's the truth."

She placed her hand on his arm, her eyes still connected with his as she whispered, "I-I know it might seem forward, Xavier, but… would you like to come in for a drink?"

He tilted his head to the side. "You must be tired."

"I am." Her smile was rueful. "But I think I need a nightcap."

Was she coming onto him, or genuine in her need for company? It was her first night on foreign soil, and not just foreign soil... she was in a palace, one of the oldest palaces in Europe no less—some of the castle walls dated back to the eighth century.

"Of course. I'll gladly keep you company."

Her smile was relieved and all the more charming for it. She opened the door and slipped inside, letting him trail in after her.

It was called the Tulip Room based upon the over-flowing vases that dotted every surface of the room. The sweet, earthy scent permeated the very air. Staff members refilled the vases every few days with fresh tulips, varying in colors.

They were every-damn-where.

Something she'd shortly be changing, he hoped.

The idiots of the royal household didn't seem to realize how much water they wasted, or how large the carbon footprint was on each one of these damn posies.

Sure, they were gorgeous, but so was a wall full of cacti. And cacti were far better for the environment.

Although, the 'Cacti Room' didn't pack the same punch, he supposed.

Otherwise, it was a rather grand stateroom, with a bed so large, dynasties could and may well have been formed on its surface, a fireplace tall enough for him to stand in, and a small seating area overlooking a patio door that was a silent sentinel to the city in the distance.

She headed for the seating area, and waving a hand at him, invited him to sit down. "Brandy?" she asked, veering off course for the low dresser which contained a silver tray housing cut glass decanters.

"Please."

As he took a seat, the only sounds in the room were that of the liquid trickling into the brandy glasses.

He thanked her when she handed him his, then grinned into his glass when she slipped out of her shoes and curled up on the sofa opposite him—he'd decided the armchair was safer.

For him or for her, he wasn't sure yet.

"God, I'm glad I didn't wear heels tonight."

Her sigh was so loaded with relief, he had to smirk. "I can see that. I'm surprised they're not glued to your feet. Most women wear them."

She shot him a rueful look. "I'm not most women." Perry took a sip of her brandy, and he watched as she took too large a mouthful, her eyes flaring wide in alarm, before she started coughing and spluttering.

It wasn't very kind of him, but he chuckled at her as she clapped her chest.

"Jesus," she wheezed. "What's in that? Dynamite?"

"Probably the finest brandy from the Armagnac region," he advised ruefully, studying her red eyes with amusement as she swiveled her head to gawk at him.

"You mean that's good stuff? Hell, it tastes like rocket fuel."

"Well, I can't say if that's true or not. Maybe that's Elon Musk's secret?" He raised a toast. "To brandy instead of diesel."

She chuckled. "I'm not sure which would be worse for the environment."

He winked, but grinned. Now she'd stopped spluttering, he could tell the brandy had worked its magic on her. She could sink a little deeper into the sofa, and there was a calmness about her that relaxed even him.

She hadn't exactly been agitated before, but he knew how jet lag worked.

It was like a long adrenaline spike. Out of nowhere, it could hit.

They sat in silence for a while. Xavier studying the brandy in his glass, comfortable not to speak. Perry studying him, equally content to stay quiet.

He knew her eyes were on him.

Knew it because he could feel her attention.

Had the brandy dropped her barriers? He couldn't say.

She wasn't drunk. But the jet lag with the brandy had probably combined to lower her inhibitions a tad. That was probably why he could sense her gaze on him.

It wasn't in cool disinterest either. But warm regard.

His cock stiffened at her simple charms. She wasn't direct. Wasn't aggressive. If anything, she was the opposite.

He was content to let the tension between them thicken without saying or doing a damn thing. Because he couldn't be the only one feeling this, could he?

Thanks to an attraction that had started from a first glance, but that had developed thanks to a riveting conversation and mutual interest, it was like the air was clogged with desire because their attraction wasn't singly faceted.

Deciding to see if he was right on the money, he flickered his glance toward her and saw her pupils were dilated. Her chest heaved a little with rapid breaths, and she had a rosy flush on her cheeks.

His hand clenched around his glass. "I should go."

Distress had her mouth forming a perfect O with those scrumptious pouty lips. "Go?"

"You're tired, Perry," he told her softly, swigging the rest of his brandy back. The burn had a kick to it, she was right about that, but it was a good kick.

What he needed if he was to leave this room and ignore the promise in her eyes.

Her sharp inhalation had his attention flickering to her. "What is it?"

"You don't feel this?" she asked softly, a confused frown puckering her brow.

"Oh, no. I feel it." His tone couldn't have been more rueful if he'd tried. "But you're exhausted from traveling, have had to attend a boring event, and just got kicked in the spleen by a rather potent liquor... I'm not about to take advantage of you."

She stunned the hell out of him by licking her lips, and whispering, "What a shame. Because I want to take advantage of you."

CHAPTER FOUR

WHERE THOSE WORDS CAME FROM, Perry would never know.

Anger at George for abandoning her at the event? The burn of the brandy which made her chest ache with its potency while setting fire to her blood? Or the bizarre fact that every single one of the DeSauvier heirs was so sinfully handsome? God had to have been playing a joke on womankind the day he produced them.

She'd never acted like this before.

Had never even contemplated a one-night stand, but tonight? The devil was at her heels.

His nostrils flared at her challenge. "We should talk about this in the morning."

Her courage, liquid or otherwise, would have disappeared by then. And this handsome beast of a man, a freaking duke no less, wanted her.

She was useless with anything with XY chromosomes, but even she could see the desire he felt for her. Maybe that wouldn't last the night. Maybe his 'brandy' goggles would have evaporated by then. All she knew was this had to happen tonight.

Before he could do little more than tense, she sat up and tilting to the side, began to unfasten the zip at the side of her bodice.

It sat snugly under her arm—so damn snugly she'd wanted to castrate George, yet again, for picking something so goddamn small.

How difficult was it to buy a large anyway? It said the size on the label, for God's sake!

This had to be a medium. Maybe even a small. She'd barely squeezed into the stupid thing earlier, and as she unfastened the zipper, as the teeth released, she wanted to sigh in relief.

Not that that would be sexy, of course. And sexy, or an attempt at it, was her current MO.

With each inch, she could breathe easier, and though she wanted to suck in a deep gulp of air, she couldn't. Not with Xavier looking on.

Who named their kids that, anyway?

Xavier.

What kind of woman put their son out there with a name that was going to drive the rest of her sex wild?

Surely it was just cruel.

Her bottom lip pouted as the top of the bustier sagged down, revealing the bra set that George had also taken upon himself to pack for her.

It was a bra with a strange kind of decoration under the underwire. The bra didn't end there, but a few inches along her rib cage.

The black lace was delicate enough to not have her feeling too mortified by the notion of George sending someone out to buy this stuff for her.

She was just pleased to feel the sexy lace against her skin, especially when Xavier's brown eyes looked as though they were on fire.

Just like his cousins, Xavier was gorgeous.

Where they were chestnut and dark blonde, he was close to auburn. But it was so dark, truly, it was more russet. Dark brown highlights outweighed the red, but it was prominent enough to glint in the light.

His eyes were smoky green, like hers really, and his mouth was made for kissing.

He had a bold nose, a jaw like granite, and a wide brow that puckered when he frowned. He wasn't frowning now though.

Edward was crown prince, but somehow, Xavier was more serious. As crown prince, she didn't even have a damn clue what kind of responsibilities the man would have, but Xavier looked like he had the weight of the world on his shoulders.

She ran her hands over her breasts, as she looked him up and down hungrily.

Like the rest of the men at the event, he wore a tuxedo. The white, gently ruched shirt lay flat against his stomach. He broke protocol by not wearing a bowtie unlike the rest. He just had the top button open, revealing a shadow of hair at the throat.

His tux fit him like a glove, while somehow making him look bigger. Stronger. Taller.

From the top of his head to the soles of his feet, he was as polished as George and Edward, but he had more rawness about him.

She knew George and Edward didn't mind playing the game. They'd been born for it. But Xavier minded.

He minded a lot.

He didn't want to be here tonight. Not at the palace anyway. Her bedroom, on the other hand, she figured he was A-Okay being here, if the inferno blazing across the room was any indication.

She sucked in a shaky breath as she squeezed her breast through the delicate lace, and he licked his lips.

"Perry," he warned.

"Xavier," she retorted huskily. "Come here."

"I-I... you should tell me to get out of here."

She shook her head. "Now, why would I do a silly thing like that?"

Her free hand, she held out. Beckoning him closer with the siren's call of her body.

She'd never felt sexy before. But then, she'd never worn lingerie like this, or a dress that made her feel like Cinderella, or been at a party where a king and queen were in attendance.

It was a night for new experiences.

And she wanted to experience Xavier.

Everything he had to give.

Even if, after the clock turned midnight, she suddenly regretted it, she decided she wouldn't. That if regrets did come her way, she'd chide herself, because for one night in her life, Perry deserved to act her age.

Not her bra size. Well, technically, her boobs were huge, but that was neither here nor there.

He swallowed but got to his feet and took a step nearer.

Another one.

Another.

Until finally, he was there. In front of her.

She bit her lip, loving the heat he was throwing off. It fired her up, empowered her, and as he approached, she saw the thick bulge at his crotch and felt her mouth water in response.

With a squeak of shock, she watched him bend down and lift her from the sofa. She hadn't expected that, had expected him to sit beside her, but he didn't.

With her in his arms, carrying her like she weighed nothing, he headed for the bed.

He was all heady man. Aroused lusts and strong passions. He was breathing fast and hard, his nostrils flaring like a stallion in heat.

God, the things he did to her insides.

He pressed her to the bed, but before he could get up again, she quickly threaded her legs around his waist and her arms around his shoulders.

The move had her loose skirt slithering down her thighs to accommodate him. And her body welcomed him eagerly.

She clasped him to her tightly, loving the feel of him against her body and between her legs.

A shiver rushed through her that made her back arc, pushing her breasts against him.

The invitation was too much for him to ignore it seemed. He bowed his head and pressed kisses to the ripe swells, and with a shudder, she ran her fingers through his hair, holding him hostage.

She had a duke on her bed.

A duke kissing and caressing her breasts.

This was more than Cinderella.

She didn't know what the hell it was, but she didn't want it to stop.

Another shudder rushed through her when he loosened one cup of her bra and tugged her breast out from inside the confines.

When his lips pursed around the tip, pleasure soared through her in such a rush, she let out a whimper.

The strength of that simple caress was too much for her to bear. She clenched her eyes shut, choosing to revel in the moment as he made her experience things she hadn't experienced in too long.

With a mewl, she lifted her head, urged his upright with the strength of her clasp in his hair and united their mouths.

She arched her hips, rocking them against his cock. He was thick and full between her legs, and she loved the heavy presence of him. Her movements were almost frantic, and that was because, in essence, they were.

She felt a desperate need unfurling inside her. One that threatened to overtake the very air she breathed if she didn't feel him closer to her soon.

Her hands released their clasp on his hair to tug at his jacket. Their lips tore at one another, seeking and discovering the other's hidden secrets as they explored one another's mouths.

It was like something from a movie, and Perry knew that if she were to view this as an outsider, she'd never have believed it was her.

Perry Taylor. Doing this. Doing a duke.

Shuddering, she bit at his bottom lip, tugging it away from his teeth as she jerked his jacket off his shoulders. She managed to get it halfway down his back before his position and damn good tailoring stopped her in her tracks. She let her nails dig into the thick corded muscles of his shoulders, and he grunted then reared off her.

She cried out at his loss. The loss of heat and his weight was more than she could bear. Her lips parted—he couldn't think to leave her, could he?

Horror whipped through her as he stood there, breathing heavily, staring down at her with eyelids so thickly lidded he was peering at her through slits.

Then, just when mortification began to stir, he dropped his jacket like it was burning oil touching his skin and began to unfasten the studs on his shirt.

Slowly.

In total control.

Internally, she was a shivering wreck at the sight of that control, because his eyes branded her in a way that made everything in her clench down with hunger. She watched as he unbuttoned the cufflinks on his cuffs, then shrugged out of his shirt. Next came his belt. Then, his fly.

He didn't grab his cock, didn't pull it out, just freed himself and came over to her again.

If his kiss had been enticing before, now it inspired a ravenous hunger in her. He forged their lips together with the same brand that had sealed her gaze to his form as he undressed. She couldn't breathe, didn't want to. Just wanted him.

It overtook her. Swelled inside her like nothing else had ever done. She needed him in her body.

Nothing else made sense.

Before she knew where she was at, he'd rolled them over so she was above him. The move liberated her from his weight, but he used the new position to grab at her dress, tug the bodice down, and slide his hands up her legs to hitch her skirt at her waist.

She could only imagine how she looked, but damn it, she didn't care.

His hands settled on the curve of her ass, and he pulled at the fabric bisecting her cheeks.

She'd never been more grateful that her best friend didn't understand that it was icky for him to have bought her underwear. She'd thank him tomorrow for getting her a thong.

Xavier slipped his hands under the fabric, then cupped her ass. His palms against her sensitive skin made her jittery. They were callused. Not the soft hands of a pampered aristocrat.

This man worked for a living.

She felt it. There was the proof, and it raked against her nerve endings like nothing else could.

When a finger slid against her sex, she moaned into his mouth. When that finger pumped into her, stretching tissues that hadn't been invaded in a hell of a long time, she clenched down around him and did the same with her eyes.

Letting him take her mind off how small she was with the kiss that just about knocked her socks off, she threw herself into the passionate embrace and let him stretch her down there.

He seemed to realize that was a necessity too, because another finger joined the first. She was crazily wet, so that helped. But he scissored the digits inside her, stretching the small passage.

Moaning into his mouth when he pulled out and used his slick fingers to caress her clit, she began to hump his hand. It was embarrassing, degrading, but it had been nearly six years since someone else's fingers had touched her clit.

Six. Years.

Yeah, she'd hump him. Jesus, she deserved it!

The orgasm, when it came, appeared out of the blue. A startled shriek escaped her, because she'd never come that fast before and hadn't expected it to blindside her.

His slippery fingers caressed her clit with a practice that should have pissed her off, but she felt churlish being jealous because damn, that experience made her come like no other man had.

It was fast and quick. Almost like a burst of adrenaline that had her soaring up to a level she'd never reached before. He kept her there, plateauing, by immediately sinking his fingers back inside her greedy pussy.

The sounds of her juices were so embarrassingly loud, she pulled her mouth from his. "No. More. I need more."

His laugh was in his eyes as he rolled them back over once more so she was on the bottom.

The bed was so goddamn huge that even lying on it horizontally, they had a football field still to play with!

She planted her arms on either side of her for balance and tried not to groan as his cock settled against her core, her juices staining the front of his pants.

She reached between them, felt the tip of his cock as it had slipped under the waistband of his briefs, and cupped him.

Jesus, he was thick. Long, but thick.

She gulped at the notion of taking him and realized that his girth was the reason why he'd kept himself tucked in his pants.

Yeah, she could imagine some girls could sob and run off at such thickness, and she would have been no different if the man hadn't wreaked the impossible...

An orgasm with his fingers?

With just a kiss?

He obviously had magical extremities, and if his cock was a magic wand too, she'd be churlish to throw this wizard out of her bed.

With a shudder, she wrapped her fingers around him and used the pre-cum to comfortably jack him off. He shuddered in her hand, thrilling her.

"In me," she whispered. "Come in me."

"You're too small," he said with a grunt, then levered up on to his arm by planting his hand at the side of her head.

She stared between their bodies and saw for herself just how thick he was.

Blowing out a breath, she whispered, "I guess I'm just not going to be able to walk anywhere tomorrow."

A snort escaped him, and she grinned up at him. A mischievous glint in her eye.

"Do you know it's very uncomfortable to laugh with an erection?"

Her mouth rounded. "It is?"

"Yup." He spoke with a casualness that flipped something inside her, and his hand came down to grab his shaft to, just as casually, jack himself off.

Her eyes widened in response, and her gaze glued itself to his cock. He milked his dick of pre-cum, and her mouth watered with the need to taste him.

She'd never given a blowjob before.

The idea that tonight she could, had her mouth watering harder.

"Do you have a condom?" he asked, jolting her from her stupor.

Blinking, she shook her head, disappointment whizzing through her at a rate that left her lightheaded.

He grunted again, levered himself off the bed.

Before she could even let out a cry of distress, she watched him take the two steps to the bedside table and began rummaging inside them.

He let out a happy, "Aha," and turned back to her with several foil packets in his hand.

"They stock that stuff in the bedside cabinets?" she asked, mouth gaping.

He laughed. "They stock everything for their guests. Just in case."

"Well, I'm very, very, very grateful for their overzealous hosting skills."

They being—hell, she couldn't see Marianne popping out to the local drugstore for prophylactics.

Couldn't even imagine it was something the king and queen had requested their staff do...

Shoving off the thought, because she was anal retentive enough to wonder just who she ought to be thankful to, she watched instead as he covered himself with the sheath.

It didn't contain the beast much.

She bit her lip, hoping against hope that the condom-bringer of Veronia also provided ones that were lubed up.

"It will fit," he reassured her softly, with his other hand reaching up to cup her chin. When his thumb rubbed her cheek, she grabbed his wrist and held him captive.

"I know."

Her simple retort had his lips twitching as he came down between her thighs once more.

This time, however, his cock touched her clit. The slick tip rubbing over her. She cried out, the pleasure making her close her eyes as she processed it.

She lifted a hand, pressed the base of her wrist to her forehead.

"Jesus," she whimpered as he carried on teasing her like that. Small thrusts of his hips that maintained the contact and had electrical sparks shooting along her nerve endings.

She loosened up, her legs parting, her body opening to his confident touch.

When the tip of his cock slipped down deeper, she felt it burrow into her warmth and knew that tensing up was the last thing she ought to do.

He coated himself in her juices, and she opened her eyes and saw him sliding his hand around his cock, making the condom slick with more of her arousal.

Hell, that sight alone was enough to blow her brains.

The tip entered her once more, and she blew out a breath and forced herself to relax.

This was kind of like being a virgin again, she realized as he edged his way in.

She froze when the first inch popped inside her. But he took her mind off it by coming down to his elbow above her and pressing their lips together.

She didn't know how he could be so controlled when she felt the exact opposite. But he took her lips with all the fire she knew he was quelling down below. His tongue thrust into her in a way they both wanted his cock to be doing to her pussy. He tore the breath from her lungs, stole her energy with his hunger.

Another inch slipped inside.

As her hands came up to grip his hair once more, another two thrust in deeper.

She clenched around him then forced herself to relax as she began to fight back, her tongue plunging its way into his mouth, parrying with him there.

Another inch.

Another.

Then he was there.

His pelvis brushing hers and her every part feeling splayed wide open, now he was inside her.

Impaled, kind of described it. Uncomfortable, another.

He seemed to realize she wasn't breathing and pulled his lips from hers.

"Breathe, Perry," he whispered, dotting kisses along her cheeks, moving down to nip at her earlobe before doing the exact thing she needed—kissing her neck.

The minute he did that, she knew it was game over.

A roar sounded in her head as all her delicate nerve endings in that most sensitive of her erogenous zones sent off flares of warning.

She clenched around him again. Not out of panic, but in need.

His tongue worked at her throat, massaging it and teasing her. She felt him nip and then suck, didn't even care if he left a hickey.

Her hands slipped down his spine, and this time, she dug her nails in hard as she flung her head back.

"Move," she gritted out, rocking her hips, loving the friction that came as a result.

His thickness did something to her clit. Made it pop out of its hood? Hell, she didn't know what it did, didn't care, just knew that when she rocked her hips, it nudged her clit against his pelvis, which had more fireworks going off at the backs of her eyes.

He made to pull out, but she quickly wrapped her legs around his hips. Burrowing her heels into his ass, she lifted her own and began to pump onto him from below.

She caught his gaze with hers when he peered down at her, but she was merciless as she fucked him.

Her ass ached, her thighs too, but hell, it didn't matter. None of it mattered, as long as whatever was going on with her clit carried on.

She felt the muscles in her face spasm, felt her nerve endings twitch in her eyes as orgasm approached.

Just when she was on the brink of tumbling over, he bucked on her, pulled out to nearly all the way, then thrust in.

The move, so unexpected, had her screaming.

She couldn't contain the shriek. Didn't want to.

He did it again.

Three more times, and that was it. She was done.

Her pussy clamped around his with a force that had his eyes widening, and with a low groan, he came too.

Their mutual orgasm, with their gazes as tightly joined as their sexes, was the most intense thing she'd experienced in her thirty-three years.

As he pumped his seed into her, the condom getting in the damn way, she flared to life around him...

And only when she could breathe again, when his cock softened inside her and he slumped on top of her, did she question what had just happened.

Because Perry, in all her years, had never felt so alive as she did at that moment. And that was a feeling she didn't want to lose. One she wanted to experience again, and again, and again.

CHAPTER FIVE

GEORGE OPENED his eyes the next morning with a groan.

Too much champagne, he chided, but then simultaneously forgave himself.

His first night on Veronian soil in years, the first time he'd seen Edward and Perry standing close to one another, the first time he'd revealed his big plan to his big brother...

It had been a heady day.

Today looked to be headier still. Where all his plans, all his dreams looked to be coming to fruition...

"I think you've had too much to drink, Perry."

She squinted at him, somehow managing to look utterly adorable, rather than pissed as a newt. "I'm not drunk," she slurred. "I'm lubricated."

He snorted. "Lubricated?" Fuck, he'd like to lubricate her. He beat down the need surging through him. It was hard, but he managed to contain it. The last thing he needed was an erection in public.

"Yes," she hiccoughed. "I need to be too."

"Why?" he asked, cocking a brow at her. He rarely saw her drink this much, and if she did, it was usually when they stayed in. Never when they went out.

She put a finger to her lips and blew out a breath.

"A secret?" he asked, trying to figure out why she immediately cascaded into giggles at his question. Considering Perry didn't have secrets, not from him anyway, he asked, "What kind of secret?"

"A secret girl friends don't tell boy friends." She snorted out another giggle, then slurped down tonight's cocktail disaster of choice—a crème de menthe digestif into which she'd plunked an Alka seltzer to combat tomorrow's headache. He loved her, but she had crappy taste when it came to anything remotely alcoholic.

"Is it about sex?"

Her eyes grew huge, and she shushed him once more. "That's a swear word."

"Since when?" he asked, amused.

"Since forever." Her eyes rounded. "Oh, no. Wait. That's fucking. Fucking is a swear word. Sex is used in school." She nodded sagely, then whispered, "Yes, it's about fucking. I mean, sex."

He hid a laugh as he drank down his draught beer. On the rare occasions Perry did let loose, he never drank too much. She was a lightweight, and he usually enjoyed the entertainment she provided when drunk.

At this moment, her rather loudly declared statement had invited the attention of the three tables around them. A testament to how loud she could be, considering there was a DJ playing chill-out tracks behind them as they slumped on the low, squashy sofas.

"What about it?" he asked, when she started squinting at the still fizzing crème de menthe pre-hangover cure. "Is it supposed to do that?"

"I don't know," she told him. "It tastes weird."

"It's crème de menthe—of course, it tastes weird. I'm surprised they even had it here."

She huffed. "I read it online."

"So, it must be true."

"The other stuff online is true."

"Like what?"

She peered around, managing to look more *Pink Panther* than spy extraordinaire, and dug out her phone. He watched her open an app, tap in a few words—that took far longer, considering her fingers were all over the place—and when she passed him it, he felt his cock harden, his brain melt, and everything that he thought he'd known about Perry tilt on its head.

"What's this?" he asked woodenly, trying hard not to start scrolling through the images before him.

"It's a blog site," she retorted, managing to be helpfully unhelpful.

"I can see that. Why are you searching for this stuff?" He sighed again when she raised her finger to her lips and blew out a shushing sound. "Why is it a secret?"

"Because it's two men. And one woman." Her eyes were big again. "At the same time."

He swallowed thickly. "If anyone's eyes aren't working here, it's yours. I know what I'm looking at."

"You do?" Her mouth gaped. "You've seen it before?"

He curled his lips inward. "Maybe," he hedged. "What made you search for it?"

"I read something about it."

"Where? Cosmo?"

She snorted. "Since when do I read Cosmo?"

"I don't know, Perry. Since when do you look at porn GIFS of threesomes?"

Perry hissed out a breath. "Omigod, you said that so loud!" she moaned, glancing around and dramatically clapping her hands to her cheeks. "Everyone heard."

"No one heard," he dismissed. "Tell me, Perry. When did you start looking at stuff like this?"

She bit her lip. "When I found this book on Amazon."

"What kind of book?"

"It had lots of men on the cover."

"So?"

"It's this new thing."

Impatiently, he gritted out, "What new thing?"

"OMGee," she wailed. "You're mad at me. Are you ashamed to be my friend?"

He scowled. "Never." When she carried on wailing and slurping crème de menthe down, he grabbed her hand and snatched the drink from her fingers—this conversation was way too important to be blurred by more alcohol and aspirin poisoning. He didn't approve of the concoction, but hell, he'd drunk worse in his glory days. "Perry, focus. I'm not ashamed. I'm curious."

"You are?"

"Yes." He sought patience, but it was hard. This felt like... Okay, so a dream might sound exaggerated. But this was starting to feel heaven sent. "Now, what's the new thing you've been reading?"

"It's where a woman has lots of men as lovers and partners. It's not just about the sex though."

His nostrils flared. He'd bet it wasn't about the sex—ha. "Where does it say that it's bad if it's about the sex?"

She squinted at him again. "I can't tell if you're being a prude or not."

George laughed. "I'm not a prude, Perry."

"You're not? I don't think I am," she declared. "But I might be."

"Would you like to be one of the women in those books?" he asked, trying not to sound too eager.

"I think so. But it seems complicated. I'd just like an orgasm," she screeched out of nowhere, and this time, definitely gained the attention of the tables around them. "George, is that so much to ask? Maybe if I have a whole team of guys, they'd get me off. I mean, it can't be so hard, can it?"

Of course, he'd chosen that moment to take a sip of lager, and he sprayed the table at her declaration. Coughing, he reached for his handkerchief and dabbed at his mouth. "I'm sure if you had a few men tending to your needs, you wouldn't have a problem," he soothed.

She gulped. "Some women don't need to be tag teamed to have an orgasm," she mumbled peevishly.

"No," he said consideringly. "But each to their own." As her words salsaed around his head, he had to ask, "Perry, have you never orgasmed before?"

His best friend clapped her hands over her face. "No," she said, wailing the word again.

For a second, he just gawked at her, then, as he processed that, he clicked his fingers to gain the attention of the waiter nearby. "Vodka shots, please. Bring the bottle." He passed the crème de menthe disaster back to the server. "You can take this away too, thanks."

Perry pouted. "I liked that drink."

"You didn't a minute ago. And that wasn't a drink. It was poison waiting to happen."

"I don't like vodka."

"You will in the morning," he promised her, watching as she scowled at that logic. Did she but know it, the last thing Perry would appreciate in the morning was any recollection of this conversation.

She'd die of mortification if she even remembered a smidgen of it.

As her best friend, it was his duty to get her drunker to deaden a few brain cells.

As the man who'd loved her for too many fucking years, as the man who'd been pining for what could never be, well, it was time to get to work...

The work, of course, had been months in the making. But he was so close now. So fucking close, he could feel it.

Perry was almost his. Orgasms were almost hers. And those naughty little desires she'd been troubled about, were on the brink of coming to fruition...

George rubbed his chin as he squinted out onto his bedroom—a room that hadn't changed since he'd redecorated at fifteen. He hadn't bothered to alter it since, though he'd stayed here often before moving to America after finishing his undergraduate studies at Cambridge, but now as he peered around, he found it hard to believe he was back. And with Perry in tow.

Choosing a college in America had been a decision based more on personal reasoning than for his career. As the spare heir, not a lot was expected of him. He could have been a playboy if he'd wanted, so long as he went to enough events and galas and helped buoy the DeSauvier name, rather than help it drown in anti-royalist muck.

His MBA hadn't been necessary. Not technically. But personally, it had been imperative.

Separating himself from Edward, putting an end to their odd... He winced at the word *fetish*, though he knew many would call it that.

How was it a fetish though? He didn't get off on being with his brother. It wasn't incestuous. Not one bit.

It turned him on to share a woman with Edward. To see her totally overwhelmed, gluttonous on a pleasure that turned her insensate, a pleasure that he and Edward could give her by focusing all their time and effort on her.

For men, sex was usually a selfish act. About them getting their rocks off. For he and Edward, it was the exact opposite.

Denying that for all these years had been...Well, hard was understating the issue.

He'd left when Edward had married. Knowing his brother wouldn't share his wife, as well as the fact George didn't want to share Arabella—who'd made the South Pole look warm in comparison—had made it easier to decide on Harvard for his MBA.

Then, when he'd met Perry...

Down the rabbit hole he'd fallen once more.

He'd opened the drapes last night before he'd crashed in bed. That was the only reason why the morning sun was piercing his retinas. Normally, the staff closed them at night, so that had to explain it.

Staggering out from between the silk sheets, he peered down at himself and saw he was in his briefs—he really didn't remember stripping off.

Grabbing the top sheet from his bed, he wrapped himself up in it, covering his shoulders too as he hunched over and headed for the windows.

As he approached though, he decided he didn't want to go back to bed.

He wanted to see Perry.

Barefoot, he headed for the door, and though it would be frowned upon for him to leave his quarters dressed inappropriately, he also knew his parents weren't going to scold him. Not after so many years away.

Taking full advantage of that, he stayed huddled in the sheet and headed into the hall.

Because he didn't give a shit about being caught, naturally, the hall was empty. Had he cared, his mother would have walked down the corridor... Murphy's law sucked sometimes.

Rolling his eyes, he headed two doors down for the bedroom where they'd stashed Perry.

Yesterday, before they'd been shown to their quarters, he'd rearranged the sleeping plan. His mother had put her in a guest suite outside their private quarters. But Perry wasn't a guest.

She was his family.

Had become that after the years they'd shared together in Boston. He wanted more, of course. But that link would never die. He'd never let it.

He knocked on the door and didn't bother waiting. If she was half-dressed, then he'd get an eyeful—good. If she was in her PJs, it wasn't like he hadn't seen her that way before either.

It was probably a jerk move, but though he didn't care if he got caught dressed like a hobbit out in the corridor, he'd prefer not to get a bollocking.

Stepping inside and quickly closing the door behind him, he turned to face the 'tulip' room and reared back at the sight before him.

Eyes widening, his mouth worked when he saw a dozing Perry cuddled up beside his cousin Xavier.

Outrage flushed through him.

She was his.

Fuck, didn't she know that?

He ran a hand through his hair, messing it up further—not that he cared. All his plans were... felled. At the final hurdle, it seemed. Had Edward been on the bed, he'd have been happy. But Xavier? He loved the bastard, but... he wasn't supposed to be a part of this.

Perry was supposed to be his and Edward's. And Xavier was just enough of a geek to be exactly Perry's type. She'd fall for him.

He could see it all. His wishes and desires, hopes and needs, unravelling before his very eyes.

When...? How...?

Xavier hadn't even been expected to attend! He'd have introduced them otherwise.

George hadn't strayed from her side all evening, save for at the end... he'd left her to talk to a few politicians. She'd glowered at him, but had seemed to understand his position. The Prime Minister, Luc De Montfort, had wanted to speak in Veronian, even though it was the height of rudeness, and he'd felt compelled to appease the man, who was usually a thorn in his father's side.

De Montfort was anti-royalist and hated the royal family. But, the DeSauviers were beloved by the people, so De Montfort had to grit his teeth and bear it.

The family made it a point to always accommodate him, even if he was irritating as fuck.

When he'd gone back for her, Perry had been nowhere in sight, and he'd figured she'd returned to her rooms. When he'd been dragged off by another politician intent on bending his ear about a financial situation in the stock markets, his thoughts had drifted off.

It would seem she had come back to her bedroom.

With Xavier.

Tears pricked his eyes. That was how hard the knowledge Perry had slept with Xavier hit him. It was like a punch to the gut. The horror, the *hurt*.

He sucked in a deep breath, trying to quell the stupid emotions from dancing around his veins.

He wasn't the type to cry, but he'd...

He closed his eyes.

George had pinned everything on Perry. He'd known she'd get to Edward. Had known, if anyone could do it, Perry would make it happen... He and Edward could fulfill the fantasies that both liberated and imprisoned them, all through her.

Was it fair to put so much on her small shoulders?

No. Of course not. But George knew Perry.

He knew her in ways some husbands didn't know their wives. He knew the little and the large, the embarrassing and the amusing... She would flourish in their care. He knew it like he knew his fucking face in the mirror.

Xavier stirred on the bed, dragging George's attention to him.

They were both semi-naked. Perry's legs were splayed, her beautiful body half covered by the dress he'd handpicked for her—all her new clothes had been chosen personally by him. Did she but know it. The gown's skirts were tugged up around her waist, the bodice lowered to reveal the luscious swells of breasts he'd wanked over in the shower.

A shaky breath escaped him, then as he looked away from his cousin's bare ass, his gaze was caught by Xavier's.

His cousin had been laying on his belly. A position that told George he'd practically fallen asleep on top of Perry after climaxing.

Xavier frowned at the sight of him. "George?"

His voice was low, and Perry didn't stir.

George swallowed, his gaze switching to Perry. Xavier shifted, covering her slightly. The gentlemanly move had him clenching his jaw.

At least Xavier wasn't a playboy. If she had to fuck anyone, it was someone who wouldn't hurt her. His cousin was more likely to forget about her, thanks to some weird botanical experiment he was holding in his greenhouses back on his estate... not through cheating on her.

Breath soughed from his lungs.

It was why he and Perry would be perfect for one another.

She was a scientist too. Xavier and she could discuss...

"George?" Xavier said a little louder this time, jerking his attention back to his cousin. "What are you doing here?"

Perry wriggled on the bed, letting out a sleepy, pleasured sigh that had George cringing. She snuggled into Xavier.

"Why are you talking to George?" she asked sleepily.

"Because he's in your bedroom," Xavier commented wryly, his own voice still gruff from slumber.

She stiffened, then relaxed. "Don't be silly," she giggled, turning her face into Xavier's arm.

The move nearly broke George's heart.

"I'm not," Xavier retorted.

"He's not," George said grimly.

The time to leave the room had gone the moment he'd closed the door. He could have sneaked out, neither of them would have known he'd caught them together.

But that time was long gone...What was he doing?

Why hadn't he left? He didn't know the answer to either question, just knew he couldn't move. Couldn't take his eyes away from this tableau of sensuality.

Perry sat up, revealing her surprisingly long spine. For someone so short, it seemed disproportionate, but hell, he'd still spread kisses down each nodule if he could. Disproportionate be damned.

Over her shoulder, she peered at him. Her eyes flared wide in distress when they met his.

"George? What are you doing here?"

It interested him that she didn't try to cover up—even though he couldn't see anything from this angle, a fact she had to be aware of, but still...

"I was going to order breakfast in bed for us," he said a little gruffly, his voice strained with emotion.

Xavier cleared his throat. "Are you okay?"

He clenched his jaw. What did he say to that? *No. You just fucked up a plan that has been nearly six years in the making.*

In a flash, he could see everything derailing, and for the life of him, he couldn't allow it.

Edward was nowhere near ready to deal with this, Perry wasn't either. He'd never prepared her. Never mentioned his predilections to her... never even mentioned that he thought of her as more than just a friend.

He was the only one in way over his head here.

"Perry, I need to talk to you." He cut his cousin a glance. "Alone."

A scowl flashed across Xavier's brow, but Perry spoke first, "George. Now is not the time."

He shook his head. "I know. But that doesn't change things. I need to speak with you. Five minutes."

The plea in his voice stunned even him, and it had Perry's eyes widening further in her distress.

It didn't escape his notice that Xavier didn't offer to leave—this was no coyote ugly for his cousin, it would seem. He had no intention of sneaking off after a cheeky one-night stand.

Gnawing at his cheek, he repeated, "Just five minutes. In the dressing room."

She sighed, turned back to facing forward and did a little shimmy. He'd have wondered what she was doing, but he saw her fasten the bodice of her dress and realized she was making herself presentable.

The last thing he wanted was her to be that.

Not wanting to embarrass her in front of Xavier, more than he already had at any rate, he strode on ahead, passing the small seating area with its spindly gilded framing and heavily embroidered upholstery to the dressing area of the quarters.

Opening the door, he strode in and waited for her to join him.

He kept his back to the door, choosing to look onto the empty rows within the walk-in closet—the capsule wardrobe he'd bought her was tiny in comparison to the cavernous area. He'd handpicked each piece, though he knew she believed he'd passed off the task to his PA. Had dreamed of watching her slip into some of the items that would cling to her skin rather than drape over her lush form in baggy swells.

When he heard the door close behind her, he remained with his back turned, his gaze glued to one dress that had been the recent star of some of his wet dreams.

"What's going on, George? Jeez, this is so embarrassing." She sounded flustered, and he disliked himself for having caused that, but... She needed to know this.

Was it selfish? Perhaps. But he'd waited all these years and couldn't bear the idea of maintaining his need for her a moment longer.

"I have to tell you something that you're not going to like."

He heard her suck in a sharp breath.

"W-What?" Before he could speak, she bit off, "He doesn't have a disease or something, does he?"

His eyes widened at that, and he turned to gawk at her. "No! Jesus, Perry, your imagination is nuts sometimes."

She scowled at him, folded her arms across her chest with a huff. "Well, what's the bad news if it isn't to do with his health?"

He ran a hand through his hair. "I-I know it's totally inappropriate, but I've been waiting for the right time."

"The right time for what?" she prompted, her beautiful green eyes squinting at him.

He sighed. "You didn't take out your contacts last night."

Her scowl deepened. "Don't change the subject."

He clenched his jaw. "That's part of the subject. How do you think I know that? Because I know you. I know everything about you. How you chew on dry spaghetti before you dump some in the pan. How you resole the same damn black flats time and time again, because they don't pinch your toes. How you smile at Tom and Jerry like they're the most hilarious characters ever."

"Well, they kind of are," she mumbled.

"I know all that," he said, ignoring her and sucking in a sharp breath. "Because I love you."

EDWARD TAPPED Flair with his heels, urging the stallion from a gallop to a canter. He clicked his tongue, patted the beast's heaving neck, and let his favorite horse calm down.

He had access to the entire household's stable, but he favored three.

Flair was his favorite, as he'd seen him being born. It was a moment he'd never forget.

It hadn't been the first birth he'd witnessed, but something about watching Flair come into the world and almost leave it within the space of a few hours had wrought a connection between them.

Edward—much to the surprise of the stable hands on staff, if not the husbandry director—had helped care for the colt as a fever had claimed the tiny creature. Had helped feed him. Had tended to him.

For that care, Flair was devoted to him.

Would follow him around like a pup, if the stallion had a say in the matter.

Edward's lips twitched at the notion of being stalked by the Palomino. It would certainly have tongues wagging in court.

Not that he wasn't used to that, he thought wryly.

In his early twenties, he'd raised hell. A lot of which had been kept buried, thanks to the country's media laws, but gossip still spread. One couldn't stop word of mouth, even if one could stop a photo being created and being spread around.

When he'd married, he'd determined to stop the wildness in its tracks.

Arabella had been a safe choice for a wife. She'd have made a fine queen. She had all the titles, the appropriate education. She'd been reared, gently, toward being a rich and powerful man's partner.

Well, partner was too generous a word, but at the same time, it was far too frugal.

She'd been raised to be a queen. Yet that gave her very little abilities in the real world.

Still, he'd grown fond of her. Had hurt when she'd passed.

She hadn't been right for him, just as he hadn't been right for her, but her death had saddened him. Had made him recalibrate his life, wonder if he was heading on the right path.

Two years after Arabella's death, he had to wonder if he'd come to any decisions about that.

He'd epitomized the gracious crown prince of this glorious nation. Had focused all his efforts on being what his country needed with his own needs being shoved aside, as any man in his position was accustomed to sacrificing his own wants for the greater good.

Yet, here George was. Back again. Mischief at hand. A promise in his presence.

Edward clenched his jaw as he peered around the fields surrounding the palace that had been his home since birth.

He'd been born here, held aloft on the palace balcony at the christening. He'd played with toy trains here, dealt with teenage acne, learned how to protect himself in case of a kidnapping attempt, suffered at the hands of Veronia's enemies, and had married and become a widower all while living within the walls of the castle.

It was a grand old dame, he'd give it that.

Tall and proud. Ancient and glorious with it. Huge walls were covered in swathes of ivy, and the windows glinted in the warm morning sunlight.

He smiled. The palace had been more than a home, and was, in many ways, a gilded cage. A thought that had his smile dying.

Acres of green fields surrounded the palace. The luscious grasses shone like shamrocks against the bright cerulean sky. It was like a blanket, so heavy and warm. That alone told him it was going to be another beautiful day in his kingdom.

Behind, he could hear the galloping of his guards' horses. They tried to give him space, and when they forgot, he often raced ahead to attain some for himself.

It was unfair of him and stupid too, but sometimes, a man could only fear his passing so much without it overtaking everything.

He spent half his time worrying about state affairs as he did his death.

At forty-one, he was too young to fear that, but he did. He had no heir, save for George.

Arabella, for all her perfection, hadn't done her duty in that regard. Her broodmare of a womb had never born fruit, and the kingdom was still disenfranchised as a result.

Edward wouldn't even contemplate getting remarried, were it not for the fact he needed an heir, as George reigning as king was too ludicrous an idea—a notion his brother would wholeheartedly concur with.

His lips twitched at the very idea as Jameson muttered at his side, "You promised to stop doing that, sir."

He shot the angry Scot a look. "You promised to give me some space."

"And we give as much as we can." Jameson cast his partner, Vazquez, a look. "But there's been some threats of late—"

Before he could carry on, Edward rolled his eyes. "When aren't there threats?"

It was a rhetorical question. Mostly.

Threats to their safety was as part and parcel of life as it was living in a palace and wearing a crown at state events.

After a while, the vague air of danger merged into the rest of the slush pile that was life.

Jameson heaved out a breath. "This one is more serious than most, sir."

Edward pursed his lips. "Do you remember how long it took me to get you to call me sir?" In his world, sir was considered the height of informality—a notion that had him hiding an eye roll.

Jameson grimaced at the question, well aware of where Edward was heading with this line of questioning. "Five years, sir."

Edward nodded. "And you've been working for me how long?"

"Eighteen years, sir."

"Exactly." Time was a relative concept for them.

Jameson huffed. "You can't.... *we* can't afford to get soft in regard to your security, Edward. Dammit, you know how the nuts can be."

His lips twitched. "Dear me. An 'Edward.' My father didn't mention a kidnapping attempt." For Jameson to drop all formality, that was the only thing it could be.

"No. He decided against it," was all the Scot said.

Edward pursed his lips. "I'm about to gallop back to the castle. If you can't keep up, it's your own fault." He tapped Flair into a gallop and took off over the rolling hills of the royal estate without a backward glance.

He heard Jameson curse, then the thundering hooves of the guards' beasts as they followed him.

Clods of soil shot up around Flair's legs as they raced toward the stables. To his left, he saw a deer in the royal forest that surrounded one half of the castle. The natural shield had been a defense in the days of Napoleon and the scene of grand wars. Not only did his ancestors take shelter behind the thick trees, they also hunted amongst them. But now, hunting was banned. Stags and does, the natural flora and fauna Veronia were famed for, had claimed the forests back.

When they were about to verge onto cobbles instead of grass, he slowed Flair down and let him catch his breath gradually before they walked into the courtyard.

The stables were bustling, and a hand appeared to grab Flair for a brush down. Gone were the days when he could care for Flair himself. Now, riding his favorite pet was a fiercely guarded moment in a day.

His secretary, Marcel, tried to insist he didn't have enough time, but Edward put his foot down. Often, he wondered who the prince in their relationship was. Marcel certainly seemed to forget his place from time to time.

To the timid girl holding Flair's reins, he murmured, "Thank you. I rode him hard. Give him a treat from me."

She smiled at him, the corners of her eyes crinkling in a way that spoke of a heavily outdoor life. "I'll do that, Your Highness," she told him cheerfully, squinting up at the sun as she monitored the blue sky. "Nice day for it, Flair," she mumbled to the horse, forgetting about Edward's presence once he'd jumped down and the horse's reins were in her hand.

He hid a laugh at her lack of regard—horse people were the same the world over. It was why he loved being around the stables. Only new staff were surprised to see him. The regulars knew the stables were more of a home to him than Masonbrook Castle itself.

Edward tapped Flair's behind, gently stroking the beast's heaving flanks just as his guards made an appearance in the courtyard. Striding away from them once they had him in their sights, he headed for the family's private entrance to the castle on the east side of the estate.

As he walked, he reached for his cellphone and called his father. "Where are you?" he asked.

Edward, George, and Marianne were probably the only ones who didn't revere Philippe. Their mother had taught them well—respect him, love him, treat him with all the rights a good father deserved, but never forget Philippe was Father first. King second.

At least, in their private lives.

"In my study. Why?"

Philippe's voice was wary, and Edward narrowed his eyes at it. Behind him, he heard the thundering feet as Vasquez and Jameson caught up. Though they were fit, their breaths were as thunderous as their pace. There'd been a large gap between them and him.

"Because I need to talk to you about a security issue."

Philippe sighed. "You know?"

"I know something," he amended. "I want to know more."

"I'll be in my study until twelve."

Edward's brows rose. "So long?"

"A cancellation in my morning."

That was unheard of.

Edward frowned. "On whose part? Yours or theirs?"

"Mine. I had business I needed to tend to."

His frown deepened, but all he said was, "I'll be there shortly."

"Fine, son."

The king cut the call first, leaving Edward to ponder what the hell had happened.

He'd known of only a handful of occasions when his father had a whole morning free. Usually, when he was ill. That was it. And never did he cancel events unless the doctors insisted he remain in bed.

Even then, his father only complied if he was contagious.

Rolling his eyes at his father's obstinacy, he pressed his personal code into the private entrance at the east wall.

It was innocuous. A wooden door that looked as though it had been there since the days of the castle's construction. A little battered, and with bolts the size of his fist on it, it was a ruse.

The door was made to appear ancient. Instead, it contained some alloy that made it bullet and battering ram-proof. The code automated the door's opening sequence, and he strode into the dim hallway.

The corridor was long and relatively bleak. There was no need for decoration here, as this had once been a servants' walkway before the days of high security.

Now, the family used it for expediency. Nothing more, nothing less.

The white walls were unadorned, the floor a rough tile as he strode toward their private quarters, which were right at the end of the corridor at the west side of the castle.

He pressed his code into the next door, a further two were required before he reached their personal living space.

The opulence made a swift reappearance, but he'd long since ceased noticing it. A grievous shame perhaps, but this was his home. Not a museum or a place of exhibition.

As he passed the first few doors on the way toward his father's study right at the end of the hall, he heard a shriek of sound.

Realizing it was coming from Perry's room, his step faltered.

"You did not just say that!"

The shriek was Perry... he'd never known anyone to shriek. Not in the castle, anyway. He wasn't sure if his mother was capable of more than a gentle grimace of annoyance.

She certainly never argued with his father. At least, not as far as he or George knew.

Their parents always presented the most united of fronts. But even united fronts had cracks in their shells from time to time, he supposed. He had to imagine they spent their anger in private, but if they did, he'd certainly never overheard it.

As she yelled something again, something he couldn't quite make out, his lips twitched.

So *American*.

Her loudness was almost appealing. But then, everything about Perry was appealing. It was why his brother's words irritated him.

She should not have been their type, and yet, Perry was obviously deeply under George's skin, and Edward knew his own body too well to fail to realize there was something about her that worked under his defenses too.

He'd barely spoken to her yesterday. Had listened to her converse with his parents, interjecting here and there when polite. She had a brain on her shoulders—no surprise there, considering her doctorate. But more than that, she was the kind of woman who...

Arabella had been cold. In every aspect of their life. Hell, in their bedroom, she'd been positively frigid.

There was a reason she hadn't been able to do her duty and provide an heir... touching her had been as unpleasant for him as it had been for her. Sperm didn't do much fertilizing when they were frozen solid in a man's ball sack, and Arabella had certainly never made him thaw.

Perry, on the other hand, made him burn.

She was vivacious. Her face was animated, her brows mobile, her lips quick to smile. She talked with her hands, unashamed to throw passion into her speech. She was the very opposite of the woman who'd once been his wife.

When another yell came from the bedroom, and he heard a low murmur that sounded like George, he headed to the door and knocked.

When Xavier opened it, Edward reared back. "What are you doing here?"

"Good to see you too, Ed," Xavier said with a sheepish grin.

Edward grunted, and then as he took his cousin's presence in, he felt a spark of...What was that?

Jealousy?

No. He couldn't be jealous. *Could he?*

Envious of Xavier's mussed form, the love bites on his throat. The air of satisfaction he carried like an expansive shield... The man had recently fucked.

And as he was in Perry's bedroom at eight in the morning, Edward didn't have to work hard to figure out who his cousin had slept with. As rage swelled through him, Edward had to accept one single, stunning fact.

George was right.

CHAPTER SIX

"BECAUSE I LOVE YOU."

For a second, Perry felt certain she'd lost control of her senses. George couldn't love her. He didn't love her. But he was looking at her like he did.

So, her ears and her eyes were in on the conspiracy, because they were working, but were obviously malfunctioning.

After a friendship that had endured six years, after a friendship that had endured more than half of that time with one of them secretly loving the other—her, and not him—he was telling her that was a lie?

That he loved her, too?

The dressing room was, as with the rest of the palace, over the top. There was a wall of empty hangers, but a chaise longue sat catty corner to one wall, with a dressing table complete with a huge ass mirror diagonal to it.

She staggered back to sit on it, and sat so hard, she inadvertently pushed it back. The scraping sound jolted her even further as she shook her head and sank into the plush chair.

"Why?"

The question surprised even her. Why was she asking that? Why did she need to know why? How come she didn't need to know how long or when or what had changed?

Just... *why?*

He stared at her blankly. Wrapped up in a bedsheet so he looked like a mummy in a movie from 20's Hollywood rather than today's cinematic wonder, he wasn't the male model hunk she was used to seeing.

Not that she hadn't seen him worse. Hair scruffy from bedhead—although, granted, he'd looked cute as fuck all mussed and tousled. Looking green thanks to the flu—not so cute. Head to toe in mud after a game of rugby.

She'd seen him at his best, last night in that sexy as hell tux, and at his worst... well, not this morning. Even in a bedsheet, he looked tousled and hot, even if he also seemed unsure, frightened, and—though it beggared belief—vulnerable.

It was the latter that made her believe. The latter that made her think this wasn't some elaborate prank he was playing because he'd caught her with his cousin.

Oh God, Xavier.

She pressed a hand to her mouth.

What would he think of her just skipping out on him like she had?

Before she could let the embarrassment swell, he murmured, "Because you're you."

That wasn't the answer she'd expected. Maybe her confusion showed on her face, because he jerked his chin in the air.

"You eat cereal for dinner not breakfast. You work too hard and get so lost in your experiments that we can be talking about the day, and all of a sudden, you'll do a mental wander. You're gorgeous, even though you think you're fat. Your hair is like silk. When you smile, you make my heart feel too full. Your tears make that same heart break." He blew out a shaky breath, then with a rueful smile, said, "I understand Elizabeth Barrett Browning now."

She blinked, bit her lip. Quoted, "How do I love thee?"

"Let me count the ways," he replied softly.

"Why now?"

"I brought you here for a reason."

"I know." She scowled. "The drought."

"That, and other things."

"What other things?"

"I wanted to introduce you to Edward."

Okay, so that was strange, Perry thought. Not so she could meet his parents, but his brother?

"Just Edward?" she asked, seeking clarity.

He nodded.

"Why?" came her wary answer.

"I don't think you're ready for that answer."

"You did not just say that!" she shrieked, her hard to rouse temper suddenly stoked.

His nostrils flared, but he murmured softly, "I know I'm throwing you in the deep lane here."

"More than that," she snapped. "Jesus, George. All these years, and you wait until today to tell me." With Xavier in the bedroom, probably listening to every damn word of their argument?

"I didn't expect you to sleep with Xavier," he snarled. "Dammit, Perry. I never thought that would happen in a million years."

A part of her was so damn delighted, she wanted to pull a victory dance. Another part questioned his timing. Why now? Why was he telling her this only when he'd seen that she'd been with his cousin?

"Why, because I'm not good enough for him?" she spat.

"Are you insane?" He reared back. "He's a duke. I'm a fucking prince. My brother's a goddamn prince and the future king. How can you be not good enough...?"

She held up a hand. "What the hell are you bringing your brother into this for?"

He gritted his teeth. "You dragged my timeline forward by fucking Xavier. That's why I'm telling you now. I need you to know before you make any decisions about..." His lips curled in disgust. "Him."

She blinked at him again. Was he being serious?

Shaking her head, she let her shoulders slump so she could press her head to her knees.

This was too much. On the one hand, she was hearing words she'd never expected to hear. A declaration of love. Of intent.

More than that, she heard the hope in his voice which, more than anything, was like a knife through her shaky defenses.

After wanting him for so long, it seemed too good to be true that it was all being handed to her on a plate. A 24ct gold one nonetheless. And because they were royal, undoubtedly studded with freakin' rubies too.

"I need to think," she said, her tone calm, even though she was feeling anything other than calm.

She had to process everything that had just been said, but the way he kept mentioning Edward was nagging at her.

"Why do you keep talking about your brother?" she demanded, unable to hold the words back.

He clenched his jaw again. "You're really not going to like the answer."

"Goddammit, George, don't prevaricate now. You've just spilled out your damn heart, why not round it out?"

His shoulders straightened at that, his back stiffening. "I need to go."

She narrowed her eyes at him. "I've loved you for years," she bit out, the words loaded with an emotion that was bitter, not loaded with the sweetness that should have come naturally with such a declaration. "I've pined and hoped and dreamed for way too long. I've watched you date other women, I've watched you take them home, and knowing that you're with someone else has been killing me for years. And you're trying to tell me that you love me? *Now?* After you put me through all that? I need a lot more than words to suddenly believe this is anything other than a joke, George.

"Men in love act like they're in love. You've never been in love with anyone but your title and what it brings."

His eyes flared wide. "That's not fair," he spat.

"Isn't it? Granted, you don't laud your title about and use it for your own good... until it comes time to pick up some stupid bitch who's only interested in your crown."

"I don't wear a crown," he retorted sullenly.

"I know that, you know that. Tell that to the women you fuck. They're too stupid to realize that."

Silence fell between them, but it wasn't comfortable as it usually was when they debated something, be it gun control or the best way to make ragu. This was heavy, fraught with tension. With emotion.

In fact, she wasn't sure she'd ever seen George emote so damn much. Hell, when his sister-in-law had died, he'd just looked stoic.

Now?

He looked like his entire world was on a fault line that had just decided to crack open.

"Do you have any idea what it's like to be different? To want different things from the rest of the world?"

She reared back at that. "You being a prince is hardly a handicap," she sneered, not willing to listen to him play the pity party over being goddamn royalty.

Boo-hoo, he lived in a palace. Drank the best champagne in the world. Flew on private jets, and used a non-existent crown to get all the pussy he wanted...

Yeah, she felt *so* bad for him.

But he quelled her thoughts with a single shake of his head. "I'm not talking about my name. I'm talking about my needs." He closed his fist and rapped it against his chest. "What I want. What fulfills me!"

For some reason, fear flushed through her. "What are you talking about, George?" she asked, hating the quiver in her voice.

He narrowed his eyes at her. "I was seventeen when I knew I was different."

"Different how?" she demanded, feeling like she'd just been thrown into a *Twilight Zone* moment and Rod Serling was about to start lecturing her on weird phenomena.

But he ignored her, carried on talking, almost as though she hadn't spoken. "I saw Edward with a girlfriend. He didn't always used to be so fucking staid and stoic. He was a wild child. Mother and Father despaired of him for a few years, but nothing they said seemed to work."

His brother? They were back on that again? She opened her mouth but closed it when he shot her a frustrated glare.

It was like he knew he had her attention, that she was listening, was as receptive as she'd ever be, and he needed to get this out before the words choked him.

His words weren't exactly rushed, but they fell swiftly from his lips.

"He was fucking her in Father's study, of all the goddamn places. I think he just wanted to rebel, break the rules. I went to see Father, came upon them. I stood in the door watching him fuck this woman I'd never seen before, and he saw me. He didn't tell me to get out, didn't even stop fucking her. Just carried on, letting me watch. Then, he said, 'Elizabeth, do you want to suck my brother's cock?'"

Perry froze. Whatever she'd been expecting him to say, it hadn't been that.

A smile curved his lips, and his eyes had turned dreamy. She saw that, processed it all, then whispered, "Did you join in?" Perry didn't know why she asked when she already knew the answer, but he'd fallen silent. Fallen into the memory, it seemed.

He nodded. "That was the first time we shared a woman. But it wasn't the last."

"You did it often?" God, how she hated how her voice squeaked.

"Often enough," he replied, his gaze finally catching hers. There was no shame on his face. If anything, he'd straightened up. His attitude that of 'accept me as I am or don't accept me at all.'

"What does this have to do with loving me, George?" she asked, shakily.

"When Edward married Arabella, he said that was it. That we weren't going to share again. He was thirty-six. Too old to play the role of wild child and family rebel. He was going to settle down, make heirs, and become a better prince." He clenched his jaw, remembered anger flashing on his face in a way that told her how much his brother's words hurt.

"That's normal, isn't it, George?" she asked softly, treading carefully because he was quite evidently still pained by his brother's rejection.

"It might be, but it didn't stop my feelings."

"You love... Edward?" she asked, trying not to be hesitant, just trying to understand what the hell he was telling her.

Revulsion marred the perfection of his face. "Good God, no! Hell, Perry. Is that what you were thinking? I had some kind of incestuous love for my brother?" He shuddered. "That's disgusting."

"Well, how was I supposed to know! This is the first I've heard of anything like this," she barked, embarrassment whispering through her. She'd read about it in books, but in real life? With royalty of all people?

He narrowed his eyes. "You know me."

"I thought I did. I never thought you'd be into... that."

"Sharing?" He cocked a brow. "You can say the word. It's not poisonous, just unorthodox."

She lifted her chin, refusing to be cowed into saying anything too revealing. "Why are you telling me this, moments after you tell me you love me?"

The door opened, making both of them jump. Edward, looking as impeccable as he'd done yesterday, but dressed in a shirt with breeches and riding boots, stepped into the dressing room.

"I think I can answer that, Perry."

George's eyes flared wide at his brother's presence, but that was nothing to Perry's astonishment, which only grew when Edward murmured, "George has told you about our..." He hesitated. *"Tastes* because he wants you to love me, too."

CHAPTER SEVEN

XAVIER STARED at the dressing room door as he watched it close for the second time that morning.

With Edward in riding gear, George in a bedsheet, and Perry dressed in last night's ballgown, he wasn't sure what in the hell kind of meeting was going down in there, but he had his suspicions.

Rubbing his chin, he tried not to eavesdrop. Every now and then, one of them would make an outburst he couldn't avoid hearing, but he hurriedly scribbled a note for Perry with a sheet of paper he found in her bedside cabinet, righted his clothes, and got the hell out of there.

His cousins always had been unusual.

He didn't think anyone aside from him and their security team knew how unusual, and for that, he was grateful. It would do no one any good to learn that the Crown Prince of Veronia and his brother were into threesomes.

Imagining the stink bomb that would cause, he wrinkled his nose as he headed down the corridor on his way out of the private area.

When his Aunt Marianne appeared, she frowned at him. "Xavier? What on Earth are you doing here?"

He cleared his throat. "I drank too much champagne last night."

"You stayed?" She cocked a brow. "That's unlike you." Her confusion turned to glee however as she slipped her arm through his and pulled him close. "Your uncle wants a word with you."

Xavier groaned. "I want to go home."

"Then you should have made your escape last night," she chortled.

"This will take the focus off me for the morning. You know last night is the third time you've rushed off without talking to any of the cabinet?"

He lifted a hand to rub his nose. "Only the third time? I thought it was more." When she smacked his arm, he just hid a smile. "Anyway, what have you done now?"

Marianne and Philippe weren't exactly demonstrative. He couldn't imagine them rowing, but he knew they had disagreements.

"He isn't happy about my upcoming visit to Lauverne."

He frowned. "Why not?"

"Says I'm needed here."

That was unlike his uncle. "Is it for fun?"

She gave an unladylike snort. "Since when do we travel for fun?"

There was a sad truth to that. Fun was found at home, in private, away from the public eye. "True," he conceded, narrowing his eyes as he contemplated what that meant.

"There's a new children's charity opening there. They want me to be a patron." She sighed. "How could I say no? It focuses on treating trauma. PTSD and the like."

Xavier winced. Considering Edward fit that bill as a child, there was no way Marianne wouldn't take a huge interest in such an organization. Philippe too. Which made it stranger that the king wasn't happy about his wife's visiting the charity in person.

Before he could pepper her for more information however, he found himself in front of Philippe's office. "Are you really going to throw me to the sharks?" he demanded of his aunt, even though he knew the answer.

"Without a doubt," she told him cheerfully.

As she opened the door and led him to his doom—an hour lecture on why they had to make nice with the politicians—only one thing made it worth his while.

Sure, he could have sneaked off last night and avoided this conversation in its entirety. But if he had, he'd never have met Perry. And *that* was something he would never regret.

"Philippe, look who I found sneaking out of a bedroom…"

When his uncle's raptor-like gaze caught his, Xavier just sighed and slumped into the chair opposite Philippe's desk.

Time to pay the price for a fabulous evening, he supposed.

―――

PERRY STARED AT EDWARD. Then she gawked at George. Her gaze flashed between the two of them for so long, her mouth was dry because it was hanging open.

"Are you guys for real?" she asked, her voice a croak when she could eventually speak.

Edward sighed. "I know it might seem a little unorthodox."

"A little?"

He firmed his lips. "A lot."

His correction had her narrowing her eyes at him, but otherwise, she relaxed. His concession soothed her. He wasn't going to just blanket over her reactions.

She was allowed to have a damn opinion, after all. Especially on a matter such as this.

Because, even though it seemed laughable, they were being serious. Deadly, so.

She'd never seen George so tense outside of work, and Edward, though she barely knew him, looked like he was the proverbial cat on a hot tin roof.

She blinked. "So, what? You just want me for my body?" Her derisive snort had both men glaring at her, a look she caught when she shot an equally derisive glance down her body.

A Victoria's Secret Angel, she most definitely was not.

It had been outside of the realm of her understanding to have landed Xavier. A fucking duke. Now these two were saying she was hot enough to attract a prince and a crown prince.

And said princes wanted to double team her?

"My life is a porn flick, isn't it? Why didn't you just come in with a pizza box? Tell me you had a delivery?"

Edward frowned, confused, but George snorted. The heaviness that had overcome him in the last few moments dissipating somewhat.

"You're nuts," he told her with a sigh, and she eyed him cautiously as he stepped away from the dressing table he'd been leaning against and headed to the chaise where she was seated.

He made no move to come close to her. Sat at the foot while she was at the head, but his proximity made every part of her stand to attention. She wasn't sure she'd ever been so hyper sensitive, and that was after a night like last night where she'd experienced things she'd never experienced before!

The atmosphere was so turbocharged, the air seemed to be draining of all oxygen. It felt curiously suffocating, but not enough to make her panic— a contradiction in itself.

How could she be starved for air but not scared? He wasn't the air she breathed... even if some nights, at her most fanciful, she felt certain he was.

"Explain this to me, dammit," she burst out finally, when neither man seemed like they were going to say another word. "I need to understand this. You can't just throw shit like this at me and expect it to stick."

Edward stiffened. "I suppose not."

George snorted. "Ignore him. He has a stick up his ass when he's not happy about something."

"What isn't he happy about?"

"I sprung you on him?"

Her eyes widened, and she pointed to herself. "*I* was sprung on *him*?" she squeaked, umbrage flushing through her with enough force to make her turn pink with it.

George leaned forward and grabbed the finger she was pointing at herself. "You'll poke yourself in the damn eye if you're not careful," he chided, then sheepishly looked at his brother. "I explained the situation to you, Perry."

Her head whipped from side to side so fast, almost like it didn't belong on her fool neck. "No, you didn't."

He sighed. "I did. Edward decided when he married, we weren't going to... do the things we'd done in the past. We haven't done them since."

She frowned. "So what? What's changed?"

"You changed everything," George admitted, sitting forward so he could rest his elbows on his knees. "I knew you'd be perfect for both of us."

"As what? A sex toy?" she squeaked again. "What would you do? Shove me in the background to keep me out of the press's gaze?"

"Of course not. People don't have to know about that, but they'll know about your relationship with one of us."

The way he hedged his words had her scowling. "One of you?" She covered her face with her hands. "Why am I even entertaining this crazy topic of conversation?"

"Because you want me as much as I want you," George said softly, sinfully. His voice like silk and with the power to completely decimate her control.

She shuddered because he wasn't wrong. She did want him. Desperately.

Pressing her fingers against her eyes, she whispered, "This can't be real. Am I still asleep?"

"You know how I feel, Perry," Edward said softly.

"I don't think I do," she snapped. "How do you even know you want me? We've barely talked. Or is this just a man thing? George loves me while you just fuck me? Is that it?"

Her own words pained her, made her feel like she'd stabbed herself in the side with a knife.

George grabbed for her hand again, and when her fingers were shielded in his, he squeezed them. "That's not how it works. Edward knows plenty about you, Perry. I've told him a lot over the years."

"Hearsay," she said softly. "That doesn't count as the real thing."

"Maybe not, but I'm not suggesting we leap into anything here. I wasn't even going to mention this for..." George sighed. "A long time, but seeing you with Xavier quickened the timeline."

"The timeline? You make this sound like you had it planned!"

"I did. I never thought you'd..." His jaw flexed, and she knew he was jealous of his cousin.

Jealous of what she and Xavier had done together last night.

"I like him," she declared recklessly. Maybe it was churlish to say it now after he'd just declared his love for her and she'd declared her love for him, but it was the truth.

She did.

The way she and Xavier had interacted last night had been outside of her comfort zone. And she wasn't even talking about sex.

On the terrace, in her bedroom... the conversations they'd had? She'd rarely felt that kind of comfort outside of her time with George.

Then, there was the inferno they'd created together in bed.

Said inferno had her jerking her chin up stubbornly. "If you're saying Edward can have feelings for me over-damn-night, why can't I have them for Xavier?"

George frowned. "Why are we even talking about that?"

"Because the man I slept with last night is outside in the other room, dammit. I wouldn't have slept with him if I didn't want him." Granted, she'd been a little tipsy, a lot jet-lagged, and kind of pissed at George for dumping her to talk politics, but she *had* wanted Xavier.

There was no way a woman couldn't want a man like Xavier.

She narrowed her eyes at Edward. "You know how crazy this sounds, don't you?"

He nodded. Once.

"So why are you taking part? How did you even know to be here now? Did George call you before he came in?"

"No. Of course not. I overheard your conversation outside."

Her eyes flared in distress. "People can hear us?"

"No. Only when you were shouting."

She wasn't sure whether to be relieved or not. Their conversation, despite its crazy topic, had been enacted in a relatively calm manner.

No one would have overheard that much. It wasn't like they'd had a screaming match.

"Still, you barged in. Why?"

"I didn't intend to." He ran a hand through his silky blond hair. Jesus, he was gorgeous. A slightly taller, lot more somber, and older George.

He was mature and sensible. That was what made this conversation so insane.

"I heard you yelling, came to see if you were okay, and then I saw Xavier." His chin jerked up, mimicking her earlier posture.

"And what? Birds suddenly appeared, and you realized you wanted me?" she scoffed, jerked her thumb at George. "Just like Buster here?"

"You don't know what possessiveness and jealousy does to a man," George growled, turning to the side so he could face her better. "Fear of loss too."

"George wants you, Perry," Edward pointed out softly, his hands coming to rest on his trim hips, which were perfectly visible in his gorgeously tailored jodhpurs. She almost wished he'd turn around so she could see his ass.

The man's thighs were like tree trunks, and God help her, she wanted to climb him like she'd ascended the old oak in her childhood home in Tennessee.

Rolling her eyes at her own silliness, she murmured, "Apparently you want me too."

His nod wasn't as firm as George's, but it was a nod nonetheless. "I'm intrigued."

His words didn't match up with his gesture. "Explain."

"George never picked the women we shared," Edward said softly, but his voice was gruff with discomfort. "That he picked you makes me wonder why you're so special. It makes me want to learn how you tick so I can understand you better, as well as understand his reasoning."

His logical response, in the face of such nuttiness, helped calm her down. He was being rational. She could appreciate that.

Cutting George a glance, she eyed his miserable face and knew that her feelings for him hadn't gone anywhere because of the last twenty-four hours.

It put her in a spot she didn't appreciate. If she didn't agree to fuck Edward, was that it for her and George?

George was the one she wanted. Had always wanted. God, she loved him. With more love than she knew how to handle some nights.

But if he was saying he and Edward came together or not at all, then she didn't want to say goodbye to Xavier.

If he was still hanging around, that is. The way they'd talked? They could be friends, and she wanted that. He'd been interesting, interested in her, and had made her laugh. What more could a woman ask for? Not only that, he was gorgeous and kind. Amusing and, more importantly, he had a trait that was her kryptonite.

He was curious.

Just like she was.

Loving George didn't mean she couldn't see the potential out of hanging around a man like Xavier.

It didn't make her blind. If anything, the fact she could sense potential spoke loudly when George was sitting here, a hangdog expression on his chops, telling her he loved her. But that love kind of came with the desire to fuck her with his brother. It was conditional. At least, it seemed that way to her addled wits, and in her mind, love should never come with conditions.

She gnawed at her bottom lip.

What had he said earlier? Edward had been screwing a woman while she'd sucked George off? Was that what they wanted from her? She gulped. Could she do that? She wasn't exactly experienced. How was she supposed to see herself in that role when she'd barely had an orgasm until last night?

"Say something, Perry," George said softly.

"Can't you just want to be in a relationship with me like a regular guy?"

George shrugged. "I do want that."

"Yeah. You just want your brother in our bedroom."

He cleared his throat, but there was a red tinge to his cheeks that surprised her. Just her saying it had his responses flaring hotly.

"Why?" she asked, curious as ever. "Why do you need that?"

Edward sighed, drawing her attention his way. "When a woman is being pleasured by two men, it's easy to overwhelm her. To drive her to a brink she won't experience alone."

They were saying that what she'd had with Xavier last night was basically the tip of the iceberg?

Her eyes widened at the prospect.

"So, it's not about your pleasure but mine?" Edward jerked his head in a yes. His eyes were dilated, and she could see he was reacting as strongly as George.

Suddenly, it became hard to breathe in the dressing room again. The small space was so clogged with pheromones, it was a wonder she wasn't choking. What were they talking about though?

Overwhelming her with pleasure until what...? She was insensate?

Was that even possible?

Feeling her throat tighten, she whispered, "Why does it excite you so much?"

George caught her eye. "Can you tell me it isn't arousing you?"

She hesitated for a long moment. "Your reactions are—" Perry broke off. "Oh."

Edward cleared his throat. "I'd like to get to know you, Perry. See what George sees. I can feel the potential here. Can you tell me you don't?"

She stared at him, saw the tension on his face, and wanted to sigh at the sight of all that male beauty being aimed her way. Should she be questioning her good luck? Or her sanity?

What woman could turn down two hotties when they wanted to arouse her so much, she was nothing but a limp mess in bed?

And when those two hotties were princes? Wasn't that like topping the cake with a crown, not just a cherry?

Was she insane to say, "Yes?"

Maybe she was. Maybe the fairies had come and stolen her brain cells after a night in Xavier's bed.

She just knew that the way he looked at her, the way they *both* looked at her, was something she'd be a fool to discard. And Edward was right. That potential wasn't something she could throw away.

Xavier included.

GEORGE AND EDWARD approached their father's study in tangent.

Though he'd spoken only to Edward, when George had discovered their father had cancelled the morning's meetings, he'd wanted to join too.

Even if joining meant leaving Perry alone for a while.

Alone to think. To process. To change her mind.

Edward had waited outside George's room while he went in to change into a pair of jeans and a tee.

A few minutes later, and he'd rejoined his brother, not exactly dressed to impress, but with more decency than a bedsheet.

"What do you think this is about?" he asked.

"I don't know," Edward told him, his ignorance genuine. George knew his older brother too well not to discern his lies; so he knew that Edward was truly unsure.

"Are you concerned?"

Edward hesitated, his stride faltering a second. "A little."

"Are you concerned about Perry?"

Edward cut him a glance. "A lot."

Nodding, he murmured, "Understandable. I was as surprised as she was when you came into her dressing room." He cleared his throat. "What happened?"

"I saw Xavier."

The simple answer was remarkably complicated. "Me too. I had a similar reaction."

He'd meant it when he'd told Perry that his intention hadn't been to share his predilections with her for a while. But Xavier's presence in her bed had upped the ante, meaning he had to leapfrog ahead too fast, too soon.

It came as no surprise at all that Edward had felt the same pressure.

Perry might not be Edward's type, but there wasn't a man alive who would fail to be charmed by her utterly.

Especially since she was blind to those charms. She could have had a menagerie of men traipsing at her feet if she'd noticed them. But that was something Perry was incapable of doing.

Her head was in the clouds. Her work or her hobbies. Never on a man, and males, being the fragile creatures they were, soon withered and disappeared at her inattention. George, not being particularly fragile in nature, had persevered and had discovered the best friend a man could ever hope for wrapped up in the tiny curves of a pocket rocket from Tennessee.

He'd never intended to date her at first though. She wasn't the one night-stand kind of woman, and when he'd arrived in America, with Edward's rejection of any future trysts firmly in his head, one-night stands had all he'd been willing to entertain.

Then, friendship had blossomed over the years into a love so strong, he'd known that he'd have to act on it.

"I don't want you to hurt her, Edward," George said softly, a few feet away from their father's study. "You don't have to do this. I'll be with her without you. I just know she'll make you happy, too."

Though some brothers were jealous of one another, envious of the other's possessions or such nonsense, that had never been an issue between the two of them.

Maybe because there was enough of an age gap for there to never have been any bitterness over parental affection. Or maybe because they knew the world outside these walls was filled with jackals, and that trusting someone who lived inside the circus was easier than anything else.

Either way, George had only ever wanted the best for Edward, and knew his brother felt the same.

Edward's life was filled with more duty than George's. More chores and tasks. There were more expectations, and he shared a burden with their father that George wasn't expected to carry.

For that reason, he'd always wanted Edward to find his happiness where it could be found... it was why he was willing to share Perry.

The only woman he'd ever loved. And all because he knew she'd make them both happy.

A fanciful notion, perhaps, but not to him. It was a belief. Resolute and irrefutable in his mind.

"You know we'll have to say she's my partner, don't you?"

Edward's low voice caught George's attention, but aside from a nod, he revealed no other emotion.

He wasn't a fool. He'd known that when he'd made the suggestion. Still, his pride didn't have to like it, even if he understood and accepted it.

"You're okay with that?"

George heaved out a sigh. "What do you think? I'm not going to do cartwheels about it, Edward, but I know the score."

His parents might pressure him to marry at some point, but an heir from him wasn't as imperative as Edward's need for a child and a wife.

He could live his life single, if he so chose—parental disapproval aside, that is.

Edward couldn't.

He had a duty to fulfil. A duty that, if things worked as well as George believed they could, Perry would share.

Edward shook his head. "I don't understand why you're doing this, George. Not when you love her."

He told Edward the truth, knowing his brother could accept no less. "Because she can make us happy."

"Happiness... you've always been obsessed with that." He sighed wearily.

"And you've never been obsessed enough with it," George immediately retorted. "What was that hideous decision to marry yourself to a woman like Arabella about? Punishment? We both knew from the start you'd be a disaster together."

Edward's jaw flexed. "Now isn't the time to talk about my dead wife."

"No? There's never a time. She was your wife. In name only. She didn't love you, and you didn't love her. You could love Perry, Edward. She's so easy to love."

"Love has never been something I'm interested in."

"You think I wasn't the same? You think I didn't believe love was bullshit?" George grunted. "I've seen more catty bullshit from courtiers than I ever believed possible. They wrecked any dreams I might have ever had for romance. But Perry changed all that. You'll see once you get to know her."

He was sure about that. Had absolute faith that Perry's rather offbeat character would capture his brother's heart.

And truth was, he hoped for nothing less than that.

Edward sighed. "We'll talk about this later."

George just shrugged. "Sure."

CHAPTER EIGHT

THE PROSPECT of facing Xavier had been enough to make her feel nauseated. But in the end, she hadn't had to worry about it. There'd been a note left on her bed, a precise scrawl that spoke of a scientist, as well as someone who'd been taught that neat penmanship was important.

One of my experiments almost exploded, Perry. I'm sorry to leave, but here's my cell phone number. I look forward to hearing from you. Maybe we can talk about ethanol explosions the next time we meet up?

Of course, the prospect of that filled her with delight. She could talk to George about anything. Well, anything other than science. Still, was it wise to see Xavier?

Wise, no, but apparently, she'd left her brain back in the States. Her wisdom too.

Not only had her best friend propositioned her with an offer that would probably make most porn stars blush, she'd actually accepted.

Questions about wisdom were definitely off the cards, because here she was. Three days later, a coffee date arranged with the man who'd rocked her world two nights before.

She took a seat in the coffee shop where she'd been directed to sit.

Perry had arrived five minutes earlier than when they'd agreed and had found two bodyguards waiting to chauffeur her to the table they'd selected for their date.

Dead on the hour, Xavier arrived. He wore a baseball cap and shades, and actually managed to blend in rather well, thanks to a ratty pair of jeans and a hoodie that made him look like a regular Joe.

When he strode in, he looked around. Not for her, but his bodyguards. Some kind of communication went down, but it was done through body language as his lips didn't budge an inch, and he used that to discern her location at the back of the coffee shop in a booth that sheltered them pretty well from sight.

He saw her, and his lips curved into a smile that had butterflies dancing in her belly. She wasn't sure what to do with her hands, so she laid them out on the table as she waited for him to approach.

"Hey," she greeted.

His smile was warm. "Hey yourself." He hovered at her side of the booth, leaned over and pressed a kiss to her cheek.

Before she could decide whether or not to move her head, to let him press a kiss to her lips or not, he'd already moved. Rounding the booth, he took a seat opposite her, sliding in in a way that pulled his hoodie taut against his lean length.

She'd touched that. All of him had been against her. His hard tautness had pushed her into the mattress, and his cock had been inside her, making her feel things no woman could ever forget.

Maybe he saw the heat in her eyes, because his smile turned wicked. "You'll have to stop looking at me like that, Perry," he chided softly, but his own gaze started to glint with wickedness too. "You'll give me ideas."

She licked suddenly dry lips. "Well, we wouldn't want that."

His grin was fleeting. "Minx."

She'd never been a minx in her life, but she liked the fact he thought she was. Now, she just had to make sure she lived up to it.

"I didn't expect to hear from you if I'm being honest," he murmured after a waitress had popped up to take their orders.

His bluntness should have come as no surprise. They were scientists, after all. Dealing in cold, hard facts day in and day out. It changed people, having to live so frigidly with words.

"I wasn't sure if I should, but I wanted to."

"Well, that changes things," he said.

"It does?"

"It does. Wanting to see me again can only be a good thing, surely?"

It depended… when George found out, he'd undoubtedly be hurt, and Edward would likely be angry.

Was that worth a coffee date with a man she didn't know in any way other than biblically?

And even if George and Edward weren't happy at her having coffee with their cousin, they didn't own her. She wasn't their peon.

"May I ask you a question?"

"Sure," she said, shrugging her shoulders. "I don't have to answer, right?"

He chuckled. "True." Xavier fell silent when the waitress came with her latte and his Americano. She also laid out a croque monsieur and a palmier for Xavier. "Are Edward and George wanting to share you?"

On the brink of pouring sugar into her coffee, she nearly knocked the tall glass mug over. Only his quick reflexes righted the beaker and with barely a drop spilled.

"Excuse me?" she asked, her voice a croak.

She knew, from her cheeks alone, she'd given the game away. Never mind her clumsiness and squeaky voice.

Jesus.

She'd need to get better at hiding in plain sight. Well, if she was going to go through with this crazy scenario, that is. She still hadn't decided, and it wasn't like her to be so indecisive.

In her defense, few women were ever propositioned by two men. And by two princes? Yeah, that was more of a never. She figured she deserved a moment to catch her breath.

Xavier's lips curled as he murmured, "I'll take that as a yes." He dosed his own small coffee cup with sugar, and then reached for the cutlery to start on his croque monsieur. "I thought they'd stopped doing that."

"You knew?" she asked, voice low as she looked around them, but the booths behind and in front of them were empty, save for Xavier's bodyguards, and most of the café's patrons were up front, not in the back.

"I did. Of course."

"Of course?" she squeaked. "Is it like a national secret that everyone knows or something?"

Xavier huffed out a laugh, finished chewing a piece of bread, then answered, "No. But we were close before George left for the States and Edward married. Very close."

Her eyes widened. "Did you share too?"

Never in her life had 'share' felt like such a dirty, dirty word, but in this context, it took on a whole different kind of connotation.

He shook his head. "No. But I knew what they were into. Knew some of the women they did it with. They were good at hiding it, and they never let things end sourly with their partners, so they were always content to keep the secret."

The world's best kept secret, huh.

She pursed her lips, wondering how much money it had taken to keep their fetish quiet.

Xavier eyed her. "You're not their type," he told her, somewhat brutally, she thought with a huff.

"No? Apparently, their type has changed then."

He smirked. "I said you weren't their type, not that they didn't have good taste."

That stopped her feathers from bristling. "Why are you asking me this?"

"Because I'm curious. After what happened the other day, with George storming into the bedroom the way he did..." He shrugged. "I'll be honest. If I'd known you were his, I wouldn't have approached you."

"I wasn't his then, and nor am I now," she said with another huff. "I'm my own person."

He caught her eye. "You know exactly what I mean."

She did, so she just took a sip of her latte.

"Do you love him?"

She nodded.

"Then why did you sleep with me?"

"Because I didn't know how he felt for me. He decided the morning after sleeping with you was the time to tell me that."

Xavier frowned. "That was the first time he told you how he felt about you?"

"Yes. Perfect timing, no?"

He rubbed his chin. "You know we connected, don't you?"

She swallowed, keeping her attention on her cup, not daring to lift her gaze to look him in the eye. "I know."

He let out a sigh, and she could tell he was relieved at her admission. "I wasn't sure if you'd try to lie to me about it."

She hunched her shoulders, wondering what she was doing here, then wondering when her life had turned into some kind of soap opera. X-rated, of course.

Swallowing thickly, she murmured, "I don't know what to do, Xavier."

He reached over and grabbed her chin, urging her to look up at him. "Do you want to talk about it?"

She bit her lip. "Where could we go?"

"My car? It's only around the corner."

"Finish your food first. No need to waste it."

He laughed a little. "Conservationist to your bones, huh?"

She grinned, finally feeling like she was on level ground, because conservationism was as important to her as her own love life.

Both were, sadly, equally as complicated.

He finished up his croque monsieur in a few bites and took his coffee like it was a shot. Her latte had cooled enough for her to drink the majority of it.

He picked up the palmier, the sugary, crisp puff pastry wrapped in a napkin, and motioned her with his hand. "Come on. Let's get out of here."

She frowned. "What about the bill?"

"One of my guards will pay."

Her eyes widened. "Wow. Don't you carry cash or something?"

He snickered like the idea was a crazy one. "No. Not usually."

She edged out of the booth and let him tuck her hand through his arm as they stepped out of the shop.

As they moved, she knew the coffee shop's patrons' attentions were on them. Not because they realized who Xavier was, but because they were the odd couple.

She hadn't known what to wear for coffee with a duke, so she'd worn a business outfit George had picked for her. A neat, tailored skirt, a bright silky cerise shirt, and low-slung flats she could just—only just—walk in.

In comparison to his kind of slouchy look, they were a definite mismatch.

As they headed outside, a slight movement caught her attention. She wasn't sure what it was. Maybe the glint of light against a key? Something tiny like that, but she saw the three men on the street.

Dressed in innocuous black suits, earpieces in their ears and shades on their eyes, they somehow managed to fit in and stand out at the same time.

Veronia's capital, Madela, was as cosmopolitan as Paris or London. Hippies walked side by side with suits, chic businesswomen sat on benches homeless people had been sleeping on earlier that day...

The city sprawl was as glossy as New York, but here, there were a heaping mound of super rich who enjoyed the fact Veronia was a tax haven. She'd never seen as many sports cars or as many Rolexes on people who looked ordinary.

It was kind of cool, actually.

"My guards," Xavier murmured as he guided her down a street where a black sedan was hovering.

"You have five guards?"

Xavier shrugged. "I'm a rich man. Third in line to the throne. Plus..."

She cocked a brow at him when he fell silent. "Plus?"

"A lot of Veronians don't appreciate some of my recent experiments."

She scowled at him. "Why not?"

"We're a modern country, but sometimes, we just don't like change." He shrugged it off, then opened the back door to his car. As she slid in, she realized there was a privacy screen between them and the driver.

When Xavier rounded the car and got in beside her, she pointed to it. "How good is that thing?"

"Good enough I need a microphone to tell Dustin where he needs to take me." He demonstrated, pressing a button and murmuring, "Dustin, can you take us to the castle?"

"Sure thing, sir." That came through a speaker next to her head and made her jolt in surprise.

"Why are we going back there?" she asked with a pout.

"Because that's where you're staying," he teased. "What the movies don't show you is that when you want to go anywhere, it has to be planned a good twenty-four to thirty-six hours in advance."

"Because your security has to check it out?"

He nodded. "Fact of life."

"It seems so safe here," Perry said with a scowl, rubbing her arms which, through the silk, felt chilly.

"It is. But we have to take precautions." He cleared his throat. "Plus, the castle is secure."

"Why aren't you taking me to your estate?"

His eyes flashed. "Do you think that's wise?"

Her shoulders hunched. "I guess not."

"Exactly." He blew out a breath. "We're just about as private as we can get, Perry. If you want to talk, now's the time to do it."

The last three days had been... difficult.

She'd needed to talk this out, but the person she usually spoke to—George—was involved, so she'd felt verbally trapped.

The idea of being able to talk to someone who knew about the brothers' predilections was remarkably freeing, though she was still aware of the need to be cautious.

"Are you friends with them now?"

Xavier blinked at her question. "I speak with George twice a week no matter where he is in the world. Edward, less so. We usually meet up instead."

"What do you do when you meet up?" she asked, curious. George had never mentioned his cousin to her. She'd known of Xavier, in an offhand way. Not to look at, but by name. She'd have known more if George had made her privy to their conversations.

His lips twitched. "Sure you want to know?"

"If it involves titty bars, no, I don't," she snapped, her temper appearing out of nowhere.

He smirked. "It involves a basketball court, Perry." Xavier reached out and cupped her chin, and when she let out a shaky breath, he murmured, "You're as tightly wound as a spring. "

She closed her eyes. "I feel like I've stepped into a bad porn movie."

"I can see why you'd feel that way."

"Are you laughing at me?" she demanded, eyes popping open to study him through narrowed slits.

He grinned. "A little."

She scowled at him. "It isn't funny. This is all coming out of nowhere, dammit. Everything is on its head, and I hate it. George has always been my confidante, but now, he's the reason I'm so confused."

"Tell me what's happening. Have they approached you in the past couple of days?"

She rolled her eyes. "What do you think?"

Edward hadn't, but every meal she'd had with him and his family, he'd practically devoured her with his eyes, instead of his dinner.

Jesus, what that man could do with a look.

She'd thought he was handsome before. Now, he was deadly. She'd never realized it was possible to expire from the promise in a man's eye, but she was getting close to an expiration date of her own.

George wasn't pressing her, but it had been pre-arranged that he visit with her. She'd seen Veronia's main dam yesterday, and this morning, had spoken with some key personnel in their government's Environmental Agency.

George had been at her side throughout, but nothing was the same.

The easygoing flow of conversation that had always been between them, even if there were chunks of silence as they pondered whatever was on their minds, seemed to have disappeared.

More than anything, she found she was mourning that.

It scared her.

He scared her.

His wants. His needs. His love.

"I've loved him for six years," she told Xavier shakily. "I met him on the Harvard campus. I was meeting a friend for lunch who was taking the same class as him, and when I saw him leave the study hall, I was amazed by him. He took my breath away."

"Did you meet then, or did you just love him then?"

She peeked at him. "The latter. Even though I know it's stupid to say that. I guess it was a crush, but it didn't feel like that. My friend saw more of me that semester than she had all the year before because I kept popping up to meet her so I could see him." Perry pulled a face. "Stalker alert."

Xavier chuckled, revealing strong, white teeth. Not American white, where teeth were almost blue with bleach. But European white. More natural, less superficial.

She'd noticed that she could discern Americans from a group of people by their dental hygiene alone since arriving in Europe.

"He always did have the ladies panting after him."

She glowered at Xavier. "I did not pant."

He snorted. "Sure."

Huffing, Perry carried on, "I was waiting for Jessie, and George came out earlier than intended. He fell over, and I realized he was sick."

"His guards weren't there?"

"George doesn't have many guards. Not as many as you."

Xavier grunted. "Wait until I tell Philippe that. Jesus, he's always avoided his security detail."

She shrugged. "I don't know anything about that. I just know I've seen maybe one guard tailing him. Not five like you have."

Xavier pursed his lips. "Never mind. What was wrong with him?"

"He had the flu of all things." She shook her head at the memory—Perry had been so astonished that something like the flu could fell such a man. "I helped him up, but he was already punch drunk, and I got him into a cab. He passed out by the time I was ready to tell the driver his address, so I took him back to my place."

Xavier's eyes widened. "You took a strange man into your apartment?"

She winced. "I know. Bad, right? But I was just… it all came as a shock, and there was no way he was faking being ill."

"Why didn't you contact the campus security? They'd have known where to take him, surely?"

She huffed again. "Look, you do know this was six years ago, right? I know I was stupid, and I wouldn't do it again, but because I did do it, I found the best friend I've ever had, so I can't exactly complain about my stupidity."

Xavier's horrified look said he begged to differ.

She rolled her eyes. "Anyway, when George woke up after two days of being sick everywhere and lots of other grossness, he thought I'd kidnapped him." Her lips curved into a grin at the memory. "It took me ages to calm him down."

"I'll bet," Xavier said dryly.

"Nearly called the cops on me when I gave him the phone and told him to call whoever he wanted to get out of there."

"You're lucky he didn't."

She scoffed at that. "My apartment is small."

The non-sequitur had Xavier frowning. "So?"

"So, when he got up, he saw the huge pile of laundry on the floor and draped all over the furniture. He saw where I'd been sleeping—on an armchair—and…" She shrugged. "He seemed to realize he'd been sick."

"I'd like to know how we can fast forward six years to him declaring his love for you in a bedsheet."

She shrugged again. "That I can't answer. He left my apartment that day, and I was sure I'd never see him again. He was kind of mad that I hadn't called anyone, but to be honest, everything happened so quickly, and he was puking all over the place that I was so busy, I didn't have much time to think about anything other than helping him."

"You paint a pretty picture."

She snorted. "I do my best."

"I don't understand why his guards didn't cause an international incident to hunt him down." He scratched his forehead. "I never heard anything about him going missing for a short time."

"I think he pulled stunts like that a lot. Plus, there was a time when he fired them all."

"You're telling me the guards still didn't trail after him?" He cocked a brow, disbelief written plainly on his face. "You don't know what royal security is like, if you think that."

"No. I guess not. But I think he used to take advantage of his new guards and would sneak out. Plus, to be fair to them, I think he made a habit of sequestering himself in women's apartments... I don't think they'd have found anything out of the ordinary in his behavior. For a while, he was a bit of a man whore by the sounds of it." She jerked a shoulder. "Anyway, the next day, he sent over some flowers. Did that for a week. Then, he arrived at my place and asked me out for coffee. We've been hanging out ever since."

Xavier's lips twitched. "That has to be the most bizarre way of meeting somebody I've ever heard."

"Story of my life," she admitted ruefully. "You don't even want to know how I met my ex."

"Oh hell, you can't say that and not tell me."

She shot him a cheeky grin. "If you're a good boy, maybe I'll tell you one day."

He sighed. "Meanie."

A laugh escaped her, and Jesus, it felt good to laugh. It felt even better to remember how she and George had met, and how their friendship had developed out of a strange genesis.

It reminded her of the good and the bad times. Of the love that her crush had developed into.

George was offering himself, his love. And she wanted that, she really did. Perry craved it with a desperation that made her wince, but the truth was, George's love seemed to come with ties.

He didn't just want her love. He wanted her to love his brother too.

"Why would George want to share me if he loves me?" she asked quietly, turning her head to stare out the window. Veronia was beautiful on a dull day, but in the sun, Madela gleamed like a new penny.

Not that her attention was on the rolling fields that appeared once they'd made their way out of the city limits and back onto the road that would take them to the castle.

No, her mind was on George. As it had been for the past seventy-two hours.

Was there something wrong with her? Something that made him think she'd be so desperate to be with him that he could get her to do anything he wanted?

Xavier reached for her hand and squeezed it on her lap. "George and Edward are far closer than you could imagine."

She blew a raspberry. "No shit."

His chuckle was rueful. "Yes, no shit. But I meant something else."

Perry turned away from the window, and searching Xavier's gaze, frowned. "What are you talking about?"

"When George was three, he was very sick. Measles. It should have been nothing, should have been routine, but he almost died. Edward was ten at the time," he murmured, pursing his lips. "I was eight. We're the heirs to the throne, so as measles is contagious, we weren't allowed to visit him."

She stiffened. "What are you talking about?"

"We live to different rules in more ways than just wearing a crown and having fancy titles, Perry. Edward and George can never fly on the same plane, because if Edward's plane crashes and he dies, George can take over as crown prince."

"That's horrible."

He jerked a shoulder. "That's life. For us, anyway." He licked his lips. "Edward hadn't been fond of his brother. What ten-year-old is happy to share his parents' already limited attention? He had to share Marianne and Philippe with a country... a baby brother was too much. And they were delighted too, because Marianne had found it very hard to carry a baby to term. She'd miscarried twice before Edward, and twice more before George appeared—of course, at the time, I didn't know any of this.

"All I knew was George was sick, and from the hushed whispers of the staff, they thought he was going to die.

"Like I said, Edward didn't like George from the get-go. But I told him what I overheard from the stewards. I think I told him more because of my own shock than because I thought Edward wanted, or even needed, to know. He didn't really care, not that Edward was very cruel or cold, but because we're raised to be so stoic—to hold any and all emotions inside, he just didn't react the way normal children did. Except that day."

The leather creaked underneath Xavier as he shifted backwards into his chair. His eyes were faraway, as if remembering that day in extreme detail. "Edward started crying, I couldn't believe it. But once he started crying, I started crying. The next thing I knew, we were plotting ways to sneak into

George's room every night." Xavier shifted his attention back to Perry, his gaze warm.

Smirking, Xavier shook his head. "Aunt Marianne found us in the morning, curled up next to George. After that, whether you want to attribute it to us or not, George took a turn for the better. And Edward... well, he had a tantrum every time they tried to get him to leave George. Screamed like hell.

"Once George was better, they both did it. Couldn't bear to leave each other's side."

"That's so sweet," she whispered softly, not wanting to break the hazy air surrounding Xavier as he imparted tales of a past she knew George would never share with her.

"It was, I guess. But it was just the start. They got closer after that. We all did. I was their cousin, but we were like brothers. Then, when George was five and Edward was twelve, their nanny..." His mouth worked, but no words slipped out.

His horror, less comedic now and definitely genuine, bled into the small backseat. It choked her, made her slide across to sit beside him. His hand reached for hers, and his grip was tight. "Their nanny's partner used his connection with her to... George and Edward were abducted. They were gone for three days."

A gasp escaped her. "I never heard anything about that!"

His laughter was grim. "We could never let a story like that leak. I was only ten, but I remember it. It was horrible. My parents had to move from our estate and into the castle. We were on lockdown because I was suddenly the heir to the throne." She saw him bite the inside of his cheek. "That goddamn throne. Like it's the only thing that fucking matters." His nostrils flared, his outrage evident. "It felt like a lifetime. They were gone so long and yet, barely any time at all in the end."

Silence fell between them as she collected her thoughts, and he was left to think back to that horrendous time when his cousins had been snatched away from their family.

Her mouth felt dry as she croaked out, "They were closer after that?"

His nod was more of a jerk of his head. "Edward changed. Became moody. Angry. He was very, very mad. All the time. When he became a teenager, it just got worse. He rebelled constantly, and Uncle Philippe and Aunt Marianne were at their wits' end. But there was nothing they could do. Nothing anyone could do. Then, George turned seventeen, something happened. Something changed."

Her eyes widened as she recalled what George had told her. At seventeen, he'd come across his brother with a woman, and Edward had invited him to share her.

"He got better?"

"Better?" Xavier whistled. "It was like he was a different person."

"George told me that he started sharing women with Edward when he was seventeen." Xavier didn't seem all that surprised by that, so she carried on, "Why would that calm Edward down?"

Xavier let out a small laugh. "Perry, you don't know my world yet. You don't know the rules or the regulations. Nobody does, until they're in the inner circle. I just told you that my cousin was dying, but we couldn't see him just in case we caught the sickness too. We live in a different world to yours. Where children can be kidnapped, and all that seems to matter is a throne. No one wants it. Not really. I certainly don't, and yet, if George and Edward hadn't come back to us, I'd be waiting to be king one day. All that mattered was my family, but to everyone outside the family who knew what was happening, it was all about securing the lineage…

"When your world is like that, Perry, don't you think sharing a woman, even if it's in secret, is like the ultimate rebellion? Don't you think being a part of something that, if it ever came out, would rock the very foundations of the goddamn establishment you've been forced to live around… well, don't you think that's one of the most liberating things a man can be a part of?"

When he put it like that, Perry could do no less than sigh in understanding.

She herself had had a cloistered childhood. Rebellion… Xavier was right. Nothing was sweeter.

CHAPTER NINE

GEORGE WASN'T RELIEVED when he saw Xavier's car pull up outside the palace from his mother's sitting room.

No, relief wasn't an emotion that could describe the complex mélange of feelings flooding his system.

This afternoon, when he'd gone to Perry's room and found she'd left without leaving a note, he'd thought...

Well, he wasn't sure what he'd thought.

Watching her alight from the car, seeing Xavier cup her elbow as he guided her into the palace, he had to curl his hands into fists.

"Your brother likes Perry."

His mother's words had George frowning and spinning away from the window. "So?"

The disapproval in Marianne's tone was hard to handle. Perry wasn't perfect. Nobody was. But Marianne's idea of perfection came in the form of women like Arabella, who she'd married off to Edward.

Arabella made Perry look perfect in George's eyes. It didn't matter that Perry hadn't attended a finishing school, or that she only knew how to use two forks on a table setting.

None of that crap mattered. Not where it counted.

"She's hardly appropriate," Marianne said softly, but a smile curved her lips. "Charming though. In her own way. Very..."

"American?" George supplied with a smile of his own.

Marianne laughed, the sound as charming as it had been when he'd been a little boy, completely unaware of her flaws, and when he'd thought she was a fairy princess. Of course, back when he'd been a boy, she'd been a princess. Not a queen.

"Yes, she is rather, isn't she?"

He smirked, turned back to the window.

"I thought you were interested in her, if I'm being quite truthful. Thought this visit was a pretense for us to meet her at last."

At his mother's perception, he shrugged. "She's a friend."

A friend he wanted to worship, but his mother didn't need to know that, did she?

Marianne sighed. "Sometimes, you're so like your father, I could scream."

He grinned. "I do try."

"I'll just bet you do." A huff escaped her.

"Would it bother you if she and Edward did... become friendlier?"

"After the disaster that was Arabella and his marriage, hardly," his mother scoffed, stunning the hell out of him. "But I'd have preferred someone who didn't take off her shoes upon first meeting royalty. Good God, I thought my eyes were going to pop out when I saw her toe nails." She sniffed. "At least they were pedicured, I suppose."

He spun around to gawk at her. "What do you mean the disaster that was their marriage?"

Marianne stared at him like he was a fool. "She made him miserable. I mourned the girl when she passed, and wish she was still here with us, but they were heading for a divorce. Even your father, as blind as he can be, realized that." She shrugged. "He'd already engaged someone to handle the aftermath."

"The aftermath of what?"

"When news broke, of course. Edward kept on asking us certain things, carefully trying to hide the truth." She pulled a face. "Arabella wasn't the sort to leave in peace, for however much a cold fish she was. We knew we'd have to engage the best to combat any filth she spilled."

He gaped at her. "You would have been fine with him divorcing her?"

"I'd have preferred for him to have been happy with her, but as that wasn't possible, a divorce seemed far better than having him suffer. The days of 'til death us do part' are long since passed, George."

"You don't have to tell me that. I just wasn't sure you knew it."

She rolled her eyes. "How old do you think I am?"

"Old enough to care that Edward could have an American girlfriend," he pointed out wryly.

She squinted at him. "That's different."

"How is it?" he argued.

"She's totally underprepared in all ways. There's no way she could be happy with the kind of life she'd have to lead here. Hers has not been a life of service and duty."

His jaw clenched because, though it killed him, he knew his mother was right.

"She cares. A lot. Her duty might not come in the shape ours does, but she cares about the earth, about the environment."

Marianne winced. "I suppose the fact you're fighting me on this suggests Edward is very keen on the girl." She sighed. "A mother knows, I suppose." She tapped her nails against the armrest. "I was just hoping you wanted her instead."

A mother knows...

She wasn't exactly wrong.

"She's a friend, mother. That's it." He turned his back on her. "And if she makes Edward happy, then that's all that matters to me."

Marianne just hummed under her breath, then, after he carried on peering out the window, wondering exactly when Xavier and Perry had agreed to meet, and what the reasons were for such a meeting, Marianne asked, "Is there a reason you're visiting me today? Or is it just to glower at the garden?"

He spun on his heel, embarrassed that she was right. The roses had been on the receiving end of some rather nasty looks in the past ten minutes or so.

"Is it wrong to want to visit with you?"

"No. But you could try sitting down so we can call for tea."

He grunted. "I don't want tea."

"Coffee then," she retorted. "I'm certain you weren't this difficult before you left for college."

He grinned. "I was. You were just used to it."

"Distance makes the heart grow fonder, not more irascible."

He grimaced as he took the side of the sofa nearest her. As he settled, he murmured, "I missed you, *Maman*."

Her eyes were twinkling as she replied, "I missed you too, child. But I don't know why you took a seat. The bell won't ring itself, you know?"

His lips twitched as he went to press the bell that would have a maid coming to attend them.

Life at the palace was surprisingly hard to acclimate to.

Staff on hand to attend his every whim, ears constantly around to listen in on every conversation. During his childhood, he'd never noticed it. The staff, as mean as it sounded, became a part of the furniture. But having been away from it for so long, it was cloistering.

Suffocating.

How Edward had stood it all these years, without even a taste of freedom, George wasn't sure. But after he left his mother's sitting room ninety minutes later, well fed and watered on her favorite Danish pastries and coffee, he had to commend Edward for his patience.

When he and Perry hung out, they might be interrupted twice. His cell ringing and hers. Marianne had been called away twice, had had to deal with a call she'd taken at her desk, and had spoken to one of the staff about a gala the palace was holding next week.

Maman was right in the fact that Perry hadn't been raised for a life such as this.

Was it selfish to bring her into it? Into a world that was completely alien to anything she'd ever known? Where considerations she'd never even have contemplated in the past were suddenly priorities?

He rubbed his chin, heading toward Edward's study in the west wing of the palace.

He'd seen little of his brother over the past few days. Not altogether surprising, considering his schedule and the one George and Perry were adhering to, thanks to her research project.

Still, he felt certain Edward was avoiding him, and that would never do. Not when Perry's happiness was at stake.

After years of pushing his desires aside, of pretending they didn't even exist, what had changed, and so swiftly?

It had to be Perry. Perhaps she'd stunned Edward as much as she'd always stunned George? But he didn't know that for certain, and he intended to find out.

If his brother hurt Perry in even the tiniest of ways, he'd have George to damn well answer to.

EDWARD STARED OUT THE WINDOW, wondering why fate had prompted him to look out at that exact moment to behold Perry alighting from Xavier's car.

The hand his cousin held to Perry's elbow had his own fisting at his side.

She smiled up at Xavier, laughing as he murmured something to her. Edward's left eye twitched at the sight of her so free and at ease when she barely glanced at him, and if she did, she did so mournfully. Ill at ease.

His jaw worked, but he purposely put the situation and her from his mind as he returned to his desk. He had a lot of paperwork to handle, and a meeting at four as a deadline.

When a knock sounded at the door, he didn't bother looking up, just called out, "Come in."

"Edward, I need to talk to you."

The sound of his brother's voice had him scowling as he raised his head. "I don't have time, George."

"Then you're going to have to make time. You've been avoiding me."

Had he? Edward didn't think he had. "If I have, it's unintentional. I have a lot of work to do. Life doesn't stop just because you visit and bring a woman you want to upturn our world with to the castle."

George narrowed his eyes as he stepped further into Edward's office, taking an uninvited seat in the tubular steel design.

Unlike the rest of the palace, Edward's office was to his specifications. He'd ripped out the ancient fittings, much to his family's horror, and made this place a modern haven.

It was the one place where he didn't have to sit down on chairs that had once supported ten kings or look at family portraits that were older than some nations.

The walls were a blessed white. His desk was glass. The furniture was white leather—a sofa and two armchairs for guests he didn't wish to visit with at his desk. Visitor's chairs opposite him were tubular steel propped together with black leather.

He had inbuilt filing systems so as not to mar the minimalist nature of the room. Wires, too, were things of the past thanks to miracles his interior designer had wrought with an engineer.

Everywhere was sleek, white, elegant.

This place was his respite from over the top gilt and Renaissance art.

There really was such a problem as too much of a good thing.

The chair George sat in bounced with his momentum, and his brother murmured, "You know we need to talk."

"We really don't."

"You laid down the gauntlet the other day when you came barging in to Perry's dressing room."

Edward snorted. "The gauntlet? That's a little melodramatic, George, don't you think?"

His brother glowered at him. "You inferred you wanted Perry. I want to make sure you're not setting her up for hurt. I'll have her myself, Edward. I love her, but I think she can make us both happy."

Edward's jaw flexed. "You can't know that. I don't know that. I hardly know the woman."

"And yet, you stormed into her room and made it clear you were interested in her."

There was no denying that he had, in fact, done that.

Edward sighed and sitting back in his low-slung white desk chair, rocked a little as he ran a hand through his hair.

Could he say he hadn't known what he was thinking?

Maybe with someone else, but not George.

George knew him and knew him well. Even with many years of distance having separated them, no one knew him better than George. Except maybe Xavier. A fact that didn't escape Edward's attention, nor made him want to punch his cousin any less for making Perry smile.

"I reacted rashly."

"So, what? You regret what you said?"

"Did I say that?" he spat, glaring at George. "I just said I acted rashly. That I should have had more caution."

"That's because you acted on instinct."

George sounded far too satisfied for Edward's own good. "Don't look so smug."

His brother shrugged. "Why? I'm feeling smug. You buried your instincts away when you married Arabella. It's about time you started living again, dammit."

"I live. See?" He sucked in a breath. "I breathe."

George rolled his eyes. "You know how to party."

Edward huffed out a laugh, then his smile faded as George's presence here made him question things he truly didn't have time to question. With a sigh, he murmured, "I heard you arguing. I didn't think anything of it, until she yelled again, and I wanted to make sure everything was alright. Seeing Xavier there, well, it changed things."

"You're preaching to the converted," George pointed out. "You don't think I already know how you felt?"

"You love her, George. I don't."

"Not yet," his brother said softly, soft enough to make Edward's throat close. "But you will."

The prophetic tone pissed Edward off. George always had been an arrogant bastard. When it came down to it, Edward was often the one wondering exactly who the elder brother was in the family, when George always seemed to have all the fucking answers.

Agitated at George's prediction, he demanded again, "Why are you doing this, George? Why not just be with her yourself?" He knew he'd already asked, but Edward just couldn't compute why someone would put the woman they loved through the ringer. If Perry had known the score from the start, then he'd be able to get his head around it. But she hadn't. She was a relative innocent. And that was when he thought about life in the royal sphere, sex notwithstanding. He scowled at his brother. "She can't be happy being mine. You and I know that. There's too much of a chasm between her current job and that of being the girlfriend of the Crown Prince of Veronia."

He said girlfriend, but they both knew he meant wife.

Veronia was a little more antiquated than the rest of Europe when it came to the romantic lives of their royals.

They expected them to live like nuns and monks, and when a girlfriend was outed to the press, the people waited for news that a marriage was on the cards.

With a foreigner for a girlfriend, such expectations would hit soon.

"Perry needs me," his brother said softly, plucking at the crease on his trousers. "She probably needs me far less than I need her. Some days, I swear to Christ, she's the only reason I get out of bed on a morning. When I'm down or just feeling pressured at work, she's my breath of fresh air.

"But I know I'm that for her too. She tells me everything. I'm her confidante, her best friend. Yes, life in the spotlight isn't ideal. And I wish to hell it would never have to be an issue, but I wish that for more than just her, Edward. I wish it for you too. For me. For Mother and Father, Xavier as well. I wouldn't wish this life on our enemy."

"So, why wish it on the woman you love?" Edward retorted with a snap.

"Because with Perry, this life won't be misery."

"That sounds very fucking selfish, George. You're bringing her into this shitstorm for our benefit, but what happens when she burns out? When it gets too much for her?"

"It won't. I'll make sure it won't. Perry will have us. She'll have the pair of us as her support and as her shield. We'll make sure she never regrets being with us. I'll spend the rest of my goddamn life making up for the fact we live in the spotlight." George shot him a look. "Why settle for being happy when the three of us could be delirious? *Together?*"

Edward grimaced. "Delirious? You always did exaggerate." He scratched his forehead, trying to process his brother's words. In many ways, George was an idealist. That blazed through his comments like a fire. "There is no being happy in this world of ours, George. Haven't you realized that yet?"

George narrowed his eyes. "If I didn't think you were being a tad dramatic, I'd say you were depressed."

"I'm not depressed." He gritted his teeth. "I'm a realist."

"Why deny something that could lighten the misery then?" George argued. "Perry will certainly do that. She makes me happy."

"You're you. You're not me."

"What? Because you're crown prince, it's impossible to find someone who won't turn that frown upside down?" he scoffed. "Bullshit. Arabella burned you. I know that. A lot of shit has happened before and since, but there's no reason whatsoever to turn your back on someone who could make you happy."

"Just because she works miracles on you, doesn't mean she can do the same for me."

"How do you know? Have you spoken to her?"

"Not outside of meals."

"Why not? Don't you think it's cruel to have gone to her the way you did, then to ignore her?"

"I suppose, but I've been busy." He sought George's gaze. "Genuinely. There's a situation with Monaco." He rubbed his forehead again. "An international incident."

"Inciting?" George asked with a scowl. "We're not going to war with them, are we? Or are our tax evaders and theirs about to square off on the football pitch?"

"Of course not, but it requires me to lick a lot of diplomatic arse."

George grimaced. "Exactly."

Edward sighed. "Plus, there's what Father told us."

"That does change things, I suppose."

"You suppose?" Edward barked. "The guards find evidence Arabella was murdered, and you only think that changes things?"

George held up a hand. "I'm sorry, I know it does."

Edward released a slow, aggrieved breath. "Why would anyone target her, George? If not to get to me? To us?"

"I don't know," George said softly. "They'll figure it out. They always do."

"It's taken them three years to uncover this," he snarled. "What makes you think they'll find any more evidence that isn't long since buried in the past?"

"Because they managed to find this. That says a lot. Plus, if you're in danger, then this is their priority from now on. The guards aren't going to stop until you're safe."

"I'm not the one who was targeted, George."

"You're scared Perry might be caught in the crossfire."

Edward caught his brother's eye. "Aren't you?"

"No. I'm not." George shrugged at Edward's aghast expression. "I disliked Arabella. I was sorry when she got sick, and I'm sorrier still now we've found out she was murdered, but her unfortunate passing doesn't make her a great human being.

"She was a bitch. She was cold. She treated you like shit. Nobody liked her. Not really. The public were in the dark, mostly, but that was only because you'd been married for such a short time. If she'd been around longer, news would have spread about her tantrums and horrible nature. Such gossip was bound to become widespread."

"Aside from slandering her name, is there a point to this?"

George ignored Edward's snappish tone. "Yes. I'm saying that Perry is the exact opposite. She makes friends wherever she goes. Hell, her spirit animal is a Golden Retriever. She's just one of these people that others love."

"What the fuck is a spirit animal?"

George grinned. "It's the animal you embody. She says I'm a drop bear."

"A drop bear?" Edward blinked, wondering if his brother was on an acid trip.

"Yeah. She says I look pretty and cuddly like a koala, then if you piss me off, I'll bite." At Edward's confused look, he continued, "Koalas are actually aggressive. They're not cute and cuddly as you might think. But drop bears are more of an urban legend." He snorted at Edward's puzzled look. "Google it."

Edward merely sighed. "And you don't mind her thinking you're a type of legendary koala?"

"No more than she minds it when I say she's like Marley."

"Who the hell is Marley?"

"A Golden Retriever in a movie," George huffed. "Jesus, Edward. Don't watch much TV, do you?"

"Yes, George, because I have plenty of time to watch stupid movies." He patted just one of the piles of papers on his desk—one of four, each half a foot thick.

George just shrugged. "Anyway, in comparison to that barracuda, Perry isn't going to make any enemies just by breathing."

Edward clenched his jaw. He knew he should defend Arabella, but... it was hard when his brother spoke the truth. She might have been gently reared, attended the best schools in Europe, and had been friends with some of the wives of the continent's most powerful businessmen, but that didn't make her a good woman.

She had been snappish, and her treatment of the staff had made him apologize on her behalf to them countless times.

He'd been grateful when, every month, her period had come. Having a child with such a temperamental woman was his duty, but not a fate he actively wished for. Of course, with every passing month she wasn't *enceinte*, her mood swings and bad temper had only been exacerbated.

"Look, I'm going to say this again. You don't have to be with Perry. But I want you to at least try to make an effort."

"Why, George? Why is this so important to you?"

"Because the minute I make it official, the minute Mother and Father know I'm with her, that's the moment *you* can't be with her anymore. I've held off all these years because I know she's perfect for you too. I can wait a little while longer to make her mine. Being with her will make me happy, but it's never going to be as fulfilling as sharing her with you." He rubbed his temple. "Don't you think I didn't wish I was like this? That I didn't *need* this? I've made things with the woman I adore a thousand times uncomfortable, could potentially have knocked us off track and destroyed our relationship in the process, simply because I *need* this. I don't know why. I've never understood it. It's just in my blood. But..." His nostrils flared. "Xavier's waiting too. I saw him with her today. He brought her home. There's a timeline now."

Scratching his jaw, Edward nodded. "I saw too. Just happened to catch a glimpse of them coming back in his car."

George scowled. "I don't know what Perry's thinking meeting up with him. I thought she was still thinking about what we discussed."

Edward sighed. "Maybe she's burying her head in the sand like we are?"

"I'm not," George retorted. "You are. I think you should talk to her."

"I can't. Not yet." Before George could argue, he held up a hand. "I seriously have too much business to handle. But I promise, I'll talk to her soon."

The promise almost choked him, but George had put his life on hold with the woman he loved for him. Would continue to do so, if Edward just gave him the word. That George was thinking so far ahead made Edward cringe inside.

He truly expected Edward to take Perry as his own. To marry her.

Because he couldn't stop himself, he whispered, "You'd be willing to live back in the palace to stay with her? What about your life in the US?"

"I stayed as long as I did because of her." He shrugged. "When the situation with the drought cropped up, I thought about bringing her in for a consult. She truly is an expert in the field. But something happened at her lab a few months ago, and it just cemented the idea in my head."

"What happened?" Edward asked with a frown.

"Her grants suddenly came under threat."

"From whom?"

George shrugged. "It happens. There's nothing shady going on, if that's what you mean. I checked it out. It's just academic politics. If she doesn't bow and scrape enough, she can lose funding."

"So you thought bringing her here would... what? Cement her position by bringing some prestige to her name and her university's if I decided I didn't want her?"

George grinned. "You know me so well, brother."

Edward rolled his eyes. "You're a pain in my ass, George."

He winked, then got to his feet. "The feeling is mutual."

CHAPTER TEN

"PERRY."

She jolted in surprise at the silken lash of Edward's voice. Turning in her seat, she peered at him in the doorway, wondering what it was about him that put her so on edge.

George was a prince, and Xavier was a duke. They were both powerful men. Both handsome creatures that would make most male models weep in envy.

But Edward? God, there was just something about him. Something that stirred her up and scared her.

She bit her lip. "Edward," she replied, politely.

Something flickered in his eyes as he waved a hand in front of him. "May I come in?"

"Of course," she told him, though she didn't particularly want him to enter her office. Still, it wasn't like she could refuse.

He tilted his head to the side as he approached her, studying her like she'd just been studying the statistics before her. According to the data, Veronia had forty years of drinking water left.

Forty years might seem a long time, but it wasn't.

The notion that a European nation, as cosmopolitan as this one, could be without water in her lifetime was...Well, to be frank, it was terrifying. The very idea had her stomach churning with nerves, and she dealt with this kind of information on a daily basis.

Cape Town had been plagued with these woes recently, but it was Africa. Africa was hot. Most people associated Africa with drought and a lack of water. Few would even think Europe could eventually suffer similar consequences.

It wasn't exactly prejudice, just what people associated the continent with. Only southern Europe was warm, after all. The center and northern regions were frigid come winter, and barely temperate in summer.

It was an attitude that wasn't exactly fair, but perceptions weren't always just, were they?

"I've lost you without even starting to talk," Edward murmured, a wry smile on his lips as he broke into her thoughts.

She jolted. "Sorry. My mind's elsewhere."

"On your work?" He frowned at her in sudden concern, and she felt it sweep over her in a great wave. He perched his ass on the side of the desk. "The statistics aren't good, are they?"

"They couldn't be much worse, Edward, if I'm being honest."

He ran a hand through his silky hair, then placed it on the table. As he did, a welter of brochures scattered about, and she flushed. "Sorry. I'll just clear that."

He picked one up, cocked a brow at its contents. "You like butterflies?" he asked, eying the exhibit at the country's national science museum.

She cleared her throat. "They're just things I thought I could see while I'm here. In my own time, of course," she said stiffly.

He sighed. "I never doubted it, Perry." He eyed her tiredly. "Do you mind if I take a seat? I don't want to make more of a mess." He waved his hand at the chair opposite her desk.

Philippe had given her a small office just off the private quarters. It was neat and well-appointed with a desk made of walnut that gleamed—she could even see her face in it.

The moldings on the wall were gilded—she was about to die of gilt overdose—and opposite her desk was a picture window with a view of the Ansian mountain range where Xavier lived, and to her left, an honest to God Rembrandt.

She was working in an office with a Rembrandt. It beggared belief.

"Is there any way you can help us?"

"We're talking massive overhauls of infrastructure, Edward," she murmured, leaning back in her seat. Where she'd been uncomfortable a few minutes before, now she was well at ease. *This* was her world.

He was asking for her expertise, and she was more than willing to impart her knowledge to save the nation from suffering down the line.

"I'm talking trillions invested here."

He shrugged. "We're a wealthy nation, and we're discussing projects that can occur over the span of decades. We have time and the funds."

Because he was right, and she'd seen Veronia's very, very healthy GDP, she murmured, "Your sewerage system is atrocious. Your reservoirs and dams are outdated." She shrugged. "Certain parts of the country are going to be uncomfortable for a while."

His lips twitched, but his face was somber. "Uncomfortable?"

She sighed. "That's the nicest way I could think to phrase it." She rested her elbows on the armrests of her antique desk chair that came with a cushioned backrest decorated with embroidery—of a bouquet of roses.

This place wasn't to her taste at all, but she was charmed by it nonetheless.

"Have you seen our underground in the capital?"

She shook her head. "I'm due to visit next week. You're fortunate that the Romans constructed the aqueducts, as it means you can work without having to totally dig up the cities, but improvements to them over the past two thousand years would probably have been advisable," she said wryly.

"Not every part of them is Roman," he retorted, but she could see he was teasing.

"No? What's the youngest part? Two hundred years old?"

He wrinkled his nose. "It's not like other capitals are any better. I know London has a Victorian sewerage system."

She shrugged. "They're not running out of water, are they?"

He sighed. "No."

"I'll list it all in my final report. I'm still collating data, and I haven't visited half the dams and reservoirs in the nation."

He nodded. "I'm looking forward to reading it."

Her brows arched. "You'll be reading it? I thought it would go to some bored minister."

"I'll be sure to CC him a copy." When she just stared at him, he shrugged. "The family takes a heavy interest in topics such as these. We haven't handed over all our powers to the government, more's the pity in their eyes."

"George says your Prime Minister is anti-royalist."

He nodded. "He's right. But the nation isn't. They're very proud of their heritage."

She pursed her lips as she caught the bitter edge to his words.

Ever since Xavier had spoken to her of Edward's past, she'd not deny, her thoughts about the crown prince had shifted somewhat. Her curiosity burned hotly, and she'd admit, *morbidly* when it came down to what had happened to him as a child. But his intensity still disturbed her. Not in a negative way. He just set her nerves on edge, and she wasn't used to that.

Or, that's to say, men like Edward didn't usually give her the time of day, so she wasn't used to being in their spotlight.

"George seems to think I've been avoiding you. Would you agree with that?"

She blinked. "No. We see each other three times a day."

He laughed a little. "That's quite enough of me, is it?"

She was taken aback by his amusement. Perry cleared her throat. "I'm a little uncomfortable, Edward. I'm sure you'll understand why."

He leaned back into the high-backed visitor's chair. "Uncomfortable or disgusted?"

That had her brow puckering. "Disgusted? Why would I be disgusted?"

"I've shared women with my brother, Perry. Most women would find that repellent."

"Well, I don't. I'm all for living and let live."

"Just not with yourself?" he asked archly.

"I've never thought about it before," she replied, honest to the last. Hell, she'd read stuff. But *everyone* read stuff. They didn't imagine themselves in the 'act'. "It's never cropped up."

"Until now."

She nodded. "Until now." When he stayed silent, she felt like he was asking her a question she was supposed to have understood without him voicing it.

Their gazes caught and held for what seemed an eternity. His avid cerulean eyes were more blue than green when his trapped and ensnared hers, and suddenly, she felt her body temperature spike. Her heart seemed to skip a beat as her lungs burned with the need for more air than she was inhaling. Her lips began to tremble.

"It's okay," he soothed.

It was? It was okay to feel like this? To feel so overwhelmed and lost over the sudden appearance of not one, not two, but three men in her life?

She raised a shaky hand and covered her face.

"Do you love my brother?" he asked softly.

"Almost as long as I've known him," she replied, shifting her hand so one eye peeked out to once again be caught by his.

"Are you angry at him for..." He waved his fingers, indicating the two of them. "...bringing this topic to light?"

Was she? She hadn't really had time to be angry. Confusion had taken over everything else like kudzu. Twining, coiling, climbing over everything in its path, leaving her lost amid the roots.

She swallowed. "I'm not angry. I just don't know what to do or what to say. George is looking to me to make a decision, but I don't even know how to go about formulating a response."

He nodded, seeming to understand where she was coming from.

"That's exacerbated by the fact I don't know you. You don't know me.

George seems to think his opinion will sway both of us. Like his judgment is all that matters. He thinks I'll like you and you'll like me, so that's it." She rolled her eyes at his arrogance, a gesture that seemed to amuse Edward.

"You know he's usually right when it comes to judgment calls on the people he knows, don't you?"

"Yes. I do," she grumbled, because she did. George managed people better than an HR manager could with a genie in his hand. "Doesn't mean that in this instance he's right." She narrowed her eyes at him. "Why would a man like you want a woman like me?"

He blinked. "That's rhetorical, I assume?"

She huffed out a laugh. "Don't be coy. I know you don't date when you're in the country. There's barely any press of you here with anyone on your arm save your wife. But when you're in London or Paris, New York or Moscow, your dates do not look like me."

His jaw worked. "You're not my type. I make no bones about it, but types aren't the be all and end all."

Though she knew that was the truth, it surprised her how much it stung.

"No? So what's the point of even talking about this?"

"Because, as I said, types aren't always concrete," he bit off, and she realized she'd angered him. "Those women are... arm candy for want of a better word. Do you think I get serious about arm candy?"

"Depends how much of a sweet tooth you have, I guess," she snarked, and he shot her a sharp-eyed glance.

"Are you jealous?"

Her chin shot up. "Of course not."

"Well, you're doing a good impression of coming across that way." Out of nowhere, he smiled.

That smile was dangerous. Sweet Jesus, it was like being blinded by a megawatt spotlight. Her heart skipped another beat, and she could feel, deep in her core, some kind of internal shuffling going on.

God help her, was she wet?

She licked dry lips. "You have a big ego."

He grinned. "Plenty of other big things, too."

"Ha-ha," she snapped, peeved by his ease when she felt anything but.

For a second, he said nothing, let the silence settle between them until she wanted to squirm in place. Then he murmured, "Would you like to go out to dinner with me?"

Her eyes widened. "Like a date?"

His nod came slowly. "Yes. Like a date."

Did that mean he wanted her like George seemed to believe Edward would?

She rubbed at her temple.

"Does George even understand how complicated he's made things?"

"George knows what he's doing. He's fighting for what he believes is our future happiness. It makes him—"

"Arrogant."

He scowled a little. "That too, but he'll go to any lengths to make his desires come true."

His words had her frowning. She sat up, leaned her elbows on her desk. "What do you mean?"

He shook his head. "Will you come to dinner with me?"

She gnawed at her bottom lip, and though she hated herself for being a pushover, knew there was only one answer she could give him.

"Yes."

"WHAT ARE YOU DOING?"

The sound of George's voice nearby had Perry shrieking. As she did, she covered a hand over her mouth and demanded, "What the hell are *you* doing here?"

He frowned. "I asked you first."

"Yeah, but we're in *my* bedroom. My *bathroom* to be more specific." Damn, was nowhere sacred?

His lips curved into a smirk she felt like smacking. "Are you waxing your mustache?"

She grimaced. "*Bleaching.* I'm bleaching..." A cough escaped her instead of an admission.

He folded his arms across his chest and leaned against the doorjamb. "I wondered what you were up to."

Narrowing her eyes at him, she demanded, "Why?"

"Why what?"

"Why did you wonder what I was doing?" Ever since he'd made his stunning revelations, they hadn't been hanging out as much as usual. And though she missed him like crazy, the solitude was doing her good.

She needed to think, needed to reason this all out in her head. She couldn't do that when he was there confusing the life out of her.

He shrugged. "Wanted to know if you fancied watching TV with me?"

"Can't."

"Why not?" He frowned at her, and she could tell, her rejection stung.

She really shouldn't have been satisfied by that. But she was. Call her a bitch or just a she-cat, she didn't care.

"I'm having dinner with your brother."

His eyes widened in surprise. "Edward?"

"Yes. Edward. Have another brother you want to share me with?" she snapped angrily, unable to contain the bitterness in her tone, even if said bitterness wasn't even necessary.

Before he could reply, she deflated. Holding up a hand, she apologized, "That was uncalled for."

"You're confused," he immediately forgave.

"Not confused enough to take my bad mood out on you."

"That's unusual for you to be in a bad mood. You're normally quite cheerful."

He was right, and that was exacerbating her temper. Because the truth was, she was nervous. *Nervous.* It was why she was bleaching her damn mustache, had shaved so close to her skin her calves were itching, and she had more cream on her body than in the tub—hydrated wasn't the word for her body now.

She was scared to put make up on because she didn't do make up, but if Edward wanted to take her somewhere fancy—and he was a prince, so why wouldn't he? She'd need to do *something* with her eyes, right? Lipstick, too?

Then there was the age-old decision. Should she or shouldn't she Spanx it up?

The only decent clothes she had for a date were the ones George had bought her, and they all felt a size too small. On her visit into the city, when she'd met with Xavier, she'd hared off before the date to buy some 'wonderwear'. But, if things got frisky between her and Edward tonight—and she wasn't going to lie to herself, there was a distinct chance that would be the case—did she really want control pantyhose to spoil the mood?

"Perry?"

She blinked as George said her name. "What?"

"Where did you go?"

"Nowhere?" she huffed. "Aside from you pestering me, why are you here?"

"I told you. I wanted to see if you were game for a TV marathon."

Oh, shit. He had told her that already. Christ, she needed to get her head in the game.

Running a hand over her forehead, she murmured, "What's wrong with me, George?"

He was part of the problem, not the solution, so she wasn't entirely sure why she was asking him, but he was also her best friend. The keeper of all her secrets...

"You're anxious about being with Edward. Alone."

"I've been alone with him before," she denied.

"I know. But not on a romantic setting." He shrugged. "It changes things."

"Are you jealous?" She knew he was of Xavier, but Edward?

"A little." That surprised her; he seemed to notice because his lips twitched. "I'm only a man, Perry. But just like our relationship has had a chance to develop and grow, yours needs to have the opportunity with Edward."

Despite herself, his words settled in deep and made her feel calmer. It disturbed her that he repeatedly told her he loved her, all while wanting to share her with his brother. That didn't compute in her mind. Knowing he was jealous? Well, it eased things for her. Made stuff seem a little more normal.

Although, nothing about this situation was normal.

The horse had already bolted after the stable door was firmly closed.

His smile was gentle as he assured her, "You'll have a great time. Edward isn't always serious. He can be lighthearted."

She frowned. "I know that." And she did. He wasn't like George—quick to laugh. But she noticed how he behaved when he was amused. Had come to read those quirks of his that were unique to him alone.

Unlike George, who would freely chuckle, Edward was stingy with his laughter. But deep in his eyes, a twinkle would blossom if he was amused. She knew she amused him. She saw that twinkle there often, and each time she caught sight of it, it filled her with a warmth that discomforted her.

Why? Because it was a reminder.

That, for as much as she wanted to be testing the water with this crazy proposition for George's sake, the way Edward made her feel was… Confusing, to say the least.

That confusion didn't abate after George left, an amused curve to his lips as he kissed her cheek in farewell and wished her well. It didn't disappear when she did without the Spanx—just in case—and throughout the journey into Madela, she still felt perplexed.

Especially as she was alone on that car ride. Having expected to meet with Edward at the palace and drive into the capital together, being alone came as a nasty surprise.

The palace was surrounded by Veronia's countryside. At the back of the castle, it was sheltered by a mountain range, and the front was cossetted by cliffs that overlooked the ocean. One side of the building looked onto a forest, and the other side, in the distance, the city itself could be seen.

As they drove along the coastal road into the capital, she was once again enchanted by how old-world the place was. Sure, Ferraris were a common sight, but so were ancient buildings. Centuries-old churches that peeked out of modern areas, somehow managing not to stick out like a sore thumb. Skyscrapers scratched the sky, while plaques decorated street corners, small bronze squares dedicated to men and women who had died in their fight to safeguard Veronia from Nazi rule during the Second World War.

For every kiss of modern life, there was an outright hug from the past.

Truth was, finding those little quirks kept her occupied on the drive. And she needed that. Her nerves hadn't dissipated. Not one bit.

She felt sick by the time the car pulled up outside a large building. She frowned, wondering what it was. There wasn't much of a clue, considering they were definitely at the back of the edifice; the dumpsters were stored here, and the old stone walls were covered in signs for the personnel to adhere to. Everything was in Veronian.

A man appeared at the side door, and he walked to the limo, lifting his hand to his mouth to speak into some kind of communication unit, and then opened the door for her to climb out.

He helped her to her feet, though it wasn't necessary. She'd stayed in flats and wore trousers that did good things to her butt without needing Spanx.

The black pants were silky though, and swayed about her curves in a way that added fluidity to the outfit. Topped with a sparkly camisole that danced with beads, she looked simple but dressy. The blouse was super heavy, thanks to the beads, but they were the sole decoration on her outfit.

She hoped she was neither under- nor over-dressed for wherever the hell they were.

"Please, follow me."

They walked down narrow, darkened corridors, until a blast of light appeared at the bottom of one. When they walked into the atrium, she blinked, then grinned.

Edward was sitting on a blanket in the middle of the space. He had a picnic basket to his side, a champagne flute in his hand, and his feet were crossed at the ankle. All the while, the Veronian Natural History main exhibit surrounded him.

It was only 6 PM, which told her this place had been closed off for their date. Despite herself, she was impressed. As well as gleeful.

And charmed.

Damn him.

She'd only said the other day at breakfast how she'd wanted to see the latest exhibition at the country's largest museum—a collection of Mayan art that was on loan to the nation. It depicted their industry, how they'd lived and worked and loved.

He'd listened. She was impressed.

He didn't get to his feet, which surprised her. Instead, he reached up with the flute in his hand and offered it to her. The lack of formality pleased her, and she slipped down to the blanket, kneeling at his side for a moment.

She tilted the champagne flute at him, and he carefully clinked them together.

"This isn't the date," he informed her sagely.

"No?" she asked, peering around the place.

"Well, it's the first part," he conceded.

"What's the second?"

He smiled. "A first glimpse at their next exhibit."

"Which is?"

"That butterfly conservatory you were interested in."

Astonishment filled her. "But it's not for another week."

"I know. There are perks to being royalty. The butterflies are in place for the first time. I thought you'd like to see it before the event goes live."

As her eyes caught his, she figured she'd be nervous. But those nerves had withered away and died. Not only at his generosity, but at his kindness too.

"Play your cards right," she said huskily, "and this could be the best date I've ever been on."

He smiled. "I play to win."

She let out a shaky breath. Why didn't that surprise her?

CHAPTER ELEVEN

"I WONDERED when you'd come and see me."

Xavier turned to face George, who was flicking a leaf between his fingers. "You want to be careful with that. It has thorns."

George shrugged. "I know. They're Mother's favorite flowers."

Xavier's lips twitched. "Of course, I remember now." Marianne always had appreciated acacias.

George stepped back and shoved his hands in the back pockets of his jeans. As he did, he peered around, murmuring, "You've changed this place a lot since Uncle Sebastien died."

Xavier shrugged. "You can do that when you're no longer the heir but the duke."

Xavier had loved his father, but the man made myopic seem short-sighted.

Months after his father's passing, he'd had this greenhouse built. It was half the size of the family manor and where he spent a lot of his time, developing new fertilizers that wouldn't pollute the ground water while also tackling pesticides that wouldn't leech nutrients from the soil.

The greenhouse was his lab as well as his office.

"You always did want to save the earth," George murmured, his tone fond. "Just like Perry."

"Smooth segue, George," Xavier pointed out wryly.

His cousin shrugged. "I want to know why you're still seeing her."

He turned his back on his workstation, where he'd been making notes about his latest experiment—an organic pesticide aimed at greenfly.

"You're asking about my intentions?" His question was rueful. "Are you her father?"

"No. I'm the man who loves her. Who she loves too."

Xavier didn't stir at that. "She called me."

"She did?" George frowned, then lifted a hand to run his fingers through his hair.

His cousin looked tired as well as confused. Xavier could well imagine George would lose his temper shortly—he always could be cranky. It came from being the youngest of their trio.

He wasn't a brat, but old habits die hard when reintroduced into a family dynamic as old as the man himself.

"She's confused, George. Overwhelmed."

His cousin blinked. "About what?"

Xavier's lips curved into a half smile. "I've always known, you know?"

"Known what?"

He rolled his eyes. "That you and Edward share, of course."

George clenched his teeth. "She told you."

"No. She didn't," he replied, calm where George was enraged. "I knew when you were twenty that you'd been sharing with him for years." He shrugged. "It wasn't that big a problem, and I figured if you wanted me to know, you'd have told me."

Frowning, George shook his head. "That doesn't make any sense."

"What? That someone as close to you as I was couldn't figure that out?" He rolled his eyes. "Jesus, George. You can keep shit like that from most of the family and the staff, but not me."

George just stared at him. In consternation or confusion, Xavier wasn't sure.

"If you know so much, you'll know we haven't shared in years."

"Since Edward married the harpy."

George's eyes widened, but he banked the smile that started to twitch into life.

"He was trying to be respectable, I imagine." Xavier shrugged, leaned over to add a notation to the margin of his work book—a thought occurring to him about a tweak to his pesticide. Calmly, he murmured, "We all have those moments where we think we need to grow up." He smirked, a far less studious thought occurring to him. "Plus, can you imagine Arabella's reaction to the idea of being spit roasted?"

He caught George's eye, and the two of them grinned at another.

George cleared his throat. "I think I'd have paid to witness that conversation."

"You and me both," Xavier retorted with a chuckle. "Does he want her?"

It was hard to keep his tone of voice calm when he wasn't feeling calm. Perry was...

Different. Different enough that she'd broken his long spell of celibacy.

He hadn't taken a vow or anything. He was as red-blooded as the next man—who just happened to be his cousin. But ever since he'd become duke, a certain type of woman had been hunting him.

It was easier to take oneself out of the hunt sometimes rather than deal with the aftermath. He had no intention of being snared in a trap by a money-hungry gold-digger.

"Edward is on the fence."

"That doesn't sound like him."

Edward was one of the most decisive men Xavier knew.

"She'll change his mind."

"How?"

"By being Perry." George stepped closer to Xavier's work-bench. "What are you working on?"

"A new pesticide," he said absentmindedly. Then cutting a glance at George, asked, "What if she doesn't want him?"

"Then she doesn't want him."

"And what if she wants you and me, and not Edward?"

George reared back at that. "What?"

Xavier just shot him a look. "I want her, George. And as trite as that sounds, like she's some goddamn piece of chattel, I don't want to say goodbye to her."

Where the words came from, Xavier wasn't altogether certain.

This entire situation was more convoluted than any relationship he'd ever been in, never mind simply contemplated.

"But..."

"But what?" he asked softly, turning and leaning his ass on the workstation. "She wasn't a one night stand. I had no intention of sleeping with her, then cutting and running in the morning."

George looked floored a second, then he let out a shaky breath. "No. She's Perry. You couldn't do that to her."

Xavier's lips twitched at his cousin's stalwart impression that Perry was female perfection personified. He guessed if he'd been panting over her for as long as George had, he'd be as goggle-brained as him too.

"You want to share," Xavier prompted. "Why not with me?"

"Because we've never done that before."

Xavier shrugged. "You never asked."

George's mouth worked. "Are you being serious?"

He laughed. "Yes. Deadly. When have you known me to be anything other than serious?"

"True." He conceded that with a scratch at his temple. "Why would you want to though?"

"Because you've got your claws hooked in Perry, and that means once she gets over how sudden this all is, she'll let go of me and fall back into your arms."

A dopey grin curved his cousin's mouth. "You really think that?"

He rolled his eyes. "Yes. And that might make you feel better, but it doesn't make me feel great."

"Sorry, man," George said ruefully. "I just... she's got me so fucked in the head. I swear, any other woman, I wouldn't stand for it. But she's..."

"Perry," Xavier supplied helpfully, a grin appearing when George just nodded as he used her name as more of an adjective than a noun.

He'd ask what the hell he saw that had those stars in his eyes, but Xavier knew.

There was just—as trite as it sounded—*something* about her.

Perry was like taking a breath of fresh air after wading through cow shit.

And though it wasn't nice to refer to the ladies of the court as cow shit, they spilled enough BS to make the stench cling. Plus, they were relentless. As dogged as any wildcat with their teeth burrowed into the hind of a gazelle on their hunt for a husband.

Perry, on the other hand, didn't seem to notice he was a duke.

Maybe because she was used to being around George, but he wasn't sure if even George's position was all that grandiose in her mind.

"Do you know what she did when she met Mother and Father?"

Because of the amusement in his cousin's voice, Xavier turned to him with a grin. "No. What?"

"Took her shoes off."

For a second, Xavier gaped at George, then with their eyes entangled, the pair of them burst out laughing. "I'd pay to have seen the look on your mother's face."

He shook his head, unable to release the image from his imagination.

"It was as hilarious as you can imagine," George confirmed with a snicker. "I made her wear heels."

He remembered that she'd worn flats to the ball. "They were too high?"

"Anything above half an inch is too high for Perry," George grumbled with a half-hearted eye roll. "She did have to walk a fair distance in them, but she said she'd either fall over or start sobbing in the middle of the reception room. Mother didn't know where to look."

"I'll bet." His grin sobered a little as a thought occurred to him. "If Edward does..."

"Yeah. I know." George ran a hand through his dark hair. "She's not exactly queen material, is she?"

Xavier winced. "Maybe not. Well, not in comparison to someone like Aunt Marianne. But a modern queen?" He pondered that a second. "Who's to say that this generation wouldn't be more at ease with a queen who knows how this planet works… I love your mother, but Marianne is—"

"As much use as a chocolate teapot?"

He snickered. "Yeah. That. She's not exactly made for anywhere outside a palace. Arabella was of the same stock, and we all know how the public responded to her."

George pulled a face. "I was out of the country for the most part, but even I know she wasn't popular."

Xavier hooted. "Popular? The tabloids are never kind, but they were worse than usual with her. The only thing they could agree on was the fact she had great taste in clothes, but society needs more than a clotheshorse."

George blinked. "You say that like you think it's a possibility."

Xavier shrugged again. "Edward will… If he hangs out with her more, outside of chaperones like your parents, he'll see her worth. Not for the throne—like that's worth a damn, anyway. But for himself." Xavier cut his cousin a look. "You were away a long time, George. You probably don't even realize how much he's changed."

"No. I do. He's a lot quieter, far more somber."

Xavier nodded. "It goes deeper than that. He's stopped playing football, barely does anything for leisure, save ride."

"I noticed he went out the other day."

Xavier murmured, "If it's not for the state or the family and a ride every now and then, his life is…dull. And for a crown prince, dull takes on totally different meanings. The rest of the world might think it's all VIP sections at clubs and fancy suits, but Edward grew out of that shit a long time ago. If Arabella had been a better match, I genuinely think he'd have been able to settle down with her and be content."

George glowered down at the workings out Xavier had spread across several sheets on his desk. "Content? Where does it say we can't be happy?"

Smiling at his cousin's naiveté, he started, "George—"

"No! Don't 'George' me. You're both the same where this is concerned. It's like Veronia owns your happiness or something."

"Not mine. But your brother is a whole different kettle of fish. Veronia is his responsibility, his duty, once Philippe passes."

George growled under his breath. "So? Where does it say that duty means no happiness? Edward needs to share. It's what we do."

Xavier snorted. "It's not like being gay, George."

"Yes. It is, dammit! Or as near as can be. Just because it's kinky as fuck doesn't mean it doesn't work."

The younger man's earnestness had Xavier shoving his hands in his pockets. "Want a drink?"

"Yeah."

Xavier jerked his chin up and strode toward the small glass door that was the single point of entry in the glasshouse. There were smaller escapes for fire purposes, but they were openings in the glass rather than full apertures.

He'd worked to code, but had made sure that the code hadn't disturbed his intentions of creating a constant temperature within these walls.

The glasshouse was attached to the main building of his family's noble seat via a brick verandah. He toed out of his boots when the floor switched from gravel to tile, and George followed suit. The verandah housed a small seating area that was one of his favorite lounges. The family seat had over forty bedrooms and countless sitting rooms...yet, he usually used this one for ease, as it was close to the greenhouse, but also comfort.

This was designed to his specifications and not a great, great, great, great uncle who'd once ruled in Xavier's position.

He brushed off his seat to make sure he had no soil clinging to his ass or thighs, and then headed for the leather sofa which looked onto a large screen TV. Beside it, there was a small console table housing a drink's tray.

"What's your poison?"

George murmured, "Whiskey."

Xavier's eyes widened. "You've changed. You used to be all alcopops and IPA."

He chuckled. "Meeting Perry changed that."

"I'm sure she'd love knowing she upgraded you from soft to hard liquor."

George's grin was rueful. "It wasn't intentional. I just...I was fighting myself. All the damn time. It grows tiring."

Silence settled between them, broken only by the squelch of the leather as George took a seat on the sofa and the splash of the alcohol in a clear tumbler.

Pouring himself a brandy, he grabbed the glasses and offering it to George, he sank back into the sofa with a sigh.

For a second, silence fell between them, but it was a nice silence. Not brooding or loaded with anger, just a nice, relative calm that came between two men who'd known each other a lifetime.

"What are we going to do, Xav?" George eventually murmured on a deep sigh.

Xavier didn't need to be told they were talking about Perry, and no longer about Edward. He twirled his glass in his hand, watching as the amber liquid spiraled around the crystal in golden waves.

"Nothing we can do."

George grunted. "I refuse to believe that. I refuse to let this lie in the hands of Fate, not when I've been doing that all these goddamn years."

Xavier pulled a face. "What made you wait so long? It's not like you to prevaricate."

"Perry's different."

He scoffed. "You keep saying that; and I know she is, but it's not very... well, it doesn't make a whole heap of sense. She's totally inappropriate for a prince's wife. Never mind the crown prince."

George snorted. "But she's great as a duchess?"

The grin Xavier shot his cousin had George rolling his eyes. "Now that you mention it..."

George grunted, but didn't deny it. "I don't care about her as a crown princess. I care about Perry. As the woman that can make things right between Edward and me again."

Xavier frowned. "What do you mean?"

George fell silent, but from the way he gritted his teeth, Xavier knew he wasn't telling him something.

"He's punishing me," the younger man said softly, doing as Xavier just had—swirling his whiskey around the glass, watching as it caught on the divots in the crystal.

"Why would he do that?" Xavier scoffed.

"He blames me for wanting what he does," George murmured.

"What? For wanting to share?" he clarified, totally failing to comprehend what the fuck his cousin was talking about.

George's nod was solemn. "He thinks he's a pervert. And that I'm part of the problem."

CHAPTER TWELVE

PERRY HUMMED under her breath as she spooned out a too large mouthful of ice cream.

So, the palace was great. She could order pretty much whatever she wanted, and she'd get it. Whether that was a freakin' muffin or smoked salmon on freshly baked rye bread—it was like they had one of those replicators in *The Hitchhiker's Guide to the Galaxy*. Program it in once, there forever. Because how they always had whatever kind of bread she wanted freshly baked, was beyond her.

The waste had to be astronomical.

Truth was, having such a kitchen at her disposal was nifty. But, though their ice cream was made on the premises, it didn't beat Haagen Daaz.

She pressed the tub between her tits and held it to her chest like she was holding a baby.

The door to her office opened after a sharp knock, and she spun around, spoon in mouth to face the intruder. Her gaze clashed with Edward's, and she flushed. Immediate mortification hitting her as she pulled the spoon from between her lips and shoved the tub behind her back.

Edward froze, then his head tilted to the side. In his hand, he held a thick file loaded with papers, which he wafted at her. "Don't stop on my account."

She gaped at him. "No, it's okay. Is something wrong?"

It was the first time he'd visited her in her temporary office since their date at the butterfly conservatory.

And to be honest, she hadn't been all that perturbed.

What he and George wanted was both so alien and yet, so intriguing that it blurred in her head.

She was scared, she'd admit.

Scared because George—in his usual elephant-clomping way—had opened up a whole new world to her.

It was like being a dedicated football fan, not realizing any other sport existed, and then being told baseball and basketball were options too.

Could a diehard football fan also become a diehard fan of another sport?

Just the thought had anxiety stirring in her belly. She knew the answer was yes, even liked the answer, but it was wrong.

So, so wrong.

Wasn't it?

She did as his wafting hand had suggested—raised her tub of ice cream, and cuddling it to her chest, murmured, "What's wrong?"

"Why should anything be wrong?"

"You're here, aren't you?"

He narrowed his eyes at her, making those beautiful turquoise orbs glint. "I wanted to talk about the report you gave on the Isdena Dam."

"What about it?"

"You're recommending building another one in the Ashe Valley. You do realize how much that's going to cost, don't you?"

She huffed, and then shoved her spoon into the mound of creamy goodness. "Considering I put costs in the report, I think you'll find I know how much it's going to cost. Plus, you said money was no object, if I recall." She shoved the spoon in her mouth and began chomping.

"You have to know we don't have the funds to construct a whole new dam from scratch in the allotted time you're suggesting."

"Bull," she retorted, her words a little dulled thanks to her numb tongue. "You can't afford not to build it. If you do as I suggest and construct three major dams in the next thirty years, you'll stave off forty per cent of your droughts.

"You have serious infrastructure issues—the Isdena Dam has the worst. So much so, I don't understand how you haven't had serious accidents there. It's under-maintained."

Edward frowned. "I don't understand why. It's not like any of them are all that old."

She shrugged. "Nearly a hundred years old, with a century old technology. Major changes now prevent major calamities down the line." A thought occurred to her, one that had her pursing her lips. Feeling the top one flatten into a disapproving line, she quickly covered her mouth with her spoon and ate some more ice cream.

"What?" he demanded, eyes narrowed at her once more. "You were going to say something."

She shook her head. "Nothing."

"Now who's spouting bull?"

Dipping a shoulder, she murmured, "Do you realize, with this one palace alone, how much waste you're propagating?"

He frowned. "We run a very streamlined household."

A snort escaped her, one that had her wincing. Rubbing her temple, she grumbled, "Brain freeze," at his concerned glance. Wafting him away with a spoon, she backed up to her desk and leaned against it. Crossing her feet at the ankles, she told him, "Veronia is an arid country. You run on the dry side. But you wouldn't know it from the palace gardens. I know for a fact your grandfather introduced the damn concept of lawns to the country."

He scowled. "It's a lawn."

"Do you have any idea how much water is wasted on unnecessary ornamental gardens?" She shook her head. "Before his renovations, the palace yards were used for vegetables or fruits. Where the rose garden is now, it used to be an herb section." She pointed her spoon at him. "That was functional. Useful. The produce you grew was used in the kitchens. And don't let me get started on the kitchens."

"Why not? If you have something to say, say it," he retorted stiffly.

"Do you realize that whatever I want, I can have?"

He blinked. "Excuse me?"

"If I fancied sticky ribs Korean-style or a goddamn Jell-O salad, your kitchens would find a way to get it for me?"

"They serve the most powerful people in the land!"

"Am I one of those people?" she retorted. "I'm just staff. I have no idea why I'm even in your private quarters, and hypocritical though it might be, I'm really glad I am. But... that's a level of production that's entirely wasteful and unnecessary."

"Are you trying to tell me that economizing in the palace will pay for this new dam you say we need?"

His exasperation had her glowering at him. "I'm saying, it's an attitude shift. Everyone needs a lawn now, when before, they didn't.

"Look, not everyone in your pretty country is rich, you know? There are a lot of people who still live hand to mouth. Just because you're a tax haven for the bone idle, doesn't mean you don't have to implement changes that will affect life from the top to the bottom. If anything, to prove to the bottom they can convert their useless yard back into something functional should start from the top."

He reared back. "You can't be serious?"

"Why not? Why have something pretty but useless, something that drains a resource you're struggling to conserve, when you could make the land work for you? Makes sense to me. But then, I'm not constrained by decades of antiquated rule."

"Did you just say what I think you said?"

She smirked. "Yup. George didn't tell you I have a mouth on me, did he?"

Edward's nostrils flared. "No, he didn't."

She jabbed her spoon in the air. "I'm not a yes man. Never have been, and never will be. I've spoken to key staff at that dam, and all of them tell me about how they're having to patch it up more and more, and that twice, they'd had issues with conserving the little water they contain. One of the walls started to crumble last year!

"I've spoken to your Environmental Agency, which is absolutely useless, by the way. They barely realize that solar power is even a thing." She rolled her eyes. "I mean, who did you hire? A friend of a friend of a duke? I mean, Jesus."

Edward scowled at her, then, he stopped squinting and asked, "Can I sit down?"

She shrugged. "If you want."

He surprised her by sitting on the sofa opposite the unlit hearth, and not in front of her desk. The move put his back to her which meant she had to shift over to the sofa too.

With a huff, she did, but she didn't sit beside him on the couch; instead, she went to the armchair and perched on there. Curling her feet under her, she carried on eating, watching him watch her.

The weird thing was, she wasn't intimidated by him.

Perry had figured she would be, especially after George had messed with her head where the brothers were concerned.

But he was just a man. Philippe was too. Maybe she was too American to understand the concept of royalty. Either that, or she was just too difficult.

As far as she was concerned, they both used the bathroom like she did—just because theirs had fancy gilt flushers didn't mean their clichéd shit didn't stink.

Sure, it made them richer. And yeah, they had more power. But better? Nuh-huh.

"What did George tell you about me?" That probably wasn't the wisest thing to ask, but she was curious.

He'd been surprised by her comments, by her outspokenness. Considering that was half her personality, George couldn't have told Edward that much.

"He told me enough."

She heaved out a sigh. "Well, that's informative."

He shrugged. "It wasn't as though he told me a great deal about you, but about your interactions with him, yes. I learned a lot about you that way."

"So why were you surprised that I have a voice?"

"I'm not."

"Liar."

His mouth firmed at her retort. "I'm not lying. I wasn't surprised at that. I just thought you'd be uneasy around me... too uneasy to be so outspoken."

"I am uneasy around you." She wriggled her shoulders. "If anything, that makes me more vocal. Defense mechanism," she admitted.

He perched his elbow on the armrest, then propped his head up on his fist. "George just had to force the issue, didn't he?"

Perry's lips twitched. "George does that."

Edward frowned. "Excuse me?"

"He's like a bull in a china shop. I don't know how he gets anything done." When Edward's eyes widened in surprise, she smirked. "You can't tell me I'm the only one who realizes what he's like?"

"It's been a long time since he's been home."

"What does that have to do with anything?" she demanded. "This can't be a new trait."

"Maybe America changed him," came his cold retort.

"What? Gave him a personality transplant?" Perry grunted. "He's delicate when it comes to work, but in everything else, he's way too ebullient."

Edward pinned her with a stare. "You're attracted to him."

"Very." Her confession came without artifice.

He scowled at her. "Then why do you want me?"

"I don't know that I do," she told him with a huff, that had his scowl deepening. Feeling mean, she grumbled, "Okay, well, that's a lie."

"What do you mean?"

"I mean," she said slowly, "I didn't want you because I didn't know about you. And now George has opened up this world of endless possibilities, and he's messed with my head." She used the handle of the spoon to scratch her temple. "You haven't made it any easier by telling me you want me too. Oh, and then backing off. Shit, you might as well have gone on a state visit to Switzerland, Mr. Neutral."

Her retort had him blinking. "You need to watch your mouth."

Her shoulders stiffened at that. "Excuse me?"

He wafted a hand. "If you're going to be my girlfriend, you can't be as blunt as you're being now."

"Who said I wanted to be your girlfriend?"

A laugh escaped him, and it wasn't a particularly nice one. "The minute there's even a whiff of my interest in you, it will be all over the papers. Not necessarily in Veronia, but around the rest of the world? Definitely. You'll be pulled apart and dissected until all your secrets are revealed to the hungry maws of the public. They'll want to know your shoe size, your favorite designer, and how you intend to win world peace—"

He broke off, nostrils flaring, and Perry could tell his own words pissed him off.

In fact, it was like showing a red rag to a bull. Cliché, she knew, but the truth regardless.

He was pissed off. Genuinely. On her behalf. The notion had her taking her spoon and digging deep into the ice cream. When she pulled it out, loaded with gloopy goodness, she offered it to him. "Do you want some?"

He blinked, smirked. "Peace offering?"

"I don't know. But it's good. Shame not to eat it all."

A sigh escaped him as he leaned forward to take the spoon from her. He slipped it between his lips, humming a little at the taste, then pulled it out and handed it back to her.

To pass him the spoon, she'd leaned forward so she could reach him. She'd stayed in that position, not because she was stuck, but because the sight of him licking the spoon, of his strong throat working as he swallowed had glued her in place.

Sweet Lord, what had the DeSauvier family done to earn not only a kingdom, but the kind of genes that could get a girl hot when one of them was eating ice cream of all things?

"Perry?"

Hearing her name repeated at least three times had her jolting in place. She cleared her throat, accepted the spoon. "Want some more?"

He shook his head, but his smile was kind. "Thanks, but vanilla's not my flavor."

She chuckled at that. "I'd never have guessed. Ya know, what with the fact you like sharing your girlfriends with George?"

His lips quirked into the first genuine grin she'd seen from him.

Sure, she'd seen him smile. She'd even heard him laugh, and his chuckle was so nice, even thinking about it made her warm.

But this grin?

It was genuine.

It hit his eyes, made them sparkle. The lines at the side of them crinkled in response, and his grin revealed sparkling white teeth that spoke of a great dentist.

He shook his head as he finished laughing, and then murmured, "You definitely need to watch your mouth."

"George wouldn't like me if I did that. He says I'm the only woman he knows who isn't a bottom feeder."

"That sounds like something George would say."

"He gets a lot of pussy that way, so I'm not sure why he complains."

Edward sighed. "Are you doing it on purpose?"

Her eyes were twinkling as she looked at him. "Doing what?"

Her innocent tone didn't fool him. "I didn't come here to talk about personal matters," he confessed.

"No, you came here to question my professional opinion." She pursed her lips, pointed her spoon at him, then jabbed the air. Twice. "You can question many things about me, but never that. Conservation and preservation is a subject close to my heart. I'd never suggest anything because it was politic to do so. The earth deserves more than that.

"We've already spent generations wrecking it with our crazy advancements that rape our resources and damage our wildlife." She shuddered, the subject matter hitting her square in the gut.

"I'm sorry," he told her softly, apparently seeing her passion and realizing it was genuine.

She shrugged, but unease still slipped through her. "Everything in there is my opinion. You can have it backed up by someone in my field, and they'll tell you the exact same thing. I haven't come up with those figures out of a hat. They're all from reports separate agencies in your government made. I'm using statistics that are home grown.

"You need a new dam. Hell, you need several. But that's the good news. Your drought isn't as severe as you feared. You're not going to be waterless, unless you don't heed my advice."

He pulled a face. "You just want me to find, what is it? Ten billion euros?"

She grinned. "Yeah. Small fry for you, huh?"

"Sort of. We have the funding, but it's getting the government to back your findings and act on them." He lifted the file and used the edge to scratch his chin. He fell into a contemplative silence, then, as he watched her, asked, "Would you have dinner with me again?" When she froze, he sighed. "Perry?"

Biting her lip, ice cream now forgotten, she stared over at him, and at that moment, felt so acutely vulnerable, Perry wasn't sure what to do with herself.

Truth was, this man was attractive to her. He was. There were no two ways about it.

He was gorgeous, he was studious. He was mature, and he cared...and yeah, he was a crown prince, too. And she guessed that for many women, that would have been the icing on the cake. Or, maybe the cake itself, she wasn't sure.

For her, it wasn't. He'd said it himself; she'd be under scrutiny if she was with him. But to be fair, she would be if she was dating George too. Maybe Xavier as well.

All three of them lived in the public eye, and even if Xavier and George avoided it as much as they could, they still had to do the whole function thing. Hell, that's how she'd met Xavier, after all. At a function he hadn't wanted to attend.

These were not nobodies, and to live this kind of weird ass lifestyle, didn't the member of said lifestyle have to be nobodies?

She gnawed at her lip, graduating from biting to grinding her teeth into the tender morsel.

"What are you thinking?" Edward asked, breaking into her thoughts with the accuracy of a bullseye.

"That I find you attractive, but things got complicated because George has given me an option. Apparently, it's not good to give women options over these things."

Edward snorted. "There are always choices."

"Yeah, but some break the bounds of society. If George and I had started dating and then I'd met you, I wouldn't be thinking about the potential between us. People don't do that. Not normal people anyway."

"What's normal?" Edward questioned, and when she scoffed, he scowled at her. "No. Seriously. What's normal? I've never known normal. My life is anything but."

"Not in a good way."

He cocked a brow. "You don't think?"

"Nope. Sure, you can eat some weird food at four AM because the kitchens are open, and you get to wear a crown and stuff, but I mean, it's really not that great.

"George dismissed most of his security a few years back, but before he did, I saw them. They were always hanging around. It was invasive, and they were so obvious too—" She broke off when something in his eyes had her frowning. "What? What did I say?"

Edward's gaze was slitted. "Nothing."

"What?" she demanded, aware that she'd missed a nuance in this conversation, and she had no idea what it was.

"If you tell George what I'm about to tell you, I'll deny it."

She reared back. "Excuse me?"

"You heard me. I'll deny it."

Her mouth rounded. "Why?"

"Because it concerns his safety."

She gulped. "Seriously?" His nod had her nodding in return. "Okay, then. If it's for his safety, I won't tell him. I promise."

He eyed her a second, then trailed a finger over the file in a random pattern that had all her nerve endings leaping to attention.

Oh, to be that file, she thought whimsically.

"If you think we allowed George to cut his trail, you're both deluded."

Her shoulders stiffened. "But they dropped out of sight."

"Exactly. Out of sight, not mind. He's being guarded by a different team, that's all."

She blinked. "But security is more effective when it's obvious, surely?"

"Effective, yes and no. When you have an idiot for a brother who spends most of his time skipping out on his guards, then efficacy gets called into question," he said wryly.

She pondered that a second, thought about how, when George had thought he was free, he hadn't been.

Or had he known? Deep down?

When she'd helped him recuperate from the flu, that first time they'd really met, he'd demanded to use the phone when he'd been well enough to do more than just puke. His family hadn't been his first call, but a man called Drake.

Almost like he'd read her thoughts, Edward murmured, "George will know, Perry. I just don't want to rub it in his face."

She bit her lip again, then because it was starting to hurt, picked up her spoon and slurped down melting vanilla sauce.

It curdled in her stomach, though.

Poor George.

"Do you know somebody called Drake?" Perry wasn't sure why it was important, it just was.

Edward's brow puckered. "Yes. He's the head of our security. Why?"

"You must think I'm a real idiot," she whispered, her voice hoarse. So, George *had* known about the guards being there. She'd almost caused a diplomatic incident and hadn't even realized it.

Stupid, stupid, *stupid.*

He frowned. "Why must I?"

"Because I believed they'd gone when he said so."

"That's not idiocy; that's just a different mindset. You're American, Perry. Security comes with a price tag. You figured if you cut off the source of the funding, you cut off the end product. But we're not a CEO or a billionaire magnate... we're royalty. We have whole bodies of agencies set up to protect us.

"If my father had tried to gain their cooperation and have the guards removed, those agencies would have ignored him. There are protocols in place.

"As much as the government would like to avoid believing we're of any use, the Prime Minister in particular, a lot of key parliamentary acts only occur with our approval." He shrugged. "If anything happened to me, George would be crown prince. Do you think he could avoid that fate?"

She'd never thought about it. Not really.

George in Boston wasn't...

He wasn't a prince.

Sure, she knew he was. At the back of her mind. But when they were doing day to day shit like watching movies or hanging out and watching the newest Star Trek episodes...?

Everything just blurred.

"He'll have to come home eventually," Edward pointed out softly, and she lifted her eyes to catch his.

"Why?"

"Because this is his rightful place."

"He'll never rule."

"No, but he has duties."

"Like what?"

"He does. It's a fact of life. Well," he said on a sigh, "a fact of *our* lives."

"If anything happens to Father, I'm the next king. Until I have an heir, George is the heir. That's why he has to come home at some point. When the inevitable happens, and I hope it isn't for another four decades at least, he has to be ready," he commented, sadness filling him. And her, if she were honest.

Imagine having to actively think about your father's death and what it meant for you? Perry thought.

Before her thoughts could deteriorate further, Edward carried on, "...when George is the heir to the throne, he can't maintain his current lifestyle."

Feeling sick, she put the half-eaten tub of ice cream on the ground.

Edward's words hit her hard, because it meant that at some point, unless she did date George, she would lose him.

Not 'lose him' lose him, but he'd have to come back here. She'd have to... her throat closed.

Live without him.

He was her best friend, and had been for so long now that she didn't know what the world would even look like without him a twenty-minute walk away.

They hung out four times a week. Minimum. Outside of that, they had lunch, usually went out for dinner.

A frown puckered her brow as a thought came to her...had they been dating all along, and she just hadn't realized it?

Sure, there'd been no kissing or sex to give the game away, but they lived like a married couple.

She knew his freakin' kitchen better than he did! She certainly cooked there more than him. If her car broke down, she called him first, and he came and did his 'manspection', then deigned to allow her to call the roadside assistance on her insurance. She didn't do his laundry, but he often told her to bring her stuff over so it could be washed by his staff. Three nights a week, she usually found herself in his spare bedroom too. On Fridays and Saturdays, but at some point, during the week as well.

Feeling sicker than she even had a moment ago, she whispered, "But I need him."

Something in Edward softened. She didn't know what, but he just seemed to relax before her. His eyes—though not necessarily hard—grew gentler, and the smile he sent her was kind. Not patronizing, but empathetic.

"I know you do. He needs you too."

"Why does he want to share me with you then?" Why wasn't she enough?

"Because he thinks you'll make me happy."

"But why is he even thinking about that? Men don't normally think that," she snapped. "They think about conquering and hording things for themselves. Not sharing the spoils of war with their brother, too."

Edward sighed, lifted a hand and rubbed at the side of his throat. Perry felt his tension, and was apologetic for it, but she needed answers.

She needed to understand, because none of this was making any sense. She'd been George's partner for years without even realizing it.

Why? Why hadn't he taken that final step toward making them a real couple?

Because he'd been waiting to introduce her to Edward? What the fuck was that about?

"George loves me," Edward said softly.

"Most brothers love their siblings. Doesn't mean they want them to fuck their girlfriend."

"I know. Trust me, I know."

"You don't know. You can't know how alien this is for me."

"You'd be surprised." He closed his eyes, then opened them again, but this time, there was a flame buried within that scalded her, leaving her gasping for air. "Did you hear about what happened to George and me—"

"The kidnapping. Yes. I'd never heard of it before. Not until I came here."

"You know how tight our privacy laws are, and when it happened, the country came together and rallied around us." His smile was frigid. "Amazing how a singular event can do that. We have a group of extremists who disapprove of our being ruled by the monarchy... before our kidnapping, they were gaining traction with the people. After? Support disintegrated instantly."

"The security of your family's reign rested on the danger you were placed in. That's hardly a fair trade."

He clenched his jaw. "You've got that damn right." She watched as he tried to regain control of himself, but that harsh hiss was, to this point in their acquaintance, the angriest she'd ever heard him.

Edward seemed to be perennially calm. She wasn't sure whether she was relieved to see the rupture in his control or not. She had a feeling that where George was like a duck on a river—unruffled but his legs flapping away like crazy under the surface. Edward was like a dormant volcano. Any eruption could have devastating consequences on anyone close to him.

"What happened, Edward?" she asked quietly. Gently. She needed to know, Perry realized. Somehow, she got the feeling that all the answers to the many questions she had about both men could find their source *here*.

"Has George never spoken to you about it?" he asked tightly.

"No." And that hurt. She'd told him her worst, her deepest and darkest secrets, and he'd never shared this with her. Xavier had. Their cousin had been the one to break the news of this particular tragedy to her.

He reached up and scratched at his temple. "We were beaten." His nostrils flared. "Touched. Humiliated. They did things that..." Edward closed his eyes, but the pressure of his jaw made the skin bleed white around his lips. "I'll never forget. George, thankfully, doesn't seem to remember much."

"But you do." A statement. Not a question.

"I remember everything," he seethed, eyes popping open to catch hers with his. "Every minute of it, I can replay it. From when they snatched me from my bed, to when our security found us in that squalid little house in Heldafort. And every second in between."

She cleared her throat at the rage burning away before her, and was once again reminded of the volcano analogy... if she wasn't careful, she'd be swept up in the outpouring of lava. The threat didn't stop her from stating, "Xavier said you were wild afterward."

A single nod was her answer.

"I can't blame you," she whispered, and as shutters fell down over his eyes, barring her out, the way he severed the connection between them—even if she'd been in danger from the explosion—*hurt*.

"If you're looking for a reason for my being a pervert," he snapped, "then you're looking in the wrong place, Perry."

"I'm not. I'm just trying to understand."

"Understand what? Me?" At her nod, he carried on, "It will take more than an armchair psychologist to figure me out. All you have to know is George feels guilty, Perry."

"Why?"

He shrugged. "For forgetting. For being the younger brother and for my being the elder... I protected him. Shielded him from..." Edward swallowed. "He loves me and wants me to be happy. That's why he wants you for me. For us.

"We all have those moments in our life, Perry, when we figure out what we need. Some people need shoes, others need to gamble. Some like to be spanked, some want to be pegged."

Pegged? What the fuck was that?

"George and I like to share. It's not unusual. Most guys do it at some point, if they're lucky. At college, or when they're in their twenties. During my wild phase, I discovered it, and inadvertently involved my brother. For me and George though, it stuck. Really, really stuck. Denying that need is hard." And it sounded it. His voice had become brutal. His words crystalline as he explained, and she sensed how tough it was. Felt for him in that moment, even as she could still feel confusion. "It's like not having sex."

She reared back. "Excuse me?"

He nodded. "Yeah. Exactly. Fucking by myself is like jacking off in the shower. It's nice, I get off, but that's it. When I share a woman..." He gritted his teeth. "It's like fire."

And those flames were still burning in his eyes, giving her a taste of what he offered. What he promised.

"I didn't just share with George. I managed to do it with a couple of friends in college, but with George, it's easier."

"Creepier, too," she grumbled, and was surprised when he laughed.

"I'm not looking at his dick when I'm with a woman, Perry," he chided. "The other guy's presence is almost irrelevant. Because, like I told you the last time we spoke of this, it would be about overwhelming you with pleasure. The pleasure two men can give *you*."

Her throat closed. "Me?" she squeaked, wondering why they'd gone from impersonal 'woman' to the very personal 'you.'

"Yes. You. I know you want me. I've seen you looking. Watching me. I know because I do the same with you. George is a bastard. He's the snake in the Garden of Eden. He's offered us both the apple, and he's waiting for our own needs to work against us."

She gulped. "George isn't that manipulative."

"Maybe not with you, but with me, he is. He knows dangling temptation in front of me is the only way he'll make this happen." She watched as he leaned forward and pressed his elbows to his knees. He bowed his head, stared down at the ground, and then murmured, "He got it right this time. He knew I'd want you."

She let out a shocked gasp. Shocked because the way George, Edward, and Xavier talked, she was like Jessica Rabbit. But she wasn't. She was short, more than a little round, and had a mouth that wouldn't quit, too.

Yeah, okay, she was pretty. Passably, so. But she'd seen Edward's late wife. Arabella DeSauvier had been like beauty incarnate. So porcelain pristine, she'd been almost creepy in her perfection.

How could Perry, ordinary American Perry, ever compete with that?

And yet, the heat in his eyes belied that concern. As he stared at her, she could feel the flush soaring over her cheeks, cresting her throat and breasts with the power of it. She gulped. "What do you want from me, Edward?"

His smile was slow, sexy. God, it hit her in places she couldn't even begin to imagine.

"Everything."

CHAPTER THIRTEEN

"WHAT ARE WE DOING?"

George squinted at Xavier as, later that afternoon, he headed off the estate grounds and drove them out onto the road which would lead to the highway.

Xavier, of them all, had the best estate. The main house was Palladian in style, tall and proud, elegantly slender with copious windows that overlooked acre after acre of tilled land.

When George's uncle had died, the first thing Xavier had done was make the estate pay for itself.

In Uncle Sebastien's time, the estate had always functioned at a loss, but Xavier had converted all the garden areas into farmland, and he'd constructed the greenhouse for his mad-hatter experiments.

Truth was, he could see why Perry was attracted to Xavier. They were two peas in a pod.

Both of them were scientists. Both of them thought analytically, and shared opinions on conservation and environmental issues. If he'd been thinking about it, approaching Xavier would have made more sense than Edward! But it was about time his brother stopped being so goddamn stoic and actually lived a little.

Perry was going to make that happen. And yeah, he knew he was putting all his eggs in one Perry-shaped basket, but when a man found his soul mate, what other alternative did he have?

He grimaced as he realized making Perry conform to *his* desires was exactly the opposite of how a man should treat his soul mate, but he knew her.

He knew her so damn well.

She was a kinky little minx when it came down to it.

He'd heard her talk when she was drunk. Had seen her, back in the early days, kissing one of her boyfriends at a party. She'd been half-sozzled on some of the ghastly punch on offer, but it had worked wonders on her—she'd practically been humping the lucky bastard in public.

She spoke freely about sex, discussed things with him that no other female friend had ever talked about...

No, she'd never mentioned the desire to be shared while sober, but neither had she admitted to him her love of kinky books! And he'd seen the stuff she read on her Kindle. Anything from BDSM to, yes, ménage. He'd made a point of looking at her reading material when they'd had that illuminating conversation over shitty cocktails followed up by vodka shots.

That, did she but know it, was why they were here today. Why he was putting them all through this...

Whoever Perry thought she was, deep down, wasn't the woman she wanted to be.

And as a friend, he pondered sagely, it was his duty to help her realize her potential.

He was the King of Generosity.

"What are we doing, dammit?"

Xavier's voice broke into his self-deprecating thoughts. "Isn't it obvious? We're going to the castle."

"Yeah, that part's obvious. I just don't know why I'm here."

George cut him a look. "Because you want to be with Perry, that's why."

"Have you given up on Edward? Is that it?"

George shook his head. "No. Not entirely. But I'm not totally selfless. As much as Edward needs to share, I do too."

Xavier frowned. "This isn't a fucking free for all, George."

"I know! I never said it was. But Perry likes you." He shrugged. "She doesn't like many people."

Xavier preened a little at that. "She doesn't?"

"Nope." That was why her sleeping with Xavier had messed so entirely with his plans.

As he drove out of the countryside and toward the ocean where the main seat of the DeSauviers was found, he narrowed his eyes against the sun. It was the end of summer, but they had very pleasant autumns. Regardless of their location, which should have had them enduring wet and soggy Falls, they didn't. But their winters were cold.

Frigid, sometimes.

Although, after Massachusetts, his idea of frigid had certainly changed.

"I want to show her her options," he said after a moment's contemplation as he asked himself exactly what it was he was doing. "Truth is, Xav, I don't have a fucking clue what to do. I've messed things up, and I want to rectify it. All I know is I can't lose her, and I'll do what I have to to make sure that never happens—that she never leaves me."

Xavier reached over, and with his fist, knocked George's arm gently. "She loves you, idiot."

"I know. But it might not be enough. I just… she's scheduled to leave in two weeks. I've wasted ten days by letting her waffle over this, and I can't let her go back to America without having a heart to heart."

Xavier grimaced. "Is it really fourteen days since she came here?"

"Yeah. She's been busy, granted. She packed so much work into this trip, it's insane."

"You sound proud."

"I am. She's amazing." He blew out a breath. "If she stays, finding a place for her to work wouldn't be hard." Trouble was, he needed to know what her decision was, because when he officially claimed her as his girlfriend, that was it.

There was no going back.

The situation with Edward would never be able to be resolved.

That was why he was under such pressure.

As the spare heir, he could marry pretty much whoever he wanted and not worry about heirs himself.

Edward had to worry about that.

It was his damn duty, and that was why he wanted Edward to have Perry. She'd lessen the burden of that duty. She'd make him and George so fucking happy that even thinking about it, had the power to make his throat thick with emotion.

She was the gift he'd never known he'd even asked for. Now it was time he proved that to her.

―――

HER BREATHING WAS HEAVY. In his peripheral vision, he saw the fast jiggle of her breasts and wanted to groan at the sight.

"Y-You can't have everything," she told him, trying to sound self-righteous and failing.

Miserably.

His cock hardened as she licked her lips, and in her lap, where her hands had fallen, he saw her fingers curl in on themselves. She was fighting this. Fighting them. And he couldn't blame her.

But he would convince her.

George was right. This desire, perverted or not, wasn't going anywhere.

He wanted Perry, and he wanted her to be so overwhelmed with everything they could gift her, that she never questioned, ever again, why she was doing this. The realization that this was right, that this was exactly how it should be, filled Edward's senses.

It was like suddenly taking in a clean breath of fresh air after decades of inhaling smog.

Everything felt clearer, everything made sense. Even the crackpot shit his brother spouted... it all made sense.

He needed Perry, and she needed them. He was exhausted living this half-life. Denying himself what he needed just to make his people happy. His people were happy with their own lives, making their choices and their own decisions.

They'd have to be content with that.

He wasn't their king, yet. He still had a life to lead, and he intended to lead it.

He knew it would piss her off, knew it would agitate her, but he cocked his finger and beckoned him to her.

His grin appeared when she jerked back, outrage slaloming across her features. Her eyes narrowed even further at the sight of his smile. "I'm not a dog," she told him stiffly.

"I know," came his calm retort. "But there's no way in fuck I'm making the first move, not when you're still undecided. I won't coerce you into this. You have to accept whether it's something you want or not. And you need to make a decision quickly..."

He sat back in the uncomfortable sofa, aware that his cock was tenting his pants, doubly aware that she knew he had a hard-on too. He didn't mind her knowing though, especially when it caused that hectic color to appear on her cheeks.

She gulped, and it looked hard—like her mouth was dry. "This is too much pressure," she whispered.

"There's no pressure at all," he immediately countered, wanting her to know that. *Needing* her to know that.

"Then why do I feel like I'm drowning?" she huffed.

"Because you're melodramatic?" He cocked a brow at her, enjoying her growl of annoyance. "You do understand why..." His own words agitated him, but she had to understand. "You have the right to say no to this, Perry. There will be no recriminations from me. That I swear to you. But once you do that, and you stick with George and that goes public? There's no going back." He stared at her. "Do you understand that?"

She bit her lip. "Maybe."

"There's no maybe about it." Trying to appear more relaxed than he felt, he rested his arm on the sofa and propped his chin up on his fist. "If this is to work, then you have to be mine in the eyes of the public."

The biting of her lip became downright gnawing. "I know."

"Do you, though? I will have to marry at some point, Perry. If we do this, and you're publicly George's partner, then there is an end date. If you become mine, George doesn't have the pressure to wed that I do... there's no end date." When she made to respond, he murmured, "But this is a decision that you need to come to by yourself. It's not now or never, Perry. It hasn't reached that point yet, but it's getting there. And the sooner you tell me, *us*, what you want, the sooner we can make that happen."

Even as he dropped the ultimatum, he prayed she'd say yes. It was like a switch had flipped in his head, and the notion of her saying no to this was more than he could stand.

George trusted Perry, and Edward hadn't trusted someone outside of the family for a long time. He was trusting her with so much here, and though he didn't like it, he knew they were both as vulnerable as the other when it boiled down to it. Both equals in their hesitancy and their uncertainty. Although, he'd managed to overcome his in this short conversation. George was right. There was something about Perry that just fit.

She was smart and beautiful. Witty and acerbic. Unafraid to be opinionated, strong and self-assured when it mattered. As a consort, she was also a nightmare waiting to happen, but he wasn't thinking about her in a formal setting.

The formal didn't matter. It had mattered for so long, all the way before he'd proposed to Arabella, and what had that got him?

A placid wife, more broodmare than woman. Except, that broodmare had liked sex with him about as much as he'd enjoyed it with her—hence their lack of an heir.

Perry stared at him, and he sensed her panic. He hated that he'd caused it, but he was relieved to see the turbulence of her response. It made him believe George was right to have seen this in her. She wanted him, but was fighting it. Was fighting it because society said she should, not for any other reason.

The silence had fallen thickly between them, and he decided to break it —not with another ultimatum, but with, "Why does George think you'd want this?"

She blinked, apparently surprised he'd backtracked. Licking her lips, she whispered, "I don't know."

He tilted his head to the side. "You're lying." He wasn't angry, if anything, he was amused enough to smirk.

"I am not," she said on a huff.

"You are. Why?" It came to him then, and he quickly dampened down his amusement. "There's no need to be embarrassed."

Her jaw clenched, and she stared down at her lap. He watched her fingers pleat her trousers and wondered if she knew how telling that was. Wondered if she was also aware of how telling it was she hadn't immediately discounted the notion of her being embarrassed.

"What does George know about you, Perry?" he asked softly, quietly. *Gently.* He didn't want to scare her or get her back up. He wanted her to share.

"I don't know... because, I didn't think he knew."

That cryptic comment had Edward cocking a brow. "About what?"

"I like to read," she said on a huff.

"As do I."

She glowered at him. "Romance?"

A snort escaped him at her irritation. "No. As you can imagine, that's not my genre of choice."

"Yeah, well, it's mine." She wriggled her shoulders and stuck her neck out. Agitation rippled from each pore. "Erotic stuff, okay?"

"Okay." He kept his tone bland and made sure there wasn't a hint of a smile curving his lips—he didn't feel like being eviscerated.

"I didn't realize George knew, but I guess he must have seen my Kindle." She wriggled her shoulders again, as though trying to slough off the unease. "I read at his place, so I guess I shouldn't be as surprised as I am."

"What do you read, Perry?" he asked, his voice calm.

"Ménage stories," she said on a squeak. "I-I just found them last year. They're quite good."

Triumph roared through him at the admission, but her prim tone had him biting his cheek to withhold a grin. "I see."

"I doubt it," she snapped.

"No. It's something you enjoy. So why do you fight this?"

"Because this isn't a ménage romance, Edward," she snarled. "This is life. And you're not two rich playboys, or a CEO and a bodyguard. You're princes. You live in the public eye, and you have different rules to live by. As you've already told me. This is real life, not a wet dream."

"But you're curious about it..."

She gulped. "Yes."

"Then, why don't we let you sample exactly what it means to be shared by two men who care about you... and you can make a more informed decision about what your next steps will be. We have two weeks until you're scheduled to leave, no?"

She bit her lip, nodded. "No strings?"

It surprised him that her question stuck in his craw. "No strings," he confirmed, his voice rough with distaste at the notion.

He very much wanted strings, he realized. And then, asked himself how George had known Perry for so long and had managed to hold back. Had somehow stopped himself from diving into this headfirst...

He nodded again. "No strings," he confirmed.

She stared at him, bug-eyed and yet, glorious in her beauty too. Then, she smiled, and even the non-sensical suddenly made a whole hell of a lot of sense.

CHAPTER FOURTEEN

XAVIER FROWNED when Philippe appeared in the private suites' hallway.

Not that the king didn't have a right to be there; hell, more of a right than even Xavier himself—it was his uncle's castle after all! But the scowl on his face had Xavier wondering what was wrong.

Philippe was one of those men who could be at war, and he'd still look placid. He just had that kind of face. A face he'd passed on to his sons, too.

Xavier figured it made a difference when the men were leaders... added an air of confidence he hadn't inherited from his mother's side of the family. People followed where the reigning DeSauviers led because they were cool, competent, and collected. At all times. Even when life was chaotic and stressful as hell.

"Father?"

George appeared as surprised by Philippe's worried façade too.

"Where's your brother?"

George paused. "I don't know. He was in meetings all morning, as far as I'm aware."

"He didn't go out with you?"

"No. Haven't you spoken with Marcel?"

If anyone knew Edward's schedule, it was his PA.

"Of course, but he doesn't know where he is either." A shallow breath slipped from Philippe's lips, one that had Xavier tilting his head in surprise as he noticed it. Followed swiftly by another, then another, he realized his Uncle was breathing like he'd been running.

"What's going on?" Xavier demanded, when a frantic light appeared in his perennially calm uncle's eyes.

"I don't know," he said, his voice thick. Lifting a shaky hand, he ran it through his neatly styled hair. "He was due to meet with me twenty minutes ago, and he isn't picking up his phone."

"Has he gone riding?" George asked, seeming to pick up on his father's concern and adopting it himself.

Xavier, completely in the dark, just murmured, "It wouldn't be the first time."

When neither man appeared reassured by that statement, he sighed. "What's going on? It's not like Edward hasn't done this a hundred times before."

"Not for years! Not since he married Arabella," Philippe snapped. "He calmed down, started handling his duties with the seriousness required."

Xavier shrugged. "So he's having an off day."

George cut him a look, and his unease transmitted itself to Xavier. "The UnReals are at it again."

That statement alone had his stomach tightening. "What?"

George clenched his teeth. "There are two newly formed branches in Saxe and Heldafort," he explained, detailing two of Veronia's upper most provinces where anti-royalist sentiment had always been a problem. The UnReals were so called because *real,* pronounced ray-al, was the word for royal in Veronian. Anti-royalist sentiment had decreased of late; the royal family had gone to great lengths to be more open and in touch with the 'common' folk.

One of the major turning points had been when George and Edward had been kidnapped as children. Marianne's sobbing on national TV had done what nothing else could—bridged her to every other mother across the nation.

The families of the country had cried with her, sobbed at the lack of updates on the princes' whereabouts, and shouted with relief and joy when the boys had been returned to the castle. The people knew of the kidnapping, but their strict media laws had prevented the story from leaking outside the borders in any way but word of mouth, which was why Perry hadn't known about the abduction.

It wasn't common knowledge.

In the subsequent years, the UnReals had been quiet. With no dissent to sow in a country content with its leaders, they'd fallen out of favor. Until Arabella happened, that is.

She'd been a clothes' horse, nothing more, nothing less. Had about as much personality as a mannequin too, Xavier had always thought.

"They're violent again?"

Some groups of the UnReals were more violent than others; it tended to depend on the leaders.

"Of the two, one is definitely more militant."

Xavier rubbed his chin. "The guards are searching for Edward, correct?"

"Of course," Philippe snarled.

"Then they'll find him, *Papa*," George said softly, reaching up to grab his father's shoulder and to squeeze it. "All will be well."

Philippe choked, "If they've taken him... it will kill your mother."

"Why would they take him, *Papa*?"

Xavier shook his head. "He'll be somewhere in the palace." He cut George a look. "Where's Perry?"

Unfortunately, George was still scared too because terror flashed in his gaze. "You think she could have been taken too?"

Xavier boomed, "No! Of course not. He might be with her. You know how close they've been of late."

Philippe reared back, then stared at George. "I thought you and she...?"

George shuttered his eyes. "It's complicated." To Xavier, he murmured, "She should be in her office."

"Have you checked in there?"

"Why wouldn't he answer if he's in the castle?" Philippe demanded, but Xavier and George knew why.

"Let's see if he's there before we worry further," Xavier tried to soothe his uncle, hating how jittery the man looked.

He'd never seen him this panicked. Even when George and Edward had been taken as boys, he'd held it together. He remembered hearing his own mother whisper at her brother's fortitude in the face of what he was dealing with; declaring to Xavier's father that she wouldn't be so brave in the same circumstances...

Now?

It seemed the façade of old was crumbling, and who could blame Philippe for it?

He'd been on the throne for thirty-eight years. That was a long time to live with constant threats, and Veronia—more than most nations with royal families—had dealt with the repercussions of those threats.

No other royals in Europe had been abducted successfully by extremists. It was why, after the kidnapping, Veronian security had been overhauled to such an extent that they'd had to fill in a lot of positions with foreign workers.

"Where's her office?" he asked George.

"It's close to the private area but near Mother's sitting room."

"The Chinese suite?"

George nodded, and as a trio, they stormed out of the private area, down a set of stairs that were lined with some of the best pre-Raphaelite works of art outside of a museum, and toward the administrative area where Marianne dealt with matters of state.

That Perry had been given the Chinese suite spoke of how well George's opinion was respected. He'd suggested Perry for the job, and his parents had concurred that she could be of some use to the nation. By putting her in an office close to the queen, it was another nod of respect to the woman who was probably clueless about how she'd been honored.

He liked that about her though.

She wasn't used to dealing with all the BS of protocol, and it didn't bother her.

When they reached the suite, he knocked on the door to warn her they were coming in—just in case—and opened up without waiting for a reply.

His delay wasn't necessary; the couple in the office weren't doing anything dirty, but the three of them had definitely interrupted something major.

The intensity in the air was almost palpable... he just wasn't certain if Uncle Philippe noticed in his relief at seeing his son, safe and sound.

"Thank God!" he whispered in Veronian, then strode deeper into the room. When he approached Edward, he hesitated, and Xavier sensed his uncle's uncertainty.

Undoubtedly, he wanted to hug his son like there was no tomorrow. But Edward was in the dark and didn't understand.

His cousin frowned up at his father. "What's wrong?"

Philippe closed his eyes, and his relief was almost as palpable as whatever they'd disturbed in the office. "I thought you'd been kidnapped."

Edward jolted, his reaction so intense he jumped to his feet. "What?"

Perry sat upright, and Xavier caught her eye and shook his head, silently asking her to stay quiet.

If she made so much as another move to grab his uncle's attention, they'd take this elsewhere, and Perry needed to know exactly what was happening if she was to make an informed decision about her future.

Whatever they'd broken up in here, Xavier was no dummy... it had been pertinent to their relationship. The way they wanted it to manifest, or not to as the case may be. She nodded slightly, telling him she'd received his barely there message.

"Why would you think I'd been kidnapped?" Edward demanded hoarsely.

"Do you remember I told you about the two groups of UnReals?"

Edward nodded, but he looked dazed, and Xavier couldn't blame him.

That time, after the abduction, was long ago. But worse than that, the distress had made his memories hazy.

All he could truthfully remember about that period was his terror at the prospect of never seeing his cousins again, but also, his horror at being the next in line to the throne.

He'd been a child, not ready for such responsibility, and it shamed the adult in him to admit that he'd probably been more relieved for himself than his cousins when they'd been returned alive, shaken, but otherwise healthy.

"Yes," Edward was saying, breaking into Xavier's thoughts. "I remember. A militant faction and a more peaceful one."

Philippe nodded. "The militant faction divided a month ago. I just received intel on this update. Our police found a site where they're training recruits and also planning some kind of terror attack at Parliament."

Edward raised a hand and wiped at his mouth. Rather than drop his hand, he tugged at his lips as he fell back against the sofa.

"On the opening ceremony?" he questioned, mentioning the event that saw Parliament start up again after summer break, then hissed when Philippe nodded. "Bastards."

The King grimaced. "Understatement. But it makes sense. That's when Parliament House is at its most full." He grunted. "There were also plans of…"

Edward gritted his teeth. "I can imagine. Another abduction plot."

Philippe nodded. "And it was as we suspected… there is a mole in the castle. They have information that could be from no other source than a guard or someone in security who works here."

George hissed. "We have a leak?"

"There can be no other reason as to why they'd have the codes they do, the intel they have on our exit strategies and safe rooms." The king's hands curled into fists. "That is why I was so scared. Some UnReals escaped the raid; they'd been spotted in the capital. I feared…"

Edward reached over and clapped his father on the arm. But Philippe grabbed him, hauled him upright, and held him in an embrace that made even Xavier's throat thick.

He'd always known his uncle loved his family—truly loved. Not an ounce of duty marring that affection—why else would he have let George have free reign in the US? But to see his horror and relief mingling as he embraced his son warmed Xavier's heart, and when he looked over at Perry, knew she felt the same.

The fear was there. The news the king had imparted couldn't be more divisive—they'd caught some UnReals in the raid, but more were missing, and they were desperate.

Desperate men were willing to go to lengths others weren't. That meant they were all in danger. And by association, Perry would be too.

Especially if she agreed to become Edward's girlfriend.

CHAPTER FIFTEEN

WHEN PHILIPPE APPEARED in her office, he looked shaken and frail.

Perry was stunned to note the difference between the usually vital man and the one who'd entered her office looking scared. The brothers were no different, nor was Xavier. They were all affected by the news, and all of them turned to look at her save for Edward who was staring at the floor.

He seemed as frozen as Philippe, and who could blame him?

He was in danger. Again.

Her fingers curled in on themselves, her nails biting into the fleshy pads of her palms as outrage swept through her at his despondency.

Xavier had told her about the brothers' abduction. Had told her how it had changed both boys forever.

"Were the UnReals the guys who..."

Xavier caught her glance. "Yeah." His voice was rough with remembered misery, and she hated herself for having stirred that to life with her question.

The UnReals? What kind of fucking name was that anyway?

It was like... hell, she didn't goddamn know, but rage coursing through her, after days of indecision, suddenly felt good.

It felt right. And she knew that was weird as hell, but it was fact.

These guys were...she gulped. Hers.

Nobody, and she meant no-fucking-body could threaten them. *Hurt* them. Goddammit, no.

Maybe she could have taken this the other way—been scared for herself too. If someone could get to kids as well guarded as two princes, then that was some major planning, but she wasn't thinking about herself.

She was thinking about them.

She was thinking about two small boys who'd suddenly been ripped from their family's arms for profit and to make a statement.

She was thinking about two kids who'd grown into adulthood, knowing what it was to feel fear, to know that their safety was borrowed and never totally secured.

The men standing here at that moment had all simultaneously aged and grown younger... As though their natures were unable to comprehend the news Philippe had just imparted. The child in them that had been kidnapped was out in full force, while equally, the men were older, wearier at the news they would have to follow different protocols to stay safe.

Philippe murmured, "The head of the guards will need to speak with both of you. Your security will have to change, tighten up, and the force increase." His sigh was heavy. "No more solitary rides, son."

The news hit Edward like a bullet. He jolted back, like guys in movies did after they'd been shot in the chest.

"Solitary?" Xavier snapped. "He has two guards with him at all times."

Philippe shook his head. "You know that's not enough."

"I know this is bullshit," Xavier retorted. "We can't play scared, or that will just make them feel like they've won, dammit. They want us to be scared, they want us terrified and so over-protected we don't get to live our lives."

The king closed his eyes, and that act told Perry the old man knew the truth in his nephew's words but was too riddled with fear to let them sway him. "It's imperative," Philippe said hoarsely, "that they are protected. They are the future of this nation, Xavier. You are too. Don't think you're not involved in this updated security protocol." Philippe shook his head at George, whose nostrils flared, almost like he knew exactly what his father was about to say... "And, for the time being, I think it's wise to stay in Veronia, son. Returning to the US is unwise with this current threat hanging over us."

Perry staggered back and sat heavily on the sofa she'd only left moments before.

Moments in which she'd been postulating over whether or not to dive headfirst into the wackiest relationship she'd ever contemplated. Being not only with two men, but with two princes. Being shared by them, fucked and loved by them...

It had seemed such a crazy concept. Hot as hell, but crazy nonetheless.

Now, her worst fear was being realized.

Edward had said that George would, one day, have to return, but that couldn't be today. Could it?

She wasn't sure why she said it, didn't know if she'd regret it months down the line, but a soft sound escaped her lips and drew the attention of the men in the room.

Her bottom lip quivered as she whispered, "We should tell them, Edward."

The crown prince—for at that moment, that was who he was—turned bruised eyes to her. That he wasn't his usual suave and assured self hurt her so intrinsically, the pain was sharp in her abdomen.

Edward was strong and borderline cocky—enough to make her want to slap him when he revealed that side of himself. He was debonair and so goddamn cool that it was like having a conversation with James Bond sometimes... Then, throw in the fact he was sexy as hell and there was the potential for him to screw her brains out?

Yeah, his overall hotness blew her mind.

But this? The pain in his eyes, the deep abyss within those golden orbs that spoke of memories too heartbreaking for her to even think about...it just affirmed what she was about to do.

"Perry?" Philippe prompted, a confused scowl on his brow. "Tell us what?" he added when neither she nor Edward said a word, just stared at each other. A visual connection forming between them in the time they took to stare one another down.

She tilted her chin, jerking it upright with a staunch pride that would set the tone for the rest of her life.

"I think I'll need guards too, Your Highness. Edward and I have been dating for a while now... If he's in danger, I might be as well."

CHAPTER SIXTEEN

THE KITTEN HAD CLAWS.

George had always known it. Had always sensed his Perry was a tigress when it boiled down to it. Sure, she was soft in all the ways he loved. So different to the courtiers who were hard and grasping, but in that moment, he knew he'd never loved her more than now.

Her chin was propped in the air like she was expecting a fight with his father, a fight she'd have no problem joining if push came to shove. There was a militant gleam in her eye, a challenge—she was daring the king of a large and wealthy nation to question her statement.

To doubt her word.

At his side, Xavier stiffened, but what worried him more was Edward's lack of reaction. He'd retreated inside his shell, and George wasn't certain if that was for good or ill. For ill, because he knew exactly where Edward's mind had taken him.

He was too young to truly remember what had happened, but his elder brother wasn't. The mind being what it was, George's had blanked out huge chunks of what had been done to them. Sometimes, when he was stressed, he *would* have dreams. Or, he supposed, nightmares were more apt a term, but he didn't remember them. Just remembered the haunting sense that came with them, and reminded him of that time.

Edward, on the other hand, remembered everything. Not that they talked about it often, but when the well of pain in Edward's eyes grew too deep, George always knew where he'd gone. Where memories had taken him.

The only way his turning inward could be viewed in any kind of positive light, was that he wasn't refuting Perry's claim. And that was exactly what it was. She was claiming him, claiming *them*.

The knowledge was like an embrace from her, and it sucked that he couldn't stride over to her and kiss her until she shook in delight at that claiming. But that was the path he'd chosen.

He was granting Edward the public side of her, not the private. When Philippe left, he'd tug her into his arms and show her exactly what she meant to him.

Perry, unlike Edward, looked like she was ready to charge into war. He loved that about her. Loved that she was willing to fight for his brother, because Arabella sure as hell hadn't.

"How long have you been hiding this relationship from us?" Philippe asked of his elder son. Then, to George, he questioned, "And did you know about it?"

He blinked. Nodded.

"How long?" Philippe repeated.

Perry licked her lips, faltering for the first time. Semantics, George knew.

He didn't know Edward's schedule, didn't know when he'd been out of the country... didn't know how to make it seem like they'd been seeing each other for a while.

"Long enough for it to be serious."

The words had everyone turning to Edward. He still looked internally bruised and so goddamn tired, George wanted to scream his fury at what those bastards were putting his brother, hell, and his family through. Because the minute his mother learned of this, she'd be terrified too.

Perry swallowed, caught Edward's gaze. A connection between them burned to life, stunning George with its ferocity.

When he'd met Perry, he hadn't thought that much of her in a sexual way. He'd been screwing someone at the time, someone he was content to hook up with, and he hadn't been looking for anyone else or even for anything serious.

She'd started off as a friend, and as that friendship had blossomed, his attraction to her had swelled.

Regardless of his initial reaction, she wasn't their usual type, and he and Edward had similar tastes when it came to women—only natural considering their inclinations. He'd known, at first glance, Edward wouldn't see Perry's charm and beauty for what it was, but that with time, she'd grow on him.

And grow she had.

Like something in one of Perry's experiments, he thought wryly—

knowing that only to his beautiful, wacky woman would that be a compliment.

Being compared to a spore wasn't most ladies' ideas of sweet talk, but Perry wasn't like other women. A fact he was inordinately grateful for. Seeing the blaze between the two of them, he knew he was right. A fact that made him feel rather smug. This would work.

He would make it work, he told himself, the ferocity of his own belief surprising even him.

Perry was too good a friend to lose to a whim, and now, because of this situation, the three of them were all-in.

Xavier was an anomaly they'd have to explore.

George had never shared with two men before, wasn't even sure it could work. Especially not with his cousin, but hell, if Perry wanted him, who was he to question?

A man couldn't ask a woman to allow herself to be shared without expecting some unforeseen circumstances to arrive as a result of that request. The interesting thing was, he wasn't jealous. Maybe with anyone else, he would be. But Xavier was… he sighed. As much of a brother as Edward.

"This changes things," Philippe was saying, his voice breaking into the sexual tension arcing between Edward and Perry. But his tone was rueful, telling George he too had seen the responsiveness of their reactions to one another.

There was no mistaking the feelings between the pair. A blind man would have sensed the connection.

"Of course, it does," Edward said, his tone bland, as he cut the cord and turned to look at him. "She'll need to go through training."

Perry's eyes widened, and George had to hide a grin. "Training? What kind of training?"

Perry was anti-exercise. Mostly because she had two left feet and was one of the only people he knew with the ability to fall up stairs rather than down.

For her own personal safety, she'd told him once, she'd decided that being a slob was in her best interests.

"There are things you'll have to learn, responses you'll have to cultivate…in emergency situations."

She settled back, and for the first time, George saw a tremor rack her spine.

Xavier saw it too, and surprised George by striding toward her, kneeling at her feet as he simultaneously reached for her hands. "It will be okay, Perry."

Philippe looked between his sons, and George knew he was confused. Who could blame him?

This situation was beyond complex; Xavier's response to Perry was as strong as Edward's and George's. And how Perry looked at Xavier was just as revealing.

At that moment, he was a lifeline.

Philippe cleared his throat. "We need to speak with Drake."

George grimaced—Drake was head of security, and had been a pain in his ass throughout all his teenaged years. Even though the man had only ever acted in George's best interests, a fact he could understand now, his dislike of the bastard was irrational and totally adolescent.

Philippe seemed to spot his disgust and for the first time since he'd made his revelations, chuckled. He cuffed George on the back of the head. "You never did like Drake, did you?"

"He was the only one who made sure you couldn't get out of the castle at night," Xavier retorted with a grin, turning back to look at the three of them.

Even Edward warmed at the gentle teasing. "I'm glad he wasn't in charge when I was eighteen."

George huffed. "If only I was so lucky." He watched as Xavier's hand tightened around Perry's, and noticed her response was to grab hold of his with both of hers.

His father saw it too, and frowned. He'd never been certain how aware Philippe was over their 'activities' when they were younger.

Their security detail couldn't not have known what they got up to, and usually, that information had a way of trickling back to the king.

If Philippe did know about it, he'd never mentioned it, and George highly doubted he'd have shared that information with Marianne.

Philippe caught his eye a second. Though his mouth tightened, he just said, "Why didn't you tell me they were dating?"

"Not my place to share," he rejoined immediately, grateful that he didn't have to give an outright lie.

He'd never liked lying to his father.

Philippe, for all he'd been busy with the duties of his position, had actually been a bloody good father.

Fair and kind, generous with what little time he had to spare. Even going so far as to make time for them on an impossible routine. Their childhood had been different to any other kid's, but for years, both the king and queen had made a point of tucking him in on a night. They'd had nannies, but that final duty had been theirs alone.

Only when they'd been out of state on travel duties had they been unable to do so and even then, there had been a nightly call to check in.

The king and the queen had truly shown their children they were loved, and as a result, the respect both sons had for their parents was without surfeit.

Lying to Philippe was one way to completely destroy that respect.

"You shouldn't have hidden this from us," he was chiding Edward. "Even going so far as to pretend to never having met when Perry arrived..."

Edward shrugged. "I didn't want to embroil her in something she wasn't ready to handle."

"What's changed in two weeks?" Philippe said, a scoff to his words.

"I have," Edward said calmly, and their father blinked at that.

"You have?"

Father and son met each other's gaze. "Yes. I wasn't ready, but now I am."

"Ready for what?"

"Ready to officially out ourselves as dating. You know what the press is like. Even though they're controlled here and we have some privacy, Perry's life is in the US... their journalists are different to ours."

Philippe shook his head. "How are we supposed to protect her when she's over there? I can't sanction a Veronian detail guarding her when she has no ties to you."

He shrugged. "That shouldn't be a problem. Perry's staying in Veronia to oversee the construction of three new dams."

Though Perry's eyes widened at that news, telling George that was the first she'd heard of this story, it was the perfect distraction for Philippe.

"Three new dams?" If the man's voice could ever be so low as to be a squeak, then that was his pitch now. "Three? That's totally impossible."

"Not if we want to combat the drought and stop it before it becomes a major issue." Edward slapped the file he had in his hand against Philippe's chest. "Read the report. It's a compelling read, and the statistics don't lie."

Philippe narrowed his eyes but grabbed the file and flipped through it. He grunted after a few minutes and said, "I don't have time to read this now. Drake will be waiting, and even I don't like to waste his time."

George grinned at the idea of his father, the king, being afraid of their head of security. Considering Drake made the term 'brick shithouse' seem kind, George guessed it was fitting.

"Am I needed?" Xavier asked softly, his attention still on Perry.

Philippe sighed. "Yes, but I know you'll ignore my words. If only my nephew was as obedient as my sons."

That had Xavier whipping around to grin at his uncle. "You tried your best, Uncle."

"My best wasn't good enough with you," Philippe grumbled, but he waggled a finger at him. "Drake will be talking to you at some point. If I hear you've given him the run around, I will not be happy."

Xavier shrugged. "I won't put myself in any undue danger. What harm can I come to in my greenhouse?"

"I don't know, but if you can find trouble, you'll find it. You always were mischievous, boy."

He rolled his eyes. "If you say so."

George grinned because he could well remember the many rounds of 'mischief' Xavier had undertaken as a child.

There'd been the time he'd stolen his mother, Lisetta's glasses, and he and Edward had switched places for the day. George remembered that one as Xavier had used his mother's confusion to sneak off their estate and to go into the forests.

He'd been found, hours later, curled up by one of the ponds where the stags and does went to drink. Yes, Xavier's mischief always had a distinctly geeky edge to it. Unlike Edward, who had been a rebel of James Dean proportions.

"Come, sons," Philippe directed. "We must go."

Edward nodded. "I'll be in your office in five minutes, Father. I just want to talk to Perry."

Philippe cut him a look but didn't complain, just grabbed George's arm before he could try and stay behind, and dragged him out the door. It killed him to leave. He wanted to know what Edward would be saying to Perry, what Xavier would say too, but that wasn't to be.

He'd have to be patient and find out what had been discussed later. Shame that he'd never been renowned for his patience.

CHAPTER SEVENTEEN

PERRY PEERED at her new wardrobe and groaned at the sight of the many, many clothes that had made an abrupt appearance without her even knowing it.

George and his minions at work again, she supposed with a grumble. Then, scratching her forehead, she stared at the dozens of rows of hangers that were loaded with designer couture, and headed for the three drawers she'd unpacked herself from her smaller cabin bag, having left the clothes George had bought her to be unpacked by the staff.

There was a comfort in finding her sloggy sweats and beaten up Harvard tee scrunched in a pile in the drawer, and she picked them up, pressed her nose to the material and smelled the scent of home.

Was it weird to find that scent of home in a fabric softener? It was just so different to what they used in the palace.

She hadn't thought she'd gone for a cheap brand of cleaning products, but having stayed here and had her panties washed by the royal laundry, yeah, she'd learned otherwise.

Even her scratchy panties were like silk now, and she had no idea what the people in charge of her laundry did to them to make them that way, but they should sell their secret.

They'd make a fortune. Perhaps even enough to pay for the dams she was insisting the country needed.

Her lips twitched at the thought, but not enough to curve into a smile.

Boy, she was tired today. Really, really tired.

She switched out of her more formal office gear, which for many women would be basic as hell but was way too rigid for her tastes—a white shirt and tailored pants, and found comfort in her slob clothes.

As she unfastened the knot her hair was tied into, she headed out of the room and found Xavier there. She blinked in surprise, not having expected to see him.

Ever since she'd told the king she and Edward were dating, and that it was serious, she hadn't seen him.

He'd stayed with her after George and Edward had left to talk to the security detail, but he hadn't really said much, had just made sure she was okay before he'd taken off himself—to the meeting with the rest of his family she'd assumed.

"What are you doing here?" she asked, her tone more curious than sharp at finding him in her personal space.

"I wanted to talk to you," he admitted, pushing his hands into the pockets of his jeans.

"What about?"

"What you told Philippe the other day?"

She'd expected as much.

Sighing, she ran a hand through her hair. "I'm tired."

His eyes softened. "You've been pushing yourself too hard."

She lifted her chin. "How can I not? Your stupid Parliament is being stubborn."

Edward had given her proposal to the Environmental Agency, but they had declared her report far too sketchy to be trusted.

Sketchy.

The fucking nerve!

As a result, whether she wanted to or not, if she wanted to protect her professional name, she had to stay here.

Oh, the irony.

She'd declared to the king himself that she was in a relationship with his son to stay here, when she'd have had to remain in Veronia period.

Was that irony, or just fate working its bizarre hand?

She headed for the sofa and slumped into it. It wasn't comfortable. At all. In fact, she wouldn't have been surprised if behind the cushions, there'd been horsehair or some shit like that too.

A notion that didn't exactly please her, but it wasn't like Barcaloungers would fit in with the whole regal-ness of the room.

Wishing like hell they did, and that there was one, she curled her feet underneath her and said, "Sit. You look as tired as me."

"I've not been sleeping," he admitted. "In the middle of an experiment, you know how things are."

Because she did, her lips curved. "It's different though. That's a kind of nervous excitement..."

He grinned back. "Yeah." Taking a seat on the sofa opposite her, he murmured, "So far, my hypothesis is standing strong. A few more tweaks, and the pesticide I'm working on will be ready for testing on a larger plot of land than what I've been working with. I need to increase the variables to see how functional it is."

She nodded; he'd discussed his new ideas for organic pesticides. Ways and means of combatting the bugs that could destroy whole crops without wrecking the nutritional value of the fruit or vegetable the chemicals were supposed to be protecting, but also without leaching 'goodness' from the soil.

"I'll have to take you to my greenhouse one day," he told her, his voice strumming with excitement. "You'd love it in there. A little piece of heaven amid the chaos that is this castle."

Because she understood what he meant, she let out a sigh. This place was calm to the point of weird. It was peaceful and strict with it. But though there was a bizarre façade of gentility, to her, and to him as well it seemed, there was a chaos to it.

A kind of madness that she was relieved to know didn't just affect her.

"That would be really nice," she told him, and meant it. Leaning her head back against the high back of the seat—the only good thing about the damn piece of furniture—she asked, "Hit me with it, Xavier. Don't keep me in suspense."

He blinked, and his lips twitched into a half-smile. "I do like you, Perry."

Surprised, she stiffened in her seat. Whatever she'd expected him to say, it hadn't been that.

"I like you too, Xavier," she replied cautiously. "I-I'm sorry about the other day."

They'd not spoken of seeing each other since that one night together, but she felt it had been cruel of her to make such a declaration in front of him.

He held up a hand. "I understand why you did it."

She bit her lip. "You do? That's weird, because I don't. Not really.

"Before the king arrived, we were just saying that we were going to try this... thing—" She cleared her throat. "—out. And then, Philippe barges in, tells us about the threats and..." She jerked a shoulder.

"The rest, as they say, is history." His lips quirked in a rueful smile.

"Yes." She blinked at him.

"Do you think you made a mistake?"

"Why? Do you?"

"No. Not really. I'm just curious about what you think."

A sigh escaped her, and it was curiously liberating to be talking about this with someone who knew the full story. Who didn't judge. Who, not necessarily understood, but didn't think it was completely outlandish and nuts.

"Do you know what's strange?"

He blinked. "What?"

"That the only one of the DeSauviers I've slept with is you."

"That's because you've got great taste," he joked, and she huffed out a laugh.

Raising a hand, she rubbed at her temple. "Before Philippe came, Edward was telling me how eventually, George would have to come home."

Xavier nodded. "Yes. He was always on borrowed time in the States. I'm surprised he wasn't called back sooner. After Arabella died, to be truthful. I know Aunt Marianne and Uncle Philippe had to work hard to curry favor. A lot of people in the government wanted him back here and working for the country."

She tilted her head to the side. "How? In what position?"

"Probably what he does now, but for Veronia." He shrugged. "He was fortunate he got to stay away as long as he did."

She lifted a hand and began to tug at her bottom lip. "Do you think I'm strange for hemming and hawing over this?"

He reared back. "No. Why would I?"

"They're princes. They're gorgeous. They're rich. They're kind and polite and have table manners. I should be humping their legs in gratitude for picking me. Shouldn't I?"

He grunted. "The reason they picked you, as you so elegantly phrased it, is because you're not like the others. You're not like most of the court's ladies who would literally swoon if they thought they had the chance to ensnare one of them into their beds."

Her eyes widened. "Seriously?"

"Seriously." His smile was grim. "They're animals. In their own polite way, of course." When she stared at him, goggle-eyed, he explained, "You haven't been to enough events to understand."

"Thank God for that. I've managed to avoid most of the ones that have been going on since I arrived here."

He pulled a face. "You know that will have to change now, don't you? If Edward attends, and he usually does, you have to make an appearance."

She blew out a shaky breath—that was a conclusion she'd come to herself. Hence the sweats and sloggy T-shirt. She really needed the comfort of home before the insanity truly struck and she was trapped in the maelstrom.

Pressing her elbow into the sofa's armrest, she propped her head on her hand and murmured, "I want them, Xavier."

His eyes were calm, free from turbulence. "I know."

"I want you too." The words weren't torn from her, but they were a rough admission, regardless.

There was a reason she'd slept with him when she never engaged in one-night stands.

There was a reason she found it easy to talk to him when she could count on one hand the number of friends she had in the world. Most of whom she couldn't talk so freely with.

"I want you too, Perry."

There was a calmness to his words that had her frowning. "Was I mad to do what I did?" She felt like it was mad now she'd done it. But the prospect of having to return to the States without George was something she couldn't abide.

The prospect of leaving Edward behind while he dealt with this situation with the UnReals, was something she couldn't abide.

The prospect of cutting and running on Xavier, of not hearing from him again or discussing one of his experiments, was something she couldn't abide.

There was a whole lot of 'not abiding' going on, but it was how she felt. There was no evading it.

"This is crazy," she whispered, as she'd been whispering of late.

"It doesn't have to be."

His simple retort had her eyes widening. She got to her feet and began to stride. From one end of the room to the other, she walked. And it felt good, felt right to burn off some of the energy.

"Next weekend, we should go to my estate in Lauverne."

"Where's that?" she asked, turning to look at him as she carried on loping from one side of the room to the other.

"In the South. It's on the sea front, and you can swim and relax. Get some sun."

"I'm not the kind of woman who sunbathes, Xavier," she pointed out, disappointed he hadn't realized that.

But he snorted. "I meant while you worked. There's a nice verandah that overlooks the Mediterranean. You can work on whatever hoops the government want you to jump through, sit in the warmth without being cooped up in this mausoleum, and then go in the sea. It's still warm enough to swim."

She bit her lip at the idea; it sounded like heaven to her. She hadn't swum in an age, and getting out of the palace was exactly what she needed.

"I already told George and Edward," he said calmly. "They told me if you want to go, then we'll all go."

"All four of us?" she asked, eyes widening at the ease in his tone.

"Yes." He caught her eye, and the look they shared had her swallowing in response.

For a second, she froze, then her mouth worked. "All four of us," she repeated, this time, even she wasn't sure if she was asking him or making a statement.

He nodded. "All four of us."

Her hand flew to her throat as her brain processed exactly what he was telling her with that one comment, but her body came to her aid.

She knew what he was saying... knew it, and couldn't be scared of it. She did want him. She did want them.

And it seemed they were willing to let her have her way. Even if that way wasn't something she'd consciously thought about.

Until now.

She couldn't cut the image out of her damn mind.

"As for tomorrow, I want you to come to my estate here in the city."

Her eyes widened as she processed the offer of two... what? Dates?

"Why?"

He grinned, reached for her. As he looped his hands around her waist, he hauled her toward him. A whoosh of air escaped her as she collided with him. "Does there have to be a reason?"

She blinked up at him as a smile curved her lips. He leaned down, his head moving toward hers, his gaze intent on her mouth as she whispered, "No. You're right. There doesn't have to be a reason."

CHAPTER EIGHTEEN

A KNOCK SOUNDING at his door dragged George from the book he was reading. It wasn't the sharp, yet gentle knock of a member of staff who needed to get his attention but didn't want to irritate him at the same time.

It was brisk and demanding.

Perry.

He grinned, rolled off the bed, and strode toward the door. Opening it, he was about to greet her, but he saw the hectic flush on her face and stayed his mouth.

He stepped back when she strode forward, and as she slammed his door, she leapt at him.

The move stunned the shit out of him, and he had no choice but to catch her.

"What the—"

He didn't have a chance to finish his sentence. Her mouth was on his before he could take his next breath, and then her tongue was between his lips.

The kiss was nothing like he'd imagined the first melding of their mouths to be.

This was primal. Raw. *Desperate.*

The emotions battered him, and he didn't understand them. Didn't understand why she felt that way, but his love for her demanded that he make it better.

That he take away the unease, the uncertainty, and replace it with something that would never change—his adoration of her.

He let their tongues whisper across the other, let her bite into his bottom lip, fucking his mouth as she held his cheeks between her hands. She switched between aggressive tongue fucks and gentle love play that had his heart beating like a drum.

Her hips began to rock, and though he knew he had a hard-on, had had one since she'd stepped into his room wearing nothing but one of the peignoirs he'd bought her and, he assumed, some lingerie beneath. But she realized it now, and used her position atop him to drag her core down his length.

A whimper escaped her, and it turned into a low mewl as her desire caught up with her.

She kept herself attached to him with the strong thighs she had glued to his hips, so he kept a hand on her ass to steady her, while moving the other up to her hair to drag it out of the way of her throat.

He used his grip on her hair to tug her head back, and the minute their lips were separated, he dove for her.

His lips plied the tender flesh, sucking and slurping in a way that would have her cursing him in the morning. He intended to mark her. Intended for her to know who she was and what she was—his.

Just because he wanted to share her with his brother didn't diminish that.

She was his. As she was theirs too.

But their bond was unique, strengthened only because their connection was a force to be reckoned with. Empowered by years of friendship, years that had been leading to this moment.

He'd always imagined the first time to be gentle. A tender seduction. In fact, he'd been nervous of how to broach it. Though he'd been hard as nails for her for years, and though she'd opened herself up to the idea of being shared, he'd been scared to approach her.

Scared because he hadn't wanted her to reject him. But Perry being Perry had decided to take control of things on her own. He loved that about her.

Loved that she was so strong, so self-assured in some things, then so vulnerable in others.

He knew her too well. Knew this wasn't born out of the confidence she had for her work, but out of her vulnerability.

She was scared, and she needed to take charge to combat that fear.

That meant she had to seduce him. Prove to herself that she was enough for him.

As if she could ever be less.

Her knees tightened about his hips as she began to rock her own. The drag of her pelvis against his shaft was more than he could stand, and he nipped at her throat and bit off, "Fucking behave, Perry."

A throaty laugh escaped her, and he reveled in the sound—it meant she was calming down. She ignored him, of course, and instead, carried on. Only, she moved slower, taunted him and teased herself as punishment for his command.

He bit down hard on her shoulder, enough to make her hiss. But she didn't chide him, only grabbed a hold of his head, ran her fingers through his hair, then forced his lips back to hers.

"Fuck me," she demanded, her tone almost angry, but it wasn't born in rage. Just in fire.

Their passion was off the charts, as he'd always known it would be, but the proof that he was right was almost enough to make him weep.

With a groan, he let her bite his bottom lip, then staggered over to the bed where he carefully seated himself.

"You want to fuck me?" he gritted out against her lips. "Then fuck me."

She moaned, and he loved the tender sound as it whispered across his mouth. She delved between them, parting the folds of the peignoir to reveal her body—her naked body. A body he'd dreamed about for fucking years. A buxom form he was astonished to find free from lingerie and all the more enticing for it.

She was perfect. Ripe with curves, slender where it counted. He loved the marks on her breasts, their jiggle, and the fleshiness of her hips. She was real, she was beautiful. She was his.

He grabbed her waist to steady her as she reached between them again, this time aiming lower. Her hand moved beneath his waistband, and his pajamas were loose enough that she could easily grab his cock without strangling the crown jewels in the elastic.

When she held him, he closed his eyes and let out a slow, long breath that was more of a hiss than anything else.

Her hand shaped him, carefully at first. And with each stroke, he felt like grunting.

His head tipped forward against hers, their foreheads touching as their breaths mingled—surging the intensity between them to heights he'd never known before.

She whispered, "This belongs to me," as she jerked her hand upwards, his cock tight in her first.

His grin was quick. Sly. And his hand was too. It slid between her parted thighs and didn't stop until his thumb was notched in her gate.

"And this is mine," he retorted, watching the passion glaze her eyes as he fucked her with his thumb.

For a second, they were immobile, and then he nudged her clit with the back of his hand, and she arched up, almost tumbling off his lap.

Before he could grab her, she steadied herself, grabbed at the condom he handed her, and covered his cock with the sheath. Then, using the momentum to better position herself, she let her pussy slide over his shaft. Quickly moving his thumb away, he felt her cunt grasp the tip of his shaft and strangle it in a choke hold.

They both gasped, and the gasp brushed over the other's mouths as they finally came together.

Him claiming her, her absorbing his claim—Perry-style.

A low groan escaped him as she carefully lowered herself onto him, and he loved how she whimpered with each claimed inch. Loved how she mewled and groaned and moaned as she took all of him.

He alternated between staring into her hazy eyes and looking down between them. The muscles and sinews on either side of her pussy were taut with a tension that came from her position. A position that had her pussy spread apart.

Her lips were forced apart by his thickness too, and the bud of her clit peeped out. He reached up and dragged his thumb over her lips. There were juices on the digit, and she let her tongue drag over it, sucking it into her mouth until he wanted to groan at the way she worked him over.

Jesus, when he got his cock into her mouth, he'd be a happy bunny.

As she sank down all the way, impaled on him fully, he reached between them, and with his thumb, began to tease her clit once more.

Gentle flickers at first, then harder rubbing as she began to ride him. Her knees clutched his hips, and she used the mattress to ground them both as she moved quickly. Barely letting him out of her pussy, keeping him deep inside, but maintaining a friction that about blew his goddamn mind.

With each frig of her clit, she let out more small whimpers until they were an endless moan that serenaded his ears.

He felt her pussy clutching at him, knew she was close, and he didn't want to climax without her, so he quickened his pace.

When her head flung backward, the sinews in her marked throat tense with the strain, he moved his hands and grabbed her hips.

Before she knew what he was about, he dragged her down over his shaft, filling her overfull in a way she couldn't have managed without his brute strength.

The cry that escaped her lips was magic in its intensity, and he knew he'd never forget that moment. Knew he wouldn't be able to.

That sound alone would forever be imprinted on his mind.

And as the long, seemingly endless cry of wonder filled his ears, the clutching of her internal muscles dragged release from him... All George knew at that moment was that he had just had the best sex of his fucking life.

"WHAT MADE YOU COME HERE?"

Perry squinted at George. She slapped a hand over her face. "It's too early for this."

"Too early for what?" he asked wryly. "We haven't even slept yet."

She gaped up at him. "We haven't?"

"No. Just napped," he told her, laughing as he peered at them both, then at the windows which were bare to the night—he hadn't closed the shades yet.

After she'd climaxed, he'd dragged them both into a more comfortable position and together, they'd napped.

He'd awoken first, and had sensed her wakefulness too.

"Whatever, it's still too early to dissect this," she grumbled.

He laughed, reached down to kiss the crown of her head. "You're a pain in the ass, do you know that?"

She shot a look at him. "*Your* pain in the ass?" she joked, playing on his words.

"Yeah." He smirked. "That sounds pretty cool to me."

Her bottom lip was scored by her teeth as she processed that, but the cocky smile that appeared soon after told him she liked his train of thought.

Not that she told him that, of course. She simply murmured, "I need chocolate."

"Cigarettes are more customary in the post-coital glow."

She pulled a face. "I'd prefer chocolate. But will accept ice cream."

"Want me to get you some?"

Her eyes widened. "You have some here?"

"I have a fridge just off the dressing room."

"You have a fridge?" Her mouth dropped open, then she scrambled off the bed. "Show me!"

Chuckling as she hopped down, still half dressed in the mostly-open peignoir that was now stained on the back, thanks to the wet spot the silk had been unfortunate enough to catch, he had to hide a smile at her simple earthiness.

She wasn't ashamed of the recently-fucked look, and he loved that about her. It was raw and real, and that was what he needed from her.

She grounded him. Always had, and now, she always would.

After what they'd just experienced together... there was no way he was ever letting her go.

His bedroom was bigger than hers. There were several areas within it. The bed stood on the back wall, and it was far less grand than hers, which was antique—his was more for living rather than peering at in astonishment.

Then, there was a small seating area over by the windows that overlooked the gardens on the back half of the building and the Ansian mountain range.

Besides that, there was a TV and a sofa with two armchairs.

Opposite the bed, there were two doors. One led to his connecting bath, the other to his dressing room and the small kitchen he had there.

He strode after her, and with his hand on her shoulder, guided her to the kitchenette. She whistled when she entered the marble-countered room with its copper finishing.

"This is your idea of a kitchenette, huh?"

"Get used to it," he advised, reaching around her to open the fridge. "This is your life now."

She gulped, suddenly nervous. "Don't say that."

"Don't say what?" he asked, cocking a brow at her.

"That." She blew out a breath. "I'm already nervous."

"You are?" It was his turn to whistle. "Why?"

"Because this is so much more than I ever thought it would be."

He narrowed his eyes at her. "Why would you say that?"

"Why wouldn't I?" she retorted with a huff. "Look, whatever I expected from this working vacation, it wasn't to hook up with the youngest generation of the DeSauvier clan!"

It was his turn to snort. "True. I'll let you have that one."

"You're so generous."

His lips twitched as he passed her a water bottle he'd opened for her. She took a deep sip, then admitted, "I'm in over my head here, George. You have to see that."

"I don't. I think you were made to make this crazy world of ours saner."

"Now I know you're reaching," she chided. "When have I ever been considered sane?"

"You're my sanity," he informed her softly, reaching over to pinch her chin between thumb and pointer finger. "I mean that. You are."

She bit her lip, and he used his hold on her to stretch his thumb and tug the mistreated morsel away from her teeth. "Stop it. You're perfect, Perry. You always have been. I've been the one wasting time. I should have spoken to you years ago about this, but I was scared."

Her chin jerked up in the air. "Why did you? Why now?"

A small smile curved his lips at her mutinous expression. "You want the truth?"

"No, George. I want you to lie to me." She rolled her eyes.

He sighed. "You're such a brat sometimes." He reached for the water bottle he'd handed her moments ago, then took a sip for himself. "I saw your Kindle, and suddenly, there was hope."

The simple statement had her cheeks blossoming with heat, then she blew out a breath. "I knew it. I knew that was why."

"You did? Then why ask?"

She shook her head. "No, I don't mean it that way. I was talking to Edward before your dad came in and dropped his bombshell on us... I told him that I'd started reading this stuff, and it was definitely interesting. I-I just can't believe..."

"It was like a sign," he assured her.

She turned away from him and hopped up onto the marble counter. As she did, she grimaced. "Ew."

"Wet spot?" he asked commiseratively.

"Yeah." She pulled a face. "I really didn't plan this well."

"What made you come here tonight, Perry? Why tonight?"

"I had to figure out if things were right between us. If we could make this work."

He smirked. "I was right, wasn't I? We're perfect for each other."

She blew out a breath, and just as her silence started to worry him, a wide grin creased her lips. "Yeah. You're right. That was..."

"Mind blowing?" he teased, placing his hands on her knees.

She grimaced but her fingers came to play with the ones he'd settled on her lap. "Yeah. It was. Don't rub it in."

"As if I'd dare," he managed with all the affront he could muster.

"Ha. Ha." She stuck out her tongue at him. "Xavier complicates things though."

George's brows rose. He'd expected her to say his brother complicated things—not his cousin.

"He does? Why?"

Perry ran a hand over her face. "I think he'd..." Her brow puckered. "I think he'd actually want to join this weird little harem we'd have going on."

His nostrils flared at the word she'd used. Harem? Is that how she considered what they'd be to one another?

Unsure if he approved or disapproved, he murmured, "And when did you have this conversation?"

"About an hour before I came and jumped your bones."

The timing of that was key, and for the life of him, he wasn't sure why she'd chosen to make her move at that exact moment.

Almost like she could read his confusion and wanted to ease it, she murmured, "I needed to see how our connection was in bed, George."

"If it was shit, you'd have gone with him?" Just the notion had him bristling.

She shrugged. "I don't know. If I'm honest, I never expected this to be like this, and yet at the same time, I've loved you and had a crush on you for so long that even in the back of my mind, I couldn't see it being anything other than spectacular. But..."

He cocked a brow. There was always a but.

"I like him, George. He gets me, and I get him." She fidgeted on the cold counter, and he smiled at the sight of her. He could see the curves of her breasts peeping through the space where her robe parted, and her hair was all over the damn place.

Sexy and rumpled, with her heavy, sloe-like eyes that made his body harden just by being around her.

"Focus, George," she said, and her tone was amused, so he grinned at her.

Sheepishly.

"I wasn't sure if I'd ever get to see you like this," he admitted softly. "It's a treat."

She sighed, reached forward, and placed her hand on his jaw. Her gentle touch got to him in ways he could barely stand... she had so much power over him. Such an ability to fuck with his head. Worse, his heart.

"Do you know how much I've dreamed about being in this situation with you?" She grinned too, but hers was rueful. "So many times, it was getting boring. And painful," she admitted after taking a long, deep breath. "I never thought it would happen. Thought I'd been relegated to the friend zone."

"Never," he said, stepping into her space, not stopping until he was between her legs, their bodies touching, the breath they inhaled coming from the other's mouth.

She pressed her forehead to his. "I've wanted this for so long, George. It's not a dream, is it?"

"No. It's reality. And we're going to make this work. We've been dicking around for too long."

"We have," she admitted shakily, and she looped her arms around his waist. "I love you, George. You have to know that."

"I love you, too," he whispered back, needing her to know she wasn't alone with these crazy feelings.

If anything, they were standing side to side as they faced the chaos ahead of them. Chaos he'd forged by bringing his brother into the situation. And something that was only going to be exacerbated if she brought Xavier into the equation too.

The thought had him closing his eyes. "I wish I was normal."

"You're wonderful," she told him softly, gently anointing his lips with a kiss.

"You know what I mean."

A sigh escaped her. "I do. But..." She shrugged. "Maybe your normal and my normal are closer than we ever thought."

"What do you mean?"

"I mean, I've just said that I want Xavier, George. Maybe you've opened a door for me, and I've just had to get used to the idea of being able to walk through it. Last month, back home, I would never have even imagined that we could be here. In the kitchen off your bedroom, where we'd just made love. And yet, here we are." She sighed. "Nothing was ever going to be the same after we finally did this."

"No. But it's a thousand times more complicated because of what I need."

She shook her head. "No. It's a thousand times more complicated because of who you are. Because of who your brother is. That's something you can't hide from, George. Your stature in this world was something I knew from the beginning, and unfortunately for you, it's as intrinsic to you as anything else.

"You were raised knowing you had power and wealth that few could even imagine. You were raised knowing that you were in danger because of that, and that if anything happened to your brother, you could rule one of the few sovereign states in the world. That changes a man, and it's as basic to your nature now as your sexuality." She shrugged. "That Edward is the crown prince is what fucks this up. But..." Perry blew out a breath. "Again, I've been confused. So confused. Unable to understand why you'd want to share me, and why you'd want to share me with your brother, which seems kind of icky to me." When he made to argue, she held up a hand to stall him. "But, it's just what you need. I understand there's nothing sexual between the two of you."

He grimaced. "God, no."

She grimaced back. "Yeah. It's about me." She scraped her teeth over her bottom lip, and when she next spoke, her voice was decidedly breathy. "How can I not find that so damn enticing it makes me want to crawl all over you?"

Surprise held his tongue for a second, then he murmured, "Feel free."

She laughed a little. "Behave. You know what I mean."

"I do. And it is. All about you, I mean." He shrugged. "This... *tonight*... it was mind blowing. I want that for you every time we're together. I want to break your self-control. Drag you to limits you never even knew existed. I can't do that alone."

Huskily, she whispered, "You don't have to convince me. Not anymore. I want this, George. I really do."

He could tell from her words that she meant it, but he could also hear her confusion.

"There's nothing wrong with you for wanting that, Perry," he told her calmly, brushing his lips over the corner of her mouth. "You want everything we have to give you. And if that involves Xavier too, then why not?"

He wasn't sure what Edward would have to say on that matter. Wasn't sure how he'd feel. But this wasn't about Edward. It wasn't even about George or Xavier.

It was about Perry.

If the three of them wanted her, all that mattered was what she wanted. What she needed.

Once he'd opened the door to her being shared, he'd realized that the situation with Xavier would complicate things. Perry wasn't the sort to fuck around or have one-night stands, which meant she'd felt a connection with his cousin. He was just grateful that had happened with Xavier, who knew the score when it came to court.

"What about Xavier?" she asked softly.

"If you need him, then we'll understand."

She bit her lip. "How does this work, George? How do we make it work?"

"Do you want it to?" he asked seriously.

"Of course. I wouldn't be here if I didn't. Things changed the minute I slept with Xavier and you told me the truth, but really, we could have come back from that. We could have stepped back, and returned to being friends. It would have been awkward, I guess, but manageable. Tonight's what changed things. And I knew that when I came here. I knew that, and did it anyway because I needed you. I needed to know this connection between us was as powerful as what I've always known in the back of my mind." She closed her eyes and shook her head; the move rolled her forehead against his. "It was a thousand times stronger. I need this to work, George. I need you, and I need them." She gulped. "Not just Xavier. Edward too. There's something about him. It calls to me. He needs me, George. I don't know how I know that, but I do."

He smiled, his Perry always had been empathetic. He reached forward and pressed his nose to hers. Rubbing gently, he whispered, "You feel the call like I do."

That had her frowning—he could feel the pucker of her brow against his own. "What do you mean?"

"Edward is..." He pursed his lips, tried to figure out a way to make sense of the duty he'd always felt toward his older brother. "Veronia is kind of old-fashioned."

She snorted. "Not that old-fashioned where the heir and the spare aren't getting it on with the same chick."

He couldn't bite back his grin at her waspish retort. "Edward hasn't 'gotten it on' with you yet."

"Semantics," she jibed.

He grinned, but it died a little as he explained, "Most other monarchies in Europe are basically just figureheads. My father isn't. He's actively engaged in the politics that shape this country. No law goes down without his approval. Veronia is still surprisingly feudal when it comes to certain things. I've always known that's Edward's future, too. He won't change the way the nation's ruled. He can't."

"That's why the Prime Minister doesn't like the DeSauviers, isn't it?"

The side of his mouth quirked up in a grin. "Yeah. That's why. If anyone's the puppet, it's Luc De Montfort. He has as much say as my father will allow him to have, and considering the man's liberal, that hurts his ego."

"That's also why the UnReals are so unhappy, right?"

He pulled a face. "Yeah. It's why we take them so seriously."

"Why don't you just give a bit more power back to the people then?"

It was so simple to the American mind, he realized on a sigh. "It's not in our constitution. There's protection for the population if one of the reigning kings goes off the rails and starts trying to create an authoritarian rulership; ways and means the government can prevent that from happening, but the DeSauviers have never been like that.

"The majority of Veronians are happy with the status quo. If I do say so myself, we've done a bloody good job of ruling the country."

"How big a majority?" Perry asked suspiciously, pulling back to look at him as he replied.

"Over eighty per cent, I reckon." The statistics backed him up on that too.

The people of his country loved his family.

Opinion often swayed one way or another when it came time for certain laws to be implemented, but at their heart, the Veronians wanted to remain with their monarch. That didn't stop radicals from wanting his family out of power, however. Declaring their need for independence from a monarchist state.

"Seriously? So high?"

He nodded. "We're a very popular family. Things changed a little when Arabella was crown princess." He grimaced. "She wasn't very warm, and though my mother isn't either, Arabella looked like a deep freezer in comparison. The prospect of her being queen didn't please a lot of people, especially as she's considered old guard. Her father is very conservative, and really old fashioned—with her as queen, the people believed she and through her, her father, would have more of a say."

"You run middle of the road now, don't you?" she questioned.

"Yeah. Pretty much. My father's liberal-minded. We only get conservative on certain issues like gun control and..." He grunted. "The last time we had a real problem was over prisons. A large part of the population wanted laxer prisons, wanted to focus on rehabilitation rather than punishment."

"Wow, that's totally the opposite to what I'm used to in the States," she murmured, wide-eyed.

"I know."

"What did your father want?"

"He saw the recidivism laws... he wanted to promote rehabilitation like the majority. But there was enough of a stink in parliament to soften the laws that went through. He wasn't happy about it, but he allowed the democratic way to reign."

"The people voted?"

"No. The government did."

"That sucks."

"Yeah. A lot of people view the monarch as having their voice, which I know is really alien to what most people believe.

"The parties wanted more control, harsher prison sentencing, and they won. My father only has so much sway. He can veto a law, but he decided not to. Not when it would cause such a stink."

"That was very diplomatic of him."

George smirked. "This government has another year of power before there's an election. My father has staying power. I guarantee the first law the new government puts into practice will be a change to prison laws."

She laughed. "I think I like him more than I did before."

George grinned. "I'm glad. He's going to be your father-in-law."

She froze. "What?"

He cocked a brow. "What?"

Perry hit his arm. "Don't even joke about that."

"If you think I'm letting you get away now I've got you right where I want you, you're nuts." He huffed to compound the ridiculousness of her statement. "You're mine. Ours," he said softly, urging her to understand, needing her to accept that.

"I-I can't be queen, George. Don't be silly. Edward hasn't even slept with me yet—he's sure as hell not going to want to marry me."

George hid a smile. "You don't know what you set in motion the other day by declaring you and he were dating, do you?"

Her eyes rounded. "What did I do?"

"It was as good as saying you were close to engaged."

If her eyes had rounded, it was nothing to the way her mouth gaped. He tapped her bottom lip.

"It's too late to back out now, baby doll." He wrapped his arms around her waist, hauled her against his chest and squeezed her. "You were made to be mine. You said he calls to you, that's exactly what he does to me. He needs us, Perry. He needs us to support him when the time comes for him to be king. Can you do that? Can you be there for him?"

She was shaking as he asked the questions, and he hated himself for overwhelming her, but these were questions he needed her to ask herself, questions he needed her to answer.

"I-I can't be q-queen, George," she whispered faintly, her pupils pin pricks. "I'm a scientist."

"You're exactly what we need you to be. That's all that matters."

Her glassy eyes seemed to focus at his words, and she gulped. "You'll help?"

His smile was wide and proud and, he admitted to himself, relieved.

"I'll be at your side every step of the way."

She sagged into his arms. He pressed a kiss to the top of her hair, wondering how it was that the future of the Veronian royal family rested squarely on this woman's shoulders.

CHAPTER NINETEEN

PERRY SUCKED down a breath of air and tried not to think about the smell. Rancid? Yeah. Rotten? Without a doubt.

If she could have pegged her nostrils shut, she would have, but at the same time, Xavier's experiments were fascinating.

She turned to look at him, and saw he wasn't focused on his work, but on her.

A smile creased her lips at his focus, something that was most definitely a compliment, and she murmured, "Hey."

He grinned back. "Hey yourself."

"Whatcha starin' at?" she teased.

"A beautiful lady. It's not often I let one into my secret lab."

Laughter bubbled from her lips. "Oh yeah, I'm sure."

His smile turned into a seriously somber frown. "No I mean it. Most people aren't interested in what I do unless I'm paying them. Though I'm sure some of the court's ladies would really like that, deep down, that's not going to happen in my life time." He rolled his eyes. "It's just nice to have you in here. You pretty the place up," he said, then winked. "And, more than that, actually seem interested in what I'm doing."

"I am." No word of a lie, either. He was working on some fascinating shit here.

Literally. That was probably where the stench came from.

She'd known that when she'd come here, and the scientist in her respected his experiments and his goals. The woman? She just wanted to get the hell away from whatever was stinking the place up.

Jeez Louise, it was strong. A bit like someone had died mixed with someone who'd been eating bad Chinese food.

Her throat closed at the thought. She'd had Chinese food two nights ago—had almost been stunned shitless to be served cordon bleu Chinese takeout on golden platters and crystal goblets.

Takeout royal-style was surprisingly hard to get used to.

"I lost you."

Her glance focused on him a second. "No. You didn't," she said softly, aware his rueful smile was loaded with disappointment. "My mind wandered."

"Wandered is a synonym for lost."

She stuck out her tongue. "Perhaps, but not in this instance."

He stepped away from his workbench, which was in the back quarter of the epic glasshouse he'd brought her to just over an hour ago.

She'd never seen anything like it, save for in a documentary she'd seen once of old British noble estates. Where one of the family's ancestors had created a conservatory, a literal *Wintergarten*, for rare and difficult to yield plants.

All of this edifice was made of glass, save for the brick wall that attached it to the family estate.

It was reflective, so there was privacy. The temperature on Veronia was always pretty mild, but in here, it was humid and sticky. She didn't mind though, mostly because she wore white linen shorts and a black camisole as he'd told her when he'd called to ask if she wanted to hang out, to dress casually.

Of course, when she'd seen his idea of casual, that had brought on a few uncomfortable moments.

In his designer jeans and an expensive linen shirt, he'd looked casual too. Just rich. Very rich. His elegant bloodlines seeping from every pore, whereas she felt sure she just looked like the southern belle who'd never really understood the appeal in mint juleps and had never had any of the requisite manners or capability of wielding a fan.

"I was just thinking that the last time I ate takeout, George and I were camped out on his living room floor. We'd taken over the coffee table, and it was loaded with aluminum dishes and paper boxes. I was drinking beer, and he had some fancy ass red wine. In the background, we were watching *Dirk Gently's Holistic Detective Agency*, but we were bitching about some crap I can't remember."

He blinked at her. "That's remarkably specific."

"There's a reason," she teased, amused at his response to her wandering. "I was thinking about how this place stank of someone's stomach contents, a someone who'd eaten leftover takeout that had gone bad."

His nose wrinkled, then he nodded. "As gross as that is, you're right. Now I think about it, I can smell it too."

She laughed. "It's a yeasty smell, isn't it? I guess it's something in your fertilizer."

He rubbed his chin, his eyes turning distant as he nodded. "Weird how I've only just smelled that. I wonder if in the fermentation process there's..." His words trickled off as he scrambled to reach for a piece of paper where he made copious notes about whatever his realization meant to him.

She left him to it. Well aware how vital those epiphanies could be, and content to let him work it out.

She turned away from him and stared at the beautiful plants filling the glasshouse.

There were eight narrow rows of plots. Long, thin lines that were loaded with so many different types of species, that Perry wished botany was her field too so she could recognize them.

They were not only beautiful, but with Xavier's wealth and status, she had to assume she was looking at some very rare, and some very difficult to grow plants.

Trees soared thirty, forty feet in the air. Huge leaves provided a dark canopy overhead, which made the glasshouse far less bright than it ought to have been.

Each of the rows was lined with a fancy stone border, before a pleasant white pebble path added a clean brightness to the dull ground before being segmented off into soil once more and the next row.

She peered overhead and saw a tree that looked like a weird palm tree had shot thirty feet into the air. Wondering what he'd do when it overshot the glasshouse's roof, she turned back to him and saw he'd stopped writing and was instead studying her once more.

"You miss the simplicity of that moment, don't you?"

His insight wasn't altogether surprising; her wistful tone had said it all. But she appreciated the doggedness in not letting the topic drop.

She nodded. "I had the Veronian royal version of Chinese food the other night."

Xavier snorted. "That's only because Marianne won't let Philippe have too much MSG. If you were eating with us, we could just buy the regular stuff."

"Panda Express dishes?" she teased, and he grinned.

"Whatever floats your boat, milady."

Perry sighed, rubbed a finger down her nose. "I just never figured this would be my life."

"Who does figure that, Perry?" he asked gently.

She narrowed her eyes at him, then taking him at his word, nodded.

"You're right. I'm not complaining, Xav. Not at all. I just... sometimes, it's a lot to process. In Boston, I have to get a visitor's pass to see these kinds of gardens. Here? I get a personalized tour from a duke."

"A duke who thinks he's falling in love with you."

His comment had her jerking to a halt.

Only she and George had spoken of love thus far, but they'd known each other so long, that it was a natural extension of their relationship. At least, that was what she was telling herself.

Edward and she hadn't really even talked about lusting over one another. Though the attraction between them burned so damn hotly, she wasn't sure she'd survive it when they eventually did get down and dirty together.

As for her and Xavier, they'd had a less than normal course. She'd heard of Edward, George had mentioned him a lot. But Xavier?

He'd been conspicuously absent from all of George's talk of family.

In fact, the notion had her frowning.

"Xavier?" she asked softly.

He nodded.

"I'm going to change the subject, but I don't want you to think it's because I'm avoiding what you said. You already know that you've spun my world upside down. All three of you have. I don't know whether I'm coming or going."

"More coming than going, one would hope," he said with a wry edge to his tone. She knew she'd hurt him, but he was taking it on the chin because she could sense he was aware of how overwhelmed she felt by all this.

In less than three weeks, her entire world had toppled on its head. In a good way, granted. But still. Her life was turning into a gangbang.

Yeah, that was a lot to take in. She grinned at his comment though, because it wasn't often his humor bled through.

Like her, he was serious and focused on his work. That was one thing they had in common, but she wanted to see the softer side of him too. The playful edge.

"Why didn't George mention you to me?"

He blinked, and Perry knew she'd really surprised him with where her question had taken him.

"He didn't mention you at all." She shook her head at her own remark. "I'm surprised, because as far as I can tell, you get on great."

"We do. But we had a falling out."

Perry could sense from the stiffness of his tone, he felt awkward. This was a topic he didn't want to discuss, and yet, she was close to them both, and he was aware that her curiosity had to be answered.

Another joy of being with a fellow scientist. They understood how curiosity worked. That if her need for answers wasn't fed, it wouldn't do them any good.

"About what?"

He pulled a face. "Women, of course."

Ah, that was why he was feeling so awkward.

She bit back a grin, then her brow puckered in confusion as she processed that. "I'm surprised. I've never seen George be willing to fall out over a woman."

"He'd fall out over you," came the swift assurance, and she could tell he was dead serious. Despite herself, that made her feel better. George was so damn gorgeous, Victoria Secrets' Angels would drool over him—hell, they probably had at some point or another. He'd been a partier in his early twenties, or so he'd told her.

In comparison, she was just plain old Perry. The aforementioned southern belle without the belle part.

"So, what was special about this woman then?" she asked, trying not to be jealous. She didn't own the man's past after all.

"My mother died when I was twenty-two. Father only passed two years ago. He was a bit of a roué, I'd suppose you'd call him. Darted from woman to woman after my mother died, who he genuinely loved.

"Anyway, he liked one particular woman. Caroline L'Argeneaux. They got engaged, and I wasn't very happy about the match as she was thirty years younger than him and a terrible gold-digger. But for the first time since Mother's death, he seemed to actually care about someone other than himself, so I was happy for him.

"When the engagement was announced, the family gritted their teeth. George wasn't there though. He was finishing up university, if memory serves, in Britain." He scrubbed a hand over his jaw. "He returned home, found out who his soon to be step-aunt was going to be, and the truth came out."

She frowned. Whatever she'd expected it hadn't been this. "What truth?" she demanded.

"He and Caroline had been at university together."

"Boy, she *was* young, wasn't she?"

Xavier's grimace said it all. "Far too young. He was a fool, but by the end, he was a hurt fool." He sighed. "George told him of all these things she'd done while at university. She'd been a drug dealer, for God's sake. Some bloody gang had used her to get to her rich friends.

"My father knew that the Duchess of Ansian couldn't have that kind of past, but he was stubborn. Refused to believe it. George told my father that she'd cheated on her finals, and that there was proof she'd paid off a professor…" He waved a hand. "The list went on and on. Truthfully, it couldn't have been worse, and my father was more of a fool for being stubborn about it. He should have just dumped her and gotten on with things.

"Only, he couldn't. So, George, being the clodhopper he is, decided to take matters into his own hands. He seduced Caroline and took pictures. Showed my father."

"Oh shit," Perry breathed. She winced too—it was such a typical George thing to do. Step right into the shit and not think about how to get out of the pile of crap without staining everything around him.

"Yeah. Crap is the word. My father was devastated, and I was furious. I wanted him to leave Caroline, but he would have done. Given time. He was a fool in love, but not a total idiot. The duchess of this house has to be beyond reproach. He knew that." He scrubbed a hand over his jaw. "Anyway, I was very angry at George. We came to blows. I broke his nose, and he sulked over it. For a very long time."

She blinked. "Whatever I'd expected to hear, it wasn't that."

He pulled a face. "We have colorful pasts."

Perry studied him a second. "Far more colorful than mine. The only exciting thing I'd done before this trip was to have a prince as a friend. Now?" She flared her eyes with amusement. "Well, colorful isn't the word."

He chuckled. "How about varied?"

"Yes," she joked. "Varied certainly seems like it would fit better." She tilted her head to the side. "What about this place, Xavier?"

"What about it?"

"Edward isn't the only one with a duty to his lineage."

He blinked. "Oh."

"Yes. Oh," she retorted, amused. "You need to be out hunting for a wife, not messing around with me." She said the words lightly, but they weren't as light as she'd have liked.

The idea of him being with another woman made her wish she had claws so she could tear the hypothetical bitch's eyes out.

And how irrational was that?

She almost sighed at her idiocy, then shrugged.

She was past the point of apologizing for her feelings. She felt what she felt, and she wasn't alone in it because Xavier, George, and Edward were all willing to be a part of this quartet. So, it figured that they were as nutty as she was.

"I have an heir," he told her easily.

"You do? You have children?"

"No," he retorted with a snort. "I have no kids. But I have a cousin on my father's side who would inherit if I provide no heirs."

She wasn't sure where the question came from but she had to ask, "What if the child was a bastard? Could that child inherit?"

He narrowed his eyes at her. "What are you thinking about?"

She couldn't answer that; didn't even know the real reason she'd asked such a loaded question. It had just appeared at the forefront of her mind, and she'd had to utter it. Had to know.

Shrugging, she asked again, "Does the heir have to be legitimate?"

He frowned, then shook his head. "No. Illegitimacy isn't as much of a problem in the Veronian royals as it is elsewhere. We've had too many kings who were bastards, and too many who were some of the best monarchs we've ever had."

She hadn't known that, and she vowed then and there that if she was going to hook up with Edward, she'd better know all there was to know about his damn country.

Xav's answer, however, settled something inside her.

It was crazy to even mention the word 'kids' in front of any of these guys, except maybe for George. But the question had needed to be asked, and now she knew.

Brightly, she turned to him and asked, "So, where are you taking me to on our date?"

She saw in his eyes that he knew she was distracting him, but he allowed her to.

Smiling, he murmured, "We're going to one of the lakes on the property."

Her eyes widened. "You have more than one lake?"

He shrugged. "It's a big estate."

Jesus. His big and her big were obviously measured differently.

"Are they small lakes?"

"No. Not really."

"Which one are we going to?"

"The largest of the two." His eyes grew soft. "There's a nice place to sit, and it's actually warmer than the other because it's just off some hot springs."

"Oh wow, that sounds perfect."

He held out a hand. "Did you wear a swimsuit like I told you to?"

She nodded. "I did."

"Good." And so saying, he led her from his workstation, throughout the grand house, and out onto the driveway.

When she'd arrived here two hours before, it had been empty of cars. Now, there was a quad bike standing pride of place in the middle of the gravel.

She laughed. "Oh man, we're riding that way, huh?"

He winked. "Edward will set you to training on horseback. He enjoys riding too much for him to not want you to go with him. Until then, we can take this."

More laughter sparkled through her when he handed her a bright pink helmet.

"You're not a girly girl, but I couldn't resist," he joked.

She stuck out her tongue. "Just wait until it's my turn to get you a gift."

He huffed. "Bright pink is far less offensive on women than men."

"How very old-fashioned of you to say," she said teasingly.

"Oh, boy. Have I started something here?"

She could tell he was amused by the notion that he might have done. And there she had it. His playful side.

She'd seen glimpses of it that first night, when he'd teased her about playing games at her first boring royal event. Since then, they'd only met to talk about serious circumstances, so neither of them had felt particularly jovial.

The truth was, with all her men—because there was no doubting that was what they were now—she wanted to see the good, the bad, and the ugly.

Not because she wanted to figure a way out. She just wanted to know them. Their flaws and their woes.

This wasn't just about sex. It played a huge part—Perry wasn't about to lie to herself on that subject.

But it was about far more too.

The way Edward called to her was more than just about sex, she knew, as she wrapped her arms around Xavier's waist when she settled in for the cross-country ride across his estate.

She pressed her nose into his back and snuggled into him as best she could. In the clear air, his scent was strong in her nose, and he smelled divine.

She smiled as the freedom of the moment flushed through her, realizing just then that the way Xavier called to her was just as strongly as Edward, and that wasn't about sex either.

In fact, though the attraction was there, it came in many layers. So many that she wondered if that was where her initial confusion in accepting them all had stemmed from.

They were men she wanted to screw, but they were men she wanted to understand. Men she wanted to befriend. Men she wanted to *know*.

The terrain changed under the ATV, and she blinked, realizing they'd gone from rolling hills to woodland, almost in the blink of an eye. She peered around the dark shadows and huddled up closer to Xavier as the change in environment brought about a change in temperature.

She cuddled into him, feeling the bite of the chill on her arms as they seemed to go higher and higher—he was the duke of a mountain range. The only way wasn't up with a guy like him around.

The air grew fresher and lighter, but also colder, and by the time they stopped, she was relieved as hell that there were hot springs to warm the water. Otherwise, no freaking way would she have even thought about dipping her damn toe into the lake. Never mind her body.

Still, as the rumble of the engine came to a halt, and the silence of the clearing surrounded her, she closed her eyes in wonder at the peace.

It was... *Liberating*.

She hadn't realized how tense the palace was. How living there was stressful, and that was before she was even a person of relevance. When it became common knowledge that she and Edward were dating?

God help her.

Sucking in a breath, she squeezed Xavier's waist and climbed off. As she did, she peered around, then her eyes widened in astonishment.

"What are *you* doing here?"

Was it dramatic to say that the lake was glorious in its beauty, but it was nothing to the two men standing there waiting for her?

She'd never seen them look so casual, so relaxed, in surf shorts and nothing else. Maybe they felt the different atmosphere here too. Maybe she wasn't alone.

The urge to go to them, to have them hug her, was a need she couldn't fight. She strode toward them and hurled herself into George's arms. He pressed a kiss to the top of her head.

"You surprised me," she said, mumbling the words against his chest. She'd only seen him that morning, but it felt like a lifetime ago.

His chest vibrated with laughter. "Then we did it right."

She scowled at him as she pulled away and turned toward Edward. It wasn't as comfortable with him. She wasn't sure why either.

George was light-hearted, so easy to be with that it was like breathing with him. Just a natural extension of herself.

Xavier appealed to her brain. He fired her up, challenged her, and she'd admit to falling for him for that alone. It took a lot for her to meet a man who was her equal, and considering his mad scientist ways, she figured she'd found one.

Edward, on the other hand, was less of a connection, more of an anomaly, and yet, the lines developing between them were all the more surreal because of it.

He was like a magnet. Something about him, maybe *everything* about him, was magnetic.

She slipped into his arms too, but unlike with George, she didn't bury her face in his chest. She looped her arms around his waist and stared up at him. His hands knotted into fists at the small of her back, and they supported her as she leaned away from him so she could stare into his eyes.

"I'm surprised you could be here," she whispered, feeling the burn of the links between them as they cuffed them together in ways she couldn't begin to understand.

"You're worth making time for." He let out a sigh, and some tension bled from his handsome face.

Edward looked beyond her, out onto the magnificent lake that belonged in the *Sound of Music*. In a valley surrounded by mountains, it was astonishing to behold. Bright, crystal blue water reflected the sky above, and all around, there were bushes and trees that swayed somnolently in the chilly air. The mountains acted like guards around them, and it was hard not to feel like they were the only four people alive at that moment.

"This is my favorite place in all the world," Edward told her with a gentle smile, his gaze capturing hers once more. "Why wouldn't I want to share it with you?"

She smiled back, then reached up on tiptoe to kiss his mouth. They sighed into the kiss, gently breathing the other's air, then she pulled from his grasp to dance over to a swim-ready Xavier who was also in board shorts now. Well, her 'dance' was more of a skip, if she was being honest.

Before he knew what she was about, she rushed into his arms and squeezed him tightly. It was a hug that was a bizarre mixture of the one she'd shared with George, one that encompassed love and familiarity, but also the stirring connection of two equals who called to one another that she'd shared with Edward.

Maybe that was fitting.

The three of them were, after all, unique.

She smiled as she accidentally rubbed her nose against his nipple. Before he could do more than jump, she tilted her head and quickly nipped the nub. He yelped, then laughed.

"Minx!"

She grinned up at him, and then danced back out of his arms. She turned in a full circle, raised her arms, then let out a holler. When the echo reverberated around the clearing, she let out a whoop, and began to strip out of her clothes.

Perry let her gaze fix on each man as she got nakey. It wasn't sexy—it wasn't supposed to be. This wasn't about the sex—at least, they'd soon learn it wasn't. But she made sure they knew what she was about as she raced toward the lake that lapped at the shore.

Sure, she'd worn a bathing suit, but she'd had no intention of keeping it on. Not since she'd seen the crystal clarity of the water.

The minute it brushed her toes, she moaned at the glorious silk tickling her ankles.

Staring overhead, uncaring that she was butt naked in the middle of a mountain range with three of the hottest guys gaping at her ass, she launched herself into the water with a whoop.

Perry knew she'd regret it later, but she sank down, letting her hair get wet. The water felt too good, like liquid gold against her body, and she swam and played in the shallow end, peering above the surface to watch the men as they stripped off too.

When they all walked to shore with their boxers on—was it a royal thing to wear boxers under surf shorts?—she hollered out a laugh. "Chickens!" she cried.

They shot each other a glance, and snickering, stripped out of their sexy briefs.

Biting her lip, she studied them all. Making sure she didn't focus on their cocks was one of the hardest things she'd ever done, but if she did, this would quickly devolve into some sort of orgy, and she really didn't want that.

Of course, her body disagreed. But her mind just wanted to get to know them better. For now.

It was the first time they were all getting together without there being some kind of outside pressure. She didn't want to lose that.

George was the first one to reach her, but she pushed off the sandy shore and swam away from him. "Oh no," she warned. "Keep your hands to yourself."

George pouted. "I knew you'd be difficult."

She snorted. "When aren't I?"

Edward laughed as he finished swimming toward them. He rolled over onto his back with a deep moan of pleasure and floated atop the surface. Xavier stayed close to the shore. Sitting on the sandy base, the water slipped over his legs and hips, covering him to the waist.

She broached the difference by moving halfway toward him, then murmured, "I have a challenge for you."

Edward laughed. "You can't challenge us when we're naked."

"Why not?" she joked, then chuckling, corrected, "It's not that kind of challenge!"

"Okay, what kind is it then?" Xavier asked, his brow raised.

"I want you each to tell me a fact about the other two."

George frowned. "Why?"

"I want to know you better."

Her request was simple, and though the men looked squeamish, because it was so basic, she knew they wouldn't wiggle out of it.

Xavier sighed. "I'll go first."

"You get points for volunteering," she assured him, but she wasn't surprised he was the first to go. Though Edward was the leader of this royal trio, it was only by title. For all his quirky ways and the burning curiosity that fed his research, Xavier was a duke to his marrow.

He smirked. "Points accrue. I'm sure I'll need them in my favor at some point in the future."

She laughed, but stayed silent, urging him to open up.

Perry had pushed them all into a situation they weren't comfortable with. George and Edward were the duo; a trio was a whole other ball of wax.

She was hoping that a trip down memory lane would help them open up to her, enable her to learn more about the men she was diving headfirst into a relationship with, but also, clear the air between *them*.

"George used to play the violin." When he paused, she waved a hand, urging him on. No way was that enough information. His lips twitched at her twirling hand. "He was terrible at it. Tone deaf, and his playing used to reverberate around the palace."

"Hey! I wasn't so bad!"

At George's complaint, Edward laughed. "You were, George."

Perry knew Edward was well aware of the secret Xavier was about to share and was totally amused by the memory—*it's working*, she thought, hugging herself happily.

Xavier grinned. "Uncle Philippe agreed, but Aunt Marianne wanted you to persevere. Philippe, Edward, and I got together and figured out a way to get rid of the violin once and for all."

George's mouth rounded. "How?"

"Uncle Philippe spoke to your instructor. Said he wanted you to learn some of the hardest pieces." Xavier grunted. "The instructor didn't understand, but he wasn't going to argue with the king, was he? So, he had you playing advanced music when you could barely play 'Old McDonald had a Farm.'"

Edward heaved out a laugh.

But George was outraged. "You do realize you totally ruined my confidence after that? I felt like such a dick for not being able to play those parts!"

"We deserved a break from your playing," Edward retorted. "Mother was so tired of hearing you squeak and screech that poor instrument, she decided to switch you over to judo. Said that was of more practical use in the future. And she never knew we'd sabotaged you."

Xavier smirked. "That was funny as hell. Our private conspiracy. Uncle Philippe was really fun back then."

"He's not too bad now," Edward remarked. "Just been under a lot of strain recently. You know how it is."

The men sighed, and the levity of the moment appeared to be close to rupturing so she quickly added, "Edward? Your turn."

He didn't move from his floating position, and from her spot, she could see the curve of his mouth as well as the fact his eyes were closed. "Xavier was thirteen when he kissed his first girl. Charlotte Llewelyn. She was an immigrant's daughter. A rich Welshman who was escaping the cold. She laughed like a horse and smelled like one too."

Xavier huffed. "She was pretty. You can't deny that. And you stink of horses too sometimes."

"Yeah, because I ride them!" Edward retorted. "She was scared of horses."

"How can someone smell like a horse and not go near them?" Perry demanded, perplexed.

"Hell if I know," Edward murmured, then tilted his head in the water to look at his cousin. "Admit it. You know I'm right."

Xavier heaved out a sigh. "I guess."

Edward's grin flashed. "Anyway, because she *was* pretty, she had such a stinking attitude. I knew Xavier liked her, but I also knew from another friend, Marcus, that she'd kissed him as well. So, I asked her to the palace through my mother. Which meant her mother would come too." He snickered as the memory played out in his head. "They were all sat there, drinking tea and eating cucumber sandwiches, when I walked in. Charlotte, on cue, turns bright pink and starts sidling up to me. I blanked her at every turn. Mother was mortified, and kept shooting me warning glances, but I ignored her and was uber polite to Charlotte's mum. Then, I asked, out of the blue, what her intentions were toward my friend.

"They all laughed, but I was persistent. I asked her why she'd kissed Marcus when she'd also kissed Xavier, and why she was being so nice to me if she already had two boyfriends." He grinned. "I turned to Mother and asked, "Mother, it isn't normal for a girl to have two boyfriends, is it?"

The four of them started snickering.

"Too appropriate, Edward," George said around his laugh.

"I know. Perfect, right?" He grinned, then lifted a hand and scratched at a water droplet that had landed on his cheek. His chuckling had disturbed the stillness of the lake around him, and little ripples were spreading out around them. "Anyway, she was mortified. Her mother was too. By the end, Mother didn't even reprimand me. Just told me not to embarrass young ladies, even if they were intent on damaging my cousin's self-esteem. Her words, verbatim," he said on an amused sigh.

The laughter had broken down more walls, and Perry was content with the hazy laziness of the atmosphere between them.

Still, George had yet to speak.

"George, your turn. But start with Xavier. You told me nothing about him in all the time we were friends. Time to rectify that."

"Jesus, you're as bad as Edward with your brutal honesty," he complained, rubbing his chin. "I only didn't talk about him because we weren't speaking."

Xavier's mouth pursed, but she sent him a warning glance that told him to keep it pursed.

"Go on. I want a story."

She swam over to Xavier and took a seat at his side. He curled an arm over her shoulder as she huddled closer to him. For a second, she reveled in the press of naked skin to naked skin, but it was overwhelmed by the glory of being naked out here.

She knew there was no chance of anyone seeing them. This territory was private, and there was no way the men would have stripped off if there had even been a chance of being spotted by the public—she didn't have to fear a long lens would snap her bare ass, either. Journalists could go to jail here for invasion of privacy.

Cuddling into Xavier's side, she felt his tension as George started, "Xavier was never as busy as Edward. Not that that was Edward's fault. My parents had him so busy with duties because he was intent on fucking wrecking the DeSauvier name with his crazy stunts, that I felt sorrier for him than I did for myself."

Edward sat up at that. "Why did you feel sorry for yourself?"

Perry tried not to drool over his washboard abs, which bulged at his motion, and instead, focused on the concern on his face for his younger brother.

"You remember when they moved me to that new school? One where my identity was secret?"

Edward nodded. "Xavier attended too, didn't he? Probably caught his last year there, right?"

"Yeah. Well, without the crown, and because I was so fucking skinny, apparently, I was open season. There were these three kids who were bullying me. I went to Xavier, and he didn't laugh. Didn't tease me. Just asked me to point out which kids. He went to them, whispered something, and then strolled back toward me. They never bothered me again. But he refused to tell me what he'd said.... I was always curious."

A smile played about Xavier's mouth. "I remember that."

She nudged him in the side. "Well? What did you say?"

"I told him our family had ties to the mafia, and that anyone who messed with us had a habit of turning up dead."

George gaped at him, then roared with laughter. "Why the hell didn't I think of that?"

Perry shook her head in amusement as George strode back toward the shore and sat down beside Xavier. He rested his hands on his bent knees and with a smirk, demanded, "They thought because of our accents…?"

Xavier nodded. "Yeah."

The Veronian tongue reminded her of a more romantic version of Portuguese. There was distinct Cyrillic accent, but at the same time, the sweet song of a Romance language softened the tones.

George's smile was smug. "They left me alone after that."

"Good. I had a friend in the year below warn them after I'd left. Said he was the son of my father's right-hand man." Xavier snorted. "They believed it."

At his words, George began peppering Xavier with questions, and Perry knew the tension she'd sensed from them—a tension that stemmed from a stupid, years-old fight—was slowly dispersing.

One thing she'd seen was how protective they were of each other. How they defended one another, and she was glad she'd reminded them of that shared trait. That exercise had done exactly as she'd hoped—created a new bridge between her men. One forged on the past, but one that would help them in the future.

One thing she'd realized from all that?

The love between them was a powerful bond. If they let her inside that tightknit union, she knew she'd be the luckiest woman on earth. The longing that came with that desire surprised the hell out of her. But what about her time with these three didn't constantly befuddle her?

CHAPTER TWENTY

EDWARD STEPPED INTO HIS OFFICE, relieved to be away from his PA, and also intrigued by the report he was reading.

Perry's ideas on water conservation were fascinating. Her expanded report on why Veronia needed new dams, a report their shortsighted Environmental Agency had requested, made for interesting reading. She had a clear and concise voice, and was unashamed of her opinions on the previous administration's inability to maintain the dams.

He guessed he shouldn't have been surprised. Before she was George's friend, she was a professional. And though George had recommended her to his father, had said she was an expert in her field, Edward knew Philippe had run a thorough background check on her credentials.

They were unsurpassable.

As he closed the door behind him, reading more into her suggestions of how to successfully encourage the Veronian people into saving water, he heard a slight noise and jolted to attention.

Peering straight ahead, he saw Perry seated at his desk.

Behind it.

He couldn't stop the smile from curving his lips at the blatant disregard for decorum as well as her rudeness.

She wasn't even sitting in the damn chair properly. Had her legs swinging over one side.

He shook his head at her antics. "You're a nightmare, do you know that?"

"A nightmare who might be queen one day," she mocked, her eyes narrowing at him, daring him to hide from her, daring him to prevaricate.

But he had no need of the dare.

She was right. He just hadn't realized she was aware of that yet.

Rubbing his chin, he murmured, "You'll hate the classes you'll need to take on decorum and royal protocol."

"Classes, I can handle. It's the whole 'putting classes into action' thing I have an issue with."

He smirked. "Yeah. That's pretty much what I meant, if I'm being honest. Still, the people won't like you if you have a stick up your ass. Trust me, I've seen the dislike they have for people like that. You'll be a breath of fresh air to them."

She narrowed her eyes as he took a seat at the side of her. Perching his ass on the edge of his desk, he placed the report behind him and watched her track his movements.

Her chin jerked up into the air. "What did you think?"

"I think it's very informative."

She huffed. "I've rehashed everything from the first report, but stacked it with shit loads of statistics to shore up each and every argument I had. Let them try to bullshit us now."

His mouth quirked up in a half grin. "I actually like this version. It's much more you."

"It is?"

"The other was informative and educational. This has everything backed up with statistics, like you say, but your opinions spill through. You were angry when you wrote it," he predicted, and though he knew he was right anyway, saw by her sheepish and rueful grin she wasn't too ashamed to admit to it.

"They pissed me off."

"I know they did," he sighed. "I'm sorry about that."

"It's okay. George has been explaining some things to me."

Like he hadn't been able to figure that out.

"Like what?" he asked instead of saying that and probably pissing her off again.

But, she surprised him by pursing her lips and stating, "You're not an idiot. I'm sure you can hazard a wild guess and come up with the answer."

He folded his arms across his chest. "Yeah. I could. But it would probably be better if you told me rather than have me guessing and getting it wrong."

She narrowed her eyes at him, squinting. "When are you going to kiss me?"

His eyes did the opposite of hers and grew wide in further surprise. "When the time's right," he told her carefully.

"And who makes this grandiose decision?"

His lips curved again. "Both of us, I suppose."

"A mutual decision, or does one have the power of veto?"

He blinked. "Mutual."

"Yeah? Well, I call your bluff."

"What do you mean?"

"I mean, I veto your decision to wait on kissing me."

He stilled. "You do, do you?"

"Yes. I do," she replied, so utterly confident at that moment, and so goddamn cute with it, that she was sweeter than sugar to him.

"You'd better put your money where your mouth is then, hadn't you?"

She grinned. "I guess I had." Perry crooked her finger at him, then murmured, "Come here."

"You do know I'm not used to being bossed around, don't you?" he told her, even as he bent at the waist and rested his hands on the armrests of his desk chair.

"That's because you've been without female company for too long," she teased, staring him square in the eye, not letting him back off or evade her.

"Ah freedom, thy true name is bachelorhood."

"Ah bachelorhood, thy true name is aching hard-on. Or should that be aching fist?"

He chuckled at that. "Carpal tunnel hasn't become a problem as yet. But yes, it does ache after a while," he admitted, lips twitching.

"I can believe it aches. Womankind is fortunate. We just get crabby when we're horny. The ache isn't as acute." She snickered. "And I'd know. I've had a long dry spell that seems to be looking up."

They were inches away from one another. His mouth hovered over hers, his body shielded hers from the room. They were close as could be without physically connecting, and then she made a connection.

Her hand slipped between them to cup his cock.

Whatever he'd expected, it hadn't been that. Stunned by her move, he tensed, then his nostrils flared as she shaped him through his pants.

"Yes," she breathed against his lips. "My dry spell is certainly over."

He swallowed. Thickly. "You know what happens to teases?"

"No. I'm not a tease. I back up words with action." So saying, she fiddled with his fly, managed to get the zipper down, then slipped her hand into the gap she'd made.

He let out a long, slow hiss as she touched him. Skin to skin.

A slow chuckle escaped her. "Commando. Interesting. I never took you as the sort. Especially when you were wearing briefs under your board shorts when we went skinny dipping at the lake."

He'd have grinned, but was too busy focusing on what she was doing to him with those clever, nimble fingers of hers.

He hissed when she squeezed his base, then shifted her fingers to grab his balls and gently tug on them. In response, his hips jolted forward, and he groaned.

"I bet you taste like fine wine, and trust me, I've only tasted the good stuff since I got here. Earthy, potent..." She trailed her tongue around the line of his mouth, and his lips parted when she pushed into him. Her tongue tangling with his as she squeezed him, not moving her hand, keeping it in place.

He shuddered, lost in the gentle aggression that was so contradictory, it suited her down to a tee. She was acting on her desire, but not being forceful, and the combination was enough to bring him to his knees. He wasn't used to this in the women he dated or, of late, fucked. He wasn't used to their taking the first step, making the first move. He guessed it made sense that Perry would break that particular rule too.

As she fucked his mouth with gentle parries of her tongue, tasting him and sampling his flavor, his fingers further tightened around the armrest. The muscles in his belly strained as she stroked him, taking him to the edge with only her touch.

Jesus, it had been too long since someone had touched him like this.

As though they had the right.

As though he was hers and she his.

Arabella had been useless in bed. More worried about mussing her hair. The last time he'd had a decent fuck was back with George—a woman they'd shared long enough for it to be considered serious in the real world, not that he and George inhabited that kind of sphere.

Mara had been sexy and sinful, and thankfully, fully aware of who they were and with no desire to be a part of the game that was life at court.

She'd touched him with tenderness and affection. Had loved everything he and George had wanted her to experience... Perry touched him like that, but this was better. This wasn't secret. This was open and, dare he say it, happening. He and George were about to pull the biggest con on the country, and he didn't care about the lies.

George was right. Edward did need him. He needed his brother's support. Edward did need Perry. He needed her steadfast manner, her blunt ways and frank talk. He needed her to cut through the bullshit, to ground him.

He shuddered and finally, leapt into the fray. And when he did, she shivered and tension flooded from her, making him realize she hadn't been sure if he'd pull away.

He thrust his tongue against hers, loving the drag and the shivers that slid down his spine as a result.

He pressed his hands to her waist, and with one move, jerked her up to a standing position. She squeaked in surprise, but was surprisingly docile now she'd garnered a response from him.

He grunted against her lips when she molded herself to him, her full-length lining against his to perfection. But not for long.

He pushed against her the desk, grabbed her legs so she had no choice but to lean against it, then perched her ass on the edge when he boosted her further.

Thanking God she was wearing a skirt, he shaped her legs, sliding his hands down their short length and letting the skirt fall back and down to her hips. He spread her legs by hooking his hands under her knees, then pulling them wide.

Moving into the space he'd made, he bit her bottom lip, then pressed his forehead to hers.

"You wanted to play, *carilla*," he whispered against her mouth, teasing her with the Veronian word for 'tease.' "Play."

Her hands had fallen back against the desk where she'd used them to support herself, but now, she left one hand there and slipped the other between them.

Their bodies were close and their clothes got in the way, but the intensity of the fire sparking between them was insanity.

He groaned when she grabbed his cock, then grunted as she squeezed him.

"Don't tease," he warned. "I want to be inside you."

Her laughter should have stirred his ire, but instead, it fired his blood. With a grumble, he bit her lip again, aware that he'd done that hard enough to mark.

The desire to mark her throat, to cover her in hickeys was a childish urge, but he acted on the urge nonetheless.

As he nipped at her throat, licked here and there, then stroked across sensitive flesh with his tongue, flesh that had already been marked by his brother, he slurped down against her skin as she pressed his shaft against her panties.

Fumbling the fabric aside, she wriggled, jerked her hips up to loosen the fabric and to create enough give to work his cock into her pussy.

When the tip was inside her, she let out a strangled moan as he sucked down hard against her throat. Her head fell back as he thrust his hips, letting all of his cock fill her as he slowly invaded her every inch.

Her hand moved between their bodies, and his blood heated with the knowledge she was touching herself.

He wanted to touch her too, wanted to own all her pleasure, but he enjoyed keeping her legs splayed with his arms, loved the feeling that she was open to all his passions.

He could feel her fumbling fingers brushing the front of his pants, loved how frantic they were as they worked at her clit.

"Move," she groaned huskily, rocking her hips and trying to urge him into thrusting. But he didn't, he let her work herself up, loved the struggles of her legs as she tried to nudge his ass with her feet.

He laughed as he carried on sucking at her throat, needing to mark her, needing—in the most adolescent of ways—to see proof of his possession of her.

Only when he pulled back and saw the dark mark there, only when he could smirk because he knew how furious she'd be when she tried to cover it and that he'd be reminded of this moment for days after, did he pull back.

He enjoyed the way her eyes widened then grew slitted as he pulled almost all the way out, then fucked back into her. Hard. Fast. Deep. A low sound escaped her as she touched herself, her eyes glued on his all the while.

He wanted to pull away, wanted to watch her fingers touch the pretty pink cunt he couldn't wait to mark with his seed, but she ensnared him.

And as a result, the blaze in his blood turned into a wildfire. He had to have her, had to burn her with his heat, brand her with the blaze that was a part of his soul.

The low wail became louder, harder. Enough that he knew someone would hear in the hall.

It pained him to do so, but he leaned forward and kissed her. Robbing her of air, stealing the sound from her lungs.

As he tongue-fucked her, he kept up the intense pace. Maintaining the deep and fast thrusts that had her on fire for him.

He felt the telltale clutch of her muscles. Knew release was imminent, and felt like a fucking king when she clenched down around him so hard, he felt sure his cock was going to turn purple with her ferocity.

As she milked his shaft, her hands came up to grab his shoulders. Her fingers dug into him, the nails tearing into the luxury silk-blend covering his back. She didn't rip the fabric, but he felt the points and couldn't wait to feel them dig into his muscles.

Skin to skin.

Tension filled her as she soared, her hips carrying on rocking as she experienced the bliss he'd given her. One she was intent on returning.

As release came to him, aided by the milking muscles, the relentless squeeze of her around his shaft, urging his cum from him, he pulled back from her mouth. He nipped at her bottom lip once more, then, as release poured through him, he realized this wasn't enough. That this would never be enough. She was fire, she was flame. She was his. And it was about time she knew that.

For the rest of his fucking life, he wanted to wake up to this woman. Wanted her to *want* to wake up beside him. Emotions, unusual and powerful, overwhelmed him and yanked at his vocal chords as he gritted out, "Marry me, Perry."

PERRY & HER PRINCES 191

HER HIGHNESS PRINCESS PERRY

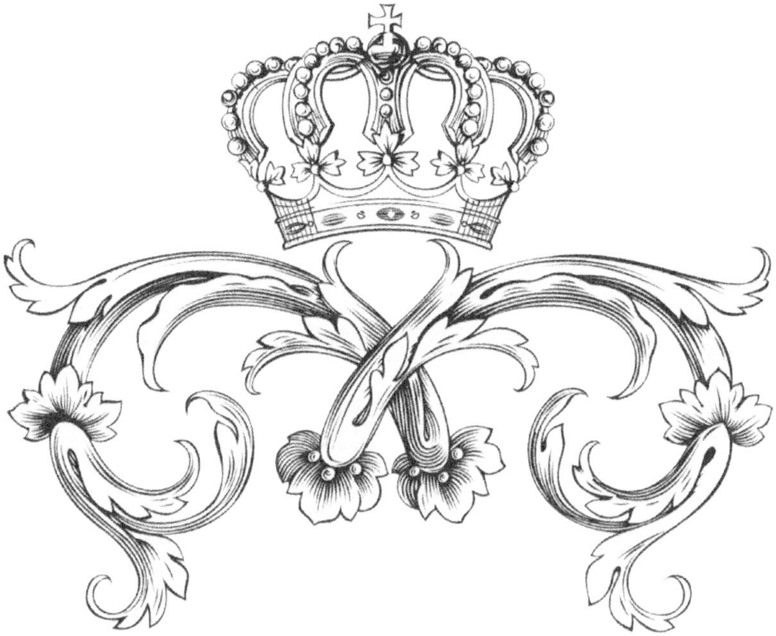

CHAPTER ONE

LIGHTS, everywhere.

They flashed, they scorched, they burned into her retinas.

They slipped into everything, sliding between her and Edward DeSauvier like sinuous snakes intent on constricting them to death.

Which, though fanciful, was pretty damn accurate.

Those lights, after all, shielded photographers from them. The bright, unapologetic glares came from the cameras intent on painting a portrait of the soon-to-be Crown Princess of Veronia, a country with one of the last true monarchies in Europe.

At her side, the Crown Prince Edward DeSauvier, stood tall, ridiculously handsome, and utterly disinterested. He wore a pleasant mask on his face, one that Perry had come to know as being his "public" look. It hid any and all expression from his features, putting a halt to the mobility of his brow and mouth, shielding any opinion, positive or negative, from the intrusive flash of the cameras.

She stood there with a version of her own. One that she hoped was hiding her true boredom as the dozens of men and women stood there taking endless rounds of the same image over and over again.

She wanted to scratch her nose, and the wedgie that hadn't been a problem earlier, suddenly was.

As those trite and middle-of-the-road thoughts flashed through her mind, she wondered how it was that one day, she could ever be queen.

She doubted that Arabella, Edward's late wife, had thought about wedgies and itchy noses on the day the world learned of her engagement to him.

She doubted that Marianne, Edward's mother and the current Queen of Veronia, pondered anything other than sensible matters that affected the country at large when face-to-face with a wall of photojournalists.

Yet, here she was, little Miss Hick from Hicksville, USA, wondering why she'd bothered to wear the thong George had laid out for her that morning.

Why hadn't she worn the panties she'd bought in a fit of pique? The bikini-style underwear wouldn't have found a home for itself in the crack of her ass. But she'd stupidly gone for the thong, and the only explanation was that she'd been nervous.

"Robotic" was the only word that summed her up this morning as her anxiety levels soared alongside her desperation for caffeine. It had been easier to wear what George had laid out for her—when he got such a kick out of dressing her—than it was to even think about raiding her drawers for the secret stash of granny panties she owned.

Delicious white cotton. High bikini cut, with no fear of the gusset slipping up her ass and mining for gold in South Africa...

She wanted to grimace at the thought, but remembered—at the last moment—that she had to wear this mask until their press officer declared they'd suffered enough at the hands of the media.

Borrrring.

She'd already had to pose with her hand splayed "just so" for them to catch the whopper of an emerald on her finger. Then had come the sickly-sweet stances where she'd cuddled into Edward's side, where they'd stared meaningfully into one another's eyes like they were Kate and Leo at *Titanic's* bow. And now this, the last shot, which would fly around the world's newspapers—her hand on his chest, her face pressed coyly into his arm.

The entire thing couldn't have been more repetitive or tedious, but then, the process of being engaged to a crown prince was exactly that.

There was none of the glitz and glamour anyone would expect. It was downright dull, and already, four weeks into the engagement, she was sick of the classes and the lessons and the goddamn useless information that she'd had to learn verbatim.

Decorum. Etiquette. Even dancing—cue shudder.

And why?

To become the perfect crown princess, one that could overcome her Hicksville past and do her birth nation—as well as her new one, because changing citizenship was also a part of becoming Edward's wife—proud.

On top of that suckiness, it also sucked—in Perry's humble opinion—

that her name wouldn't become renowned for her work, but instead, for the fact she was marrying Edward.

Anything else she accomplished would undoubtedly be forgotten.

Sure, she'd make it into some history books somewhere, but not for being an environmental scientist with a mission. For being a walking womb that wore a tiara.

Her natural feminist umbrage wasn't enough for her to call off the engagement, but it did piss her off. Especially since she wasn't marrying Edward for his position. If anything, his being crown prince put a major dent in her sex life.

Had he been a normal SOB, she could have just had her cake and eaten it too. Instead, she was having to go through this bullshit just to make sure the three men she loved would be a part of her life for the duration of their relationship. Whether that would be for forever or fourteen months. Being Edward's wife kept her on Veronian soil where her other lovers lived, but it also meant that Edward would no longer have to seek a wife which could, ya know, wreck the little harem she had going down at the moment.

But, all that aside, she'd agreed to marry Edward for one reason and one reason alone—he needed her.

And while it was too soon to even contemplate getting married, because they barely knew one another, hadn't had a chance to really come to terms with the relationship they'd be having in the future...none of that mattered. He needed her, and the girly part of her nature, the one that believed in soul mates, amongst other sappy shit, truly felt his soul called to hers.

Ugh. She wanted to cringe at even the thought, but it was the only way she could explain this burning sensation to be with him. Had it been farther down, she'd have thought it was a UTI. Instead, it was in the region of her heart.

She'd already ruled out heartburn and indigestion, so, nope, Perry was left with the conclusion that he was her freakin' lobster.

She felt like every day, Edward was suffering. Like he was dying inside somehow. And yeah, she knew that sounded freakishly melodramatic. He was a future king, after all. He was about to rule his own goddamn kingdom! The watch on his wrist cost close to half a million dollars, and she'd never seen him wearing anything other than hand-tailored clothes. But that didn't mean he was happy. That didn't mean he wasn't suffering out of duty to his country.

It just meant he was suffering while being really well-dressed. 'Cause, boy, the man did things to a suit and tie that had to be illegal in some parts of the world.

On top of that, the marriage proposal solved a few more complications that had arisen of late. George, Edward's brother, was her best friend. He was also her lover, partner, and all-around soul mate *numero uno*.

To be with George at all, with the potential of being with Edward in the future, she had to marry Edward. If she didn't, then she'd have to return to the US where her job was, and George would have to stay here in Veronia, thanks to some crackpot anti-royalists who'd made several death threats to the DeSauvier family.

As Edward's wife, she was above suspicion. She'd be in the lofty position of the heir to the throne's princess, and though she'd be under public scrutiny, a closer than normal relationship with her husband's brother, a man known to be her best friend, would be above conjecture.

Of course, the tabloids might chitchat, but they'd never out-and-out declare it. Not with Veronia's strict privacy laws and the family history of suing any publication that reported poorly on the Crown.

No, she and Edward and George could explore this unusual dynamic without fear of reprisal if she had a ring on her finger. That was why she'd said yes.

And considering she wanted to throw their cousin into the mix too, they all needed to be above reproach.

If shit came to shit and it was a total disaster, they could always get a divorce. But for now, she was happy. A bit bewildered, a lot taken aback by the swiftness of this and the sudden scale her life had taken, but... happy about cut it.

She'd wanted George for years, and she was getting him. Something about Xavier had made her fall into his bed after less than two hours of knowing him—and Perry was *not* the one-night-stand kinda chick. Edward needed her, and she, God help her, was starting to need him too. His somberness called to her in ways she couldn't define. It was like he reached for her soul whenever their gazes caught and held—he wanted the real her to want the real him.

That was heady stuff for a nobody from Tennessee.

But more than that, it was easy to feel swept away, caught up in what she knew was the early stages of love.

The thought had her gulping, because no declarations had been made between them. Not even of "liking"— never mind of "loving." Well, that was only between her and Edward. Xavier and she had talked of "falling for one another." She and George *had* said the words. Even if they were both coyer than two lovestruck turtle doves about it.

The brothers had shared for years before Edward's marriage, and they were slowly coming to terms with her need for their cousin, Xavier. He, like George, was watching them both from the side wall, peering at the photojournalists like they were tigers who'd been parachuted into a donkey sanctuary.

"Thank you, ladies and gentlemen. I'm sure you have enough photos now. If you'd like to follow me, I can direct you to..."

Perry ignored the rest of the press officer's words. She wasn't interested in what crap they were selling the media about her past, present, and future. She was just grateful that soon she'd be able to scratch her nose and pull her panties out of her ass-crack.

As the woman spoke, Edward started to guide her across the room to the side door where her other men were waiting for her.

The gold and gilt panels bore ancient art, and the carpet was so thick, her heels almost caught in the pile with every step. Overhead, a chandelier blazed, and on the exterior wall, a dozen double-breasted sash windows overlooked a scene that belonged in a Netflix movie about Christmas and princes.

There was no doubting that she was in a palace.

There was no hiding from the fact the man at her side, and the men in front of her, were of royal blood.

And they were hers.

Jesus, Mary, and Joseph.

She gulped, then almost tripped as nerves hit her—but at the last minute, just as the ground started to wield its magnetic pull on her, Perry managed to grab Edward's arm tighter and cling to him for support.

These goddamn heels.

He reacted with a lightning-swift response. He curled into her, shielding her from the remaining press in the room so they couldn't see her stumble, then the hand closest to her tightened about her elbow while the other slid around her waist to haul her against him for stability.

When the danger of falling flat on her face passed, she happened to catch George's eye.

Glaring at him, because he was laughing and not hiding it, she pouted. "Why do I have to wear these things again?" she demanded, sotto voce to her fiancé.

Fiancé.

God help her.

"Because they do fine things to your ass," George inserted softly when she stepped nearer, but he was grinning at her like a proud mother watching her son during school play season. "You did brilliantly, Perry," he told her, and as they backed off into the corridor, away from any lingering camera hounds, he grabbed her hand and squeezed it.

Xavier smiled at her, and she was taken aback by the desire in his eyes. "He's right."

"About the shoes and my ass, or how well I did in there?"

Desire was drowned by amusement—she seemed to have that effect on them a lot, which made zero sense in her eyes. She could be described as...cute. Sexy? Nuh-uh.

"Both. You do look good in heels, Perry," he assured her.

Her lips twitched, and though she felt she could relax because for a moment, they were alone, she knew she couldn't.

They were in a public hallway, which meant any of a gazillion helpers or servants or admin or cleaners could come scurrying out of the woodwork.

There were so many, she didn't even know where they worked.

Truth was, Perry had never even noticed them before. But being at the center of their attention had changed that. Now, it simply wasn't possible to be unaware of the staff.

Although, she guessed "servants" was the right word here. And damned uncomfortable it made her, too.

The goldfish bowl of this life was something she was finding the most difficult to acclimate to.

It was no wonder Edward needed her.

He had no privacy, and she knew, somehow, that in the chaos that was this existence, she'd have to find the strength to forge a private piece of life for them.

He wouldn't do it himself. He was too tied up in the notion of duty. Too aware of his responsibilities to maintain some private time for himself.

She could understand now why George thought she'd be good for his brother. She'd done the same for George, hadn't she?

Back in Boston, when he was overworked, she was the one who reminded him there was life outside of the office. And hell, she was dedicated to her own craft. Science was in her blood, and her cause was something she lived and abided by... but there was a limit.

A line.

Both brothers had been raised with that line blurred. It was her duty to unblur it.

So, though she wished she could kiss the smirk off George's lips and cling to Xavier's hand, she didn't. She stayed with a boa constrictor's grasp around Edward's arm as she tried, with a wing and prayer, not to fall over again as they walked down the hall toward the private section of the royal residence.

When she'd first arrived here, she'd only been shown certain areas of Masonbrook. Now that it was going to be her home, she was learning more of it. The more she learned, the more in awe she was and the unhappier she became at the prospect of living here.

This wasn't a home.

And she refused to believe it was.

It was a conversation for another day, but if Edward thought they were living here after they wed, he had another think coming.

"Where's Aunt Marianne and Uncle Philippe?" Xavier asked, breaking into her heavy thoughts. "I figured they'd be watching from the sidelines with us."

"They had another function over in Madela. Unavoidable. They're in a neighborhood renowned for UnReal sympathizers, and are trying to break the borders down. You know what Mother's like with the North. Constantly trying to smooth over troubled waters with a visit and a prayer."

Perry's eyes widened in astonishment. "Your parents walked into an area known for anti-royalist sympathies?"

Edward squeezed her hand. "Their security is beyond a joke. It's an inner-city school they're visiting."

She turned to him with a concerned frown. "Shootings can happen in schools," she reminded him.

"Not here. That's not going to happen. And Edward's right, their security is so tight, it's insane. This isn't the first time they've done it, Perry. Won't be the last," George reassured her, his mouth softening as he smiled at her. Perry sensed his pleasure in her caring for his folks, and knew she'd have received a kiss right about now, if the walls didn't have eyes and ears.

Still, no matter which way she swung it, she couldn't imagine uptight-but-kind Marianne in the middle of an inner-city school, surrounded by kids who were more used to being approached by drug dealers than royalty. Whatever she'd imagined her future parents-in-law to be doing today, it hadn't been that.

"Whose idea was this? Marianne's or one of the idiot press officers'?" she asked huskily. Though Perry was nothing but an American commoner who wouldn't know decorum if it bit her on her still-wedgied ass, Philippe and Marianne had treated her with nothing but kindness and respect.

"Mother's," Edward said absently as he read from his phone.

"Marianne's?" Perry squeaked, astonished.

Xavier chuckled. "Marianne isn't as delicate as she looks, Perry."

Apparently not, because he wasn't taken aback by the news that they'd gone into what was essentially enemy territory. She was the only one flabbergasted by the notion.

"Does it work?" she questioned.

"What? Do royal visits break down borders?" George asked, brow cocked and fingers in the air as he made the quotation. At her nod, he carried on. "Surprisingly, yeah."

"Then why is UnReal sympathy on the rise?" she asked skeptically.

"Because we're talking about regions who are reared to not trust the monarchy," Xavier said softly. "Some people just don't like the prospect of being ruled by a singular family, even if that family has done nothing but right by their nation."

Edward shot his cousin a look. "You know it goes further than that. Deep into crazy territory."

Xavier grimaced. "Yeah. But let's keep it simple."

"I'm not stupid," Perry retorted. "I can handle a dive into crazy town."

Edward snorted, then squeezed her waist. "Back in the nineteenth century, there was a series of uprisings. My family quashed them, and I'll admit, they were harsh. The punishments for taking part in the mutiny were severe, and a lot of people died as a result."

"People still talk about it to this day," George inserted grimly, and she knew from his tone alone that their history still affected the present.

"But surely the people can't blame you for what your ancestors did?"

Edward shrugged. "Fear and hatred can be as inbred as red hair."

She frowned. "That makes no sense."

"You can say that when people are seeking reparations for family members who were slaves back in the day in the States? When inherent dislike of the English had the Scots seeking a referendum to be a separate country?" Xavier shook his head. "Just because it isn't rational, and just because something is ancient history, doesn't mean fear can't pervade everything we do."

"I know, but still... it just seems so extreme when you rule fairly now."

George shrugged. "Don't get me wrong. There are a lot of people who love the royal family. Who would never want to be without us, and thankfully, that sentiment is stronger than any anti-royal grudge. But that doesn't mean the minority doesn't have a way of making their voices heard.

"Over the years, the affected provinces have tried to secede and become an independent state, separate to the union. Some of those uprisings are more popular than others... hatred and fear are always at the heart of such movements."

Perry sighed, troubled by their comments. This was her problem now. She was merging into a nation's heritage, wading through the quagmire and getting caught up in the stink. There was so much to navigate that she feared...

Ugh. What *didn't* freak her out about this situation?

As they reached her rooms, their unofficial meeting ground, and she stepped inside, Perry tried to cast off her heavy thoughts—but it was hard. Her only saving grace was the scent of tulips that overwhelmed her and was an instant irritation.

Called the Tulip Room, she'd yet to enter the bedroom without being suffocated by the flowers' scent. The goddamn waste had always gnawed at her, but now that she was officially being wed into the family, she figured she could start throwing her conservationist weight around.

The room itself was grand, with a huge four poster bed, plenty of Louis Quinze furniture dotted here and there...but the truth was, it was too stately for her tastes.

Which didn't bode well for the future.

She hadn't even seen Edward's quarters yet. They'd always met here, for some reason. In fact, she'd seen more of Xavier's home than she had of Edward's apartments. Of which she'd seen his office.

That was it.

Deciding that she was going to change out of her dress, she immediately heeled off her shoes the second the door was closed behind her.

Wry, masculine chuckles had her rolling her eyes, but she didn't turn back to glower at the men. There was no point. They'd endeavor to find her hatred of heels amusing, and she'd endeavor not to use one of said heels as a weapon and one of the guys for target practice.

Discomfited by the knowledge that she'd never seen Edward's private quarters, unease slithered through her as she strode across her room toward the dressing area, the tight clothing clinging to her in a way that made her cringe.

The walk-in closet was a separate entity to the space where she could change and store all her crap—well, most of the crap had been purchased by George. So it wasn't hers, per se.

She wasn't, and never would be, a fan of shopping. Especially not for clothes.

Considering that being a royal princess meant looking pretty at least three-quarters of the time, her appearance was as much a part of the job as the huge rock on her ring finger, so she'd left her wardrobe in George's capable hands.

He had good taste, and was fearless with a checkbook where she would never be, so why not dump the chore in his lap?

Still, the reason for her discomfort was twofold. Her clothes were, as George was wont, far too tight. But more than that, Edward was her principle worry.

He was, and she feared always would be, a closed book.

Just the realization that she'd only ever seen his office before—nothing more, nothing less—made her movements jerky with distress.

He'd proposed to her in his office. He must've fucked the sense out of her on his desk, because she'd been crazy enough to say yes and get this whole nutcase of a rigmarole started.

Why hadn't he invited her back to his suite? Why had she only just realized he was hiding something from her?

His sanctum sanctorum. The place where he escaped from the rest of the world...

Surely she would have to become a part of that haven, if this relationship was going to work?

She could barge her way in there, but that was no use, was it? It meant nothing if she wasn't invited in.

Sighing, Perry glowered at the heels in her hand, which, she'd agree with the guys, did wonderful things to her ass.

Dropping them in front of the chaise for some wonderful member of staff to retrieve, she peered around as she figured out what she wanted to wear.

The closet consisted of three walls of hangers, which were mostly full now, when only days before, they'd been empty. Opposite, there was a chaise lounge and a mirror that tilted this way and that so she could obsess over how chunky her thighs looked in the too-small clothes George insisted on buying her.

Coming to a decision, she reached for a slouchy tee and pair of yoga pants she'd brought with her from the US, then immediately unfastened the zipper that ran down her side. Stepping out of the too-tight, wraparound dress that somehow made her seem more voluptuous than she was, she breathed a sigh of relief at being liberated from all the cling.

She felt like her skin could breathe again when she was naked, and though she doubted the men would complain if she waltzed out in her birthday suit, she figured it was more politic to put something on.

So, glumly, she dressed, but rather than head back to the main room when she was decent once more, she slumped down against the chaise lounge and began to pull out the pins in her hair.

A smiling stylist had appeared this morning, the smile hiding a sadistic streak as she pulled Perry's wavy, dark chestnut locks into a deceptively simple chignon.

After had come a session in torture as the soon-to-be—insert snort—"royal eyebrows" had been shaped and plucked to within an inch of the stylist's life; death would have befallen her via tweezer if she had carried on with her plucking much longer. And then, Perry's face had been made up to look exactly as it did before...

What was the point of the *au naturale* look when you looked exactly the same after hours of being primped? Perry grumbled to herself and winced with the retrieval of the pins.

Stacking each pin in a line on the seat beside her, Perry bit her matte nude-tinted lip as she recalled the day of the engagement.

It certainly wasn't something she'd forget this lifetime.

The man hadn't given her a proposal worthy of the storybooks, but memorable? He had that down pat.

Edward's voice had been hoarse from his climax, his breathing ragged, his skin sweat-slicked as he loomed over her.

Ever debonair and constantly dressed to impress, it had floored her to see him look less than pristine. But that "floored" sensation had disappeared into astonishment when he'd proposed.

He'd seen her, all of her. Had even seen the pained look on her face as she came, had heard the caterwauls that were her screams of delight as she climaxed... that the man still wanted her after all that was more than she'd been able to process.

But want her he had, because the sincerity in his tone, in his eyes, had been half of the reason that she'd said yes at all.

That had been four weeks ago, and the truth was, she'd been reeling ever since.

The moment she'd said yes, everything had changed. *Everything.* And she feared nothing would ever be the same again.

When the pins were out and her hair was allowed to fall around her shoulders once more, she stared at them for a second. Absentmindedly fiddling with one, she thought about the conversation she'd need to have with her parents soon.

Was it weird she hadn't called them? Hadn't told them she was going to be a princess? A queen, one day?

Her lips twitched as she decided that no, it wasn't weird. They wouldn't have believed her.

When she'd moved from home, moved up north, they hadn't exactly abandoned her to her fate, but they'd been displeased.

They hadn't wanted her to go anywhere. Had wanted her to stay close, marry a local boy, have local kids, and play housewife for the rest of her life.

They were simple, country folk. Nothing wrong in that. And had she not been born with the brain of a scientist, one that was ever curious and ever seeking answers, she was sure such a life would have satisfied her.

But it hadn't. Her insatiable need for answers had taken her to Harvard where, ultimately, she'd met George.

Which had led to this point in her life.

She blew out a breath. The unease of moments before was transforming into a feeling of being overwhelmed.

If her own parents wouldn't believe she was going to marry a prince without a press release to back it up, how was the rest of the world supposed to believe it?

Marianne was queen now, but only as long as Philippe—Edward and

George's father—was king. There'd come a day when she, Perry, would be queen instead.

Not just queen of the lab, but of a country.

An honest to God *country*.

Gulping, she decided that ducking her head between her legs was the only way to go. Otherwise, she'd hyperventilate.

The minute her head was between her knees, she heard the door open. A heavy sigh came next, then footsteps followed. She recognized George's scent, and knew his touch as he pressed a hand to the back of her neck.

Warmth flooded her, and she sighed, relief filling her at his presence.

"Overwhelmed again?" he asked softly, and she nodded.

This was the third time he'd found her this way, and that was mostly, she figured, because he was the one who spent the most time with her. Not because he had some kind of Perry radar that told him when she was feeling totally mind blown by the situation she found herself in. Although, experience told her he had a smidgen of that, too.

"It's okay," he told her, his voice a low, soothing rumble. "Everything will be fine."

"How can it be?" she asked, after sucking down a large gulp of air. "I can't be queen, George. You know it, and I know it."

"You don't know that. I certainly don't."

"I *do*! I can barely hold my own in the lab without being undermined," she said on a thick swallow, hating her own words for the truth buried within them. "You know Stanford and Harley always bully me. How can I be a queen?"

"You don't have to be a queen. It isn't an adjective, Perry," he retorted. "Edward doesn't need that, do you, Edward?"

Perry blinked, then jolted upright as the sight of her fiancé's polished leather-clad toes appeared in her peripheral vision.

He approached on her left, his hand resting on the top of her spine, then falling down the curve of her back as he cupped her there, relaxing her with his touch before he took a seat.

"It's okay, Perry. You're bound to be a little scared, but there's no need. I had a wife who was born to be a princess, and the people loathed her." Well, *that* was reassuring. Not. "You're one of them, Perry. That's what they want now. But more than that, *I* want you."

She blinked at him, her lashes fluttering as she processed what he'd said. "But I'm... not suitable. Even your mother doesn't think so."

"Aunt Marianne likes you," Xavier countered, and she saw him leaning against the doorjamb, staring in. She didn't like how on the outside he seemed, so she held out her hand, silently beckoning him closer.

A small smile curved his lips as he neared her, then squatted down in front of her. One of his hands came up to entwine with hers, while the other touched the ground in front of him for balance.

Surrounded to the left, right, and front with gorgeous men dressed in suits that cost more than a few months' rent in her tiny apartment in Boston, she cut them each a look. When she did, she had to shake her head in disbelief.

What the hell did they see in her?

Not just Edward, who would be king one day. But his brother, and their cousin, a duke.

One of them, okay, she could snag—her tits alone would snare one of them, she thought wryly. But all three?

She let out a shaky breath at the knowledge that she was at the center of their world, then whispered, "I *can* do this, can't I?"

Xavier was right. Marianne *didn't* hate her. Hadn't she smiled yesterday when she'd shown Perry today's schedule with the press? And Philippe usually just shook his head and smothered a laugh at the many times she almost tripped over her own feet... if her future in-laws didn't loathe her commoner self, then that was all that mattered, right?

They, and these men here, believed she had it in her.

She sucked down a breath, taking comfort from that. Because if anyone's opinion really counted, it was her men's.

Not only that, but Edward wanted her. Her, not some perfect potential princess and future queen. She felt the tug of that connection in her soul, and responded to it like the lifeline it was.

George's smile was reassuring, as was the way he gently pinched the back of her neck, rubbing the tense muscles there. "You've got this."

"You really do," Xavier assured her.

"And even if you falter, we'll be here to make sure you don't fall," Edward told her, and that, more than anything, eased her terror.

Because he was right.

Hadn't he stopped her from falling flat on her face in front of the country's press? Hadn't he supported her, kept her upright and stopped her from making a fool of herself when she'd tripped over nothing but fresh air?

Yes, this situation belonged in one of the romance novels she loved reading. But that didn't mean she couldn't live it and love it, too.

With a crown on her head, no less.

"Yeah. You're right." She smiled, sucking in a deep breath to unsettle the cobwebs of anxiety still dusting her psyche. "*We've* got this."

George pressed a kiss to her temple as he curved an arm around her waist and nestled her into his side. "You ready to go?"

She hadn't been, but she was now. "Yeah. I am."

Xavier grumbled, "Why you arranged these meetings so close together, I don't know, George."

She said nothing because she also wished they weren't traveling to one of the dams in the northwest of the country for infrastructure checks. That was why she'd dressed for comfort rather than to impress. It was a whistle-stop tour. An hour's ride in a helicopter, and she'd be dealing with some of the engineers in charge of maintaining the second-largest dam in the nation.

After the one in Isdena, it was suffering the largest losses. She needed hands-on information to pass on to Veronia's Environmental Agency, which was resisting the idea of building new dams to combat their national and dire drought.

Morons.

"It wasn't like I had a choice," came the immediate retort. "Getting the three engineers on-site at the same time was like herding a dozen cats."

Edward sighed. "Stop arguing, you two. These meetings were arranged weeks ago. And now that Perry has a vested interest in Veronia's future, it's only for the good of us all that she's seen to be caring for the nation's water supply."

"Who says conservation can't be sexy?" she said wryly.

"When it comes Perry-shaped, no one would be stupid enough to think it isn't," Xavier teased, and that, as well as their belief in her, did more than dust away the cobwebs.

It freakin' eradicated them. With a goddamn flame-thrower.

Because whatever she thought, whatever she *saw* in herself, they saw something else. They saw a Perry who could kick ass while wearing a crown, too. And if that wasn't something to live up to, she didn't know what was.

CHAPTER TWO

WITH A HEADACHE BREWING, Xavier wriggled his shoulders as he scrawled notes onto his work pad.

His PA tried to get him to use a Dictaphone, saying it would be easier to transcribe his voice notes rather than his scrawl, but no matter what he tried, he never got the same feel as pencil and paper.

Maybe it was because it reminded him of science class back in school; the nostalgia alone gave him the feels, and it was hard to break a habit that was so many years in the making.

He drew a rough mock-up of the leaf he was studying at the moment. It was a rare plant, unique to a certain area in the Ansian mountain range—a part of his territory.

It had a similar flavor profile to basil, so it was often substituted in cooking, but it also had homeopathic properties that he was studying in his spare time.

The elda plant was a renowned anti-emetic. Relieving morning sickness woes for newly pregnant women, or being the hair of the dog after a hangover, and generally being the best thing since sliced bread when it came down to anything vomit-related... it was also giving him a migraine. The distinctive smell was pleasant, but with the amount he was growing, it was overpowering. Cue headache.

A pharmaceutical company, based in the US, had approached the Veronian government with a request for a research and development facility to be constructed here, with the express purpose of further investigating the root.

Of course, with his ties to the monarchy, there were definite perks.

When Philippe had heard the company's offer, he'd come to Xavier first, offered him dibs on the early research, knowing how interested Xavier was in all things botanical.

Progress was slow of late, which made him feel guilty. The anti-emetic could have far-reaching benefits, ones that made Xavier believe it could help with the nausea woes that plagued chemotherapy patients, but he was on a go-slow because of his love life. Hardly justification to the rest of the world, but to him…?

A dopey grin curved his lips, because it had been so long since he'd *had* a love life that any guilt he felt was actually wiped away. It was about time there was more to his days than just his plants. His research was vital, but all work and no play made Xavier a lonely boy.

The sound of a throat clearing was his first clue that he was no longer alone.

His staff had varying means of breaking his concentration—throat-clearing was the most polite, and usually the one that failed the hardest.

"Yes?" he asked lazily, uninterested in being disturbed.

"Her Majesty is here, Your Grace."

That had his shoulders straightening. "The queen is here?" he demanded, standing and turning to face the entrance to the conservatory where he worked.

Over six thousand square feet of the ducal gardens had been transformed into a glasshouse where he could work year-in, year-out. This was more than just his office—this was his refuge.

It contained rare ferns he'd planted himself, housed flowers whose roots he'd spliced. There were trees that soared forty feet into the air, each inch lovingly tended by him alone.

This was where he worked, played, and generally lived.

But for Marianne to be here… it spoke of a situation too delicate for potential eavesdroppers to overhear at Masonbrook Castle.

Marianne never visited his estate; she disapproved of his work too much to come to the scene of his many crimes against the Crown—well, in her eyes, anyway.

She didn't particularly approve of the idle rich, but nor did she wish the largest dukedom to be managed by a man more interested in his plants than his people. He wouldn't say she considered him a hippie, but it was close.

"Aunt?" he murmured when he saw her standing beside his butler. Surprise welled in him at the sight of her.

On the rare occasions she'd visited in the past, she'd always waited for him in one of the estate's many salons.

The Chinese Lily Salon had always been her preference when his mother and father had been alive.

He blinked at the sight of her standing there, looking faintly bored, but elegant as always. Her pantsuit was neat and well-tailored. She showed off her slim lines as well as the regalness of her posture—no one but royalty stood so tall and proud.

After gawking at the powder blue intrusion into his office, he remembered his manners.

He strode forward, but hesitated when he came close to her. Though he wasn't dirty, she didn't know that. And seeming to understand his dilemma, she tilted her face to the side to allow him a kiss.

His lips curved in a smile as he anointed her cheek with a small peck.

"To what do I owe the honor, Aunt?"

"I wish to speak to you about… Perry."

The slight hesitation had his brow puckering, but otherwise, discomfort filled him. Perry? He highly doubted his aunt was aware of the unusual nature of Perry's relationships with her sons and nephew, but why else would Marianne come out of her way to speak to him about Perry unless the conversation was going to be delicate in nature?

He nodded. "We should retire to the Chinese Lily Salon."

She pursed her lips as she took a glimpse around his lab then sighed. "That would be more comfortable."

Hearing her disapproval, he barely refrained from sighing himself.

To his butler, he murmured, "Please, serve afternoon tea in Her Majesty's favorite salon."

"Of course, Your Grace." To Marianne, Rodgers bowed, then disappeared with a gently uttered, "Your Highness."

Xavier watched him go, then holding out his arm, offered, "We shall walk there now."

"I think I'd prefer to walk around this monstrosity of yours for a bit, Xavier. I feel the need for some greenery to soothe my nerves."

At that wistful reply, Xavier's unease soared. Marianne liked greenery as much as he liked life at court.

She had a fondness for acacias. That was pretty much it. She was useless at flower arranging, even though that had been an important skill for her generation at the finishing schools she'd attended. And though the royal household could consult with her over the gardens of Masonbrook, they never did.

Marianne simply wasn't interested.

"Is everything all right, *Tanta*?" he asked softly, using the Veronian word for "auntie."

"No. It isn't," she admitted, equally as softly. She tucked her arm through his in what was, for her, a particularly affectionate gesture.

Though she was warm with family—could even be gentle and tender at times—as a queen, she wasn't known for it. She was seen as a little demure, a lot detached.

The Veronian royal family was popular with most of its people, save for the scant few who were totally against the notion of a monarchy. But Marianne's chilly disposition hadn't won the DeSauviers any fans over the years.

George's supposition that having Perry for a queen would ease public opinion, and have them sway over more to their favor with her down-to-earth nature, wasn't totally ridiculous.

That being said, Marianne's emotive display on national television, when Edward and George had been kidnapped, had destroyed the dissidents' support in one fell swoop... she *was* capable of affection, was even loving, but was always a little aloof.

"What's wrong?" he asked, trying to be patient when he wondered why she wasn't just stating what the problem was, here and now.

"It's your uncle."

Xavier frowned. She was here to talk about Perry. Wasn't she? "What about Philippe?"

"He's keeping something from me."

Tension filled him. "*Something*... like what?"

She shrugged, wriggling her shoulders in a way that was distinctly unlike Marianne, who was always cool and calm in a crisis.

Imagined or otherwise.

"I'm not certain. But he's being secretive. I don't like it when he's being secretive."

Xavier cleared his throat. "No, I can see why you wouldn't appreciate it."

She let out a small laugh. "The last time he was secretive, I found he had some slut holed up in a penthouse in Bayera." She pursed her lips as he let out a shocked splutter that petered out into a cough. "Come, Xavier, don't be childish."

"Childish?" Xavier retorted, still astonished at the idea of his uncle cheating on his aunt. And *her* knowing about it. "Are you certain he was having an affair?"

Marianne's jaw tightened. "Sadly, yes, I'm certain. However, after the last debacle, he promised he wouldn't do it again. I fear he's broken yet another promise to me."

Xavier shook his head, and despite himself, tugged free of her gentle clasp on his arm. He didn't do it to distance himself from her; if anything, he did it so he could move toward the glass wall and rest against it.

The world had, quite suddenly, toppled on its head.

"No. I can't believe it," he stated dumbly, staring blindly at his aunt, almost pleading with her for reassurance.

There was a look that was close to pity on his *tanta's* face, and that alone gave him reason to believe her.

"Do George and Edward know?" he asked, his voice quite hoarse.

She shook her head. "Of course not. They adore their father." She sniffed. "He can do no wrong in their eyes."

Floored by the bitter cynicism in her words, he whispered, "You think he's cheating on you again?"

She sighed, turning her head to the side to gaze at a particularly beautiful Deathcap fern. It had flowered earlier than seasonally it should have, but it was flourishing in the tropical and steady temperatures of the glasshouse. It was one of his pride-and-joy plants, but if her disinterested glance was anything to go by, she wasn't impressed. "What is that?" she asked, pointing at the fern.

Or, maybe not.

"It's called a Deathcap fern. It's native to Veronia."

Her head tilted slightly to the side. "I've never seen it before."

"It's quite rare. They don't always develop properly and need a perfect climate to flourish." He shrugged. "With global warming being as it is, the perfect climate can only be found in places such as these."

Her mouth tautened with distress. Then she surprised the hell out of him. "Such a shame. It's really rather beautiful."

The deciduous tree *was* beautiful. It was tall and grand, with arching branches that spread wide like long fingers, and each one was dosed with millions of tiny fronds.

It could have been mistaken for a Christmas tree with its shape and coloring, but when it flowered, it took on a whole other life. The fronds became almost fluffy, making the tree look like the branches were loaded down by feathers.

"Still, I'm not here to discuss your projects, pretty though they may be." She cut him a look, stared him dead in the eye, and said, "I'll assume whatever secret he is keeping from me isn't to do with a woman. Considering you look pole-axed at the notion of Philippe being adulterous, I would further assume you are not aware of what I'm speaking, which means it must be to do with Perry." Her mouth tightened. "Totally unsuitable." Then, she relented enough to sigh. "But I've not seen Edward smile so much for a very long time. Too long. So, I suppose she's worth the hassle for that alone."

Had he not been pole-axed before, he certainly was now. "I-I know UnReal sentiment is on the rise, Marianne. I know Philippe's intent on protecting the family from their reach. But that is all I know," he told her earnestly, needing to meet her truth with hard facts, while choosing to ignore her comments regarding Perry.

His aunt was a prideful woman. Too prideful, his mother used to say. But for all that, he'd always liked her. She was strong and brave. Tough, yes, but at her core, she was gentle. She could be hurt, and he found himself inordinately enraged at the notion of his uncle cheating on her.

No one knew the truth of a relationship behind closed doors, and he himself could imagine Marianne being rather cold... it was why she'd liked Arabella, Edward's first wife. They were two peas in a pod. Similar heritage, similar schooling, and similar future... until Arabella's death, of course.

Still, there was a softness to Marianne that was found in the love she had for her children. Xavier had always appreciated that about her.

"I wish I knew more," he told her truthfully. "But if there are secrets, they pertain to the UnReals."

She narrowed her eyes at him. "What kind of activity?"

"Are they engaged in, you mean?" When she nodded, he sighed. "Edward might be at risk again."

A wrinkle appeared between her brows. "Again?" She raised a hand and cupped her throat—the protective and self-comforting gesture didn't escape him.

He winced at the sight, wishing he hadn't hurt her, but also knowing that keeping Marianne out of the loop was beyond ridiculous.

His uncle had acted foolishly by not sharing such information with her.

They'd get nowhere if one of them was misinformed.

They all needed to be on their guard—especially the queen, as she had more duties outside the palace walls than the rest of them combined. Unlike Philippe, whose work kept him inside for the most part, and Edward, who had always handled the family's ties to governing the nation.

A soft breath escaped her lips. "I think I'd have preferred for him to be cheating on me again," she whispered, her eyelids drooping as she bowed her head and stared at the pebbled path beneath her feet.

"I'm certain all will be well," he said, trying to reassure her and moving away from the wall to approach her once more.

Now that the notion of Philippe cheating had settled in, albeit uneasily, Xavier found he was firmer on his feet again.

Well, he thought he was, until the idea of Philippe in such a position bewildered him all the more. He'd always believed in his uncle. Though he'd never thought him to be perfect, or even an angel, he'd never imagined Philippe would be a serial adulterer.

It was totally out of character.

Unless it wasn't, and Xavier had only ever seen what he wanted to see.

As he reached for her, he tucked his arms around her, pulling her against his chest to try and transfer some comfort to her.

That she didn't pull away or complain about the smell of the earth on his clothes from his work told him how emotionally frail she was at that moment.

How hurt she was.

Both about the secrets her husband was keeping from her, as well as the fact her son was in danger.

But then, when *hadn't* Philippe kept secrets from his wife? From them all? And when hadn't Edward been in danger? George too?

Those three issues were part and parcel of being Queen.

A king always kept secrets, and the heirs to the throne were in constant peril...

Still, that didn't make it hurt any less. And though it could never be said that Marianne was anything other than a wonderful queen, she was still a woman. Still a wife and a mother, and capable of being grievously hurt.

He sighed, pained on her behalf. "*Tanta?* Are you all right?"

She propped her chin in the air as she stepped back out of his arms. "I'll be fine, Xavi."

That she'd used his childhood nickname told him she was the exact opposite.

"Would you like some tea?"

"Not particularly." Her smile was tight. And he saw the same militant look that often appeared on Edward's face when a matter of great importance was suddenly up for discussion. "What do the UnReals want this time?"

"Who knows?" he said softly. The trite answer was the dissolution of the monarchy, but that was a ridiculous prospect. The monarchy would not be dissolved just because a pissed-off group of a few hundred had decided that was what they wanted.

It's all so bloody pointless, he fumed inwardly.

So much terror, so much suffering and heartache, and all for nothing. The foolish wants of some idiots who didn't realize the only thing they were messing with was fire.

"I think I should return to the castle. I postponed a meeting to come here."

Considering how dutiful Marianne was, he frowned. "Why?" he asked, knowing something must have triggered her suspicions for her to have canceled a meeting.

"Philippe was being more secretive than usual this morning. George had disappeared with Perry somewhere, and Edward was busy. But, regardless of them all, you're the only one who'd answer me anyway. You always were a good boy."

"Good is a relative concept," he muttered dryly.

She peered around the greenhouse, her smile wry. "Your parents wouldn't be happy with the addition to the estate, but your mother always did have appalling taste."

The catty statement seemed to perk her up. His aunt and his mama had been exactly that—cats. Two angry cats whenever they were locked, figuratively, in the same space together.

Christmases and Easters had been a nightmare, he recalled with some fondness.

"I'll speak to you later, Xavi." She reached over and pressed a kiss to his cheek. "Don't judge your uncle too harshly, child. He isn't the only one who's made mistakes in our marriage."

With that, she departed, leaving Xavier sputtering.

What the hell had that meant? Had she cheated on Philippe too? Or had she done something to make his uncle cheat?

Of course, that started an internal moral debate on whether one person in a relationship could ever make the other cheat…

As he pondered those thoughts, he retreated to his workspace. After scrawling down some notes that had more to do with sociology and the psychology of marital relations, his butler cleared his throat.

Again.

"Dammit, Rodgers! Not another intrusion."

A soft snort was his butler's answer as Xavier spun around irritably. Spying Perry, he blinked. Then to Rodgers, he nodded briskly but with an apologetic narrowing of his eyes, and when the butler had disappeared with a stalwart glance and a faint, "Tea has been served, sir," Xavier turned to Perry.

The woman who had turned his world on its head.

He folded his arms across his chest, and he grinned as she mimicked his posture.

"What's this I hear about tea?" she demanded, slouching back and angling herself against the back wall in a way that reminded him of MC Hammer back in the day.

"Marianne was here."

She stood up straight at that. "She was? Why?"

He shrugged, hiding a smirk as she peered around, checking to make sure the queen was no longer in the vicinity. "She left, Perry. Don't worry, she's not here to reprimand you for slouching." When she rolled her eyes, he stopped hiding his smirk. "She wanted to ask about the UnReals."

"Why did she ask you?"

"Because I don't treat her like she's made of kid gloves, that's why."

She shot him a knowing look. "That's the scientist in you. I do love that about you."

He cocked a brow. "The scientist in me purrs with approval. The man, less so."

She snorted as she stepped toward the workspace. The distance between them displeased him, even when she rested against the desk, further mimicking his posture.

Said distance put him on edge, and he wasn't entirely sure why.

"I didn't expect to see you here today," he said casually.

"No? Then you're in for a welcome treat, aren't you?"

Her witty retort had him snickering. "Welcome? I wouldn't say you've been particularly welcoming," he finished with a sniff.

A wicked glint appeared in her eye. "How would you like me to greet you?"

"Rodgers is part of the furniture," he said softly, his tone musing.

She frowned. "Huh?"

His segue had confused her, so he clarified. "You can pretend he's not there."

"I can? Won't he gossip? Look, I've seen *Downton Abbey*, ya know. The staff talks."

He laughed at the notion of Rodgers unbending enough to discuss anything improper about the duke's taste for date and walnut cake—never mind his love life. "Perhaps, but never Rodgers."

"Why not?" she asked, her distrust evident. That alone saddened him. A few weeks ago, she wouldn't have even cared, but now that she was in the public spotlight, everything had changed.

Only a week ago, she and Edward had declared their impending nuptials to the public. Seven days in which her life had forever changed, and that were already starting to tarnish her with the insidious ways their lifestyle had a tendency of doing.

They were rich, powerful, and more fortunate than most could comprehend. Yet things like privacy, security, and loyalty were more fiercely guarded than the crown jewels.

Well, on a personal level, anyway.

Her privacy had already been invaded by the press—who were actually kept on a leash by the Veronian Constitution and tight privacy laws. If she journeyed out of the country, she'd really learn what a breach of privacy felt like—something he certainly didn't want for her.

Her security was at risk by the sheer fact she was going to marry Edward. Thus, guards were on her wherever she went.

And loyalty? She hadn't been around long enough to inspire it in the staff. He knew that only George, Edward, and Xavier were the ones she felt she could trust. Although the king and queen would never do anything to hurt her, they would always be more on Edward's side than Perry's, thanks to parents' needs to shield their child.

She was adrift, in truth.

Lost to a strange new world, within an even stranger relationship.

At that moment, he felt incredibly lonely for her, and he determined that he would always, no matter the circumstance, be her port of call when times grew tough.

As the legendary Enrique Iglesias had said once upon a time, "I can be your hero, baby." Inwardly, he laughed, even though it was true.

He'd be her hero. And more.

"So, basically," she grumbled, breaking into his little dive into post-Millennial pop music, "you're saying I can just jump on you in front of Rodgers, and he won't bat an eyelid?"

"He's well-paid to maintain my secrets," was all he said, but the truth was, it was a disservice to Rodgers.

The words were ones that Perry, American and capitalistic to the marrow, would understand.

But Rodgers had been with the family from birth. Well, almost. His parents had served on the staff here, and his grandfather had also been a butler to Xavier's great-grandfather.

His line ran parallel to Xavier's, in a way.

It was beyond his own rather wild imagination to even consider Rodgers selling out the family—it would be like the butler betraying his blood relatives.

Because she was American, the notion of a high salary had her nodding her head in understanding. However, it didn't stop her from asking, "What if the press offers to pay more than you do?"

He snorted. "Rodgers is well-rewarded for his work here. But more than that, his very family is a part of the bones of this estate. We're all intrinsic to it, we all have our part."

She cut him a look. "Does that part include turning a blind eye to the future queen's shenanigans with the lord of the manor?"

His grin was like quicksilver. "Most definitely."

She laughed at the satisfaction in his voice, then stepped away from the workspace to approach him from the front.

He sighed when she curved her arms around his neck, and he settled his hands on her slim waist. On tiptoe, she reached up to press her mouth to his, and the taste of her was like a mug of hot chocolate after a night on the piste.

There was something about Perry that made a man think of long nights in front of an open hearth. Not just her ripe form, which was made for exploring in front of the licking flames, but because it would be a joy to sit and just be with her.

He hadn't had that with her yet.

All of this had happened so quickly that just chilling out with one another hadn't exactly taken precedence.

George's fault, of course.

He'd shifted the timeline leagues ahead when he'd told Perry his desires for his future with her. The idiot always had gone more with "less haste, more speed" than was good for him.

She too, sighed into his kiss, as he speared her mouth with his tongue, gently thrusting against hers. He was content to savor, content just to taste, and it seemed she was too.

The generous swells of her body sank into him, merging against his hardness until they were one entity as they stood there, in his greenhouse, the scents of his favorite place in the universe filling his nostrils.

A voice cleared, and Perry tensed. He opened his eyes as he gritted out, "Rodgers?"

"Apologies, sire. Their Highnesses are here."

He blinked. "Which Highnesses?"

"Princes Edward and George, Your Grace." Rodgers looked anywhere other than at the woman in the Duke's arms. "They are in the Tulip Room, sire. I thought it wise to avoid a scene."

A shocked and very anxious giggle burst from Perry, and she burrowed her face into Xavier's throat.

"Oh my God. Let the earth open up and swallow me whole."

Xavier, trying not to laugh, arranged his expression into somber lines. "Rodgers, you're aware of who Perry is?"

"Of course, sire," came the grave retort. "I'd have had to be a fool to miss last week's announcement."

"Then, you'll need to be kept in the loop." Xavier caught and held his butler's eyes. "Perry isn't cheating on Edward."

Confusion laced the older man's stoic features, and Xavier finally had the answer to an age-old unspoken question he'd had floating about his head.

Exactly what could break the man's stoicism?

Apparently, talk of the future queen, while in the duke's arms, being faithful to the crown prince...

Xavier couldn't blame the man for being confused.

Rodgers cleared his throat—this time not to seek attention or to break into a private moment, but out of genuine perplexity.

"I think I understand, sire," he said after a moment, though it was quite clear he didn't. "I shall keep the staff from intruding when Her Grace is at the estate."

"While I would appreciate that, Rodgers, this is my home. I will not limit my activities with the woman I love here. And," it was Xavier's turn to clear his throat, "you should probably be more accustomed to the princes being here too."

Rodgers's eyes widened. "Being here? Overnight?"

Xavier nodded, and had to hide a smile when Perry groaned and burrowed her face into his linen shirt.

"Of course, you are the only member of staff who will understand the delicacy of our situation."

Pride and bewilderment fought a battle on Rodgers' face. His mouth popped open then sank closed. "I am, sire?"

"Yes. Both here and at the castle. I trust you with my life, man. Therefore, I can trust you with Perry's too."

For a second, the butler looked more floored than he had a moment before. Which was really saying something. "I think I understand, Your Grace." In his black tails and white gloves, Rodgers was a walking, talking embodiment of an establishment that no longer existed.

He had the morals of a man from that same era, but he was his duke's attendant through and through, and would never betray him. He nodded and made to depart, but before he could, Xavier murmured, "Get used to seeing Perry around here, Rodgers. She's the mistress of the estate now. In action and deed, if not name."

Rodgers' shoulders stiffened, but that was nothing to Perry's reaction.

"Excuse me?" she demanded, when the butler's steps had faded out. "The mistress of the estate?"

Xavier grinned at the fire flashing in her eyes as she peered up at him, the tips of her fingers digging into his chest as she pushed herself away and brought distance between them.

He didn't let her move far. Keeping his hands looped about her hips, he murmured, "You are one of the family. Rodgers understands family like nothing else. If I say you're the mistress of the estate, he knows to protect you and shield you and serve you as he would me."

For a second, she stared at him blankly, her crisp aquamarine eyes slightly unfocused until she clenched the lids and shook her head.

"This is..."

"Don't say it," he warned. "I'm sick of you declaring this situation crazy."

"And what else is it?" she snapped. "This situation... you guys, your status? I mean, it just makes no sense to be tempting the fates the way we are. We're going to get caught, and we're going to create a huge scandal."

She looked so pained he had to kiss the tip of her nose. Not to shut her up or to undermine her concerns, just to connect.

He felt her stress, wished there was something he could do about it, but that just wasn't to be.

"We're not going to get caught. We're not going to cause a scandal." With the knowledge that his uncle had somehow managed to have enough affairs to upset his *tanta*, and all without it becoming public knowledge, Xavier knew well and good that the royal family could have secret lives with no one being any the wiser.

It was all down to the staff one trusted with those secrets, and there was no one more trustworthy than Rodgers.

"I didn't realize they were coming to visit today as well," she told him, and he realized her tone was apologetic.

He frowned. "You don't have to sound guilty, Perry."

"Don't I?" She bit her lip. "I wanted to spend some time with you."

He smiled, touched by her words. "I'm glad," he told her, his tone grave, as serious as the situation required.

She reached up and cupped his cheek. "I don't want you to feel like a fifth wheel because you're not at the castle."

He snorted. "Trust me. I don't feel that way," Xavier told her, amused at the idea. "If anything, I have the most freedom at home. The privacy we'll find here is beyond compare."

She let out a shaky breath. "I must admit that when the driver brings me here, as soon as the gates close behind us, I feel safer."

While he was pleased by the notion, he didn't want her to feel like she was in danger.

Though she technically was, he didn't want her to live her life in constant fear.

There was already one DeSauvier who led his life like that, and being married to him was more than enough for any woman to stand.

"We'll keep you safe," he informed her gently, tilting his head so he could nuzzle his chin into her palm.

She smiled at the affectionate gesture. "You don't have to say that. If the guards couldn't keep George and Edward safe when they were boys—"

Her voice broke off, but not before he started shaking his head. "Different times, Perry. Surely, you must see that. The technological advancements are more than even I can even understand, and I'm more at ease with the need for security than you are." He pointed to three separate places in the foliage behind her. She twisted around to see where he was gesturing.

"Cameras. They're always watching." When he sensed her tense, felt the way in which her body was cuddled into his, he teased, "If the guards ever sold their story, they'd be thrown into Veronian jails for treason."

"Holy shit," she breathed. "That's hardcore."

"Which part of the Veronian way of life makes you think we don't take our security and our privacy seriously?"

She gnawed at the inside of her cheek. "I guess it makes sense."

Xavier nodded, his brow arched knowingly. "You Americans are so obsessed with the freedom of the press that you forget how invasive that freedom is. Our press has the right to print whatever it wants about genuine news pieces. But about whoever it wants? No. That's when the privacy laws bang into place.

"But with the guards, it's different. They sign official documentation that binds them to us forever. Even if they retire, resign, or are fired, they can never reveal anything they might learn while in our employ. To do so would invoke the strictest laws of the land. Worse still, it would be an act of defiance against the royal family."

"Hence the treason." She gulped. "Is Veronia a capital punishment country?"

Xavier grimaced. "Sadly, yes."

"They'd be executed?"

"Depends on the secret they leaked," he said after a while. "And, let's face it, one of this magnitude could rock the royal family... there's no way any guard would survive the telling of such a secret."

"I'm not sure if you've made me feel better or worse," she complained.

"He has a habit of that," George said, his voice breaking into the hushed environs of the glasshouse.

Xavier turned to look at his cousin. "What are you doing here, pipsqueak?"

George scowled at the old nickname, but Perry laughed, turning her head to stare at her best friend and lover.

Of them all, Perry and George had known one another the longest. They'd met at university in the US and had been friends ever since. The drunken recounting of a secret, a glimpse at a Kindle, and George had guessed that Perry's predilections ran parallel to his and Edward's when it came to sharing and being shared. Luckily for them all, he'd been correct.

Xavier had only been thrown into the mix thanks to a simple twist of fate.

When Perry had come here, on her first night, there had been a banquet. She and Xavier had met there and had consummated the attraction that had flared to life between them.

Upon seeing Perry—the woman George had loved secretly for years—in Xavier's arms, the truth had come tumbling out.

And now, close to two months later, they were all caught up in a net that had appeared out of nowhere, yet was entirely of their own making.

"I wanted to start eating, but Edward said it was poor manners."

Xavier snickered. "Never stopped you before."

"No, but Edward isn't usually around preaching about decorum."

"Since when has he cared about that?"

"Since he was yelled at this morning by one of the Guardians of the Keys."

Perry's mouth rounded. "What's a Guardian of the Keys?"

"You know what a chatelaine is?" Xavier asked her quietly, surprised she hadn't come across a Guardian of the Keys in one of her many lessons.

"The woman of the keep," Perry said, "had all the keys on a chain about her waist. She was the lord of the manor's lady, and their home was her domain."

Xavier nodded, impressed at her knowledge of old lore. "Well, the castle is too large and Marianne's duties too numerous for her to be the chatelaine. The Guardians of the Keys are positions held by the highest-ranking nobles of the land."

"Like the queen's ladies maids?"

"Exactly. Guardian of the Keys is a more Veronian way of phrasing it." To George, he asked, "What did Edward do?"

"He was caught feeling up Perry in one of the hallways."

Perry stiffened. "Oops."

Xavier laughed. "If you're allowed to be felt up by anyone in a hallway, it's Edward."

"Apparently not, if it shows a lack of decorum," Perry said, but she didn't sound peeved, just glum.

"It's their job to preach about a lack of decorum," George told her ruefully. "But that doesn't mean it's our job to lead our lives by it. We're in charge, after all."

Xavier laughed again. "If you think that, it's no wonder Murielle Harlington loathes you. Knowing you, you've probably shoved that in her face."

George sniffed. "Irrepressible busybody. We're already constrained in public. The castle is our home first, then our seat. I see no need to be totally restricted."

"Edward, it would seem, doesn't agree," Xavier pointed out, amused at George's rebellious streak.

He watched as his cousin folded his arms across his chest. Obstinacy radiated from his pores, and he wondered if it was because he was the baby of the family

"Actually, Edward does agree with me."

"Why's he bitching at you about eating the sandwiches without my approval then?"

"Because he's being a bore."

Xavier frowned, but Perry beat him to it. "Why do I feel like I'm missing something?" she asked, and pulled away from Xavier's hold on her hips.

Though he wanted to haul her back, he didn't have to. She didn't move far, instead just turned around and leaned back against him so she could look at George without craning her neck, while maintaining a close contact with Xavier.

George noticed the move, and the smile on his face was as close to beatific as could be.

The sight pleased him.

Xavier didn't particularly understand George's kink. Nor did he understand Edward's, or even his own. He just knew he needed Perry in his life.

She was the first gulp of fresh air he'd had in too long. After years of being hunted by the women at court, a misfortune his cousins shared with him, Perry's very nature was appealing.

She was smart. A creature who worked on instincts—not that she realized it. She was open and warm, affectionate, and had a desire to help for the sake of helping rather than for what good it would do her or her family name.

There was a selflessness that called to Xavier, and he knew it called to his cousins too.

They were powerful men. Could have anything they wanted whenever they wanted—nothing was outside of their means. And yet, the one thing none of them had was a steady relationship.

He and George were in their thirties, Edward was forty-one. All of them were old enough to have settled down by now, and yet they never had.

The world might think it was because they were consummate bachelors, but that wasn't the case. Before he and Perry had slept together, he hadn't been celibate, exactly, just disinterested in the women he'd met in his small circle. This usually only involved ladies from the court, as the only time he left his lab was to answer the queen's summons that he attend a ball or gala at the castle.

He knew Edward was the same. Only George had had more freedom than most when he'd left Veronia to study and then live in the States. But even he hadn't settled down.

Well, that was what Xavier believed until George had brought Perry home.

Three men, all accustomed to getting their way in whatever they wanted, and yet, they were willing to share Perry.

Why?

Because she was unique.

Special. In ways Xavier couldn't really explain.

He could only liken her to an unpolished diamond. Amid a treasure chest of emeralds and rubies, she shouldn't have stood out. And yet, she did. And when she was cut, she'd be larger than the Hope Diamond, and more beautiful than the Ugly Duckling post-transformation.

"You're missing nothing. Edward can just be a pain sometimes. Look, can we move to the Chinese Lily Room or what?" George was grumbling now. "It stinks of cow shit in here."

"I'm experimenting," was all Xavier said, well-accustomed to the stench. Although, it explained why Marianne had looked so uncomfortable in the glasshouse. Not enough to leave its confines for their conversation, mind. Just enough to wander deeper into the wilds of his specially cultivated plants, where the scent from his experiment was farther away.

"It does stink in here," Perry admitted ruefully, peering over her shoulder at him. "And I could eat."

George looked her over with a weather eye. "You haven't been eating that much of late, have you?"

She moved away from Xavier so he could stand, but he saw her shoulders stiffen, and her head tilt—she was bristling.

"Since when do you watch what I eat?"

"Since I noticed you dropped about five pounds that you can ill-afford to spare," George snapped back.

His highhandedness had Xavier shaking his head. "You catch more flies with honey than vinegar, George," he retorted.

"Not with Perry," he said mulishly. "She needs vinegar. Just like I do. We're two peas in a pod."

Perry stiffened again, then blew out a breath. "Dammit, stop being right."

George's grin, when it beamed Xavier's way, was smug.

Damn his hide.

―――

AGITATED AND UNEASY, Edward paced the length of the Chinese Lily Room.

Unlike the rooms at Masonbrook castle that were named after flowers, this place wasn't loaded with furniture topped with vases of their namesake.

Instead, great murals had been painted onto the walls. Edward easily remembered how much his aunt had loved this sitting room, and when meeting with guests, Xavier's force of habit was to seat them in here.

The man had had a busy morning between his arrival and George's, alongside Perry's too. Plus whoever the tea had been originally intended for.

Considering that the tea was Tienshe Flower, he had a feeling it was his mother. Only Marianne drank the delicate tea in their family. If that didn't help identify the tea's original intended recipient, the exact brand of honey was further clue.

He rubbed his chin, wondering why his mother had visited with Xavier.

They were close as a family. Always had been. Though George and Edward's *Tanta* Lisetta hadn't been friendly, she and Marianne had been loyal to one another. Family first, and all that.

Xavier had been at the castle as much as Edward and George had been as a boy. It was why the three of them were so close; Xavier had always been welcome in Masonbrook, and for a long time, before the troubles had befallen them, Xavier and Edward had been the best of friends.

In truth, if Edward thought about it, he still considered Xavier his closest confidante.

It was just that, of late, he hadn't had much confiding to do.

With his back to the murals of Chinese Lilies, endless rows of them that had graced this room for close to two centuries with its aged patina, he stared out onto the Ansian mountain range ahead.

One couldn't go far in the city without spying Xavier's ducal territory, and as he looked on, he couldn't help but feel jealous.

Xavier had the freedom to do whatever the hell he wanted with his days, while still remaining tied to the family.

He, on the other hand, had no choice but to dedicate his life to a throne he'd never particularly wanted.

He'd never liked strings... and being a DeSauvier meant strings were par for the course.

Behind him, the door opened. George and Perry were bickering over how badly the Guardians of the Keys would react if Edward and she had been caught doing far more than just kissing.

Edward sighed. "You told her." Why had George done that?

Honestly, the man had the mouth of a gossiping old hag.

He ran a hand through his hair, uncaring that he was unsettling the pristine style he kept it in. By nature, he wasn't a groomer, but necessity had shown him how always presenting a perfect image facilitated him.

The ways were numerous and pathetic.

"Of course, he did," Perry retorted as Xavier closed the door to the sitting room behind him, shutting them all in.

She surprised him by striding over to the window he was still half-facing, and slipping her hand around his waist.

Tenderness wasn't alien to him. His mother, though she was by nature not the most affectionate of creatures, did hug him and always kissed him farewell—whether it was for a short, out-of-town visit, or just to bid him goodnight. His father was a hearty back-slapper, and George had inherited that trait. But Edward's late wife had made a can of tuna seem warm and tender, so Perry's generosity with herself came as a surprise.

A welcome one.

Still acclimating to that side of her, he allowed himself to react spontaneously—sliding his arm around her waist so they were mutually linked.

"You should have told me. It's not down to you to take the blame for everything I do wrong. And we both know I started that kiss."

Desire flashed through him, and he knew she saw it in his eyes. The wicked grin curving her lips told him exactly how amusing she found that.

He sighed, recalling the incident two days ago.

She'd stunned the hell out of him by pushing him against the wall in the West Wing as they strode away from an interview with the royal chronicler who was commemorating their nuptials in the family records.

She'd grabbed his hands, pinned them to the wall, and had kissed him. Thoroughly.

Of course, he'd had to cooperate.

Perry was tiny in comparison to his six feet four inches, and there was no way she would have had the strength to keep him in place unless he had wanted to stay there.

Sadly for him, well, both of them, Murielle Harlington had caught them in the act. She'd merely cleared her throat and made her disapproval known before sweeping away to her office.

He'd had the misfortune of greeting her on his own this morning.

"You started it, but I wanted it to happen," he told his fiancée calmly. A part of him was still amazed she'd said yes, mostly because he didn't understand her reasoning for it.

She didn't love him. Of that he was well-aware.

He wasn't a lovable man.

George was easy to love, with his teasing nature and wicked and wide smiles. Xavier might have spent most of his time with his head buried in a book or his eyes squinting over some noxious vapor he'd created during an experiment, but he, too, was witty and charming.

Edward, on the other hand, felt certain he was dull as ditchwater.

Had she been anyone else, he'd have believed she'd said yes because of his title. But if anything, that title terrified Perry.

The responsibilities and duties were akin to a nightmare for her.

So, no. There was no reason to believe she'd said yes to become the next queen of this glorious nation.

Which meant he had no real logical explanation for her behavior.

Sometimes, she was standoffish, abrupt and almost aghast when she was processing the many aspects of her new role as his fiancée. She didn't sink into him like he'd seen her do George or Xavier… but she did attack.

Not in a bad way, of course. But in a way that seemed unique to him.

She had a habit of grabbing his hands and shackling his wrists with her own when she kissed him. Almost like she was frightened he'd touch her.

He wasn't sure why that was. She liked his touch, that he knew. He'd given her pleasure, and knew far too much about a woman's body to think she could be lying about climaxing in his hands.

He supposed it might have been a control thing. She was as unsure about him as he was about her…but it wasn't derailing their plans.

"You think too much," she said softly, breaking into his thoughts not only by word but by deed too—her finger came up to stroke along the pucker between his brows.

"The lot of a prince, I'm afraid."

"Before I met you and George, I'd have said that was the last problem a prince had to deal with." She smiled ruefully, and it was aimed at herself. "Truth is, I've never seen two people work so hard for so little appreciation."

"That award has to go to my mother and father," George retorted, clearly amused at Perry's frank remarks. He took a seat and grabbed a sandwich. Studying the teapot with interest, he said, "You think what Edward does is thankless? You ain't seen nothing yet."

Edward sighed. George, for all his smarts, could be an idiot sometimes.

"You mean the roles Edward and I will fulfill at some point in the future, George?" she asked, but he was relieved to hear the teasing note to her tone.

His little brother, as always, was unapologetic. He brandished the sandwich at her, wagging it around so that bits of grated cheese fell to the floor. "I'm honest, Perry. You know that. I never said it was going to be easy, just that it would be worth it."

"That Aubusson rug will be worthless if you get more cheese in its weave," Xavier said mildly as he poured himself a glass of juice from the carafe on the tea tray.

George peered down at the rug and grimaced. "Sorry, cuz."

Their cousin just chuckled and turned to face the tray. "Do you want something to drink, Perry?" he asked, changing the subject with an ease Edward envied. "It would seem Rodgers has provided a veritable feast."

"He would, wouldn't he?" Edward asked blandly. "If my mother was visiting..."

From behind, Edward couldn't discern his cousin's expression, but he could see the sudden tension in Xavier's shoulders.

"Yes. She was here," he said softly, not turning back to look at them as he spoke.

"Why?" George asked, frowning at his sandwich before he took a large bite.

"Because she wanted to speak with me, of course."

George huffed. "I managed to figure that one out, Sherlock. What about?" He enunciated his words carefully.

"She thought your father was keeping something from her."

Edward winced. "She always was too smart for her own good."

"Wait a minute," Perry broke in. "You mean to tell me Philippe hasn't shared news of the UnReal's regrouping?"

Edward squeezed her waist. "My mother's reactions to that news wouldn't be..." He cut off his own words. Marianne was a grown woman; they all had a tendency of trying to protect her, but the truth was, she was, like the rest of them, a survivor.

It was an intrinsic part of being a leader—the instinct to survive. To wend through political drama and fuss with little difficulty.

"She should have been told," he admitted softly, and he felt Perry relax at his words.

Inadvertently, he'd managed to say the right thing.

"Well, she wouldn't leave until I told her, so she knows now."

George finished his sandwich and reached for another. "How was she?"

Something passed over Xavier's face, something Edward couldn't understand. Xavier took another sip of his juice, then murmured, "As you would expect. She took it badly. But she composed herself before she left."

"That bodes well," George pointed out. "If she was too distraught, she'd have had to take to one of the rooms and rest here."

"I can't imagine your mother being that delicate," Perry confessed.

"She isn't. Unless it comes to us," Edward admitted quietly.

Perry rubbed his side with her hand, then detached herself from his grip.

The ache that bloomed inside him at her absence surprised him, but he tracked her movements. He watched as she placed a hand on Xavier's back, then peered at the tea trolley that would feed an army.

The irony was that his mother rarely ate any large meal. Maintaining her figure was paramount in her eyes.

Still, the kitchens would try their best to impress and would, ultimately, be disappointed, he thought wryly. Now, he was grateful that he'd had the urge to come to the estate, even if all it achieved was saving Xavier's chef's pride from the tray returning untouched.

There were jugs of two different juices—the colors telling him one was apple and the other cranberry. A carafe of milk, a pot of coffee, and a teapot of his mother's favorite tea were all stacked on the trolley, surrounded by several types of mugs, cups, and glasses. There were dishes piled high which were loaded with scones and sandwiches, and a cake stand topped with petit fours.

The urge to come here had been spontaneous. A desire to escape the castle, to flee the many eyes that watched over them, had filled him with the memory of Murielle's chastising ringing in his ears. On his way out, his brother had caught up with him, and they'd decided to visit Xavier together.

Only on the road over here, when George had called their security team, had they both realized that Perry had fled to Xavier's estate, too.

Will this always be our bolt hole? Edward asked himself.

Their safe haven from the prying eyes of court?

He didn't know, and only time would tell.

Striding over to her side, he reached for a plate and loaded it with petit fours and a sandwich, as well as taking a dish of a posh fruit salad.

As he turned back to the room, he saw everyone was gaping at him. Well, everyone save Perry, who was watching his brother and cousin gape at him.

"What?" he demanded with a scowl.

Xavier cleared his throat. "Nothing."

George hunched his shoulders. "Yeah. Nothing."

Edward's nostrils flared irritably. "If you have something to say, say it."

Perry, an éclair in hand, murmured, "I don't get why they're staring at you, Edward, but I'd hazard a guess that it's because you never seem to eat outside of mealtimes. And even then, you eat very little."

"I eat. Just not in front of people."

That had Perry blinking. "Huh?"

George and Xavier were nodding sagely, as though that was the answer to one of life's mysteries.

"Why don't you eat in front of people?" Perry asked when he took a seat. His stomach began churning now that he realized he was about to do what he hadn't done in a long time. But the petit fours looked good, and it felt, well, *different* to relax.

He was among friends, family, and his lover. It was time to unbend a touch.

"You know I was kidnapped, Perry," he told her smoothly, though his insides roiled with anxiety. When she remained silent, he managed to whisper, "The men enjoyed starving us, then giving us a feast. Then they'd watch us puke it all up when we realized it was either bad or dosed with sleeping pills." He clenched his jaw. "Of course, we were not only young, but starved, too. We had no choice but to eat, and then to continue the vicious cycle as they watched and laughed."

George cleared his throat. "I don't really remember it."

"Good," Edward retorted succinctly. "I wouldn't wish those memories on my worst enemy."

Perry stared at him a second and carefully placed her éclair down on the plate. A thoughtful look appeared on her face and she murmured, "These UnReals?"

Cautious, he asked, "The ones who kidnapped me or the group itself?"

"Your kidnappers," she clarified, then asked, "They were executed, weren't they?"

Apprehension filled the room. He, George, and Xavier all shared uneasy looks—she might approve, she might disapprove. Who knew with Americans?

He forced himself to pick up a petit four and take a bite. It churned in his stomach, then settled, and he took another bite, well aware that neither George or Xavier would answer in his stead.

By the third bite, he knew he wouldn't be sick, and knew all the more that he could continue eating everything else on his plate.

"Yes," he told her, after a good two minutes had passed.

Tension seemed to bloom in the room like a mushrooming cloud of toxic air that had the power to poison them all. Then it disappeared, as if a huge swell of wind blew it away, when she murmured, "Good."

A surprised laugh burst from George. "Bloodthirsty wench."

She grumbled, but didn't deny it. Instead, picked up her éclair and took another bite. As she did, her gaze remained fastened to his. Each bite was slow, calculated, and he realized she was trying to entice him to carry on eating.

He gulped, touched by her consideration, then picked up a sandwich. As was always the way, the first mouthful was like sawdust.

But it dispelled.

As did some of the shame he felt for being so weak as to allow a childhood incident to still affect him this late in his life. That she'd noticed his eating habits at all, that Xavier and George had been surprised by them, embarrassed him. He hadn't realized they were so evident to those close to him.

His stomach still churned, but it eased as conversation swelled once more, and Xavier and Perry slouched on the sofa beside his brother. When the focus was no longer on him, the food actually started to taste of something other than wet pencil, and he managed to do the plate of food justice.

As he placed the dish down, over three-quarters empty, Perry caught his eye, and the pride on her face both amused and disconcerted him.

He wondered what he'd do to keep on seeing that look aimed his way, then he stopped wondering. Because he already knew the answer...

Anything.

He'd do anything to make sure she was happy.

Even if it meant squashing his own demons to please her.

CHAPTER THREE

PERRY GNAWED at her thumbnail as she whizzed through the open tabs on her browser. She wanted to bite all ten fingernails, but managed to contain herself to the left thumb.

It was hard though.

Very, very hard.

And not just because Marianne would start bitching at her for biting her nails again.

Until yesterday, she hadn't really wanted to know more information about the ordeal her lovers had endured as children. But after Edward's revelation, she was compelled to know it all—everything she could get her hands on.

When she'd found herself diving headfirst into this relationship—"down the garden path" as her grandmother would have said—she justified it with an ingrained knowledge that Edward needed her.

She didn't know how she knew it, didn't even know why the thought sprouted to life in her brain. He was the most self-assured man she'd ever known, after all. His confidence was built into his very bones. As was his poise, charm, and elegance.

He was debonair, charismatic, and so well-read that she'd heard him discussing everything from the experiments at CERN to the pros and cons of relying on electric vehicles.

Nothing fazed him. Or nothing *seemed* to.

But only when George and Xavier had watched him, stunned when he'd picked up some snacks, had she realized why they'd been astonished.

She thought back to every meal, every afternoon tea or snack she'd had with Edward present, and not once did she remember him digging heartily into his meal.

There'd been a girl in her English class in college who, whenever she'd eaten, had grazed. Moving each item of food around on her plate so many times that it made everyone around her assume she was eating.

Edward did that, too. But his reason wasn't because he was anorexic. It was because of what those bastards had done to him.

She felt sick to her stomach at the cruelty inherent in taunting two young boys into eating poisoned and tainted food to ease their hunger.

It was no wonder Edward only ate when he was alone.

And it filled her with pride and warmth to know that he'd taken a small step yesterday. Even if she had no real idea as to why.

Some women, Perry felt certain, needed to be needed. It was like it was a part of their biological make up. While Perry would never have considered herself as being nurturing, being here, in this unusual situation, she was discovering sides of herself she hadn't known before.

And she had to wonder if those instincts were what had prompted her to say yes, and to agree to become Edward's wife.

She bit down hard on her nail, enough to wince at, when she read a particularly detailed report on how the men behind Edward and George's kidnapping plot had been shot by a firing squad.

The method seemed particularly antiquated, but it wasn't like she could judge. The States' supposedly "contemporary" ways of electrocution or lethal injections that didn't always work, weren't exactly the height of modernity.

And it wasn't like capital punishment could ever be considered a new thought process. It was as old as time itself to beget an eye for an eye, and for the first time in her anti-capital punishment life, she found she was glad for it—glad to know those men were no longer wandering around this Earth. Even if that Earth was a six-feet by six-feet jail cell.

George was right. She *was* bloodthirsty. Where those assholes were concerned.

It wasn't just about Edward, either. The notion that the UnReals could hurt any of her new family made her want to froth at the mouth in outrage.

Which was why the whole nurturing thing was bewildering her.

She'd never felt like this before. This expanse of emotion was more than she was used to dealing with.

As she continued to gnaw at her nail, occupying one hand, the other was on the mouse, scrolling through the myriad nasty details of a crime she didn't particularly want to know more about, and yet felt totally compelled to learn everything available to her.

The contradiction set her nerves on edge, so when her cellphone rang, she nearly leaped out of her seat in surprise.

Heart pounding, she took a second to gather herself. Only family, work, and George knew this number, and she didn't particularly feel like dealing with any of them at the moment.

Even though that conversation with her parents was long overdue, she thought guiltily.

Reaching for her cell, she let it dial off. There was no need for her mother to pay the exorbitant long-distance rates. It wasn't like Perry had to worry about paying her bills anymore, was it?

Though she huffed in amusement, the notion was still more than she was accustomed to. As she dialed the number that hadn't changed in all the years of her existence, she kept on scanning the computer screen, staring with hatred at the men who had robbed the childhood from Edward and George's lives.

When the call connected, she was still reading, and her mother, Janice, heaved out an exasperated breath. "Aren't you going to say hello?"

"Oh, sorry, Mom," Perry mumbled absentmindedly. "I was just reading an article."

"Let me guess—about animal poop and how it's going to save the world?"

Perry blinked, then sighed at her mother's shortsightedness. "If anything, Mom, it's going to be to our detriment. Well, that is, if we don't reduce the number of cows on the Earth. Did you know big meat is literally pumping millions of gallons of sewage into the ocean? I mean, can you think of anything more disg—"

"Perry! You are not talking to me about global warming, are you? Not when I've just found out from Jessie-Ann from the co-op farm that you're getting wed?"

Oops.

Perry bit her lip. "It's not that big a deal, Mom."

"Not that big a deal?" Janice screeched. "It would be a huge deal if it was the boy next door, but you're marrying *royalty*, Perry. Royalty. That is, if Jessie-Ann wasn't stirring mischief."

The hope in Janice's voice pricked Perry's pride. She wasn't sure why. Did her own mother not think she had it in her to be queen?

Hell, Perry agreed with her, but it sucked that her mom felt that way too.

"No. She's not messing with you. It's been an overwhelming few weeks. I'm sorry I haven't been in touch sooner."

Silence welled down the line, and Perry, who knew her mom better than anyone, reckoned the tears had started.

Grateful that she didn't have to worry about silent long-distance phone call rates, she went back to reading the news articles on her laptop.

Maybe it made her heartless, but she knew her mother too well. Janice was melodramatic to her core. She'd never made any bones about her wanting Perry to settle down a few farms away with one of the local boys, and she'd been quite ashamed of the fact Perry hadn't wanted to grow up to be a housewife like her mother, grandmother, and great-grandmother before her.

For all that, Janice loved Perry. And the feeling was mutual. It was just… well, talking to her mom was like talking to Jane Austen.

Or, at least, Perry hoped Jane hadn't been as myopic as her mother.

They weren't Amish or anything like that, but her family was seriously anti-anything modern. Growing up, she'd never been able to watch TV, and even the radio was frowned upon.

If they'd been religious, Perry might have suspected them as being part of some obscure sect. But they weren't. It was just her father's way.

He was like her, really. A scholar. He wanted peace and quiet to read at night, while he spent his days tending to his land. A land that had been a part of his family for generations, property that the government couldn't snatch from him, and that he'd protect with his life, if anyone came a-calling.

It was a pre-Civil War kind of attitude to have, and whenever Perry visited, she felt suffocated by the vise of her parents' choices.

She loved the city. Loved technology. Coping without Wi-Fi was just something she couldn't do, but at her parents' home—though they didn't understand what 4G was—they fully expected her to do without.

And as a result, the last time she'd been home was, she counted guiltily, four years ago.

"I should come and visit soon," she mumbled, her self-reproach making her blurt out the words into the silence.

"You should have visited sooner. That boy needs to ask your father for your hand!"

Janice's screech had Perry rubbing her temple. Was it any wonder, with parents as antediluvian as her own, that Perry really was ill at ease with this whole three-men-one-woman situation?

Perry wasn't about to change it. She was finding her place for herself in this unusual household of four, but still, it made perfect sense why she couldn't get her head around it.

Even if she could get her body around it.

It being them, of course.

Several times.

A night, if they'd let her.

A wicked grin had her smirking at the screen, but she sobered up as she murmured, "It's the twenty-first century, Mom. Men don't ask for permission for their girlfriend's hands in marriage anymore."

"Well, they do in this family, young lady."

"Edward's a crown prince. What do you want him to do? Hop in a pickup rental and come and feed the goats with Dad and ask him out on the range?" Perry scoffed.

Janice blew out a breath. "You never could do anything easy, could you?"

"Most moms would be tickled pink that their daughter was marrying a prince," Perry said with a grumble, even though she knew that to be utter BS.

She highly doubted any mother would be content with the notion of their child being swept into a royal family. Why would they?

The child was being dragged toward danger, led into a constricting lifestyle, and though they'd never have to want for anything, it wasn't exactly a walk in the park.

For a woman who led a simple life, Perry knew her mother would never understand the complexities of what her child would face, but that she'd instinctively disapprove of it regardless.

"I think it's bad form for him not to come and meet his future parents-in-law."

Perry grimaced because, deep down, she knew Janice was right. "We're organizing something," she lied. "Things have been a bit crazy here after the announcement."

"I'll bet," Janice retorted, sounding remarkably wry for once. Then, she blew out a breath. "I'm hurt, Perry. Real hurt."

She bit her lip. "I'm sorry, Momma. I didn't mean to hurt you, I just...I didn't really know what to say to you. I knew you wouldn't approve, and I guess I've been putting it off and off until *boom*. This, you know?"

"Surely you must have realized someone would have told me?"

Considering the rest of Perry's hometown was as backward as her parents, preferring the slow and quiet country way of living to the hardcore rat race of everywhere else in the United States, Perry had hoped for more time.

She rapped her fingers against her desk, hoping to quell some of her nervous energy.

It didn't work.

"I didn't really think about it, Momma. It was unintentional. I just needed some time to process. He proposed out of the blue, you know?" Hell, that was no lie.

He'd asked her to marry him while he was still inside her. Fucking her on his desk, no less.

Not that she'd tell her mother that.

Jesus.

Janice probably thought she was still a virgin.

Wanting to snort at the notion, Perry managed to refrain. Barely.

"Does Papa know?"

"No. Not yet. He's wrapped up in a new book he got the other week." Janice sighed. "I don't have the heart to tell him."

"Don't," Perry told her softly. "Honest truth, Momma, I don't know if we can leave Veronia at the moment. There's been some local trouble and the royal family needs to stay close to home. But that doesn't mean Edward can't call him and ask for my hand that way."

Janice exhaled deeply. "I guess that's better than nothing. You know what your papa's like. He won't know if no one tells him."

Perry nodded, even though she knew her mother couldn't see the gesture. "I figured as much. I'll talk to Edward and make sure he calls within the next day or so."

Janice huffed. "What about me? Will he talk to me?"

"Of course. If you want to talk to him," Perry murmured quietly.

"He's going to be marrying my daughter, ain't he?" came the gruff retort, and Perry saw her mother, deep in her mind's eye, fiddling with the hem of her housecoat.

Janice could be beautiful if she tried a little. But neither her momma or her papa were all that interested in appearances. Beauty was skin deep in their eyes, and therefore, not worth bothering with.

Truth was, she'd been raised that way, too, and it was why dressing up in fancy clothes was alien to her.

She wasn't averse to it, aside from the heels, but she needed help. Desperately. She was well out of her comfort zone, and George, thankfully, wasn't. He loved buying her clothes.

The tighter the better, she thought disapprovingly, as she felt the pinch of the skirt at her waist. It fit. Just.

Comfort meant very little to George, she'd come to find.

"I'm not going to see all that much of you anymore, am I?" Janice said feebly, her voice more a whisper than anything else.

Perry blinked, surprised by the question. They didn't exactly see each other a lot now, so what Janice meant, Perry wasn't certain.

"I'll call more, Momma. I'll have more time." That was a lie, but she wouldn't be as tied up with her lab work, that was for damn sure.

Though she refused to give up her studies, would even join with Xavier if it meant that was the only way she could keep her toes dipped into her experiments, her life wasn't going to be the same ever again.

Speaking with her parents would do something no one else could help her with—they'd ground her. Remind her of her roots. Simple roots, base farmer roots that were founded in the soil, and not a grandiose house like the DeSauviers, who'd built their dynasty on the blood shed by thousands of strangers fighting under their banners...

"You won't. You always say you will, but you never do, and I'm not one to pester."

That was true, actually. Janice might be a nag, but she didn't call Perry all that often. She seemed to realize that Perry would phone when she had something to say.

"No. I mean it, Momma. I won't be as busy with work, and I'll need you to keep me grounded. I didn't mean to cut myself off. I really didn't."

"It's okay, Perry. I know you're ashamed of us."

For a second, white noise blasted between her ears, then she blurted out, "Ashamed of you? I thought you were ashamed of me?"

"What are you talking about?" Janice demanded, sounding irritated. "Stop talking nonsense, Perry."

"I'm not! You're the one who goes on about me marrying Abe Grantham every time I *do* visit."

"Because I want you to be happy. Not because I'm not proud of what you're doing," Janice retorted.

"B-But..." Her mouth worked blankly, but there was no real argument if Janice meant what she'd said. "I thought you hated that I was a scientist."

"I hate that it's taken you so far away from us," Janice corrected. "But I'm proud of you, Perry. What on earth would make you think otherwise?"

Perry scowled at the computer screen. "*You* made me think otherwise, Mom. I'm not hysterical or irrational. I don't just feel things because I've made them up." Then, because she still felt guilty, she sighed. "I know you love me. I know both you and Dad do."

"I should hope so," came the tart response, and it was sour enough to make Perry's lips curl. She could just imagine her mother glowering at the toaster oven.

"But I just always felt out of the loop. I don't think it's something you guys did intentionally, but you live about thirty years in the past, and I want to live three decades ahead." Slight exaggeration, but her mother only seemed to understand extremes. "That being said, you're right. I should have called and told you the news first. I didn't, and I hope you can forgive me for that?"

"Of course," Janice said, surprisingly easily—Perry had half-expected her to drag out the apologies for a lot longer than the instantaneous forgiveness she received. "Just, please, get the boy to call your father. Make that right for him."

Perry's lips curved again at her mother calling Edward "the boy." The Crown Prince of Veronia wouldn't be able to get too big for his boots when it came time for Thanksgiving, that was for certain.

She thought about that a second. Wondering if Thanksgiving with her family would ever be possible...

Weird how she suddenly wanted it to be, when she hadn't been home in so long.

It was reckless and rude and really poorly timed, but she made the promise anyway. "Set the table for two extra this year, Momma," Perry murmured.

"Huh?"

"For Thanksgiving."

Silence fell. "You're coming home?"

"Of course."

Janice sucked in a sharp breath. "I'm glad."

Perry smiled at the less-than-effusive response that nonetheless meant a hell of a lot.

"You'll come to the wedding, won't you?"

Refusal shouldn't have even been a possibility, but who knew with her parents?

They didn't like fuss, and they certainly wouldn't like the rigmarole of a royal wedding. And, for as much as she considered herself different from them, in that, they'd raised her right.

The whole parade wasn't something she was looking forward to. A lot of girls would probably kill to be involved in a royal wedding. Not even as the bride, but just to be a part of the congregation! Not Perry.

She was, quite frankly, dreading it.

Not the marriage part, oddly enough.

She wanted that. And having seen more reports than she cared to regarding the kidnapping plot, she wanted to be Edward's wife with a ferocity that stunned her.

"Do we have to?" Janice said eventually, and Perry realized she'd been quiet so long that she'd almost forgotten the question she'd posed to her mother.

Because she couldn't be offended when she herself didn't feel like attending either, and it was her damn rigmarole, she murmured, "You kind of have to, Momma. Or there'll be talk."

"Think I'd prefer the talk," came the blunt response.

Perry laughed. "You would because you wouldn't hear it. I, on the other hand, would never hear the end of it."

She ruefully recognized that whether she'd like it or not, within the upcoming weeks, her men would have realized she hadn't yet informed her parents so would have had no choice but to share her news... arrangements would have to be made, after all.

"Perry, I'm not certain we can afford the getup we'd have to wear."

"I can afford it."

"I'm not letting your husband pay for our clothes," Janice retorted, sounding both stiff and prideful at the same time.

"You don't have to let him pay for anything," Perry snapped. "I can afford anything you need to wear. I'm not a pauper, Mom. I've done quite well for myself, thank you very much."

Sure, her apartment back in Boston wasn't as big or as grand as George's, but hell, nobody's was. He lived in a freakin' New England palace in comparison to the average apartment, and her place, though small and simple, was above average.

"We don't like charity. You know that," Janice replied.

"I know you don't. But this isn't charity, is it? It's from me. We'll have to make arrangements to get you guys over here, but let's not get ahead of ourselves. I'll talk to Edward today and have him call Papa." Perry coughed. "I'll also try to call you more, keep you in the loop about what's going on."

"I'm not sure I'll be much help, Perry. What do I know about organizing something like that?"

The simple lives her parents had always led, the simplicity of her own life before she'd met George, washed over her then.

Nothing would be anything less than complicated from now on.

A visit home wouldn't constitute worries over whether she'd be able to take the paid time off without her boss getting mad, and there would never be fears about being able to pay for the tickets—although, that hadn't happened since her student days. She wasn't lying when she said she made a nice living from her career.

But that was neither here nor there.

From now on, her life would be a welter of complications, most of which she wasn't and would never be prepared for.

Going home would involve security protocol she couldn't even begin to imagine, and just going out with her mother to buy the dress she'd wear to the wedding would undoubtedly require more bodyguards than Rihanna at Coachella.

Perry pursed her lips as she contemplated the best way to answer her mother's question. "You know as little about organizing this kind of thing as I do, Mom. So, you know what? We leave it to the pros."

A small laugh sounded down the line. "I knew my daughter was smart, I just didn't realize how smart."

And Perry, taking that for what it was, beamed happily at the compliment.

CHAPTER FOUR

"PUT IT ON SPEAKER," Xavier prompted.

Edward pulled a face but complied, and the ringing tones on the other end of the cell suddenly echoed quite loudly in George's office. The three of them shared glances, and George whispered, "Are you nervous?"

"A bit." The way he wriggled his shoulders told George his brother was lying. But that didn't surprise him. Edward did, after all, have a way of stretching the truth.

Before George could call him out and cry bullshit, the line connected.

"Hello?"

Part of him wanted to laugh at the voice of the woman on the other end of the line. It was an equal ratio of suspicious and accusatory. From what Perry had told him about her parents, both made sense. Neither her mother nor her father liked technology.

That apparently included landline telephones, if Janice's tone was anything to go by.

He couldn't say they hadn't been warned. When Perry had asked Edward to contact her father, she'd told him her parents were a little unusual.

Considering they'd created her, that seemed about right, he thought with an amused twitch of his lips.

Edward cleared his throat — only "a bit" nervous, his ass. "Mrs. Taylor? This is Edward DeSauvier speaking. I believe your daughter, Perry, has spoken with you today and has informed you of our nuptials..."

George gaped at his cousin, who gaped right back. Shooting a glower at his older brother, one Edward missed because he was too busy scowling down at his desk, George shook his head. There was being formal, and then there was being 1820's formal.

Janice cleared her throat too — seemed she was nervous as well. "Mr. DeSauvier, is that what I call you? Or Your Highness?"

"That isn't necessary, Mrs.... may I call you Janice?"

"Please, do."

"Before anything, I'll be your daughter's husband. It's only right that you call me Edward."

"I appreciate your clarifying the situation for me," Janice said. Quite formally too, George thought. Although, this entire conversation looked set to be more conservative than a morning spent in Parliament.

"Perry expressed your wishes to me, and I'm ashamed that I had to be prompted. There was no disrespect intended in my oversight." Edward reached up and rubbed at his temples. "I hope you can believe that."

"We're an old-fashioned family, Edward. I know such customs are dying out, so there's nothing to forgive. But I'm grateful for your calling. Would you like to speak to my husband?"

Edward's tone was grave. "I'd like that very much."

A pleased hum sounded down the line. "I look forward to meeting you, Edward."

"The feeling is mutual, Janice. Do you have a pen?"

"A pen?" There was the sound of rummaging around in the background. Then, the telltale click as a retractable ballpoint pen was discovered. "Yes, I do now."

Edward recited the private number to his office. "Janice, that's a number very few people have. You can call me anytime of the day or night, whether you're concerned about the wedding, or about Perry's safety, or whatever. I'm here. I intend on being a very good son in law."

George could sense Janice didn't really know how to answer that. Her silence was heavy and long, then she murmured in a soft voice, "I appreciate your saying that, Edward." She coughed. "I'll get my husband now."

The landline was placed on the counter, then shuffling steps sounded in the near distance. Xavier leapt on Janice's absence to grumble, "You sound like you belong in a Dickens novel."

Edward frowned at him. "Perry said they're old-fashioned."

"Janice didn't sound like she disapproved," George pointed out quietly, surprised too.

"You're going to marry into the family, not be their king," was all Xavier said next. "Are you going to be the same with her father?"

"If it isn't broken," Edward murmured, shrugging.

"Still not nervous?" George mocked, having watched Edward's shoulders wriggle more in the past five minutes than in the past five days.

His elder brother shot him a disgruntled look. "Shut up."

A clicking noise sounded on the speaker, and the three of them sat upright like damn meerkats who knew they were in a hunter's sight.

"Sir?" Edward asked carefully.

"Yes. Who is this?"

He shot George and Xavier a wide-eyed look, then after blowing out a breath, murmured, "I'm Edward DeSauvier."

"My wife said you wanted to speak with me?"

"Yes. It's about Perry."

"My daughter?"

George covered his mouth to hide his laugh.

"Yes. Your daughter."

"What's she done now?"

"Well, nothing, sir. I'm her partner."

"Her partner," came the stunted reply. "Like in business? At that fool laboratory of hers? You a scientist too?" The man's tone was suddenly loaded down with suspicion. "What are you calling me for? She in trouble? If she's blown up that lab of hers again, I can't be held responsible for it."

Edward's mouth gaped. Hell, he wasn't the only one. George felt flabbergasted too. Perry had blown up a lab before?

"No. Nothing like that. I'm not a scientist. I'm a... well, I'm her partner, as in, we're in a relationship."

"A personal relationship?"

"Yes." Edward frowned, rubbed his forehead. "We've been seeing each other for quite some time."

"You have?" Nathaniel sounded doubtful. "Since when?"

Edward widened his eyes, and George held up two hands. Nodding, Edward mumbled, "Eight months."

"That's a long time. Has to be the longest she's kept a man. Never did understand why she didn't take up with Abe Grantham. He'd have put up with that fool science of hers."

George barely withheld a snicker. Casting Xavier a look, George saw his cousin was equally as amused. Only Edward looked bewildered.

"Well, I'm a very lucky man. She makes me happy, sir."

"That's good, that's good. There a reason you're calling, Edward?"

"Well, I'd like to marry her, sir. And I'd like to ask you for her hand."

Silence fell, then came, "You know she's in her thirties, don't you, son?" came the kindly retort. "I love my daughter, but she's a willful girl. Not exactly the marrying sort. She won't wash your dishes, and if you ask her to do your laundry, she's the type who'll put a red sweater in to discourage you from asking her again."

George couldn't help it. He laughed aloud. Edward wafted a disgruntled hand at him, but even he had amusement firing up his eyes.

Perry would be mortified if she'd heard this call. Though he found it funny, George knew full well she wouldn't. Relieved she wasn't here to hear this, he watched as Edward struggled to find a response.

"Well, I can afford to have someone else clean my dishes and do my laundry."

George shot him a thumbs up, and Edward looked relieved to have fielded it.

"And I'm forty-one, sir. Perry's a lot younger than me."

"Still, a man can have children at any age."

"I want her for more than just her ovaries," Edward said stiffly.

"Nathaniel, what are you trying to do? Discourage the man? He's my one shot at grandbabies. You shut your trap." The discontented grumble sounded loud and clear—Janice, apparently, wasn't happy with her husband.

"I'm just being honest, Janice. Heck, I don't want Perry getting a divorce just because she's not the most house proud of women."

"Like that matters anymore. I told you. Edward's important," came her hissed retort.

"My wife says you're important, son. That true?"

"Yes, sir. Relatively speaking, anyway."

"Who are you then?"

"Well, I'm Edward DeSauvier."

"He's a prince," Janice whispered, but her tone was quite audible down the line.

"A prince?" For the first time, Nathaniel sounded truly surprised. "Which country?"

"Veronia, sir."

Silence fell.

"Are you all right, sir?"

Nathaniel cleared his throat. "Do I have to call you anything special?"

"Just Edward will do."

"Then I suppose you'd better call me Nathaniel." The older man hummed a little. "Well, I wouldn't say Perry is princess material, but she'll certainly keep you grounded, son."

Edward laughed a little, for the first time sounding a touch more relaxed than usual. "That's for sure, Nathaniel. She's already doing that. She makes me very happy."

"Even though she wasn't reared for that kind of life?"

"I don't know what you know of my past, but I've been married to someone who was reared for this life. She didn't make me happy. She made me miserable. I know the difference. Perry's a breath of fresh air, and it would be my honor to serve as her husband."

A gust of air sounded. "Well, it's good of you to ask. Not many would. Folk are so rude nowadays."

George and Xavier grimaced, but Edward winced—he hadn't acted without prompt. Perry had had to ask him to call. "That they are, Nathaniel. Your opinion is important to me. I'm sorry to be doing this over the phone, but Perry says you're a man who understands responsibilities, so you'll appreciate why I can't leave my post here on a whim."

"I'd say our ideas of responsibilities are two entirely different things. A whole country isn't about to fall apart if I wake up late and don't milk the cows on time," Nathaniel said gruffly.

"No, but a man's land is his own personal kingdom."

"That's very true," came the bright response. "And I do understand why you can't be here, though I do wish I could meet you first."

"Don't be difficult, Nathaniel," Janice grumbled.

"But yes, of course, you have my permission to ask my daughter to marry you," Nathaniel said quickly, and George could easily imagine that Janice, who seemed like an older version of Perry, had given her husband the stink-eye until he'd conceded.

Edward blew out a relieved breath. "I can't tell you how much that pleases me, sir."

"Less of the 'sir.' Nathaniel, remember?"

"You're right. Of course. I promise, I'll do right by your daughter, Nathaniel."

"Just love her and care for her. Nothing more a man can ask for his only baby girl."

"I have no intention of waiting a long time to wed Perry if she says yes. So, I'll be in touch with the arrangements for the wedding. You'll walk her down the aisle, won't you?"

More silence. "I'll assume this won't be a small affair?"

"No, sir. It will be taking place in Yorke Abbey."

"On the TV?"

"Yes, sir."

"Jesus wept." A long breath gusted down the line. "We're simple folk, Edward. Not used to that kind of thing."

"No, but if it's any consolation, I *am* used to that kind of thing, and I'm nervous."

"Not sure if that makes me feel better or worse," the older man grumbled.

"Hush now, Nathaniel. You'll walk Perry down the aisle, make no mistake. If she says yes, that is," Janice said with a huff.

"My wife apparently has no worries about me making a damn fool of myself in front of the cameras. Considering she'll undoubtedly be waiting in the wings while I'm the one on show."

"Technically, Perry's on show."

Nathaniel chortled. "You know she trips a lot, don't you?"

George covered his mouth to hide his laughter.

"Yes, sir. It hasn't escaped my attention." Edward chuckled a little.

"Well, if you know that and want to marry her anyway, who am I to put a spanner in the works? I'll prepare myself for the madness, Edward. Don't be a stranger, will you? And have Perry call us if she says yes."

"I surely will," Edward replied. "It's been a pleasure speaking with you, Nathaniel."

"Likewise. Be good to her, son. You might be a prince, but you'll be her husband first and foremost," Nathaniel murmured, his words mimicking Edward's earlier ones.

"We're on the same page there. You don't have to fear that."

"A man always fears for his baby girl. You sound like good people, and I'm too American to be afraid of your title. If you hurt her, being a prince won't stop me from hunting you down with my shotgun," he said cheerfully.

So cheerfully it was impossible to take offense.

"Consider me warned," Edward joked with a laugh.

"Good. Best of luck with Perry. I'll be rooting for you."

"Thank you, Nathaniel. Good day."

When the men cut the call, George let out a whistle. "Perry's just like them, isn't she?"

"Guess we shouldn't be too surprised," Xavier replied, but his grin was wide. "I like them. I'm looking forward to meeting them."

Edward rubbed his chin. "Same here. Let's not mention any of what he said though, eh?"

George snorted. "She'd be mortified."

"Exactly. He didn't sell her in a nice light, did he?" Edward mumbled.

"Nope. Like father, like daughter," Xavier said, and the three of them shared a glance, then burst out laughing.

"YOU DO REALIZE this is bullshit, don't you?"

George's nostrils flared with amusement—it was the only way he could hide his need to laugh. "Stop bitching," he said gruffly.

"You can't reprimand someone while simultaneously trying to stop yourself from laughing," Perry retorted as he zipped up the back of her dress. "It's like, the law or something."

"I've never heard of a law like that."

"It's a parenting law, dummy," she retorted, wriggling and wiggling as she tried to settle the dress more comfortably on her torso.

He watched with great interest as she slipped her hands inside the neckline of the dress, cupped her breasts, then jiggled them around while watching her reflection in the mirror.

The move was made out of practicality, not one ounce of intended enticement, and yet, his cock was as hard as nails at the simple gesture.

"I can feel your hard-on."

He cocked a brow. "That a complaint or a request?"

She snickered. "Would be a request if you hadn't bought this dress for me."

"What's wrong with it?" he demanded. "You bitch about everything I buy, so you know what the solution is? Buy stuff yourself."

She huffed. "I hate shopping."

"Tough," he retorted, tone succinct as he cupped her hips, then slid his arms around her waist to tuck her close to his chest.

She molded against him in a way that spoke of how she'd been made for him. He loved that about her. Her softness and his hardness came together like white on rice.

Perfection.

"Anyway, what's bullshit?" he asked softly, dipping his head to press his lips to the curve of her throat.

"The dress is, silly," she grumbled, tilting her head to the side to give him more access.

Smirking against her throat, he continued to trace his tongue along the sinews there, to nip and tease with his teeth and lips until she was shivering against him, her nerves a thing of the past.

"What's wrong with it?" he asked softly, loving how she shivered when his words washed over her skin. As he held her in place, he slid one hand over the silky fabric covering her belly and cupped her breast through the dress. "It looks and feels perfect to me."

She let out a soft sigh. "You can see everything in it."

"No, you really can't," he groused after a few moments of trying to figure out what the hell she was talking about.

The silk sheath fit her to perfection. All her ripe curves were embraced so she looked like walking, talking sex on goddamn legs. The bright blue silk was cut on the bias and it draped over her in a way that would have every man at tonight's event drooling over her.

Not that they'd ever get a taste.

He'd share with his cousin and his brother, but with no bastard else.

Perry wasn't some free-for-all.

She was his.

Theirs, he corrected himself, with no small amount of satisfaction.

His hand was pale against the bright cyan. The starburst of crystals that were sewn onto the bodice could have looked tacky on someone else, but not on her. Instead, with her creamy paleness and dark Stygian hair, the diamond-like accents looked like she'd been bathing in the starlit sky.

The boat-neck led to long sleeves, and a tight-waisted bodice. The two combined made her look svelte, then her curvy hips got in the way, before giving way to a frothy aquamarine, white, and silver skirt.

Truth was, she looked like a damn mermaid. Either that, or a siren. And hell, he'd never wanted to be led to his doom as much as he did at that moment.

Sighing at the sight of her exquisiteness, and at how right he'd always been when he'd recognized her gorgeousness underneath the ratty tees and yoga pants she wore way too often, he stated the obvious. "You look perfect."

She winced, but beneath the crass words and pouting looks, there was a vulnerability there. He saw it, and was sensitive to it. Tonight was a big night, after all.

"You really mean that?"

He nodded. "Of course, I do." He rubbed his nose along the line of her jaw where her perfume was strongest, yet didn't overwhelm. She always smelled like linen and lilies. One overtook the other, and he could never decide which did. She was never cloyingly floral though, so he figured the clean linen scent won.

"You look like the Queen of the Sea. That's why I bought this dress for you. It's frothy enough to make you look like you're rising from the waves itself."

A soft laugh escaped her. "You're such a romantic sometimes, George."

"Well," he complained, "someone has to be."

She snorted, but raised her hands. One, she rested against his on her hip, and the other, she used to cup his jaw and hold him to her, keeping their faces pressed close. She tilted her head and rested hers against his as she whispered, "I'm nervous."

"You don't have to be. You'll knock 'em dead."

"With boredom? Maybe," she said on a grimace.

"Now *that* definitely is bullshit. There's no way they're not going to be eating out of your hands tonight. You just watch."

She pursed her lips. "I doubt it, but I'll settle for not making a fool of myself."

He nuzzled her again. "See, that's why this dress is perfect. You can wear flats. That's why I bought it. The skirt covers your feet. You don't have to worry about tripping over or falling."

A laugh barked from her. "I never thought about that. You really did think about this dress when you bought it for me, didn't you?" she murmured, her tone amazed with the prospect.

He shook his head. "I didn't think about the dress, I thought about you inside it and you owning it." He grunted. "You surpass my expectations, Perry," he told her softly. "I never imagined that dressing you like a princess would be my personal version of porn."

She hooted. "No way do I look like a porn star."

"That's because you're not standing in my position." He shot her a cheeky grin, then changed the subject and asked, "Did you get the jewelry Edward sent you?" His brother had requested that some basic pieces be sent to her for the early visits and interviews—earrings and the like.

She nodded, then bit her lip. "It's very…"

"What?" he asked, cocking a brow when she seemed to take an age to put the words into a sentence.

"Regal, I guess, and I know that shouldn't come as a surprise," she admitted on a long, deep breath. "Considering I'm going to be regal soon."

He turned his hand so that he could clasp hers, then bringing their joined fists to his mouth, he kissed her knuckles. "You've always been regal, Perry."

She closed her eyes against the sight of them in the mirror. Their arms crossed her chest in a feudal salute, and the image of their union would forever sit with him as he watched her try to run from a future that had been hers from the moment they'd met.

"I'm not like that though, George. You know that. The courtiers… Xavier told me what they're like. They'll eat me alive."

"You think Edward will let that happen?" he demanded. "You think I or Xavier will?"

She blew out a breath. "I notice you don't disagree with Xavier though."

"No. They're bitches. The lot of them. Why do you think Edward and I haven't married from within their lot? We'd prefer to stick pins down our nails. But they have nothing to do with life here, Perry. They're part of the events, and that's it. They don't have to be a part of anything else."

"You two can't stick up for me. It will look odd."

"No. It won't. It's well known the three of us are close. Always have been. We were raised together, for God's sake. People expect it. And where you're concerned, they know we'll close ranks."

She gnawed at her lip. "Really?"

"Of course. Xavier and I will protect you when Edward has to go off and speak to someone about some boring shit that's to do with the throne." He rolled his eyes in disgust, but he loved that he made her giggle. He kissed the side of her cheek again and whispered, "All will be well, sweetheart. You were born for this because you were born for me. For us."

She sucked down a shaky breath. "You really mean that, don't you?"

He nodded, trying to look sage and not just shaken. "I do."

"W-Why, George?"

"Because I just… nobody could fit me so perfectly and not be ready for this life. You're nervous because it's your first event as a part of the royal household. Anyone would be nervous—it's a nerve-wracking experience for someone not accustomed to this way of living. But after tonight, you won't be. It's boring, Perry. More than anything, it's dull and tedious."

"Xavier says that."

"Xavier's right. Just don't tell him *I* said that." He winked at her in the mirror, and smiled when she chuckled. "It's dull, and the only anxiety you'll really feel during these events is when you think about how long you still have to go before you can come back to your quarters."

"They can't be that bad," she reasoned sourly.

"Oh, I promise, they can be." When she huffed, he grinned. "I told you I wouldn't lie to you, didn't I? Well, here's me not lying."

"Some lying might do well. Now, I'm not nervous, at least. Just dreading how boring it will be."

"Then my work here is done."

She hooted and shimmied against him. "Your work here is *not* done."

"If I hadn't watched that magnificent work of art being put together," he told her, eyeing her updo, "I'd lean you over the dresser and take you right here and now."

At the promise in his words, her color soared. She gulped, then her breath came quickly, and her breasts heaved in response to his words. "Y-You could anyway."

He snorted. "And have you scalp me later? Not bloody likely. You need your war paint on, Perry. I'm not going to weaken your stance by sending you in there anything less than pristine." But even as he spoke, he reached between them and tugged at the zip that ran down the length of her side, hidden from view by her arm.

"What are you doing?" she breathed as she watched the fabric slacken from its taut caress on her curves, and viewed the hand sliding between the gap he'd made with curiosity. "I thought you wanted me 'pristine'?"

"I do. That means you can't move," he whispered in her ear.

She let out a moan when his knuckles made an appearance through the silk of her dress. He really hoped he wouldn't crease the fabric, but didn't see why he would if he kept his hand flat against her body.

He wanted her to be ready for battle where her appearance was concerned, but mentally? He needed her to know, point blank, that she was his. To have the pleasure that he gave her ringing through her body, making her senses sing as she dealt with the tedious formalities that came with her introduction to court.

A whimper escaped her as he slipped a hand over her mound, but it was no less shaky than the moan he uttered when he realized she was bare beneath. "Tease," he said on a grunt. "You're not wearing panties."

"VPL, George. Look it up." She'd have sounded tart, if her voice hadn't been breathy as hell.

He ran his fingers over the smooth mound of her sex, then slipped two through the slit of her lips. She was wet. Already.

Fuck.

He sank those two digits down low, coating them with her juices before he rose and began to caress her clit.

She clenched her thighs about his hand, and sank heavily into him, so he was supporting her totally.

That was his right.

This here, all of it, was his right.

She was his. His to love, his to please. His to cherish and adore.

He shared, willingly, and always would, but there was a part of her that would always be his alone. Just as she'd have parts that belonged to his brother and cousin, too.

She shuddered when his slick fingers rubbed the bud of her pleasure, and a keening cry ricocheted around the dressing room as she rocked her hips back and forth, riding his hand as they both worked for her pleasure.

She wasn't quick to orgasm, usually. But now? He knew the situation was working against her.

She could watch herself as she came in the mirror, with them both fully dressed as he worked to give her everything she needed, as he strove to calm her down before tonight's main event. She could see the contrast of their readiness: their elegance, but also the basic earthiness of his hand as he claimed her on a visceral level.

Her cheeks were flushed, hectic with color as she watched him please her. Her gaze darted from the bulge of his hand through the fabric at her groin to his face as he worked her over.

She let out a sharp gasp, her legs rocking beneath her, but he kept her up, using the grip he had on her to maintain her position.

She swung her head from side to side, once, twice, until he whispered sinfully in her ear, "Don't move. Or everyone will know what you were doing before the event."

Her eyes flared wide with mortification. They met his in the mirror, and then, the delicious act of anguished delight came cresting over her features as she burst in his arms. Climaxing over his fingers as he taunted and teased her clit, letting her ride out her desire as and when it came to her.

A low, breathy moan spilled from her lips as she collapsed in his embrace, and with a final, gentle caress to the delicate nub, he retreated.

His wet fingers slid along her belly, and she shuddered at the delicate kiss of her juices against her skin. When he pulled free of the gaping silk, he murmured, "You're beautiful, Perry," and then swirled his tongue around the fingers that had rubbed her.

She moaned again, this time in half despair as she watched him. "You're a wicked, wicked man," she whispered, her pupils like pinpricks as her gaze fixed itself to his fingers.

Though her words weren't intended as a compliment, he grinned nonetheless. "That's why you love me."

Her gaze softened in an instant. "I do. You know that, George, don't you?"

His smile was just as soft. "I do. And I love you."

Breath whooshed from her lungs. "I can't believe we've reached the point where we can say that to one another. I-I've dreamed about it for so long," she confessed, and at that moment, he fell harder for her.

Slumped in his arms, her juices in his mouth, the delicate scent of her pleasure in the air, and her languid smile gracing the beautiful curve of her mouth... she was perfection.

He nuzzled her cheek once more. "Never doubt my love, Perry," he told her, whisper-soft. "I might enjoy things that seem strange—"

But she cut him off, swiping her head decisively to the side. "No. They're not strange. Not anymore."

His smile widened. "My little hellcat," he told her silkily. "Where've you been all my life?"

"Waiting, just waiting."

He snorted. "You've never waited for anyone, ever."

The languid caress of her eyes turned battle-ax hard. She pouted. "How do you know?"

"Because I know you." With his clean hand, he bopped her on the nose with his fingertip. "You're not a person who waits, my darling."

She squinted at him. "Don't spoil it. You were being so nice to me."

Laughter fell from his lips, and he couldn't stop himself from rocking forward, his cock nudging her ass as he whispered, "I think I've been very nice to you."

Before she could answer, a knock sounded at her door. She let out a mournful groan, then whispered, "Probably for the best."

Her rueful comment had him grinning; he knew she wouldn't have let his challenge fall by the wayside without rising to the occasion.

He winked at her. "*Entrez*," he called out as he quickly zipped up the side of her dress and headed to the sofa in the dressing room that was just off the bathroom.

"Perry? It's me. Marianne."

Perry's eyes widened as she glanced at him, but he waved a dismissive hand. He'd never outright tell his mother what was going on with Perry, because she'd never approve. But his *maman* knew Perry and he had been close friends... she'd just have to get used to the sight of him in situations that might seem unusual but could be construed as friendly visits.

The sight of him on the sofa in Perry's dressing room wrinkled Marianne's smooth brow. "What are you doing here, George?" she demanded, her intonation of his name, as always, French.

"Watching Perry get dressed, Mother."

His lover cleared her throat. "He means he's been watching me have my hair done."

Marianne shot him a look, and he could see the wry irritation in it as she murmured, "Your English hasn't improved much from your time in America, my son, if you can make such a mistake in meaning."

His grin widened. "Perry was nervous. I've been keeping her company."

If Marianne thought that was odd, she didn't say so. But the purse of her lips told him she hadn't missed his ease in Perry's dressing room.

She dismissed him a second later, however, and proffered a royal blue velvet box to Perry.

It was most definitely a jewelry box, and curious, George sat straighter on the chaise. "Which pieces?" he asked, out of curiosity.

Marianne tutted. "Let the girl see them first before we spoil it with their history."

George huffed out a laugh. "Spoil it? The history, not the gems, will pique her interest more than anything, won't it, Perry?"

Her eyes sparkled as she nodded. "He's not wrong. May I please see?" she asked politely.

Marianne smiled. "Of course. Edward picked them for you specially. Unlike the pieces he gave you before, these will have to return to the vaults, though."

As George pondered why Edward had picked them but hadn't delivered them himself, Perry opened the box with a glee that only Pandora could combat.

Of course, there wouldn't be the disastrous consequences afterward.

Her mouth rounded, and curious himself now, he got to his feet and sauntered over to where he'd made her climax mere moments before.

His brother, for all his faults, had good taste. And he'd actually listened when George had informed him of the dress Perry would be wearing this evening.

Perhaps it was unusual for a beau to play such an intrinsic part in a woman's wardrobe, but considering Perry didn't have a clue and had no care to educate herself in anything high fashion, George saw no problem dressing her up in things he wanted to see her in.

There had to be some perks to the job, after all.

For over five years, he'd seen Perry in yoga pants, black trousers, white shirts, and bland, overlarge tees— so overlarge that they'd have swamped *him*.

He reckoned she owed him a bit of skintight silk from time to time after drowning him in loose fabric and blandness for all the years he'd known her.

Of course, he'd loved her, regardless of her shitty fashion sense. And her crappy taste in clothes didn't detract from her beauty...but that didn't mean such a status quo should continue, did it?

He wanted to see her sparkle. And that was the damn truth of it. Especially when it came to approaching the ladies of the court on their own battleground.

George noticed, as he examined the chandelier earrings laid out on the velvet pad before him, that Edward apparently felt the same way about the "sparkling."

"I've never seen you wear those, *Maman*," he said softly, staring at the four rows of ornate beadwork that came together in a shower of gems. There was a row of sapphire, aquamarine, a frothy kind of quartz that was tinged the faintest blue, and then shards of diamonds.

Literally hundreds of them.

"It's not my style," Marianne said simply, but there was no offense intended. His mother was suited to the less intricate pieces. Of which, in the royal vaults, there were few.

In the glory days of the royal family, when they didn't have to worry about anything other than maintaining their seat on the throne at all costs, lavish jewels were a sign of prosperity.

George knew his father had had a lot of presents made from repurposed old pieces to gift his mother.

Perry, on the other hand, was suited to the frivolity.

She had a heart-shaped face, creamy skin, and eyes like almonds. When her dark hair was knotted at the top of her head as it was today, she looked like the queen she would one day be.

"They're beautiful," she whispered as she reached for one and placed it in one ear, then quickly added the other one. She whistled as she swung around to face herself in the mirror. "They're so heavy!"

George smirked. "What do you expect? You've got about ten carats of diamonds alone on each earlobe. They're doing the ear equivalent of bicep curls."

Perry snorted, then whacked him on the arm. "Shut up, you."

Marianne cleared her throat, drawing the attention back to her. Perry's cheeks turned pink as she realized she'd fallen back into old habits with him while his mother was there to see it.

Apology tinted her gaze as she peeked at him from under thick lashes, but it wasn't necessary. The family knew he and Perry were close. Now that she was becoming a part of the DeSauvier clan, thanks to his brother's proposal, they'd just have to get used to seeing it.

The friendship side of his relationship was one thing he refused to hide—even if it stirred gossip. Being Perry's friend wasn't illegal. And there was nothing wrong in it. He was okay with not being her lover in public, but he absolutely insisted on their being able to be themselves together. As they always would have been if George hadn't suggested this madcap relationship Perry had with his brother, cousin, and himself.

"Edward has picked well, Perry," Marianne murmured kindly, and George knew the double entendre was intended. "That blue matches your dress perfectly. But we also have two other pieces."

Both his and Perry's attentions were well and truly pricked. Underneath the royal blue box were two smaller boxes, cupped in Marianne's fingers. And George realized he'd mistaken the earrings as having come from the larger of the three.

She placed one of the smaller duo down on the table, discarding it now that Perry was wearing them, then held out another.

Perry opened it and let out a deep sigh at a cuff that, while not a matching set with the earrings, did in fact suit her down to a tee. It was large, and thanks to the three-quarter length sleeves that clung to her forearms, the cuff would be perfectly showcased there. Filigreed gold and silver came together to form a lattice-style pattern. He remembered seeing that on his mother's arm when the palace had been hosting a bunch of Greek diplomats. The style was an old tradition in the smaller Cypriot villages, and Marianne had worn it for that reason.

Thousands of strands of silver and gold were woven together to create a truly, uniquely delicate piece. One that suited Perry's dress but also herself.

With the frothy earrings and the fancy cuff, she looked elegant to a fault.

Knowing what the third and final box contained, he folded his arms and leaned against the mirror, amusement setting in at the prospect of Perry's next reaction.

She let out a soft squeal at the sight of the tiara, and though she didn't realize it, she was being honored.

Veronia had odd traditions when it came to the females they allowed into their ranks by marriage. The headpieces were usually only presented to women after matrimony. Arabella, for example, Edward's late wife, had been presented on her wedding day with access to a few of the simpler, smaller tiaras that belonged in the family vaults.

She'd certainly never worn the diadem resting on the velvet pad.

Made of platinum, it was similar in style to the cuff. The filigree work was exquisite and so delicate that she'd look like Titania wearing it, not just a princess-to-be. With diamonds and tumbled pearls decorating the four points of the headdress, and a large sapphire cabochon in the center, he couldn't decide whether she'd look pagan or fairy as he took in the piece when his mother helped her wear it.

When it was settled atop her head, Marianne shot him a look. One that he simply blinked at.

They both knew what Edward's gifts meant, and it was a further clue as to why the man himself wasn't here to present the jewels to Perry—he'd wanted their mother to deliver them.

Edward's selections were perfect for his wife-to-be. Not only down to the gown she wore, but for the woman herself.

Edward had, did she but know it, informed their mother of the depth of his regard for Perry.

And Marianne now knew it.

"Oh my God," she whispered, when she turned to face herself in the mirror. "Oh my God."

The litany repeated itself a few times as she gawped at herself, and George had to curb a smile at her response.

Even his *maman* looked amused. "You look like what you are, and what you will soon be to the rest of the world, Perry," she told her kindly, resting her ringed fingers on Perry's shoulders. "A princess."

She gulped, caught Marianne's gaze in the mirror, and whispered, "Thank you, Marianne. I appreciate the vote of confidence."

And with that gentle and humble retort, words spoken with no avarice and no intent, George realized she'd done the impossible and won Marianne's approval for the match.

"YOU LOOK NERVOUS."

Edward grimaced at Xavier. "I'm not."

"No? Well, you look it," he retorted, eyeing his cousin as he settled his tails and fiddled with his white cravat for the tenth time.

"I'm just curious, that's all."

"Curious about what?"

"I sent mother with some jewelry for Perry."

Xavier frowned. "You did?" That was an unusual means of declaring war. "Why?"

"I wanted her to know that Perry wasn't..."

"An American strumpet who happened to bare her bewitching ankles before your rapt gaze, and you were instantly captivated and imprisoned by her greedy hooks?"

Laughter bellowed from Edward, and Xavier's lips curled in response. His cousin slapped him on the back and jibed, "Yes. That. Although, I'm not certain if Perry would appreciate her ankles being labeled as the only part of her body that are in any way bewitching."

"Well, we can tell her differently. *Tanta* Marianne and Uncle Philippe never had sex, after all. You were both born by immaculate conception."

Edward just pulled a face. "We're too old for such thoughts."

Xavier shuddered. "You're never too old for those thoughts," he retorted quickly, especially as he had far more intimate knowledge about his aunt and uncle's love life than he'd ever wanted before.

Knowing Philippe had had affairs tainted Xavier's opinion of the man, he had to admit. And though he wished he didn't know the truth, pulling the wool over his eyes didn't make the situation any better.

Maybe it could be said that a man in Philippe's position would always have *affaires du cœur*, as the French would say, but Xavier had always genuinely believed that the king and queen were in love.

Learning otherwise bruised his outlook some.

He was quiet when they wandered down the private royal quarters toward the ballroom where the party was being held tonight.

In Perry and Edward's honor, it was a unique blend of personal and private. But of course, when that was done to suit the court's lavish tastes, that meant there were at least four hundred people here.

One couldn't offend the important nobles of the country. Even if they loathed the royal family and were loathed in return.

The pomp and ceremony bored him senseless, but he had to be here tonight. Not just in an official capacity, but for Perry.

Not only did he want to see her in the dress George had shown him, but he also wanted to be with her in a public setting.

The last time they'd been at an event of this stature, they'd stolen away together and had spent the night in her room.

That, had they but known it at the time, had triggered a chaotic tumble of events they could never have predicted. One which led to the here and now, where Perry was marrying Xavier's cousin, while he was content to be one of the future queen's secret beaus.

"You'll have to go in by yourself," Edward told him as they approached the private entrance to the ballroom. "Perry and I will be announced by the master of ceremonies."

Having realized this already, Xavier clapped his cousin on the back. "*Bonne chance*," he told him brightly.

Edward grimaced. "Is it bad that I'm more nervous about her wearing heels than anything else?"

Xavier chuckled, jolted from his troubled mood by Edward's serious tone. It was one that was reserved for crises at court or international economic problems... not for a woman's footwear.

"Considering she almost fell arse over head in front of the press on the day you announced your engagement... and that her own father warned you of her habit of tripping over air... no. I'd say your concern is viable."

Edward pulled a face. "George wouldn't be so foolish, would he?"

"Yes. He would, but not in this instance."

It was the woman herself who made such a declaration, and as he and Edward turned to face the dazzling creature who was both of theirs, they sucked in sharp breaths at the sight of her.

She looked like...

Titania and Poseidon's Queen Amphitrite combined. Ethereal yet solid, with a vibrant elegance that was unique to her alone.

"I do think you've made them speechless," George told her, sounding proud as punch at the prospect. "And all without a heel in sight."

She snorted. "I'm surprised you were intelligent enough to let me wear flats, George. Why they wouldn't be surprised too, is beyond me."

His younger cousin pouted, "Why do I feel insulted?"

"She called you an idiot. You should be," Xavier retorted with a grin, but he strode over to Perry and, with a caution he hated but was imperative thanks to their location, pressed his lips to either side of her cheek in a friendly but light greeting.

On the second kiss, he whispered, "You look divine. And you look like mine." When he pulled back, her eyes were sparkling brighter than the diamonds on her head or swinging from her ears.

"You mean that?" she demanded, her hand coming out to grab his forearm, holding him close.

"I do," he told her, his tone formal in response to the uncertainty in hers.

She let loose a shaky breath then whispered, "I'm glad."

It wasn't like her to be tentative, although he knew their situation had shaken her more than most. It didn't surprise him. She was about to dive headfirst into a swimming pool loaded with piranha... she'd have been foolish not to be agitated with the secret she was shielding from everyone—her love of three of the four highest-ranking males in the kingdom.

A mutual love that was being explored in a relationship that was so beyond outré, the scandal that would hit the nation would... well, he couldn't even contemplate it.

They were walking a fine line, and they all knew it. But he, George, and Edward knew how to play the game. Perry was new to it.

She was the weakest link in that regard, but he had faith in her.

She was tough when it came down to it. She'd need that when push came to shove.

Perry let go of her clasp on George's arm, and like Aphrodite floating to shore on her seashell, swept forward toward her fiancé.

Edward look starstruck. There was no other word for it. There was more emotion in his eyes than Xavier remembered seeing in the past twenty years.

The truth was, even though Xavier wanted Perry for himself, Edward was... he needed her.

The nation needed Perry for that reason alone.

Edward would be a good and fair king if he ruled alone. But with Perry as his queen? He'd be one of the best Veronia had ever seen, and, Xavier believed, the pair of them would see the nation through this recent unrest.

With a commoner for a bride, groups like the UnReals couldn't deny that the monarchy was evolving. Change, it seemed, was exactly what such radicals wanted to see.

Perry was the harbinger of so much, and she didn't even know it.

Protective instincts he'd never felt for anyone before flared to life, but they were unnecessary at the moment.

All three of them would shield her from what was to come for as long as they could. There would be a day when she'd have to stand on her own two feet, but tonight was not that night.

―――

"YOU LOOK LIKE A GODDESS," Edward breathed, and Perry felt her cheeks burn brightly for the millionth time that evening.

His words were so sincere, she bit her lip. The paint on her mouth was like goddamn glue. It wasn't going anywhere, but it tasted and felt like crap against her tongue.

The nastiness grounded her, and boy, did she need that.

When Edward looked at her like she'd painted the stars in the night sky, it was hard to remain on planet Earth.

But it was a huge confidence boost.

On the other side of the grand, gilt-edged doors, there were a few hundred people who'd all want a piece of her.

Here, before they made their grand entrance, she had a chance to breathe in air that was redolent with the heady desire her men felt for her.

Because of that, she knew that whatever the courtiers thought of her, whatever the women jealous over her ensnaring their future king thought, none of it mattered.

At that moment, to her men, she was perfect.

That was all that counted.

She pressed herself against Edward's front. He was wearing a tuxedo jacket that swept down into two elegant tails that flapped against the backs of his thighs, reaching his knees. His black trousers were pressed just so, and the white shirt combined with the white waistcoat and cravat should have made him look like a walking, talking piano, but he didn't. He looked fucking gorgeous.

Over his shoulders, in a move that beggared the laws of gravity, he wore a chain that must have restricted the movements of his upper arms. The heavy gold links were loaded down with emeralds. In the center of his chest, there was a large pendant styled out of gold that looked ancient, and housed, she noticed with interest, the DeSauvier family seal.

His hands curved around her waist as she pressed herself against him, and they slid down to cup her ass with a possessive hold that made her nostrils flare with desire.

Something about Edward did this to her.

He was so straight all the time. So rigid in his posture, in his stance... but with her, it was like she was the only one who could break that a tad. And she meant a tad. But where he was concerned, it was like letting the floodgates open.

"Thank you for the jewelry," she whispered against his cheek as she reached up to kiss him on the lips.

"It's yours, Perry," he told her softly as he tilted his head and brushed the crown of her cheek with his lips. "You look like my queen," he continued. "Like you were born to stand at my side."

Gulping at his heady words, she had to whisper, "Not three paces back?"

He heaved out a laugh. "Like mother? No, certainly not. We rule together, or not at all."

Despite herself, and despite the responsibilities that would entail, she brightened. "We rule together, or not at all," she repeated softly.

"Exactly," he told her, sounding so satisfied that tears pricked her eyes.

Edward wasn't broken. She couldn't describe him as such. But he was...

Well, his past made her think of Humpty Dumpty. Only in his case, all the king's horses and all the king's men actually did manage to put him together again. But the cracks were there, and those cracks housed a thousand hurts she wanted to heal.

When she felt his kiss on her forehead, she let out a deep sigh. At that moment, everything truly felt all right in her world.

Even if there was a whole ton of crazy going on right now.

By the time she righted herself, she realized George and Xavier had disappeared. Edward noticed her disappointment and dragged a finger over the line of her jaw. "They need to be announced separately to us. We're the final guests."

She nodded. "I know. George drilled the rules into me today." She really didn't know how some of the new royals coped when they didn't have three men teaching them the ropes.

Xavier was going to help her learn to dance, and was going to be her partner in the coming weeks as she learned how to schmooze dignitaries.

George was helping with all the mind-numbing protocol she also had to learn.

Edward was like a solid wall for her to lean against when it came down to it. He didn't have as much input as her other men at the moment, but she had a feeling tonight was where he'd shine.

And she wasn't wrong.

When the master of ceremonies swung open the immense doors and they opened onto the grand ballroom, Edward kept her tucked into his side.

Marianne had informed her that they needed to stand as two separate entities. That the affection between them had to remain "barely there." But Edward was of a different mind, it seemed.

When the master of ceremonies bellowed their name into the throng, Edward had his hand possessively placed on her hip, his fingers curving down toward her sex, making her very, very aware of her decision to go panty-less.

Of course, that was exacerbated by the fact George had brought all of her brain cells down to biological functions earlier.

As she stood there, overlooking the mob, she was indelibly marked in every guest's mind as Edward's.

And she loved that.

Hell, screw that. She fucking adored it.

The ballroom was vast. Underfoot, parquet floors gleamed with the patina of old age, as the room itself had seen a thousand such events over the centuries. The walls were loaded with ancient brackets that had once held logs that blazed with naked flames, but were now tamed with honest-to-God candles. There were thousands of them, and she really felt for the guy who'd had to light them. Hopefully, there was a team of them, because that was a thankless task. The candles added a heat to the room that brought out a kind of hazy sensuality to the formal event.

Maybe it was because the warmth exacerbated the guests' natural scents? As this wasn't Elizabethan England or pre-revolutionary France, everyone showered and tended to wash up prior to these parties; the heady warmth strengthened the perfume and aftershaves people were wearing in a way that wasn't cloying but was, strangely enough, sensual.

Or that could just be because she was breathing in Edward's personal scent, and she was drowning in his pheromones.

As they stepped down the thirty stairs toward the ballroom, she was amazed by the expansive, frescoed ceiling that seemed to merge into the walls, bringing the cherubs to life in a way that made the shining cream and gold beings dance into the party itself.

Here, there were only people. Endless reams of them as they awaited her and Edward's attendance. Next door was where they'd be eating.

She'd actually already been in there. The dozens of bright red-covered tables with silver linen napkins and central floral displays that further encompassed the DeSauvier colors with touches of royal blue, was a grand banquet she'd never thought to see in her life.

But she was doing more than seeing. This was for her.

All for her.

The notion was staggering, and as Edward and she alighted into the crowd, they were swarmed upon. Ambushed like thundering wildebeest on a stampede as people bowed and curtsied before her, begging her attention, desiring Edward's focus.

Through it all, he kept her clamped to his side. Not in a creepy way, but in a way that declared to one and all that she was his and there would be no parting them.

Twenty minutes in, the whirl of faces hadn't let up. She was overwhelmed and resenting the inferno blazing from the candles and the mass of body heat. Edward kept her upright, but she almost sagged with relief as George and Xavier appeared like beacons of hope.

They also came sporting gifts.

Of the champagne variety.

She grabbed the flute from Xavier's outstretched hand with little decorum, and drank half without blinking.

"Thirsty? Or desperate?" George murmured in her ear, snickering when she whacked him on the arm.

"Both," she retorted with a snap.

He just chuckled, but she growled at him. "How many more people?" she asked Edward, who looked more stoic than ever.

Had they been following Marianne's distinct orders and had been separate throughout this torture, she'd have felt out in the cold. But though he looked disinterested, even bored, by the events playing before him, the hand clamping her to him was ferocious.

Truth was, the way he looked and how he held her was an insight into the man.

She vowed never to forget this night. Not that that was possible, considering the circumstances, but for his touch alone, the evening's events would remain solidly in her memory bank.

She realized that just because the man on the outside looked cold and unfeeling, inside, he was a turbulent mass of emotion. Emotion that, for good or ill, he'd decided to focus on her.

"Almost there," Xavier informed her kindly, when he seemed to sense Edward wasn't going to answer.

He looked over his cousin with a weather eye, and Perry read his concern. She wondered about it, but didn't ask. Still, when Xavier inadvertently caught her gaze, he just blinked at her and smiled. It was a dismissive smile, though. One that told her, without his meaning to, that something was wrong.

She studied Edward a second, but he seemed his usual self. Sure, he was stoic, but all the royals were in their own way, weren't they?

They had that "bored shitless" air about them, even if they were trying not to.

As she stood there, bored shitless herself, she figured she'd best find out a way to replicate the look.

And fast.

When Edward's hand released its hard grip on her hip, she was almost surprised at being relinquished. Then, he surprised her further by hugging one of the women who had just approached them.

"Cassie, it's wonderful to see you. I had no idea you were in the country!"

"Oh, Edward. It really has been too long," the other woman was saying, a bright smile on her face that was, nonetheless, a little teary, too.

Perry eyed the woman, who was closer to Edward and Xavier's age than her own. She was dressed in a simple black sheath that, of course, she wore like a million dollars.

On Perry, it would have looked both funereal and like she was a lumpy sack of potatoes. Cassie, whoever the hell she was, looked slender and lean.

She was also hugging Edward too intently for her liking.

Still, jealousy became no one, so she plastered on a bright smile when

Edward, after murmuring, "I didn't expect you here," pulled back to encompass Perry in the greeting. "Perry, this is Cassandra Whitings. She's married to an old friend of mine."

Cassandra's married?

Call her petty, but that amendment made Perry blow out a relieved breath.

"It's a pleasure to meet you, Cassandra," she said cheerfully—and meaning it, now that there was no need to be jealous.

The other woman turned kind eyes on her. "And I you." She placed her hands on Edward's shoulders, but the move was, somehow, not proprietary. Perry wasn't even sure how that was possible, but it wasn't.

Cassandra just looked square into Edward's eyes and declared, "You look happy."

At her side, the four women who'd approached them alongside her tittered uncomfortably, while shooting Perry half-jealous, half-false smiles.

As with the rest of the courtiers, this was standard behavior. The men either ogled her breasts or ignored her totally, and the women just looked at her like she was the luckiest woman on Earth or like they thought Edward had gone blind overnight.

So, Cassie's reaction was actually really nice. At least one person around here was genuine, she thought, watching as Edward's cheeks turned faintly ruddy in response to her declaration.

"I am happy," he said a little stiltedly, and Perry couldn't help it...

She burst out laughing.

Cassandra looked at her in surprise, then, with a mischievous grin, joined in.

Edward pulled a face. "Why are you laughing at me?"

"Because your mouth was speaking English while your body was speaking French."

George, at her side, piped up, "What does that even mean?"

"It means, Big Ears," Cassie retorted, relinquishing her hold on Edward's shoulder and turning to kiss George's cheek, "that Edward sounded anything but happy."

George grunted. "My ears aren't even big anymore."

"The joys of a nickname," Cassandra retorted, her tone gleeful. "They never die a death."

Xavier laughed. "She's right, George." He swept down and tugged Cassandra into a hug too. "It's great to see you, Cassie. I didn't know you were back here. Thought you were still in New York because of Marcus's work."

A look shuttered over Cassie's face, one that no one save Perry seemed to pick up on. "He'll be here shortly. I returned first with the children." As she approached Perry, she murmured, "Sorry I left you until last, but it's been an age since I've seen the boys."

Perry, unable to help it, grinned cheerfully at her. "I understand. They're too delicious not to hug, aren't they?"

Cassie shot her a conspiratorial wink. "You've got that right." As the two women kissed cheeks, she pulled back and said, "I'd really love to catch up sometime. Get to know the woman who snared one of my oldest friends."

"If the children are here, does that mean you're staying in Veronia long term?" Edward asked.

That odd sadness swept over Cassie once more, and Perry wondered why her men, usually so empathetic, failed to sense it.

"Yes. We're back here permanently. I couldn't stand New York a minute longer." She reached for Edward's hand, and shocked Perry by grabbing hers too. "I want to catch up with you both."

As she squeezed their fingers, the one voice Perry had been dying to hear since the rigmarole began, called out.

"Dinner will shortly be served," the master of ceremonies boomed, and en masse, people turned and began to head toward the ante-room where the banquet would be held.

Cassie's eyes sparkled as she took in Perry's relief. In the melee of the crowd's distraction, she leaned in and murmured, "We need to work on your po face."

Perry blinked, then curled her lips inward to hide a smile. "That obvious?"

"Definitely." Cassie winked at her. "Edward has my number, Perry. Call me. I'd love to go out for coffee sometime."

"I'd like that," she replied, meaning it.

Cassie smiled, then hooked her elbows through two of the women's arms, women she recognized from an online blog about court life as Lady Helene de Mastin and the Marchioness of Grasse-Beau.

Of course, the blog was strictly illegal, considering the nation's privacy laws. But Veronia didn't believe in outright censorship, especially of the internet, and George had been using the blog to show her some of the cats at court.

His phrasing, not hers.

"I like her," she told Edward as they strode toward the banquet.

"I'm glad," was his simple reply, as a path opened up before them, letting them head directly to the other room without being jostled in the crush.

Sometimes, being a princess-to-be had its perks.

CHAPTER FIVE

GEORGE STARED over at Ferdinand L'Argeneaux and tried not to grimace.

Of all the men to meet, this was the last one on his list.

"Your Highness," Ferdinand said curtly, sounding not in the least gracious.

George's smile was tight. "Ferdinand. It's good to see you." A lie, but what else could he say?

Ferdinand didn't bother with such politesse. Just motioned to the seat opposite George and asked, "May I?"

Considering he'd half-expected the man just to take a seat without asking, the question was more than a kindness coming from a snake like L'Argeneaux. "Of course."

Ferdinand was, what would once upon a time have been called, a kingmaker.

He knew the right people, held all the cards, and had the bank balance of a sheikh. He was also Edward's former father-in-law, and had used his daughter as the ultimate pawn by ingratiating her into the royal family.

For that alone, George would never like the man. Arabella had done nothing other than make Edward miserable throughout their short marriage. A marriage that would never have happened without her father having made the political play.

It was the new millennium, and yet both her father and Edward's had arranged the match. Ferdinand with an end game only he knew, Philippe because he'd wanted Ferdinand's support in Parliament.

Which was exactly where George was now. For Parliament to open a session, a DeSauvier needed to be there. Philippe could have pawned it off on a lesser DeSauvier, a second cousin or the like, but he took pride in playing a pivotal role in the country's laws, and eight out of ten times sat in on the session himself. He'd only ducked out of today's because he and Marianne were due to visit Monaco for a meeting with the crown prince there.

And now George was back, the mantel didn't always have to fall on Edward.

Sharing the load sucked, even if it was only fair.

"How can I help, Ferdinand?" George asked briskly when the man just slouched back in one of the leather club chairs, studying him like a cobra eyeing its charmer and captor.

It was no use in thinking that he simply wanted to talk. Ferdinand never did anything without a purpose. Life was one huge game of chess to him.

George loathed the man.

"I found your presence here interesting today."

"Why? I've returned home. I have duties to attend."

"You didn't care before."

"I was younger, and foolish before." He cocked a brow as he took a sip of his whiskey.

Seeing his drink, Ferdinand nodded at a waiter who approached and ordered. "My usual." The server almost dropped into a dead run to attend the man.

Life goal, George thought ruefully, *make the staff tremble in their shoes by the time I'm fifty.*

Not.

The DeSauviers had never ruled by fear. It wasn't their way. Still, to command such clout without so much as a title spoke of Ferdinand's power plays.

"That's an interesting choice of phrasing," Ferdinand murmured softly, as he sipped at what looked like a gin and tonic that the server returned with surprising speed. "*Foolish.* Would you say your time abroad has made you a wiser man?"

"One would hope so," he retorted. "Otherwise, few life lessons have been learned."

Ferdinand's rare smile made an appearance. At that moment, the familial connection between him and his daughter was so apparent, George had to hide a grimace.

Arabella had been a celebrated beauty, but she'd always left him cold. Ferdinand had that same way about him. Being in his presence was like sitting next to a freezer with the door open.

"What did you think of today's session?" Ferdinand asked after he'd taken another sip.

To tell the truth or to lie, that is the question, George thought wryly.

Considering the man made diplomacy look like a game of Monopoly, George thought the truth would rattle him. "I thought it was bullshit."

Ferdinand cocked a brow. "How so?"

George thought back to the pointless one hundred and twenty minutes he'd spent in the DeSauvier seat, watching over proceedings.

Half-throne, half-chair, he'd lounged opposite the Speaker of the House —the man who maintained order when the bickering between parties grew too loud. On either side of the raised dais upon which their seats were placed were rows of padded, maroon leather. Twelve rows deep, the seats had all been filled, as today there had been important laws under dispute— one of Philippe's pet causes on prison reform.

Between him and the speaker, there were three podiums. One for each party in the House.

The grand lecterns were tilted at an angle that made it seem as though they were talking directly to the man or woman seated in the DeSauvier throne, but it also angled them at the party opposite, ensuring their argument was heard by all the right people.

As he'd watched the eight hundred strong members of Parliament in action, he'd asked himself how it came to be that those morons were in charge of running the country.

And considering Ferdinand was one such man, George's use of the term "bullshit" took the insult to another level.

"I thought Philippe would have sat in today, considering this particular reform has his stamp all over it." Ferdinand's sneer told George exactly what he thought of Philippe's "stamp."

"If the issue with Monaco hadn't arisen, I'm certain he would."

"Why were today's proceedings bullshit then? If it wasn't to do with the topic."

"Because you were bickering like spoiled children. Crying and screaming when you dropped your rattles," was George's curt reply as he took a sip of his own drink. "We all know the prison reform will happen whether you agree or not."

"Because your father wishes it," Ferdinand snarled disgruntledly.

"Yes. There is an advantage to being king of your own country," George said wryly. "That's a position few of us can aspire to."

Ferdinand narrowed his eyes. "And you think it's fair that because your father wishes it, that makes it so?"

"I think it's stupid to question and argue over a status quo that will never be undone in our lifetime." George sipped at his drink. "Don't you?"

"Maybe it's stupid to believe the DeSauvier line will never end. Few other nations are fit to maintain a monarchy."

"That's because they don't rule like we do. Say what you will about royalty, you can't deny that my father's a good king."

"I don't. I'm just saying, tides can turn."

"While he's alive and my brother, who was raised in his image, is, I'd say we're safe."

Ferdinand didn't reply to that, merely asked, "And you, George, now that you're back on home turf, and seemingly so dutiful, is marriage your next step? Or are you leaving that to Edward?" Ferdinand's mouth pursed. "He called me about his new engagement."

"He did?" George cocked a brow. "That was polite of him."

"He was a polite son-in-law."

Though it was underwhelming, George felt certain that was the highest compliment Ferdinand was capable of bestowing on anyone.

God help his children.

It was no wonder Arabella had turned out colder than a frozen ready meal.

"Perry's a good woman."

"Arabella was a better one."

George held his tongue. "That I can't argue," he said quietly, proud of the play on words which neither confirmed nor denied Ferdinand's intent. "But Perry isn't to be compared. She has to make her own place for herself."

"That's naïve. Everyone will compare, and when she falls short, that will humiliate the DeSauviers." He ran a finger over the lip of his cut glass tumbler. "I wonder if Edward is prepared for that. Even Arabella, with all her training, often felt the pressure of her position."

Perry was nervous, George knew. She felt overwhelmed. But that was because this was new to her.

Maybe it was hubris on his part to think once the ring was on her finger, she'd settle down. With him, Edward, and Xavier at her back, surely she'd find her feet?

"Is there a reason you wished to speak to me today?" he asked, rather than comment on that.

After a session, it was tradition for the government to gather in the club located within the same grounds as the House of Parliament.

As with the session, a DeSauvier maintained a presence here too.

Unfortunately for him, that meant staying here until the rest of the politicians had disappeared off into the ether—which couldn't come a moment too soon, as far as he was concerned.

"Georgiana is of an age now," Ferdinand remarked softly, and George's eyes widened.

The man couldn't mean…?

"How fast they grow up," was all George said, his tone faint with the surprise he felt.

"Indeed. She's twenty-four, and recently home from finishing school. She's expressed a desire to meet you."

He cleared his throat. "I'm certain I shall make her acquaintance once more at Edward's wedding. You'll be attending?"

Ferdinand nodded. "Yes. But I'm certain she'd like to meet with you before then." His smile turned into a sneer. "I'm sure you know how it is with daughters. A man must accommodate their every whim."

George almost snorted at that. If Ferdinand's daughters dared have any whim, that characteristic was soon weeded out.

"As you can imagine, my schedule is rather full at the moment. I'll be certain to pass on Georgiana's request to my social secretary."

Jesus. The man was only trying to palm his daughter off on George —*another* daughter on the royals! The bastard had gall, he'd give him that.

But George and Georgiana?

Even if he'd been in the market for a wife, two Georges in any house was one too many.

Ferdinand bowed his head, but from the steely glint in his eye, George could tell he wasn't pleased.

"Tell your father I asked after him," he said as he got to his feet.

One thing that could be said for him was that once he'd made his point, he didn't hang around. And the fact that he headed off after a curt nod told George that his main intent was to push Georgiana on him.

Shuddering at the very idea—because if she was anything like her sister, then George's cock would drop off from frostbite—he watched as the Prime Minister approached.

Of *course*, he had to deal with both of them today.

His sitting here was simply a formality. Even when his father was in state, it didn't mean any politicians approached him. Naturally, he had to deal with the PM and L'Argeneaux—the father-in-law from hell.

Talk about rotten luck.

"De Montfort," George said briskly when the Prime Minister gestured at the seat Ferdinand had left moments before.

"Your Highness," he replied as he settled into the club chair. "I wished to speak with you in regard to your duties, now that you're back home for good."

George stiffened. "My duties will be ascertained by the royal household."

"But Parliament has some say in that. Unless you'd like me to quote the letter of the law, of which I'm quite capable, you'll listen."

George stared at him. "I'll gladly listen, but my acting upon whatever it is you have to say isn't guaranteed."

"Spoken like a true DeSauvier. I wondered if America had softened that self-righteousness, but it would seem not even the Land of the Free can wreak such miracles." His top lip curled. "More's the pity."

"The US and Veronia may have two different kinds of government, but we're both a democracy."

"Ours is one that's chained to an outdated rule. How can progress be made when we're forced to cede to tradition?"

George scoffed at that, even as he was unsurprised by De Montfort's stance—his dislike of the royal family and royalty in general was well-known.

That he and his party had been voted into power at all had spoken of a turn in the tide towards the old guard of the nation.

A response, George wholeheartedly believed, that had been triggered by Edward's marriage to Arabella.

The public might not have been in the know of all the power plays that went down in the House of Parliament. However, they weren't so blind not to see that with a man like Ferdinand married to the crown prince, his spider-like presence would begin to shadow the family's movements.

Now that Arabella was dead, the ties cut. Once Edward was wed to a liberal American, next year when the election rolled around, George fully expected another party to win. De Montfort was far too conservative for the average Veronian.

"You try to wield the term 'tradition' as though *your* own opinions are not old-fashioned. Father's interest in prison reform is in line with the Scandinavian preference of rehabilitation over punishment. That makes him a modern thinker. Ahead of the times.

"You, on the other hand, want to punish, regardless of the statistics on how often our prisoners reoffend. Who's the one with their feet firmly fixed in the past?" he chided.

"It's short-sighted to think that just because the king wants it, his people do too," De Montfort retorted, his back up now he'd been called out.

George shrugged. "Perhaps it is. Perhaps it isn't. The king will be around a lot longer than you or I, Luc. Maybe you should have realized that before you took your seat of office."

De Montfort's mouth tightened, but in the face of George's argument, there was little left to say.

The office of king was timeless. The man holding the title was bound to the chains of time, but the title itself wasn't.

Edward was formed in their father's image. They had similar ideals, similar goals for the shape they wanted the country to be in...

If anyone could outlast such a dynasty, it wasn't George, and it certainly wasn't De Montfort.

The Prime Minister leaned forward, and pressing his elbows to his knees, asked, "What did L'Argeneaux want?"

Edward's former father-in-law and the Prime Minister were a part of different political parties. Though De Montfort was conservative, L'Argeneaux was considered almost a radical. A bare hairbreadth away from nationalism... which, in George's opinion, was too damn close to fascism.

The last thing they needed was a goddamn Nazi in Parliament.

"By the sounds of it, he wants to marry me off to his youngest daughter."

De Montfort's eyes widened, and George knew he'd surprised the man with his candor.

Cocking a brow at that, the Prime Minster murmured, "Why on Earth would he do that?"

"The ties that bind, I guess." He shrugged. "What better way to make sure those ties are like concrete? Marriage is the only way."

"I'll assume you'll need to discuss this with the king?"

George, unable to help himself, snorted. "No. There'll be no discussion. And you can tell L'Argeneaux himself that, too," he declared, knowing that by proffering the words, De Montfort would hold his tongue.

That was the nature of politics.

Whatever you didn't want discussed would soon spread around the party like chlamydia. What you didn't care about being under discussion was boring as fuck and as safe as a nun's chastity.

"You changed during your time in the States."

"Had to," George replied, hearing and disliking the musing note in the other man's tone. "Part of growing up, I suppose. The Americans don't really care if I'm a prince or a pauper. We're all equal there."

"Bullshit. Like your title didn't open doors."

"Oh, it opened the doors, but they didn't stay open for long if I didn't swiftly prove myself."

De Montfort's disbelief was evident in the cynical twist to his lips, but he didn't further his argument. Instead, he asked, "Your father told me you wish to get involved with the country's finances. Was that true?"

The truth was he didn't have much of a goddamn say in the matter. But that was something he wasn't willing to disclose. "I haven't decided yet."

De Montfort narrowed his eyes. "I need to be kept in the loop on this, Your Highness."

"I'm well aware of that. As it stands, I haven't decided what I'll be doing with myself now that I'm back." His smile wasn't exactly warm when he continued, "I might even decide to be a layabout. Just to fulfill your expectations of the idle rich royal."

The politician's mouth tightened. "I see you haven't grown up enough not to be childish. This is no laughing matter."

"Do you see me laughing?" he retorted silkily. "I'm not laughing at all. But I won't be pressured into a position I don't want. I'd prefer to go private before working for some middling governmental department you deign to stick me in."

De Montfort frowned. "You're aware that will sow dissension? If the public see you go private, they'll assume my government and the DeSauviers aren't…"

"In sync?" He cocked a brow. "I wonder how they'd figure that out?"

De Montfort glowered at him. "What do you want?"

George's top lip quirked in amusement. De Montfort knew he was on the way out—his policies weren't liberal enough for Veronia's current general population. If George was a gambling man, which he wasn't—outside of playing the markets—he'd have bet his fortune that De Montfort would lose next year's election, and the socialist party would be in power.

If he wanted his party to retain any seats in Parliament, it was best for De Montfort to cozy up to the royal family rather than alienate them.

"Like I said, I haven't decided yet. But once I know, I'll be sure to pass the message on."

De Montfort's jaw clenched, a sight that made George smile with good humor—he did so like pissing the right people off.

The Prime Minister got to his feet, and without another murmur, disappeared.

The break in protocol didn't go unnoticed. As he wasn't crown prince, it wasn't required that everyone bow or curtsey when they left his presence, but it was still tradition that they use his title.

It was a petty piece of tradition that hadn't died a death. Though it didn't bother him, the impolite behavior caused titters of interest which George weathered with a bland smile.

Rubbing his chin, he wondered what Xavier, Edward, and Perry were up to, and more than that, he hoped they were having a damn sight more fun than he was.

CHAPTER SIX

"I REALLY DON'T CARE."

George heaved out an aggrieved sigh. "You have to care. It's your wedding cake. Also, this stuff is supposed to be more important to you than it is to us."

Xavier snorted as he absorbed the sight of George, surrounded by cake samples, lace swabs, and various other items of wedding regalia. When he took in the room at a glance, there were also cards, different styles of ribbon, and pictures of hairstyles in a large folder.

"I didn't take you for a wedding planner," Xavier murmured as he stepped into the room.

Satisfaction filled him at the sight of Perry cuddled into the sofa in his favorite sitting room. She wore an overlarge rugby jersey that she must have purloined from George's wardrobe, and those weird yoga pants that looked oddly like jeans. She was barefoot, her hair was in a high ponytail, and her nose was buried in a book that, after peering at the title, he saw had nothing to do with weddings, royal or otherwise, and everything to do with water conservation.

Considering that she'd come to Veronia in the first place to help with their severe water shortages, it could almost be considered fitting.

Well, it would be, if George didn't look like the bride in this scenario and she the groom.

"I'm not a wedding planner, but Perry won't make any decisions," George grumbled.

"I told you already, I don't care." She hummed under her breath as she stole a piece of cake from a plate George had propped on a sofa cushion to her side. "Although, the banana cake is really nice."

"And totally untraditional, of course," Xavier declared, delighted by how difficult she was being.

Well, difficult wasn't the word. Not really. She wasn't purposefully being a pain. But her disinterest would soon make George blow his top—always an amusing sight to behold.

"We can't have banana cake at the wedding, Perry," George groaned. "I don't know why they even included that in the taste testers."

She scowled at the page in her book. "Why can't we? It's my wedding, isn't it? The one thing I'm interested in, and you're not going to let me have it." She huffed. "That sounds about right."

For a second, his cousin looked pole-axed, then he closed his eyes. "If you want the banana cake, then I guess we can say it's an American tradition."

She hooted at that, deigning for the first time to look up from her book. "I want to be around to watch you sell that. Somehow, I think Cassandra Whitings might smell a rat. Living in New York will do that to a girl."

George waved a hand. "Cassie won't snitch."

"How backward is Veronia if you can pitch them that lie?" Perry asked herself the question more than them, Xavier thought. But before they could reply, she asked, "You're old friends with Cassie, aren't you? All of you, I mean."

Xavier nodded as he took a seat beside her. Lifting an arm, he slung it behind her shoulders, and smiled when she snuggled into his side. She was a tactile little thing, and he, Xavier noted with quiet astonishment, was equally as tactile when it came to her.

"She's an old friend. And we went to school with Marcus."

"Does she know about how you and Edward like to share, George?"

His cousin snorted. "No. Of course not. If anyone knew, it would be Marcus, but I doubt he does." George shot Xavier a look. "Although I was surprised to realize you knew, Xav. Do you think Marcus is in the dark?"

He pondered it a second, then nodded. "I only knew because of how reckless Edward was back then. Marcus wasn't totally clueless, but Cassie was giving him the runaround in those days, and his family was having problems with their debts. Remember?"

George pulled a face. "I do. Shitty times all 'round, really." He forked up some cake, and pulled another face. "God, I didn't think I could get sick of cake, but I am now."

"Let's go for the banana cake, then," Perry said mulishly. When he scowled at her, she huffed, and changed the subject. "Why did Cassie look sad the night of the ball?"

Xavier pursed his lips. "You caught that, too?"

George looked up from a display of wedding invitations to ask, "She looked sad?"

"Yes," Perry retorted with an eye roll. "She did. Twice. When you mentioned her husband."

"It's weird too, because I called Marcus a week ago. He never mentioned the family was returning to Veronia."

George frowned. "You don't think their marriage is in trouble?"

Xavier scoffed. "No. Not Marcus and Cassie. They were always like two peas in a pod."

"Things change," Perry pointed out softly.

"They do, but not Cassie and Marcus. I swear, they're one of the only love matches in our circle. Everyone else, if they're married at all, has gone for the money. But Marcus's father lost the family fortune in the stock market crash ten years ago, and Cassie never minded. If anything, she supported Marcus throughout that time, and it was bloody hard, too."

"God, I remember that. When they had to sell the family estate?" George winced at the memory. "And they wouldn't let anyone help them either, would they?"

"Bloody pride. Marcus and his father were too alike in that regard."

"You'd have helped shore them up?" Perry asked, eyes wide.

"To keep the house in their family? Of course. It's not like we couldn't afford it," Xavier said dismissively. "But they wouldn't even contemplate the notion. Their pride definitely came before the fall."

"That's sad."

"Yes. It is. And now, we have some idiot pop stars living in a noble house that had been, until that point, in the family for close to half a millennium. Marcus' family is as old as ours, and they were our first standard bearers back in the day when Napoleon was threatening our borders."

She blinked. "It's insane that you're all linked to this, I don't know, strange interconnected universe. Where history and the present seem to collide."

George cocked a brow. "That's a weird way of putting it."

"No weirder than hearing you talk about Napoleon on a personal level," she said wryly. "Let me guess, one of the DeSauviers was friendly with him at one point?"

Xavier grinned. "How do you think we kept him out of our land? Well, we had a prince who was chummy with him... Our forest barricades and natural defenses also helped."

"Exactly! That's my point." She blew out a breath. "Your family is walking, talking history. It's kind of overwhelming."

"Your family soon, love," George pointed out.

"Is there a reason you've camped out in my sitting room?" Xavier asked, smirking at the tableau before him when Perry began fidgeting beside him, her discomfort evident to everyone with eyes. Well, save for George. "Not that I mind, but... you have plenty to go at in the castle."

Perry shrugged; the move jostled him a little, but had her settling deeper into his half-embrace. "I like it here."

"Meaning, you don't like Masonbrook Castle?" he asked, cocking a brow at her.

He expected her to be embarrassed, to shoot George an apologetic look when she replied—but she didn't. She blatantly grumbled, "No. It's horrible."

George huffed. "Say it how it is, Perry."

"It *is* horrible. And you know it, George. It's way too big, and everyone can listen in on even the quietest of conversations." She shot him a narrow-eyed glance. "And those Guardians of the Keys? They give me the goddamn creeps, wandering around clanking. It's like living with Peeves."

"Who the hell's Peeves?" Xavier demanded, when George just snickered.

"Don't watch much Harry Potter, do you?" she retorted.

"Considering it's for kids, no."

She sucked in a sharp breath. "You'd better be messing with me. Have you read the books?"

"No." He scowled at her. "I'll assume you have."

"Both of us have," George replied, grimacing. "They suck you in, cuz."

"They're for kids."

"They're totally not," she barked. "Right, that's it. We need a Harry Potter movie marathon night." She tapped her chin with a finger. "Do you think I could convince Edward to come and watch it?"

Xavier whistled. "Might as well test the limits of this relationship from the very start."

She froze. "What's that supposed to mean?"

He nudged her. "I was only teasing. But I think the last time I actually saw Edward sit down in front of a television was..." He frowned. "In fact, I don't even remember when."

George peered down at some ribbon samples—whatever the hell he was doing, Xavier didn't have a clue. "He's not a fan of TV, Perry. Still, for you, he'd probably watch the movies."

"What are you doing, George?" Xavier asked, eyeing his cousin askance.

Perry answered instead. "Marianne gave me a list of things a wedding planner needed from me. I gave that to George, considering this is all his fault."

"'Fault' has negative connotations," George immediately retorted, wagging a finger at her.

"This is a negative situation," she blustered. "I'd be happy getting married in the town hall, but oh no, God forbid we don't get married in a goddamn abbey." She rolled her eyes. "That's your fault, bud. You have to pay the ferryman."

"But I don't even know what half this stuff is for," he said on a wail that had Xavier snickering.

"You think I do?" She pointed a finger at him. "George, who is the least girly girl you know?"

His cousin grumbled. "You." There was such little dithering over the answer that Xavier's snickers turned into outright laughter.

"Exactly. So, since you get such a kick out of dressing me in all those way-too-tight dresses, why don't you make yourself useful and pick my wedding dress too?"

"Sounds perfectly logical and reasonable to me," Xavier said smoothly, grinning hard when George flipped him the bird.

Perry stuck her nose back in her book. "When it comes to important things like the food, I'm in. Dresses and shit?" She scoffed. "I've the Veronian water supply to save, so don't think you can waste a crap ton of it on stupid bouquets at the wedding."

"It's traditional," George retorted. "How the hell can we cut down on flowers?"

"We're bringing the royal family into the modern age, aren't we?" she jibed. "Modern age means not destroying the Earth just so some tables can look fancy. And don't think I didn't notice all those flower arrangements at the engagement party." She shuddered. "I almost cried when I saw them being tossed out."

Xavier squeezed her arm. "They're not tossed out. They get sent to the local hospitals."

"Well, the staff didn't look like they were handling them with care." She pursed her lips. "I made a point of watching."

"We're not screwing you enough if you have time to sneak out and watch the staff clear up after balls," George grumbled.

"I couldn't sleep," she admitted. "It was a big night, and none of you were with me. So, yeah, there was no screwing to be had."

Xavier sighed. "It would have been impossible to have sneaked in and out."

"Oh, I know. I'm not complaining, just saying it how it is. Which is why, when we're married, we're moving."

George's eyes widened. "Beg pardon?"

"We're moving," Perry said, with no small amount of satisfaction.

"Where to? A terraced house in the city center?" George snapped, his shoulders hunching in agitation.

"No. To Grosvenor House." Her eyes sparkled. "I saw it in one of those long, and bloody boring books Marianne gave me."

"I've created a monster," George wailed, eyes aimed heaven-ward.

"Not a monster. Just someone who wants some privacy while she's got it. There's no reason we have to stay at Masonbrook," Perry argued. "I double checked the protocol, and even asked one of the ghost keepers. They looked as surprised as you do, but they answered."

"Jesus, you mean you asked the staff?" George's mouth fell agape. "Please tell me I misheard you."

"Nope."

He ran his hands through his hair. "News will have spread to Mother."

"It already has," she told him calmly. "When the Guardian of the Keys said there was no real reason why we couldn't live there, and she asked someone in the royal library who concurred, I told your mother. She said it was a wonderful idea. And it is. It's two estates away from this place, Xavier, so we can be close, and requires a quarter of the staff needed at the castle. It really is too much to have such a residence being used when things are so dire on an ecological front." She wagged a finger at him. "And don't accuse me of being an eco-warrior, not when I'm only here to save Veronia from itself!"

For a second, George was speechless, and Xavier couldn't blame him.

"Does Edward know?" he managed to utter after a few silent moments.

"Nope. I thought I'd let it be a surprise."

Laughter barked from him at that. "It will certainly be that, Perry."

In fact, a surprise would be an understatement.

Still, he was coming to learn that when it came down to Perry, most things were a definite understatement.

Veronia was about to be shaken up. Xavier just hoped the nation was ready for the earthquake.

CHAPTER SEVEN

PERRY SMILED THROUGH HER NERVES. It was ridiculous to be nervous now, but meeting a woman who was considered a friend by not just one of her men, but all three of them?

Talk about pressure.

Of course, pressure was a relative concept these days. With Marianne, George, and even Philippe nagging her about wedding preparations, and a gaggle of staff that seemed to hover around the queen before creating satellite gaggles around her, Perry had never been so popular.

It was with relief that she fled to The Grange, a hotel that had been in Veronia for over a hundred years and was as renowned as The Ritz in London or The Four Seasons in New York. The only downside to her escape was the fact she was meeting with a stranger who, technically, knew more about the three men who had totally turned her life on its head than Perry did herself.

"Perry!"

Cassie's voice was overly loud in the quiet tea lounge—yeah, it was *that* kind of place. Had a tea lounge and everything for the "little women."

When she'd been guided in here by a fawning concierge who she had nearly tripped over because he was bowing so low, she'd smuggled herself into a corner booth where she could hide from the interested stares of the ladies in the salon.

The place was all red chintz and gilt touches. Everywhere she went of late seemed to be gold-plated. It was starting to drive her crazy.

Her minimalist apartment in Boston looked like an empty space in comparison to the overdressed and over-decorated rooms she was having to adapt to.

If Edward wasn't careful, she'd take to camping out in his office. It was the only place she'd been in the castle that didn't have cherubs as accents.

"Hi, Cassie," she murmured when the other woman approached the booth and slipped in. She shot her a nervous look. "Thanks for meeting up."

She'd never been that great with the same sex. They never seemed to like her, and of late, she'd hung out mostly with guys anyway because of George. It was probably why being with three men at once didn't bother her.

George had more friends than she did, but he'd always included her like she was one of the guys.

Huh. Had he been training her from the start?

The notion had her lips twitching, and she quickly hid her amusement, lest Cassie think it was aimed at her.

"Sorry. I should have waited to call you Cassie." She grimaced. "That was rude of me; it's just that's what the guys call you."

The other woman waved a hand. "Please do. I'm only 'Cassandra' here in Veronia. It's like stepping back a hundred years sometimes. My husband's name still packs more punch than mine does."

Perry's brows rose. "Really?" Considering Xavier had told her that Cassie's husband's family had lost their fortune, that was a double blow to the feminist cause.

"Yes. Really." She grimaced as she settled her purse beside her on the red pillowy chintz. "It's very annoying. Although, New York, while it is far more level over there, still has its moments. My husband's firm—he works in venture capitalism—treat its female staff members abominably, in my opinion."

"What do they do?"

"Hire fewer women around our age because we can get pregnant. Stuff like that. I only know because Marcus tells me, and then regrets telling me when I try to make him talk to his other partners about it. He just says it's industry standard stuff, but that doesn't mean it's right, does it?" she complained with a grumble.

"No, it really doesn't." She pulled a face. "I'm fortunate, I guess. I've never experienced anything like that. The guys in my lab can be douches, and they walk over me sometimes, but that's probably my fault for letting them."

"Different industries. When you play the stocks, it's a high risk, high turnover process," Cassie explained. "A lot of people don't stay in the game long. Their hearts won't let them."

Perry widened. "Why won't they? They feel guilty about making so much money?"

Cassie hooted, her hand coming up to clap her chest. "No, Perry. Dear God, no. They have heart attacks, silly. It's too much stress and tension. High pressure. It's a nightmare situation."

Perry laughed too. "Oops. Of course, that makes far more sense."

"Venture capitalists don't *have* hearts, according to some. So they certainly don't feel guilty for getting richer and richer." She winced. "Not that I'll be giving my children that insight into what their papa did for a living."

"Did?" Perry asked carefully. "Is that why you're moving home?"

Cassie sighed. "No. We're moving back because Marcus was one of the unfortunate ones. Again."

"In what way?" Perry asked, trying to be careful, as really this had nothing to do with her. To make up for sounding like a snoop, she murmured, "I know Edward's concerned. Xavier too. Xavier said he spoke with Marcus recently, and he never made any mention of coming home."

"That's because he had no intention of moving home, until I made the decision for us." Cassie's tone was so grim in contrast to her usual joviality that Perry's eyes widened in surprise.

"Is everything okay, Cassie? I'm really not prying, but you just seem a little stressed."

The other woman shot her a look. "That's very perceptive of you. But I need a drink first."

Taken aback because it was only two in the afternoon, Perry watched as Cassie clicked her fingers and a footman appeared. In another place, at another time, she'd have said the guy was a waiter or a server. But with his honest-to-God breeches and a queue hairstyle, along with a tightly-fitted waistcoat and jacket, he looked like a Comic-Con visitor who'd managed to mix up a comic with the Beauty and the Beast cartoon.

She could even imagine the dude belting out, "Be Our Guest."

Within ten minutes, they had a platter of sandwiches, a high cake stand loaded down with cakes and scones and fancies, as well as a bottle of champagne and a tray of tea.

Cassie fell on the champagne like a dog scarfing down meat after being on a vegan diet for two months.

"God, I needed that." Cassie pulled a face as she practically hugged the champagne flute to her breasts. "You must think I'm a drunk or something. But I'm not. It's just...the children are being nightmares. They didn't want to move, and I can't blame them. They were born in New York, but they're still Veronians, and I refuse to stay in Manhattan."

"Kids can be difficult after a big move. They're just getting used to a new place, I suppose."

Cassie sighed. "Oh, I know, but that doesn't make any of them less of a monster for it. My eldest, Sebastien—he's eight—this morning declared that he wanted to divorce me so he could return to New York. He said he felt certain our old nanny would take him in." She rolled her eyes. "The same nanny who wouldn't come with us, even though the situation was urgent, and I offered her twice the salary for a year just to get her to make the transition with us."

Perry's throat choked. "Twice the salary?"

Cassie nodded. "Louise had been with us for six years. She's the only nanny Jessica and Robert have ever known. But she wouldn't come." Cassie shrugged, but Perry saw how irritated she was. "They're all struggling, but Robert is finding it the hardest." Cassie pronounced the name the French way. Almost like she was saying 'Row-Bear.'

The Veronians had an odd accent. It was like a hodgepodge of all the Romance languages, but the names tended to either have an Italian edge or a kiss of French. Like George and Xavier. Only Edward's name sounded very English, and quite stilted with it from time to time.

"Is he the youngest?" Perry asked softly.

"Yes. He's the baby." She sighed into her champagne. "It's very difficult to…"

"To?"

"Have your children pine so hard for another woman. I suppose it's my fault for having a nanny, but when the children came—and so close together—I was out of my depth. My husband hired our first nanny, and then when I had Jessica, my mother hired Louise. Can you imagine? We had two!

"I fired the first one because I didn't like how she handled Sebastien's tantrums, and stayed with Louise. I should have fired the pair of them and been a mother myself. Now, I have three children who don't know what to do with me, and who have zero relationship with their workaholic father."

Perry blinked. Going instantly from sharing nothing to sharing everything, Cassie apparently was a lightweight when it came to champagne.

"Maybe this is why you needed to return to Veronia," Perry stated gently. "So you can reconnect with your family. It sounds like that's something you want."

Cassie winced. "It is. My mother thinks I'm mad, but the last thing I want is to have a relationship like ours with the children.

"We're about as close as the North and South Pole. She only calls to dictate something to me like a tin pot Hitler." Cassie clapped a hand over her mouth. "Oops. I'm sorry, Perry. I'm sharing too much."

Letting out a little laugh, Perry had to admit, "I didn't expect you to tell me so much at first, but it's okay. I won't speak a word to anyone."

Cassie eyed her. "No, I think I recognized that from the off anyway. Plus, Edward wouldn't be marrying you if you were a tattletale. He had that once—Arabella was a frightful gossip, you know? The last thing he needed was a repeat of that!" Before Perry could mine for more information about Edward's late wife, Cassie carried on, tone mournful. "It's been such a long time since I've been back here. I barely recognize my old friends. They're all Botoxed to the max and can barely open their mouths from all the collagen fillers.

"I thought New York was bad for that. Then, there's the fact they won't talk about anything other than you and how you snared Edward. I forgot how incestuous life at court is, but it's not like I can avoid it. Being back here means I have certain roles to fulfill once more." She grimaced, toasted her glass. "The duties of being a marchioness."

"Is that why Marcus doesn't want to be here? He's the marquis after all. He'll have more duties than you, surely?"

"That's the half the reason."

"What's the other half?" Perry asked wryly. "It's okay, Cassie. You can tell me. I really won't share it with anyone. Not even Edward, if you don't want me to."

Cassie picked up a sandwich and took a deep bite—she swallowed the whole thing in close to one-and-a-half mouthfuls. Then, she fluffed at her bouncy bob of golden curls—hair that anyone would be jealous of. "You know how I said venture capitalism was bad for the heart? It was bad for Marcus's."

"He had a heart attack?" Perry asked, aghast.

"Yes." She pursed her lips as she poured herself another flute. When she waggled the bottle of champagne at Perry, Perry shook her head and motioned at her teacup, which was still full. "I told him that he was going to kill himself with work, and I was half right. He almost died. Then, when he decided that jumping back in the saddle a few weeks after he was released from hospital was a smart move, I told him I'd divorce him if he didn't take a step back." She firmed her jaw. "When he didn't take *that* seriously, I moved here."

Perry's mouth gaped at the serious ultimatum. "God, Cassie, I never..." What could she say? She didn't know the woman, so couldn't say it seemed out of character or surprising. In the end, she blustered out a truth. "That took balls."

Cassie froze, then snorted. She caught Perry's eye, and the pair of them burst into a flurry of giggles.

"Where are you from again?"

"You mean more specific than the United States?" Perry asked drily. "Seems like that's all anyone hears, anyway."

"Veronia is the center of the world, didn't you know?" Cassie retorted, tongue-in-cheek.

She laughed. "Yeah, I'm figuring that out as I go. I'm from Tennessee originally. Place called Billier. Tiny craphole of a town," she added fondly.

"Do you miss it?"

"Hell, no. I lived in Boston ever since college. That's where I met George, and," she coughed, "how I met Edward."

Cassie pursed her lips. "I wondered how you'd met. You don't seem like his regular kind of woman, but to be fair, Edward doesn't have a regular kind of woman. Not for a long time. Knowing Marianne, I bet she was scared he was gay or something. It's okay to be gay everywhere else, just not in the royal family."

Her mocking tone had Perry's eyes widening. "People seriously thought he was gay?"

She wrinkled her nose. "Probably not. To be honest, I just thought he'd been turned off women by the ice queen. And I don't just mean his late wife."

Surprised by the cutting remark, Perry felt herself stiffening up in defense of her soon-to-be mother-in-law. "Marianne's always been really kind to me."

"She's kind. To a fault," Cassie murmured softly. "Just to everyone else and not to her boys. But then I remember the old days, when she really did make a freezer look tropical." Running a finger around the rim of the glass, she continued. "Things changed when Edward and George returned from…" She choked a little. "You know."

"The kidnapping, I know."

Cassie kept her eyes down-turned. "Does Edward ever speak about it?"

"No. Not really." Not since he'd told her of how the kidnappers had manipulated the boys' hunger, anyway.

"I'm not surprised. He never did. It was all the chatter at court back when we were kids. I only know because I overheard my mother and father talking about it. She was friends with Marianne back then, before she moved to Switzerland with her new husband." She used the fancy silver tongs to plop a few sugar cubes into her teacup and, pouring herself some Darjeeling into the bone china, she followed that up by serving herself a scone, too.

"As far as I'm aware, no one knows what happened to the boys, not really. George was too young to figure it out, and I think Edward protected him from the men who took them. But Edward kept his mouth shut ever since."

"Really?"

Cassie nodded. "Really. I mean, look, Perry, I like you. I really do. And I think we could be friends, you know? So, I don't say this to get you mad or upset or anything but... we used to be really close. All of us. Marcus and I with George, Edward, and Xavier... there were a few others too. Jessica LeSaux, she's who I named my daughter after, but she died in a boat accident, and Jane Lewison was a friend for a long time before she became famous in Hollywood but..."

Jesus, talk about another world. Perry was about to merge not only with royalty but Hollywood royalty too!

"But what, Cassie?" she asked warily, uncertain if she was about to be warned off or something. The other woman's tone certainly didn't sound friendly.

"But... I've known them a long time, that's all. I know a lot about them. If I tell you something, I don't want you to get jealous. That's all."

Perry blinked. "That's all?"

Cassie nodded. "Why? What did you think I was going to say?" she asked, buttering her scone before taking a huge and wonderfully indelicate bite from the sweet treat.

Sweet, baby Jesus. Had Perry stumbled upon an actual woman with the potential to be a friend and not a Stepford Wife-cum-Real Housewife of Veronia? One who ate honest-to-God calories and said too much when squiffy?

"I don't know. I thought you were going to demand I treat Edward right or you'd go to the papers or something weird."

Cassie snorted out a chuckle then covered her mouth with her hand. "Well, I took that as a given."

Her wry tone told Perry she was joking, and she let out a sharp laugh. "I think we'll get on just great you and I, Cassie."

The older woman reached for her champagne flute and raised it over their afternoon tea. Perry picked up hers too, and touched brims with Cassie's.

"Here's to the start of a new friendship," Perry murmured softly.

"Hear, hear."

THE SMILE on Perry's face more than made up for the whirlwind morning Edward had endured in order to make this happen.

He was tired, a little cranky, and a lot hungry.

Not just for food, either.

But when she saw the car waiting outside the hotel for her, he watched her distracted expression turned focused as she peered into the windscreen to ascertain the driver's identity.

Her grin bloomed wider when she saw it was him, and God help him, his heart tightened in response.

Such an honest reaction was more than he ever expected anymore. In a world of intrigue and lies, where deception was a cold, but the most *common* of bedfellows, such earnestness wasn't seen often. Nor was it usually appreciated.

But Edward appreciated it.

Perry's candor was so utterly refreshing that some days, it was like sitting in the desert, thinking you'd seen a mirage, then discovering that you'd just fallen into Lake Titicaca by happy accident.

As she approached the vehicle, he reached over and opened the door for her. When he did, Xavier murmured from the backseat, "Why, Edward, I think you have a crush."

He shot his cousin a quelling glance, but stayed silent until Perry hopped into the passenger vehicle.

She was still beaming as she turned to him and murmured, "I didn't expect to see you today."

"What about me?"

Her surprised shriek had both men chuckling, and she turned to scowl at Xavier. But the scowl quickly turned into a rueful smile. "You're not supposed to make me jump."

"Why not? Where does it say that in the small print?" he teased, and sitting forward, he cocked his cheek to the side in expectation.

She bit her lip, shot Edward a look, then murmured, "Can I?"

Her hesitance hurt him. Not just because she was being cautious when he could sense she had no desire to be—it was the need for caution itself that upset him.

This was his life. The goldfish bowl hadn't changed, but he was seeing the new parameters since her arrival in his world.

And he didn't like it.

Hence today's visit.

He cleared his throat. "Xavier's an old friend in public, Perry. A part of my close family too. You can greet him."

"That means you can kiss my cheek but not my mouth. And don't slip me the tongue, not unless you want to start a riot."

Xavier's dry tone had Edward smothering a laugh, but Perry didn't smother anything. She chuckled, leaned between the seats, and pressed a kiss to Xavier's cheek. "Just because I can't, doesn't mean I'm not thinking about it."

Her husky tone had Edward's cock hardening, and he was already fighting his self-control.

Today had been… wearisome.

There was no other way to describe it.

He needed some space from the palace, he needed some space from the government, and he needed some privacy.

Just for a short while. Some normalcy.

Well, as normal as it got for a royal, anyway.

With a deep sigh, she sank back into her seat. But he quirked a brow at her. "No greeting for me?"

Her eyes flared. "You probably couldn't handle my greeting." She darted her gaze to the street ahead. A doorman was trying desperately not to look into the windscreen from the hotel's entrance, and pedestrians were also trying to ascertain the owner of the sleek Bentley.

He'd learned a long time ago, back in the folly of his youth, that the sports cars he loved inspired only more avid curiosity from the public. Sleek and more sedate sedans caused less of a thrill, but still caused a stir.

Especially as his car was armored like a damn tank.

It was the only compromise he'd been able to earn from his father.

Either he had to have a driver and guard ride with him, or he drove the civilian equivalent of a tank.

In his opinion, this caused more of a stir than a regular Bentley. After all, people were well aware that this vehicle was different, and different inspired inquisitiveness. But privacy was what he'd wanted, and privacy was what he had.

Of a variation.

Perry swallowed thickly as she leaned into him. Her lips brushed his in a soft, innocent touch, but it was the way she breathed out as she kissed him that fired his blood.

She stayed there, her lips touching his, no further caress to entice them…but that spoke of her need. Her hands came up to his shoulders, and the tips dug through his fine linen shirt until he felt her nails prick his skin.

"Jesus, that has to be the most innocently carnal kiss I've ever seen," Xavier said huskily, breaking into the moment.

Edward knew what he meant. How could such a delicate kiss be so dangerous? Perry, that's how. She somehow made the innocuous seem tempting.

Her sensuality streamed from every pore until it dosed the very air he breathed.

When she started to move away, he pressed his forehead to hers. "I have a surprise for you."

"You do?" she whispered throatily. "Does it involve a bed?"

"It involves several, actually."

Edward growled at Xavier's interruption. "Don't spoil the surprise."

"Hey, I'm the one that came up with it."

Edward snorted. "I'm sure Perry will thank you for it later."

She bit her lip and kept her gaze swept down as she retreated to her seat. "I'm sure gratitude can be expressed far more comfortably when we're not being gaped at by hotel staff."

Edward saw another doorman had appeared, and a man in tails with a bright cravat that spoke of a concierge service.

He blew out an irritated breath and wished that, like the passenger windows, the windscreen could be tinted too. But hell, a man had to see to drive. Though the reasoning made sense, it didn't make it any less irritating.

Grumbling, he started the engine and headed out into the busy flow of Madela traffic.

Like any cosmopolitan capital city, it was busy twenty-four hours a day. Like its neighboring Mediterranean countries, there were lags when the city dozed for an afternoon nap. This traditional time was when he and Xavier had collected Perry from the hotel.

As such, heading out of Madela and toward Brixan took far less time than he'd originally anticipated, and before he knew it, they were on the open road to the countryside with Perry chattering happily away at his side.

"You sound like you and Cassie got on well," he commented upon hearing her discuss Cassie's opinion on Veronia after having lived in the USA for so long.

"We did, actually. I'd like to get to know her better, let's put it that way."

"I'm sure that can be arranged." He cut Xavier a look in his rearview mirror. "It would be a good friendship to cultivate, wouldn't it, Xav?"

"It would? Why?" Perry demanded suspiciously.

"Cassie is a court favorite thanks to her lineage, and you'll be needing a lady-in-waiting of your own."

Perry pulled a face. "Why would she want to be that? She has three kids. That's enough 'waiting' in my mind."

"Because it's an honor," Xavier chided, but he was amused. His grin was barely concealed at Perry's total lack of understanding. "Jesus, trying to make Americans understand royalty is surprisingly difficult. We don't have to make sense for it to be a way of life."

She huffed. "That's very inefficient."

"You'll need your own Guardian of the Keys, Perry," Edward pointed out softly. "They're your allies."

She frowned. "Hang on a minute. Your mother chose hers from her friends? But they're battleaxes."

Her astonishment had both of them chuckling. Xavier was the first to point out, "And Marianne isn't?"

Her scowl puckered her brow. "I wouldn't have said so, no."

"Mother's tough in her own way."

She shot him a look. "Cassie said she's cold."

"Cassie's tendency for brutal honesty hasn't died a death, it would seem." He grimaced.

"You didn't deny it."

"What's to deny?" he asked, shrugging. "It's the truth. Mother was never very demonstrative when George and I were growing up. If we wanted affection, *Tanta* Lisetta was where we went."

Xavier smiled broadly. "Mother was a pain, but she knew how to dole out tea and sympathy, didn't she?"

Perry turned in her seat, putting her back to the glorious rippling fields ahead of her, as well as the Mediterranean to her left.

"Marianne's always been kind to me."

"She's softening in her old age. Plus, she probably never thought Edward would marry again," he retorted wryly, but Edward's shoulders stiffened. Of course, Xavier noticed. He clapped him on the back and murmured, "You and I both know it."

Perry shot them both considering looks. "You'd have had to have married, surely?"

Edward's nostrils flared. "Do we have to talk about this? I *am* getting married now. To you. There are no 'what ifs' anymore."

Her grin was cheeky. "Yes. I'm well aware of that. As were all the waiters and staff in the hotel."

"Princess bride in the making," Xavier joked. "You'll get sick of it by..."

"Last week?" she mocked, snorting. "I'm not exactly a fan of all the attention, but I guess it has its place."

"What's that supposed to mean?" Edward asked, curiosity urging him.

"It means I know how much Veronia earns from having a royal family. This is all part and parcel of it." She pursed her lips. "I don't have to like it, but I can endure it."

But how long *could* she endure it?

She hadn't been raised to be a princess. Worse still, she hadn't been raised to be a queen.

He swallowed back the nerves he felt at the prospect of her... what? Leaving him because she couldn't cope with her new role? Would she do that to him? To George? To Xavier?

"Hey, what's wrong?" Her hand, so soft and delicate, slid onto his lap. It wasn't a sexual touch, but an affectionate one.

"He's worrying. When he looks constipated, he's worried."

Xavier's blasé tone had Edward letting out an irritated hiss. "Remind me again why I brought you along?"

"Because he's so pretty," Perry mocked, shooting Xavier a dark glance that, Edward was half-amused to note, was loaded with warning. "Why are you worried, Edward?" she asked quietly.

"Because there will come a day when you can't endure it. It never goes away, Perry. Ever. This life is a constant. It's a duty."

"I can handle duty," she retorted. "I grew up on a farm."

Silence fell in the car, then Xavier broke it by hooting out a laugh. "What the hell does one have to do with the other? We don't milk many cows in the castle, Perry. It would kind of ruin our image."

She glowered at him. "Shut up, you. I just mean, you have duties to attend to, and if you don't, one, the animals will die. Two, your business will burn to dust. I understand duty, guys. Even worse than being a royal is being a scientist. The Earth is my major responsibility. At least as a crown princess and then a queen, I'll get Parliament to listen to me about the dams. "

Xavier's ears pricked at that. "They refused to listen again?"

"The so-called Environmental Agency that's so un-environmental it's a joke, rejected it. Said the country can't afford to rebuild."

"We can't afford *not* to rebuild either," Xavier retorted. "I know someone in the agency. Let me speak to them."

Interest piqued, Edward cocked a brow. "Who do you know in the EA?"

"Laurenne Jonquil."

Perry's eyes narrowed. "You know that stuck-up bitch?"

Xavier cleared his throat. "I was friends with her brother at school."

"She means biblically," Edward put in, ever helpful. When Xavier grunted, Edward just smiled.

Sometimes, it was nice shoving the shoe on the other foot.

The remainder of the twenty-minute journey took place with Xavier and Perry bickering, and Edward chuckling here and there. One thing he enjoyed about Perry was her ability to make him smile.

He'd been called a stick in the mud before now. Stoic to the point of tedious, and that was exactly how he preferred it.

While stoic, he was at least in control. It was when he was lost control that the problems started.

Growing agitated at the thought that the one woman with whom he could be out of control was his future wife, because there was a vein of trust blossoming between them, he ran a hand through his hair. Perturbed to notice that his fingers were shaking, he clenched them into a fist.

Perry's nature invited him to be true to himself, and he hadn't been that for a very long time. It was disconcerting to realize that he didn't know who he was anymore. That he'd have to relearn himself before Perry could truly have all of him.

"Anyway, where are we going?" she demanded, after asking if Laurenne Jonquil's bite was worse than her bark.

"We're going to Grosvenor House." Edward cut her an amused look. "Apparently, our residence after we wed."

She licked her lips. "I can explain that." To Xavier, she hissed, "You told him? I was waiting for the right moment."

"Of course, I did. There's protocol. That manor house hasn't been lived in for close to five years. It will need a lot of work done on it before it's ready for staff."

"I don't want staff," she said on a groan. "I want an empty house."

"You can't, Perry. That's not the role you're going to be playing. Whether you live at the palace or at the manor, there will be events you'll have to host. At home or at Masonbrook. The place needs staff, and it needs some care before it's livable once more because, knowing Edward, he's let it go to rack and ruin."

"Hardly. It's maintained," was all he said. "Where do you think I've been disappearing to all those weekends when Mother and Father can't get in touch with me?"

Silence fell. "Why didn't your guards tell the crowns?"

Perry's brow turned rumpled. "You call Philippe and Marianne 'the crowns'?"

Xavier shrugged. "Sometimes, they're more crown than parent."

At that, she winced. "That seems rather harsh."

"It's fair. I love my parents, Perry, but sometimes, they have no choice but to be king and queen above mother and father."

She huffed at that. "I hope you know that's total and utter bullshit, and if we're lucky enough to have kids, and I can't believe we're having this conversation right now, but if we do, then... Screw that. I'll be a mother first, queen second." She harrumphed to underscore her point.

Xavier laughed. "I wouldn't argue with her, Edward. She sounds like she means business."

Edward, on the other hand, didn't laugh. As he pulled into the sweeping manor driveway, he reached for her hand and squeezed her fingers. "I know. And I couldn't be happier about that."

Silence fell at his words. But he meant every single one of them.

He and George had been blessed with Marianne. Perhaps she was a little chilly, hardly demonstrative, but she loved her children. A veritable tigress when it came to her family and her defense of them. But she was always the queen. Always contemplated the importance of her position, put her duties at the top of the list of her priorities.

She was a marvelous queen. Edward couldn't fault her that. And as a mother, she was wonderful too. But for Perry to put their children first?

That was what he wanted.

More than anything.

He wanted their children to be the priority. As king, he was honest enough to admit to himself, at least, that he probably wouldn't be able to do that. The position was too taxing, too all-encompassing to not overtake their family life. But he'd fight to make sure Perry had enough time for their children.

Perry cleared her throat. Almost as though she could read his thoughts and wanted to dispel them, avoid them for the moment. But there would be no avoiding such thoughts when they were wed.

Part of her role as his wife, princess, and future queen was providing the next heirs to the throne.

He wondered if she felt as overwhelmed by that task as he did.

CHAPTER EIGHT

XAVIER RAN a hand through his hair as he stepped out of the car.

Grosvenor House had been in the family for generations, and upon their grandfather's death, Edward had inherited it at a very young nine years of age. Long before Edward had started to use it, however, the family had often visited during the summer.

Xavier recalled holidays in the long, summer days. Where the sun never seemed to stop shining, and the sky never failed to be anything other than periwinkle blue. George at his and Edward's heels as they trundled all over the estate, adventuring and causing mischief in the rare time they had to themselves...

That had been back when their Grandfather had been alive and had been king.

King Xavier, for whom he'd been named, had been a tough bastard, but he'd been better at finding a work/life balance than his son or grandsons.

Though the drive had been short, he still felt cramped. Stretching out his arms, he grunted happily as his muscles responded to the gentle heat of being warmed up. A soft hand fell at the base of his spine, jolting him. He turned and caught Perry's quick wink, which was as fleeting as her gentle touch to his back.

Kicking himself for jumping like she'd frightened the life out of him, he murmured, "This is one of my favorite places in the whole world."

"Seems like you both have a lot of those," she teased, making Edward laugh.

Xavier cocked a brow, confused by the reference. His cousin just cleared his throat. "Your lake. Acquaevit, it's one of my favorite places. I told Perry that the last time we were there."

Considering the four of them had been swimming naked in Xavier's ancestral land, he understood the snickers.

Grinning, he nodded. "You'll find we're all contradictory."

Perry snorted. "Why doesn't that surprise me? But tell me more. In what way are *you*?"

He shrugged. "I can guarantee, we all love each other's inheritance more than our own."

Edward, for once, laughed without sounding like he was in pain. The genuineness of his amusement had Perry's eyes flaring wide with delight. She pressed her hand to Xavier's back once more, her fingertips digging in slightly as she half-turned toward Edward, taking in his laughter like a flower preening in the sun's rays.

Xavier couldn't find it in himself to be jealous of the attention she was giving to his cousin. Not when she made sure she was connected to both of them.

That simple, basic touch of her palm to his lower back was a union of a different variety. One he could appreciate just as much as her attention.

He wished like hell he could reach for her wrist, to hold those frail, fine bones in his palm, and feel the pulse of her heart against his fingertips. But that wasn't to be.

Not when they were outside, anyway. Not with the staff, undoubtedly looking on.

Instead of doing as his instincts clamored, he remained rather rigid before her.

"That kind of belly laugh means he's right," Perry pointed out with a quick smile.

Edward shook his head but said, "Yes," making the pair of them laugh at the contradiction.

"Well? Which is it?" Perry demanded.

"George loves Xavier's family estate. I'd have Haversham House in a heartbeat."

Perry blinked, so Xavier, sensing her confusion, explained, "Haversham House is George's seat."

"George has a seat?" she asked carefully, and his lips twitched at her bewilderment.

Not that he found her confusion in any way amusing—it was just how she processed things. He could almost see the whirring cogs in her brain as she tried to figure out the extent of George's life that was outside her ken.

They'd been best friends for so long that she'd expected, he knew, for things to never change. But Xavier, though he would have loved for things to be different, knew better than most.

No one could be trusted outside of the family.

It was why it was such a big leap being with a woman who didn't believe that. Truth was, he could only envisage someone being hurt at the end of this.

And, knowing his luck, he'd be the one doing the hurting.

Still, now was not the time for thoughts of such matters. Perry had a way of surprising him. He'd imagined himself being left out in the cold as the relationship between the princes and the future crown princess developed, and yet, she continued to bring him into the fold. To make him know that he was important to her.

Why?

Maybe the answer wasn't one he'd ever learn... but the question would always burn on the tip of his tongue.

"George has a seat. We all do. Several. Edward more than the rest, of course." This was said without jealousy; there never had been any kind of envy between the three of them.

It was that, and Perry's nature, which gave him some small hope for the future.

"Because he's to be king? I know that seems like an obvious question, but I figured he'd get less 'seats' because he'll have the biggest of them all someday."

Edward's lips twitched. "If our ancestors had thought like you, Perry, I'm certain we'd be far richer than we are today."

"Yes. Common sense and battle strength aren't necessarily two things that go hand in hand. At least, not in the DeSauvier lineage."

She smirked. "I guess it's not to my detriment to be aware of this before I spawn another generation."

Xavier barked out a laugh. "Spawn? Beautifully phrased, Perry."

"I'm known for my scientific brain, Xav. Not my romantic, English-lit origins." She winked, then turned to look over the house before her. "I've only seen this in pictures, but it's more beautiful than I thought."

Edward murmured, "I'm glad you think so. It's to our benefit that you like it here. It will cause less of a fuss if we're seen to be spending more time here than at Xavier's estate."

Perry frowned. "But that's where he works. He'll need to be there."

Xavier placed a hand on her shoulder. "I can run my experiments there and come visit here."

But she shook her head. "No."

Edward cocked a brow. "No? No to what, Perry?"

"I don't know," she retorted, folding her arms across her chest, managing to look more mulish than outright stubborn.

"Then how can you refuse when you don't know why you're refusing?" Edward demanded, grimacing at her logic.

"Because Xavier will feel like he doesn't have a place, that's why. How would you like it if you had to make excuses to come and see me? You're the only one who won't have to, and George has an inbuilt reason to be close to me—he's my best friend. If anyone questioned it, they could research our background, dammit. I've practically lived with him for almost half a decade! But Xavier has no reason. I don't like that. It's not fair."

She was close to pouting, and Xavier, for all his thoughts, had taken a swift dark turn upon leaving Edward's car. He found that Perry had lifted his mood, and he should have had faith that she would do exactly that.

The connection between them was special. He was relieved to know that he wasn't the only one feeling that.

It meant he wasn't out in the cold, and that was what mattered.

For this to work, all four of them had to remain tight-knit, and it seemed Perry was the staunchest supporter of that.

"It's okay, Perry," Edward was telling her now. "Xavier and I have always been close. And considering your background in environmental science, and the fact I reckon you'll be playing an even bigger role in our ecological issues than before... it fits for us to be a tight-knit circle."

She pursed her lips. "I suppose. But I like Xavier's estate too. I just meant for us to live here rather than the castle. I don't like it there," she admitted, ducking her gaze from Edward's as though concerned he'd be upset by her revelation.

"Neither do I," was Edward's answer, and Perry's head darted up as she gaped at him.

"Then why the hell do you live there?" She stacked her hands on her hips, irritation bubbling from her pores.

His shrug was easy. "Tradition."

"Tradition can suck my ass." She sniffed.

"Why, Perry, if I'd known you were into that, I'd have fallen at your feet sooner," Xavier retorted silkily, grabbing her around the waist and dipping her to the ground.

She shrieked out a laugh and whacked him on the shoulder. "Put me down, dingbat," she retorted, but she was chuckling when he helped her back upright.

Edward, benevolently holding court, just smirked when she patted her hair. "He's right, Perry. George would have helped with that particular fetish too."

She let out a hiss. "You know exactly what I'm talking about, and it has nothing to do with rimming."

"Aha," Xavier declared. "The lady does know more about these things than she cares to let on."

Perry shot him the stink-eye, and propping her chin in the air, jibed, "And there's a reason why I want to spend more time with you? Must be a glutton for punishment."

He laughed, and swept his arm through hers. "That's one way of putting it."

"I'm sure there are several," Edward remarked as Xavier began walking toward the pillared portico.

The sound of the car alarm beeping was followed by the noise of gravel spilling as another vehicle came down the drive.

Edward groaned. "I thought I'd lost them for a little while longer," he admitted, as they strode up the four marble steps toward the entrance of the house.

It was grand, but small for their standards. With only fourteen bedrooms, he could see why Perry would prefer such a seat instead of the castle.

But, living in places such as Masonbrook was what she'd have to adapt to.

When Philippe passed, that was where they'd have to live.

Either there, as it was close to the capital, or in any of the three other royal residences dotted around the country—each which was just as large, but without the facilities Masonbrook had.

"I wondered where your guards had disappeared to," Perry confessed as they stepped inside. She peered up at a domed hallway that had the scene of a battle raging up in the heavens gloomily looking over them as she found her bearings.

"Cheerful," she said, pointing up at the ceiling. "Don't you just wish, sometimes, that you could get some paint and...?"

Edward laughed. "All the time. Remember my office?"

She blinked. "You mean that was like this?"

"It caused quite a stink. There was a fresco in there that had to be removed. It's at the National History of Art in Freju now."

Perry's mouth rounded. "I like your style, Edward. Although, I guess I'd get more of a fix on that if I'd seen your damned room." She cut Xavier a glance. "I haven't seen his *or* your bedrooms, for that matter. I think that's so wrong."

Edward and Xavier just smirked at each other, and that smirk had Perry glowering at them.

"What's that supposed to mean? Do you both have dungeons in them or something?"

"Or something," they repeated at the same time.

She chuckled. "You're nightmares. You know that?"

Before she could reply, one of Edward's staff, Jamieson—his head guard—marched toward them. If the vein bulging on his forehead was anything to go by, he was pissed as hell at Edward's giving them the slip.

"Sir. We agreed. You'd take the Northbound exit." Jamieson gritted his teeth, and opened his mouth to continue the barrage, but Xavier grabbed Perry's hand and tugged her away to one of the smaller sitting rooms off the hall.

"Let's leave Edward to be ass-chewed in peace."

"We're obsessed with butts today, aren't we?" she observed ruefully, peering over her shoulder as she watched Edward, appearing totally unapologetic, as his guard tore into him.

"Why he persists on avoiding them is beyond me. It's easier just to give in," Xavier admitted. "It's one less battle to have to fight on a daily basis."

"I'm surprised. Considering his father was so concerned when news spread about the UnReals' numbers having increased," Perry admitted, her gaze taking in the bright red paneled walls. Cream and matching blood-red brocade surrounded each panel, and gilt trimmed each plate, creating an over-the-top explosion of color.

This room was known as the Music Room for a reason. Where there would ordinarily be artwork and pieces to boggle the mind, there were instruments. Anything from a two-hundred-year-old baby grand, to a Stradivarius on a perch, with a bow tilted just so to entice anyone to play.

There was a cello, a trumpet, and a saxophone too. All held in place by specially crafted stands that held them aloft in a way that made them seem as though the instruments were being played.

"Wow," she said on a low whistle as she took in the twenty different instruments. "Can you guys play any of these?"

Rather than answer, he headed for the cello, took a seat on the ornately tapestried-stool behind it, and picking up the bow, began to play a particularly favored piece of his—"Paint It Black."

"Rolling Stones?" Perry demanded, eyes wide as she chuckled. "Sacrilege!"

He grinned and carried on playing. "It doesn't all have to be Bach and Beethoven—though I'm sure the house's very foundations mourn such days. This place was a firm favorite for a lot of the royals back in the day. They invited the greatest composers here.

"It's said Mozart wrote some of his most beloved pieces on this estate when King Gerard invited him to recuperate here after a nasty bout of influenza. Austria's winters could be very harsh on the delicate artistic temperament."

She snorted. "Wine, women, and song also didn't help I'm certain." She perched on an uncomfortable sofa that was high-backed and stuffed with horse-hair. "Why does Edward fight his guards, Xavier?"

"He doesn't always," he admitted. "Just sometimes. It's a little rebellion, I suppose. Does us all good from time to time. And we *were* safe. Jamieson knows that. Otherwise he'd never have let Edward into the car alone anyway."

She pursed her lips as she stared over the room's contents then looked out onto the gardens ahead. A small, low maze had been crafted out of reams of herb bushes.

Lavender, mint, basil, oregano... they'd all been shaped into tight square blocks. But nature won out here. The odd frond of lavender bobbed and swayed in the wind, as did a rebellious tower of mint as it grew at a faster rate than its neighbors.

"Xavier?"

Her softly-posed question jolted him as he fell into the music. Though he'd teased her with the Rolling Stones, he fell into a darker piece of his own making—its somber tones were underscored by lilts and bouncy crescendos that filled the room with a levity which was unusual in such a serious composition.

"Yes?" he asked, allowing his mind to drift into the piece.

"I love you, you know that?"

With a screech, he stopped playing. Whatever he'd expected her to say, it hadn't been that.

He blinked at her, his head tilting to the side as he took in her deliciously awkward posture—she looked as uncomfortable as could be. Not just because of the horsehair-stuffed cushions that did nothing to pad one's butt, but also because she was ill at ease.

He smiled at her though, touched by her words, even though her drifting into sentimentality obviously made her uncomfortable. "I know."

She frowned. "You do?"

Amused by the frown, he nodded. "I do. You show it in many ways." And that was no lie. She did, by including him where it would be easy to exclude him.

"Oh." Her frown lightened. "Well, I'm glad I do."

"And I feel the same." He caught her eye, trying to imbue those words with the depth of emotion she inspired in him.

She licked her lips at that. "I-I just... I didn't want you to think that my wanting to stay here meant anything bad, you know?"

"No, it means you're trying to find your place in this life and—" He blew out a deep breath. "Perry, as much as I want to make this easier on you, staying here won't do that."

Her scowl made another reappearance. "Why not?"

"Because Masonbrook is the main seat. You need to grow more comfortable being there."

He watched as she ducked her gaze and began biting her bottom lip. Under his watchful eyes, she raised a hand and began gnawing at her thumbnail in a way that would send his *tanta* Marianne's blood pressure soaring through the roof.

"There are too many people there."

"I know. It's difficult. But you'll grow used to it. With time. You can't do that if you're here and not there."

She blinked. "But surely…"

"You can do whatever you want, Perry. That's not under discussion. If you want to leave Masonbrook, you can. I just think it would be easier for you in the long run that you grow accustomed to the castle."

"Are Edward's quarters like his office?" she asked, sounding hopeful.

"You mean three-hundred-year-old art isn't your style? Perry, you wound me," he teased.

She stuck out her tongue. "I just want to have somewhere I don't need to be terrified about spilling tea over everything." She propped her elbow on the armrest, and glumly murmured, "Somewhere I don't need to worry about knocking over a Ming vase. There's a reason my home is nearly empty… I can't be trusted with tchotchkes."

"I broke an irreplaceable Limoges salt and pepper cellar when I was a child," he told her, his tone reminiscent. "My mother didn't speak to me for a week save for scoldings. Then my grandmother, who you would have loved, told her that these priceless artifacts were as entwined with our daily living as they'd been for our ancestors, and that to punish a small boy for such a mistake was unfair when we lived in a museum." His smile deepened as he remembered his grandmother's wrinkled hand when it came up to run her fingers through his hair to settle the mop of curls he now kept tamed with a short cut. "Mother soon had most of the delicate items put in storage. Where they remain to this day."

She blinked. "But your house has lots of stuff in it."

"Of course. But not my rooms. Or the ones I use more than most." He shrugged. "When you're the queen, you can do what you will with Masonbrook. As it stands, when you marry, you'll get different quarters. You can be the queen of those until the time comes for you to take your place."

She winced. "That had better be many moons in the future."

His smile was tight. "I pray you're right."

His somber words caught her attention, but before she could ask him anything—her intention was written into the lines that made up the scowl on her face—Edward stormed in.

He wore his anger like a damn cape that swirled about his feet as he took in the room on the whole. Spotting Xavier on the cello and Perry on the sofa, he retreated to the violin. Before anyone could say another word, he'd pressed the instrument to his chin and out poured a furious tumbling of Mozart.

Xavier caught Perry's eye, shot her a quick grin, and joined him in the madness.

———

SHE DIDN'T PARTICULARLY like classical music. In fact, she'd have said she loathed it. But watching Xavier and Edward play was far more entertaining than it should have been.

They were somber men in public. Quick to smile, granted, but their shoulders were always tense. They were rigid with their duty—as though each moment was loaded with the impossibility of their forgetting, even for a moment, the severity and strictures born within their station.

But here, now, they flowed.

That was the only way she could describe it.

For these endless, timeless moments, they were at one with the music she usually hated, but now loved. If it meant seeing them this way, then she had a new favorite.

Touched to the depths of her soul at their ability to relax with her, she felt her eyes burn with tears at the sight of them. Of their liberation in art.

It was... a masterpiece to her.

It was like the air around them could sigh out its relief at their having calmed down, and in turn, the music actually soothed her too. Enabled her to sit back in the seat with more ease.

Of course, now that she'd told Xavier the truth of her feelings for him, she felt like she could breathe easier too.

When she'd thought about love before, she'd never envisaged it could be this way.

So all-encompassing. In a way, she felt like she could drown in it. Like it could overtake her.

Perry knew that if she was to be with these three men, she'd have to be strong. Love needed strength anyway, but with George, Xavier, and Edward, it was different.

Their way of life presented issues normal mortals didn't usually touch upon. And Perry, until George, had been the most ordinary of mortals.

Now, she was going to be a princess. Strength and fortitude were going to have to be her keepers in the days, months, years ahead.

Her eyelids closed as the men slipped from one piece to another. It felt seamless to her, but they had to be communicating the change of composition somehow. But she wouldn't let herself be swept up in such matters; she slipped out of her shoes and curled her feet under her on the sofa.

However she'd imagined passing the rest of the afternoon, it hadn't been like this.

She slept, eventually. She didn't even know for how long, just that she awoke no longer on the uncomfortable cushions but in someone's arms.

She sucked in a breath and smelled Xavier's musky aftershave. With a yawn, she reached up and curled her arms about his neck. "Did you know that musk deer are on the protected register?"

The man holding her stilled a second. "Yes. I knew that. Why?"

"Your aftershave has musk in it," she reasoned, pleased when Xavier chuckled. "How did you pick me up without waking me?" she asked, turning her face into his throat where more of his delicious scent could be found. She nuzzled him there, enjoying the way the muscles of his throat bobbed in response.

"With great difficulty," he stated gravely, gravely enough for her to know he was joking.

"Jerk," she said without heat. "If I had a weight problem, then you'd totally be up shit creek now, wouldn't you?"

"But you don't though, do you?" he countered.

"Most women do. We all want to be thinner or have more curves or to have a firmer ass." She shrugged. "The nature of the female beast."

"Well, your ass is divine, you have enough curves for me to drool over, and if you lost weight, your tits would shrink. So... nah. You're perfect."

A satisfied smile curved her lips as she finally opened her eyes and pulled away from the shadowy haven of his throat.

When she did, she saw Edward was at her side, moving silently with them. "Do you agree?" She hadn't meant to sound so challenging, but it came out that way regardless.

It was hard not to picture his late wife. So fragile and delicate. Harder still not to see the arm candy he'd had in photos she'd found online, of his attendance at events both pre- and post-marriage. They'd all been the same.

Svelte.

Firm.

Toned.

Bitches.

He cocked a brow at the challenging note to her voice. "I think I need to prove my case if your tone is anything to go by."

She blinked, surprised at the sparkle in his eye as he made such a vow. Then, the fact she was in Xavier's arms and not Edward's as he walked down the corridor to only-God-knew-where hit home. From scent alone, she'd known Xavier was the one carrying her, but here, that held implications, so she asked, "How come...? Where's the staff?"

"They're very well behaved," was all Edward said.

"Did you use this place as a fuck pad?" she demanded, the thought occurring to her and stirring all her petty jealousies.

Jesus, only hours—or possibly minutes—before, she'd been thinking to herself about how she needed to be strong. Yet, here she was, falling at the first hurdle.

The green-eyed monster could be a true bitch.

"A fuck pad?" Edward repeated. "That's a new one on me."

"Because you're so old," she retorted with a huff, but her arms tensed around Xavier's neck. He couldn't help but feel it, but rather than say anything, he lowered his head and pressed a kiss to her temple.

The gentle, and *loving*, touch had her relaxing against him.

"I'm not that old," Edward countered, but she could hear that he was still amused at the turn their conversation had taken.

"You're in your forties. That's positively ancient."

Xavier snorted. "You're thirty-one, Perry. Nine years isn't that long a time."

"I'm on the early half of thirty-five. I can afford to be mean still."

Both men chuckled at her teasing. Edward, however, said, "No, Perry. This isn't a fuck pad. I used a discreet apartment in Madela for such things."

A part of her wanted to raze the apartment building to the ground at his words. Maybe he saw the evil twinkle in her eye, because he reached out and traced a finger down the lower curve of her calf. "My, my, I think I like this jealous side of you."

"I'm not jealous," she groused.

"Seems like it to me," Xavier pointed out cheerfully as Edward motioned to a door to the side of them. Edward turned the doorknob to let them through, and Xavier swung her around and headed through the opening.

She gasped at the sight of the room rather than take umbrage at Xavier's taking Edward's side.

"Wow," she replied. "I'm sick of gilt and sick of antiques, but this place is fucking awesome."

As was often the case when she was with them, either individually or within the quartet, they laughed. She made them laugh a lot, she realized, and was glad of that fact.

Edward always looked so somber that she wanted to tease him out of it. Xavier, more often than not, held the look of a man whose thoughts were elsewhere.

Probably back in his lab.

Because she could empathize, she wasn't offended, but had made it her unofficial mission to make them both smile more.

The stateroom in question was epic. Maybe epic didn't begin to describe it, she thought, as she took in the majesty of this place.

It was the size of a tennis court, minimum. One side of the room was taken up by just bed.

Miles and miles of it.

Okay, slight exaggeration, but she had no fucking idea where they bought sheets for that bad boy. Bed, Bath, and Beyond sure as fuck didn't stock that kind of sizing.

Royal red curtains and a matching coverlet entwined around vine-like posts. They were the size of Xavier's rugby-player thighs, too. Thick and carved with such detail that she wanted to stroke each one, feel the grain beneath her fingertips.

Each post held different carvings. They were all unique, some with flowers, others with insects engraved into the vines.

The rich dark wood gleamed with the patina of wax and old age.

When Xavier carried her over to it, depositing her down, she quickly grabbed him by the hips and kept him in place.

"What is this room?" she asked, staring around, inadvertently catching sight of her reflection.

Overhead.

She gaped, tilting her head back to better see the mirror.

It was aged, had spots on it in the corners that spoke of it being an antique.

Xavier laughed when he saw where she was looking. "One of our ancestors was a pervert."

Her eyes flashed at the thought of seeing him above her, his ass flexing and working as he fucked her.

She licked her lips, then settled to biting the fleshy bottom one as the possibilities occurred to her.

"It's a bedroom for the king—where he stays when he's here."

"Philippe stays here?" she asked Edward dumbly; he was the one who'd answered her.

She'd known this was no ordinary bedroom. But a bedroom fit for a king? *Whoa.*

He shook his head. "Father never comes here, but tradition would put him in this room if he did. But he wouldn't. He knows this is where I sleep."

"So, I'm sitting on a bed that's held the asscheeks of royalty?"

Both men stilled at that, but Xavier was the first to break into chuckles. He reached down and cupped her cheek. "The way you view the world..." He grinned. "I love your brain, Perry."

She pouted. "It's true." Kings had habits like anyone else. Like farting and burping, and of course, fucking, she thought. Though she held her tongue.

Almost as though he'd read her mind, Edward came and sat next to her on the bed. Her temperature immediately soared at having them both so close to her in such an intimate setting.

Knowing Edward's penchant for sharing, as well as George's, it surprised her that Xavier, not George was here if this had been their intention all along.

Her breathing sped up at the endless possibilities while Edward answered, "The mattress is frequently changed, Perry. The bed has witnessed many sordid acts, I'm sure, but the mattress hasn't."

She looked at him, wide-eyed. "How did you know I was thinking that?"

"Because when you have an inappropriate thought, a special kind of gleam appears in your eye."

"What kind of gleam?" she asked suspiciously.

"I'd have said she looks constipated, just like you, Edward, when you're worried," Xavier retorted, drawing her attention to him.

She whacked him on the side. "I do not look constipated when I'm curious," she grumbled.

"You do," he teased. "Desperation for answers makes you bunged up."

She couldn't stop herself from laughing, but it died a little as she looked around the room.

"Christ, this is a bedroom for kings," she breathed, more to herself than to them.

"It's just a bedroom," Edward countered softly "Nothing more, nothing less."

The look she cut him was wry. "Bullshit."

"Whatever it is, it's built on perfect proportions for more than two people," Xavier commented. "This bed... it's held more than a king and his queen."

"Maybe deviancy is in the blood," she remarked sweetly, giggling when Edward reached over in the blink of an eye and took her mouth.

"Deviant, am I?" he growled under his breath before he speared her lips with his tongue. She moaned into the kiss, loving the rapidness of it, the spontaneity, as well as his means of punishing her for her wicked words.

She smiled though, when Xavier shifted between her thighs. She loved that he was close, loved that he was seeing this.

"Seems like Edward isn't the only deviant in the here and now," was what he said as his hand came to her thigh, and she felt him move his thumb in a circle that made her wish he'd head farther north.

She bit off a sigh when Edward pulled back, nipping her bottom lip as he did.

Her breathing was heavier now, and her eyelids had shuttered to a close in response to the magic the man could work with his mouth.

She wasn't sure why, but ever since it had been taken as granted that the four of them were in this for keeps, they'd barely touched.

With three guys to satisfy, she'd kind of figured she'd be sore as hell. Instead, she was dying here.

She rocked her hips, needing friction and not getting any, thanks to the way her thighs were parted because Xavier was standing in between them. Her hand snaked down, curling over her thigh, her aim evident, but Edward grabbed it.

"Now, why would you do a silly thing like that when we're here to see to anything and everything *you* might need?"

She pouted, though his words sent her blood pressure soaring. Jesus, was this how a pasha of old had felt? Knowing he had hundreds of women to serve him? To give him pleasure?

"You haven't been 'seeing to' much recently."

"Is that a complaint, I hear, Xavier?" Edward asked his cousin, though his eyes were fixed firmly on Perry.

"It sounds like it. In fact, it sounds like the time we gave her to get used to this new situation has been sorely underappreciated."

Her bottom lip popped out. "I didn't say I didn't appreciate it. Just..."

"You're horny?" Xavier asked, humor in his voice.

"Maybe," she retorted, peering up at him from under her lashes. When wide grins were her answer, she had to hide a snicker. Instead, she threw herself back against the mattress and nearly scared the shit out of herself when she came face-to-face with her reflection overhead. "Jesus," she whispered.

There was a lot of her to see.

Her cheeks were bright pink, and her hair had clung to her brow. With just a kiss, he'd managed to make her body temperature skyrocket.

Her eyes were dark and stormy, and her lungs were starved for oxygen, which, of course, meant her breasts were jiggling like Jell-O salad.

"It's intense, isn't it?" Edward said softly, lying beside her, his hand coming to cup her breast as he stared up at the pair of them in the mirror.

"Very," she whispered. "How do you sleep in this thing?"

He chuckled. "You get used to it."

"Pervert," she commented, but there was no heat to the word. "Although, considering I'd like to watch you jack off, I can't blame the mirror for wanting to play dumb witness too."

Silence fell at her words.

"You'd want to watch me jack off?" Edward asked around a croak, but she knew he was amused.

Shit, sometimes it was great that they found her funny, but at times like this, it was mostly annoying.

"Yes," she gritted out, placing her hand on his flat belly and letting her fingers splay against the sharp white shirt he wore. "I do. Very much."

His nostrils flared. "Another time, but I'll hold you to that."

She swallowed at the promise. "You will?"

"Gladly."

She turned her head and stared up at Xavier. "Is this what I think it is?"

Xavier's smile was gentle but earnest. He had a way of smiling with his eyes that warmed her up from the inside out. It was like his heart and soul were involved in each twitch of his lips when he bestowed them on her.

She loved them. They made her feel like she was being granted something very few people were lucky enough to receive. They made her feel unique, and yes, loved, in return. God, what had she done to deserve such good fortune?

"It's whatever you want it to be."

She cut Edward a look, her brow puckering a little as she did. "What about George? I thought this was his..."

"He had other duties to attend to today."

That was a non-answer if ever she'd heard one. She turned to Xavier. "Do you want this?"

"Do you?" he countered, his gaze steady and measured. Free from anger and irritation.

She licked her lips, nodded. Whenever she'd imagined being shared, it hadn't been with Xavier and Edward. She'd always pictured George being somewhere in the threesome.

That he wasn't, jarred her. But what jarred her more was the fact Xavier wanted this too.

"Are you sure about this?" she asked him.

He cocked a brow. "Why wouldn't I be?"

"I didn't realize you were into this kind of thing," she whispered hesitantly.

"I wasn't. But I'm into everything where you're involved."

She gulped, taken aback by that. What had she done to make these men, powerful and rich individuals, look at her the way they did?

It was like they saw someone else when they looked upon her. Like she was Claudia Schiffer or Bella Hadid or someone crazy insanely gorgeous. Not her.

She wasn't gross, by any means. And after her evil stylist was done with her, she looked really nice, but Edward, George, and Xavier nice?

Nuh-uh.

"Why are you looking at me like that?" Xavier asked, but he didn't sound irritated, just perplexed.

"Why me?" she asked hoarsely, emotion bleeding into her voice and making her sound as overwhelmed as she felt. "Why are you willing to do this? T-to change?"

He tilted his head to the side, but Edward caught her attention as he reached for her chin and turned her head to look at him.

"What do you see when you look at yourself in the mirror, Perry?" He turned her back so she could look up at her reflection. Then, he watched her study herself.

Perry shrugged, her eyelids dipping down to shield herself from her reflection which was so, so, *so* there.

"Perry," Xavier urged gently, and she knew he wanted to hear her answer to Edward's question too.

She licked her lips. "Someone plain. Someone not worthy of..." Of them? No. That wasn't it. But... "Not worthy of being a princess."

"But worthy of us?"

Hesitantly, she nodded, wincing as the exact copy above her did the same.

"If anyone knows this, Perry, it's you—we are more than just our station. I'm more than just a crown prince. I'm Edward. Xavier isn't just a duke."

"I know that," she snapped angrily. "I don't understand what you see in me, but I don't have to. Beauty is in the eye of the beholder. I don't question *that*, I don't even question why. Not really. And yes, you're more than just your station. I get that. I know that. I do. But your station is a pretty big fucking part of your lives, Edward. I can't get away from it.

"Marrying you, I'm more than just Mrs. DeSauvier. I'm a crown princess. Marrying you puts me in a whole other stratosphere. *That's* what makes me nervous. What puts me on edge.

"You're going to make me a princess, and if anyone *wasn't* born for that role, it's me."

"And that's where I disagree," Xavier said smoothly, and he reached over, not stopping until his weight was half on her, his forearms coming to rest either side of her head so there was no avoiding his gaze. No avoiding him. "You're beautiful, Perry. Maybe not like a model, but who wants a model and not a real woman? Your eyes are like gemstones, your skin is like cream. I want to kiss the tip of your nose, and make sure that you're always smiling, because a smile from you can bring me to my knees."

Considering she'd been thinking the same about him just moments before, his words made her melt.

"You fill a dress like no one I've ever seen, and you're short enough to bring out all my protective instincts. In heels, I want your legs wrapped around my hips, those damn stilettos digging into my ass. I want to fuck you, I want to love you, I want you to be mine, *ours*. And though it's too much for you to take in right now, the duke wants the same. Because I am the duke. And he is me."

She swallowed, her blood thundering with the fire-licking at those words. "I know that, silly."

"I don't think you do. I'd make you my duchess in a heartbeat, Perry. Because for all I want to fuck you and make love to you until you don't know whether to scream or sob, you're a wonderful woman.

"You're kind and gentle. Generous with yourself. I've never seen that miserable bastard next to me laugh as much as he does when you're around. You bring peace and happiness to my days. Why wouldn't I do anything to keep you in my life?"

"But 'anything' involves sharing me," she whispered.

"Sharing you with two men I love. With two men who need you just as much as I do. You don't know our world, Perry. And I hope to God that the more at ease you become with it, you don't let it affect you. I never want you to change. I want you to always be yourself. Even when you're queen. I never want you to watch your words, or guard your tongue. Just be yourself, Perry, because more than a queen or a princess, you're ours. And we need you. We need you to be Perry."

His words made her mouth tremble and tears prickle. She reached for him, her hand cupping his jaw as she stared deeply into his eyes.

"Thank you."

His smile hit his eyes, but he didn't reply, just reached down and pressed a kiss to her nose.

"Do you want me and Edward to share you?" he asked after he'd kissed her there, then dipped his mouth to her lips.

She gulped.

"Do you want us both to give you pleasure?" Edward questioned, and she turned her head to look at him.

"I-I do."

His mouth curved at her response. "There will come a day when you say those words to me, and they'll change your place in this world. But, nothing else matters but this. Do you understand me, Perry?"

She nodded. Shakily. But it was a nod nonetheless. "How could I not?"

CHAPTER NINE

WHEN XAVIER'S mouth captured hers, Perry immediately shuddered. His weight atop her was like a heavy blanket that pressed her into the comfortable feather-down beneath her. It was like being surrounded on all sides, and though it could have been claustrophobic, instead, it made her feel grounded. Like she was connected in an intrinsic way to him.

That connection was something she needed to feel.

Hell, she needed it with all of them.

This was such an unusual situation, one she had no experience with outside of books, and they never really dealt with the minutiae of day-to-day-life anyway.

They were the run-up to a happily-ever-after, but what came after... that was anyone's guess.

How did a woman keep three men entertained? How did she maintain the ties between them? Binding them closer and closer so there was no distance, nothing in that space between them that could separate and knock the bond out of sync?

Xavier was the first of her DeSauvier men she'd slept with, and touching him like this was a reminder of the heaven he'd made her feel.

She moaned into his mouth as he speared her lips with his tongue. His aggression wasn't a turn-off. She wanted him—needed him—with all that she was.

She lifted her arms and pulled him closer to her by his neck, running her fingers through his hair. The thick russet locks were like silk between the digits, and her hips bowed into the mattress as her lower body clenched with the memory of that silk against her inner thighs.

He tilted her head to the side, and she followed, uncaring, then realized why. Edward was there. He had appeared like a phantom, his lips ghosting along her throat, making her shiver and shudder as his breath skimmed along the tender flesh. Then, his lips were there, his tongue prodding and tasting. She moaned harder when she felt him begin to suck down, and the breath soughed out of her lungs as her eyes popped open.

She'd always been a neck girl. Her boobs weren't all that sensitive, but her neck sure as hell was, and the dual torment of Xavier making love to her mouth and Edward's tender teasing made her melt from the waist down.

She dragged her lips from Xavier's, gripping his hair tighter to pull him back as a whimper escaped her. "Oh God," she bit off, her ass clenching so she arced off the bed a little when Edward sucked down harder. "Oh God," she repeated, her eyes blind as all her nerve endings went to war with her body.

"I think she likes that," Xavier pointed out wryly, and traced the curves of her lips with his tongue.

Beneath him, she was awash with sensation, and they hadn't even touched her. Not properly. This wasn't even second goddamn base.

Holy shit, how was she supposed to survive this when just their kiss was making her feel like she was losing bone mass and was about to turn into primordial goo on the ancient bed?

She focused when Xavier's weight retreated from her chest, but before she could complain, his fingers worked at the few buttons on her shirt. As he parted the sides, he revealed the delicate silk lace of her bra.

One of Edward's hands came up to palpate the tender flesh, while Xavier's fingers nudged the lace out of the way. Before she could do more than squeal, he'd grabbed one of her nipples and had pinched down hard.

Her ass rocked up off the bed in response, and she mewled, "Ouch."

Dark laughter fell from the men, but she couldn't take umbrage. Anyone who could make a woman feel like this without groping her all that much deserved to laugh. Deserved to be fucking triumphant because, sweet Jesus, this felt good.

Better than good.

What had Edward told her? George, too?

That they wanted to overwhelm her with pleasure. That sharing a woman was about her, not them. That they wouldn't stop, didn't want to stop, until she was a wriggling, writhing mass of sensation.

Until now, she hadn't believed them.

Well, they'd made a theist out of her.

Her hands were enfolded in one of the men's strong fingers, and her arms were raised until they were above her head. The movement lifted her shoulders, making her breasts rise higher. Before she could process the new position, Edward's lips trailed down from her throat to her breast, and he sucked down on her nipple through the delicate lace bra.

She clenched her eyes shut as her throat closed too. His lips were like fire against her skin. They set her alight in a way that made her crave him like Perry had never craved before.

She'd sensed the deep, dark desires in him when he'd made love to her before his proposal. She knew he wanted her to submit to him. Not in a BDSM way, just a dominant way.

This man wasn't in charge of his life. Not really. But in this? He was the freakin' king, and he wanted her to know it; he spent the next few moments making her understand that she was a puppet on his strings.

Not in a bad way. Just in a way that made her wonder how he knew her body so well.

Every single one of her pores seemed to surge to life into a well of goose pimples wherever his lips touched. And they touched everywhere. His mouth caressed almost every inch of her torso, but he left her breast alone after that gentle slurp. He had her so hyper-sensitive that she felt like she could jump out of her skin, and the only thing that grounded her was the press of Xavier's cock against her core, and the way his hands were massaging her thighs, gripping her skin as though he were refraining from touching her elsewhere so Edward could work his magic on her.

She knew they hadn't shared before, couldn't even begin to understand what had made Xavier agree to this, when it had always seemed like George and Edward were the ones who wanted to share her. But the truth was, she didn't really give a damn. She just needed them. Needed them in a way that stunned her. Made her question everything she'd ever known about herself.

Then, all thoughts disappeared as Edward retreated. She felt the bed jostle as he left the mattress, and her dazed eyes stared at him a tad blindly as she tried to figure out why he'd stopped.

A gentle smile curved his lips as he took her in. He was amused, but not cruelly.

"Why?" she complained on a soft, husky breath.

"Because we're wearing too many clothes, *carilla*," he whispered, using that Veronian word she always forgot to ask about, but the one he called her when he kissed her goodnight.

Chastely.

God, she was tired of chaste.

She was tired of sensible.

She'd accepted three men into her life, and now she needed them in her bed.

Every day.

Every night.

Call her greedy, but hell, she didn't give a fuck what anyone thought.

She loved these men, she realized, with a ferocity that would burn anyone who dared to argue, that would raise hell if anyone dared to endanger them. From the depths of her need, she knew that to be the truth. She could only be this way with them, crave them like this, because her heart trusted them.

With them, she could be free, and she couldn't wait to soar, to explore the liberation they offered her with each kiss.

When he began to shrug out of his jacket, she watched greedily, then his shirt came next. As his hands went to his belt buckle, she licked her lips, the desperate need to taste him so urgent at that moment, it was like she'd been denied breath.

After he dropped his pants, stepping out of them and his socks and shoes at the same time, she came face to face with an Edward that was totally nude.

She hadn't seen him completely undressed. He'd fucked her in his office while they'd both been clothed, and while it ranked as one of the hottest experiences of her life, it began to pale in comparison to the sight of him in the raw.

Dear God, the man was hung. But more than that, he was hard and taut in all the right places. His skin was supple and golden as it flexed over hard muscles. She licked her lips once more at the sight of his happy trail, craving the taste of him against her mouth, needing to drive him as wild as he'd driven her moments before.

She cut a look to Xavier, whose hands were still massaging her thighs. His gaze was fixed firmly on her, and when he realized he'd caught her attention, he rocked his hips, dragging his cock down the length of her pussy.

Thanking Christ for skirts, she whispered, "You're wearing too many clothes."

"The same could be said for you," he teased, but with a squeeze of his hands, he lowered her thighs and stepped away.

Though she wanted to pout, she also recognized that this was the quickest way to see the two hottest men on God's green Earth get naked.

He stripped, revealing paler skin than Edward's, a creamy gold that made her want to lap him up like a kitten given a saucer of milk. She fell in awe at the sight of both men as they revealed themselves to her.

Not that they stood there for her perusal. Edward was already back on the bed, and he'd taken Xavier's spot between her thighs.

Against her pantyhose, she felt his naked cock rub against the nylon and whimpered at the pressure.

"Do you want to be naked, baby?" he whispered as he unfastened the front clasp of her bra. When her breasts spilled out, too big as goddamn usual, he grabbed them in his meaty fists and began to squeeze them.

Her eyes widened as he squeezed to the point of pain, until the flesh turned an angry shade of pink. Then, with a careful hand, he tapped the skin with his fingers.

Unable to speak, she watched as he repeated that twice more, tapping different spots, making her doubly sensitive in those primed areas.

Breathless, she watched as he lowered his head and tugged her nipple between his teeth.

In every other aspect of his life, Edward was charm itself. Debonair and charismatic. Controlled in a way that couldn't be healthy.

But here?

She knew this was where he ran wild, and she loved that the liberation he made her feel was something they could share.

Then, she clenched her eyes shut as he bit down hard on her nipple. She grabbed his head as she squealed, her nails dragging over his scalp as she disturbed the tight waves of his hair.

"Ow," she whined, then whimpered when he sucked it harder between his lips. "Oh, damn, don't stop."

Xavier chuckled, and she realized he was watching. Before she could even be embarrassed, he climbed onto the mattress at her side, where Edward had been before, and with his change in position, something caught her eye.

Their reflection.

Her mouth gaped at the sight above her.

Two naked men—like Adonis reincarnated, the pair of them—were tending to her. Worshipping *her*.

She was dressed, but she was splayed out wantonly, and from the way they were staring at her, caressing her, loving her, it was evident that though she was outnumbered, she was the center of this deliciously sordid little display.

At this moment, whether they knew it or not, they'd made her their queen.

And that realization ignited her senses.

She tried to study the little she could see of Edward's expression in the mirror, but all that was really visible was her bright pink breasts where he'd squeezed and tapped. She'd have marks there tomorrow, and maybe that should have upset her, but it didn't.

It further fired her blood.

She wanted their marks on her.

She wanted hickeys all over her goddamn body. She wanted to know who she belonged to... but more than that, she wanted to return the favor. Wanted them to know she was their queen as they were her kings.

It was a driving need that inspired her into action.

Before either man could complain, she reared upwards, using momentum to sit up and knock Edward out of the way. She'd had enough of being worshipped—now, it was time to get in on the action.

She scrambled onto her knees, quickly tugging off her shirt and flinging her bra off her half-naked form.

The speed of her actions had caused them concern, she knew. They'd thought she was rejecting them, when she was doing anything but.

God, she wanted them. Inside her, claiming her. The only thing missing was George, but that was for another time. Another day. And because of her decisions, each one of which had brought her here, to this moment, they had all the time in the world.

She reached behind her and unzipped the fastener at the back of her skirt. Then, sweeping her legs out from under her, she wriggled out of it and flung that to the ground as well. Which left her covered only in pantyhose, and she'd never loathed them as much as she did right at that moment.

Before she could do more than squeal, however, Edward reached for their waistband, then slid his fingers down the seam at her crotch. Within seconds, they were torn. A gaping hole right above her sex, making the red lace of her panties burn brighter now they weren't shaded by the tan hose.

His fingers dug down, not stopping until he reached the gusset, and then he slipped a digit underneath and touched her. Finally.

The shock had her jerking backwards, and her arms flailed back to stop herself from slamming into the mattress.

Of course, that wasn't necessary, not when Xavier was there to catch her. He supported her, the pair of them watching as Edward, using his free hand, tore a larger hole in the hose, and used the new slack to pull her panties farther aside.

The sight of his fingers exploring the crevice of her sex was a revelation. She whimpered as he slid through her juices, not stopping until he'd penetrated her, thrusting two more fingers inside her as they watched.

Xavier's hands moved around her body, one reaching for the swell of her breast, the other joining Edward. She whimpered as he rubbed her clit, taking the pearl and nipping it between finger and thumb.

They were being rough with her today, and she loved it because she knew it meant they were on edge.

But so was she. Her hips began to rock of their own volition, back and forth at a pace that made her belly muscles ache, as both men tormented and teased her. She felt close to detonation when Xavier reached down and nipped the side of her throat.

Close, so close, she realized. With barely any foreplay, she was so damn near to completion, it beggared belief.

Then, though she was too dazed to figure out what the hell was going on, both men looked up, and she knew they were peering at each other.

Silently communicating *something*.

She tensed, preparing herself for whatever that something was, and she was right to.

With a squeal, she was rearranged. Xavier swiftly moved his hand to her hips, and with a smooth motion that spoke of his damn strength, she was suddenly pushed forward and onto her hands and knees.

The position put her face remarkably close to Edward's cock, and Xavier's dick deliciously near her pussy.

Her hair tumbled loose of the clip she'd put it in hours before, and she felt hot and sweaty, over sensitized in a way she'd never felt before.

She wanted to look up, wanted to see herself bent over for them. The desire was addictive. She'd thought she'd be nervous, shyly embarrassed at them seeing all of her, but Perry realized she didn't give a damn.

They didn't care about her weight, didn't care about the silvery stretch marks on the sides of her breasts, the dimples on her ass.

They just wanted her.

All of her.

And the notion added to that glorious sense of freedom spinning through her veins.

Their queen.

That was what she was. And this just hammered it home.

THE SIGHT of her on her hands and knees was enough to make Xavier sweat. His cock was hard, pounding with his pulse as the desperate urge to fill her swept over him.

He watched his cousin with heavy-lidded eyes, enjoying how Edward grabbed Perry's hair with one hand, and guided his cock to her lips with the other.

Perry's eagerness was evident, and enough to make him smile even through the exquisite pain of his arousal.

Seeing Edward in this way wasn't how he'd expected the evening to pan out. But when Perry had fallen asleep on the settle downstairs, when the two of them had played more music together than they had in twenty years, their old tenuous link had rejoined them.

A link that had slowly been crumbling ever since Edward's kidnapping.

His cousin had been returned to him, but he hadn't been the same boy.

Each year, Edward had turned in on himself more. Putting distance between him and the whole family, not just Xavier. But Xavier was the one who'd been affected the most.

They'd always been close. Like peas in a pod, his grandmother had always declared. And though he knew she'd be scandalized at the idea of them sharing a woman, Xavier didn't give a fuck.

Seeing Edward's cock was disconcerting, granted, but the feeling of the bond between them surging to life... that was priceless.

It wasn't like he wanted to *see* his cousin's dick. Because he sure as shit didn't.

What he wanted to see was Perry. He wanted to see her lost to the pleasure, a slave to sensation, forever abandoned to the heat of the moment.

That was what drove him wild.

He loved the sounds she made as she sucked Edward's cock, he adored the moans that escaped her, moans that were proof this wasn't just for Edward but for herself.

She wanted this. Every inch of her screamed it, and they answered the call.

Edward grunted, and the noise caught Xavier's attention. Their gazes clashed, and a silent conversation passed between them.

You okay?

Yeah. I need her. Xavier's eyelids lowered, shielding his expression as the truth of that hit home. God, how he needed her.

Take her then. She's yours.

Ours.

Edward's eyes flared at the last, and he gritted his teeth as he focused his attention on Perry once more.

Xavier grabbed ahold of his cock and began to slide it through her juicy cunt. God, she was sopping wet. So slick and so hot, he felt sure he'd fucking combust by the time he was inside her.

He was sheathed in a condom, had used the moments after he'd stripped to cover himself, and though he resented the covering because it denied him the true heat of her, he was past caring.

He needed to be inside her, because he felt like he was fucking dying here.

Notching his cock to her gate, he began to pump his hips, loving the way the throat of her sex caressed him, silkily squeezing him in a way that had his fingers digging into her hips. She wriggled beneath him, her hips rocking, her back arching as he maintained position. Not filling her, not even moving, just enjoying the sensation of being inside her.

He ran a hand over the curve of her spine, loving how she responded like a cat as she rounded her shoulders. Gooseflesh followed the move, and he raked his nails down her sides, hearing the whimpers escape her as she responded to the touch.

It was torture to stay so shallow when her depths called to him, but he did so for a reason. He wanted her to beg. Needed to hear her reveal her craving for him.

He wanted to fuck her so hard, they punched through time and found next week. But he stayed where he was, continued to tease and torment her as Edward grabbed ahold of her hair and fucked her mouth. He shaped his cock through her cheek, touched her mouth, rimmed her lips with his fingers as he urged her into taking him how he needed to be taken.

She was like liquid beneath their hands. Merging and reforming however they needed her.

There was no doubt here. No embarrassment or lack of surety that would put her on edge.

She flowed because she'd given herself to them. She trusted them, and that was the most priceless gift of all.

Out of nowhere, her hands came up and she grabbed Edward's hips and pushed him back. A yelp escaped her when Edward's hand tightened on her hair, but he swiftly dropped his firm hold when she shifted.

"Goddamnit, Xavier! Why aren't you moving?" she sobbed out, the breath soughing from her lungs as she twisted around to glower at him.

But it was a glare filled with frantic need. A desperation that more than matched his own.

Before she could do more than open her lips to scold him further, he slammed into her. Every inch of his hardness claiming every inch of her softness.

Her eyes rounded before a scream escaped her, and she fell face first into the bed. Well, she would have done, if Edward hadn't supported her, helped her upright as Xavier pistoned his hips into her.

"Ohmigod, ohmigod," the litany continued in panicked mumbles as he plowed his shaft into her, fucking her with all he had to give. She was shaking beneath him, her body one massive quaking shape as she took every inch of him.

But Edward wasn't content with that.

He used his hold on her to position her once more, and grabbing his cock, he shoved it against her lips.

She opened her mouth like she was parched for water and he'd pressed a glass to her lips. She slurped him down with a greed that beggared belief, sucked him, swallowed him whole. Taking everything he had to give too.

The sight of her—so eager, so needy—was like a bullet to the brain.

He let out a hoarse yell as he emptied himself inside her, fucking her harder, deeper, faster, needing to expend every ounce of his release inside her. Like his reaction triggered Edward's, his cousin let out a hoarse yell too. He pulled back though, letting cum spurt from his shaft to coat Perry's face.

She froze a second, then jerked forward, hungrily seeking Edward's release in a way that made Xavier's eyes want to cross.

Jesus, she was as tenacious in this as she was in everything else, and she milked them both dry.

But she hadn't come.

He hadn't felt the telltale clenching of her pussy muscles about him, and he knew, though he wasn't sure how, that she was so charged, release was close, but just out of reach.

He slipped his arms through hers, and used his grip on her armpits to jerk her upright. The move had his softening cock changing angle inside her, and she mewled and stopped struggling as he rearranged her atop him.

Like it was as natural as breathing, Edward dropped down to the mattress, and in less time than it took for Perry to gulp down one more mouthful of air, Edward was on her.

It should have been weird. Hell, it was, he guessed. His cousin was close to his cock. That was a big no-no. But this wasn't about him. It wasn't about Edward.

It was about Perry.

And it wasn't like Edward was even touching him. From the wails and squeaks and mewling whimpers, Ed was focused on her clit.

The sounds had his cock hardening inside her. He knew he wouldn't come again, but the fullness had her slumping against him. Then, just as she did that, she tensed, her hands gripping Edward's hair as she fucked his face. Her hips jerked back and forth as she rode his tongue.

Within seconds, her cunt was clenching down hard on him, and he felt her orgasm before she even released the keening cry that spoke of her climax.

She was, as in most things, the most beautiful thing he'd ever seen.

And she was his.

Theirs.

From that moment on and forevermore.

No more doubts filled him. No more worries for the future, or concerns about how this would work.

They'd make it work.

Or die trying.

Because Xavier refused to give this up. Refused to give *her* up.

He loved her, and she loved him, *them*. Nothing else mattered.

CHAPTER TEN

"HOW'S IT GOING, CASSIE?"

The phone call from the other woman came as a surprise, Perry wouldn't lie. But it was a good surprise. A great one.

Perry had always found it hard to make friends, and Cassie seemed so down-to-earth, so normal in a world of crazy courtiers and sniping political players, that she really hoped the other woman liked the idea of them growing closer too.

"Perry, thank God you answered."

She blinked at the relief in Cassie's voice. "What's wrong?" she asked, then gulped when the door to her bedroom opened and George popped inside. "Cassie," she mouthed, when he cocked a brow at her.

He nodded, wandered over to the drinks' tray that sat atop an antique Chinese bureau in a rich, chestnut mahogany in one corner of her Tulip Room quarters, and poured himself a few fingers of what looked like whiskey.

With one eye on him, she watched as he moved around the room. He seemed at ease to let her carry on with her conversation, so she did.

"M-Marcus isn't coming over."

A slight note in Cassie's voice told Perry she was drunk. "Ever?" she asked sadly, hurting for the woman as well as her children.

"I don't know. He told me I could send him the divorce papers, and he'd rip them up into a million pieces." A despairing grumble sounded down the line. "He said I was his, but that I couldn't expect him just to give up his life in New York because he'd had a health scare."

"Wow, that's pigheaded."

"Pigheaded?" she shrieked. "It's insane."

Perry's lips twitched at Cassie's subsequent roar of outrage. She could tell even George heard it, because his eyes widened. She just shook her head, and mouthed, "Later." To Cassie, she said, "Just give him some time. That's all you can do."

"He doesn't have time, dammit. I didn't move us halfway across the world on a lark, Perry. The idiot's doctor told me..." A quiver entered Cassie's voice. "Marcus wouldn't survive another heart attack. It was bad, Perry. Very, very bad. He might need a pacemaker, but he's putting that off, too, because there's some stupid deal about to go down.

"I told him, what's the point in earning a three-million-dollar bonus if he's dead? But the moron just told me that the doctors were exaggerating. How can one smart man be such a fucking dimwit?"

She knew she shouldn't find Cassie's despair amusing, but the other woman's no holds barred attitude, after weeks of bullshitting, was a breath of fresh air. Perry coughed out a laugh. "Oh, Cassie, you really don't pull your punches, do you?"

"Apparently, I'm not hard enough if that dick won't listen to me."

"It sounds like he's worried about money. Maybe he's focusing on the bonus. Maybe once that comes through, he'll relax?"

Silence fell as Cassie processed that. "You know about our past, don't you? Well, *his* past, I mean."

"Yes. It seems to reason that he'd be very sensitive about money if his family lost everything."

"Even if it kills him?"

"You know him better than I do. Plus," she said on a sigh, "men can be really stupid, can't they?"

"You're so not wrong there," came the grim retort. "I mean, he's always been sensitive about money."

"All I know is what you're telling me," Perry broke in. "I could be completely wrong. It's just odd that you mentioned that over everything else, you know? His bonus. It's like you didn't think it was worth mentioning, but subconsciously, you did.

"Do you want to break up with him?"

George's mouth fell open at that as he slumped into the sofa opposite her.

"No. I love him. The dick."

Perry laughed. "Well then, no more talk of divorce, eh? It's not going to make him do what you want him to."

"No. It hasn't worked so far, has it?"

"Not really," Perry said with a grimace. "Just... I know you don't think he has time, but if he's so worried about money, then, he's not going to stop, Cassie."

She blew out a breath, but for some reason, Perry thought she sounded calmer. "I'm sorry I called you so late."

"Don't be."

"I had no one else to turn to. I haven't told anyone else about Marcus, you know?" She swallowed, then, on a soft whisper, asked, "Do you want to meet for afternoon tea tomorrow? I'll understand if you don't want to because I sound like a crazy person."

"I'd love to meet up, but I have a dress fitting." Perry paused. "You wouldn't want to go with me, would you?"

"Are you sure you'd want me there?" came the cautious reply.

"I need someone on my side against Marianne," Perry teased.

A groan sounded down the line. "You just gave me a reason not to come...but how about we head out for coffee afterward?"

"It's a date."

Cassie laughed. "It is. Except I don't put out for coffee."

Laughter snorted from Perry. "That's good to know. I'll see you tomorrow, Cassie."

"Great. Thanks for listening. See you later."

As Perry put the phone down, she glanced at George. "You look like you needed that."

George scowled down at his glass—her attention might have been on Cassie, but she'd seen him refill the tumbler three times. "Bad day," he grumbled, then his scowl darkened. "Cassie filed for a divorce?"

"It's not my story to tell," she said on a sigh. "But no. It was a threat. She wants to move back here, and Marcus doesn't."

"He's ill?"

"He had a bad heart attack."

George rubbed his chin. "Edward and Xavier never mentioned anything to me about that."

"I don't think many people know."

"They'll go apeshit if that's the case."

"Then, don't tell them," Perry advised. "Cassie has already put him under a lot of pressure—and he's not caving in."

"They're having money troubles?"

"No. But Marcus won't leave New York because he's waiting on some deal that will give him a great bonus."

"Idiot," George grumbled under his breath, making Perry cock a brow. When he saw her surprise, he wriggled his shoulders. "Marcus is Edward's age, Cassie is mine."

"So, what? She's more your friend than he is?"

"Yeah." He grunted. "She used to be, anyway. Before they moved to New York...then, everything changed. Still," he said, his tone brightening a little, "it sounds like you two are getting close."

"Maybe."

"I'm glad. She's a good friend to have. Very solid, stable, and she gives a crap about life outside of court."

Perry tilted her head to the side. "I'm glad you approve," she teased. "Now, what's wrong with you?"

"Nothing. Just..." He sighed, then pressed his own head back so he was staring up at the frescoed ceiling. "It's been a long day."

"Why?" She hadn't seen him since that morning at breakfast, so wasn't all that sure what mischief he'd been making.

"Another session at Parliament. God, it bores me shitless."

She grimaced because she knew how much he loathed politics. "Do you have to do it?"

"No choice. Now that I'm back, I have to take up my responsibilities, but that doesn't mean I have to like them." He took another sip of his whiskey, then peered at her, "I spoke with Xavier this afternoon."

"So? I imagine you do most afternoons."

"Yes. But he told me what happened two days ago. You kept that to yourself."

Her cheeks flamed with heat. "Oh."

He snorted. "Oh? Is that all you have to say?" He sat upright, and she could tell the topic excited him. "Did you enjoy it?"

She narrowed her eyes at him. "What do you think?"

"I think you did. More than you thought you would."

Her nod was stiff. "You realize how smug you sound?"

"I do," he joked. "Still, I can cope. Would you do it again?"

"Yes."

"My, you're a woman of few words at the moment."

"I just... I'm a little uncomfortable talking about it."

"Why?"

"Because..." She hesitated—was that why? "I don't know really."

He eyed her over the brim of his tumbler. The ice clinked together as he did so, and her mouth watered with the sudden need for a whiskey of her own—that would make this conversation easier, right? "Because I wasn't involved?"

"Maybe."

"You don't have to worry about my being jealous, Perry," he told her softly. "I'm not. I wish I had been there, of course. I wish I'd seen. But there will be plenty of other times, plenty more fun to be had." His grin was wide and true. "I just wanted to check in with you... I knew it was strange you hadn't told me about it."

She wriggled her shoulders. "I don't always want to talk about things like that."

"I know, but you have to. We have to be open with one another, sweetheart. You see that, don't you?"

"I do, but, *that?*"

"That more than anything," he told her wryly, cocking a brow. "The minute you stop enjoying being with us is the moment we have to sit down and reassess everything."

Because she guessed he was right, she nodded. Slipping from her armchair, she padded over to the sofa where he was. Curling up at his side, she pressed her face into his arm after she'd tucked her feet under her butt.

"I did like it. A lot," she whispered softly, the heat in her cheeks flaring to life once more. "I want to do it again."

"I'm glad," he murmured, not pushing the subject, not asking her for more than she was ready to give as he rested his head once more.

"I love you, George," she told him, needing to make the affirmation, even though there was no reason to fret.

He pressed his lips to the crown of her head. "I love you too, Perry." He let out a soft, amused laugh. "Even if you are making me help with the wedding arrangements."

"You know you love it, really."

He sniffed. "I love *you*," he corrected. "And I know you're not only crap at that kind of thing, but you loathe it and it bores you shitless. For me, I'm bored senseless. You trump my boredom levels. However, expect to wear the sexiest goddamn lingerie as you walk down the aisle as payment."

She couldn't withhold the laughter that burst from her lips. "Don't ever change, George, please?"

He sniggered before he took another sip of his whiskey, and as they fell into silence, both just enjoying being together, the warmth of the early autumnal night surrounding them as well as the soft tunes of Damien Rice's O album playing in the background, she knew they were both at a peace that was of their own making.

And it was a peace that was a thousand times more powerful because of that.

CHAPTER ELEVEN

THE SIGHT of future in-laws waiting by the door should inspire terror in anyone. But for Perry, her in-laws-to-be were king and queen of a nation that commanded the respect of some of the world's heavyweights. Why?

Because Veronia was hardcore.

They had a military to be reckoned with, a GDP that rubbed elbows with Norway—thanks to oil fields in over two-thirds of their territory—and more than that, they were a haven for the super wealthy...

Veronia might be small in stature, but it was one of the big boys on the playground, and its two leaders were standing in her doorway, smiling pleasantly at her.

In the month since the announcement of her engagement, she'd come to distrust that particular smile.

It usually meant they wanted her to do something, and as they were the fucking king and queen, it wasn't like she could refuse them.

As a result, she'd had deportment lessons, been trained in the various ways of sitting—because yes, there were hours-long classes on the right way to put your asscheeks on a chair—and had been prodded and poked in ways that even with three men in her bed, she wasn't accustomed to.

Those smiles meant business, she'd come to realize.

And business wasn't something she liked.

Sighing at the sight of them, she let her shoulders slump before she remembered that Marianne would smack her hand when she slouched. She quickly straightened up while asking, "Yes?"

They'd also told her off for calling them "Your Highnesses," but she didn't feel sufficiently at ease to call them their given names.

Not that they weren't nice to her.

They were.

They just always wanted her to do shit.

And Perry's to-do list was ridiculously high without them adding nonsense classes to it. Anything from how to greet POTUS properly—yeah, that visit was going to be in her future at some point, *yikes*—to the disconcerting number of ways she'd be expected to spearhead charitable campaigns, all while being able to waltz better than a *Dancing with the Stars* pro.

"Perry, we've come to take you to Drake," Philippe told her cheerfully, that untrustworthy smile still gracing his lips.

Drake was the head of security, and that they were there, not Edward, had to bode poorly for the subsequent hours ahead of her.

Gulping, she asked, "Drake? I didn't realize I had an appointment with him today."

"You didn't, not officially. This is one that Philippe and I arranged. We want to discuss something with you." Marianne swept out a hand, inviting her out into the hall.

Despite herself, Perry took note of the gesture. The way her mother-in-law was smiling was still an epic tell—something unpleasant awaited her. But how Marianne managed to make something an order with a simple sweep of her hand?

Jesus, that was priceless.

She eyed Marianne's fingers. There were more rings on there than usual, and she was wearing a man's Rolex. The bulky piece was surprisingly elegant on her slender wrist.

"It was a gift," Marianne informed her, when she saw where Perry's gaze was trained.

Blushing, Perry cleared her throat. "I wasn't looking at your watch."

Marianne frowned. "Then what were you looking at?"

"Your hand." She mimicked the pose. "How did you do that?"

Marianne sighed—a sign she was losing patience. It was something Perry was getting used to hearing. "How do I do what?"

"With a wave of your hand, make something compulsory."

Philippe, though he'd tried to remain stoic from the moment she'd started gawking at his wife's hand, snorted. He cut Marianne a look, who shot him a disapproving glower, then shrugged. "She's funny. You can't deny the girl is humorous."

Marianne sighed once more. "I don't. But the future queen isn't supposed to be humorous, Philippe."

The king grunted. "I don't see why not. This is a different age, Marianne. You and I both know it. The young people don't want stiff formality. They want someone they can aspire to be."

Perry blinked. "Nobody is going to aspire to be me, Philippe."

There was a kind twinkle in his eye. "Now, we both know that's not true. Harvard is one of the best schools in the world, and you managed to not only study there on scholarship, but worked there for a time before you moved onto MIT... you're an expert in your field, and you're going to be royalty soon. You're a strong, capable woman, Perry. That's something any parent wants their daughter to emulate."

Though she was touched by his words, the idea of any small child emulating her made her nauseated.

Still, she smiled through the torment. "I'm glad you think so," she said, choosing diplomacy over the truth.

A fact Marianne seemed to be aware of, if the approving look she sent Perry's way was anything to go by.

Perry kind of hated herself for perking up at Marianne's obvious pleasure in her. It made her feel like a six-year-old again, tugging at her father's jeans as she begged him to teach her how to milk their small herd of Friesian cows.

He'd never been an overly affectionate father—more like one of those men who lived by the earth and died by it. Who knew how to stare at the sky in the morning and configure the weather for the next week. Who could figure, with a few touches here and there, what was going on with a nursing mama whose calf wasn't faring well. The man had no diplomas, didn't have a lick of university schooling to his name, and yet, he was one of the smartest men she knew.

Because she'd never wanted to be a farmer, she'd felt guilty for most of her childhood. Overcompensating had made her pester her dad, and he hadn't particularly appreciated it... the same went with Marianne.

So, when she received one lick of approval from the queen, it always made her stand a little taller. Grimacing, she focused on the royals in front of her. Marianne's coveted approval was disappearing as Perry lingered in the doorway.

"Well?" she asked softly, but there was steel lining that one word.

She gulped. "Of course." Closing her bedroom door behind her, she stepped into the hall and found herself being shepherded to a section of the palace she'd never been to before.

Considering Xavier had taken her on a guided tour, she was kind of miffed at being in new territory.

Still, she hadn't missed much.

These were definitely staff quarters. The hallways were painted gray, and notice boards lined the walls. Each panel was for a different section of staff. Some notes for the groundskeeping staff, others for the kitchen.

She took it all in under the light from a flickering, and irritating, fluorescent bulb. Their heels tapped against the painted concrete as they headed down a long corridor. The door at the bottom, the only aperture in the hallway, was their apparent destination.

If she'd been escorted by police, she'd have felt like she was being guided to a torture chamber, for there was something very prison-like about the hall. No windows, dark, grim. And was it her imagination, or did the corridor seem to be growing narrower? Shorter too. Like the door to enter Willy Wonka's factory or something.

She bit her lip when Philippe strode two steps ahead to open the door for them both.

Perry was pretty happy to see a big, bulky man behind a desk—the bulk was offset by a cheery smile that further relaxed her. The windows at his back revealed a pleasant section of the garden ahead, and the lack of torture devices in the office filled her with relief.

Whatever this was about, it didn't involve them sticking pins down her nails.

Chiding herself for being fanciful—the Veronian Inquisition, which had happened around the time of the Spanish one, was far in the past—she watched as the king and queen took a seat in front of the desk, while the man behind it remained standing.

Uncertain of what to do, or where to sit, she stared at the man, head tilting to the side as she studied him.

"Are you Drake?" she asked, unable to hold her tongue when the silence continued.

He nodded. "Heard much about me?"

She grimaced—George had complained, frequently, about Drake's high-handedness as he rearranged a new security detail about the Prince's person.

Now, whenever she, Edward, George, and Xavier got together, there was a team of twelve people guarding them.

It was bordering on the ridiculous. She felt like she was on a football team sometimes.

"I take it from that grimace Prince George is still whining?" Drake didn't sound too displeased by such a prospect, a fact which made her lips curve.

George was one of those people who, with a smile and a word, could wangle almost anything from someone.

He didn't do it maliciously—it was just a part of his nature. He was one of those sunny people who could charm the birds from the trees.

Most of the time, that ability irritated her. He could switch it on and off depending on his mood. Though she knew it wasn't intended as a falsehood, knew it was a part of his princely persona, it made her feel like he was playing a role. She never wanted that when she was with him. She wanted him to be himself.

It had taken years for her to break down those walls. And it was why he spent most of his time with her teasing her or being a snark. Because he could. Because she'd worked hard to get him to stop being a prince in her presence.

So, when someone else appreciated that side of his nature too—and she could tell that Drake most definitely did by his satisfaction at George's grumbling—she found she liked being in similar company.

"He doesn't understand why they follow him to the pool," she told him, folding her arms across her chest. "Says they want to perv over his muscles."

Drake and Philippe chuckled in shared amusement, though Marianne gasped in horror.

"He didn't imply such a thing?" she declared, making the words half a question and half a statement.

"You know our son, Marianne. What do you think?" Philippe retorted. "The boy's incorrigible." He didn't sound too displeased by that fact, either.

Drake shot her a grin. "Well, I'll be certain to reassure him that his new guards are, most definitely, married. To females. They're not interested in his package, or anything else he has to offer."

"Giles!" Marianne complained.

Drake merely rolled his eyes as he took a seat again, and Perry found herself slightly overwhelmed. Considering that the man was staff, an employee, he certainly behaved casually.

Even with the Guardians of the Keys, women who were supposed to be her friends and allies, Marianne was formal and polite. It always made Perry feel uncomfortable, put her on edge. But it also helped her understand why it had been so hard to break down George's walls.

They were ingrained.

Even with people who weren't necessarily staff—like the Guardians of the Keys, who were nobility and hand-picked by the family to work in the most intimate aspects of their lives—the DeSauviers maintained a strict distance...

It was like sharing a house with strangers, and it was one of the reasons why she didn't want Masonbrook for her first marital residence.

Once he was rocking in his chair, seated behind a desk that was neat to a fault, Giles still managed to tower over the wide surface. He was a tall man anyway, but he was wide at the shoulder, and beneath his jacket, there was the bulge of a holstered weapon.

Considering he rode a desk and didn't work active duty, the gun seemed unnecessary...but what did she know?

Some people were obsessed with being armed. Her daddy was one of them.

"Perry," Marianne started, sounding pained. "Drake wants to discuss your situation once you're wed."

"What kind of situation?" she asked warily, finding it odd that she was still standing. It reminded her of standing in front of the principal, and most definitely being found wanting.

It was incredibly difficult not to cross her arms over her chest or to fidget.

"Edward has indicated that you wish to live in Grosvenor House?" Drake asked.

She bit her lip. "Yes. Just for a while. Until I find my bearings." Though she'd taken Xavier's words to heart, every day she spent here at the palace sucked at her soul. It helped that she and her men were spending more time together, forging the bonds between them whenever they could, but it didn't chase off the chill that came as part and parcel of this way of life.

It was cold and formal, and though she'd never lived in such luxury, it didn't bring her peace. In fact, she'd only found that in two places.

One, her office.

Helping to resolve Veronia's developing ecological crisis was coming to be a means of escape for her. Though she'd always put her all into everything she worked on, now, her time was precious. Over half of it was being wasted on learning the useless crap that would make her a perfect princess.

As a result, the time she could spend on her work was a source of comfort to her. In a world where nothing made much sense, where having to learn that one ate asparagus with one's fingers and never used a knife to cut a bread roll at the table was deemed important, her position as aid was imperative to her very sense of self.

Her other source of comfort was bed.

Well, comfort wasn't the right word.

The way George, Xavier, and Edward had been of late... she was lucky she could walk at all. Never mind pitter-patter around in the ridiculous heels that were her new uniform.

"That's fine," Drake was saying, jolting her from thoughts that had taken on a decided X-rating. "But you are aware you'll require staff of your own, correct?"

"Edward has enough guards to cover me, surely?" she asked, utterly discomfited by the notion of having even more men hovering around.

The guards had to know what was going on between her and the DeSauvier men, surely?

But when she looked at Giles, his beefy features expressed no disgust or distaste, just a pleasant blandness that she knew was to make her feel she had no say in the matter.

Not by one inch of the twitch of his brow did he indicate there was a means of persuading him otherwise.

She sighed, ceding to him. He *did* know better than her. But the idea of even more guards hanging around made it seem likelier they'd be found out.

She bit her lip, wondering who'd bust the biggest gut when they discovered she was sleeping with three men—not just the crown prince.

"Was there something else?" she asked quietly, feeling her stomach twist at the idea of someone knowing their secret. And because she felt like she was on trial, as the only person standing here, it was hard not to feel like she was being judged.

"Yes. The arrangements have been made for you to fly over in the jet to Tennessee. You are aware you'll have to remain on the jet, and that your parents will have to be chauffeured to the airfield, correct?"

She bit her lip. "I'm aware. But would it really do any harm for me to go home for the night?"

"Yes. It requires more staff. Staff we can't afford to send over to the States when all hands-on-deck are needed in the run up to the wedding." Drake cut her a look. "Edward told me you agreed with all this when he came to me with your request."

"I did," she said sullenly. "I-I just felt like visiting home."

His eyes softened. "I understand, and ordinarily, it wouldn't be an issue. But they'll be arriving a few days before the wedding. We'll be stretched to our limits, and considering the recent circumstances... I don't want to take any risks."

"In the future, I'll be able to visit them?" she asked eagerly, surprising herself with how badly she wanted him to say yes. Ironic, considering she hadn't been home in four damn years.

"Of course," he told her, surprise lacing his tone. "Although it would be easier for them to visit Veronia."

She shook her head. "Their work wouldn't allow it." She didn't mention the fact they were farmers; Marianne always looked on the brink of passing out whenever she happened to mention her folks had a farm.

Her deportment teacher had already informed her that she was supposed to say, "My parents invest heavily in agriculture," whenever someone asked about her family.

Cue eye-roll.

"Will Edward be coming with me?" she asked. Though Perry knew it was strange not to be asking her fiancé that particular question, some things were out of his hands.

Prince or not, she was coming to realize that their head of security often had more say in their lives than she'd have liked.

Drake shook his head. "You'll be traveling alone."

She gnawed at her lip, trying and failing not to be angry about his softly uttered words.

"On another matter of business, Drake has agreed to act as witness on our behalf, Perry," Philippe murmured softly, after the silence fell and grew so loud that it had a volume all of its own.

She frowned. "Witness to what?"

"A prenuptial agreement."

Marianne said the term as though she'd just dropped an F-bomb in front of the Pope.

Perry frowned at the tone, but shrugged. "Okay. Where do I sign?" she asked, heading over to the desk, atop which Drake had slid a very, very, *very* thick file of paper.

She grimaced at its thickness. "Look, I know I should read this. I really know I should, but if we get divorced, I'm not going to end up owing you anything, am I?"

Philippe blinked. "No. Why would you?"

"Don't you know how prenuptial agreements work, Perry?" Marianne asked kindly.

"Of course, I do. I was being facetious," she said on a huff. "I don't want anything other than what I'm bringing to the marriage. Which, in comparison to Edward, is buttkiss." She shrugged again. "I just don't want to sign and then learn that I'll owe you my kidney if we split years down the line."

Philippe's lips twitched. "No. Your kidneys can remain your own. Although, if at some point down the line we do get ill and are in need of a kidney, I'll know to knock on your door to see if we're a blood match."

She grinned, charmed by this teasing side of Philippe's nature. He'd always been pretty somber around her. This was the first time she'd seen him laugh freely.

Maybe there was something in her DNA that acted like weed around DeSauvier males. She always seemed to make them chuckle.

Uncertain whether that was an advantage or a disadvantage, she murmured, "Do you have a pen?"

Drake placed one in her hand, and she quickly scanned the sheets, seeking the dotted line. There were many places her signature was required, but just as she poised the pen on the first line, the door burst open.

Startled, she jolted and dropped the pen. Seeing her fiancé standing there like the Angel of Death, she frowned as he burst into a flurry of infuriated Veronian.

It was a funny language. Romantic edges, but with a heart made up of Balkan-like syllables.

Hearing him rail at his parents in such a barrage had her feeling like each word was a poorly aimed bullet, and she was caught up in the spray.

Though he stunned the shit out of her, he also managed to look utterly magnificent. His hair gleamed like bronze in the light from Drake's garden-view window, and his eyes were like storms as he raged on. In his tailored suit, he was sin personified, and he was hers.

Wonders never ceased, but she was so utterly aware that she was his too.

That was why he was here.

For her.

Now she just needed to figure out why he'd had to bring out the big guns.

"Edward," she said softly, breaking into his tirade with the gentle utterance of his name.

He jerked to a halt like he'd been slapped, and though he was breathing heavily, his nostrils flared, he stopped railing at his mother and father.

"It's okay," she told him with a calm smile. "I don't want anything from this marriage. You know that. The money means nothing to me."

Marianne stiffened, Perry noticed from the corner of her eye, but whether the older woman believed her or not didn't matter. It was the truth, and that was all that counted.

"You don't know what you're signing, Perry," he retorted, shooting his parents a glare. "There will be information in there about any issues we may have. You're signing away your rights to raise them."

Issues? She frowned. "I am?"

"Yes," he exploded. "That's why I'm so mad. They chose to do this without my being here because they knew I wouldn't agree to it. My children need their mother," he snarled at them. Then, so saying, he strode over to the desk where Perry was standing, picked up the prenup, and with his other hand, grabbed hers.

Sliding her fingers through his, she allowed herself to be dragged out of the office and back through the grim tunnel. But before she left Drake's quarters, she shot Philippe and Marianne a hurt look.

They hadn't needed to pull the wool over her eyes like that.

The unfairness of it stung, even though she recognized they were doing their level best to protect not only their son, but any future grandchildren they may have.

When Edward carried on pulling her down the corridor, she dug her wobbly heels in and tugged him to a halt. "Edward! I can't walk so fast in these stupid shoes."

In less time than it took for her to inhale a gulp of air, she was flying through the air, and landed solidly over his shoulder.

For a second, she could do nothing more than just gape at the floor.

Had he done what she thought he'd just done?

Was he seriously *carrying* her? Caveman-style?

The bitch of it was, she knew she should be pissed. Instead, she was impressed. Jesus, she wasn't exactly light, and the man hadn't even grunted when he'd taken her weight onto *one* shoulder, then started hauling her ass down the endless tunnel-like corridor.

When her wits returned, she reached down and bit his ass.

"That's for scaring the crap out of me," she retorted, feeling her hair fly loose from the clip and start to dance over her face.

He didn't yelp, just reached up and tapped her butt. "You bite me again," he warned, "you'll get a harder smack."

She grumbled, then grimaced at the bob of her head. "This isn't comfortable, you know? I could have just taken off the shoes."

He let out a pained sigh, one that sounded more irritated with her than anything else.

Despite herself, she had to grin.

Talk about making him react!

The man was so fucking perfect all the time, it was nice to see him out of his shell.

Yelling at his mom and dad, then doing this?

Shit.

She was rubbing off on him.

And not just in a sexy way, either. In a way she'd known she would, a way George had known too.

She was lightening him up, lightening his load.

Even though the blood was starting to pound in her head, the very idea made her incredibly happy. Especially when they passed a few members of staff on their way out. Staff who went from chatting and giggling to dead silent as they watched him cart her off down the hall.

She twisted to look up at them, and couldn't stop the swift grin on her face at the sight of the women's gaping mouths—similar reactions to her own—and the men's delight in seeing their prince and future princess in obvious disarray.

She grinned at the women, knowing from their looks that they were as caught up in Edward's swarthy handsomeness as she was.

One of them shot her a cheeky grin back, then gave her the thumbs up. Deciding that she liked her, and recognizing her from one of the many classes Marianne was giving her on event planning, Perry decided she liked the woman more and more.

Ten minutes later, having strode through a public walkway, passing three guards, a Guardian of the Keys—identifiable by the swaying chatelaine's belt and heavy bunch of keys he wore around his hips—and at least four more staff, they made it to the private section of the palace.

They didn't stop at her quarters, as she'd expected.

Oh no. They carried on. Down the hall to where she'd never traversed. Past George's room. Onwards. Onwards. Until they came to a door.

When he opened it, she sucked in a sharp breath.

This was his room.

His goddamn room! *Hell, yeah!*

She knew she shouldn't be so giddy about seeing his quarters, but she really was.

She'd been engaged to the man for over two months, and had yet to see his personal space.

Perry wasn't sure why he was revealing it now, but revealing it he was.

With a grunt, he tugged her over his shoulder, swaying her into his arms before he steadied her hips and helped her stand.

She winced, her head light and her eyes pounding from the prolonged stay upside-down.

Lifting a hand to her forehead, she grumbled, "Caveman."

With his hold on her hips, he dragged her against his body, and she felt his raging hard-on against her belly. "You loved it," he whispered, bending down and whispering the words in her ear.

Then, he further surprised her by not starting something. And he had to want *something*. There was no way his cock wasn't ready for her.

Her mouth watered at the very idea.

Eyes flaring wide with sudden arousal, she inadvertently took in more of his quarters than intended as he strode off towards a sofa that took up a large space of the room. It was same size as George's, which meant it was almost two to three times the size of her enormous stateroom, and there were very few antiques in here, just like in his brother's.

The bed was a solid frame, and obviously old, but that was pretty much it. It had simple dark mink drapes swathed around the posts, and she could easily imagine him closing himself inside the bed like a child would cover her head with the blankets to protect herself from the monsters in the closet.

She sucked in a sharp breath as the thought occurred to her. It hurt to think of him like that. To think of him scared.

But from the little that was available in the press and online searches, and mostly from what Xavier had told her, he'd been snatched straight from his bed by his kidnappers.

What did that do to a person?

To know that during sleep, when one was at one's most vulnerable, was the moment someone had taken advantage.

When someone had dragged him from his rest, snatched him from his home, and taken him captive.

She gnawed at her lip, hating where her thoughts had gone. Now wasn't the time. Not when he was acting so deliciously out of character.

He dragged her attention from his bed and back to him by shifting on the sofa. The dark brown leather squeaked as he settled himself deeper into the L-shaped section, and she caught a glimpse of him—knowing he was watching her look at his bedroom.

A desk, less busy than the one in his office, took up a space by a set of French doors. It overlooked the waste of water that was the fountain Masonbrook was named for, she'd learned when she'd tried to get them to shut it down. The spout soared tens of feet into the air and was channeled by water pressure. She didn't dislike the fountain because it wasted energy... she just thought it was a waste of goddamn water.

And, if she couldn't shut it off, she intended on diverting the water stream somewhere else.

At some point in the future, at any rate.

The desk was also a fancy affair. Wide and strong, it looked like Edward wasn't the first DeSauvier to sit behind it.

A music station hovered in another corner, and a quick glance revealed hidden speakers dotted here and there. Considering there was no TV, it must have been his entertainment of choice.

The only music she'd ever heard him listen to was classical—in the car. Then he'd played the violin with Xavier that one magical, crazy-good night.

A treadmill peeked out from behind a screen—ornately carved rosewood, by the looks of it. Indian in design if the many-armed God, Vishnu, was anything to go by.

More curio, dotted here and there, revealed more of the man to her than she'd expected.

Sure, she'd known seeing his space would show her facets of his nature she'd yet to come across, but she was seeing more than she'd hoped.

This, unlike his office, wasn't uber modern. It was traditional, yes. But there were pieces in here that were selected out of choice.

The screen. A tapestry depicting sunlight falling over an estate she didn't recognize—thousands of tiny stitches somehow creating an evocative piece that spoke of a beloved place in Edward's heart.

There were the random pieces of art. Some he had propped against the wall on a console table, others were on the wall. Some hung from large pieces of corded rope because they were so heavy. Portraits, landscapes...

the selection was eclectic. But that was nothing compared to the framed photos.

She was dying to dart around, look within the frames and see what he'd deigned important enough to capture forever and commemorate, but he cleared his throat, and she dragged her attention away... away from the other side of this man. A side she'd been dying to see.

How she'd held her patience, Perry wasn't sure. Only knowing that he'd open up to her eventually had helped.

With a sigh, she slipped out of her heels and strode over a thick, plush rug that felt great against the soles of her feet, and took a seat by his side.

She jolted when he hauled her closer, not stopping until her hands were pressing into his chest for support as she steadied herself, barely refraining from tumbling headfirst into his lap.

Not that she'd have been averse to such a position, but she could tell he wasn't exactly in the mood for that.

With a whooshed exhalation, she glowered up at him. "Stop dragging me all over the place."

He stared at her, totally unrepentant. "Can I help it you don't move fast enough?"

She rolled her eyes. "I thought you were supposed to be charming?"

"I am," he joked. "Just not *Prince* Charming."

She huffed out a peeved breath, then stared past him at a table behind the sofa. Butting up against it, she could see a simple black photo-frame that housed a single image: a hand, reaching up to grab a door knocker that was as ornate as it was ancient.

"That was in Malta. A place called Medina," he informed her, seeing where her attention was and explaining—for once, without having to pull teeth.

"What's in Medina?" she asked gently, wanting to reach out to touch the door knocker. From a wolf's mouth, a god and goddess hovered, their arms curled into carved stone drapes to support themselves but their feet entwined, their calves, too, as they clung to each other, creating an elongated circle.

The woman's breasts were bare, her face turned away, gaze lowered. The man's beard looked like it swayed in a breeze; his glance was more direct as he stared ahead, but it too, was averted.

Another wolf's paws crossed over their legs, holding them in place forevermore.

"It's a citadel," he explained gently. "A walled city. It's ancient. I was there a few years ago on a royal visit when the Pope went to one of the oldest churches in the nearby town."

"You've met the Pope?" she asked, her voice a squeak. Then she wondered why that came as a surprise.

Veronia was a Catholic country, after all, and Edward *was* a prince and the future ruler of said nation.

Although, the family wasn't Catholic. Not practicing, anyway, because they hadn't had her convert for the marriage ceremony. Unless that was on their to-do list too, she thought glumly.

"Will I have to convert to marry you?" she asked, curiosity urging her to ask as she peered at the knocker. It was a crystal-clear shot, so detailed that she could see the god's belly, taut with defined stone-muscle.

"That would have been a wiser question to ask nearer to the time I proposed, wouldn't it?" he retorted, sounding amused.

She stuck out her tongue. "Maybe. It's not a big deal to me. I just wondered." Although, he was right. If converting had been necessary, that would have been one of the many lessons on her schedule.

"No. There's no need to convert. The abbey where we'll wed is non-denominational, and it won't be a priest overseeing the ceremony but a kind of..." He pursed his lips. "I've never had to explain it before," he said wryly as he rubbed his chin.

"Like an officiant? In a civil ceremony?"

"I guess," he murmured, lifting her leg onto his lap until she was as close to him, as nestled, as could be. He ran a hand down her calf and said, "But it's a religious ceremony, too. We have too many religions here for the royals to align to just one."

"That's remarkably forward-thinking," she joked.

"We're a remarkably forward-thinking nation," he teased back. "My ancestors saw how religion created wars and disturbances hundreds of years ago, and rather than add themselves to the fray, they created a haven for all, rather than just one."

"I like your ancestors more and more."

He grinned. "I'm sure they'd like you too."

"I doubt that," she said brightly. "I'm a commoner."

"We all were at some point. It just takes one person to slaughter the right man and to take his place."

She rolled her eyes. "Well, that's cheerful."

He laughed. "You haven't been absorbing much in your history lessons if you haven't learned of the family's roots."

"I process, I just don't absorb. History was never my thing. Plus, there's so much other crap I have to learn," she complained. "How to make sure I don't upset a British royal by sitting them near the French president and other crap."

"That crap's important," he chided, but he was smiling as he leaned into her so he could cup her cheek.

"No, it's not. There are like, forty event planners here. They all know that shit. Why do I need to know too? It's called delegation. Your mom needs to get better at it."

He grimaced. "You're right. She does." Then, he eyed her. "You should be grateful for those event planners. George says you're not as involved as he'd like."

"Like you are, too," she retorted, but her cheeks heated. "Anyway, it's your fault there's so much pressure. We're getting married very quickly. I swear, that scene today was because your mom thinks I'm pregnant. She thinks it's some kind of shotgun wedding."

A snort escaped him. "She doesn't think that." He sent her a wary glance. "Does she?"

"You tell me," she groused, throwing her hands up. "You know her better than I do."

He snorted. "If you think that, then you don't read between the lines." He reached up and traced a finger down the curve of her cheek. "It's important to me that if we have children, you play a substantial role."

She cocked a brow at him. "Well, duh."

He bit back a laugh. "This isn't a joke, Perry."

"I never thought it was," she told him, deadly serious now. "What made you think it would be? I'm not sure I want kids, but I intend on having a lot of sex in my life… children tend to happen as a consequence." She shrugged. "Just because I'm not maternal now, doesn't mean I won't be when I'm knocked up."

He sighed, tapped her chin. "You're one of a kind, you know that?" Before she could answer, his cell buzzed. He reached for it, rolled his eyes at the screen and flashed it to her so she could see the caller ID. "What's wrong?"

She snuggled into his side, ready to be amused at whatever George had to say. He answered the phone, and the voice on the other end sounded exasperated.

"Do you have any idea where Perry is? I've got four damn cakes, and she needs to try them."

"I don't need to try anything," she retorted, loud enough for her voice to travel down the line. "Edward has to try this shit. Here I am, starving myself to get into that freakin' dress, and you're trying to stuff me full of cake. Cake that I don't want—I told you, where's the banana one?"

"Like you need to lose weight."

Though she appreciated George's scoff, she pouted. "You haven't seen the dress. I'm sure Marianne did it on purpose. It's tighter than an elephant's asshole." And just as horrible, too.

She was not looking forward to walking down the aisle in that monster.

Edward blinked. "Stunning image there, and just as I was starting to look forward to you sashaying down the aisle."

"Now you'll look at me and see elephant anus. Brilliant. My work here is done," she told him cheerfully.

"Bring them to my room, George. I'll sample them."

She huffed. "How benevolent of you."

George didn't wait to reply, just cut the call—apparently not one to bite the hand that fed. One minute he was there, the second he wasn't.

"That brother of mine..."

"A liability?" she joked, grinning widely at him. "You want to thank him. He's the reason the wedding's happening on schedule."

Edward tilted his head to the side. "Is that because you don't really want to get married? Is that why you don't want to get involved in any of the arrangements?"

She pondered that, saw the roots of hurt begin to spread. "No. You know those girls who have a binder at four and have planned every last inch of their ceremony, down to the last detail?"

"Yeah," he asked warily. "Not personally, but I've heard the stereotype before."

"Stereotype, my ass," she pshawed. "There really are women like that. But I'm not one of them. It's just never been that big of a deal to me."

"So, let's say you were marrying George... would you be as disinterested as you are now?"

"Probably more, if I'm being honest, Edward," she admitted sheepishly. "The vaguest smidgen of interest here is because I don't want to make an ass out of myself. This is happening on a sphere that still boggles my mind. But I can't be enraptured by something that bores me shitless."

Though her response was artless, it seemed to satisfy him. He settled back into the sofa with an ease that pleased her.

"Before George interrupted, we were saying... I know the prenuptial agreement's terms. I wasn't happy about it the last time, but she signed it. I didn't want you to."

"If I'd known about that clause, I wouldn't have. I-I just thought it would be about money, I guess. Stupid of me," she said on a sigh. She rested her chin on his shoulder as she looked over it and beyond to the windows that peered onto the neat yard ahead.

This room could be her new home, if she'd let it. If she wasn't dead-set on not living at Masonbrook for the near future.

Here she was, in a palace, cozying up to a prince, as they discussed children. Kids who wouldn't just have to worry about college and measuring up—they'd have to worry about a nation and the duties that came with their positions.

Jeez, and *she'd* thought being thirteen sucked.

Her kids, if she were to have any, would have it a thousand times suckier.

"Naïve," Edward corrected gently. "Not stupid. They played on that."

"I'm surprised they did. I thought they were warming up to me." Was she hurt that they'd tried to pull that score on her? But… if Perry was trying to protect her own son and grandchildren, wouldn't she pull dick moves too?

She had to admit she would.

Perry was learning she was a bit of a tigress when it came to the people she loved.

"They are warming up to you," he told her softly, reaching up to shift a lock of hair that had tumbled over her forehead. "But we're talking about grandchildren. That changes things."

She pondered that, then pondered something else he'd said. "Arabella didn't care if the children stayed with you in the event of a divorce?"

He sighed, shook his head. Taking that as a sign he didn't want to discuss it, and because she didn't either, not particularly, she just cuddled closer to him.

He was hurt. Arabella's decision had wounded hm…

What did that say about the serious man at her side?

One who was so bound in duty, so tied into it, that he barely enjoyed the life he'd been given, yet fretted for the lives that had yet to be born…

She fell a little bit harder in love with him then.

For a man who could be so protective of children he hadn't even created yet, his character was just as she'd believed it to be.

Her instincts hadn't failed her when she'd thought he'd needed her. She wouldn't let him, or any mini-hims, down.

Or mini-Georges, or mini-Xaviers, she guessed, biting her lip.

"How does that work, Edward?" she asked softly. "I mean. George wants this long term, and Xavier seems to as well…"

"You mean children?" When she nodded, her cheeks burning, he just jerked a shoulder. "It doesn't matter. We're all DeSauviers."

Her eyes widened. "Really?"

He shot her a look. "Really."

At that moment, she knew she couldn't contain the words. They spilled from her lips. "I love you, Edward."

His eyes flared wide, his surprise evident. But he reached for her, his hand grabbing hers. He squeezed tightly, then in an almost angry tone, bit off, "And I love you, Perry. You do know that?"

Before she could say another word, the door opened and George appeared. Four large boxes were in his hands, hiding his torso from view. From his waist to chin-height, he was loaded down with the thick containers.

Though she was singing inside at having finally told Edward her feelings for him, and having heard them returned, she couldn't find it in herself to be angry at George's intrusion.

It was wonderful to see him, even if his timing was shitty.

"What are you even doing in here?" George demanded. "I've been looking all over for you."

"Calm down, Bridezilla," Perry retorted, swinging her legs out from under her and getting to her feet. She strode over to him and helped unload two of the boxes. As she did, she reached up on tiptoe and puckered her lips.

His irritated huff came shortly before a kiss landed on her mouth. She quickly nipped his bottom lip and murmured, "You do realize you're turning into a TLC special, right?"

He focused a steely eye on her. "Those women were planning small ceremonies. I'm worried about entertaining presidents and other royals!"

She grinned. "First world problems."

"You forgot the hashtag," he grouched. "Otherwise it means buttkiss."

Snorting, she returned to Edward's side and stacked the boxes between them.

"What did you settle on in the end?"

"The ones that you actually sampled," George said wryly. "Ten different flavors, and you wouldn't eat half of them."

"They were gross," she retorted. "That fruitcake was like a brick."

"It's traditional," Edward murmured softly, but his lips were twitching as he opened the box. As he stared at the buttercream-coated concoction, he looked up at George. "Shouldn't Xavier be here for this?"

Perry, God help her, melted a little more at that.

George blinked. "I didn't think. Stupid," he said on a sigh as he reached for his cell. When the call connected, he grumbled into the phone, "Dude, get your ass to Edward's room. There's cake to try."

A groan sounded down the line. "Not more fucking cake."

"Be warned, you're on speaker," Perry warbled in a singsong voice.

"I don't care if I am. You didn't even try those damn cakes. George and I had to."

"Jesus, you boys would think I'd dumped the weight of the world on you! It's just cake. And I totally tried the banana one. Which I want. Which

Bridezilla isn't letting me have because it's not 'traditional.'" She imbued as much loathing as she could into that one word.

Damn, it wasn't even feigned. She was totally sick and fucking tired of tradition.

"You dumped more than just cake on me. You dumped table decorations and bridesmaids' dresses too!" George declared, his eyes a touch wild. "What the fuck do I know about rose satin?"

She snickered. "More than me. You did a great job with my wardrobe."

"Only because I picked everything I wanted to strip you out off."

She reared back at that. "You're kidding."

Edward laughed. "Surely you knew that? You didn't think it was out of the kindness of his heart, did you?"

"Is that why everything's three sizes too small?"

George's grin was unrepentant. "Of course. You should pick your own damn clothes if you don't want me to imagine stripping you to your skin."

She groaned. "You've perverted my entire wardrobe now."

"Hardly. I wanted to fuck you when you were in ratty yoga pants. At least now I don't have to wonder if you're wearing boring white panties underneath them."

"No, I just have thongs stuck up my ass-crack," she growled. "I'm sick of the constant wedgie."

"Buy your own bikini-style panties, then."

She gaped at him. "How do you even know what they are?"

"Because I read," he declared, then sheepishly admitted, "And I might have dated a bikini model for a short time when I was younger, and all she talked about was bloody underwear."

"Guys, guys," Xavier boomed down the line. "We're digressing here."

"Only because you're procrastinating. This is as much your wedding as it is mine," she said snippily. "Your input is required."

When none of the men responded to her statement, she glowered at the two in the room with her. "What? What did I say?"

George cleared his throat. "Nothing."

Though she narrowed her eyes at him, she just murmured, "How long until you can get here, Xav?"

His voice was husky as he murmured, "Ten minutes. I was driving to the palace as you called."

"Why?" she asked. "Did you have a meeting? You should have told me. I'd have arranged for lunch."

"It was a spur of the moment decision."

George grinned. "That means he missed you."

"Fuck off," Xavier retorted, but he didn't deny it.

Pleased, she sat up straighter. "See you in ten."

"Feel free to start eating all the cake without me," he grumbled, cutting the call before anyone could say another word.

She grunted. "You guys, I swear. This is the best decision to be making! Cake. Guys love cake."

"I *loved* cake," George said gloomily. "Until I had to figure out what the hell frangipani flowers were."

She smirked. "Now you know what women have to go through when they get married."

"It's a good job this is only happening once in our lives. I'll never get over it," he declared gloomily, and she burst out laughing at his shell-shocked face.

"There, there," she told him, patting his knee in commiseration. "I'll make it worth your while," she finished, her tone teasing.

"Oh, I intend on working off my dues on your ass," he rejoined, sounding remarkably cheerful now. He leaned over and tapped her on the nose. "You'll like it, I swear."

What the hell did it say about her that she hadn't doubted, for one second, that she'd love every goddamn minute of whatever he had in store for her…

CHAPTER TWELVE

"XAVIER, DID YOU SEE THE NEWS?"

"Could hardly miss it," he snapped on a grimace as he stacked his cell-phone between his ear and shoulder. "What the fuck's going on, Edward?"

"I have zero idea."

"Bull. What's Drake have to say?"

"Remarkably little."

Xavier frowned at the plant he was potting. The fern had outgrown its starter planter and needed to be moved so it could flourish. "That doesn't sound like Drake," was all he said.

"No. I thought that, too."

"He's no idea who the guy is?"

"No. Just that, according to the papers, he's a top member of the UnReals."

With the wedding less than four weeks away, the timing of this was beyond a nightmare. Xavier rubbed his hands together to shake off the soil that had gathered there.

Only practice stopped him from running his fingers through his hair to ease some of his agitation.

"We've no idea that the papers are right," he threw out, aware that the solution was weak at best.

"They sold the copy on the fact that the Prime Minister is meeting with a fucking rebel, Xavier. They're not going to get that wrong. Not when they know we'll have them in court faster than I can curse out their managing director.

"They know better than to put false information in print."

"You say that, but the media isn't something we can always control."

"You're wrong," Edward rejoined, his tone gritty. "And you know it. You're reaching because you don't want this to be the truth. But it *is* the truth, and there's no evading it." He blew out a sharp breath. "It's just a matter of time until we figure out who the man is. Drake's already ascertained where the image was taken."

"One of the usual rebel neighborhoods?"

"Yeah. Up in Helstern." He cleared his throat. "I have more news. None of it good."

"Hit me with it."

"The medics who tended to Arabella when she was..."

Xavier winced. Arabella had been found comatose on the bathroom floor in the suite she'd shared with Edward.

On the journey over to the hospital, she'd passed away.

"What about them?"

"They're all dead."

Stillness overcame him. "What?"

"You heard me. They're all dead. The EMTs that tended to her, the doctor who declared her dead upon arriving at the hospital. Even the doctor who held the post-mortem. All of them, Xavier."

"That can't be possible."

"Well, it is. I'm looking at their death certificates as we speak."

"Explain," Xavier demanded curtly.

"The doctor who declared her dead died in a car crash in Vancouver. A few months after Arabella passed, she emigrated."

"So, it was an accident."

"Yeah, it looks that way. But the EMTs? One died on the job. The ambulance drove over a section of the road that was being maintained and hadn't been properly signposted. It went nose-first into half-set concrete."

"Jesus Christ."

"Yeah. I'm looking at the pictures. It was bad business. The front end of the ambulance was completely smashed up, and the back end of it didn't fare much better."

"As they were on their way to an emergency, they were all seated up front. They didn't stand a chance."

Xavier rubbed the back of his neck, uncaring of the soil dirtying his fingers. "And the rest?"

"One died on a beach, of all places. A jet ski veered into waters that were designated for swimmers. The pathologist died on site at a restaurant—he was allergic to peanuts, and his meal had been contaminated."

Unease filled Xavier. "They're all plausible."

"They sure are. That's why they're fucking clever. Separately, you wouldn't think anything of them, would you? Just bad luck. But together? When you think of the connection?"

"But Arabella was sick, Edward. There's no reason to think there's some kind of conspiracy going on where she's concerned."

"Well, these death certificates tell me otherwise. And it's not like I even know. I wasn't here, was I?"

"No," Xavier whispered softly, getting to his feet now so he could begin pacing. He needed to do something, anything to burn off this energy that was overwhelming him. "What does Uncle Philippe say?"

"I don't think Drake has told him yet. I only found out because he was with me when he got the call on the last death. I knew something was wrong, so I asked him. He was so surprised by the coincidence that he told me."

Jesus, for a man like Drake to be perturbed, that meant there was more credence to Edward's shaky supposition than Xavier wanted to believe.

"But why?" he repeated, staring down at the floor as he tried to process why someone would kill four medical professionals who'd been in contact with the crown princess.

"I don't know. But Drake's investigating." He sighed. "Not that it feels like enough. I have my own people looking into it. And if you combine it with what he uncovered before, gossip that Arabella might have been murdered, this just stinks even more."

"Gossip is gossip. It isn't fact. He was stupid to have told Uncle Philippe that. It wasn't relevant to anything, and all it did was stir up the old man's unease. You know how protective he is of you."

"I do, but not even Drake can avoid a king's dictate," Edward said wryly. "If Father wants to know something, then he'll find it out, one way or another. Drake might have the balls to stand up to him, but his assistants don't."

Xavier smirked a little at that. Philippe hid his tenacity behind a benevolent façade. But the man made a bulldog look lazy.

When he went after something, there was no getting in his way. And where his children were concerned, he was even worse.

"Jesus, this is a lot to take in," he said slowly. "De Montfort meeting with a goddamn UnReal, and now this? Is it connected, do you think?"

"I don't see why."

"Who else would kill Arabella?"

"To get to her father? You know, L'Argeneaux is a man with as many enemies as friends."

Xavier stared uneasily at a tree in the near distance. "No. I disagree. His enemies are too damn frightened to do anything against him. And if they did, it would be in a business setting, maybe a political one. Nothing like this.

"There was no reason to kill Arabella. She was useless. A pretty bauble." He should have felt guilty at dismissing his cousin's dead wife that way, but it was the truth, and there was no point in hiding from it.

Edward sighed. "She had connections. You can't hide from that."

"I'm not. I just don't understand why those connections might be what got her killed."

Silence hovered between them a second as Edward processed that. Then, he gritted out, "I need to tell Perry and George."

Surprised that George hadn't been the first one informed of this news, Xavier couldn't deny the warmth that filled him at his cousin's revelation.

Learning that he was Edward's first port of call deepened his voice with emotion as he murmured, "You know they'll freak out."

"George might. I doubt Perry will," Edward said, his tone considering.

"What makes you think that?"

"I usually think about a normal woman's reaction to something and then flip it on its head. That tends to be how she'll respond."

Xavier's lips twitched because there was no denying the truth in that statement. He grunted. "She'll be frightened."

"Maybe. But I can't keep it from her." Edward grew quiet, then he said, "You scared she'll call things off?"

"No." The word fell from his lips without him having to give it a moment's thought. "Are you?"

"No. I just wondered if that was why you were against my telling her."

"I'm not against it, per se. I'm just... it seems foolish to tell her something that we're not certain about."

"Nothing is certain, Xav. You know that. And keeping her out of the loop is one great way to piss her off. If I tell her this, then at least she'll know I'm willing to share."

"Why are you?" he asked quietly. "Willing to share, I mean. You weren't with Arabella. I know because you two barely talked, even weeks after you were wed." The telltale signs of intimacy had never manifested between his cousin and his late wife.

There had always been an invisible wall between them.

Sometimes, when he'd watched them interact, Xavier had wondered if they'd even had sex. It was like they were two wraiths passing through each other's lives, intent on not disturbing the other too much.

It had upset him to see that, if he was being honest. Edward was too good a man to be wasted on a vapid woman who was more interested in her appearance and idle court gossip than anything else.

Not that he'd not been saddened to hear of her passing. But he wouldn't deny that he'd known Arabella's death had freed Edward in a way that divorcing her wouldn't.

And he was well aware how that thought process made him seem. It was why he kept his opinion to himself.

"Perry's different," Edward said after a few moments. "I know she thinks she'll be a terrible princess, but we both know that's bullshit. She cares too much. About everything. She won't fail. If anything, she'll use her new position to help her achieve her goals. That makes her night and day to Arabella."

Xavier murmured, "I agree. The DeSauviers are about to be up to their eyes in charitable organizations."

Edward snorted. "I can see it now. She'll singlehandedly transform our reputation."

"It's a delicious kind of irony, really," Xavier murmured, lips twitching.

"What about her isn't?"

―――

THOUGH SHE KNEW George shouldn't be there, and from the disapproving glances Marianne and the rest of the staff kept shooting his way, she could tell they concurred...but she wanted his opinion.

Ever since he'd told her that he'd picked her wardrobe with the intent of getting her out of it, she'd wanted him to see the dress.

Which, up to now, was the only aspect of the wedding he hadn't actively been involved in. She'd liked the idea of the three men seeing it for the first time together, on the day itself...but now?

She wanted him to see her in the swathing folds of lace and silk and only God-knows-what-else. Why? She needed help telling his mother she loathed it.

And yeah, she knew that made her sound like a big fucking kid. Ballless and lily-livered, but... Marianne, for all her icy politeness, was a she-devil sent to terrify Perry.

Well aware there'd come a day when she'd have to stand up to the older woman, Perry had decided it was for the best not to come to blows over the dress, and to just get George involved.

Especially after the prenup debacle.

Perry hadn't sulked, even though Marianne had tried to screw her over, but she was aware that any complaints about this dress might be construed as her being a diva over what had gone down in Drake's office.

That totally wasn't the case, of course. Still, Marianne wasn't to know that, was she? It wasn't like women couldn't be petty over the most stupid of shit, after all. And Perry was capable of being petty too, just not when she could understand her in-laws' motives.

She'd freakin' kill to protect her men. Why wouldn't Edward's parents?

This was the fourth dress fitting. The first had been a nightmare, and she'd ceded to Marianne far more than she should have. But what did she know about wedding dresses? Royal ones that were fit for a princess, at that? She'd listened, and now she was paying the price for it.

The dressing room was white and bright. It showed all a woman's flaws, which made it her idea of a nightmare.

Around the large space there were low sofas, and Marianne and one of her friends, a Guardian of the Keys and marchioness, Louisa Patrice, was seated at her side. George filled another seat, as did Cassie. Perry had invited her new friend to the second dress fitting, in the vain hope that two of them could bulldoze Marianne's sway...

It hadn't worked.

Still, having Cassie here made the torturous event fun. She hadn't exactly seen a lot of her since they'd met up for coffee, save for these dress fittings, but she felt the stirrings of a friendship regardless.

And it helped that George, Edward, and Xavier liked and knew her well, too.

Perry stood on a low platform in the center of the room, which only enhanced the idea that this was her version of hell on Earth.

There was no escaping the fact that she was the center of attention, and that every eye in the room, including those of the four dressmakers, each wearing neat pinnies that had pins and needles tucked into the thick cotton aprons, some with pens tucked into smart buns, was fixed firmly her way.

Two of the dressmakers had helped her into the dress, and now they were pinning it in place so the end look could be envisioned. Each appointment, she'd had to be taken in a few notches more. The stress of the upcoming wedding hadn't helped her appetite, and for once in her life, she'd been losing rather than gaining weight.

Who knew that getting married to a prince would be the best diet aid in the land?

When the dressmakers stood back after she'd been pinned and prodded, the dress finally falling into place, she turned around and stared at the back wall which consisted of nothing more than a mirror.

She grimaced at the sight of herself.

George, in the reflection, got to his feet, and walked around her.

The silence in the room was almost deafening, then he folded his arms, turned to his mother, and glowered at her.

"You've made her look like one of those dolls they used to put on top of toilets."

Perry coughed. "How do you know what they looked like? I can't imagine the royal potty was decorated with tat."

"I've watched movies," he retorted grimly. "What the hell is this, Mother?" His demand included a wave of his hand that encompassed the entire frou-frou disaster.

And, boy, he wasn't wrong.

The dress was so, so, so *BIG*. Capital letters big.

Like a meringue and a tutu had exploded and had babies that were really fucking ugly.

"She looks regal," Marianne declared, getting to her feet and managing to look better than every single woman in the room, despite being double some of their ages.

Dressed in a demure pale mauve pantsuit, she looked like class.

Perry wished she could say the same.

"She might do if she was your size, Mother, but Perry's…" He eyed her breasts. "Well, she's not you."

She had to curl her lips inwards to hide her smile.

With the meringue-tutu skirt, the sweetheart neckline made her already large boobs look like pillowy mountains.

And not in a good way.

She dreaded to think what she'd look like when it came time to add a train to the disastrous ensemble.

"No, quite simply, no," he declared, and Marianne huffed.

Was it wrong that Perry wanted to climb him like a tree at that moment? God, he was so fucking sexy when he took charge, making a damn queen bend to his will.

Ugh, now was totally not the time to be feeling horny.

Focus, Perry. Focus! she told herself.

"And who gave you the decision over yes or no? This dress has taken weeks to make."

"Well, it will take hours to unmake. I wouldn't let an enemy walk down the aisle in this monstrosity—never mind a dear friend!"

At her back, Cassie started hiccupping. Perry shot her a concerned glance, then rolled her eyes when she realized the other woman was trying, and failing, to hide her laughter.

To the seamstresses, George was kindness itself as he murmured something gently in Veronian. They nodded, bobbing their heads as they studied the skirts, looking wherever he pointed, pulling at the dress and peering at him to see if they'd gained his approval.

"A princess has yet to walk down the aisle with that style," Marianne retorted crisply.

"Well, it's time for a change. Some women suit this kind of…" His eyes grew hazy as he tried to come up with a word, "whipped dessert of a dress, but Perry isn't one of them." The best friend a woman could ever have, and one of the loves of her goddamn life, peered up at her, confusion in his eyes as he demanded, "Why didn't you say anything?"

Shit, he knew her too well.

Ordinarily, she'd have been all over this. The first to complain about the ridiculousness of having a short-ass in a dress that was taller than she was. But Marianne was…

Well, she was kind, but she was also really fucking strict. Saying no to her was like saying no to the principal. Or the dean at her college lab.

So, so, *so* hard.

She pulled a face. "I didn't want to disappoint anyone."

"Aside from yourself, you mean?" he declared gruffly. "Perry, you do realize the world's cameras are going to be upon you. We might not court the press usually, but a royal wedding can't not be publicized. You'd have been photographed looking like…" He blew out a breath as he took in the whole Pavlova effect. "…*this!*"

Cassie's hiccups cascaded into outright laughter now, but George just stacked his hands on his hips as he turned to her. "And you. I know you've been coming here with Perry. Why the hell didn't you say something?"

Though she was still snickering, Cassie pointed to Marianne. "Your mother didn't want to know."

The queen folded her arms across her chest. "I asked Perry repeatedly if she was content with the design."

Feeling a little helpless, because Marianne really had asked, Perry murmured, "She did, George. Honest."

"Then why didn't you say anything?"

"Because whenever I pointed out styles I liked from the magazines I was looking through, she said they weren't appropriate. And hell, what do I know? She's the one who's done this before. It would have been stupid not to take her advice into consideration."

Marianne sighed, apparently bored with the conversation, then reeled something off in Veronian. One of the seamstresses disappeared from the room and returned with a notepad. The pencil that had been sticking out of her bun was now in her hand as she scrawled something onto the page.

She passed it to George, who studied it, pointed at some lines on the drawing, which the dressmaker promptly addressed, nodded with satisfaction, then gave it back to her.

She guessed she should have been pissed at his highhandedness, but hell, she was relieved. It wasn't like she'd passed this first Herculean task, was it?

She'd pretty much failed at the first hurdle.

Staring at the design, though, she felt tears prick her eyes. "It's perfect," she whispered, and was grateful he'd come along this morning. He'd used the excuse that they hadn't hung out in ages because he'd been too busy with organizing the wedding, as well as the new duties his family were imposing upon him.

Four times this week he'd taken a seat at Parliament—a task he loathed. He'd also had to host an event in one of the palace ballrooms, and had been sent out on an official visit to open a hospital.

George was not a happy bunny.

Still, happy bunny or not, she wanted to ride him into next week.

"You like it? Genuinely? I'll tell them to change it if you don't," he prompted as she stared down at the clean and simple lines of the dress.

Shoestring straps connected to a simple bodice that was shaped and boned in at the waist before gently flaring out into a mermaid skirt. Before him, she hadn't realized she was suited to tight-fitting skirts, but she was. The skirt would cling to her thighs, but she had freedom around the feet.

The dress was angled so she could see the back, and saw the train flared from the top of the bodice rather than from the skirt itself, which simply pooled around her feet.

"Do you like the colors of this dress? The fabrics?" he asked, and when she nodded, he told the seamstresses something.

Perry knew it could be constituted as rude, but she also knew it wasn't meant that way.

Veronians had two national languages. Veronian and English—thanks to all the rich ex-pats who took advantage of Veronia as a tax haven. Everyone always spoke English in her presence unless they wanted to adapt a more compatible tone.

"We can have the train in the Seville lace, ma'am, and the rest of the dress in the silk," the seamstress said, smiling at her.

Perry was amused to note the woman was relieved—the owner of the fashion house apparently didn't want her name attached to this monster of a dress either.

"That would be perfect," she told the designer, who beamed with delight.

Marianne tapped her foot. "How long will all this take? We don't have time for this, George. If you were going to be so fussy, you should have come earlier."

"Perry usually has a voice in her head," was his waspish retort. "I didn't think she'd need backup to deal with you, Mother."

Marianne rolled her eyes. "She's quite at ease with me, child. Just not when it comes to the wedding."

Perry grimaced, because her future mother-in-law wasn't wrong.

In her mind, Perry believed she had no right to argue when she didn't have a damn clue about what was going on.

Marianne, on the other hand, had not only been through this herself, but was guiding her through the assault course... to ignore her seemed churlish.

"Well, that doesn't excuse your eyes. Do you need to go to the optician or something?"

Marianne turned pink. "My eyes are fine."

"They're certainly not if you think that dress is beautiful."

Marianne glowered at him, then turning on her heel, nose pricking the air, stalked out of the room.

Louisa Patrice heaved a world-weary sigh, shook her head at George, then took off after the queen. As far as Perry had seen, the woman rarely said a word. And it wasn't because with Marianne she couldn't get a word in edgewise. She was just perennially silent.

When Marianne had disappeared, tension flooded from the room and everyone remaining breathed a little easier. Well, not George. He seemed as unaffected as usual.

With the queen having departed, Cassie climbed to her feet and strolled over. She whistled at the sight of the design and crooned, "Much better."

George elbowed her gently in the side. "You should have told me Mother was being harsh on Perry."

"She isn't being harsh," Perry instantly countered. "If anything, she's being very nice." Which was the truth.

If you didn't take into account the woman had tried to sneakily snatch custody away from Perry of children she didn't even have yet...

"Marianne is set in her ways," Cassie muttered, her eyes still on the design. She murmured something to the seamstress who nodded, and a panel of lace made an appearance at the front of the dress. "That's better," she declared.

George, head tilted to the side, studied the design, too, and nodded, sporting a beatific smile as he did. "Perfect."

Cassie snorted. "I didn't realize you had such an interest in fashion, George."

"It's amazing what one picks up in the US," was all he said, his reply lofty.

Perry laughed, then joked, "He's the best friend a girl could have, Cassie. I swear, he could only be better if he was gay."

When both women collapsed in laughter at that, George just grunted and declared, "I've just saved the day, and you're picking on me. How's that fair?"

"Who said life was fair, bud?" Cassie retorted, a wicked gleam in her eyes.

"Jesus, the day you two met was a day Edward will rue, won't he?" came his wry rejoinder.

Cassie and Perry glanced at one another and smiled. Widely.

He was right, Perry realized.

Incredible though it seemed, she'd made a friend. One with as slick a sense of humor as her own.

A new dress, the need to ride George like he was a horse, and the realization that Cassie wasn't just an acquaintance with an interest in her because of Edward... could the day get any better?

CHAPTER THIRTEEN

A HAND TRAILED over his shoulder, delicate fingers trickling down over the length of his arm until they captured his wrist.

"What are you doing?" he asked, amused when she clung and wouldn't let go.

"Saving you."

"Saving me from what?" George turned to Perry with a cocked brow. "Didn't realize that *I* was the damsel in distress this time."

She huffed, and her eyes narrowed. He knew her squeaky voice was about to make an appearance—as it usually did when he wound her up. "I wasn't a damsel in distress."

"No. You were a damsel in 'this dress,'" he teased, loving how her eyes sparkled with both merriment and exasperation. "You needed me to save you," he continued in a singsong voice. "Don't lie."

She scowled at him. "I don't lie. Not to you, anyway."

The amendment had him snorting. "What about Edward and Xavier?"

"Nope. I don't lie to them either. To your Environmental Agency, on the other hand, I will."

His eyes flared in concern. "Why are you lying to them? Don't they need to know facts?"

She huffed again. "Like I'm going to tamper with evidence, George. I simply meant that though I want to tear them all, individually, a new one, I shall lie and smile and be polite when I want to tell them they're all morons and need to find new jobs."

George squinted at her. "You do know that's just being two-faced."

She jerked a shoulder. "Two-faced, lying, all means the same thing."

"Well, the most important lesson they'll never teach you... to be a royal, you need to be two-faced as fuck."

She grunted. "Like I didn't guess that."

"Talking to boring politicians, dim-witted diplomats, and stroking everybody's ego all the damn time..." He groaned, then dramatically flung his hand up to his brow and whimpered, "I do declare, it's a hard lot being a prince."

"Okay, Scarlett, let's calm this down." Perry giggled as she propped her chin on his shoulder. "Whatcha doin'?"

"Trying to figure out what I can do while I'm here. If Mother sends me on another hospital tour, I won't be responsible for my actions."

Perry whacked his arm. "That's not nice. Those kids loved meeting you."

He grunted. "I loved meeting them too. It was the goddamn shadow Minister of Health that ruined it for me."

"What was he doing there?"

"Exactly," he retorted angrily. "He had no place there. They made my visit into a political movement, and even though I understand why, it still pisses me off."

"Okay, you might understand why, but I don't."

"Next year's an election year. If I'm not careful, every visit I attend will suddenly have a shadow minister popping up out of nowhere."

She dipped her head deeper over his shoulder so there was no evading her scowl. "Why would they do that?"

"Because they want the public to see we have ties to the Socialist party."

"And the Conservatives are in now, right?" she asked, seeking clarification.

"Yes. But the names don't make much sense. Our Social party is like the US Democrats. The Conservatives are Republicans, and then we have the Liberals who are very much like Liberatarians."

"That's not too difficult for me to make sense of," she jibed, then her brow cleared as she asked, "So, basically, the Democrats want everyone to know they're best buds with the DeSauviers."

"Yes. And considering De Montfort just made a political stand, I guess it's more important than usual."

"I read about that in the papers last week, and I meant to ask you what it meant. You guys never raised the topic with me so I didn't think it mattered, then 'wedding dress-gate' happened and I got sucked into some reports..." She shrugged— there was no denying Perry had been busy of late.

George knew because he'd helped her mock up a schedule that reminded him of a school timetable.

"The Prime Minister getting chummy with the head honcho of our major extremist group doesn't exactly inspire confidence in him as a leader next year. Not when public sentiment is purely on our side."

She tensed behind him. "Surely that's not allowed."

"Ya think?" he said with a snort. "I'm not sure what the hell's going on. How they even got a snapshot of that is beyond me."

"Doesn't that break your anti-privacy laws?"

"No. Politicians aren't as covered by those laws as most. It's a part of the office they're voted into—they're supposed to be available to their voters at all times."

"Well, that sucks," she retorted.

"The pay's good though," he mocked, then grimacing, continued. "Drake's been investigating ever since, but the man De Montfort met with has gone underground."

"What about De Montfort? He's resigned, hasn't he?"

"Not yet. It's on the cards though. His party's certainly starting to make those demands, but he hasn't heeded their call."

"Well, this is a clusterfuck."

"You're telling me," he said on a laugh that held zero amusement. "And here's me bitching about the opposition inviting themselves to my visits… I just don't like being used."

"What about if I use you?"

He turned his head to the side. "Is that a promise?"

She laughed, and her hand slid over his belly, then aimed downward to cover his shaft through his pants.

"Does that feel like a promise?"

He pondered that a second. "I don't know. I think it feels more like action."

She rubbed her cheek against his; the move was distinctly feline and had him shuddering in response as all his nerve endings flared to life. Her lips trailed a hot path over his jaw, along his chin, until they reached his own. When their mouths could finally connect, they breathed into the kiss, and that breath was loaded with a sense of relief as well as a sense of homecoming.

Almost as though that was too much for her, Perry pulled back and pressed her forehead to his temple. "God. I sometimes wonder how I survived without this for so long."

He swallowed, because he could empathize. "We were stupid."

"You were holding out on me."

"I was," he confessed. "Do you hate me for it?"

"Hate you for holding out for your brother?" She let out a deep sigh. "How could I? When I love him, too."

He stilled. "That's a new development."

"Not really," she whispered, rubbing her forehead against his so that wispy strands of her hair tickled his jaw and throat. "It feels like it's been building forever. With Xavier too."

Relief swelled inside him. "I knew Xavier was different. You're not the one-night stand kind of girl."

She huffed. "Whatever gave you that idea?"

"Years of friendship?" he teased. "That was the biggest clue. I don't think, in all the time I've known you, you slept with anyone as fast as him."

She shrugged. "We connected."

"You never connect."

"I was mad at you. You'd left me to the masses to go and talk to boring politicians."

"I had no choice," he countered waspishly. "You think I want to talk to those boring bastards?"

She snickered. "'Want'? Don't you mean 'wanted'?"

"The tense is relevant for today or four months ago," he retorted, but his lips twitched. "I never want to talk to those boring fuckers."

"I was mad at you, regardless of whether you deserved it or not, and I was tired of feeling so messed in the head about you. It's irritating. All those years of unrequited love? Of lost passions? It hurts after a while. Then Xavier was there, and he made me feel...different."

"Bastard. Charmed you out of your panties."

She chuckled. "I wouldn't go that far. I was the one who charmed him out of his briefs."

George stilled. "What does that mean?"

"It means he was a perfect gentleman. I was the one who came onto him." His mouth rounded, but she popped his bottom lip with a finger. "Don't look so astonished. I am capable of making the first move."

His eyes flared. "I need to see this. The patented Perry seduction."

She flushed. "Shut up."

"Never," he teased, reaching for her mouth and groaning with delight as their lips met.

He sank into the kiss, not needing to take it further, not needing it to go anywhere it didn't need to.

He just fell into her. Fell into the warmth of her, the depth of her love. Knowing she felt the same for Edward, and Xavier too—though, granted, that had been a miscalculation on his part—filled him with a relief so deep, it felt like it touched his soul.

He'd never loved a woman like he loved Perry. He wanted to give her the world. Wanted her to look down and know he'd give her everything, all that he was and ever would be, just to have her at his side.

As her tongue tangled with his, twining and teasing, the door at his back opened. The slight whoosh of sound acted as a trigger. He immediately pulled back and Perry shot upright.

She wiped her mouth quickly before she turned around. George peered over his shoulder and saw his mother was scowling down at her cellphone.

"George, do you know where Perry is?" she asked, sounding almost absentminded—considering his mother was never absentminded, the tone was decidedly unusual.

He cocked a brow—but inwardly, he was so relieved her focus was elsewhere that he felt sick. Jesus. "Look up. She's here."

When Marianne did as bade, Perry waved a hand at her, and cheerfully asked, "Everything okay, Marianne?"

There was an irony to the fact he, Edward, and Xavier were more pissed at Philippe and Marianne than Perry was about the prenuptial agreement, and how they'd tried to trick her into signing away her parental rights in legalese so long and drawn out even a contract lawyer would be cross-eyed at the end of it.

None of them had raised the subject though. Mostly, George thought, because the three men knew Perry would never divorce Edward, so the prenuptial clauses would never come to light.

Still, that didn't make it right. It was just a sign that his parents were willing to be devious when it came down to protecting their sons. And as Perry had told him before, her understanding still boggling his mind a little, who could blame them, considering their past?

His mother blinked, smiled vaguely, looked down at her cellphone once more. "Yes, yes."

"Then..." Perry shot him a look. "Why were you looking for me?"

Marianne was lost once more to her phone until George cleared his throat. "Playing Candy Crush again, Mother?"

Perry snickered, and that seemed to draw Marianne's attention for a small pucker marred her brow. "Dear, I've told you about that. And snorting too. It isn't ladylike to do either."

Perry heaved out a sigh. "Yes, Marianne. I remember. I didn't think it mattered in private."

"What becomes second nature in private will become first nature in public," she recited, and George knew that must have been one of the many bullshit lessons she'd received at finishing school. "Anyway, dear," Marianne murmured, sending a warmer smile to the pair of them. "I need your help."

"You do?" Perry asked warily.

"Yes. Come," Marianne beckoned, holding out a hand.

Perry shot him a beseeching look, but he ignored it. He just grinned at her. "*We* can talk later," he said, mock-severely, but she glowered at him over her shoulder as she strode over to the door where his mother was waiting for her.

"I'll get you back for this," she mouthed.

His grin widened. "Can't wait," he returned, then blew her a kiss.

As the door closed behind him, his attention reverted to the information in front of him. He'd done well for himself in the States. Had made a name in certain markets, and it was a name that wasn't tainted by his family or his status.

He was damn good at what he did, and the contracts in his hands proved that.

Four investment brokerages had contacted him. The hedge funds they managed handled billions of euros, and truth was, working in Veronia would probably do his reputation good.

The number of wealthy elite here, per capita, was staggering. For every two people with average incomes, there were eight more living affluent lifestyles.

Veronia was, putting it frankly, stinking rich.

Which was why Perry was pissed when the EA claimed they couldn't afford to repair the dams.

There was no doubt about it—the government needed more involvement from the DeSauviers. His family wasn't Veronia's sole protection against the incompetency of democracy, but it was a start.

George wasn't an autocrat. But having viewed close hand that the democratic way inspired nothing but idiocy, he wasn't entirely sure how to best rule a nation with the most efficacy.

All he knew, from his bird's eye view of governing a nation, was that every new government that found its way into power made a bigger mess of the job. Without the royals to protect the people, he'd despair for Veronia.

Which was what made the whole situation with the UnReals totally remarkable.

They were so besotted with the past, they were blind to the future.

Shaking his head at his own musings, he wondered if he was being selfish by trying to find a private sector position.

Lifting a hand, he rubbed at his temple. Duty, it was everywhere he damn went. The only place he'd been free of it was the US, but even then, he'd been on borrowed time.

Sighing, he pushed away the latest job offer he'd received via snail mail. He stacked it with the others on his desk and viewed the little skyscraper he was making with the damn proposals.

Working in a hedge fund was what he wanted to do. The *last* thing he wanted was to work with the Minister of Finance. Even in an advisory capacity, most of the ministry would spend their time trying to give him the runaround. But that didn't stop him from being able to access everything they were doing… from being able to make sure funding was appropriately arranged.

Though he'd prefer the Veronian Democrats to be in power than De Montfort's Conservative League, he trusted neither.

With a heavy breath, he switched his attention to something that was actually useful—the table arrangements for the wedding reception.

Neither Perry nor Edward seemed willing to take responsibility for it, so George had volunteered.

Hell, maybe he should go into event management. Seemed like he had the knack for it, and with the royal wedding on his resume… talk about the right kind of references to have.

He grinned at the thought, then buried himself in the diplomatic nightmare ahead of him. Better that than to worry about a life tucked away in the dingy halls of the government because duty compelled him to think with his head and not his heart.

CHAPTER FOURTEEN

THE SOUND of another jet landing shouldn't have been all that disconcerting. But they'd arrived on the private airfield twenty minutes ago, and unlike major airports, there wasn't that much traffic.

She could hear the birds tweeting outside—that was how quiet it had been since they'd cut the engines to the private jet.

Strange, wasn't it? How she'd been living in a palace for the past five months, and yet, what really made things hit home was this jet.

Luxury had become a part of her life. As ridiculous as that sounded, it was the truth. She slept on a four poster that had, once upon a time—and she really hoped they'd changed the mattresses since then—comforted and sheltered royalty. She drank food that came from royal estates, ate on Limoges plates... even her panties had designer labels.

And as terrifying as it sounded, what had once perplexed her, now was just a part of life.

Still, this wasn't.

This plane?

Nuh-uh.

This was terrifying because she, Little Miss Nobody, had access to a private jet.

What the hell was that even about? Perry asked herself as, for the millionth time, she gaped at her surroundings.

It was a small plane, she guessed. Nothing like what she'd traveled on in the past. And she had it to *herself*. Maybe that was why this was even more impressive? Or wasteful?

She wasn't sure which.

Even her conservationist heart was bewildered at being able to have this kind of luxury on call. And though it didn't improve matters much in her head, Drake had explained to her that she wouldn't just be putting herself in danger if she traveled on a regular flight, but all the innocents on board, too.

That, more than anything, had given some semblance of peace about the situation. But the peace had come with a kind of terror of its own.

The only reason those innocents would be in danger was if she was in danger.

She was now a person who could endanger those around her.

The mind boggled.

Enough that she wished George was here to tease her out of her funk, or that Xavier was there to hold her hand. She'd sit in Edward's lap if she could. And no mistake about it, she'd do anything to find some kind of normality in this crazy new reality of hers.

She was only here because she'd insisted on coming. Had refused to let her parents travel to Veronia alone. Drake's compromise had been that she travel by herself, and even though Edward hadn't been happy about it, he'd let her make the decision while railing at the head of security all the while.

Once again, however, Giles had won.

It amazed her how much power he had over the rulers of a nation, but safety was everything. It was paramount.

And this jet was a reminder of the kind of world Perry was diving into.

The leather was soft beneath her, the color of a café latte. The bucket seats were plush and cushioned, and she could lay down in the space between this seat and the next—that was how much legroom she had.

Coach, this was not. Cattle, she'd ceased to be.

A bouncy carpet underfoot cushioned her feet, the walls were paneled in a gleaming mahogany, and the light fittings were uplighters. Soft pools of gold bathed the ceiling, not dark enough to fall asleep, but light enough to not get eye strain.

A sofa ran down the length of one side, and opposite it, there was a narrow table in matching mahogany—for business meetings, she assumed.

Even the air smelled rich. Like incense, of all things. And that horrible squeak that came as part and parcel of traveling in the air? Yeah, that wasn't there.

She'd eaten five-star fare on honest-to-God porcelain dishes, and had been shown to a small bedroom with a connecting bath that would have put a seven-star hotel in Dubai to shame.

This?

It just beggared belief.

Of course, the one thing to spoil it were the two men sitting on the sofa. Yeah, she hadn't mentioned them because they weren't exactly people she wanted near.

Guards.

Two of them. Of a team of ten.

The numbers were astonishing.

How could she, one tiny person, need so much protection? Hell, they just had to shove her in a small hidey-hole, and she'd be fine. There had to be some joy in being a short-ass.

Apparently not.

The remaining eight guards hadn't needed to come because she wasn't actually leaving the plane.

She was here to make sure her parents, her salt-of-the-earth folks, didn't balk at the sight of the private jet.

They were already hesitant about coming.

She heard it every time she'd called her mom the past month or so. Perry had been making an effort to be more in touch with her, but every time she did, she wondered if she wasn't making it worse.

Janice, like most mothers, had the nasty habit of finding a reason for her daughter's unease and picking it apart until the matter was resolved.

Only trouble was, some of these situations couldn't be resolved by a mother's loving advice.

The EA still wasn't listening to her, wasn't taking her seriously. How could Janice help with that?

The ball held in honor of the Ukrainian president? The Veronian courtiers had still snubbed her. Had still peered at her as though she was shit on their shoes.

How could Janice rectify that?

Then there was the nightmare of the wedding itself. Every day closer to the event of the century, according to the Veronian press anyway, and there was more to do. More to worry about.

How could Janice help with that?

Perry bit her lip, praying as she'd been praying for the past few hours, that her parents wouldn't balk further. That they'd come.

In a normal situation, she had no doubt they'd be at her wedding quicker than a NASCAR rally car around the track. But this wasn't normal.

And the jet was just further proof of that.

It had all the makings of the nail in her goddamn coffin.

When a cellphone rang, she jolted in surprise. The silence since the jet had landed had been pretty nice. She'd closed her eyes, had taken the moment to just breathe. To prepare herself for the many, many questions her parents would have for her when they boarded.

As the guard started talking, however, she opened her eyes and studied him.

He was remarkably short for a guard. A few inches taller than her. His head was shaved and shiny on top, and he plucked his eyebrows.

Why did men do that? Perry asked herself, tilting her head to the side as the Veronian guard's voice raised.

She didn't have to speak the damn language to know he was cursing.

"What is it?" she asked, raising her own voice to be heard over the man's curses.

The guard, Gerard, clenched his jaw. But that was the only response he gave her. He got to his feet and headed for the door. At his approach, one of the stewards stood and frowned.

More Veronian, confused this time, went down, but the door opened. She sat up, wondering what was going on and irritated as fuck that she didn't have a clue why Gerard was angry.

Soon as she was married, goddamn Veronian classes were on the huge list of things she had to do.

After solving the nation's drought, of course.

A woman, even a princess, needed priorities.

Still, Gerard wasn't concerned... he was angry. That meant her safety wasn't compromised, surely?

The guards stood to attention in a way that pricked Perry's curiosity all the more. She went from sitting straight to getting to her feet, too.

When Gerard saluted, she knew the person on the other side of the door had to be a royal.

Her lips curved at the notion, but what astonished her more were the tears that burned her eyes when Edward appeared in the doorway.

His smile was tight when he shot something back to Gerard, who was mumbling his displeasure, but Perry interrupted and said, "He might not be pleased to see you, but I'm relieved as all hell that you're here."

Gerard sighed, knowing he was beat and when to quit mumbling, but Edward grinned as he stepped nearer to her.

He looked divine. His bronze-like hair dappled in the golden lights onboard. His skin was creamy now that summer was mostly over. He'd also grown paler because he wasn't being allowed out to ride as much as he usually was.

His eyes were like peridot, facets of light making them sparkle and glint gold. His lips—full and almost rose in color—curved with a genuine warmth that eased her more than she could say.

She hadn't realized she'd been cold inside. Not until then.

Fear, she guessed. Concern and disconcertion over being here, in this jet, over waiting for her folks...

But his presence soothed that. Let her breathe a little easier.

She didn't care that his suit was tailored, that the fabric of his shirt was an exquisite silk blend. When he brought her into his arms, she clenched her fingers in the fine tailored jacket, and pressed her cheek to the soft caress of the silk.

Letting out a shudder of relief, she whispered, "You're not supposed to be here. Drake said you would be in danger if you came."

"Is that a complaint?" he teased.

She rubbed her cheek against his chest, wishing it was bare, wishing she could smell him, just him. "No. Never." She paused. If Gerard had been that angry, how mad was Drake? "Are you in trouble for coming?"

He shrugged. "I'm the crown prince," he murmured. "Trouble is my middle name."

A laugh escaped her at that. "You rebel, you. Should I call you James Dean now?"

He chuckled, pressed his lips to her hair. "No. Edward suits me fine. Although James is one of my many names, so I'd answer to it."

She stilled at that, then pulled back to stare into his eyes. "Many names?" she asked, seeking clarification.

He winked. "I have about eight."

Her lips parted. "Eight?"

"Yes. One for each of our allies. Or so it seems."

"What does that mean?"

He shrugged. "Queen Victoria is a great, great, great-grandmother. For all the nations where her bloodline sowed a seed, we're unofficial allies."

"So, like England and Russia?"

He reached down a traced a finger over the curve of her cheek. "Yes. Greece, Finland. Yugoslavia, Romania, et cetera."

"So what are all your names then?" she asked, tilting her head to the side so he could better cup her cheek. Her eyelids fluttered closed as she sucked in air that he shared.

"You'll find out on our wedding day."

Her eyes popped open at that. "Meanie."

He grinned. "We don't have time. Your parents are five minutes away."

She gulped. "You were supposed to wait in Veronia."

"There are many places I'm supposed to be today, and the only one that mattered is here. I've already let your father down by asking for your hand over the phone. I couldn't let my relationship with him deteriorate further."

Her stomach, so tightly clenched with nerves, eased some at that. The butterflies stopped dancing, and she sagged into him, tightening her arms around him once more. "Thank you," she whispered, voice thick with emotion.

"Oh, Perry, *carilla*, you never have to thank me for being here. This is where I'm supposed to be."

And that, God help her, was better than any vow he could speak in church.

It meant the world, and from a man intending to give her just that, it meant even more.

CHAPTER FIFTEEN

"YOU CAN'T BE SERIOUS."

At her side, Cassie pressed a hand to her mouth.

Perry glowered at her. "Don't you dare laugh."

"I'm not laughing, I'm not," she retorted, but she had to cough a few times to dispel her mirth.

"Seems like it to me," Perry grumbled as she stacked her hands on her hips and studied the three different vehicles before her.

In a gust of Chanel No. 5, Marianne appeared from one of Masonbrook's side entrances. There were many, and the queen had taken a different one than Perry and her newly appointed Matron of Honor, Cassie.

"I see you're ready, Perry," Marianne said gaily.

"Ready to commit murder," she bit off under her breath, making Cassie snort.

"Stop making me laugh. She already thinks I'm rude."

"That's because you are," Perry said on a chuckle of her own when Cassie elbowed her in the side.

Sweeping her hands out in a graceful gesture—one of many in her repertoire—Marianne murmured, "This is your last lesson before the wedding."

"We've already gone over how to get in and out of cars, Marianne," Perry complained, folding her arms across her chest.

"Do these look like regular cars to you?" the queen snapped, mimicking Perry's pose. "We have a low sports car, that's the one you'll be climbing in and out of after the reception, and Edward will use it to drive you to the airfield. Then, the first carriage. This is the covered one you will travel to the abbey in with your father. The open-top carriage is for after the ceremony."

Perry cut Cassie a look. "What am I missing?"

Marianne's nostrils flared with irritation. "Edward and George have rightly pointed out how clumsy you are, and that it would be remiss of me to fail to cover this potential hole in your education."

Well, wouldn't she just make them pay for that pleasant little suggestion later?

"It can't be so hard, can it?" she asked brightly, eyeing the formal gold and powder-blue cab that reminded her of a moving Fabergé egg, and the open carriage that looked like it belonged in a Disney movie. The car was an E-type Jaguar. It was low, looked mean and fast, and would suit Edward down to the ground.

"In your wedding dress, you'll be maneuvering with a hefty weight of fabric around your legs and ankles," Marianne pointed out. "For the Jaguar, you'll be changing into a simpler dress for the reception so you won't have as much to worry about, but there are still concerns."

"There are?" Perry asked doubtfully, her feet crunching on the gravel as she approached Marianne and the three luxury vehicles. Each of which spoke of a completely different époque in Veronian history.

"You could end up flashing your boobs or your panties, depending on what you're wearing," Cassie advised quietly, nodding at Marianne. "You have to be careful. It can be really embarrassing, especially if there are paparazzi following you, Perry."

The turncoat.

"I thought you were on my side," Perry groused.

"I am," Cassie joked. "That's why Marianne's right. You do need to know this, Perry. You'll regret it if you don't."

She winced. "Okay, so where do you want me?"

So began a tedious two-hour class on how to climb into and out of the carriages, tips on how to sit straight even if the horses were making the ride rocky, as well as the perfect wave—Marianne even slapped her hand a few times when Perry found the motion difficult to mimic.

Of course, the instant she did that, Perry knew immediately what to do.

She was starting to think she was a glutton for punishment. Either that or one of Pavlov's dogs. A simple slap on the wrist from the queen, and like clockwork, she immediately started behaving.

If it wasn't downright weird, it would have been damn funny.

"We'll have footmen on either side of the doorway. They can either help your father and Edward, or just one can, but I'd recommend you grip both their hands with your own and allow them to guide you to the ground,

Perry," Marianne murmured as Perry stood in the open-top carriage, two bored servants standing in front of her.

Half sure she'd been less mortified at her first pool party after her boobs had popped up overnight, she placed her hands into the men's and transferred her weight onto them so she could climb down the steps with ease.

Really, it wasn't rocket science, but Marianne had her practice a handful of times.

Then, when she was deigned fit for purpose, Marianne opened the Jaguar.

"I've seen your dress. There's no need to worry about your panties, and you'll certainly not be wearing anything that short in future..." Marianne pursed her lips in disapproval, but before Perry could defend her future self of any wrongdoing, the queen stepped into the car and faced the windshield.

At that moment, it was impossible to think the woman was almost seventy. Not only was she spry, but in her neat pantsuit, and with elegantly coiffed hair and made-up face, Marianne was so damn perfect, it was almost sickening.

With the sunlight beaming down on them and flushing her cheeks pink, the sky a pleasant, if strong, blue that had her squinting at the brightness, and a piece of gravel stuck in the tread of her shoe making her toes ache, Perry felt the exact opposite of perfect. Between the sweat gathering at her brow, and a wedgie—a constant state of affairs now—lodged in her ass crack... the last person she was emulating was Marianne.

Blowing out a breath to move a piece of hair that had glued itself to her brow, she watched as Marianne motioned to the footmen standing beside the car. He closed the car door, sealing her into the low vehicle.

"I'd best show you, Perry. Forewarned is forearmed, and you can be surprisingly hapless for a scientist, dear child," Marianne murmured, with the same shade as a southern mama could throw when hollering, "Bless your heart," at someone she loathed.

"Thanks," was all she mumbled, and she shot Cassie a despairing look.

The other woman hid a smile. "Watch. You'll appreciate the lesson."

Huffing, Perry did as bid.

With great flair, the footman opened the car door. Marianne kept her knees tucked together, pinned her ankles close, too, then swept her legs out, while using one hand on the seat to pivot.

"I'd advise you carry a clutch purse, dear," Marianne carried on. She held out a hand. "Imagine I have one in my hand. You place it here," she advised, resting it between the slight swells of her breasts, "and it covers your cleavage so that when you bend over to climb out of the vehicle, there's no chance of any mishaps." She placed her weight on the hand burrowed in the cushion, then propelled herself upwards.

Considering that the part about the clutch purse was actually sound advice, even if the rest was quite mundane, Perry tilted her head to the side and nodded.

The rest of it couldn't be that hard, could it?

Of course, she was proven wrong.

Somehow, what she'd been managing to do since she was a child was surprisingly difficult in "princess mode." It was difficult not spreading her legs, placing one on the ground and then using that to propel herself upwards. Mostly, it was about breaking the habit.

Again, easier said than done.

Cassie huffed out a breath. "Jesus, Perry. Concentrate. I'd like to see my firstborn sometime before he has to leave for college."

Perry squinted at her. "Remind me why you're here again?"

"Moral support," was the retort.

"Next time, remind me to invite George."

"There won't be a next time, dear," Marianne said, her tone like steel. "This is the last comportment class we'll be having. You'll be moving onto more important subjects after the wedding."

Perry scowled. "Like what?"

"Politics, history. Culture."

"I've already been having those classes!" she complained, her tone more of a wail than anything else.

Christ, it was like being back at school, and the only light at the end of the tunnel was the idea of the wedding bringing an end to the classes.

But Marianne broke her heart. "No, indeed. There's plenty to learn. Philippe and I will be watching over those lessons, dear. We've covered the basics these months past; next, we'll be moving onto the things that actually matter."

Just when Perry thought she'd burst—because if all the crap she'd been learning didn't actually matter, why the hell had she had to waste so much time on it?—Edward appeared.

With him in sight, and like a shining beacon of hope that spoke of escape, she motioned to the footman to open the door to the Jaguar. She climbed out of the car to her husband-to-be, her savior, her end destination.

Of course, the minute she had both feet on the gravel and was striding toward him, applause sounded behind her.

"You did it!" Marianne boomed contentedly.

She had?

Edward jerked at his mother's holler, then grinned widely. Perry blinked. Had she just mastered the princess equivalent of first grade?

Spinning around to spy the wide grins on her friend and mother-in-law's faces, she realized that, holy shit, she had!

Huh.

Maybe this princess shit wasn't too hard after all?

———

"LOOK, I know you don't like me. You don't have to like me to realize that my statistics are right. My conclusions are right. And my forecasting is right."

Xavier hid a smile. Perry's arrogance might have irritated the ruling council of Veronia's Environmental Agency, but the truth was, her words *were* fact.

He'd looked over her speech, over the presentation she was giving today, and had to concur with her facts, findings, and forecasting.

For whatever reason, the ecological crisis that was affecting Veronia and Veronia alone?

It didn't exist.

Xavier was still scratching his head over it. But Perry's findings were concrete, and there was no denying that what she was saying was the truth.

The dams were at fault. The infrastructure was at fault. Every experiment she'd run, every fact-finding mission she'd been on, and every interview with key personnel onsite at the dams confirmed it.

The dams were old. Crumbling. There were many issues with them. However, something else was exacerbating the issue.

"Your reputation precedes you, Dr Taylor. However, you must understand that we require a national to go through the evidence you have uncovered."

"I'm marrying your crown prince," Perry said on a huff. "I guess I'm not a national yet, but surely you can see that my future here is as on the line as yours is.

"I don't understand what the problem is," she continued, glowering at the vice president of the EA who'd countered her arguments. "Everything I uncovered is good news. Manmade problems can be resolved. Naturally occurring problems? Yeah, not so much."

"We appreciate the time and energy you spent on researching this issue for us—"

Perry held up a hand. "You paid me. Fair and square. And I'm telling you, you might want to believe that this issue is environmental, but that's nonsense. You're pulling the wool over your eyes, and causing untold damage, by perpetuating this belief."

The vice president narrowed his eyes. "As I was saying, we appreciate your input, and now have other means of investigation we need to put into practice."

"What does that even mean?" she snapped, slamming her hand on the table in front of her.

Xavier's heart sped up at the sight of her all fired up and practically vibrating with energy.

She was a pocket rocket in the staid meeting room.

Around a black ash round table, in a white room that screamed administrative block, and surrounded by a bunch of no-hope bureaucrats with no real interest in their posts save for the fact they'd been put into their positions by the current government... Perry was the only one truly impassioned by what she was discussing.

In her neatly tailored, cream silk suit—another one of George's investments, if the length of the skirt was anything to go by—she looked bright and vivacious. Her shirt was bronzy, and it offset the dark locks that bounced on her shoulders as she throbbed with each passionate word she uttered.

He watched her stand there at the head of the table, her hands out, her body language imploring and... "Enough."

He had to speak.

The words wouldn't stay contained.

The vice president, on the brink of saying something else moronic, no doubt, jerked to attention. "Excuse me, Your Grace?"

Xavier narrowed his eyes and scanned his gaze over the eight-strong team the EA had sent to watch this presentation.

"Enough," he repeated, this time silkily, getting to his feet and striding to the foot of the table where Perry was standing.

At her back, there was a blank wall loaded with the projections and diagrams she was using to back up her conclusions.

As he approached her, he saw her frown, and knew she wasn't pleased about his weighing in on this. But she stayed quiet. A fact he was infinitely grateful for.

"What's the politics here, Charles?" Xavier asked the vice president. "Is there a reason an 'environmental crisis' is more auspicious than the truth?"

"Don't be ridiculous Xavier," Charles bit off, but he pulled at his tie nonetheless.

A tell if ever there was one.

In a tone that was conversational, Xavier murmured, "You do know you've been doing that ever since you were at school."

"Doing what?" Charles snapped.

Xavier mimicked the VP, who was as much of a prick today as he'd been as a child. Pulling at his tie and fingering his collar, Charles flushed.

Carefully putting his hands on the table, Charles retorted, "Xavier, you and Dr Taylor are being ridiculous. It's well proven that the reason for the drought—"

"The evidence you have has been nobbled. There's no other answer for it."

Perry's words were incendiary. The minute she dropped them, in the mushroom cloud came a shower of voices, each one barking over the other.

"Enough!" More exasperated than he remembered being for a long time, Xavier half-roared the single command, but the instant he spoke, the others fell silent. "If your name isn't Charles Françoise, then clear the room."

The other seven members of the EA gaped at one another, umbrage making them bristle, but begrudgingly got to their feet.

Xavier didn't watch them trudge out, but Perry did. She folded her arms across her chest as she watched the top dogs of the EA depart, leaving them with the vice president.

"Charles, I want to know why Veronia's most pressing ecological matter isn't being handled by the president of the agency."

The other man cleared his throat. "Justin, as you can imagine, is a very busy man."

"Too busy for the nation's biggest crisis?" Perry scoffed. "Something stinks here, and it isn't your shitty aftershave."

Charles flushed once more, and Xavier had to hide a grin—she wasn't wrong. The man had overdosed on sandalwood this morning.

"Dr Taylor, I fail to understand why—"

Xavier sliced a hand through the air. "No. I fail to understand why you're here and Justin Montrail isn't. I fail to understand why you're not seeing the bigger picture, and why you're intent on trying to sell snake oil to me." He cut Perry a look. "You should have told Philippe or Edward that the EA was being so unreceptive to your conclusions,"

She blinked, but her cheeks tinged with pink. "I wanted to handle it by myself."

He cocked a brow at that, unsure as to whether or not he believed the simplicity of her answer.

Maybe that was the whole truth, but somehow, he didn't think so.

Rubbing his chin, Xavier watched Charles carefully as he spluttered, "This has nothing to do with the crown prince or the king."

"It has everything to do with them. If one arm of their government isn't working, then they need to know. Especially if that arm is actively sabotaging the nation."

Charles's eyes widened. "Sabotage?"

"Yes, sabotage," Xavier retorted. "What else do you call it, man? Perry's findings are concrete. There is no crisis."

"Well, there is. But it's artificial," Perry butted in. "And for some reason, your organization is content with allowing that particular status quo to carry on."

Charles' mouth flattened as he got to his feet. "I don't have to listen to this." He buttoned his suit jacket, his hands jerky, the motion agitated. Then, reaching over, he collected a few of his papers and stacked them together. "You think we're going to take your word on something because you're the crown princess-to-be?"

"No. I expect you to take my word on this because the evidence is right in front of your damn eyes," Perry snapped. "I've taken information from your sources, I've found my own. Everything points to the real issue at hand. Someone is purposely damaging the dams. They're old, yes. But old and, until recently, well-maintained. Something has changed that, and you're idiots if you aren't going to look into that."

Before Charles could speak, Xavier inserted, "Oh, don't worry, Perry. If Charles isn't going to look into it, I know a few other people who will."

"You think because you fucked Laurenne Jonquil you can get her to speak to the president on your behalf?"

Though Perry stiffened at his side, Xavier ignored her. That was the past, and the past had no say in his present. "I think she has a surprising amount of clout in this agency, you're right. However, I'm talking about my uncle. I think he might be able to scurry up some interest in what Dr Taylor has to say."

Charles grabbed his leather briefcase. "You're trying to create a conspiracy where there isn't one."

"No, you're trying to hide from or shield a conspiracy that's been long in the making. This is a long con," Perry spat at Charles. "If George hadn't brought me here, who knows how long you could have swept this under the carpet for? It's only because I'm totally impartial that I'm saying any of this. And it's only because of Xavier and his apparent ties to Ms. Jonquil that you even agreed to this presentation."

"I read your report," came Charles's bored reply. "There was no need for a presentation on findings that are completely ludicrous."

"I'll be sure to tell my future father-in-law that," she retorted sweetly. "I'm certain he'll appreciate your opinion."

"My job here is secure, Dr Taylor," Charles hissed.

"Secure until the next government sits in place. Well, that would ordinarily be the case. With De Montfort resignation on the cards?" Xavier shook his head. "We both know there's going to be a cabinet reshuffle. Maybe you'll be shuffled off the political playing field altogether."

Charles's jaw clenched. "You always were a prick, Xavier."

"Funny that, Charles. I always thought the same about you." Xavier folded his arms across his chest and watched as the pipsqueak shot off out of the boardroom.

When the door closed behind him, the bang resounding and impossible to mistake as being made by anything other than one pissed-off official, Perry shot to life.

However, she surprised him.

He expected her to ask him about his "ties" with Laurenne Jonquil; instead, she fell silent and began shutting down her computer. Her movements were precise, neat. They weren't jerky, but he knew her well enough to read her.

He knew she was containing her irritation and uncertainty within the everyday actions she was undertaking.

He sighed when she remained quiet, refusing to meet his eyes when he said her name.

"It was a long time ago," he told her when she maintained her stubborn stance.

"I'm sure it was." Her bland tone had him gritting his teeth. Then, she amazed him by asking, "Did you know Edward was going to come to the States to meet with my parents?" Taken aback, Xavier just studied her a second. Uncertain whether she'd be angry for admitting that he had known, he nevertheless went with the truth.

He nodded.

"Why didn't you tell me?"

"Because I only knew he *intended* to go. I wasn't sure if he'd be able to make it happen."

"Isn't it funny how he's going to be the future king, and yet, he has to answer to Drake?" she murmured, tone pensive.

He shrugged. "I suppose. But if he wants something badly enough, he'll fight. And here, it would seem, we have proof that rebellion works."

She blinked, then put the lid to her laptop down. "True. Handy for future reference."

His lips twitched, but he just asked, "How did the first meeting between him and your parents go?"

She shrugged. "Quite well."

"Only 'quite well'? I'm sure Edward will be upset to hear that. He wanted to make a good impression."

"Oh. He made a good impression. Apparently, I didn't."

"What?" Xavier demanded, as a scowl puckered his brow.

"My father told me I'm getting 'too big for my britches,' as he lovingly phrases it." She pursed her lips as she shoved her laptop into its case.

"Why did he say that?"

"Because we were discussing the wedding, and Edward was teasing me, saying that I wasn't interested in the event like a lot of women might be. Then my father said I'd always been ungrateful, and that he was sad I hadn't grown out of it."

For a second, Xavier just gaped at her, his mouth working. That, however, seemed to be all he needed to do, because after staring at him for a handful of seconds, she started giggling.

"Your face is a card."

"You're lying?" he said, somewhat relieved, then astounded once more when she shook her head.

"Nope. He's mad at me, I guess."

"For what?"

"Keeping them out of the loop. There's a lot to be mad about, I suppose. I haven't been home in four years, then when I do get in touch more frequently, it's to tell him I'm about to get married to a man they've never met. Not only that, but the man lives across the world. He's going to be king one day, and worse still, that means I'm going to be a queen." She blew out a sharp breath that morphed into a chuckle. "It's no wonder he's pissed at me."

He frowned at that, then reached over and pressed a hand to her shoulder. He wanted nothing more than to tug her into his arms and hug her, but the truth was, he daren't. Anyone could be watching through the transparent wall of glass behind him, and anyone could walk into the boardroom.

Though an embrace between him and his cousin's fiancé might not be too bizarre an idea, the sight of one might raise suspicions.

That was something they couldn't afford.

Irritated because he couldn't act on his feelings, he instead squeezed her shoulder. "He should be proud of you. Look at you, two days until the wedding itself, and here you are, working. That says a lot about the daughter they raised."

"You're forgetting," she said wryly, "This, to them, isn't all that important. They'd have preferred for me to be a happy housewife than a stressed scientist."

He shook his head. "Then, their opinion doesn't matter."

She pulled a face. "I try to tell myself that I believe that, but I don't. Not really. My dad's opinion has always meant a lot to me. Mostly because I knew, from being very small, that one day I'd disappoint him by not doing what he wanted. By not being what he wanted for me." She shrugged. "He'll get used to the idea."

Xavier's brow puckered further at how sad she sounded. "Is there anything I can do?"

"Take him under your wing at tonight's party?"

He blinked. "Of course." He reached up to tug at his bottom lip. "You all set for the rehearsal dinner?"

She nodded. "As set as I'll ever be." He watched her place a hand on her stomach. "Not that I'll be eating anything. I couldn't eat a damn thing."

"Nerves," he told her softly. "It will all be over in two days' time."

"Yeah, it will. But then it's the start of a whole lot of... something else."

He winced because she had that damn right. In this instance, she was truly falling from the frying pan into the fire.

"I can't believe it's been four months since..."

He smirked a little. "'Since' being the operative word."

She caught his eye, smiled. "Four months." She blew out another breath. "Where's the time gone?"

"Has to be a record," he told her ruefully. "No other wedding has happened so quickly."

"I can believe it. It feels insanely fast to me, too." She stacked some papers together and shoved them into her laptop case. When he reached for it, taking it from her with ease, she sighed at the courtly gesture. As he swooped in, she took advantage of their proximity to murmur, "And yes, I'm jealous as hell."

He blinked, then grinned. "There's no need to be. It was a long time ago, and it was an even bigger mistake."

"I shouldn't be happy to hear that, but I am."

He winked. "You think I want to hear about the guys you've slept with?"

"Well." She cleared her throat. "You were my first and last one-night stand."

He laughed at her hushed tone and murmured, "Glad to hear it." He placed a courteous hand at her lower back as he shepherded her out the door. It wasn't how he wanted to touch her. If anything, he wanted to curve his arm about her waist and tug her close. Declare to the whole fucking world that she was his.

But she wasn't.

As far as the world knew, she was Edward's.

And that sucked. But, at least he had her. At least she was a part of his life at all, and for that, he had to be grateful.

As they stepped into the admin block of the EA, they were confronted with suspicious glances from the worker bees hiding inside their cubicles. He barely glanced at them, but with each scornful look, Perry straightened her shoulders, strutting her stuff, ignoring the contempt aimed her way.

Apparently, she'd made a reputation for herself in the EA.

He had to hide a grin at the thought.

Xavier hadn't needed to be at the meeting, not really. Although he knew his presence had meant that prick, Françoise, had been there, Xavier had attended the meeting mostly as a courtesy, but also out of curiosity.

She'd been grumbling about the EA, and he'd wanted to see her in action as well as learn why she was so annoyed with the agency. He'd learned more than he'd expected, as well as the fact she'd been trying to handle this remarkable situation herself.

He could commend her for that, but she'd need to learn how the family worked. Especially where their pigheaded government was concerned.

After they headed through the dowdy office and found their way onto the main street, the limo was waiting for her, and she climbed in. "Aren't you coming with me?"

"My car's parked around the corner," he told her.

"Can't one of your guards drive it?"

He pondered that a second then reached for his phone. After he speed dialed a button, he said into the receiver, "Can you drive my car to the estate? I'll be going to the castle."

"Of course, Your Grace."

With the assurance in place, he climbed into the limo.

"That was relatively painless."

He shrugged. "I was going to come to the castle later on anyway."

"You were?" she asked, brows high.

"Yes. Edward, George, and a few other friends from school are having a drink in one of the staterooms before the rehearsal."

"Like a well-behaved stag party?" she asked, chuckling.

"I guess," he replied ruefully.

"I can't imagine Edward ever being wild enough to have an all-out stag party," she mused. "But then, Edward on the outside is completely different to the one he's shielding on the inside."

"You're getting to know him well," Xavier replied, approval lacing his tone. "He's insane at heart. There was a particular summer," he murmured, tone reminiscent, "We went to Ayia Napa."

"How the hell did you fool the guards?"

"We didn't. We had to fool Marianne and Philippe, but Drake knew. He didn't approve, but Edward was young and so was I. He understood." Xavier rubbed his chin as he grinned, memories flooding his mind. "It was probably the last time Edward ever really acted his age." Sadness filled him at that thought.

"I always had a lot more freedom than him, you know? I'd been to Ibiza the year before, and had passed out way too many times in Prague. But Edward? Not so much. He kept all his rebellions hidden in the bedroom."

He cocked a brow at her so she'd understand his meaning without him having to utter another word.

Her laughter was choked, but hell, he'd take it. She'd looked so sorrowful when she'd spoken about her father, and he wanted to rectify that, take that away from her, any way he could.

"So, he's not going to be attending the rehearsal meal pissed out of his skull, is he?" she asked wryly, turning in her seat so she was facing him. "I really need one of us to keep on impressing my dad, otherwise that's just going to be awkward."

"Awkward?" he joked. "That's what you'd call it, huh?"

She snickered. "Well, it's polite."

He winked. "I'll do my best to restrain him. If having his father hanging around isn't enough to dampen the party atmosphere, that is."

"Philippe's going to be there?" She smirked. "Okay, well, that totally reassures me."

"Thought it might."

She pulled a face. "Does he need one?" she asked after a few moments.

"A stag party?" He cocked a brow. "Why?"

"I don't know. Sow the last of his wild oats?"

He scoffed at that. "You think he'd cheat on you?"

"Well, no. But, I mean, does he need to go crazy?"

"I told you. Edward doesn't do 'crazy' outside of the bedroom." He pursed his lips. "Do you worry about that?"

"About Edward needing to sow his wild oats?" She shrugged, and, *sotto voce*, murmured, "Maybe. Hard not to. Three of you, one of me. Although, I guess if anyone is gonna cheat, it's more likely to be you or George." The breath she blew out was long. "He's tied to me. You guys are—"

When she broke off, he asked, "We're what?"

"Out in the cold."

He squinted; making out her mumble was harder than it ought to have been. "You really think that?"

"No. I'm scared that's the truth. But I don't let it rule me. Otherwise I wouldn't be going through with—" She broke off. "That's a lie."

"It is?" he asked, even though he knew it was.

"Yeah. I wouldn't have said yes to Edward's proposal. But that was then. This is now. I love him, Xavier."

"I know you do." His smile was heartfelt. "And I've never been happier about that. He's eating more, sleeping more. Been less stressed. He's happier. Jesus, I haven't seen him this happy in a lifetime, Perry."

He shot a look at the driver and the guard at his side, but their attention was on the road. Using their inattention, he reached for the hands she had laying in her lap and threaded his fingers through hers.

"I'm relieved to hear it," she confessed.

"Do you have any idea how grateful I am for how you've brightened up his life?"

"I don't want your gratitude, Xavier," she said playfully, but her fingers squeezed his.

"No. But you have it. And if you think I'm going to repay that by—"

"There's nothing to repay," she told him. "Nothing."

He knew she meant that, but still. "I wouldn't do anything without telling you first, Perry."

She screwed up her nose. "I guess that's the most anyone can ask."

He smiled, then turned to look ahead. In the near distance, he saw Masonbrook. Jerking his chin at it, he murmured, "Almost there."

"Great." She grunted. "I'm having a last-minute session with the dressmaker."

His lips curved in a smile. "You do know who the dressmaker is, don't you?"

"Luisa Raziona," she said disinterestedly. "Marianne said she's very good. Well, she is, considering how quickly she managed to sort out that travesty of a dress Marianne helped design."

"George told me," Xavier murmured. "He was very unhappy with the state of it."

"*He* was unhappy? God, can you imagine how badly *I* felt? Even with as little fashion sense as I have, I knew that dress was a disaster." Her grin was sharp. "The new one looks gorgeous, but unlike Edward who's eating more, I'm eating less. I'm nervous," she admitted. "She keeps having to pin the waist in."

He sighed. "After this is all over, will you start watching your diet?"

She wrinkled her nose. "Is it terrible to admit I like being this skinny?"

His lips twitched at her scandalized tone. "No, it's not terrible, but it is a shame. You were beautiful the day you walked onto Veronian soil, and you're still beautiful now. But all that matters is you're healthy and happy with how you look, you got me?"

"*Capiche*," she jibed.

"You going *Scarface* on me to put your point across?"

She laughed. "If that's what it takes." Perry let out a small sigh. "I promise though, I'll start eating normally once this is all over. I'm trying not to let it get to me, you know?"

"I do know. You've done a remarkable job of staying out of the arrangements, truth be told."

"Only because George has taken on a lot of the slack for me." She shrugged. "I'm lucky."

"You are. Very. But then, most brides want to be involved."

"Not me," she said cheerily. "I'm not that way inclined."

He chuckled at her choice of words. "What? Female inclined?"

She scowled at him. "Just because I have ovaries doesn't mean I have to like all the sappy stuff, thank you very much."

"No, true," he conceded.

She nodded, a little righteously as far as he was concerned. "I'll be glad, on the day, that it's beautiful. But it would be equally as beautiful in a small town hall with only you and George there for witnesses.

"I've never been the sort of chick who gets emotional or teary-eyed over weddings. It's just not in me. Still, some part of me must be affected, or I wouldn't be this nervous."

"You know everything will be okay, don't you? After, I mean."

Her smile came slowly. "I know it will be."

That smile had him settling back into his seat, ease flooding through him as he realized just how okay she was with the future, unorthodox though it may be, ahead of her.

This path was fraught, he knew, but if they maneuvered it together, as a quartet, being each other's strength when one was weak, they'd make magic happen.

And magic was exactly what he intended to make with her.

———

"TO MY DAUGHTER and my future son-in-law, may you have the love my wife and I have shared. May you find joy in the simple things of life. And may you never lose your path and be lost from one another." Perry's father, Nathaniel, peered down at the champagne in his hand like he didn't know how it had come to be there.

Considering this was the first time he'd probably ever held Veuve Clicquot, George couldn't blame him for looking overwhelmed.

Of the entire wedding party, only Janice and Nathaniel looked uncomfortable. Even Perry, who before him had been unsociable to the extreme, looked at ease at the table of sixteen.

They were in a small restaurant that had been hired out to them for the occasion.

It was his father's favorite restaurant on the Madelan port, and the public knew and loved that he came here for the freshest fish from the best catch of the day.

Giuseppe's was a local legend that had been further canonized by the king's patronage.

When George had thought about where he'd like the rehearsal dinner to happen, he'd been able to think of no other place that could compete. He didn't know Janice and Nathaniel, but from what he knew of her past, he knew Perry had been raised simply. Her childhood was honest and real as only that of a child reared on a farm could be. What was that phrase the Americans used?

Salt of the earth.

Honest and kind and decent.

He liked the term, if he was being candid. It summed up a lot, and though he'd barely had a chance to speak to Janice and Nathaniel—thanks to the crazy amount of organizing he was having to do for the upcoming nuptials—he knew those adjectives summed them up to a tee.

He watched as Nathaniel finally cleared his throat and looked over at Perry. George realized he was slow off the mark, because Nathaniel's eyes glistened with crystalline clarity, thanks to the tears pricking them.

"I wish you well, Perry. I wish you happiness. And I wish you both a love-filled future. To Perry and Edward," Nathaniel said softly, raising his glass finally. And as the rest of the table repeated the couple's names, he took a sip and seated himself a few seconds later.

George knew his mother had been a little frantic at the notion of two hillbillies being at the royal table, but she should have realized how impossible that was. Perry, though she may not have been a stickler for etiquette or courtly mannerisms, was polite to a fault. Her parents had bred that into her.

Though they were both as wide-eyed as children wandering around the everything-is-edible room in Willy Wonka's factory, they comported themselves with a decorum he was thankful for.

They were quiet, polite, and eager to learn so as not to make fools of themselves. The latter saddened him. He felt their self-imposed pressure as he'd seen Perry adapt to it over the months. It had formed her, forged her, really.

He knew his mother had wanted to bring the Taylors over earlier than five days before the ceremony was due to take place. She'd wanted to give them some basic etiquette lessons, but though Perry had extended the invitation, she'd predicted—and had been right about—their ultimate refusal.

"A woman's life on a farm doesn't stop because her daughter's getting married. Doesn't matter if that daughter's marrying a king or a pauper. Cows still need milking and fields still need tending."

She'd sounded incredibly Southern at that moment, and though his mother had been aghast at her words, George had been hard-pressed not to kiss her.

An elbow dug into his side, stirring him from his thoughts. "Penny for them?"

"They're not worth so much," he joked.

"I'm sure they're worth more," Perry whispered as she tilted her shoulders to the side to allow the waiter to serve her meal without getting in his way.

George had to smile at the gesture. Perry, future crown princess, would always be that way. Thoughtful, kind.

It was a tiny gesture, but having seen the late crown princess comport herself in public, well...

Safe to say, for a woman who had no noble blood in her veins, Perry was a lady through and through in comparison.

Not that he'd tell her that.

She was already antsy.

"You did good, George," Perry told him when he didn't reply to her scavenger hunt for answers.

"You like it?" he asked, pleased that she did. "I knew you'd prefer somewhere like this to the palace."

She shrugged. "Feels a bit more normal, you know? Not like anything we just did was normal, of course."

He hid a grin. "At least the rehearsal went down well."

She grimaced. "If you can call that 'going down well.' I nearly tripped, forgot one of Edward's names, and on the way back down the aisle, Edward had to stop me to remind me to curtsey before the king and queen."

Her glum tone prevented him from hiding his grin any longer. "Chin up, buttercup," he teased. "That's why rehearsals happen. So you can make all the cock-ups now."

She rolled her eyes. "Is that supposed to make me feel better?" she grumbled.

"Yeah. It is. Because it's the truth. You won't forget to curtsey, your dad is there to make sure you don't trip like he did tonight, and Edward has far too many names to make missing one a problem."

She blew out her cheeks as she cut him a look. "Ya think anyone would notice?"

"Probably the world, but hell, what do they matter?"

She snickered and reached for her glass of wine. The sip she took was deep, and the sigh that came after was loaded with angst. He could feel her nerves throbbing through her, and guilt flushed through him. It could be said that today was the culmination of a lot of hopes and dreams on his part. And that wasn't a lie.

But he wished she wasn't so nervous, wished that he could ease it for her.

In this entire situation, though he'd maneuvered everyone around better than a Grandmaster played chess, he'd never wanted to hurt anyone. Jesus, if anything, he'd wanted the opposite. He'd wanted to make everyone happy.

Give everyone a sliver of what they could only dream of if they went through with it.

He knew he'd succeeded, because none of this would be happening otherwise. Perry's reasons for saying yes to being Edward's girlfriend in public were a far cry from the reasons she'd be saying "I do" in two days' time, that was for damn certain.

"You doing okay?" Edward asked quietly, tilting his head so that only Perry could hear, and George, too, as they were seated beside one another.

She shot him a tight smile but nodded. Edward seemed to sense her distress, and George watched his hand move from the glass he'd been holding to his lap. Discreetly, Edward shifted it over to Perry's before he turned back to his conversation with Cassie. He could only imagine how tightly Perry clamped down on Edward's fingers.

"This pasta is lovely," Perry murmured as she forked up a bit of the tagliatelle George had recommended to her, and sparingly ate a few strands.

He sighed when she put her fork down and took another sip of wine. "That won't settle your stomach. Do you want an aperitif?"

"No." She shook her head and cradled the wine glass to her chest. "I'm fine with the red."

He snorted. "You look fine. If frantic, insecure, neurotic, and emotional is the con you're trying to sell?"

She squinted at him. "Stop being mean. You were being so nice, too. And you picked this beautiful place and managed to seat everyone perfectly."

He grinned at that. The event was a success, he had to admit.

The back terrace of Giuseppe's was where they were all seated. Under a bower of apple blossom that had to be false, and yet, looked real as hell.

The autumnal night wasn't cold—even the weather was on his side. The table overlooked the back of the restaurant, and they had the yard—normally a bustling terrace filled with diners—to themselves. The old farmhouse looked quaint and rustic, and it was the last place anyone would really think to hold a small, intimate, but nonetheless, very royal, event.

It was why he'd chosen it. He'd known Perry would love it here.

The table itself was placed in an E-shape without the central tine. In the middle were the bride and groom, beside them were their main attendants—as Edward's best man, he was at Perry's side, and Cassie as Perry's hastily selected Matron of Honor, was at Edward's. Then came a few family members, Xavier included, and on the outer edges, opposite one another were the two sets of parents.

He'd segregated them both for a reason. His parents had to have a seat of some standing, while Perry's had to be opposite them. By sectioning them off the way they did, yes, it was isolating, but it meant Nathaniel and Janice could talk amongst themselves without fear of having to socialize—a fate worse than death for her father, if Perry was correct.

It belonged in a movie, if he was being honest. Kind of a *Last Supper* vibe with a *Four Weddings and a Funeral* thrown into the mix.

And why that gloomy combo popped into his head, he'd like to say he didn't know... but he did.

His position in the center of the table meant he could see his parents easily. Which meant he could also see the three guards that had ducked down, individually, to whisper something into his father's ear.

And whatever they were whispering, it wasn't sweet nothings.

Though Philippe was good at hiding the strain that came as part and parcel of their position in Veronian society after many years of practice, he couldn't con a conman.

Or, in this instance, someone who shared the same life as him.

The worried strain on his features that tightened with each word that passed from his guard's lips. The small bites of his favorite dish that made Perry's appetite seem ravenous...

No, something was happening.

And if George was a betting man, he'd say it was something to do with the wedding and the UnReals.

Not that it took a seer to figure that one out.

What else could it be?

The eggs for the cake had all been declared as coming from a batch with chicks in them?

The dress had been stained with paint?

No, nothing made his father get that particularly pained look on his face like the UnReals.

And sadly for George, there was no way he could go over and ease his curiosity. Not without stirring Perry's interest too.

And an interested Perry was a dangerous Perry.

He'd learned that mistake back in Boston.

CHAPTER SIXTEEN

"WHY, I'm not sure how he does it."

Perry's lips curved in a smile. She couldn't help it. The pure Tennessee twang of a woman who hadn't left the state in her lifetime—save for this one trip to her daughter's wedding overseas—was blissful.

It was the sound of home, she realized.

And wasn't that just poor timing that she started connecting the dots between her folks and home and haven, when it was a little too late for her to start thinking that way?

This place was home now.

Well, it was a roof over her head until she could leave for Grosvenor House. But, more than that, she had Edward, George, and Xavier.

She had three men to help settle her into this way of life, and though she was still chewed up with nerves over what was going to happen tomorrow, a part of her was coming to look forward to it.

Why?

Because if she looked forward to it, it would be over that much more quickly. Once the wedding was over, she could slip back into the role she was learning—without a deadline.

There were certain things she needed to know now, and there were things she could learn in time. The pressure of the deadline was amping up her anxieties, but her mother's presence was, surprisingly, working wonders on her.

"You don't know how *who* does it, Mom?" she asked casually, swinging her foot over the side of the armchair.

Though her parents weren't in the private family wing, she wasn't offended on their behalf. George had tucked them away in quarters that were far more comfortable and a lot less stodgy with fewer antiques around every corner.

That meant the armchair she was sitting on was actually comfortable. And she didn't have to fear she was about to break an heirloom every time she got up to take a leak.

The simple cream walls were offset with glossy wooden panels. Bright royal blue curtains hung around the bed—because even a less impressive stateroom in Masonbrook came with a four poster—and they matched the drapes that were swathed in great loops at the windows.

A grand Persian rug was underfoot, tonal colors of rich indigo and cream and brown melded together delightfully. And here and there, there were paintings on the wall of whose signatures she didn't have to peer at to know they were Grand Masters of the field at their point in history.

Quite naturally, her parents hadn't noticed. If anything, her daddy was trying to read the Bible while her mother flitted around the room like she hadn't already been in here for two nights.

Janice's "oohing" and "aahing" over everything made her a delight to show around the palace. She had a childlike glee about her that warmed Perry up.

She'd been impressed herself, but with the same beatific zeal as her mom? No way, no how.

She'd figured, after seeing her father's reaction, why that was exactly.

She was a lot like Nathaniel Taylor. You could take the girl out of the state, could take the girl off the farm, but you couldn't take her daddy's influence from her character.

Truth was, she kind of liked that, though.

It made her feel close to him, and considering he'd been pretty damn quiet since he'd arrived here, that was something she really needed to feel.

"Philippe, of course," Janice said on a huff, after she'd stared out of the window onto the gardens for a good two minutes. Apparently in awe of them. "Philippe—I don't know how he does it. You saw him last night, didn't you? There we all were, enjoying ourselves and having fun—"

"Some of us were enjoying ourselves a little too much," Nathaniel retorted archly, but his leonine head didn't lift from its bowed position over the Bible. Because her daddy was the type of guy to read the Bible to relax...

The scientist in her shook her head.

Janice just huffed. "If a woman ain't allowed to have two glasses of that Verf Click stuff on her daughter's wedding rehearsal, then when is she, Nathaniel?"

Perry had to hide her grin at her mother's butchering of "Veuve Clicquot," a very fine champagne that Edward had poured for her parents himself.

"Yeah, Dad. You could lighten up a bit," Perry retorted, surprising herself with the criticism. Normally, she just let her dad be his quiet self.

But she knew this would be the longest she'd get to be with him for quite a while. Though she'd wanted to make it for Thanksgiving, unless her family came here for the event, this year, it was a no-go.

Drake had already put his foot down.

Being a royal sucked. And she wasn't even royal yet!

Yeah, she got to travel in fancy schmancy jets and shit, but what was the point when those jets were never freakin' used?

That particular tidbit of news was something she'd shared yesterday, and the disappointment on their faces had damn well broken her heart. But what could she do? How could she…?

A thought came to her, one that required further contemplation, as well as planning—could she find someone who'd look after the farm for two weeks? Could she encourage her folks to come to Grosvenor House for Thanksgiving?

Excitement welled in her at the prospect, but her father stanched it by grumbling.

"I'm quite happy as I am, thank you, Perry." Nathaniel peered over his reading glasses to pin her with a look. "Can the same be said about you, child?"

Janice pshawed at that. "Don't be silly, dear. Of course, she's happy. I mean, Edward dotes on her. Anyone can see that." Janice cupped a delicate peony that was arranged artfully in a beautiful glass jug on a side table. "I was the first to say that I thought you were crazy, sweetheart. But having seen him and met him and spoken with him, I can understand why you've fallen for him. Even if he does come with all this."

Considering she'd been ""oohing" and "aahing" at everything since she'd arrived, Perry was surprised by her mother's last comment.

Still, she shrugged. "I'm not doing it for anything other than Edward. He needs me."

"You certain that's the truth? Would be very easy for even a levelheaded girl like yourself to get carried away with it all."

The dampening tones, of course, came from her father.

She sighed. "Yes, Dad. I'm certain. If anything, as Momma says, these extra bits, they're more of a pain than a virtue.

"You know me, Daddy. I don't want, nor need, nor like, a lot of fuss. And what's happening tomorrow is one whole heap of fuss."

Janice's lips curved into a bright smile. "Why, I think that's the most southern I've heard you sound all day."

Nathaniel sniffed. "It's a wonder you haven't forgotten your roots, considering how long you've been away from them."

"Now, Nathaniel, you promised you wouldn't mention that."

Perry frowned as she sat up a little. "You could have called, Dad. If you weren't happy with how long I'd been gone, you should have called."

"I didn't want to pester," he said with a sniff.

"So, instead, you're going to preach at me from behind a Bible?" She narrowed her eyes at him, not willing to take another potshot from him. "I've taken a lot on the chin since you arrived, Daddy. You weren't kind to me on the plane, and you embarrassed Edward when he was just trying to make you see how happy we were together."

"It would take a whole lot more than me to embarrass that boy," Nathaniel remarked drily. "Anyone can see that."

Because she trusted his opinion, she was curious what he meant. "What are you talking about?"

"Boy works on another playing field."

"What do you mean?" She scowled at him. "Are you saying my fiancé's nuts?"

Nathaniel huffed. "Did I say that?"

"No. Not exactly. But I'm not entirely sure what it was you were trying to say anyway."

Janice, in a simple but pretty dress that George had helped Perry pick out for her, came to stand behind her husband. She pressed a quelling hand to his shoulder. "Now, Nathaniel, what have I told you about going all cryptic on me?" She shot Perry a look. "He's getting worse with old age," she complained.

Nathaniel peered up at her and shook his head. "You're just not listening, neither of you. And you—a scientist, too," he retorted, the words obviously aimed at Perry.

Swinging her feet around and off the arm of the chair, she turned to face him. "If you've got something to say, Dad, just say it."

"I'm saying, the boy ain't no simpleton. That's all."

"Well, no. I know that." She frowned. "What I don't understand is what you're getting at."

"Once upon a time they'd have called him a strategist. But it's not political nowadays for a king to be that."

"A strategist?" She frowned. "Why is that a bad thing?"

"Not necessarily a bad thing, nor is it a good thing. I'm just saying, kings and princes are more baubles now than the warriors they once were."

"And Edward's a warrior?" she asked, still confused.

Nathaniel nodded. "It's why he's lost. Doesn't know what to do with himself."

"You'll be good for him," Janice pointed out brightly, but even she looked uneasy at her husband's words. Perry saw her squeeze his shoulder again, this time, hard enough to make her knuckles turn white. "Anyway, I was saying. *Philippe*. When those guards came to talk to him, why, he did look so stressed. I wanted to go over and ask if he was okay, but your father stopped me. Said it wasn't our place."

"The guards spoke to Philippe?" Perry asked, curious now. She hadn't noticed anything amiss—the guards usually checked in with the king, or Edward, if he was the highest-ranking official at an event.

Janice shrugged. "He just looked mighty stressed out to me." She picked at the waist of her dress. "This is lovely, by the way, Perry. Thank you for thinking of me."

Still a little off-kilter because of the direction the conversation had taken, she murmured, "You're welcome, Momma. I hope everything fits."

"Oh, it does. And the suits fit your father a treat. Especially the one for the wedding." Her mother let out a giggle that was surprisingly girlish. "Top hats and tails. I never. He looks quite the gentleman."

Perry rolled her lips inward to hide her smile. Her mother looked delighted, whereas her father looked mortified.

Still, if that giggle was anything to go by, her parents were going to get up to mischief while they were on Veronian soil.

Not that she wanted to think of her parents doing anything other than holding hands, quite naturally.

She smirked at the thought, touched despite herself to see how close the two were.

That hadn't changed. Not in all the years they'd been together.

In fact, watching them interact was very grounding. And Perry hadn't realized exactly how much she'd needed that. Not until now when suddenly, it became a little easier to breathe.

Thank God for parents.

CHAPTER SEVENTEEN

NODDING AT XAVIER, Edward murmured, "Did Perry ask about what we're wearing?"

Shaking his head, his cousin replied, "Why would she?"

"Because most brides would be interested in something like that." He wasn't hurt by her disinterest though—more like, amused.

"Why are you asking me anyway? Surely she'd have talked to George about it?"

Edward snorted. "If you think that, you're mad. She's avoided any talk of the wedding with him, because she knows he'll bore her to death with the details."

Xavier shot him a wry look. "So he's been boring you to death with them instead?"

"And you, too, by the looks of it," Edward retorted, lips twitching as he tightened the chain around his hips.

"She'll be shocked as hell by the kilt," Xavier pointed out as he adjusted his own. "You never get used to the breeze, do you?"

His rueful comment had Edward laughing. "No. You don't. Imagine how women feel in skirts."

"I'd rather not. And don't belittle my masculinity by comparing this to a goddamn skirt."

Edward grinned. "What about my masculinity?"

"You're very secure in yours. You're older. I need the extra nine-hundred days to get a grapple on things."

Edward snickered, and realized how relaxed he was feeling. It was an odd sensation. He was about to get married in front of the whole world, and rather than feeling a lick of nerves, he felt like he'd downed a half-bottle of scotch—without the hangover waiting to happen.

It was a novel feeling.

"You look happy, cuz," Xavier murmured, knocking shoulders with him as he approached the mirror where Edward was standing.

Xavier had come to Edward's room for help with the cravat that came as part of the national uniform they were both wearing. He fully expected for his younger brother to make an appearance shortly.

One day, Perry would help them with this cravat...

He chuckled at the thought.

"What are you laughing at?" Xavier asked curiously.

"I'm just trying to imagine Perry helping us with the neckties."

Xavier's eyes widened. "Jesus, we'd be better off asking one of the guards." He grinned back, then studied Edward's smirking profile a second. "See, that's what I'm talking about... it's great to see you so at peace."

Edward cocked a brow. "What? In comparison to the last time?"

"You looked like you were going to attend a funeral."

Edward shrugged. "It felt like it."

"This doesn't?"

"What do you think?" Edward replied, a quick grin lightening his features further. "I haven't felt this..." he blew out a breath, "*buoyant,* I guess, for years."

"I'm glad to hear it."

"I think I deserve to drop this particular bomb..." George's voice made an appearance then, before his body did. "I. Told. You. So."

"Nobody likes a know-it-all, George," Xavier groused, sounding more bored than irritated.

George just laughed. "No, but everybody loves me because I'm the matchmaker." He pumped his fist in the air. "Although," he continued, his expression darkening, "it's also my fault we're wearing this stupid uniform."

Xavier shrugged. "You know the women love it."

"Wonder if Perry will," Edward mused, rubbing his chin as he peered at himself in the mirror.

They were all similarly dressed, the only difference being in the colors of certain parts of their uniform.

Queen Victoria had brought her love of the kilt to the Veronian empire. They were heavily influenced with the Scottish tradition, but theirs came without tartan and was black and plain.

There were few tucks, the pleats were boxy, and somber black added a gravitas to the formalwear.

The Royal Guard wore a similar outfit, but as he, George, and Xavier were high-ranking soldiers of that particular Armed Force, their attire was a little different.

They wore a chain around their hips. Where the Scottish sporran would rest, they had a medallion. Edward's was in platinum, George's gold, and Xavier's bronze. Each medallion housed the DeSauvier royal crest and was encrusted with the gem of their station. Emeralds for Edward, rubies for George, and sapphires for Xavier.

The medallion was the size of his fist, and it was guarded alongside the royal jewels. Only the Crown Prince of Veronia, a Prince of Veronia, and the Duke of Ansian were entitled to wear such a chain with the accompanying medallion.

They wore leather boots that gleamed so brightly, they could see their reflections in them, and into them, they'd tucked black socks that covered their calves to just under the knee.

The sight of his knees was an unusual thing to behold. Usually hidden behind exquisite tailoring, he was just grateful he worked out—otherwise they'd have looked knobbly. Instead, the muscles were developed, and he had nothing to fear where their virtue was concerned.

The jackets they all wore were black, tight-fitted, and dotted with more accoutrements of their station.

Epaulets rode their shoulders, their colors of platinum and emerald, gold and ruby, and bronze and sapphire carried on here in the thread that decorated the flaps. Tightly tucked into their waist, they were buttoned and only a hint of the shirt they wore underneath, white linen, was visible. At their throat, they wore cravats. Simple, without the fancy of a Regency dandy, but still damn hard to fix without help.

On the ties, they had lapel pins, miniatures of the medallions hanging around their hips.

Though they hadn't seen active duty outside of Europe, they had been conscripted at twenty-one and had served until they were twenty-eight. None of them had been required to serve in the wars in Afghanistan or Iraq, but George had almost been shipped out, much to their mother's terror.

The only reason they hadn't was because the government of the time had refused to sign off on his being deployed. This had pissed George off—he'd wanted to serve, and their father's hands had been tied by the administration. Said that the administration's decision, its control over his life, had been one of the reasons he'd headed off to America for his MBA.

Still, deployed or not, they'd taken part in missions overseas, had been engaged in active duty and wore medals that spoke of that time in service.

These were no tokens. They were proof of the pride they had in their country, the evidence that they, as was the case of every other male in the land, were willing to sacrifice their lives to protect Veronia's freedom.

"We look like dicks," George said sourly, coming to stand next to him and Xavier.

"No. We look like chick magnets," Xavier corrected. "More so, we look like Perry magnets. She reads romances, guys. Women love those Scottish highlander books."

George snorted. "How would you know?"

"When you told me what you found on her Kindle, I did some research." He grinned. "I'm a scientist. I like to have all the facts at my disposal."

"I can't see you sitting down with chick-lit," Edward joked.

"They're two separate genres," Xavier corrected, refusing to take the bait. "Chick-lit and romance aren't the same thing."

George just snorted, then, he glowered at his reflection. "Good job we work out," was all he said.

"Weird seeing our knees, isn't it?" Edward replied, understanding exactly where his brother's train of thought had taken him.

He nodded glumly, then scowled as Edward grabbed him by the shoulders and turned him to face him. As he began on his younger brother's cravat, George peered at him. "You look calm."

"What is it with you two? Do you *want* me to be a nervous wreck?"

George grinned. "No, of course not. I just didn't think you'd be this comfortable."

"He was laughing earlier. And I watched him eat breakfast, too."

George heaved out a sigh. "Aren't you the lucky one? I was too busy sorting out some last-minute arrangements for the service."

Edward laughed. "You really should open your own wedding planning business."

George's lips twitched. "If my career in the stock markets falls through, I know what to do with my life."

"You've found your calling," Xavier inserted dramatically.

George rolled his eyes, then, heaving out another sigh, he grumbled, "Go through the schedule."

Edward blew out a breath. "Again?"

"Yeah. *Again*. Until I know you've got it right."

He rolled his eyes, but knowing how much work his younger brother had dedicated to his wedding, decided he wouldn't be a jerk about George's sudden flights into tyranny when it came to making sure everything was going according to plan.

"As soon as the car comes, we'll be driving along the coast road to

Madela. The minute we hit the city streets, we'll get out of the car and the three of us will start the walk to the abbey."

"Drake must be shitting a brick."

George shrugged at Xavier's wry comment. "He knows how it works. Security is crazy, as I'm sure you can imagine."

"I'm not worried," Xavier replied, peering in the mirror and straightening out his cravat a little more. "Just making a statement."

"Go on," George continued, as Edward lifted the linen and began tucking it into place in sweeping folds and loops.

"As we walk through the streets to the abbey, we'll be saluted by my old regiment upon approach."

"Then what?"

"I salute my old regiment in return, and each soldier fires two rounds into the air apiece."

"Because that's not a disaster waiting to happen in a crowded public place," Xavier groused.

"We've done it a hundred times before, and no one's ever been hurt. Tradition, man," George snapped. "Stop interrupting. This is important."

Edward rolled his eyes again as he reached for the lapel pin George was holding out on the flat of his palm. "Once the shots have been fired, Xavier heads into the church first. He bows to the reverend, who will be waiting at the doors.

"When he's gone inside, we follow him. He leads the procession into the abbey. Xavier, the reverend, you, then me.

"As we walk down the aisle, I'm not allowed to greet any of the guests. Only when I approach Father on the throne, and after I bow, can I turn around to face the door.

"Xavier joins Mother and Father at the thrones, you stay at my back throughout the service." As he placed the lapel pin into the central fold, he grumbled, "Sad though it may be, I have done this before, George."

"As have Xavier and I, but this time, it actually matters."

"Bloody hell, George," Xavier said, wincing at his candor. "That's harsh."

"Harsh but true," was all he said with a shrug. He turned to face the mirror, straightened the cravat a little as he wiggled his neck to get comfortable, then he grinned. "Thanks. Hate doing that."

"Why do you think I'm in here?" Xavier retorted. "I hate doing mine too." He cocked a brow at Edward. "Do you need to go through the ceremony too?"

"No," he barked. "I damn well don't."

"Do you think Perry will trip on the way down the aisle again?" Xavier asked.

"No. She's wearing flats," George answered as he slicked his hair back.

"Thank God for that," Edward replied, sighing with relief. "That's a weight off. I wasn't sure if Mother would insist."

"Mother is officially allowed no say in Perry's wardrobe. Jesus, how the woman can have such taste for herself and zero for Perry is beyond me. You should be grateful," George remarked, pointing a finger at Edward. "If it wasn't for me, you'd be marrying a meringue."

"What's inside the dress is sweeter than a meringue," he joked. "I could have born up under the pressure."

George punched him in the arm. "Wait until you see her before you say another word. You think she was sweet before?" He whistled under his breath. "You owe me, brother."

Though he knew George was joking, the words took on a meaning of their own when taking the gravitas of the situation into account.

"I really do, George. For everything," he said softly, catching his brother's eye so there was no chance of either of them misunderstanding what the other was talking about.

George's smile was soft, though. Not filled with his usual gregarious ebullience. "I know you do, but you can pay me back by being happy. How's that for a tradeoff?"

Edward grinned. "I think I can manage that."

―――

"OH, DARLIN', you look divine."

"She's right, Perry. You do," Cassie murmured softly, lifting a silk handkerchief to her eyes. She dabbed carefully, not wanting to disturb the makeup that had been an hour in the making, and Perry couldn't blame her.

She'd thought the makeup she'd been having for the royal events had been hardcore? That was nothing compared to today.

She'd been plucked, prodded, and primed. Not a bit of her had been left alone. In certain areas of her person, she was even feeling quite violated.

The need for a Brazilian wax on her wedding day wasn't something she'd particularly understand. It wasn't like that area was for public consumption, which made her think it was a prank George had set her up with.

The bastard.

She grimaced as she tugged at her skirt and tried not to fiddle with the veil the dressmaker had helped set atop her head personally.

Luisa Raziona, who was so famous even her countrified momma knew who she was—leaving Perry the odd one out—had seen to the final touches herself. Smoothing out the lines of silk here, ruching the pleats of the skirt at the back.

Truth was, Perry could have worn a sack, and she'd have been more grateful than could be for not having to wear the disaster Marianne had concocted.

"It's better than the other one, isn't it, Cassie?" she asked, her tone laced with more of a plea for reassurance than she liked.

"It's wonderful," Cassie breathed, and Perry saw, deep in her eyes, that the other woman spoke the truth.

She gnawed at her lower lip, then whispered, "You ladies look beautiful, too."

More than her own dress, she'd actually had a lot of input in their outfits. Mostly because George had said it would be weird as hell if the bride didn't know what the bridesmaids and her mother were wearing.

As a result, the simple pink sheaths—that had more of a bronzy feel to them than a Georgia sweet peach—had been approved by her.

Cassie, in all her slenderness, looked divine in it. It was simple, elegant, timeless. For a hick, Perry thought she'd done really well in picking that particular dress.

Cassie was the only attendant she actually knew and liked. The rest were part of the DeSauvier clan—nobles who'd be her bridesmaids simply because of their names and ties to the family.

Why, it was enough to warm the heart, wasn't it? She rolled her eyes at the cynical thought.

On her side, she had a swarm of uncles, aunts and cousins roaming around at the wedding, but the only ones that really mattered were her momma and daddy.

Her momma looked divine in a cerise dress that brought out the blond in her hair. She'd had it touched up at the roots and now had silvery high lights roaming over her head. The bright cerise dress came to just below her knees, was paired with some strappy silvery kitten heels, and she wore a gray, with silver accents, tailored coat that fit at her shoulders, making her look broader than she was, and cut in at the waist so her youthful figure was on show.

Janice had perched a pillbox hat jauntily on her crown, and Perry knew if her daddy was as dapper as her momma had giggled about yesterday, then she was the female equivalent of dapper too.

Delightful?

Pretty?

She honestly didn't know. But Janice, the housewife, and Janice, the Crown Princess of Veronia's mother, were two different beasts entirely.

Janice patted her hair and her hat, and Cassie touched her waist self-consciously as she complimented their elegance. It was easier to compliment them than it was to actually look at herself, because, for the first time, she started to believe she could do this.

Who was the woman who looked back at her in the mirror?

These past few weeks, she'd been beset by an anxiety that had nauseated her. Not because it made her stomach churn with fright, but because she'd always believed in herself. Had always fought to make sure that even if the rest of the world had no faith in her, she herself did.

So, these past couple of weeks had been hard on her.

But as she stood there, dressed in a gown that would make any princess in Europe gasp in envy, Perry knew, for the first time, that she had this shit.

She could own it.

Because the Perry who'd been bullied at her lab by her superiors, the Perry who had waited for George to declare his feelings for her, well, that Perry was gone.

And in her place was Princess Perry.

She had no idea where that side of herself had come from. Was it from the months of torturous "How to-" classes? The smacks on the hand that Marianne delivered every time she did something wrong?

Perry didn't know exactly, but hell, it didn't matter.

She sucked in a shaky breath as she turned to face her reflection once more. Looking at the dress made her look at the *new* her, and it was disconcerting, to say the least.

Who was the woman whose hair flared out around her shoulders in a wave of mahogany silk?

Whose eyes sparkled like the gems she wore?

She didn't know, but she was rocking it, and she sucked in a sharp breath as she took in the wonder that was her dress.

Even after George's redesigns, the dressmakers had had to work on it to make it fit her shape, as his hadn't suited her either. But they'd put their heads together, and those poor seamstresses had been working like there was no tomorrow.

Like Cassie's, it was a sheath dress that cut in at the waist and dipped low in front. Not scandalously, but enough to make everyone realize that the things attached to her chest weren't melons but quite nice boobs.

From top to bottom, the sheath was covered in Sosan lace from the Sosa region of Veronia. It had been stained an antique beige, and the color offset her pearly skin to perfection.

But the dress, for all its majesty, was only the sum of its parts.

What really made her look, as Xavier said, the dog's bollocks, was the train.

There was a medieval style to it. It clung from her shoulders and draped about her like a floor-to-ceiling wedding coat. But this was no wedding coat that any bride had ever worn before.

Those poor seamstresses had created a tapestry of everything that made Veronia great, set amid the bejeweled and embroidered tableau.

This was what the queen of a new king, of a new dynasty, wore.

A reminder of all that made Veronia great.

Of all that made it powerful.

She embodied it, and such a task should have daunted her, but it didn't.

If anything, she knew she was up to the challenge.

In contrast to the beige wedding dress, the wedding coat was the purest, cleanest white imaginable. That was what made the embroidery so enchanting. It was ghostlike, because it, too, was pure white.

A glimpse of Veronia's national flower there, of the Ansian thistle here. The only bright bursts of color came from the cuff at her wrist which was visible when she moved and the coat parted, and the ringlet on her head.

Marianne had dug around in the crown jewels like it was a costume box up in the attic—how cool was that?—and had found a tiara that was medieval in fashion. The circlet sat on her forehead with a comfort that surprised her, considering it hadn't been made for her, and though it was heavy and might become a nightmare after the ceremony, it was worth it to look like this. The veil was sheer, like a whisper of silver as it sailed over her head. A simple bias-cut piece that draped to the floor and could be discarded later.

She looked, as her mother said, and as Perry, so uncomfortable with compliments, believed—divine.

"It's astonishing, Perry. You're astonishing," Cassie choked out as she carried on dabbing at her eyes. "You're going to make Edward the luckiest man in the church today."

Despite herself, Perry had to smile. Because—and she didn't give a damn if it made her sound big-headed—Cassie wasn't wrong

---

HER FATHER WAS as dapper as her mother said he was.

In the journey to the abbey—which occurred in a horse-drawn carriage—there was little chance to talk.

The screams of the crowd were too loud, too numerous for gentle conversation.

She kept her head turned to the public, a smile pinned to her face as she waved the way Marianne had taught her with one hand, like she was caressing the air, while the other was held in a tight clasp by her daddy.

She wasn't sure who clung to whom most, but they were both clinging, that was all she knew.

She was ready for this. Readier than she'd realized she could be… but that didn't mean the ride wasn't eye-opening.

Thousands of people lined the streets of the capital to greet her. They chanted her name, they cried out Edward's.

The roads were barricaded so her carriage, and the guards riding horses at front and back, could traverse with no problem. The many aspects of Madela she'd come to appreciate, she barely saw.

She was a bit blind at that moment. Tunnel vision was allowing her to see only the way ahead, and that path was dotted with people wishing her well and waving Veronia's flag as they did so.

These were *her* people now, she realized, surprised by the notion.

She had a "people." She was becoming so much more than she'd ever dreamed she'd be, and in the wide-eyed expression on her father's face, she saw his surprise at her acceptance by the Veronians, as well as his pride in her.

Not that he'd admit to that. What with pride being a sin, after all.

In the distance, she saw the abbey. It was large and daunting. Gothic in style, it reminded her of the Sagrada Familia in Barcelona, but where the Gaudi monument was freely formed, almost like candlewax melting down the candlestick, this was sharp and harsh. Fierce lines.

This was a place of worship where royals were baptized, married, and buried.

This was where the country's royal heart was kept safe.

And she was getting married there.

The tower pierced the sky with an aggression that had her eyes widening.

It wasn't the first time she was seeing it, wasn't the first time she'd be inside it, thanks to the rehearsal, but it was the first time this would be happening.

All roads led to Yorke Abbey, and it was where her fate and Edward's would unite forever.

She was nervous again by the time they made it to the front steps of the abbey. Her father climbed down first, hopping with an agility that belied his sixty-eight years, before he rounded the carriage, a guard ushering him, to reach her side.

Another guard, dressed in royal livery, more gilt and a wig this time that reminded her of the Stuart royal household, held open the carriage door for her.

He and her father then held out their hands, and she grabbed both and carefully lowered herself to the ground.

There were many phases of the wedding where she knew she could make a fool out of herself. Tumbling headfirst out of the carriage was one such instance, but she managed her exit with a panache that astonished even her.

When the gown was settled and righted, she nodded at her father.

This was the moment the world would see her dress for the first time, and Drake had warned her that she might feel blinded by the flashes.

Just as she started to take the first step towards her future, a noise made itself known to her.

She froze, then as the stench of fresh horse dung filled the air, she whipped her head around and saw the evidence for herself.

"Animals will be animals," her father whispered in her ear, and she could hear his amusement.

For herself, she wasn't sure whether to laugh or cry. Then, because if that was the worst destiny could throw at her on her journey to being Edward's, George's, and Xavier's, she flipped fate the bird.

Tilting her head back, she let loose a laugh she knew would grace the front pages, and enjoyed the moment. Her father, chuckling at her side, helped steady her as she began to ascend the steps. Her short train at her back, the longer train of the wedding coat pooling around the stairs.

Each step was a minefield, but she managed it. With her father's help.

"Thank you, Daddy," she whispered, a touch brokenly, as she made it to the top of the steps.

"Anytime, buttercup," he said roughly, and she caught his eye with a grateful smile that was loaded with the love she felt for him.

He'd been pigheaded since his arrival here, but God, she wouldn't change him one little bit. That, and her gratitude for his doing this with her, for falling into the fray at her side, must have been evident in her expression because he caught his breath at her smile.

Reaching up to cup her cheek, he bent down to kiss her there. The candid moment set off a flurry of flashes, but she ignored them.

This wasn't for the world.

This was for her.

"You ready for the zoo?" he asked gruffly.

She blew out a breath. "As ready as I'll ever be."

Straightening her shoulders, she turned to face the crowd head-on, and raising a hand, waved.

Three times, Marianne had told her. Three single times.

Each one seemed to stir the crowd into a frenzy of joy that made her throat choke at the sight.

They were happy for her, she realized. And she felt that joy down to her bones.

Jeez, it almost made her want to cry.

But the makeup had been too long and arduously set for that. And then she had the whole "seeing George and Edward at the altar" thing to contend with. Never mind Xavier, who'd be hanging out with her future in-laws beside the thrones.

Hiding her grimace as she prayed she wouldn't break down and start weeping, she squeezed her father's hand once more. Together they walked into the grand arch that had seen hundreds of DeSauviers pass through its aperture for such a festivity.

She sucked in a sharp breath as they headed into the small antechamber at the entrance, and the doors closed behind her.

The brief moment of privacy had her asking, "How do I look, Daddy?"

"You look like a princess," he told her softly, reaching over to cup her chin through the veil. "My little girl, getting married, and becoming a princess." He whistled. "It's not what I ever imagined for you, buttercup."

Her eyes pricked with tears once more. "Me neither, but he makes me happy, Daddy."

"I'm glad he does. If he ever doesn't, I've plenty of land out back where we can bury him, and the rest of these fools won't ever know."

She chuckled. "I think they'd realize if he went missing."

Nathaniel winked. "At least it made you smile. You're beautiful, Perry."

Nerves beset her once more. She clung to his hand. "I wish we had more time." Her throat closed. "I should have visited more..."

"There's never enough time, sweet pea. The years pass in a flash, and you had a life to forge of your own. A path that led you to here." He blew out a breath. "I couldn't be prouder of you."

Now, the tears seemed less of a threat and more an imminent danger. "That means a lot, Daddy."

Before he could reply, the footmen behind the grand doors to the chapel stomped their feet.

She knew that was a cue.

They'd be turning in unison to face one another as they reached for the grand iron rings that acted as doorknobs on the huge wooden doors. They were made from raw planks that had been seasoned with an orangey varnish over the years, and big bolts studded the ten-foot monsters.

A footman leaned over with her bouquet, a cascading waterfall of peonies and natural flowers that were native to Veronia—from the thistle embroidered on her wedding coat, to a delicate lily that was a sunburst of color amid the other white and cream petals.

"Ready?" he whispered at her side as she tucked the bouquet securely into her hand.

"As I'll ever be."

He raised his arm, and she settled her fingers atop it, and together, they entered the nave and walked down the aisle to a choral accompaniment—the name of which George had told her, but she hadn't really processed the Latin.

The high voices, the echoing sound as the song speared the chapel, soaring high enough to hit the ceiling hundreds of feet overhead, made shivers run down her spine.

She knew from the rehearsal that the chapel was dark and pretty dingy, the only light coming in from a domed roof and the myriad stained windows. But that gloom added to the pageantry of the moment, and with the choir? It was all the more powerful.

The aisle was studded with huge swathes of flowers, bright white thistle and elda, flowers that were embroidered on her dress. Tucked with large roses and bunches of peonies, all matching the bouquet in her hand.

The floral chaos was astonishing, though, and stayed with her throughout her journey down the aisle.

The Veronian service had the bridesmaids and even Cassie, her matron of honor, settling into place long before she even made it down the aisle. Which meant all eyes were on her and her daddy, their own gazes aimed down toward the altar where her future husband would be standing.

She didn't see the huge stone tablets underfoot that were the resting places of hundreds of reverends who had served this abbey. She didn't see the domed roof with its bright blue fresco that overlooked the festivities. She didn't see the grand thrones, ornate and studded with gems where her future in-laws were seated and beside which Xavier stood. Nor did she see her mother or her family who were close to the throne, where in a regular church she figured the choir would stand.

Here, the choir was at the back, their haunting melody chasing her down the aisle, making those chills shoot back and forth along her spine with every step.

She had no room to fear she'd trip.

She had no room to think anything other than the need to calm her breath. To steady her heart.

The aisle was long. Hundreds of feet long. She started to feel a little desperate, a little ragged, until finally, she caught sight of her men.

They were standing there, so proud, so tall. So elegant and so regal that they blew her breath away.

Only the sight of them grounded her.

Only the sight of them in their splendor let her breathe deeper, easier.

For the first time, she sought out Xavier who was standing beside Philippe on his throne. He was at attention, but he was just as glorious as George and Edward in their...

If her father hadn't been shepherding her down the aisle, she'd have frozen in place to gawk.

Because, were they wearing *kilts*?

Holy crap, were they butt naked under them?

The notion made her cheeks tinge with pink as a desperate need to find out that particular truth hit home.

And it was those thoughts in mind, not of the future or of the solemnity of the moment, that helped get her down the aisle with nary an issue.

Because when it came to the prospect of her men being butt naked under a kilt in church, not even the future could take pride of place in her thoughts.

CHAPTER EIGHTEEN

AT THE SIGHT of her sweeping down the aisle, Edward felt choked.

George had been right.

The bastard.

He'd said her glory would astonish him, and it did. *It did*. She was like something from pre-Elizabethan times. A pagan goddess come to blow his mind and to steal his heart.

Half-witch, half-goddess.

That she was to be a princess was affirmed at that moment.

She was short, there was no avoiding that. She wasn't skinny, even though he knew she hadn't been eating well. And though she might not have been anyone's idea of a princess, she was his.

And she was perfect.

Glorious.

She gleamed like an angel with each step she took toward him. And with each step, he wondered if she was questioning this. Wondered if she was uncertain about the future and the power of what they had together in the face of what she had to do to be with them all.

He had no doubt that her wide eyes weren't for him alone. They were for George, and if her darting looks were anything to go by, Xavier too.

But as she approached the altar, moving ever nearer, any qualms fled. He felt her delight in his uniform, just as Xavier had predicted. He sensed her joy in what was about to happen. Her absolute surety.

From the shaky beginnings, from a start that had more chance of crumbling than flourishing thanks to George's machinations, here they were.

The culmination of George's hopes and dreams. Of Edward's needs and passions. Of Xavier's wants and desires.

She was the living embodiment of it all, and he'd never been more grateful for her than he was at that moment.

The choir ceased singing its powerful aria as she neared the altar. With six feet to spare, utter silence befell the abbey.

The thumps of her slippered feet and her father's Oxford's were the only sounds echoing around the atrium. The whisper of her train could also be heard, but it was a steady hum that soothed him.

The aisle gave way to a clearing where they came to a halt.

As protocol demanded, Cassie descended, graceful to the last, from her perch on the penultimate step to the altar. She swept down to face Perry and began to carefully lift the veil off his fiancée's head.

The movement enabled him to see the glorious circlet atop her brow, its bright emeralds winking at him. And he knew his mother had had a hand in choosing that particular piece—emeralds were, after all, the crown prince's stone.

She looked a little white around the gills, if he were being honest, but her cheeks were tinged pink and her eyes were bright with excitement, he was relieved to note.

Cassie gathered the veil in her hand and collected Perry's bouquet of flowers before dipping into a low curtsey and retreating to her perch.

Perry shot him a look that held the mysteries of the ages, a look that had confounded greater men than he and which Da Vinci had captured in *la Gioconda*. Her father once again took her hand, and together, they turned to the left where the king and queen were seated.

Nathaniel's heels clicked as he stood in place and carefully bowed as Edward had instructed him. When he'd supplicated himself, he half-turned to Perry, and with his support, she fell to her knees.

Seeing her there made Edward's throat choke. The pool of white creamy beige against the decorated and carved stone floor was a powerful image he knew he'd never forget.

If he'd doubted his love for her, he knew at that moment he couldn't.

The rest of the world disappeared. The cameras, the congregation, even their family, no one else was there. She was it.

On her knees, she bowed her head and whispered the words that would start the wedding.

"Your Highness, I claim your son as my own. With my heart, I shall shield him. With my body, your line shall continue." She fell silent a second, and Edward's heart raced. The world reappeared, and he glanced quickly at George who also looked a little frantic.

Had she forgotten the rest?

But before their nerves could swell further, she cleared her throat, and the words came out choked. "Do you grant me leave to be the future of your house?"

"Aye, daughter, I do," Philippe said, his tone neither booming nor gentle. But it was heartfelt.

Edward knew it, and as he caught his father's eye, he saw Philippe's approval at his choice.

His father hadn't said much about Perry. But Edward sensed his relief. Not only that he was marrying, but that Perry was the bride.

With her, there was a future that included the chance of a DeSauvier heir of Philippe's direct descendance.

But more than that, Edward knew Philippe was aware of how happy Perry made him.

That, Edward realized, was what counted to his parents as it hadn't the last time.

Before Nathaniel could help Perry onto her feet, Philippe stunned them all by standing, too.

The thrones were ancient and huge. Made from solid gold and carved with motifs that Edward had long since learned and forgotten about, they were also uncomfortable as hell. Not even the red velvet cushions made them easier to sit on—he knew because he'd plunked his butt on there as a child more times than he could count.

Still, his heart was in his throat as Philippe descended the dais and approached Perry.

He looked at Nathaniel. "Your child is welcomed into my line. We shall shelter her for you and safe-keep her future."

Nathaniel blinked, and Edward recognized the appearance of a rabbit in front of headlights, as this was most definitely off-script.

Philippe whispered something which had Nathaniel nodding, and Edward watched as together, they helped Perry stand.

His father held out his arm, and Perry, white-faced and trembling now with confusion and nerves, placed her small hand atop his father's wrist as she did with her own.

The trio managed to walk the six steps to the altar in sync.

Edward caught his father's eye as he too descended the stairs. Bowing deeply, he felt his father's hand on his head. Hesitating a second until Philippe's fingers slipped away, Edward stood.

His eyes prickled with tears, and he silently thanked his father for his explicit approval of this match.

No other bride had been treated so generously in their history.

This was a first.

Groundbreaking.

Philippe smiled at him, the gentle twitch of his lips warm and loving, before he turned to Perry and further amazed anyone who knew anything about protocol, and bowed his head to her.

Perry, looking close to fainting now, gulped.

"I am relieved the future of my line is in your hands. But more than that, it warms me to my soul that my son's heart is in your safe-keeping." He stepped close to her, kissed her cheeks, then having stunned the world with the breach of etiquette, retreated to the throne.

When Edward glanced at his mother, he saw that she wasn't surprised. If anything, her smile was approving. When she realized his attention was fixed on him, her smile widened, but she flared her eyes. A silent prod to get things moving.

Amused at his mother's bossiness, he approached Nathaniel, hand outstretched. His future father-in-law shook it. With his free hand, he reached for Perry's and placed hers close to Edward's.

"Thank you," he said softly, watching as Nathaniel leaned down to kiss Perry on the cheek before he made his retreat to Janice's side, leaving him and his bride-to-be alone.

"Are you okay?" he whispered, squeezing her fingers.

"I'm fine," she said, her words almost exhaled rather than vocalized.

"You look wonderful," he told her, hoping she knew the truth of that.

A throat cleared behind him, and he looked back at a grinning George.

Unable to do anything other than share in his brother's joy for him, he grinned back.

Then, with Perry's hand in his, he guided her to the altar steps and together, they walked toward their future.

CHAPTER NINETEEN

"I NOW PRONOUNCE YOU, man and wife.

"You may kiss the bride, Your Highness."

When Edward's lips caressed hers, she breathed into the kiss, and pressed her hands to his shoulders to hold him closer.

Her fingers were shaking. And though this morning she'd removed her engagement ring and now there was nothing but a ring some ancient queen had worn once upon a time, her hand felt inordinately heavy. The gold was old, tarnished with the years, and Edward could not have picked better for her.

Applause started behind them, and they jumped.

Considering it wasn't protocol, but a hell of a lot of that was being broken today anyway, they looked around a little wide eyed, and saw Philippe was joining in. As was usually the way... if the king was okay with it, or had even started it perhaps, the rest of the world was okay with it too.

Both of them grinned around at the congregation, then Edward reached for the reverend's hand and shook it in thanks.

For a second, time stood still as she looked upon the man who was now her husband.

It seemed incredible, and yet, it was the truth.

They bound their hands, and together, they moved toward the thrones.

There, she dipped into a curtsey while Edward simply bowed before his parents.

She'd never not find that weird as fuck that he had to supplicate himself before them, but one day, if they had a child, he or she would do the same to them.

But that was a whole other load of terror, and she was still in the middle of this half-dream, half-nightmare.

Truth was, now that she was married, she wanted to be away from here.

She wanted to be on the jet to wherever Edward had cooked up for their honeymoon.

After months of living in a pressure-cooker environment, months of being in the public eye, and months of having goddamn lessons, she needed a break.

Stat.

Greedy?

Maybe. But hell, she was tired. Really, really tired.

It was an odd time for her adrenaline to drop, but she'd been hyped up all morning, so maybe it made sense. And the day wasn't even done.

There was the carriage ride through Madela that would take them past another crowd that numbered in the hundreds of thousands as they were cheered on their way to the reception. There was the meal, the after party...

But, more importantly than that, there was now.

Her coronation.

She watched as Marianne got to her feet, where, immediately, she turned to her right to find a page standing with a soft velvet cushion.

Perry gulped at the sight of it. Not because it was a particularly terrifying thing to behold, but because what it represented *was*.

Marianne gathered the cushion in her hands and then brought it to Philippe. When his father stood, Edward helped her back down to her knees—sheesh, she was getting tired of the cold stone against her shins—and he began to help lift the headdress from her brow.

As he released it, her hair fell deeper about her shoulders. She could sense his desire to gather it in his hands and sweep it back for her, but he didn't. Though the fire burning in his eyes meant one thing she was used to seeing, more than just passion for her blazed in those depths.

His love did too.

Before she could fall into that inferno, an inferno she wanted to dive into, Philippe reached for her chin and turned her attention his way.

She peered up at him, a shaky smile on her lips as he reached for the tiara on the cushion Marianne was holding and began to place it atop her forehead.

She saw little other than more emeralds, a silver metal, and an ornate filigree work that patterned the diadem. Then it was on her forehead.

And after, Philippe pressed a hand to her shoulder and in a loud voice, declared, "You may now rise, daughter. Let the nation know, and let the people celebrate, for Veronia is blessed."

And just when Perry thought her nerves would induce her to faint, Marianne, her voice softer, more genteel, declared to the congregation, "Please stand for Her Highness, Princess Perry of Veronia."

CHAPTER TWENTY

EDWARD WATCHED AS PERRY, snuggled into the limo seats, snored and mumbled in her sleep. He'd been watching her since they'd climbed into the vehicle, and the truth was, he couldn't take his eyes off her.

Onboard the jet, she'd changed from her bridal gown, and with that, she'd reverted to the Perry of old.

Out had come the yoga pants and a tee-shirt. Although, Edward had to thank his brother for the fact both were tight-fitting rather than two sizes too large.

And he wasn't complaining.

Sex on a jet wasn't the be all and end all, and Perry was as exhausted as he.

He, too, had taken the chance to get out of his uniform and to change into a pair of favored jeans and a simple shirt.

After the day's pomp and ceremony, wearing something so simple was really wonderful.

Although, he'd never look at his uniform the same way again. Not after Perry had copped a feel of him when they'd had a moment's privacy between the reception and the carriage ride to the palace.

His lips twitched at the thought.

The day had been…

He smiled. Everything a royal wedding ought to be, he supposed. Except here, there was no artifice. There was love.

He loved her, and she loved him.

The notion was remarkably freeing, he realized. It made the day, so fraught with tension, so overwhelming in its entirety, a wonderful memory that would be with him until the day he died.

He'd watched, prouder than he could admit, as his people embraced their new princess. Roaring and chanting her name as they rode through the streets and back along the coast road to Masonbrook.

He'd watched, honored that she'd tied herself to him, as she danced with his father and hers after the reception breakfast. He'd grasped her hand firmly in his, delighted when, with the other, she'd fed him a sliver of banana cake they'd recently cut to the roar of their guests. As he'd sampled the one true part of the reception that had Perry stamped all over it—the unorthodox cake—he'd rejoiced in the fact she was his.

Together, they'd climbed into the limo and headed for the private jet. She'd been so exhausted by that point, that she'd done little else other than snuggle into him on the ride to the airfield.

Because he understood and was equally as exhausted, he'd just curled her farther into his side, loving the intimacy between them.

He knew another man would think him nuts, but those private moments had meant more to him than burning off his raging lust.

The honesty of it all had touched him deeply, and he'd been honored to see that side of her because that day, she'd played a part for him. A role. Now, she could breathe a little easier before the royal charade began once more after their honeymoon.

When, beneath the limo, the sounds of the wheel's track changed, he curled a stray lock of hair behind her ear and murmured, "Perry, it's time to wake up."

She grumbled, and he had to hide a smile. "It's too early to wake up."

The mumbling was so sleepy, he barely heard it, but because he could surmise, he managed to make out what she was saying.

"We're at the house."

Her eyes opened a little at that, but she still squinted at him. "You ready to tell me where we are yet?"

"Well, that woke someone up."

Her laughter was husky. "How many times do I have to tell you? I'm infinitely curious."

He pursed his lips. "Well, I think you've shown great restraint."

"You're still evading my question," she slurred, turning her face into his side. "And I'm too tired to investigate."

"I'm not surprised, considering we've passed through a few time zones."

"We have?" She sat up at that. "Hell, how long were we on the jet?"

"You slept for eight hours," he teased, unable to hide his amusement. Amusement that only soared when her eyes widened, this time in horror.

"Are you being serious? Why the hell did you let me sleep so long?"

He shrugged. "You were tired. So was I."

She narrowed her eyes at him. "How long did you sleep for?"

"About six or seven. A little less than you."

The breath she released was relieved. "Oh, that's okay then." Her scowl returned. "Where the hell are we? And how come it's dark?"

"That has to be the oddest question I've ever heard," he teased. "It's dark because it's night. And we're in Dubai."

"Dubai?"

He nodded. "A gift from one of the Sheikhs. I saw no reason, nor did my parents, not to take him up on the kind offer."

She blinked. "We're in Dubai?"

"Yes," he repeated patiently.

"Where are we staying?"

"One of the palaces, of course."

Her mouth worked a second, then she blew out a breath.

"What is it?"

"Nothing," she replied, but he heard the false brightness in her tone, and hid a smile at the sound of it.

"They'll be here shortly."

Her eyes widened. "*They* will?"

"Of course."

"B-But..."

He cocked a brow at her. "What? You thought we'd be without them?"

"But it's important nobody suspects."

"And nobody will. Xavier managed to wangle an invitation from one of his old school friends who works here. He's tagged along."

"It still looks suspicious. But I don't care. I'll take it. What about George?"

"The old school friend's wife knows him."

She squinted. "How well?"

Edward laughed. "Not Biblically. She's a lesbian."

"Xavier's visiting a woman?"

"Yes. Why does that stun you?"

"I don't know. I'm just surprised. Are you even allowed to be gay in Dubai?" she mused.

"I highly doubt they reveal the truth of their relationship. Xavier's friend, Lucy, runs a laboratory here, and her partner, Jane, is officially her PA."

"Whether it's allowed or not, they'd always keep it a secret. Funding might mysteriously disappear if details of their relationship were known."

"That's sad," she murmured, "but no different than the secrets we'll have to keep, I suppose."

He nodded, but the strain in her voice had him frowning a touch. "Xavier thought you might like to meet them."

"Why? To compare notes on how to lead a secret life?"

He snorted. "If you want."

She reared back at that, then after studying him, her mouth gaped. "You mean I can tell them about what we are to each other?"

Edward nodded. "Laura and Jane are attachés to the Veronian court. They're as tightly bound by non-disclosure agreements as our guards. But more than that, we've known each other a hell of a long time."

She rubbed at her forehead. "How do you know we can trust them?"

"Because we can. Trust in me."

Perry blinked up at him, and he realized that once more, exhaustion had waved over her.

The past few months had been tough on them all, he knew. But Perry more than most. She'd had a hell of a lot to learn in a very short time.

It was with relief he felt the speed of the limo reduce noticeably, and a few moments later, it came to a halt.

He waited for his guard to open his door and as he slipped out, he reached his hand inside and held it out for her.

When her fingers were clasped in his, he helped her up, then the minute she was standing, he swept down and lifted her into his arms.

Laughter escaped her, and he hustled her closer so that her cheek could brush his jaw. "What are you giggling at, Mrs. DeSauvier?"

She chuckled harder. "Mrs. DeSauvier?"

"What? That's your name, isn't it?"

Perry's shoulders dropped at that. "Wait a minute. Are you being serious? How come in England they get to be duchesses, and I'm a Mrs.?"

He snorted as he carried her away from the limo and across a mosaic-tiled courtyard, complete with a fountain in the center of it.

The soft tinkling was a soothing addition to the sounds of insects in the near distance.

Lights shot out from odd angles to illuminate the inner courtyard where modern met antiquity as the two styles embraced.

There were clean lines to the palace that had been recently built, but there were the patterned tiles, the many arched walkways and mezzanine floors—and that was only on the outside—that spoke of the inherent beauty of Arabia.

"You're a princess, Perry," he chided her. "That trumps a duchess. But when we're out and about, as with now, you're Mrs."

She narrowed her eyes at him. "Does that work?"

"What? When I pretend to just be plain old Mr. DeSauvier?"

She nodded.

"Sometimes." He shrugged. "Depends how well I cover up and where I am. There's no point in even trying in Veronia. But elsewhere? America, for example? Yes."

She pursed her lips as she pondered that, then the door opened, a great beast of a thing with raised carvings on it that followed a symmetrical floral pattern in the wood. Above it, there was a domed mosaic that further extended the pattern.

"Welcome to the palazzo, Your Highnesses."

Well accustomed to having staff now, Perry didn't gape, didn't even blush at being carried over a threshold that wasn't theirs. "Thank you," she told the butler brightly. "Now, where's the bedroom? If I don't fall asleep within the next ten minutes, I might just die."

When the man's eyes widened, Edward had to laugh.

Sometimes, Princess Perry had about as much tact as Princess Peach.

GEORGE SQUINTED AT XAVIER, who was busy reading something on his cellphone.

"Did Father ever tell you what was happening at the rehearsal dinner?"

Xavier sighed. "I would have told you if he had. You know what he's like. He deals with certain things by himself."

"Certain things...?" George snorted. "*Most* things. The man needs to learn to delegate. It's beyond a joke."

"At least Edward will have us." Xavier cast George a look. "You do know we'll both have to step up to the plate. Perry won't be happy if we don't all deal with things together if Edward suddenly turns into a workaholic like Uncle Philippe."

"Xavier," George said wryly, crossing his feet at the ankle as he slouched back into the sofa with a glass of mint tea in his hand. "I just arranged the royal wedding. If you think there's nothing I can't handle now, you're wrong."

"Oh, I forgot. Being a wedding planner means you can handle Iranian diplomats and talk to the French when they start sniffing around our borders." Xavier huffed. "You organized a party, George. Don't lose perspective."

George narrowed his eyes. "It might have been a party, but it unified the nation in ways that are priceless. Don't undermine what I did for us."

"I'm not. I'm just saying, it doesn't prepare you for everything," Xavier retorted patiently, making George grit his teeth with exasperation.

"When do you think we can go over there?"

"Edward texted an hour ago. She's still sleeping."

George had to chuckle at that. "Only Perry could sleep through the first night as man and wife."

"By the sounds of it, Edward did too." Xavier frowned. "I wonder if he knows what's bothering Philippe."

They'd both picked up on the king's agitation. It had only increased when Perry and Edward had left the reception, their destination an airfield with a waiting jet.

He'd been testy, on edge. His mother, perpetually calm and impossible to ruffle, had even snapped at his father.

Something was definitely amiss.

"I doubt it," Xavier said softly. "Philippe wouldn't want to worry him on his wedding day."

"I have a bad feeling about this, Xavier," he pointed out quietly, taking a sip of the sweet mint tea as he closed his eyes—he wasn't the only one jet-lagged and feeling tired from the past few months' frenzy.

Truth was, he laughed at Perry's sleeping her first night as a wife away, but he hadn't slept long enough himself.

Unlike Edward and Perry, to sneak out of the country, they'd had to fly commercial. And as wonderful as first class was, it didn't beat private. Private jets came with wonderful luxuries like bedrooms and private bathrooms...

The thought made him laugh at himself.

A few months back in Veronia and already he was back to appreciating the royal way of life.

Luxuries were far too easy to become accustomed to.

In the living room of old friends, they'd found their accommodation for the next few weeks. Jane and Laura were workaholics and hardly ever there, plus they were about as non-judgmental as could be... which meant only the guards would truly know what they were doing when they were at the palazzo where the newlyweds were sleeping.

The guards would have informed Drake as to their location, but George had a feeling Drake wouldn't rat them out to his parents.

He hoped not, anyway.

He fully expected an irate call from his mother at some point in the next week, and he highly doubted he or Xavier would be able to stay away for as long as the married couple were on honeymoon, but something was better than nothing.

"I miss her," he said randomly, the thought popping into his head as he stared at a low leather stool, patterned with the ornate majesty of triangles and stars.

Laura and Jane had lived here long enough to make this place a home, and though they were only really a professor and an assistant, their digs were pretty nice.

Well, that made sense, he supposed. Jane was the daughter of a diplomat, after all. And Laura's father ran one of Veronia's most powerful private banking firms—one of which had offered George a position a few weeks back.

"She has a way of getting under your damn skin, that's for sure," Xavier admitted, not looking up from his cellphone.

"What has you so intrigued?" George asked, curious as to why Xavier had been glued to his phone all morning.

"You know that presentation Perry had a few days ago?"

"With the EA?"

"I'd seen the slides for her presentation, went through some of her report, but what she said put me on edge."

George blinked. "What *did* she say?"

"That the dams were being sabotaged."

He reared back at that. "Sabotaged?" he asked blankly.

"Yeah." Xavier pursed his lips but otherwise, he sank deeper into the sofa like George had, and crossed his legs, setting his ankle on his knee. "And as much as Veronia is dealing with a lot of problems at the moment, we both know there isn't a group in the land who'd damage something as basic as our water supply that wasn't the UnReals."

George rubbed his chin. "You've spoken to Father about this?"

"Yeah. The day I watched Perry's presentation. She was right. About not getting anywhere with the agency, I mean. I had to set up a meeting on her behalf through Laurenne Jonquil, because no one else was willing to give her the time of day.

"Only my presence, in the end, ensured we had the VP there. You'll remember the idiot, Charles Françoise, from school?"

George rolled his eyes. "That moron."

"Yeah." Xavier scowled. "Did you know he and Luc De Montfort are good friends?"

"No. I didn't. But they're on the same party. Those Conservatives are all pally."

"Yeah, but their wives are sisters, George. They're family."

George sat up. "What are you saying, Xavier?"

"I don't know what I'm saying. I'm just thinking out loud that's all. Can't be a coincidence that De Montfort is seen with an UnReal, then a few weeks later, we find out a high-ranking official on the EA is actively discouraging any further investigations into what Perry's discovered."

"I know Perry said the drought wasn't as serious as she thought it was," George reasoned slowly.

"Yeah. She's an environmental scientist, George. Not an engineer. She came looking for reasons for a water shortage. She found one, but in our infrastructure." He rubbed his chin, his unease evident in the taut skin about his eyes. "I spoke with Philippe the day before the wedding, and he's looking into it."

"But that has nothing to do with why he's been so edgy?" George cocked his head to the side.

"As far as I'm aware, no." He leaned forward to reach for his own mint tea. After taking a sip of the sweet drink, he murmured, "I only told him at the get together before the rehearsal dinner. The guards would barely have had any time to investigate anything."

"Do you have a bad feeling about this?" George asked softly, catching his cousin's eye.

"Why do you think I'm reading Perry's reports?" He sighed. "You went with her on some of the interviews with the dam's project engineers. What did you see?"

George pondered those few meetings that had had him and Perry flying all over the nation as they visited Veronia's largest dams.

"The engineers all seemed very friendly and helpful."

"You didn't think anything they said was suspicious?"

"No. I'd have brought it up with Perry if I'd thought so, and if she'd agreed, I'd have told Father or Edward. Or even you."

"Maybe, whatever's going down, they're not in on it?" he offered.

"Could be. But if they're actively damaging the dams, then there has to be someone on the inside helping."

"Has Father hired an outside engineer to come and inspect them?"

"Yeah." Xavier rubbed his chin. "Thing is, I'm relieved I sat through Perry's presentation. If I hadn't seen the level of disregard the EA had for her findings, I don't think I'd have put two and two together myself. She worked outside of the slides I checked over for her, and only through her voice did I really get a sense of how perturbed she was."

"She'd have come to us eventually."

"No, I don't think so," Xavier murmured slowly. "She wanted to handle things herself. And because she doesn't know the politics, she wouldn't have seen anything amiss."

George sighed. "Poor Perry."

Xavier cocked a brow. "Why?"

"She has a Politics 101 class coming up."

A chuckle escaped his cousin. "We might need it too. I had no idea Françoise and De Montfort were related."

George pulled a face. "Me neither. Still, you can't discredit a man for who he's married to."

"No, but you also know it isn't as simple as that. If the sisters share an anti-royalist background, then that's only going to push any sentiments their spouses have out into the open."

"You can't say that."

"I just did," Xavier retorted drily. "But between that and Philippe's unease, you're damn right I have a bad feeling about what's going on."

George's phone buzzed against the sofa cushion he'd perched it on. "Edward says Perry's awake and wants to see us," he stated after he'd read the message.

Xavier snorted. "She's a bossy little thing when she wants to be."

George wiggled his brows. "We'll be glad of that shortly."

"You do realize there's no guarantee you'll get more than a peck on the lips when we get there, right?" Xavier asked, narrowing his eyes at him as they both got to their feet.

"Of course." He shrugged. "Like I said. I missed her. I'm used to having her around. When she isn't, it puts me on edge."

Xavier studied him a second, then it dragged on. Long enough for him to wriggle his shoulders with unease. "You really mean that, don't you?"

George grunted. "Why would I say it if I didn't mean it?"

Xavier shook his head and slowly murmured, "You did a good thing by getting Edward involved with Perry. Hell, me for that matter." Xavier reached over and squeezed his shoulder. "Thank you."

Discomfited, George grumbled, "Don't be stupid."

"No, it's not stupid," Xavier said softly. "I know you love her. I'd have to be an idiot not to see that. But I didn't realize how much of a…" He paused, sought the right word, "sacrifice you'd be making by sharing her."

"I want Edward to be happy," he said mulishly. "Perry can do that."

"What about *her* happiness?" Xavier retorted.

"I'll die before I let her be anything other than content with her life," George half-snarled, the growl in his voice surprising both of them. "Edward's busy. He has a duty that neither of us could ever understand. We can make that easier on him, but only if we work together.

"I haven't brought her into this life for her to be miserable, Xavier. Whatever she wants, whatever she needs, we'll get it for her."

Xavier held up his hands. "I know that."

"Good. Well, as long as we're on the same page."

"And we are," Xavier replied, nodding gently.

Knowing his cousin was trying to soothe him, George rolled his eyes. "Let's get the hell out of here. We've got our woman to meet."

SLOUCHING BACK against the low sofa, Perry sipped at a glass of *qamardeen*—a thick apricot drink—as she looked over the pool in front of her.

It was a beauty.

The water was crystalline, and with the sun so hot, it looked all the more inviting with its surface reflecting the sky almost perfectly overhead.

They were tucked in the shade, in a tent that seemed to fit right in with the grander elements of the palace.

"The sheikh's wife is Bedouin," Edward told her, seeing where her attention was.

The great structure was the size of her apartment back in Boston, an apartment, come to think about it, that she really needed to move out of.

"What are you thinking?"

She smiled at him. "Thought you were a mind-reader."

"I wish I was," he said wryly.

"My dad said you were a strategist. Said that one of the reasons you weren't happy is because you couldn't put your brain to work where it should be."

She knew she'd surprised him because his knife scraped noisily against his breakfast plate. He caught her eye, looked at her a second, then quirked his top lip up in a half-smile. "Your father is remarkably perceptive."

"He's right then?" she asked, curious now.

"He's not wrong," was his cautious reply.

"You know I'm no politician. Nor am I a stranger. You don't have to watch your words with me."

He frowned. "I'm not watching my words, Perry. I'm just not sure what to say."

"Whatever was on the tip of your tongue before you blanked your mind."

"I could say the same thing for you," he retorted. "You just changed the subject on me."

"Because my subject is inane. Yours isn't. I was simply thinking I need to move my things out of my apartment in Boston. Pay off my lease, things like that. See, *boring*?"

He grinned at her. "George, with his new talent for management, sorted that out a while back. All of the things are being crated over. They'll probably be arriving upon our return to Veronia."

She cocked a brow. "Really? That was presumptuous of him... but cool." Easy, too. She hated packing shit up.

Reaching for one of the freshly baked croissants that were tucked prettily on a napkin-covered bowl, she began to break it into pieces on the plate in front of her. She was slumped back amid the cushions of the low seat she was on, in an almost Roman pose for eating—she totally understood now why they'd laid back and eaten. She was comfortable and had no desire to move.

She might have slept the night through, several nights, if the air journey was taken into consideration, but she was still feeling the after-effects of a few months of one adrenaline spike after another.

That didn't mean she wasn't happy, however.

Just tired.

If anything, being here with him, knowing Xavier and George were on their way? She was at a peace she hadn't realized she'd missed. As she popped some of the buttery pastry into her mouth, she pointed a finger at him.

"Spill."

"Dictator," he told her, taking a bite of his scrambled eggs. He, unlike her, was sitting forward, somewhat hunched over the low table before them.

He hadn't complained though. He could have moved over to one of the higher tables, the one at the back of the tent that was more like their dining tables, but she knew he didn't want to leave her.

Truth was, she liked how close he was sticking to her side. She liked it a little too much, considering when they made it back to Veronia, they'd have to be separated for the natural day-to-day tasks.

"You never said, you know, if you liked my uniform."

She grinned. "Stop fishing for compliments. You know I liked it. I thought I made that clear when we were waiting to walk into the reception."

With the four-hundred strong guest list waiting for their wedding breakfast, they'd had but a handful of moments alone between leaving the carriage that had driven them from the capital to the castle, and their arrival at the grand salon where the reception was being held.

When the groom would traditionally touch the bride up, she'd pulled his kilt out of the way to discover if men really did go bare under there.

She hadn't been disappointed.

"You just liked the easy access," he said with a mock pout firming his lips. "That doesn't tell me if you liked it."

She laughed, her head falling back. "I thought I was the one who needed to hear how beautiful I looked?"

He snorted. "You know you looked gorgeous. I wanted to fuck you, right there and then."

"In front of God and the rest of Veronia?" Her eyes widened innocently. "My, that would have been a display."

"It would have set the tone for the rest of our marriage, that's for certain."

She snickered, unable to help it. "I probably wouldn't have enjoyed it. My stomach was dancing like mad."

"You looked a little pasty at first, but then, after the vows, you seemed to relax," he remarked.

She nodded. "It was a lot easier to breathe when your eyes were on mine."

His face softened at that. Any tension their earlier conversation might have caused dissipated in the truth of her words.

"I'm a very lucky man to be able to call you my own. Do you know that?"

She blinked. "I do now."

"And you looked like..." He whistled. "I wasn't sure if I had a goddess walking toward me, or my future wife."

Her cheeks burned a little at his candor. "I was only teasing. I knew you liked my dress."

"Well, I was only teasing too—I knew you liked my uniform."

"I did. And seeing it multiplied by three?" She let out a whistle of her own. "That certainly worked its number on me."

He grinned at her. "Xavier said you'd like it. George just felt like a dick. Or so he grumbled. Constantly. Throughout the walk to the abbey."

She laughed. "I can imagine. He can be such a baby sometimes."

"A 'baby' isn't the word." He pulled a face as he set his knife and fork aside. Then, after reaching for his own juice, he took a deep sip and sank back onto the sofa opposite her.

They were in a low circular seating area, with the table in the center. Staff came and went sporadically, dipping curtsies and sending shy, polite smiles as they retrieved hot silver pots of coffee and freshened up teapots, while gathering dirty dishes and replenishing bowls of pastries and sweet treats that tasted of almonds and rosewater.

Edward had eaten a more hearty and traditional repast of bacon, eggs, and toast. She'd sampled the countless tiny morsels that were Arabic in origin. Anything from the sweet mint tea that was so sugary it was like a syrup and just as addictive as crack, to the almond and pistachio sweetmeats. But the call of a fresh croissant had beckoned, and her fingers bore the brunt of the buttery, delicious greasiness.

As he sank back, full now from his meal, he stared at her over his glass a second, and she realized then how relaxed he was.

Sure, he'd relaxed when it was just the two of them, or if Xavier and George were around. But this kind of relaxed was different.

She wasn't sure why, either.

Just liked the look of it on him.

"That uniform wasn't just ceremonial."

"I never thought it was," she murmured, taking another sip of tea. "It's well known Veronia has conscription."

He nodded. "Well, I did quite well during my service. We all did. Only Xavier wasn't too keen. He prefers his trees and farms to the army. But George and I? We liked it."

"Wasn't it a bit…" She pulled a face. "You know, nepotistic?"

He laughed. "Never change, Perry."

"What do you mean?" she grumbled.

"Always be as blunt as you are now, and we should have a very happy marriage." Though she rolled her eyes, he just murmured, "No, it wasn't about putting us somewhere and trying to make us look good while keeping us very safe.

"You should know by now, Veronia doesn't do things by halves. If we'd died in the act of service, we'd have been beloved by the people. It's a part of our society."

"George never mentioned his time in the Forces, and yet, you say he loved it?"

Edward nodded, a grim smile twisting his lips. "Just before he moved to America, Veronia got involved with the conflicts in the Middle East. We shipped out troops."

"He served over there?" Her eyes widened, unease flittering through her at the knowledge George had kept something of that magnitude from her.

"No. The government at the time said he would endanger the troops he was serving with. Soldiers would die to protect him, to keep him safe. Said that he would never be treated like any other enlistee." He blew out a breath. "War is different to the maneuverings of an army during peace time. Unfortunately for George, who wanted to serve over there, do his bit, and as irritating as it is to have Parliament control our lives, they were right. George knew he'd be putting more lives in danger by going. He went and did his MBA instead, and never really forgave the government for it."

She blinked. "How did I not know that?"

"Because he didn't tell you. And what Veronia doesn't want to leave its borders, information included, doesn't leave our land."

"What about you?" she asked, sorrow for George filling her. Although, it was hard to be sad for him when, if it wasn't for Parliament's dictates, they'd never have met.

"I had a talent for, as your father put it, strategizing. For a while, I helped the police force control corruption. We managed to send a few mafia heads to jail."

She studied him a second, heard what he wasn't telling her. "You miss it."

He didn't prevaricate. "I do."

"Can't you...?"

"Go back?" He shook his head. "It doesn't work like that. Unless we're at war, once your time is over, your time is over. And by that point, I had to take my duties as crown prince seriously."

She processed that, then blew out a breath. "Being royal sucks."

He snorted. "Lucky for you, you just became royal too." His eyes twinkled with amusement, and it surprised her because she would have expected him to wince or to try to make her see how great it was to be a DeSauvier. But he didn't.

And for that, she was grateful.

The moment of honesty warmed her. She knew, then and there, that there would be no bullshit between them.

Honest questions would be answered with the truth. For both of them.

The idea that she was working on a level playing field settled any uncertainty she might have had over how things would be.

She did not approve of how Marianne was kept in the dark about certain matters, and hadn't been sure of how to raise the topic with Edward.

If she was in danger, then she wanted to know. Not be protected and cosseted.

Their eyes met and held. A silent agreement formed between them. Surging to life as desire surrounded the moment of mutual respect.

But before the desire could take hold, a throat cleared, and they both jolted at the intrusion.

She peered over to the intruder and scrambled onto her knees when she saw Xavier and George in the open doorway that consisted of two sides of the white cloth that sheltered them from the sun, pinned up and held in place to form an aperture.

The servant, a discreet little man in black trousers and a black polo, disappeared the moment Edward nodded at him. When he'd gone, Xavier peered around the tent, while George grabbed the loops that held the swags apart and set them down to give them total privacy.

"That's better," he said jovially. "Now, where's my kiss?"

She laughed as she scrambled over the side of the sofa rather than heading for the small sliver of space that broke up the perfect circle of the low seating area, and shot toward him.

He grabbed ahold of her and spun her in a circle. Then, before she could do more than laugh once more, he tipped her down over his arm and brought their mouths together. But just as she sank into the kiss, he raised her once more, only to sweep her legs up over his arm. When she was aloft, laughing and squeaking all the while, George moved over to Xavier who bent down and pressed a kiss to Perry's forehead.

"Congratulations, darling," Xavier told her gently.

"Congratulations to you," she chided. "We're all in this together, aren't we?"

He studied her a second, then his lips quirked to the side. "We are indeed." He cut George a look. "You drop her, you answer to me."

"Drop this itty bitty thing?" He snorted, then proceeded to let go of her then catch her after a split second.

The rage on Xavier's face had Perry hiding a laugh. "Don't worry, Xavi. That's not the first time he's done that, nor will it be the last."

George pouted. "Am I that predictable?"

"Deadly predictable."

"Even I saw that one coming," Edward retorted, sliding his arm across the back of the sofa.

That sense of peace seemed to drift from his very pores again. She'd never imagined he could be so relaxed, and she loved seeing him that way.

George, after carrying her to the sofa, plunked down with her in his lap. Once seated, she resettled herself and asked, "Have you had breakfast?" When they both nodded, she asked, "Fancy some coffee?"

"No. Do they have any of that mint tea? I'm getting addicted to the stuff."

She pressed her thumb to his jaw. "When you lose all your teeth because of all the sugar, I'll still kiss you."

"That's true love, that is," he countered, but his grin exposed those white dazzlers.

She reached up a little to press her lips to his cheek, and she sucked in a deep breath, loving the scent of him. Loving that he was here.

The truth was, now they were all here, the way Edward looked, she could actually start to *feel*.

Was it weird?

Hell, yeah.

Was it the way of it?

Damn straight.

She needed the three of them. She'd needed the sight of them at the abbey to calm her. Had needed to catch them at the reception, watch them glide like sharks through the deepest seas to keep her afloat.

Just being with them let her breathe a little deeper, a lot easier.

She turned, moving in George's arms so that she was straddling him. The minute she was there, his hands came to grip her ass through the shorts she was wearing. As he palpated the skin, she reached up for his mouth and connected their lips.

The minute they touched, she breathed out, loving his taste, needing to savor more of it.

A groan escaped her, and she arched her pelvis, loving his responsiveness to her as she could feel the hard thickness of his cock between her legs.

A yelp escaped her as a sharp slap rang out—one that came from him tapping her on the ass.

Hard.

She pulled back and glowered at him. "What was that for?"

"For being naughty," he told her, relaxing back into the sofa. In fact, he relaxed so much, he was diagonal against it rather than straight up.

"Naughty? I was kissing one of my husbands," she said huskily. "How is that naughty?"

"You're tired. We all are. And there's no need to rush."

She blinked at him. "Rush?"

He quirked a brow at her. "Yeah. You know what it means? Need a definition?"

"I know what it means." She glared at him and slapped his arm with the flat of her hand. "How is it rushing? It's the morning after my wedding, and I haven't slept with any of you."

"Are you feeling neglected?"

Xavier's voice was teasing, but she focused her grimace on George. "What's going on? Don't you want me?" She made the complaint, even though she knew it was bullshit.

He snorted at that. "Can cats shit in human toilets?"

For a second, her mouth worked. "I have no idea how to respond to that."

"Think the more common phrase is, 'do bears shit in the woods?', George."

Edward's tone was bland, and she couldn't tell if he was trying to hide the humor in his voice. What humor could be found in this situation, she wasn't sure.

Her bottom lip popped out in a pout, and she couldn't stop herself from rocking her hips once more.

Another tap on her butt was the only response she got.

She glowered at him. "Stop doing that."

"Stop trying to get me to respond, witch. There's no need to take things too fast, Perry." He reached up, and with the hand that had slapped her butt, cupped her cheek. On her face. Not down below. *Sadly*, Perry thought. "The last thing I want is for you to head into something when you're still tired."

She frowned at him. "Too tired for what?"

"For the three of us."

Her eyes widened. "Three of you? At once?" Her eyes stopped widening and downright flared open. "In my pussy?"

A snort escaped George, and the men at her back chuckled, although they tried to hide their laughter by coughing and repeatedly clearing their throats.

"No, love." He tapped her bottom lip. "Here." He rocked his own hips, making her eyelids flutter with the wonder of that hardness pressing against her hot softness. "Here." And then, with his other hand, he squeezed her ass cheek. "And here."

She licked her lips. "Oh."

"Yeah. 'Oh.' I'm not ready to do that until you are. So, until then, let's just take things at our own pace. Now, we have all the time in the world."

She blinked, still taken aback by his generosity. In her experience, men didn't worry if their woman was tired.

Apparently, she had three men who were concerned about her, because neither Edward nor Xavier spoke out against George's remarks.

Which had to mean they were in agreement, too.

For a second, she just stared into George's delicious jewel-like eyes, at the handsome face that had caught her heart all those years ago, but more, at the intellect, wit, and charm that had trapped said heart and forever made it his.

She asked herself if she was ready for more. If she didn't still need to rest.

She was horny. There was no doubting that. And the need was there. But so was the need to relax. To chill. To take things at their own pace, as George had said.

She knew that any other woman, faced with three delicious specimens of masculinity like her men, would deem her crazy, but they hadn't just gone through what she had.

The wedding, the preparations, the struggle with the EA? Then, the emotional turbulence of coming to terms with the fact she wanted three men, of learning that a group of extremists wanted to hurt Edward...

George was right. It was all too much, and the chance to relax was exactly what she needed.

A moment in time to be with the men she loved without lust getting in the way.

Which it would.

Soon.

The minute she was back on fighting form, they were going down.

In the best. Possible. Way.

And that was a promise.

CHAPTER TWENTY-ONE

IT WENT on like that for two days.

A strange kind of truce between them all. The minx that was their woman teased them at will, kissed them like there was no tomorrow, and felt no shame in nuzzling up to them, but he certainly didn't mind and neither did his cousins.

Xavier loved how tactile she was. And after two nights of good rest, he could see the spark was back in her eye.

He'd been surprised at George's declaration when they'd made it to the palazzo. He'd expected his hothead of a cousin to pounce on Perry the first instant he could.

Instead, he'd been patient, and had shown a deeper understanding of her than Xavier had expected. Even if that was short sighted of him, considering how long George and Perry had been friends.

But Xavier understood.

In those shorts and a thin camisole at breakfast, it had hit home exactly how much weight Perry had lost. As autumn had drawn close, she'd been wearing long sleeves and thick fabrics to ward off the faintest of chills.

Here in the scorching heat of the desert, there was no need to cover up, and he saw her. They all had.

She'd been pleasantly plump upon her entry into Veronia. An armful, granted, and more than enough for one man to worship at her feet. Now? She was edging towards slender.

Her breasts were still large, thank God. But they had perpetuated the notion that she hadn't lost that much weight. The camisoles and the bikinis she wore disproved that.

And so, for two days, they'd fed her. Watched her sleep at the side of the pool, taking advantage of the tent and the comfortable day beds, or relaxing back into one of those pods with the retractable roofs.

They'd teased her, made sure she ate, ensured she was back on fighting form.

Xavier was a gardener first and foremost. He knew that to tend to a seedling was the way to make the most beautiful of flowers flourish and blossom brightly.

That was how they'd cared for Perry. They cherished her, bathed her in their love, and like the most delicate of flowers, she flared to life.

And in the interim, he and George had totally dropped the pretense of staying at Jane and Laura's. They were tucked away in Sheikh al-Habib's stunning palazzo. Away from their government, free from their duties... he knew he hadn't wanted to leave Perry, and neither had George. So, they'd stayed close, if not in the same quarters, and he had been enjoying the chance to simply be.

It wasn't something they often managed to do. In truth, it was the truest of luxuries. More than the exquisite palace and the delicious food, the chance to be themselves was the most glorious of wonders.

There was always trouble in paradise, of course. His worry about the dams wasn't far away, and he was sure George and Edward had their own concerns waiting for them back home, but Perry had a knack. She seemed to sense when they were getting bogged down in their thoughts and would tease them out of it.

Not for the first time, he found himself in awe of her, and felt like the luckiest bastard when she looked upon him, her heart in her eyes, and made him aware of how deeply she felt for him.

As she was doing now.

The tease.

He shook his head at her antics. "Don't think giving me moon eyes will put me off-guard."

She smirked as she moved her rook. "Who said anything about moon eyes?" Her grin was like quicksilver. "I love you. There's nothing moon-like about that. Oh. And check."

His lips twitched at her self-satisfaction.

George called out. "Watch her. She's the chess equivalent of a card shark."

"Now he tells me," Xavier grumbled.

Laughter pealed from her glossy lips. "Tell you what. If you can checkmate me in five moves or less, I'll suck you off. Right here. Right now."

He squinted at her. "You're not ready."

She huffed out a breath. "Who are you to decide that? I know my own body, Xavier. You were right the other day to be concerned. All of you. I was really tired. More than that, I was *weary*. Even though I was happy, too.

"Now I'm not."

"It's been two days. Hardly enough time at all," he retorted, tongue-in-cheek.

She growled under her breath. "Five moves. It's possible. It's not easy. But it's doable."

"What do you get if I don't win?" he asked, scanning the board and trying to find a better option than her offer of five moves.

If she offered five, then there had to be a reason for it. Either she could checkmate him in fewer moves, or she was stuck and needed him to maneuver.

"You suck me off instead."

Her words were like silk, so much so, he knew Edward and George—who were at the other end of the tent, in the circular sofa—were too far away to hear.

He eyed her a second, wondering what her game was, but that flush on her cheeks was too enchanting to ignore.

"You're on."

He moved his bishop. And she devoured him whole.

Checkmate in two moves.

He cocked a brow at her as he folded his arms across his chest. "You played me."

She grinned, bobbing merrily in her seat. "I did. It worked." She clicked her fingers. "Now, time to pay your dues."

He laughed, loving the sparkle of dominance in her eyes. "But the tent flaps aren't closed."

"Go close them then," she murmured drily.

He pursed his lips as he stared at her a second. There was something else going on here.

But, unlike before, she wasn't betraying a damn thing.

He drummed his fingers against the table and then got to his feet. It took a minute to drop the flaps, and he knew the move attracted his cousins' attention, but he ignored them and returned to the chess table that took up one corner of the huge tent.

The damn thing was the size of a small house. Had more nooks than Masonbrook, stank of incense, and Perry loved it in here.

Said it made her feel like a slave girl.

Xavier, ever dubious, wondered how the hell that could ever be a good thing... still, he'd kill to preserve that smile on her lips.

When he returned to the table, there was a bottle beside his king.

He laughed. "You totally played me," he groused, picking up the lube and tossing it from hand to hand.

Her grin was cheeky. "We've already established that."

They were seated on a smaller version of the seated circle where George and Edward were leaning back and relaxing. As such, she had only to fall back against the cushions to recline... hell, it was more accessible than a damn bed.

These Arabs knew how to live, that was for damn sure.

He rubbed his chin as he stared at her. He'd seen skimpier bikinis, barely there scraps of fabric, but nothing satisfied him like the one she wore.

With its ties at the hip, the substantial cups that supported her generous breasts, the tie-dye pattern that consisted of different shades of pink, it further highlighted the glow she'd earned while swimming and sitting outside.

"Sun-kissed" was the word, and she was delicious.

Now that she had his attention, she reached down and unfastened the knots at her hips.

"Whoops," she murmured, her mouth rounding in false surprise. "How did that happen?" she asked as she moved the scrap aside and revealed her bareness.

He watched, teeth clenching and his cock already responding, as she traced a few fingers over the soft, hairless skin.

"George's wedding present to himself," she said softly, apparently not wanting to attract his and Edward's attention.

Maybe because she knew she'd lose against the three of them.

But one on one?

Hell, he wouldn't be surprised if Edward had been fucking her at night. Even though they'd all agreed to leave her alone for some R&R.

An eager Perry, a Perry with one thing on her mind, was incredibly difficult to ignore.

He licked his lips at the smoothness he wanted to feel under his tongue, and with a grunt, sank down on the sofa at her side.

He could smell her. And Jesus, she was potent.

She was all female. His. Clean and sweet and just, Christ, *his*.

He let out a groan as she parted her legs, sliding further along the sofa so that she was flat against the cushions. She lifted a calf and rested it on the back of the low seat, parting her lips so that he could see the telltale slickness of her arousal.

The sight had his cock throbbing with need. He needed in her. Now.

Her call was too strong. Like a siren, she'd sung him into a danger he ignored willingly as he fell upon her like a drowning man offered a life jacket.

The minute his tongue was on her clit, she arched into the cushions, her ass sinking deep as she jerked her hips in response. Her hands came to his head, threading through his hair to keep him in place.

But she'd ensnared him in her trap. There was no way, no how, he was moving from this spot.

He sucked her clit, fucked it with his tongue and teeth. Then, he licked down, suckling the lips, going down, down until he could slip his tongue into the hole of her sex.

He thrust idly for a few seconds, sampling more of her taste, then he pressed a finger to her tightness and reveled in the soft moan that escaped her in response.

She clamped down on him, holding the digit snugly in her pussy as he returned to her clit. This time, he gave it an open-mouthed kiss as he treated it cruelly. Flicking it, sucking it, taunting it. Not giving it the delicate touch it needed. Instead, punishing it for her disobedience. And all the while, he fucked his finger in and out of her.

Slowly, but with intent, not stopping until he could go no deeper.

Her pelvis rocked, and her moans grew needier as he added another finger. He started to scissor the digits then, stretching her as he changed tactics. His tongue gentled as his fingers began to fuck her, and the contrast had a deep cry escaping her throat.

There was no way his cousins could fail to hear that, and in the periphery, he sensed them shifting, moving about. But he didn't move from this spot.

She'd wanted his attention, so she was getting it.

He looked up at her, saw her hands were cupping her tits, watched on as her head swayed from side to side against the cushions, as though the pleasure was too much for her to stay still.

The sight inspired him.

He removed his fingers from her pussy, slipped those of his other hand deep into her core, then, he moved down and prodded her asshole.

She fell silent then, her breathing deepening into ragged pants.

"She likes that," George remarked softly, and he stepped nearer, making Xavier realize the small chess table had been shifted away, and that both his cousins were watching the show their woman was giving them.

"She does," Edward concurred. "How tight is she, Xavier?"

He mumbled against her clit. "About to find out."

Both men laughed, then George chided, "Don't tense up, Perry. That won't make it any fun."

She moaned, and as he peered up, he saw George had moved toward her. Granting Xavier a glimpse of his cousin's bare ass—when had the bastard stripped?

In less than a second, the sounds of someone being sucked off were very evident, and God help him, his cock ached in response. Pressed into the sofa the way he was, there was no friction. Just pressure. And Jesus, he wanted.

With a moan, he doubled his efforts. Torturing her clit with barely-there flickers, keeping his fingers static in her cunt, and gently pushing into her ass, preparing her there for one of them.

A flush of heat swept through him at the idea, but that was nothing to the orgy that was going on before him. The inkling of which sent fire through his veins, but when he looked up and saw Perry's small hand clasping Edward's dick, it hit home.

He was as much a pervert as they were, because knowing that they were doing this to her, that the three of them were owning her pleasure and gifting it to her?

He'd never felt so fucking alive in all his life.

And hell, he'd thought he'd loved sharing her with just Edward.

How had he lived without this for so long?

Without the adrenaline burst, the spiking arousal?

Lightheaded, he spread his fingers inside her pussy and pressed down against the one in her ass.

And that was it, like a rocket, she went off. Her thighs reared up, and with the strong muscles, she clamped down on his head as she keened, rocking from side to side in response.

He had to laugh because he could barely breathe, thanks to her chokehold. The noise must have gained Edward's attention because he snorted. "I think you're choking Xavier, Perry. And considering he just made you come, I think that's a touch mean, darling. Don't you?"

She let out a moan that was mumbled around George's cock, but the tight grip she had on his head immediately relented.

He moved away, wiping his mouth on his shoulder, as he continued to ply her holes. Spreading her wide, getting her used to the touch in both her ass and pussy.

Edward let out a growl. "Enough teasing. Perry, let go of George's cock."

Her disgruntled moan had them all chuckling. She had her bone(r) and like a dog, she wasn't about to let it go.

"We'll make it worth your while," George said, but he panted the words, then he groaned, staggering back as she released him. "You have the mouth of a piranha, sweetheart," he said on a gulp.

Perry rubbed at her lips with the back of her hand. "But I don't bite my meals."

He groaned. "No, you'll just suck me dry." He growled at the thought, then, before any of them knew what he was doing, he reached down and hauled her up into his arms.

In less than a minute, they'd moved from awkwardly standing around the sofa, to him sitting back against it, Perry on his knee.

The move mirrored the position Perry had been in days before when George had cautioned her to take things slowly.

And Xavier didn't think his cousin had forgotten that.

A belief that was confirmed when he grunted, "Ride me, Perry."

Her mouth formed an O as she reached down, and with her small hand, grabbed ahold of his cock. With the other on his shoulder to steady herself, she sank down onto his shaft, and the pair of them groaned as she settled against his lap.

He watched them pant, their lips brushing, their breaths mingling, and knew that if he didn't free his cock soon, he'd fucking explode.

With his hand on his fly, he released himself and grabbed a hold of his shaft. A few swift wanks didn't improve his situation, but a firm hand on his balls did the trick.

Seeing the bottle of lube on the sofa, where one of the guys had obviously left it earlier after moving the table out of the way, he reached for it and coated his shaft with the liquid.

The slick glide of his hand this time was fucking torture. But, prepared now, he dropped to his knees and used Perry's position to facilitate things.

Spread open, he could see her asshole winking back at him, and that was further helped when Edward split her cheeks with his hands, pushing them wide apart.

She jolted at the move, her head turning to the side to figure out who was doing what, but George's hands came up to cup her breasts, and he rocked his hips up, grabbing her attention.

Xavier used his slick fingers to slide into her ass. She'd already told them she wasn't a virgin there, but the ease in which he slipped into her told him she liked anal. And the moan she let loose, as well as the way her head rolled back on her shoulders at his penetration, merely confirmed that belief.

"Jesus, you should feel her clamping down on me," George muttered, sounding both desperate and aroused.

"I l-love anal," she whispered, then released a keening cry as Xavier thrust another finger into her ass. Scissoring them as he'd done with her pussy, he made sure she was ready.

"Move back, George," Edward directed.

No more words were spoken as George copied Perry by slumping deeper into the cushions so he was laying back. He scrambled his legs up so he was flat out, and Xavier, avoiding his cousin's hairy thighs, bracketed them with his own as he climbed onto the sofa too.

Perry had fallen onto all fours at the change in position, and her round and curvy ass was up and bobbing in the air as he looked on.

Letting out a growl, he grabbed a hold of his shaft and pressed it to the tight pucker. "Are you ready for this, babe?" he demanded.

"Oh God, yes. Yes!" she half-squeaked. "I n-need you. A-All of you."

The words were like music to his ears, and as he slipped inside, he knew he was slipping home.

―――

PERRY SCREWED her eyes shut as Xavier filled her.

It was a breathless moment. She wasn't sure if he'd fit with George already deep inside her, and neither man was small.

Her small holes felt like they were being… fuck, the exact opposite of choked. It made her throat tight and made sweat prickle along her brow and down her back as Xavier carefully thrust inside her.

She panted, slumping against George's chest as she acclimated to the fullness.

Whatever she'd expected, it hadn't been this, but she loved it. Loved it with a passion that astonished her.

Though she was overwhelmed, it was the best kind. Like tears of joy or sad laughter. The contrast made no sense, and yet, it meant the world.

She sucked down air like the room's oxygen supply was depleting, and gradually, as both men stroked her with their hands, soothing her and gentling her, she finally found her place.

Settling back so she was no longer slumping over George, she went onto her hands and knees and felt her mouth gape at the sight of Edward, standing there, his eyes glinting like the finest diamonds, and one hand on his cock, the other on his balls.

He loved this. Loved seeing her this way. It was in his stance, the way he stood tall and straight. His legs wide, his cock held firmly. He was proud and unashamed, and she'd given him that.

She'd made him look that way.

A shudder eased its way down her spine at the thought.

Her mouth watered as he clenched his fingers down around his cock at the sight of her interest, and she pressed her own to George's chest to sit up straighter. The move did interesting things deep inside her. Her back arched, and her pussy muscles clenched around George, while seeming to release around Xavier. Which meant, to her surprise, he could slide in deeper.

She gasped, her mouth rounding at the new angles and deeper penetration. But she could tell the men liked it, if their dual groans were anything to go by.

Xavier moved up close behind her, and his hands came to her elbows. She felt his support, knew he was helping to hold her upright in position.

"Are you ready?" Edward growled, his voice deep and gruff and so keyed to her body, she felt tiny sparks in her pussy that spoke of another orgasm starting to manifest.

She shuddered at the sensation, then whispered, "I'm ready."

He stepped closer, closer. Not stopping until his cock was a few inches away. She reached for it, then jerked when he slid the head over the curves of her lips, up the slope of her chin and down the line of her jaw. She felt the wet kiss of pre-cum on her skin, and her eyelids fluttered shut in response to his decadent caress.

Her mouth quivered, need flooding her. The desperate urge to taste him rode her as she couldn't ride the men beneath her—whatever happened, she knew she couldn't move, not if she was to satisfy all three of them.

And, goddammit, this was the consummation of her wedding vows. There was no way in hell she wasn't satisfying them all.

The ease of it slid into her mind as slickly as George had filled her pussy. The rightness of the moment settled into place in her psyche, forever erasing even the smallest shadows of doubt from her mind.

She'd been born for this.

Born to be theirs.

The notion was freeing, liberating, and she stopped letting Edward tease her, snapping her head to the left to grab ahold of his shaft with her lips.

In response, he let out a long hiss, and his hands came up to slide through her hair and hold her in place.

And that was everyone's cue.

Slowly, at first, George began to arch his hips, rolling them upwards. Xavier began to push into her ass, steadily, thrusting in as George thrust out. To that motion, Edward fucked her face.

For a second, as all three of them sawed into her, she was overwhelmed by feeling. Awed by the sensation. And then, her body skewed it. Translated it so it intensified, so that her mind became frenzied with each thrust. With the rub of Xavier's cock against George's, with the taste of Edward's seed on her tongue.

It was like panicking, but in a good way. She wanted more. She needed more. She was rabid. For them. For all they had to give.

Perry tightened her pussy around George, and slipped a hand down her body so she could touch her clit. The further stimulus was like a firework exploding in her brain.

The lights illuminated shadows she'd never even known, and as she explored those dark depths, the pleasure intensified. Sweat rolled down the curves of her body. Xavier's chest was slick at her back, and the heat George and Edward emitted roasted her.

At that moment, she knew she'd never been more alive. They'd brought her to this. Had driven her to the pinnacle. Just as Edward had promised her, right at the very beginning when he'd told her he and his brother worked together to rock a woman's world.

He hadn't lied.

Her secret desires and passions born from reading smutty erotica had come to life because of them.

The tales she'd read paled in comparison though. Now she was here, now she was at the center of their love, everything seemed to explode into reality.

Her fingers quickened as George and Xavier's pace did, too. They worked in tangent, sweating and groaning, panting and pleading for completion.

Then, she felt it.

It was there. Right in the depths of her mind, deeper than even the shadows the fireworks of her pleasure had revealed.

It was dark there. Black. So deep and so Stygian that she was blind.

But she didn't need to see to feel the splash of Xavier's cum deep in her ass. She didn't need to see to feel Edward's hands tighten in her hair as his thrusts in her mouth became short, sharp, and jerky as he rode out his release. And she didn't need to see to hear George's roar of completion as he fucked his cock deeper into her, needing to give her every inch of him as he explored his own orgasm.

The taste, the slick feel of them deep in her core, was a minefield for her to dance in. And dance she did, uncaring where she trod, unperturbed of where she stepped. Until finally, the explosion of her release came.

It tore her into a million tiny pieces, ripped her to shreds in the cruelest of ways.

But as she flew apart, she was glued together again.

A stronger, fearless Perry, who knew, point blank, that the men around her were hers.

There were no more doubts.

There were no more fears.
It was done.
She was theirs, as they were hers.
Simple.

CHAPTER TWENTY-TWO

TWO DAYS LATER, Perry laughed as she ducked in from the courtyard, from the bright light of day to the dark shadows of the palazzo. Though the place was fully air conditioned, the way the shadows embraced the interior of the palace truly made all the difference when it came to moderating the temperatures.

More laughter escaped her as she heard George's feet tapping behind her. She'd ran in from the pool area... only after she'd pushed him into its chilly depths.

"I'll get you for that," he hollered out behind her, but she just chuckled harder at his curses and grunts, slipping around the courtyard while chasing her.

When she turned around and saw Drake standing there, of all people, her happy giggles died a death.

She blinked. "I heard a car, but, Drake...? What's going on?" She cut Edward a glance, saw the pallor of his face, the whiteness about his taut mouth.

More than that, she saw the agony in his eyes, the tremor of his jaw as he ground his teeth together.

He was dressed in board shorts. They'd all been hanging around the pool this morning, and she now saw how the stress from Drake's presence was actively affecting him.

His fists were tensed so tightly, his biceps bulged with the strain. And his throat? The sinews were so prominent, it looked painful.

Gulping, she turned to Drake when Edward remained silent.

Her mouth worked, the need for answers burning her tongue. But Drake stunned her. He moved towards her, and then she saw the contingent of guards at his back. A handful of other men gathered in the doorway. Men she'd never seen before. Men who suddenly made her uncomfortable when she realized she was in a bikini and nothing else.

But their head of security didn't give her time to grab a wrap, didn't give her time to do anything. At his approach, another man appeared from Edward's left. In his hand, he had some kind of scroll. His pace was quicker than Drake's. He reached her side and held out his arm for her.

She peered, confused, at Edward, then when he just stared blankly, *blindly* ahead, looked at Drake.

He nodded, the motion encouraging. Unease filtered through her as she placed her hand on the man's forearm.

As he started to guide her toward Edward, she heard the patter of George's feet, then his laughter as he made it inside the house. A few seconds later, she heard Xavier too. She also heard the punch and the "ow" as Xavier apparently punched George in the shoulder.

"That's for pushing me in too, jackass," Xavier grumbled, and though a minute ago, she'd have laughed, now, her throat felt frozen. Her vocal chords too.

At the silence in the salon, both her men seemed to realize that something was happening. That something was wrong.

Very, very wrong.

They fell silent too, and as the stranger guided her to Edward's side, she fell into place at his right. Her terrified gaze switched between George and Xavier's, who seemed to read the situation better than she had.

George let out a choked sound that had fear roaring through her, and Xavier's hand came up to cup the shoulder he'd undoubtedly punched mere seconds before.

What the fuck was happening?

Why was nobody speaking?

She wanted to scream. Wanted to rail. Wanted to demand that someone tell her what was going on. And then... she wished she didn't know. She wished it all back as the man with the scroll cleared his throat, and in a pious tone, declared to the room at large, "After the assassination of Queen Marianne, King Philippe the Fourth of Veronia, son of Xavier the Third, has abdicated the throne.

"As of this date, the sixth of October two thousand and eighteen, and with great sorrow and great joy, I pronounce King Edward the Second and Queen Perry of Veronia as the sovereigns of our glorious and proud nation."

A stunned breath slipped from her lips as the others in the room, everyone from Drake and the guards to her men—her wonderful lovers also took part—sank to their knees, almost as one, and intoned:

"Long live, King Edward.

"Long live, Queen Perry."

HER HIGHNESS PRINCESS PERRY 447

LONG LIVE QUEEN PERRY

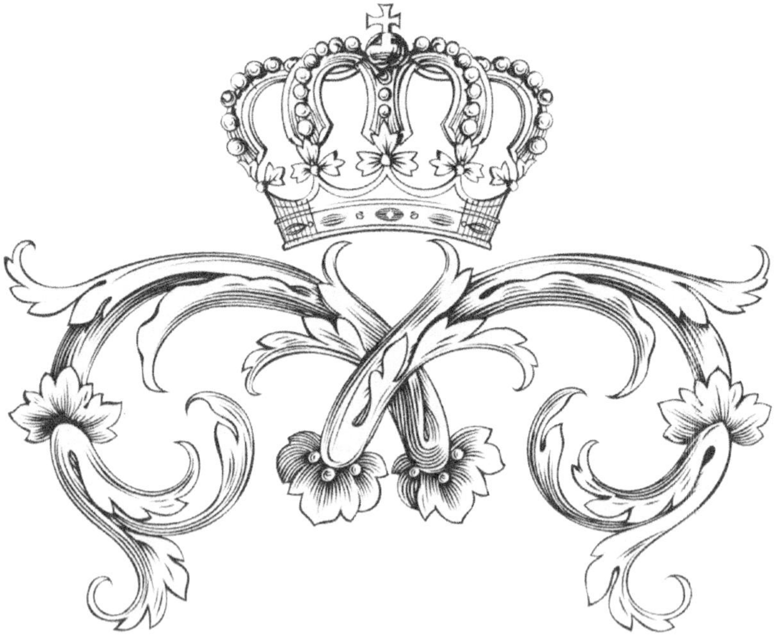

"BEING HAPPY IS BETTER THAN BEING KING."

African Proverb

CHAPTER ONE

YORKE ABBEY, although she'd been married there, was no less daunting than it had been a mere three weeks ago.

In fact, though the wedding had been the largest spectacle of her life, it was nothing in comparison to what was about to happen.

To put it frankly, Perry DeSauvier was shitting herself.

Actually, "shitting herself" in no way described the terror she was feeling at this moment.

The worst thing was, that terror had two faces.

Three weeks ago, she'd been on honeymoon, after having married the crown prince of this great land. She'd been happy. Still slightly bewildered to find herself the bride of a royal, but gradually adapting to her new status in life. A status that involved her being the Crown Princess of Veronia, as well as the secret girlfriend/lover/partner of her husband's younger brother and cousin.

She'd been in Dubai. On a luxurious honeymoon in a wonderful palace where a Bedouin tent had been set up in the Arab-style courtyard, overlooking a twinkling fountain and a pool so shiny that it made mirrors seem like non-reflective surfaces.

Those early days of her marriage were supposed to have been her chance to catch her breath. A moment in time for her to adapt, to transition from the environmental scientist of old, to the crown princess of new.

Then, her mother-in-law had been assassinated.

The king, fractions of an inch away from death himself, had been terribly wounded in the assassination attempt on his life. The bullet had spared vital organs, thank God, but it had nicked his spinal cord.

Philippe DeSauvier, on the brink of surgery that he might never wake up from, had made the decision to abdicate, i.e. to renounce the throne in favor of his son—meaning that her husband was no longer the Crown Prince of Veronia, but the King of Veronia.

Which made her the Queen of Veronia.

The *fucking* Queen.

"You look perfect, Perry," Cassie Whitings, her new friend, whispered.

The older woman's throat was definitely clogged, but the whole country had been in a state of mourning since Marianne's death and Philippe's abdication.

If the people behind the assassination, a group called the UnReals, had intended to create dissent among the people, they had failed. If anything, the public had rallied in their grief. Any anti-royalist sentiment was looked upon with outright hatred. The rebels were being vilified in the press, *anything* against the royal family was viewed with not only scorn, but distrust and disdain.

But that was too late for Marianne. Too late for Philippe as well. He'd been right to abdicate—he still lived, but he'd yet to awaken from his surgery, and they had no idea if he ever would wake up either.

"Thank you, Cassie," she whispered, her voice as weak as Cassie's own.

Nerves made her jittery. Her hands were trembling, and her throat was aching with suppressed emotion. Her stomach was in a state of terror. The butterflies were slowly being overtaken by a nausea so powerful, Perry was petrified she'd puke in front of the millions around the world who were watching the coronation.

For the tenth time, she settled her skirts about her legs, and peered down at her feet.

It was wrong, oh, so wrong, but under the terrifying gown she was wearing—a silk gown embroidered with crystals and other embroidery that was so heavy, her shoulders and back were already aching—she sported flip-flops. Fancy ones, ones that cost an eye-twitching amount of money, but flip-flops nonetheless.

They had been George's solution. She'd been so terrified of tripping or falling over her skirts as she walked down the aisle of the abbey, that he'd suggested she wear the simple coverings on her feet.

It would have been a wonderful solution if she wasn't horrified by the idea that the world would see them peeking out from underneath the hems...

That was the last thing they needed. She could see—and dread—the headlines in her mind's eye. A flip-flop-wearing future queen walking toward the man who was now king in more than just name. For Edward had already been crowned, and was the ruler of this grand country.

She'd watched the majestic procession from the antechamber at the head of the abbey. Petrified over what was about to happen—the ceremony that would proclaim her his queen—she'd found little comfort in her husband's stoic reaction to being king.

To Perry, he'd looked so at ease, so comfortable with how things were proceeding, it made her own nerves jitter all the more.

Sure, since his birth, he'd known this day would come. Whereas she totally hadn't. But he was so calm, so fearless. Even though twice in the space of a handful of months, his name had been declared to the world at large—because how her gorgeous husband could have Gottfried, Berthold and Donatus as names, she wasn't sure. Maximilian and Christoph made up for some of the others a bit, but not that much.

In the face of those crimes against humanity being revealed, yet again, she wasn't sure whether it made her love him more or made her be envious of his serenity—enough to hate him just a smidgen.

A teensy weeny bit.

Before God and his country, Edward had knelt on the cold stone slabs of the abbey's floor, had laid himself prostrate before the altar, while three of Veronia's highest clerics circled him, chanting words in Latin, before sprinkling holy water on his back.

She was surprised at how religious the ceremony was, considering that Edward himself had told her that Veronia didn't have a national religion. But the overtones were definitely here, and she supposed it made sense, considering how old the ceremony was.

Just because the nation didn't have one now, didn't mean it hadn't been religious in the past. And here was proof of that.

Her part in the ritual was approaching, and watching Edward's wasn't helping ease the fear.

With her anxiety levels shooting through the roof, she watched as two of the clerics helped him stand.

Holding out their hands, Edward grabbed a hold of them and used them for support.

George had explained this tiny action was a metaphor—a part of the ceremony that showed the people that Edward would always seek a helping hand, that he wouldn't turn his back on support in times of need. Be it from the government or another country.

The king, in Veronia's eyes, should be humble.

And considering that, to become king, Edward had to kneel on the cold floor, she didn't think he could lower himself much further.

Still, he was now on his feet, and a page appeared from the side of the nave to grab the train of his cloak.

The boy was only eight, if that, but he seemed to have more confidence than Perry herself. He wore a black suit coat with tails, knee-length black breeches that tucked into black stockings. The shirt he wore was plain, but around his neck, he had a waterfall cravat. On his feet, he wore polished black shoes with silver buckles.

The child, a son of some courtier or other, managed to look both precocious and cute as hell as he gathered the ermine train that fell in great swathes about Edward's feet. The fur was pure white with black dashes dotted here and there. It lined the cloak, which on the outer part, was a royal, rich burgundy velvet.

The cloak seemed to fall off Edward's shoulders. She wasn't sure how it stayed on, because it seemed impossible to her that it remained in place. But magic or secret fastenings kept it in line, and the deep red highlighted Edward's swarthiness in a way that made everything south of Perry's waist flare to life.

With the page holding his train, Edward turned to face the congregation. For a second, she was taken aback at how handsome he was.

Edward was one of the world's youngest kings, and at that moment, Perry knew she had probably broken a billion women's hopes because she had taken him.

And he was hers.

All hers.

Crazy though it was, her nerves disappeared at the thought.

This incredibly beautiful, smart, wonderful, charming, empathetic king was *hers*.

He stood there, facing the abbey's entrance for countless seconds. Giving her and the rest of the world time to take in just how powerful he was at that moment, and he seemed to wear that power with the same ease with which he wore his gravity-defying cloak.

He was dressed similarly to the page, with a black fitted suit coat that was cut short at the front and graduated into tails at the back. Edward, however, wore full-length trousers, and a white silk bow tie instead of a cravat.

His right breast was dotted with the myriad medals and rank insignia he'd earned during his time in the Veronian Armed Forces. His left breast was home to a large brooch that only the King of Veronia wore on state occasions—the royal lion and unicorn fighting one another in pure gold so bright and so yellow, that in the right light, it hurt the eyes to look upon.

Across his chest, he wore a sash. It was in Veronia's national color, a royal blue that was almost cerulean in hue. It spoke of Veronia's rich trading history with the Orient, back when such a color would have cost the earth to produce.

Her dress was that same royal blue, but unfortunately for her, blue was not her color.

Still, *nothing* was her color at that moment. Her skin, usually creamy, was pasty with her fear.

A fear Edward didn't seem to be feeling.

In the grand opulence of his ceremonial wear, it was hard to recognize the man she'd slept with last night. Hard to see the husband, who had shaved this morning beside her in the bathroom, as the king standing before his people.

While Edward stood at the altar, his gaze focused on a point visible to only him, three men strode sedately down the aisle.

Just like the young page in breeches and tails, these were somber-faced and dour with the seriousness of the task ahead of them. For, in their arms, they held burgundy velvet cushions which supported the crown jewels.

Like a dance, when the first page was two-thirds of the way down the aisle, Edward turned and retreated to the throne behind him. He ascended the three small steps, turned once more to face the crowd, and took a seat on the ornate gold throne. To his right, there was a smaller but equally detailed and bejeweled seat—Perry's.

As nerves once again bubbled in her veins, making her lightheaded, she watched as the same three clerics approached the pages, each one taking the ancient pieces in hand.

The first cleric retrieved a scepter. The gem-encrusted ball was topped with a solid gold, engraved cross. Edward held out his hand and the cleric placed it in his open palm.

The second cleric retrieved a chain. Even with the distance between her and the altar, a good fifty or more feet, she heard the echoing sounds of the heavy chain clanking as the cleric stepped toward the throne. Edward sat straighter as the man placed the chain over his head, settling it over his cloaked shoulders, where the centerpiece, the Royal Seal, sat over the sash crossing his chest.

Finally, the reverend who had officiated her wedding, the highest cleric in the land, clasped the crown in his hands as he too, approached the throne. With little ceremony, he placed it atop Edward's bowed head.

It wasn't as grand as the British Imperial State Crown. At least, not from what she'd seen in pictures. This was...kind of short. It didn't cover his head, but settled on his temples, so his leonine hair was fully visible. It was crenellated, but with sharp points, and each point was tipped with a gemstone so large, she could see it from here.

The clerics circled Edward once more, more Latin was chanted, and out of nowhere, the choir at the back of the abbey began to sing.

She closed her eyes, terror whirling through her as she realized the end of the song was her cue.

Perry spun around, and whispered to Cassie, "I'm not sure if I can do this, Cassie."

Cassie's bright blue eyes widened in dismay, but she reached for Perry's hands and squeezed them. "Of course, you can."

She shook her head. "If I didn't have to walk down the aisle by myself, I don't think I'd feel as terrified. What if I fall?"

Cassie sighed. "I swear, you spend half your time petrified you're going to fall. But you never do."

"Is that a challenge? I don't fall because somebody is always there to catch me," she said grimly. "Edward, George, my father… nobody will be out there to save me, Cassie."

"You're wearing flip-flops. For God's sake, Perry. How much trouble can you get into wearing those?"

She worried her bottom lip nervously with her fingers. "Do you think I should go barefoot?"

Cassie rolled her lips inward, and though Perry knew Cassie was stemming her laughter, she didn't take offense. "I think you'd regret it. The floor is freezing."

Perry slipped off her shoe, pressed her sole to the floor, and winced. Fall was almost over, and with it, winter approached. She'd been feeling the chill of the stone through her flip-flops, but hadn't noticed it because of her nerves. There was no way she'd be able to walk down the long aisle, then stand around throughout her part of the ceremony, not without her feet going numb, anyway.

She lifted a hand to her brow, but as she began to rub at her temple, Cassie's fingers came out to slap her wrist. "Stop that. You'll ruin your makeup."

Perry sucked in a deep breath when she heard the soprano soloist in the choir reach the crescendo of the song.

"Do I look okay?" she asked hurriedly, her head swiveling around to face the abbey and her immediate future.

"I already told you. You look perfect."

Cassie's earnestness eased her nerves some, and she wished like hell her friend could follow her down the aisle, but Cassie would stay here until Perry reached the altar. After, she would slip into the congregation where she would watch the rest of the service with her husband and children who were watching the coronation in the pews.

Perry peered down at herself, and not for the first time, questioned her judgment. Judgment that had brought her to this petrifying moment in her life.

She knew a lot of women would have killed to be in her position, but at that moment, she'd kill to be anywhere else.

She knew she was being selfish—her husband's mother, Marianne, was dead. A good woman, a loving mother, and a caring queen had been slaughtered, all because an angry political group wanted to make a stand. Wanted to send a message. And yet, all Perry could think of was herself.

This situation was fair on no one. Perry should be in Dubai still. Her husband should be chilling out at the side of the pool. Her lovers should be relaxing and eating as they enjoyed their honeymoon.

Instead, Xavier and George were part of the congregation, watching as she and Edward became the leaders of Veronia.

She wanted them at her side—needed them. Cassie was lovely, but Xavier and George were hers. They'd buoy her confidence, tease her out of her anxiety. Kiss her, hug her, remind her that she could do this.

She needed them more than she'd ever needed anyone.

A haunting melody suddenly whispered along the sound waves. Recognizing it, she clenched her eyes closed as the song finally came to a halt. The piercing notes ceased echoing around the abbey's domed ceilings, her cue for the next part of this ritual.

Cassie grabbed her shoulders, gently shook her, and in a half-whisper and half-snarl, hissed, "You've got this. Dammit. You own this, Perry. You hear me? You're the strongest woman I know. Rock this shit."

Licking her lips as she absorbed her friend's strident words, Perry nodded and allowed herself to be spun around. Swallowing thickly, she gulped down a long breath of air, and nodded at the footman standing at the doors.

Her nod was the catalyst.

With the click of their heels, the footmen opened the doors wide, and Perry stood, trying not to panic. The congregation turned to watch her leave the antechamber.

She knew she wasn't queen yet, not officially, but all that "God save the Queen" shit? Perry could really do with some of that right about now.

———

THE THRONE WAS as uncomfortable as he remembered.

As a small boy, he'd stolen the seat, often play-fighting over who could sit upon it with his brother, George, and cousin, Xavier. His mother had watched over their fighting with a harried smile but *Tanta* Lisetta had always been amused by their antics.

The two women couldn't have been more different, and in their too-short lives, had never been able to see eye-to-eye. It just seemed incredible that neither of them were around anymore. In fact, it was more than incredible—it was wrong. So wrong.

Lisetta had died in her forties—Edward's age, or thereabouts. Marianne had been barely sixty-five. And his father? And Xavier's? Both too young to have passed on.

Being royal and being rich was no promise to a long and healthy future. It only meant a life fraught with tension and fear, political unrest, and societal anxiety. Yet he had just dragged the woman he loved into this world. A woman who was walking toward him, her face a stony mask, a complete contrast to her usually mobile features.

Still... she was beautiful.

Astonishingly so.

He knew, that while this was a day that would remain with him for the rest of his life, he would never forget the sight of her as she walked toward him. She'd done the same a handful of weeks ago, each step taking her towards her future as his bride and princess. But now, everything had changed.

They were leaders, no longer the leaders-in-waiting.

The abbey itself was a perfect juxtaposition of the current state of their emotions. Not just personally, but as a nation. On one hand, they mourned Marianne's death and Philippe's abdication. This was represented in the swags of black fabric swathing the hundreds of dark oak pews.

On the other hand, they were celebrating the new king, a new reign, a new future for Veronia. Atop the black fabric, there were bunches of bright white lilies for rebirth and splendor, grace and sorrow.

DeSauvier banners hung from the domed ceiling, draping several dozen feet above them, creating shadows on the stone floors. There were hundreds of them, and they alternated between royal blue with the family crest, a rearing unicorn, and purple with a lion stitched in gold upon it. The gold lion represented Philippe; the royal blue with both the lion and the unicorn was for Edward.

Veronian nationals wore black, whereas visiting dignitaries wore whatever they liked. The abbey was a sea of black broken up by bright sparks of colors.

The coronation was always a difficult time.

The passing of an old sovereign raised sorrow—or sometimes joy—from the people. Both emotions had the potential to cause trouble.

The backlash for the UnReals had been immense. His mother's murder had triggered outright abhorrence from the general public, as such a deed should always stir.

His people weren't acting bizarrely by mourning the murder of the queen. But as always with terrorists, there was that bizarre sense they were all on a different plane of reality—unable to accept that the worst truly had happened.

Yet how could they feel anything else? How could the royal family and the nation's government have expected any other kind of reaction than the hatred spilling the UnReals' way from Veronian nationals?

Their attack had proven the UnReals had access to every aspect of life here. That was a chilling threat no one save the family seemed to be reacting to. Why? He'd yet to find out. But find out he damn well would.

The carved gold motifs on the throne dug into his spine, making this effort in torture even worse. The saying, "heavy is the head who wears the crown," didn't take into account how damn uncomfortable the throne was, too.

The whimsical thought was enough to make his eyes sparkle with tears.

He'd lost his mother less than a month ago, and yet here he was, having had barely any chance to mourn her passing. No opportunity at all to overcome the tragedy and horror of her death.

A single sniper's bullet had changed his life forever. Perry's too. And if he was being really maudlin, an entire country's.

As Perry walked towards him, his feelings were far too complicated to dissect. There was sadness at having brought her, far too swiftly, into this position. There was sorrow, for the last woman he'd seen wearing the ermine cloak had been his mother, at his father's coronation, when he was a boy. There was a touch of amusement at the mask on her face, a mask he knew hid her fear... not fear of the moment, or fear of the crowd. But the fear of tripping over her skirts.

Sometimes, she was too damn predictable, and too damn cute with it.

Then, most perplexing of all, when taking into account the muddle of his feelings, there was lust.

Perry wore a bustier. Royal blue, tightly fitting, making her lush tits swell over the sweetheart neckline. The bustier was embroidered heavily with gold and silver thread. Fleur-de-lis danced over her chest, around her waist. The gold and silver, as well as the rich blue, made her skin look creamier. Her chestnut hair was so dark that it looked black, especially in contrast to the rich hues of her dress, the skirts of which were long. Gathered tightly at her hips, they fled out in gauzy waves. With each step, they swirled about her feet in a timeless dance that enchanted him.

From her shoulders, a cape matching his own draped to the floor. The burgundy velvet, the white fur, were a study in contrasts that suited her coloring greatly.

She wore no jewelry. Not even earrings. Just as he had walked down the aisle bare from artifice, she did too, save for the embroidery and the crystals sewn onto her bodice. Though he highly doubted he looked as gorgeous as she did.

The three clerics, the highest in the land, moved from their positions, and as if in a choreographed dance, came to stand in front of Edward. The wall of reverends was irritating, if expected. Edward did not appreciate being denied the sight of his woman. Because no matter her title, beneath it all, she was his. As he was hers.

The thought was grounding.

With his entire world up in the air, he realized how badly he needed his wife to keep him on solid earth. His brother, George, had showed unexpected wisdom in bringing this woman to Veronia, in bringing her into their lives. Because the truth of it was, without George and Xavier, as well as Perry, Edward was not sure if he'd be able to do any of this.

Daunted by the task ahead, he focused on Perry instead.

The terror on her face had lessened now that she'd reached the altar. Now that she was out of danger of falling.

He wasn't sure why she was so terrified of tripping over all the time, just knew that she was. Those moments of insecurity tended to be handled by George, so only God knew what suggestion he'd come up with to resolve her fear. Knowing him, Edward had to wonder what kind of shoe Perry wore under the sweeping skirts of her dress—more than likely flip-flops. Or, God forbid, Crocs.

If it hadn't been the start of winter, and if the floor beneath them wasn't frigid, he reckoned she'd have gone barefoot.

The thought had him studying her face once more. There, he sensed relief, but he searched her expression for pain or discomfort as she walked... When he saw none, he highly doubted she'd gone without shoes. Although, he wouldn't have put it past her. Or George, for that matter.

"Perry DeSauvier," the reverend boomed out in officious tones once Perry had approached. She came to a halt before the wall of clerics standing in front of Edward. "You come to us a child of two nations. A child of two worlds. You hold in your hands the ability to shape this country. Do you deserve this privilege?"

She gulped. But, as rehearsed, whispered, "No."

"Do you promise this great nation that you will earn the right to shape its destiny?"

"Yes." This time, there was no nervous gulping beforehand. Her earnestness was evident, not only to Edward, but to the cameras trained on her face.

"Do you vow to stand by your husband's side, to help him lead when times are troubled?"

"Yes."

"With your body, and with God's will, shall you bear the next DeSauvier to rule over this proud land?"

"I will."

"And do you realize that you stand here before me today, with the Veronians at your back and front, with the promise of their heritage to cherish and protect for future generations, and all because of God's will?"

Edward's lips twitched at the mutinous expression that appeared suddenly on his wife's face.

An atheist, he knew she'd find that part of the oath the hardest to vow.

Veronia had no official state religion, but it was a theist nation. They were a people of believers, and whichever God it may be, that God was respected.

But though she looked particularly mulish, he could perhaps have mistaken it for zealousness; she gently murmured, without a whisper of dissent in her voice, "I do realize this."

The high cleric nodded and swept out his arms. "Then show your people the willingness to be their queen."

The other two reverends moved out, and as planned, Perry reached for their fingers and used their support to lower herself to the ground. On her knees, she peered up at the high cleric, who anointed her forehead with the cross in water that had been blessed. Two pages appeared from the side of the nave, carrying padded cushions. They came to a halt at either side of the cleric, and he reached for the crown that denoted Perry's station.

With little ado, he placed the diadem on her head. The rubies sparkled and shone in the dull light that gleamed from the stained-glass windows. The gold deepened the darkness of her hair, and with the dimming sunlight gleaming on her face, Edward knew she'd never looked more beautiful to him than she did at that moment.

He'd thought her precious on their wedding day. But today, she made these vows not just for him, but for his people. And this was her sacrifice on his behalf, because Perry didn't want this. She'd never wanted this.

The cleric reached for the second symbol of Perry's station.

This was a lighter, smaller chain that matched the one about Edward's shoulders. With care, the cleric placed it over her head and moved it so it rode the upper part of her arms. The thick links were heavy, and in contrast to the delicacy of Perry's form and dress, they were statements.

Though Edward wanted to do it himself, he had to stand by and let the clerics help Perry back onto her feet. They retained their hold on her fingers as they guided her to the throne beside Edward's. She took a seat, settling nervously at his side—but those nerves were only his and the clerics to see... the tremble of her fingers, the goosebumps on her arms. Her poker face had definitely come on in the past few months, he realized, and was saddened by the necessity for that.

He'd changed her life, and wasn't altogether sure that it was entirely for the better. Wealth and privilege weren't everything. Especially to a creature like Perry, who preferred science, who cherished knowledge over everything else.

When she was seated, the reverends disappeared, merging into the crowd of staff at the side of the nave, leaving only the high cleric alone at the altar.

Then, with the last of the pageantry, the man who had crowned Edward's father before him, declared, "Long live King Edward II, and long live Queen Perry."

And like that, his and Perry's fates were sealed.

Forever.

CHAPTER TWO

"WHAT ARE YOU DOING HERE?"

Standing in the music room of the house that should have been hers and Edward's after their marriage, Perry jolted and spun on her heel to look at her husband. As well as her lovers.

Her cheeks turned bright pink as she murmured, "Thinking." Had life not suddenly gone off the rails, Grosvenor House was where she'd be living now. Instead...

"Thinking?" Xavier strode toward her, and she allowed herself to settle into his arms with a sigh when he wrapped them about her. God, did he have to smell so freakin' good? Like sex and laundry detergent and sandalwood? Talk about a cocktail for your nose! "What about?" he asked, interrupting her internal grousing about his sexy-as-hell scent.

Choking a little on the words, Perry admitted, "About how much I wanted to live here."

She closed her eyes, feeling them prickle with tears at what would never be. Just coming to Grosvenor House had required that she have more security guys than a soccer team. She knew she'd been a pain in her protective detail's ass too by demanding this visit. But George had warned her that her guards would always try to hem her in, and she had to do what she wanted. Otherwise she'd go stir-crazy.

Stir-crazy wasn't just hyperbole now. It was a real thing. A definite possibility.

There was no exaggerating this shit. Day-to-day life had become more complicated because just leaving the palace was turning into something more complicated than a Japanese gameshow... and this was only day one on the new job.

The sound of footsteps on the antique parquet floor indicated either George or Edward were approaching. She felt a hand on her back and shuddered a little at the touch. "I'm sorry if I frightened you by disappearing," she whispered. "I just needed a place... I just had to find somewhere I could breathe."

George sighed. "You don't have to apologize. This situation is overwhelming for us all. And, though it's not happened how we imagined, we always knew the day would come where Edward would rule in Father's stead. You haven't had the years we've had to prepare for it."

She nodded, knowing he was right, but her desire to live in Grosvenor House made things harder on her. The manor house wouldn't have been her first choice for her first marital home, but it was a damn sight better than Masonbrook Castle, with its endless corridors, drafty rooms, ceilings that were sky-high, and more staff than a Hershey's factory.

Grosvenor House, by comparison, was so intimate with its fourteen bedrooms, that knowing she couldn't live here just saddened her deeply.

She rubbed her nose against Xavier's shirt, and pulling in a deep gulp of air that was loaded with more of that epic scent of his, she moved out of his arms and away from them all.

This was the first room they'd shown her at the manor—a sitting room that had more musical instruments in it than actual furniture.

And this shit was insane. Only the best Stradivariuses for the DeSauviers, of course.

Not just one, but *several*.

She rubbed her temple as she eyed one of the polished pretties that was tilted on a stand atop the baby grand piano, and tried not to feel like Alice after she went through the looking glass. These museum quality pieces were now hers to play... well, if she could play more than Chopsticks, that is. Fuck.

"Do you want some pizza?"

She blinked, taken aback at the pedestrian question. Turning away from the piano, she squinted at her husband. "What kind?"

Xavier snickered. "So suspicious."

"Perry takes pizza very seriously," George remarked as he plunked himself down on the sofa that, mere weeks before her marriage, she'd napped on, before being deliciously plundered by Edward and Xavier upstairs in the master suite. Those were good times, deserving of more "o's" than the two that "good" already contained. More like *goooood* times.

"Who doesn't take pizza seriously?" she retorted waspishly, when the men carried on snickering at her.

"I'm not that big a fan of it myself," Xavier murmured, then held up his hands in surrender when she gaped at him.

"You've never had the right stuff, then."

His lips twitched. "I've eaten it all around the world."

"You need to have it in New York. Best. Pizza. Ever."

"You do know we're across the border from Italy? I'm sure they'd argue they have the best pizza. Ever." Edward moved over to her, his lips curved in a smile. He reached for her hand and gently tugged her toward one of the armchairs. As he took a seat, he tumbled her down onto his lap. "Come on, sit with me a while."

She snuggled into him, hating herself for feeling so insecure when he, *they*, were the ones who needed help, support, encouragement—and anything else a new king required his new queen to be. She was doing them a disservice by being such a wimp, yet she just felt so... blah.

Yeah, that was it. *Blah.*

Feeling a bit like a little girl—the exact opposite of how she should be feeling in this sex God's lap—she pressed her face to his throat and murmured, "Pepperoni. Every time."

He chuckled, and it comforted her to feel his chest vibrate with amusement—he'd been so somber since that last day in Dubai, when they'd been declared king and queen. Not that she could blame him, but it did her heart good to know he could still laugh. "Pepperoni for you then. Mushroom for me."

"I'll have that too," Xavier commented.

"I'll tell the kitchens," George instructed, and she heard the sofa squeak as he got to his feet.

"It's mean to make them cook pizza at this time of the night," she reasoned—quietly, though. She really did want the pizza.

"That was a token complaint if ever I've heard one," George retorted with a snort as he made his way out of the room.

She pulled away to watch him go, and studied the set of his shoulders as he moved.

There was a tension riding him, riding them all.

Fuck. They really did *not* need to be babying her.

"I'm sorry," she whispered when he'd gone. Somehow, it was easier to say without George in the room.

He was her best friend, one of the loves of her life, and yet, he knew a different side of her. The playful side, the one who'd whoop his ass at *Mortal Kombat,* and could out-eat his body weight in donuts.

She hadn't been feeling herself for a long time.

Being with these guys... it had changed her. Not in a bad way, though. If anything, she felt sure they made her better. Like, she was the best person she could be with them at her side. But the world they'd brought her into, it was where she was at her weakest.

Her most vulnerable.

And the dichotomy was tiring.

"There's nothing to be sorry for," Edward murmured softly, seeming to discern how sensitive she was at that moment. He nestled deeper into the armchair like he was settling in for the night, and that helped her breathe a little easier.

"There is. You don't need me to be a big baby."

Xavier snorted. "Perry, do you know what you did today?"

"Managed not to trip up in front of the world?"

He rolled his eyes. "You became a queen. Now, you're *the* queen. If anyone's allowed to feel a little shaky, it's you. And Edward. George and I didn't have to do what you did today, and *we're* feeling the aftermath.

"You're entitled to be overwhelmed and scared and tired, even."

She bit her lip. "I do feel tired."

"Of course. I do too."

She peered up at her husband. "I feel like I haven't seen you in ages."

"I have to learn a lot, Perry," Edward admitted. "I don't know how... It's going to take me a long time to fill my father's shoes."

"You don't have to fill them. You have to make your own place for yourself. Make it yours."

He touched his thumb to the scowl puckering her brow. "And I will, once I know what I'm doing."

Jesus, if he didn't know what he was doing, and he'd been preparing for this all his life, was it any wonder she was feeling like a tub of cookie dough ice cream without the cookie dough?

Pointless.

"Guess that means I need to get used to you not being around for a while, huh?"

He sighed. "Maybe." She felt his nose nuzzle her hair before he murmured, "I'm sorry."

"Don't be. It's not your fault."

"Fault can't be attributed to anyone here," Xavier pointed out gently. "But it doesn't mean it's not crazy scary."

She stared at him, took him in in all his perfection, then whispered, "You really feel that, too?"

"Of course. Things are going to change now, Perry. Things *have* to change. We're... we can't be the kids anymore. We're the grown-ups."

Her eyes widened. Jesus. *That.* "Yes."

His lips twitched. "You feel the same way, huh?"

"I do. Like, with Marianne and Philippe around, we could still make mistakes. Now, I feel like we have to be perfect."

"Well, that's never going to happen. We're always going to make mistakes," he assured her.

"But some of us more than others," she said wryly, surprising herself with the ability to joke about a future that was so uncertain, and therefore, all the more terrifying.

"We'll be fine," Edward said, to Xavier too, not just her. "We'll live and learn, and if we make mistakes, then Mother and Father aren't around to reprimand us for it. And if the courtiers complain, they can go fuck themselves."

"Off with their heads?" she teased, doing her best Queen of Hearts' impression.

George slipped into the room with a snort. "I'm out of the conversation for five minutes, and when I come back, you're ready to decapitate someone?"

"Only if they deserve it," she teased.

He grinned at her. "What merits you going all Queen Redd on someone's butt?"

"I haven't been queen long enough to make a list. I'll come up with appropriate punishments for certain misdemeanors."

"She's hardcore," Xavier told George with a laugh, and they all joined in.

"Pizza will be ready in twenty," George informed the room at large.

"Want to watch a movie?"

She scowled up at her husband. "Where can we watch a movie? Does this place even have a TV?"

He blinked at her. "We're the richest people in Veronia, Perry, and you think we don't have a TV?"

"I feel like I've only seen one in the castle. In George's room."

"Mine's hidden in a cupboard," Edward informed her. "In my old quarters, I mean. There are televisions, they're just not on show."

"Okay then, movie night it is. But where is it?"

"In the cinema room."

She gaped at Xavier. "This place has a cinema room?" Her lips formed a pout. "Now I really wish we were going to live here."

Beneath her, Edward tensed. His hand came up to cup the back of her neck. "I'm sorry we're not going to," he told her quietly.

"Me too, but we'll make Masonbrook work." The smile she shone his way was tight but earnest.

"It's not all bad," George pointed out. "There are great stables, Perry. We need to get you riding."

"Because I'm not dangerous enough on two legs, you want to shove me on four?"

"I swear, you're terrified of falling over, and I haven't seen you fall once."

"Why does that sound like a complaint, Xavier?" she demanded drily.

"Trust me, she doesn't do it often, but when she does, it's spectacular."

She rolled her eyes at George. "My public misery is there for your private consumption."

He snickered. "I know. One time, we were in downtown Boston. We were just about to head into this great little bar called White Hart."

His words struck a chord with her.

God, how long had it been since they'd gone there?

Would they ever be able to go again?

Not likely.

"We were walking in, and this car, out of nowhere, drives past and through this shit-deep puddle."

"His Highness over there didn't get a mark on him, of course," she grumbled. "I got piss wet through."

"She means it, guys," George said, his tone gleeful at the memory.

"Why do I love you again?" she demanded.

"Because I rock?"

"Oh yeah, it could be that."

When he winked at her, she grumbled, then huffed out a sigh when he carried on. "So, it was scorching, hot but we'd just had this storm, and she's covered in this gray water. Ms. Braveheart over here runs into the street and starts waving her arms at the driver who totally didn't notice her as he was driving off.

"She's so busy trying to get the guy—who's on the other block by now—to see her, she forgets other cars are allowed in the road too. Huge SUV comes up behind her, toots its horn and—"

"Where are you when this is going down?" Edward demanded, scowling at his brother. "This doesn't sound very gentlemanly, George."

She preened at Edward's courteous words. "I know you wouldn't have let me do that, Edward."

"George shouldn't have either!"

The man under fire held up his hands in surrender. "She'd dashed into the road before I could stop her, then, when the SUV made its appearance, I nearly got thrown under a damn bus trying to get her out of the way."

She wrinkled her nose. "He did do that."

"Thank you," George retorted wryly. "She managed to dash off faster than I did. Anyway, as I get out of the way of the bus, she's on the other side of the road at this point. I have to rush across too, and then, lo and behold, the bus takes off, and *boom*."

Perry burst out laughing. "He got covered in shitty water, too."

George grinned at her. "I think we need to be grateful those things don't happen too often. We're the ones in danger from her clumsiness. Not her."

Edward snorted, but Xavier murmured, "We'll keep her safe from herself."

"Just throw her in a padded room." George winked at her. "That should do it."

She shot him a wide grin as the happy memory flooded through her. She'd been wicked pissed at getting wet, angrier still when the jerk driver hadn't stopped to apologize. Then, watching George almost get run over, while terrifying, had ended up hilarious because he'd been drenched too.

"I'm glad the memory makes you smile, Ms. Grumpy."

"I'm not grumpy," she argued. "Not now that there's pizza coming."

George rolled his eyes. "Are we watching a movie or what?"

She bit her lip. "Shouldn't we be doing something more..."

"More what?"

At Xavier's question, she shrugged. "Royal?"

"Royal?" Edward laughed. "No. Royals are allowed to eat pizza and watch movies, too."

"But you're too busy," she said sadly. "I'm sure there are other things you need to be doing tonight."

He grabbed a firm hold of her chin, tilted her face to his and pressed a gentle kiss to her mouth. "There's nothing more important than you tonight, Perry. Than making sure you're okay, and that *we're* okay."

She gnawed at her bottom lip. "Are you sure?"

"I'm positive." He stared deeply into her eyes. "These moments might be rare, but they will be precious."

His words had her frowning—it was indicative of the upcoming weeks, she supposed. He was warning her, he wouldn't be around much.

The notion shouldn't have left a deep ache in her soul, but it did.

It really did.

Maybe it should have scared her how much she needed these men. She'd never needed anyone before George. Having left home at eighteen, she'd barely gone back to her parents' farm through college, and after... she'd been independent, was used to that. Then, she'd met George, and she'd grown to depend on him in different ways.

But that was nothing compared to now.

She needed each man, needed them in a way she couldn't understand how other women didn't.

How did they cope with just one man?

Edward was her silent strength. The man at her back, who always would shelter her and protect her. Xavier was the light at the end of the tunnel. He would speak for her when she was wordless. When she couldn't make sense of things, he made them right for her. And George? He was her joker. He managed to make the darkest situations the lightest.

All three of them were her strength.

She could do this—be queen and their lover, and all the other things she'd need to be over the upcoming months. She knew that. Perry wasn't a total no-hope, after all. But *this* was their world. This was a universe of courtiers and royal visits. Of waving at millions of strangers who knew the most intimate of details about her and her husband's world. It involved smiling when she was sad, of being polite when she felt she was drowning.

It meant wearing a crown and being regal when all she felt like wearing was yoga pants and a smile—one not loaded with lipstick.

This world was not her own.

But that didn't mean she couldn't make it hers.

Even if she'd have to start with Edward not being as close as she needed.

She reached for him, pressed her mouth to his. "You need to do what you need to do. I recognize that."

She felt the tension release from him like an ill wind. "Thank you for understanding."

"Of course."

"I won't be far away," he promised her.

Somehow, she knew that was a lie. He could be just down the hallway in Masonbrook, and it would feel like he was in another damn town.

"I know," she assured him, cupping his chin and stroking her thumb over his jaw. "Just don't…"

"Don't what?"

She shook her head. She'd been about to ask him not to forget her, but he wasn't going anywhere.

It just felt like he was.

Xavier cleared his throat, and she was grateful that he seemed to sense her uncertainty. "Come on. Let's go to the movie room."

Edward scowled at her, then flashed his cousin a glance. But whatever he saw on Xavier's face had him nodding.

Perry leaped off his lap, then held out her hand as he too, got to his feet.

"Who's picking the movie?" she asked, forcing a smile.

Tonight was tonight, and tomorrow was another day.

George laughed. "Me!" Then, he took off like the joker he was, and damn her hide, she couldn't stop herself from rushing after him.

"Not if I get there first."

"That will be bloody hard considering you don't know where it is!" he called back to her.

"Well, shit," she grouched, coming to a swift halt, causing Xavier to bump into her.

He laughed, then scared the shit out of her by hauling her over his shoulder and taking off at swift run. Before she could do more than squeal, he declared, "Game on, George. We're coming to get you."

And while she knew he was only teasing, the words fit them all.

If one faltered, the others would approach, en masse, to help him.

Just as they would if Edward dove into his new role and drowned in the quagmire of it. Just as they would if the same happened to her.

They were a foursome, not single units.

And they would never, ever, be alone again.

She needed to remember that.

CHAPTER THREE

"WHEN IS he going to wake up?"

Xavier ran a hand through his already rumpled hair. George's exasperation bled through his demand, and it was shared by them all.

Philippe's grand suite had been overtaken with medical equipment. Amid the richest tapestries in the land, the most ornate of decorations in the former king's rooms...the modern didn't marry successfully with the past.

Philippe had been hit twice by a sniper's bullet. One had caused nothing more than a flesh wound, but he hadn't been so fortunate with the second... It had pierced his stomach, doing damage to his liver and spleen along the way as it injured his spinal cord.

Upon their return from Dubai, Philippe had already been unconscious. He'd awoken only to abdicate the throne and consent to the operation that would reduce the swelling on his spinal cord—the endgame to stabilize his spine and avoid paralysis.

Though he was clinging to life, Philippe had yet to wake up from his surgery, and had been in an unresponsive coma ever since.

While Xavier wanted to see his uncle, to speak with him, he was well aware that a healing rest was exactly what Philippe needed. The chaos in the wake of the assassination, the subsequent abdication, then the new coronation, had left Veronia in a state of flux. For a country as large, as rich, and as powerful as theirs was, that was never good thing. It was a time of stress, and with his injuries, the last thing Philippe needed was to be dealing with that.

Still... his wakening didn't promise much, but he and his cousins longed to speak with Philippe. Xavier knew that was because they were reverting to type. While they were some of the nation's most powerful men, that did not mean that they themselves did not feel fear or concern or anxiety. In Philippe's presence, they were small boys again, needing reassurance from their father and uncle. Needing to know they were safe.

But they weren't safe.

They had proof of that now.

In the face of George's anger, the doctors were uncomfortable.

The surgeon, a specialist who had been flown in from Switzerland, mumbled, "It is difficult to say, Your Highness. His Highness's injuries are severe. Rest is his saving grace. He will awaken when he is ready, when his body is ready."

George rubbed his temples. "But he was supposed to be conscious for the coronation. That was two days ago now. Surely it's a bad sign that he's still sleeping."

The surgeon, Dr. Schertz, shrugged his pigeon-like shoulders, but he flushed when he caught Perry's earnest eye. "There is no good nor bad. He needs rest. Sleep. He is healing from grievous wounds, Your Highnesses."

Perry sighed, and reached over to rub George's shoulder. She was trying to comfort them all, Xavier realized, while floundering herself. The truth was, however, they were all floundering. The only solace was in the closeness the four of them shared.

Not that Edward was here.

A fact none of them could argue about. They knew he'd be attending this appointment if he could, but his new station simply didn't allow it. In fact, that new station barely allowed any time to grieve Marianne's death or Philippe's current state, never mind anything else.

Though Edward was aware it wasn't fair, and that that route only lead to burnout, that was the way of it. It was like a trial by fire. Philippe would be the first to say that the earliest months of a new monarch's reign were the hardest. A reign, after all, always began with grief, for a new king surfaced only upon the former king's passing.

In this case, Philippe hadn't died, but every day, his life hung in the balance.

To Dr. Schertz, Perry murmured, "I'm certain Philippe's in the best care. Thank you for coming to speak to us, doctor." She reached for his hand and gently squeezed.

It was quite amusing to witness the surgeon's preening at her praise—that was, if it hadn't been so damned irritating. In her new position, Perry had been manicured in a way that they were all getting used to. Slowly.

The wedding had been the first phase in that change. The coronation had been the second.

Her nails were no longer bare, but discreetly buffed and polished. Her brows were perfect, her makeup natural and flawless. Her hair gleamed with good health after a recent cut, and her wardrobe, which had already been revitalized under George's supervision, had endured a distinct overhaul.

The Perry that had flown into Veronia all those months ago was no more. Xavier supposed, in a way, they were also mourning her loss. Perry was changing, he knew. She had to. Her new role required adaptation.

Patience.

More change.

More flux. It was everywhere.

It was overwhelming.

In his white coat, beneath which was a very smart suit, the surgeon's posturing had him pushing out his chest as he strutted out of Philippe's bedroom.

When George spoke, the doors had closed behind the small man, "Another admirer, Perry."

"Shut up." She eyed him grumpily, but the hand she lowered to George's was anything but tempered by her mood. She squeezed his fingers, Xavier noticed, with a strength she tried to imbue to his cousin.

"I don't know, Perry, they seem to be dropping like flies around you," he teased, needing to play, to jerk her chain a bit. Do anything to lighten the tension in the room.

But he could only do so much.

Philippe's silence and stillness, combined with the endless beeps of the machines that kept him alive were, draining any possibility of light-heartedness.

As always, her sensitivity surprised him. She seemed to recognize what he was doing, didn't take offense, and murmured, "I prefer 'bees around honey' than being compared to flies, Xavier." She pouted.

His grin appeared, and it was such a strange development that the muscles in his jaw ached. It had been close to four weeks since they'd been happy and on honeymoon. Smiling was something rare at the moment.

"Stop being fussy. They're all insects."

"Bees have queens," George said hoarsely. His hand closed around Perry's like the lifeline it was. "She's right. It's more fitting."

Perry ducked her head when George took a seat beside his father's bed. She pressed a kiss to his temple, then closing her eyes, turned slightly and buried her face in his hair.

Xavier understood. The need to connect was deep. It burned like a living flame between them all.

It was an unusual phase in their relationship, considering how new their being together really was. So shortly after the honeymoon, they should still have been at it like rabbits. But since Marianne's murder, they hadn't come together in that way... and it was strange. Strange not to seek union in that manner. Instead, they were growing more affectionate.

Especially Perry.

He hadn't needed George to tell him that Perry had had few romantic relationships in her life. She was very comfortable in herself, but in many ways, unused to being touched by others. It wasn't that she wasn't affectionate, but simply unaccustomed to being able to touch somebody with tenderness. In these past weeks, she'd been learning. Gradually becoming fluent in the silent language they could only utter with touch.

"Where's Edward? He should be here," George whispered, all joviality disappearing.

Xavier sighed, but it was more like a gust of air than a gentle trickle. "You know he would be if he could."

Perry straightened a little, moved her hands to bracket George's shoulders as she whispered, "He's meeting with Drake today."

His cousin shuddered. "I hope that means they have news. It's about goddamn time."

"Drake called in as many favors as he was able," Xavier noted, thinking uneasily of the offer of help Perry's former president had extended to them. He shouldn't have been surprised that there was a CIA black site here in Veronia, but he was. And that their head of security had been using it merely deepened his unease.

"Not enough," George said hoarsely. "Not nearly fucking enough." His eyes were trained on his father's pale and drawn face.

Philippe had always been hale and hearty, rarely ill. Now, to see him like this, he looked every one of his sixty-eight years.

Xavier wasn't sure if that made him feel very young or very old.

"That reminds me," Perry said softly "Edward wanted me to ask you something, Xavier."

Curious, he cocked a brow at her. "What?"

She pulled a face, and her discomfort made itself known as she bit her lip. "He was wondering if you'd sit in Parliament for the foreseeable future."

The notion didn't exactly thrill him, but he was eager to help. In times of crisis, family pulled together or fell apart. He had no intention of their quartet disintegrating.

"Of course."

Perry blinked. "Really?"

Her surprise had him smiling—twice in one hour, talk about a damn miracle. "Edward sent in the big guns, huh?" It didn't astonish him that

Edward had believed he'd say no—Xavier had, after all, spent most of his life avoiding his Aunt Marianne's attempts to bring him more into the royal fold.

She cut him a look. "Maybe. If you consider me 'big guns.'"

George snorted. "You've been Perried, Xavier."

Didn't he just know it.

CHAPTER FOUR

IN THE FAMILY, Edward was the rider. The one who found freedom on the back of a horse, who could and would lose himself on an hour-long ride. But it was George who found himself today on horseback, he who sought the gentle peace that only a stallion could bring him.

He wished he was alone, but ever since the shooting, security had begun to border on the ridiculous. Perry and Edward were followed around by small armies, and George and Xavier, even though they were lesser royals now, hadn't been saved from the miserable fate of having too many guards traipsing around behind *and* in front of them.

After the freedom of the States, George felt certain he'd go mad if he couldn't have a moment to himself. Then, when such thoughts crossed his mind, he felt inordinately guilty. How must Perry feel? She, who'd led a simple life before he'd barged his way into it? Who was unaccustomed to needing guards, never mind the depth of security they were currently enduring.

Sighing wearily, George brought his horse to a halt. Standing in the stirrups, he balanced himself on the unsteady terrain as Whisper, an Arabian stallion, shifted and settled himself.

The play of his muscles felt good, George realized. Since Dubai, they'd been inactive for the most part. Sequestered in secure locations, shielded from any and all potential dangers.

Though he understood, the brain didn't always make sense. Feelings certainly never did. These precautions were for his safety. It was the same for Perry, Edward, and Xavier. Drake wasn't a sadist—he didn't get off on making them more miserable by having them under constant supervision.

He did it for their own good.

But that particular truth didn't stop·him from feeling trapped. From feeling like he could scream and scream from within the box that was suddenly his life.

All around them, he saw DeSauvier terrain. Land and territory that had been fought over and conquered several times throughout his family's dynasty. He wondered how his ancestors would handle the current threat to the throne. Would they have allowed themselves to be curried into safe locations? Or would they have gone to war?

Knowing his heritage, his ancestors' delight in claiming more territory for themselves—a delight that had in fact inspired the UnReal's anti-royalist cause in the first place—George could well understand the desire for battle.

Only something like fighting would burn off this excess energy that was roaring through his system. Some moments of the day, he felt sure he'd go mad. Only Perry seemed to calm him. Only she, who was far newer to this world than he was, had the ability to help George breathe through the rages that threatened to drown him.

The wind whistled through his hair. It was sharp and brisk, cold too. There was just enough nip to the air to make him shiver despite his thick Aran wool sweater—the faint perspiration his abrupt ride had stirred was likely the reason for that. The sun was murky, shielded from sight by a thick blanket of clouds, mostly grayer than white, but that perfectly suited his mood.

Rain beckoned, and the truth of it was, George welcomed it. He could handle being drenched, might even feel renewed by a spiritual cleansing.

In the distance, Masonbrook peered back at him. On days like today, with moods like his current one, he hated the castle. It was so solid. So enduring. It outlasted them all. Had seen so many of his line since the first DeSauvier who had constructed the monstrosity.

It seemed to span miles—especially from this vantage point. The rolling hills that surrounded the castle didn't even impugn the building's stature. If anything, the castle dominated *them*, with its endless turrets, walls that spanned hundreds of feet.

Slivers of air were cut into some of the ramparts, holes that had once enabled archers to attack enemy soldiers, for the DeSauviers had many enemies over the years—something that hadn't changed. *Would it ever?* George asked himself sourly.

There was a garrison, cannons lined some exterior courtyards just as suits of armor were decorative fodder in certain halls inside. The past was disturbingly present in Masonbrook. There was no forgetting the brutality of their history, and considering how his mother had just perished, that brutality seemed to be without end.

"Your Highness, we'd best be getting back. It looks like rain."

George cut his guard a look. Francesco had been his 'sentry' since George had left for America years before—even when he'd fancied he'd dismissed them all, he'd known Francesco was there. Ever waiting, ever watching. He'd come to know the man quite well, had even appreciated the Italian's bawdy sense of humor.

That prior knowledge was probably the only reason he didn't snap at him. Francesco hadn't done a damn thing wrong, save for doing his job. Just because George wanted to be caught in the rain, didn't mean it was fair that his guards would share a similar fate.

The simplicity of his life in Boston was a siren's call at that moment—God, how he wished they were there instead of here.

Back in Boston, he'd only really answered to his boss and to Perry. The former he'd only done so he'd have a legitimate reason for staying there. The latter being why he needed the reason.

He didn't reply to Francesco, just seated himself and rode back to the stables. As always, the place bustled with activity. The DeSauviers spent a fortune on their horseflesh. For the family, it was more for the luxury of their station. For Edward, it was personal want—he loved his horses. The breeding program was something his brother had implemented back in his twenties, and the racehorses that program had reared were prizewinners in themselves.

Knowing he was being a brat didn't stop George from being petulant. He left Whisper to a stable hand, mumbling thanks to the young lad who looked up at him in awe, knowing full well he should have seen to the stallion's tack himself.

It was a poor horseman who didn't care for his beast after a ride, but knowing that didn't stir him into action.

As he approached the castle, he blinked in surprise at the sight of Perry in one of the smaller courtyards. She had a small retinue of staff around her, fluttering around like wild butterflies that had been let loose.

The courtyard contained a fountain and several beds of roses that were currently barren because of the season. Winter or not, the fountain tinkled merrily away, as it had done for the past two hundred years. The grand marble statue of Poseidon, complete with trident, had been a gift from an ancestor to a particularly fertile bride. If memory served, each fish that spouted water into the air represented a child. As a boy, the notion had always astonished him.

There were fourteen fish, after all.

To George, that wasn't fertile—it was madness.

Still, different times, he supposed, trying to find comfort in his heritage. Everywhere he looked were the signs of his family's longevity. They had survived worse than this threat, and they would live to see another day as they always had.

Amid the dead rosebushes, Perry stood with all the fortitude of Boadicea. Arms aloft, she pointed here and there, muttering something that had the staff around her nodding in agreement. A few faces showed surprise, so only God knew what she was planning.

He saw her delight when she spied him. Her hands came together in pleased applause, and he knew if they were alone, she'd have launched herself into his arms.

He bitterly regretted that was impossible. With his maudlin mood, he could've done with a Perry-style hug.

When he neared, however, she reached for his hands with both of hers and squeezed his fingers tightly as she stared up at him. Her beautiful face shining with a bright happiness that skewed the darkness of his own mood.

"What are you doing out here?" she asked.

If he'd needed proof of the fact he was brooding, he guessed he'd just had it. "I went for a ride."

Her eyes widened. "You did?"

He watched as she pulled her bottom lip between her teeth, he let her gnaw on it a second before reaching up to pinch her on the chin. "Why does that come as such a surprise?"

"It's not, not really. I was just thinking."

"Always dangerous," he teased.

She huffed. "Xavier told me Edward loves to ride, that's all. He half-threatened to teach me how." Her huff turned into a grimace.

Despite himself and his earlier agitation, he had to hide a grin. "Half-threatened? I offered too."

"You were only teasing. He was being serious."

"*I* was being serious," he countered drily.

"It takes all my energy to stay on two feet. You, more than anyone, know that."

He shook his head. "I know you're clumsy, but you're not as bad as you think, Perry. I swear, it's like you think you're one of the Marx brothers. You don't spend half your time on the floor, you know. And if you did, you'd find an epic way to do it."

"If I fell before, it didn't matter. Now?" She gestured at the staff behind her, who had dispersed somewhat to give them some privacy. "Now I have an audience."

"I wish I could tell you that you get used to it," he grumbled, eyeing his own protective shadows who had stopped on the perimeter of the courtyard. He peered around, a thought occurring to him. "Where are your guards?"

She shrugged. "Here and there, I'd imagine."

Concern filtered through him. He knew he'd only been mentally complaining about the gaggle of security acting as their second skin of late, but they were there for a reason after all. And that reason wasn't for goddamn fun.

"They should be here," he insisted.

"I'm sure they are," she returned, raising a hand and rubbing at his shoulder to console him.

He sighed impatiently. He didn't need consoling, he needed answers. Turning to Francesco, he beckoned him close.

As the guard approached, George asked Perry, "What are you doing out here anyway?"

"This courtyard used to be an herb garden." She smiled with no small amount of satisfaction. "I'm arranging the way I want it to be once the flower beds are tilled."

"Edward gave you free rein?"

He only asked because his brother hadn't said anything about it to him. But then, Edward hadn't been saying much of anything to anyone outside of his advisors.

The satisfied smile on her face broadened. "He did."

George couldn't withhold his snort. Why did he think Edward didn't realize the castle was about to be totally overhauled? He fully expected for the ancient edifice to be ripped to shreds to salve Perry's eco-warrior conscience.

"The queen needs her guards," he informed Francesco.

His man nodded, then spoke into his microphone. Whatever he heard had him frowning as he turned about the garden. Then, he pointed to one, another, and a final one who looked like he was doing something illegal or something definitely *dodgy* behind a bush. "They're dotted throughout the gardens."

"Who's in charge of her staff?"

"Raoul Da Silva," Francesco murmured.

"Mother's head guard?"

"Yes. Natural fit, I suppose, sir."

"Okay. Thanks, Francesco," he said dismissively, feeling more at ease now he knew the guards were there, even if they weren't entirely on show—on Edward's orders, undoubtedly. Trying not to make Perry feel like she was totally hemmed-in.

When his guard fell back, George turned to a scowling Perry. "Why herbs?" he asked, smiling a little as she glowered at where

Francesco had pointed. When she failed to respond, he repeated his question.

Though she was still glowering, he assumed because she'd thought she was free from their surveillance, Perry grumbled, "According to records I found in one of the libraries, this used to be an herb garden...before it was converted into a useless rose garden."

He rolled his eyes. "You do know Veronia is famous for its roses? Which is why we have a lot of girls named Rose." Like her new PA. The one she'd had for two minutes and didn't like, and whose mother was one of their parents' oldest friends. More's the pity.

That had her mouth rounding. "Huh, well, I didn't know that about the girls' names. Anyway, it can still be famous for them. We just don't need a dozen rose gardens in the castle grounds." She planted her hands on her hips. "You don't even like roses."

"No," he agreed. "I hate them. They're trite and cliché."

"Then why the questions?" She squinted at him, her narrowed eyes raking over him in a way that, had they been alone in one of their quarters, he'd have used to start something between them.

Pity that they were in the garden.

"Curiosity, that's all."

"You're never curious about gardens. Your thumb is only green from flicking through all the money you earn in the stock market."

He chuckled, knowing full well that only she could make him laugh in his current mood. "You do know how playing the stock market works, right? We don't actually touch the money."

"It's all Monopoly money to you anyway," she said on a sniff. "Why didn't you invite me to go out with you? We could have walked, not gone riding."

Cocking a brow at the out-of-the-blue question, he grabbed her elbow, and gently shuffled her away from the half dozen members of staff pretending not to eavesdrop on their conversation. "Because I wanted to be alone."

She shook her head decisively. "The last thing you need is to be alone. You don't do well alone. Edward doesn't either." She pursed her lips, a pensive expression crossing her features. "Xavier likes his own company. We're alike in that."

He scowled at her. "I do do well alone."

"Oh, you do do, do you?" She let out a giggle. "British English makes no sense sometimes."

"Well, I'll have you know it's American English that's crazy."

She leapt back, jumped into a boxer's shuffle, put her fists up in a fighting stance, and grumbled, "That's fighting talk."

He grinned at her antics. "You know you look crazy in front of the staff?"

"They had to learn at some point," she said dismissively, and carried on bouncing. "Come on, defend your language."

"Is this a duel?" He folded his arms across his chest and cocked a brow at her. "Pistols at dawn?"

Her mobile lips curved into a brash smile. "Screw the pistols."

"Said no American ever," he quipped.

She narrowed her eyes. "I'm deadly with my fists."

"Since when?" He scoffed at the very idea.

"Since now," she jibed, letting loose with one of her fists and jabbing him in the shoulder.

He rolled his eyes. "Remind me to get Drake to hook you up with some classes."

She huffed, stopped bobbing from foot to foot. "Well, that's just mean."

"No, the lack of force behind your punch is what's really mean. I told you back in Boston to sign up for some self-defense classes."

"You mean to tell me that with all these guards, I need to worry about self-defense?" There was a knowledge in her eyes that disturbed him. And though men were from Mars, and women were most definitely from anywhere else but there, at that moment, their minds were as one.

Self-defense lessons hadn't saved Marianne.

Nothing, no class, no martial art expertise, could save somebody from a sniper's bullet.

The thought dampened any amusement he might've found in the situation, and plunged him into the dark pit he'd been struggling to free himself from since his mother's murder.

He took a step back, ignored the hand she held out to keep the connection with him. He shook his head. Though he appreciated her for trying, he just needed to be alone.

"I'll see you later, Perry. At dinner."

Remorse crossed her features, but she nodded. Her eyes took on a wistfulness that hurt him.

He knew she thought he was pulling away. But he wasn't, not really. Coming to terms with everything that happened, the way their lives had changed, was more than he was capable of at that moment.

Not only was he dealing with the death of a beloved parent, he was dealing with a change in status.

When the average person lost somebody close to them, somebody they loved, if they fell into depression, that was okay. Well, not *okay*. But permitted.

People were allowed to crash and burn as they explored their grief.

Were allowed to sink to rock bottom as they processed a world without the person they loved in it.

George, Xavier, and Edward weren't allowed that.

It wasn't just the Brits who were renowned for their stiff upper lip. Most royal families, by necessity, had to be this way. But that they constantly had to be perfect was more than just tiring. In fact, exhausting wasn't even the word.

He strode from the small garden where Perry was declaring war on the old, *and* wasteful, way of life at Masonbrook. Taking one small step away from the past and leading them into the future, he headed for the castle proper. At the moment, he was in neither, and even the present wasn't as solid as he'd have liked.

PERRY WATCHED George trudge away from her, feeling as she had done of late—on shaky ground.

The irony was, of course, that she'd never been more secure. She was married, with two lovers. All three men had made vows to her, even if Edward's were the only official ones. Her taking the next step in becoming Edward's wife had also been a promise for more. So much more than most could begin to understand.

So, security wasn't an issue. Well, not the emotional kind.

It was the physical variety that was the problem.

Marianne was dead, Philippe was still in a coma. The entire world might not have been up in the air, but hers was. As was that of the men she loved.

She'd been in an earthquake before, but not even that compared to just how precarious their situation was.

She'd forced herself out of bed this morning, determined to do some good with her day. She had a to-do list that ran into the hundreds, one that had been compiled by her new social secretary. Because yes, Perry DeSauvier, née Taylor, had a goddamn social secretary.

She sometimes wondered if she'd entered a parallel universe. But Perry wasn't sure what kind of parallel universe would make sense of her rocketing into this position.

Staring around the courtyard, she felt disheartened. Seeing George had added a gloom to her morning—and that made her feel guilty. He was grieving his mother's passing, and she longed to help him. To be there for him. Only he wasn't allowing her to do that.

Her men were being pulled in so many ways, she feared for them. Wished wholeheartedly that she could do something to improve their lot.

But she wasn't Valium. She couldn't magic up a cure-all that would bring Marianne back to life, restore Philippe's health, all while taking away the constant threat of danger they were having to live with.

Blowing out a shaky breath, she turned to her new assistant, Rose, and murmured, "Do you have enough information from me to get this project underway?"

Rose was Perry's age, but there was a sharp gleam in her eyes that made her seem older. Edward had hired Rose without consulting Perry, but she didn't take offense at that. She knew if the task had been left to her, she'd never have hired anyone. Being served by servants was one thing, and it was one thing she found particularly difficult to come to terms with. Having an assistant? A social secretary? As well as the myriad of retainers that were suddenly following her around?

No. It was far too much.

And it wasn't even the beginning.

She still had four Guardians of the Keys to select. Speaking of which…

"Yes," Rose stated, interrupting Perry's train of thought. "The gardeners know which herbs you want planting. As you're not bothered about the design, we can leave it in their hands, can't we?"

Perry nodded. "I don't care where anything goes, but I want the herbs to take." In her mind's eye, she saw the list of produce the kitchens required. "Have them confer with the kitchens over the specifics. In two years' time, I want to eradicate the need for outside grocers."

Rose pulled a face. "That will anger a lot of people, Your Majesty."

"Like who?" Perry scowled at the thought. "Using the gardens as they were intended will reduce our expenses exponentially. As well as being more ecologically friendly. Who could that *anger*?"

"The people who provide our produce." She shrugged, and the move jostled her phone against the notepad she had in her arms. "People spend a fortune trying to attain the royal stamps, and once they get them, they don't like losing them. It's good for business. If the royals use it, then they can advertise it as such. It brings in customers."

Perry contemplated that a second, weighed it up against her wishes, and decided that capitalism could go fuck itself.

"At this moment in time, Rose, the gardens are a drain. Not only am I concerned about the water—which is still a precious commodity, but they're an unnecessary expense." The list of gardeners they had, specialists to boot, bordered on the ridiculous. "I understand we have an image to maintain. That's why I agreed not to touch the front gardens of the palace. But the back?" She shook her head. "No way. They're mine."

"I understand, Your Majesty, but I wouldn't be doing my duty if I didn't keep you informed of all sides of our position."

"Don't mistake me, Rose. I'm not mad at you. I'm grateful. But things are going to change, and if Veronia doesn't like it, then, well, tough luck." When Rose winced, Perry huffed. "That might sound really arrogant, but it's how I have to be if I'm going to force the household to take its carbon footprint seriously. Somebody has to think of the Earth and the environment. Why not the queen? It's not like I'm changing all that much," she reasoned when Rose still didn't appear convinced. "I'm just implementing things that are vital for the economy and for our environment."

Though she looked doubtful, Rose asked, "So, we're starting with this space for the herbs, and the east courtyard for the vegetable garden. That's right, isn't it, Your Majesty?"

Though she nodded, Perry grumbled, "Rose, do you have to keep calling me 'Your Majesty'? I think I prefer ma'am, and I never imagined I'd say that."

"It *is* protocol, Your Majesty."

"Screw protocol. If you haven't already gathered that I don't give a damn about crap like that, Rose, there's no hope for you."

Though the other woman's lips twitched, Perry was left with the feeling that Rose's uncertainty around her would carry on until they'd been working together for a long time.

Though that was hardly out of the ordinary, Perry wished she could fast-forward a few months so that they'd have that ease of people who were used to working together. It would make things so much more comfortable.

Still, if wishes were horses, beggars would ride. Sucking it up, she murmured, "What time is Cassie Whitings due?"

Rose checked her watch. It was proof alone that being the PA to the queen paid well — she wore a brand-new Rolex. After working at the palace for like five seconds. Either that or she had rich parents, and undoubtedly, that was why Rose was her new assistant. Edward had probably known her since they were children or something. "Twenty minutes, Your Majesty."

Nodding, Perry stacked her hands on her hips and peered around the yard. She did like roses—it wasn't as though they were her enemies or anything. They were a drain, however, and that was something she couldn't abide.

She envisaged a lot for this space. Intended on tilling the entire backyard, and making it work *for* them. The food bills at Masonbrook were astronomical. She didn't even want to think about how much waste they produced. But slowly and surely, she fully intended on implementing strict guidelines within the kitchens—where meals were prepared only with produce gathered from their own land. The money didn't matter—the DeSauviers had so much it was obscene. But Perry wanted them to have a conscience.

The situation with the water drought was, according to statistics she'd uncovered herself, man-made. But it could so easily have been real. Cape Town was running out of water, why not this small nation?

If Veronia was going to change, was going to embrace a more environmentally aware *and* protective future, it had to start from the top. The people had to see and had to know that the king and queen lived that way, and so, they should care too.

It was a long-term endeavor. That she knew. But she didn't intend on going anywhere, so had decided that starting now was the best option.

Perhaps it would seem radical to some, but it was a way of making sure she didn't lose herself.

This was who Perry was.

With the fancy hair, the crazy new "job" title, and the three lovers, it would be easy to forget who she was, which was the last thing she wanted.

Nodding with satisfaction that phase one was underway, she turned and saw that the gardeners who had been gathered around her had dispersed to different parts of the yard. Though there was undoubtedly protocol to follow, rules which involved them all bowing and scraping and tugging their forelocks—well, not all the time, but enough to make her uncomfortable—she cut Rose a look and beckoned her with her pointer finger, intent on disappearing without them having to curtsey her off.

When her PA's mouth dropped open, and the other woman looked back at the workmen then doubtfully cast a glance back at her, Perry channeled Marianne. Trying to look her regal best when it was pure theater, Perry cocked a brow and used her fingers to once more beckon Rose to her.

Rose's disapproval of her behavior was quite evident, though Perry figured there had to be some advantages to being queen. One of them being that she could sneak off whenever the hell she wanted to.

Rose was silent on the short walk back to the palace, but Perry didn't mind. Especially if Rose wanted to chastise her for failing to follow protocol.

But protocol could be damned.

She was sick and goddamn tired of the word, didn't know if she could have it shoved down her throat for even one more day. And hell, that was with her being very new to being queen. She had to start making this work for her, or she'd go insane.

It was way too soon after Marianne's death to be making such large changes, but Perry knew Marianne's formality would be to her detriment—there was no way she would be able to follow in her mother-in-law's footsteps. No way, no how. She just wasn't like that. Wasn't wired that way.

It was, she thought, better to piss people off now and get them used to her way of doing things from the offset.

She entered Masonbrook via a set of French doors that led into one of the many salons she now had available to her. From a six-room apartment, to a six hundred room estate. Her life couldn't be more different if she tried.

This salon was more comfortable than most. Though they were many and varied, very few of them were actually comfortable. With winter coming, they were even less suitable for relaxation.

The high ceilings were pretty, especially with their antique ornate frescoes painted by masters of the time, but heat flooded out of the rooms like a river whose banks had burst. The fireplaces that serviced the rooms were small, too small for such grand staterooms.

She knew royals were renowned for being impractical, but there was being impractical and there was being stupid. As far as she'd been able to tell, Edward, George, and Xavier's relatives were more stupid than anything else.

Still, it wasn't her place to judge, but to rectify the mistakes of her husband's ancestors.

As a result, she now used only the smallest of the public salons and reception rooms, as those would waste the least amount of heat.

This particular salon, she'd learned recently, had been popular with Xavier's mother, Lisetta. The woman had good taste in rooms, if not in furniture. Although, Perry surmised the other woman had been as limited with interior design as she herself was.

If it didn't have gold decorating at least some part of the piece of furniture, the DeSauviers apparently hadn't commissioned it.

No wonder the world was running out of gold. It was all in this palace.

Here, parquet floors were arranged like a chessboard, and atop the gleaming antique surfaces were equally ancient items of furniture.

Four wide, gilt armchairs sat around a low coffee table. But this wasn't a coffee-table worthy of IKEA—there were more curlicues, moldings, and detailing on this single piece than in the whole Swedish store.

Topped with gray marble, there was a tea tray sitting upon it. The tea beckoned, as did one of the armchairs. Padded with red velvet with voluptuous palm tree markings, she took a seat, and decided to be rude and not to wait for Cassie before serving herself.

At her side was a twelve-foot-long mirror. It was one of the panels in a fifteen-foot wall. On either side of the mirror were two loaded down, half chandeliers that were attached to the wall. The mirror itself reflected a dangling chandelier on the ceiling.

What had to be hundreds of lights sparkled and glistened, thanks to the pendulous crystals bobbing merrily overhead.

There was also a large armoire. Chinese, Perry thought, in design. But she'd never been interested in antiques, and figured that would make anybody who did, envy her position terribly.

Though the armchairs weren't to her taste, they were actually quite comfortable. She sat back with her teacup in hand and took a deep sip.

Like every American, she was a coffee lover, but living here had given her a whole new appreciation of tea. Especially this loose-leaf stuff the castle's kitchens served.

Glad that Rose had disappeared without being asked to, Perry enjoyed the peace of the moment.

A luxury she'd never appreciated before now.

Being alone was a precious commodity, she was coming to learn, and knew that of the many aspects of her new life, acclimating to this change of pace would be the hardest.

She was a scientist, after all. Accustomed to working by herself on her projects.

Yet another facet of life she was going to have to adapt to, she realized. Wistfully, she thought back to days that had been her own, to worries that had revolved around her poor organizational skills when it came to her apartment.

She no longer had to worry if she left the iron on. She had a whole laundry staff to see to that chore for her.

Okay, so *some* things *were* cool.

A knock sounded at the door, jerking her from her thoughts.

George really had soured her mood, she thought on a sigh, making her wish she could ease his pain, do something to stop him from brooding.

"Come in," she called out. Looking up from her teacup, she was pleased but not surprised to see Cassie standing in the doorway.

Smiling, she waved a hand, beckoning the other woman in. She was coming to know Cassie well—maybe not as well as she'd have appreciated back home, but what she did know of her, she liked.

That Cassie had been friends with Xavier, George, and Edward since childhood, as well as the fact she was married to one of their close friends, helped Perry feel more at ease around her.

Of course, she'd never be able to reveal the full truth about their unusual situation, but she could relax; very little surprised Cassie where Perry's men were concerned. Cassie and Marcus, her husband, were part of the family.

"You want some tea, Cassie? If you don't, I can order coffee."

Cassie wafted in in a cloud of Chanel No. 5. She was the only one who treated Perry as though nothing had happened, as though her status hadn't changed, as if she wasn't now the freaking queen of a whole country or something like that... All the more reason to like the older woman.

She bustled over and dipped down to buss Perry on the cheek before floating over to the other armchair and settling down.

"Tea's perfect," Cassie said. She peered at her while Perry poured the tea. "How are things?"

Perry shrugged. "Exactly how you'd expect, I suppose." She passed over the cup, its delicate china almost singing as it exchanged owners. "George and Edward are reticent, Xavier has buried himself in his lab." She pursed her lips. "The whole place is somber. It's not like it's not understandable. I just... I'm at a loss. I can't make this better for anyone."

Cassie winced. "Marianne and I didn't see eye-to-eye often, Perry. Too different. I didn't particularly like her." She quirked a brow. "I'm sure you noticed that sometimes."

Perry's lips twitched. "Neither of you kept it a secret, did you?"

"No, but, even so. I thought the old witch made an ice hotel look warm and cozy, but she didn't deserve *that*."

Blowing out a breath that disturbed the amber brew in her hands, Perry murmured, "She certainly didn't."

This wasn't the first time Cassie had visited the palace since Perry's coronation, but the conversation always began the same way. She pulled a face, because she knew she had to be a horrible person, but talking about Marianne all the time just made her depressed.

As well as fearful.

For herself, and for her lovers.

Even then, it was more for them than for herself. They spent more time out of the castle than she did. For the moment, at any rate.

"Anyway, let's change the subject. How are things going with Marcus? Have you managed to convince him to quit yet?" Marcus's job on the Stock Exchange in New York was high pressured. It had triggered a heart attack. When he'd refused to slow down, hadn't quit his job for the sake of his own health, Cassie had returned to Veronia with their children in the hopes he'd come around.

He hadn't.

He was stubbornly clinging to his job, and was making vague promises to return home once the deal he was working on was done.

Cassie shot her a considering look, one that analyzed more than Perry's words, but she did as requested—changed the subject. "I'm not sure why I'm shocked, but he's been ridiculously stubborn about all this. When I brought the children over, I just thought he'd follow." She grimaced. "Trouble is, Perry, I'm starting to like the fact he isn't home."

Eyes widening in surprise, Perry murmured, "It's a novelty. Not having to answer to anyone but yourself." She knew Cassie and Marcus had been married a damn long time. "But a change is as good as a rest. It will do you good to be apart, and make you more appreciative when you're together again." The recipient of a doubtful look, Perry had to stop herself from laughing. She lifted a hand and covered her mouth.

"It isn't funny, Perry," Cassie chided, but half-choked on the words.

Perry glanced at her, and the two immediately cascaded into giggles when their eyes caught and held. As they snickered and chuckled, they fed each other's amusement by casting surreptitious looks at one another, chortling away for only God knew how long...but the break in tension was welcome.

Cassie gasped. "God, I needed that. Everyone is so bloody serious at the moment. It's driving me crazy."

It wasn't like Perry could argue, though she felt guilty for understanding and empathizing with Cassie. "It's hard. We feel for George, Edward, and Xavier. And Philippe, of course...plus we're dealing with the aftermath and how it affects us all."

"Tell me about it," she grumbled. "Did you know Marcus is eighth in line to the throne now?" She rolled her eyes. "Can you imagine? The man can't organize his own life, never mind the country. Please, Perry, get pregnant quickly. I can't stand the extra guards."

She winced. "How do you think I feel? It's a goddamn nightmare. I can barely use the bathroom without having a guard check the bowl for somebody hiding out there."

Cassie gagged. "Gross."

Chuckling, Perry jerked a shoulder. "Gross, but true. Unfortunately. Anyway, I thought you were going to threaten Marcus with divorce if he didn't immediately move over here? It was a good sign that he came to the coronation, no?"

"His mother would have killed him if he hadn't shown his face at the coronation," came the bitter retort. "I should probably get that old witch to tell Marcus to move over here. He'd probably do as he was told. He such a mama's boy."

"Are you really happy without him?"

Cassie shrugged. "For the most part, sadly. It's just a lot easier, you know? I didn't realize, not until...

"My time is my own, Perry, once the children go to bed. I don't have to attend boring parties for his work, nor do I have to deal with him grumbling like an old man. If I want to work for a charity foundation, he can't gripe over the one I pick, because he's not here."

"I suppose I'm just realizing what a pain in the ass he is."

Perry winced. "Aren't all men? We love them anyway." She studied Cassie, trying to ascertain if her friend *did* love her husband.

Apparently, Cassie grasped her point, because she pouted. "I suppose it's lucky for him that I do."

"I guess the last thing you guys need is added pressure, Cassie." She heaved out a breath, hating that she was about to dump something else on Cassie's shoulders. But Perry's need for ladies maids she trusted was becoming vital. "I mean, I was going to ask you to be my head Guardian of the Keys, but I totally understand if it's just too much for you right now. What with the kids and everything..." Perry trailed off. Then, when her friend just stared at her, she continued, "I've been putting off asking you for ages now. But Edward hired this dragon for a PA, and Rose has been harping on at me about getting a team together."

Cassie's children were acclimating to a new nanny, and things weren't going very well. When she said that she'd understand if it was too much for Cassie right now, she'd meant it. Though meaning it and hoping to God that wasn't the case were two different things entirely.

Just when Perry had started to freak out that she'd totally messed things up, Cassie whispered, "Oh, Perry, I'm honored that you've asked me."

Blinking, not having expected that particular answer and stunned to see the tears in the other woman's eyes, she questioned uncertainly, "Is that a yes or no?"

"It's a yes, of course!" Cassie jumped to her feet, strode over to Perry, bowed down in a curtsey that had Perry freezing in her armchair. "Your Majesty, you honor me with your request."

Her friend's formality, after always having been so informal with her, didn't help defrost Perry's sudden attack of nerves.

God, there was so much for her still to learn. So much Marianne hadn't managed to pass on.

Perry should have had years, a decade, *minimum*, to prepare for this role. Instead, she was having to learn as she went, and while that wasn't a problem when it came to anything science-based...royal-based?

That was a whole other ball of wax.

Uncaring that she probably sounded like she had a frog in her throat, Perry whispered, "Please, Cassie, get up. Come on, you're making me blush here." When Cassie snorted out a laugh, Perry could finally take a deep breath. Relief filtered through her. "Seriously, don't do that to me. You know I don't like it when things are all formal."

Another snort. "You're the queen now, Perry. You're going to have to get used to it at some point."

Feeling mulish, Perry jerked her chin in the air. "If I'm queen, surely I can do whatever the hell I want."

Cassie laughed. "Well, that's certainly one way to look at it."

"One way to look at what?" The question came from the doorway, and

Perry's heart leaped at the sight of Xavier standing there like her knight in shining armor. Maybe he could help Cassie understand?

Though she longed to stand, to fling herself into his arms, she remained where she was. Cassie might have thought it was rude, but Perry didn't care. If she moved, she was falling into Xavier's embrace, and not moving an inch for a year. *Minimum.*

Cassie's laughter trickled from her, and she tilted her head to the side so Xavier could kiss it—he swooped down to do just that. "Perry has just asked me to be her Guardian of the Keys. When I curtsied, she looked like I'd electrocuted her."

Xavier shot Perry a look. "She does look rather shell-shocked, doesn't she?" When Cassie giggled, Xavier grinned. His smile widened when Perry rolled her eyes at him. "Anyway, it's about damn time you asked her. You've been procrastinating over this for ages."

Cassie pouted. "Why?"

Grimacing at having been placed in the spotlight again, Perry mumbled, "I wasn't sure if you'd say yes."

The older woman's mouth fell open. Then, she cast a look at Xavier who simply shrugged. "Perry doesn't get how big a deal it is," he said. "How large a compliment... She sees it more as a nuisance."

Flushing, because he wasn't wrong, Perry wriggled her shoulders. "I just know how busy you are, Cassie. And considering I now know what the Guardians of the Keys *do*, why anybody would want to do it is beyond me."

When Xavier and Cassie burst out laughing, Perry huffed. Cassie tried to hide her smile, but it was very evident as she murmured, "It's a paid position, you do know that?"

"For the amount of crap you have to do? It had *better* be paid. Otherwise it would be slave labor."

"It also brings with it a kind of prestige that's considered priceless," Xavier said smoothly.

"Like what?" Perry demanded, failing to see why being a glorified housekeeper and royal gofer was such a great thing.

"Things like memberships to clubs. Cassie and her family will have doors opened to them that were closed before. They'll be treated like royals. That's a big deal in Veronia," he said wryly.

She scowled. "I'm not putting her in danger, am I?"

Perry blew out a relieved breath when they shook their heads.

Cassie answered, "No, not at all. But Xavier's right.

"We're nobles, so privilege being what it is, mostly unfair, we already have the advantage over a commoner, but if Marcus comes back, for example, and joins his old club, he wouldn't have to pay a membership fee.

"Or, if there was a club he wanted to join, where he'd been blackballed in the past, then my being Guardian of the Keys will change that straightaway. It's perks like that."

"That's it? That sucks."

A laugh escaped Cassie. "There's more to it. Let's say I want my hair cutting one day. I call for an appointment and there's a three-week waiting list, then I tell them my name, and like magic, something will immediately open up for me.

"The kids—the waiting list was ridiculously long for their prep school—but now that waiting list will disappear."

Perry sniffed. "Sounds damn elitist to me."

Xavier chuckled. "The joys of a royalist nation."

Perry pondered that and fell quiet, letting Cassie and Xavier chat and catch up while she zoned out a little.

Sometimes processing the way of life here was more than she could stand.

Still it wasn't like the States were perfect. It was elitist as all hell over there. And where in the world didn't, "it's not what you know, but who," reign supreme?

As people who had known each other a long time were wont to do, Cassie and Xavier fell into conversations about times past, friends and acquaintances old and new, and things that generally excluded Perry from the chatter.

She didn't mind, knew it was unintentional. If anything, she appreciated seeing Xavier with one of his friends.

It hadn't escaped her attention that her men had very few people they considered to be that. It wasn't like she could judge, though. She'd always been a loner, and when she met George, he'd become the pal she hung around with almost all the time.

George had work colleagues that he'd socialized with, and she knew them because they'd usually gone out together. She hadn't particularly *liked* them though.

George was in venture capitalism. The rest of his circle from work were too, which meant they were all pricks.

Or, as George called them laughingly, wanker bankers.

The very British insult was too apt for her to giggle over. But he'd never seemed to have minded they were jerks. The lot of them.

After having been in Veronia for a time, she could see why. Those bankers, and the courtiers here, were of the same breed. They thought they were something special, because they'd been born with a silver spoon in their mouths.

Her lips pursed with disapproval at the thought. If, in her time of being queen, she could change that, she would.

And, though the notion petrified her, if she did get pregnant, she certainly wouldn't raise her kids to be little nightmares. They'd be the darlings of the Crown, that was for certain, but they wouldn't be monsters.

"Well, I'll be off," Cassie murmured with a laugh, and her amusement dispelled Perry's musings.

"You will? You only just got here," Perry said, sitting up and feeling guilty at having spent most of Cassie's visit zoned out.

Cassie snorted. "I've been here an hour, Perry."

She had? *Oops*.

"When will you present yourself for duty?" Xavier asked, a touch formally, Perry thought.

Cassie's pretty doll face turned contemplative. She lifted a hand to her mouth and tapped her bottom lip. "I have a few appointments I need to settle over the next week. But if I start as Guardian of the Keys now, those appointments will take barely any time at all. They'll cede to my devious wishes immediately."

Xavier frowned. "Schools?"

Cassie nodded. "Yes. As I said, the waiting lists for our first choice prep school are long. I'm finding it hard getting the kids into a class halfway through this term.

"Henley College tried to tell me I should tutor them from home for a spell, until the new term begins." She sniffed her disdain for that suggestion, making Perry's lips twitch.

"Will being Guardian of the Keys really change things so much for you?"

Xavier murmured, "Of course. It might seem like a chore to you, Perry, but like we told you, it truly isn't."

Cassie laughed, and Perry had to smile. Neither were mad at her for failing to understand why the position she'd presented Cassie was anything other than a pain in the butt.

She offered her cheek to her friend and new 'Guardian'. Cassie promptly bussed it as Xavier got to his feet, hugged her when she stepped over to him, then left them in a cloud of overwhelming perfume.

When she was gone, Perry curled her finger at Xavier. He grinned, placed his hands on the armrest of her chair, then bent down to anoint her mouth with a kiss.

He started off slow, his lips merely pecking hers until he slanted his mouth and nipped at her bottom lip, tugging it down playfully, teasing her into responding.

She opened for him, letting him sweep inside her mouth, letting him claim her and make her his in that one small way.

This was how they should have greeted one another.

This was how they should always begin every day.

The thought sent longing shuddering through her, because she knew it wasn't to be.

"Can't you live at Masonbrook?" she whispered against his mouth, sitting straighter in her chair, eagerly seeking more from him, needing to get closer, to be in his arms.

He stilled. "You'd want me to?"

"I miss you," she confessed, sad that he'd stopped kissing her, but feeling flushed at the heat in his eyes as he looked at her.

"I see you every day."

He made the statement, but she could tell he wasn't peeved by the notion. Nor was he pleased. If anything, his tone was distinctly bland.

"Not enough. I want to kiss you in the morning. I want to..." She closed her eyes as she raised a hand to her mouth, sealing his kiss onto her lips. "I need you here."

He tilted his head to the side. "I have no logical reason for being here."

The sound of the doorknob turning caused her to stiffen in place, fear flushing through her at being caught in this compromising position, but Xavier didn't shift at all. When the door opened and George headed in, her mouth rounded in an O, and she demanded, "How did you know it wasn't someone important?"

George huffed. "I'll have you know I'm very important."

Xavier laughed. "Because nobody important would just open the door without knocking. Sweetheart, there's nobody more important in the land than you or Edward. Everyone else has to knock."

She blinked, taken aback at the idea. Then, she focused on George, who'd strode in, his feathers obviously ruffled—something that had nothing to do with her faux pas. Because hell, he was used to them by now.

"What's wrong?" she asked, frowning at him as he strode in front of her fireplace, pacing back and forth. "And why haven't you kissed me?"

George staggered a step, then blinked as he turned to her. "I forgot."

His simple retort had her eyes narrowing. "Un-forget."

As quickly as that, his glower turned into a cheeky grin as he swaggered over to her, all cocky and arrogant, elbowed Xavier out of the way, and kissed her promptly on the mouth.

She wriggled in her seat as, unlike Xavier, he bit down hard on her bottom lip. The move had her pussy, already molten hot from his cousin's attentions, stirring to life once more.

She clenched her thighs as he fluttered his tongue against hers, then moaned when he retreated.

"You two are no fun," she grumbled.

"We're plenty of fun," George immediately countered, returning to the fireplace where he began striding back and forth once more.

"Yeah, you're a barrel of laughs," she complained, fidgeting in place.

Xavier snorted. "Horny, love?"

She blew out a breath. "I *wasn't*. If anything, I was out of sorts." She ran a hand through her hair, trying to soothe her own ruffled feathers after the sweeping attentions of her men—who knew having three of them would make her greedier for them?

After time, she'd imagined it would get boring. That she'd grow weary of having to juggle not just one guy in her life, but three. As it stood, she'd yet to reach that point, and considering they were all so damn elusive, she was starting to think that she'd forever be in a state of wanting them.

Not that that was something to complain about.

Xavier cut her a look, razing her defenses to the ground with that one simple glance. "Fancy showing me your new bedroom?"

She bit her bottom lip, still sore from the teasing nips her lover had gifted her. "Yes?"

He laughed. "Not too certain about that answer?"

She smirked. "Well, Prince Charming over there is obviously in a snit."

George protested, "I'm not in a snit."

"You only pace when you're in a mood or angry," she instantly retorted. "You forget, I know you too well to fall for your bullshit."

"My ego is mortally wounded."

"Your ego is always mortally wounded in my presence," she said, her tone cheerful now because he was right. "That's my job, don't you know? To keep you down-to-earth and grounded. Otherwise, you'd be such a big-headed jerk, I couldn't stand to be in the same room as you."

George rolled his eyes as Xavier snickered. "That's your job, is it? Your official role?"

She grinned. "Yup. Screw all this 'queenie' nonsense."

George shook his head, but she could see in his deep brown eyes his own humor sparking to life.

"What's wrong, George?" Xavier asked patiently, but she could see as he settled back into his seat, he was dealing with his own arousal. He crossed his legs, resting his ankle atop his knee, and grimaced at the positioning.

Yum.

All hers.

"That isn't helping," he said absentmindedly, not looking at her, but talking to her nonetheless.

"I never claimed to be helpful. Just a grounding presence," was all she said.

He heaved out a laugh, then to George, mumbled, "Spit it out, man. Perry's calendar is clear for the next two hours. Do you know how rare that is?"

George's pacing came to a halt. "Two hours?"

Xavier nodded. "I checked with the Dragon."

The Dragon was Perry's nickname for Rose—she hadn't realized they were aware of it.

Perry folded her arms across her chest. "Why do I feel like I've just been micromanaged?"

"Because you have?" Xavier said. The grin he shot her way was wicked, his intent evident.

He'd come here with the purpose of seducing her.

Wicked, naughty, wonderful man.

She licked her lips again, then murmured, "Yes, George, get on with it already. The two of you could be doing something more pleasant with those mouths of yours than talking."

"She's a minx, isn't she?" George said on a growl, but he'd stopped pacing at last, and leaned back against the wall at the side of the fireplace.

The position was an odd choice. With his shoulders hunched as he pushed his hands into his pockets, he looked surprisingly vulnerable.

"Come on, darling. Something's obviously on your mind." She knew that—he'd gone on a ride. Edward was the horseman. Not George.

"I don't want to talk about it."

"Sure, you don't," she teased gently. "That's why you barged your way in here. Because you don't want to talk about it."

He pulled a face. "I'm torn."

His wistful tone had her cocking a brow at him. "About what?"

"You still trying to decide where you should work?" Xavier asked gently, surprising her with his insight.

She tensed, displeased by the idea George was struggling with something she wasn't aware of.

Now that she thought about it, when was the last time she and George —her best friend, as well as her lover—had sat down together and had a really good chat?

She blinked because she couldn't remember when.

Outrage flushed through her at the thought, and it was aimed wholly at herself.

She'd been so focused on the nuttiness that was her new role as queen, that she hadn't sat down with any of her men and really talked about what was going on with *any* of them.

Perry didn't hate herself too badly, because they were still reacting to recent events. Reacting didn't give a person much time to deal with and process the things that mattered.

But still, now that she was aware of the lack in her relationship with all of them, she'd make damn sure to rectify that.

In fact, she'd pin Rose down and start shuffling things in her schedule.

There were a million and one things Perry had to do in a day now, but not a single one of them was more important than her men's wellbeing.

"What's going on?" she asked, frowning but otherwise not showing her displeasure at being kept in the dark.

It wasn't George's fault she hadn't been paying attention.

"George wants to work in the private sector, but feels like he should be directly involved with the Ministry of Finance."

Xavier's succinct summary surprised her. "You hate politics."

George winced at her blunt retort. "I know."

"Well, why the quandary then?"

"Because it's what I should do."

She blinked. "Why should that bother you?"

He sighed. "Duty, Perry. It comes to us all in the end."

"Not in this instance it doesn't have to," she argued. "I mean, I know Edward's pushed some responsibilities onto you…"

George immediately shook his head. "Not enough. Not as much as he should."

His self-deprecatory wince had her tilting her head to the side. "Then, if you know you're not being fair to him, why are you letting him get away with it?"

Xavier snorted. "Why change the habit of a lifetime?"

George's shoulders stiffened, but just as his mouth opened to blast Xavier, the wind dropped from his sails. He sighed. "You're right."

"I know I am," Xavier said smoothly, cutting her a look. He flared his eyes once, and she knew he was telling her to shut up.

She huffed, a little aggravated at being verbally leashed, but sank back into the armchair and let Xavier take this where he wanted to.

George, totally missing this byplay, murmured, "My working in the Finance Ministry wouldn't ease Edward's load, would it?"

"No, but it would help him to have eyes in there. It seems the likeliest place to put you, considering your expertise," Xavier reasoned. "But you know full well you can have your pick of the ministries. The government views it as us having pet projects, you know that as much as I do."

It was Perry's turn to wince.

What a patronizing way of seeing things.

As far as she'd learned, being a royal was actually one of the hardest freakin' jobs out there.

She knew other countries might only have had token royals nowadays. Where they did more waving and spending than anything else.

But here?

No way.

It was more than a full-time job. It was like a divorce lawyer in Manhattan and a cardiologist had combined to create a power-job, where there was little sleep, more work than either job could handle, and a hell of a lot of luxury.

George blew out a breath. "I'd be put to better use taking some of the tasks off Edward's shoulders. That way he can at least spend time with us."

"He will eventually. He's just finding his place. Don't forget, there's a lot of internal power plays to manage at the moment. He's finding his feet in Uncle Philippe's world. Things will settle down shortly."

Perry perked up at that. She'd barely seen her husband since they'd been crowned.

At some time during the night, he'd wake her climbing into bed, and when she awoke the next morning, he'd already be up and about.

Being king played havoc with his queen's sex life, that was for damned certain.

Xavier grimaced. "Anyway, that's why I'm going to throw my lot in, too."

George scowled. "What do you mean?"

"I finally put finishing touches on that fertilizer I was developing..."

Perry's eyes widened, and she scrambled out of her seat and plunked herself on his lap before he had the chance to do anything other than take in a breath. "Oh my God! You did it?"

He grinned as she slipped her arms around his neck and tugged him into a tight hug.

"Feels like it. It's onto larger-scale trials now. I'm working with one of our agricultural research labs over in Helstern to further develop the product, but it needs to be tested on grander scales than I can manage with my acreage." He shrugged. "That cuts down my research exponentially, and rather than looking for something else, I'm going to stick with my current projects and help Edward out."

She worried her bottom lip. "You're doing that for me, aren't you?"

He tugged at said bottom lip. "I know he's not spending hardly any time with you, and that worries me. Because he needs you just as much as we do.

"But I'm also just doing it because I'm as guilty as George of taking advantage of Edward. He puts his everything into doing something he doesn't like, and he does so because it's his duty. It's time George and I started pulling our weight too."

Perry reached up to kiss his cheek. "Thank you."

"It's for all of us," he said dismissively.

"Maybe, but still...thank you." She turned to George, who'd folded his arms across his chest as he stared at them. "What put you in that mood before you came here?"

He frowned. "Blevins James..."

"The bank you contacted about work?"

"Also the biggest hedge fund this side of London," Xavier inserted wryly.

"They've offered me a job," George said wistfully. "I want to take it... but I know I can't."

"Hence the pacing and the ride," Perry murmured, sadness welling in her. "I'm sorry, sweetheart."

He pursed his lips. "You don't have to be sorry. It's not like it's your fault." He moved away from the wall, his jeans and shirt rustling as they pulled against the silk wallpaper, then slouched his way over to her.

Turning around, he crouched down on the floor, then leaned against Xavier's legs. It meant she couldn't see his expression, but she figured that was why he'd maneuvered himself into that position anyway.

She slipped her hands through his silky hair, unable to help herself. Her nails scraped against his scalp, and he leaned back into her tender touch.

"What will you do?" Xavier asked quietly.

"If I can keep an eye on the chancellor, then it will help Ed, won't it? He needs all the eyes, ears, and hands he can get to monitor this current farce of a government," George replied, his tone stilted. "I can't help him out if I'm in a hedge fund in the center of Madela."

Duty...

It was a four-letter word, and one she hadn't shirked from in her life. As a child, there'd always been something to do on the farm, and when she'd left the farm for Boston, her sense of duty hadn't disappeared with it—her higher calling had been to protect the Earth. To keep it safe for future generations as she tried to combat the many ways humans, corporations, and governments were destroying it, little by little.

She knew what duty was. But until she'd seen how it had torn up the DeSauvier family, she hadn't truly known it on a personal level.

Blood had been spilled to preserve the Crown for Veronia. Her men sacrificed their own ways, their own needs, to rule a country where people lived who had murdered their family members.

She wasn't sure if, just then, she wanted to weep because she was proud of George for stepping up to the plate, or because she was so dreadfully sorry for both of her men. They were stepping away from their callings to fall into line for the Crown...

It was a thankless job they were about to leap into. A world of responsibilities and cynicism and unpleasantness.

And for all that, at that moment, she was just glad she was there.

There had to be some sugar in everyone's life—otherwise the lack would drive anyone mad. She could be that sweetness to soften the bitterness, and she'd take on the role willingly to give her men some semblance of peace as they maneuvered a world they'd been born into, but didn't particularly want.

George's shoulders bowed. "I'll inform Edward in the morning."

Xavier sighed. "It comes to us all, George."

Duty, Perry knew he was saying.

"I know," he said grimly. He got to his feet again, his restlessness surprising her. Then, with his back turned away from them, he carried on, "I'm going to tell him now. Get it over with. Otherwise I'll procrastinate… and he needs me."

Before Perry could open her mouth, he strode off, his pace swift. She stiffened on Xavier's lap, made to scramble off and head for George, but he tugged her firmly into his hold.

Only after the door had closed did he murmur, "No, Perry. Let him go. He needs to do this. For Edward's sake. He'll kill himself to make us happy. To let us do what we want to do while he buries himself in work." Xavier's tone was grim enough to make Perry bite her lip. "George had to reach the decision himself."

She turned wide eyes up at him. "Being king really sucks, doesn't it?"

He snorted out a laugh. "Pretty much."

———

"YOU KNOW when you know someone's gorgeous? But you don't actually realize it?"

The words came from the doorway, and George frowned at his wife's voice. Turning away from the mirror where he'd been checking his form as he did bicep curls, preferring real eye contact over a reflection, he asked, kind of dumbly, "Huh?"

She snorted, folding her arms across her belly in a way that plumped up her breasts. His mouth watered, and his dick began to harden. It was inappropriate, considering the thoughts that had been going through his head just seconds before, but then, Perry had a habit of making him hard in even the most difficult of circumstances.

"I know you're handsome."

Okay. He blinked, unsure where she was going with this. "What have I done wrong now?"

Her chuckle made him uneasy. "Nothing, Dumbo. Why would you think you'd done something wrong?"

He'd stormed off earlier, leaving her and Xavier like they meant nothing to him, but the need to think, to clear his thoughts in the mindlessness that came when he worked out had been a siren's call he'd been unable to avoid. Only when his blood was pumping, his pulse throbbing in his ears, did he seem to find any clarity.

It was one of the reasons why he'd been camped out in the gym since they'd made it back home, had endured his mother's funeral, as well as his brother and wife's coronation.

He stacked the dead weights down on the ground, carefully placing them as he bent over in a deep squat to protect his back from the strain. As he straightened up, he saw that she'd taken three steps into the gym, but more importantly, had closed the door.

His lips curved. Perry usually left doors open. It was a weird habit of hers he'd noticed when she'd camped out in his apartment back in Boston. He, accustomed to life at Masonbrook, always closed them, knowing if they were open, he wouldn't get any privacy at all.

Perry, on the other hand, who'd had a normal life, just left them open without a care in the world.

He cocked a brow as he jerked his chin, motioning to the door. "You just cut off the air flow in here."

"I did?" She tapped her chin. "My bad. Want me to open it?"

"Depends."

"On what?"

"What you do to make it worth my while?"

Her eyes brightened at his teasing, and a wicked smile gleamed his way. "Oh," she drawled. "I have to make it worth your while, do I?"

He nodded. "Without a doubt." It was his turn to fold his arms across his chest, but unlike her, he took a seat on the bench beside him. It was flecked with sweat from his workout, but he didn't mind—it still needed clearing down with antibacterial spray before he left here, and he'd only been halfway through his intended session. As he moved position, he also moved his arms, stacking his elbows on his knees as he watched her continue approaching him.

The way she moved had his cock hardening further. That sinuous sway of her hips was mesmerizing. Hell, it practically had his gaze gluing to those round, ripe swells that were made for carrying babies and for his hands to grab a tight hold of.

A growl rumbled in his chest at both thoughts. God, the day she discovered she was carrying their child was a day he was going to fuck her raw until they were both sweating and had to collapse in a pile of sweaty bones.

Fuck, the things she made him think drove him insane.

And, the wonderful thing was, with her in pricktease mode, just like with the workout, his mind was otherwise engaged.

He clung to that with both hands, grabbing the lifesaver eagerly until he could grab a tight hold of her instead.

She finally moved nearer to him, her legs coming to a halt between his spread knees. She smelled clean and sweet, a bright floral perfume that added to her musky scent. She'd changed clothes from earlier; wore a cream sweater now, thin and silky with a boat neckline that exposed her throat and collarbones, and a pair of jeans that made him want to bend her over and slap her ass for daring to give anyone, save for him, Xavier, and Edward such a sight.

They clung to her like a second skin, and he knew she'd lost weight from that alone, because the Perry he'd grown to love in Boston would never have dared to wear such an outfit. She'd been too rounded, too plump in her eyes. Definitely not his. He missed her generous curves and thought that with time, she'd grow more comfortable, more at ease with her position, and as a result, her appetite would return.

He really hoped so, because he'd had so many wet dreams over the Perry of before, and he needed to reenact them. Badly.

His hands came up to cup her hips as he'd been wanting to do since her first words had shaken him from his mindlessness. He blew out a breath as he stroked down the sides of her pants. "These are nice," he murmured.

"Only nice?" She slapped her hand on his damp shoulder. "I picked them for you specially. When Cassie and I went shopping together before the wedding. I thought you'd love them."

George grinned. "You went shopping for me?"

"Yeah." She scrunched her nose, then a thought came to her, and she licked her lips. "You're all sweaty," she whispered.

"I am." He caught her gaze, saw the heat in hers, and had to hold back a smile. "Now, what the hell were you talking about? Knowing someone's sexy but not realizing it?"

His wife blinked. "Well, yeah."

"That doesn't explain anything, Perry." He laughed.

"I just mean, I knew you were handsome and gorgeously scrumptious before, but now?" She whistled. "And all sweaty? Your muscles are bigger too." Her glance turned concerned. "How much time are you even spending down here?" She peered around at the state-of-the-art gym that was nestled in one of the subterranean floors beneath Masonbrook. "I didn't even know we had a gym until Xavier told me this was where you'd probably be hiding."

"I'm not hiding," George grumbled.

Her lips twitched. "No. Of course not."

Knowing he was being placated, he heaved an aggrieved breath, then he shook off those thoughts by slipping his hands around to cup her ass. "I want inside you," he said on a low breath. "I want to forget, Perry." His eyes caught hers. "Help me forget?"

The amusement on her face softened as she lifted a hand and cupped his sweaty jaw. "Anytime," she breathed, and he knew she meant it. The word was a vow. As much of an oath as the one she'd made before God and country to Edward on her wedding day.

Before he could whisper another word, she'd grabbed the hem of her sweater and was tugging it overhead.

"The door...?" She'd closed it, but that didn't mean somebody might not walk in. Even though he'd noticed that the gym, with hot-shit equipment the best money could buy so that the Royal Guard could train and keep fit here, had been surprisingly empty of late. Drake, their head of security, must have told them to work out elsewhere while George was using it.

Totally unnecessary, but the Royal Guard had a habit of staying separate from the family they protected. His friendship with Francesco was unusual. Although, Edward was friendly with a few of his too, a guy called Jamieson, if memory served.

"I locked it." Her words were garbled as her mouth was covered with the sweater. Then, she tossed it overhead and immediately went to work on the buttons of her fly.

His mouth watered at the sight of her ripe tits, which, surprisingly, were bare. Perry was definitely top heavy, and the large nipples were just cherries on the top of a delicious cake as far as he was concerned.

"You came to seduce me, didn't you?" he joked as she pushed the tight denim over her thighs and down to the ground, but though he was teasing, knew it to be the truth. She'd definitely come here with a purpose in mind.

Perry paused, lifted a hand to cup his jaw again, then said, "I wanted to make you happy."

"You don't need to do this to make me happy." His words were choked, because they were definitely self-sacrificing. But still, she had to know she was more than just a fuck doll to him. Jesus, was that what she thou—

Her snort intruded and she lifted her hands to cup her tits. "These make you happy," she said matter-of-factly, her eyes glinting in the harsh overhead lights of the gym. Then, she stunned the shit out of him by pushing forward, not stopping until she was straddling his hips, her panty-covered pussy and his gym shorts the only thing separating their bodies.

She writhed against him a second, her pelvis digging down to rub her core against his cock.

"I know *this* makes you happy," she whispered, a light moan escaping her lips as her movements worked on her too.

His tongue felt like it was cleaved to the roof of his mouth.

Was this Perry?

His Perry?

Seducing *him*? In the nasty white lights where all her flaws, and his, could be seen? His shy little lover who still covered her belly with pillows after they fucked, and wrapped herself in the sheets like a mummy to hide herself from them as she slept?

Who was this brave, braw lass who'd come to rock his fucking world?

He blinked.

Why the fuck was he wasting time asking questions?

He lunged at her. Well, his hands did—he grabbed a hold of her chin, tilted her head, and dove onto her lips. His tongue plunged into hers, and he began to fuck her mouth like he wanted to fuck her pussy. As she clung to him, whimpers escaping her as they kissed, he dropped his hands to the sides of her panties and tugged, hard enough for the silk to dig into his palms, as he tore them off her.

Then, he slid between her legs and felt her sopping wet cunt and knew that mindlessness he'd been seeking, was in full working order.

Her scent overwhelmed him. She was horny and hot and *his*. Fuck!

His fingers plunged through her wet folds, nudging her clit repeatedly as he moved the digits through her slick heat. The moans she made had her tongue vibrating against his, and he loved it. Adored it as she curled her arms over his shoulders and dragged him close, so that the taut points of her nipples burrowed into his chest.

Another growl hummed low in his chest, and he felt like exploding then and there as she began to wriggle, using the motions to direct his fingers.

She pulled away as a sharp cry exploded from her mouth when he rubbed her clit again. "Jesus, that feels so good!" she whimpered, then she stared at him with passion-drenched eyes. "You smell so fucking delicious." The whimper had given way to a growl of her own. "I want you to fuck me, George. I want that sweat all over me. I want to smell of you. I want *you* all over me."

He blinked at her, slowly. His brain taking a ridiculous amount of time to process her words because, truth was, 'little' brain was already in full working order.

Then, the primal beast inside him responded to the primal beast in her.

Her words were the catalyst, and with a grunt, he grabbed her hips, held her tight to him, then carefully heaved them both from the workout bench to the plastic mat on the floor. The minute she was on her back, he pulled off slightly, and looked at her, tits heaving, a red flush of delight burning her chest and cheeks, letting off enough heat to melt him.

He shoved the waistband of his shorts down, and to the audience of dozens of dumbbells, still treadmills, and silent cross-trainers, as well as their reflections on the full-length wall mirror behind him, he dove on her once his cock was free.

She moaned when he rubbed the glans over her folds once more, but as he found her gate and notched it home, she let out a sharp cry as he fucked into her.

She bucked underneath him, her hips alternating between dipping down and then rearing up. He knew she wasn't used to this. They'd always teased her before. Had always driven her crazy with want and foreplay before they took her where she needed to be.

But this was different.

He felt like an animal. A beast intent on focusing on anything but the situation he found himself in, able to concentrate his entire being on her, and not on the future.

At that moment, he drowned in her.

Loving that she absorbed all of him, that she was his comfort and his place of rest.

She screamed as he rammed hard into her, but she didn't complain. Her legs came up to tuck about his hips, and her feet burrowed into his ass with enough power to mark him later with bruises. Her heels guided him, urging him harder, deeper, faster. And the moans she made did the same.

The fire in her eyes was another trigger. It urged him on, demanding more, and her hips rose and fell to meet his.

With their gazes glued, he fucked her as she fucked him back.

He didn't know what had made her seek him out but was utterly grateful that she had.

Then, just as he felt his orgasm approach, he pulled back. She let out a shriek of outrage. "What the fuck, George?"

He smirked at her, loving her growl of pure fury as he grabbed hold of her and flipped her over. Maneuvering her so that they were looking into the mirror, he fitted himself behind her, then dragged his cock through the juicy mess he'd left behind. She whimpered as she looked at their reflection. Then, a cry echoed around the vast room as he plunged in deep.

From this angle, they could see her tits sway and jiggle, their pendulous weights slapping with the hardness of his thrusts. Her arms quivered and shook, and he saw the blank pools of her eyes as she absorbed his fast rhythm.

Then, she made a mewling noise, and her eyes closed. He slapped her ass, jolting her into opening them again, but she surprised him by resting her weight on one arm, then reaching down between her legs with the other. He felt her fingers fumbling with her clit as she touched herself and the sight of that, the sight of her face puckering with the sudden swell of ecstasy was all he needed to come.

He held off, waiting, waiting, hard but desperate for the urgent clutching of her intimate muscles around his shaft. When they set off like a firework display, he roared out his release, loving that her screams of joy entwined with his.

God, this woman was made for him.

He slumped against her, all the strength in his muscles disappearing as he fell against her, his hands sinking to the mat to stop his weight from falling entirely on her. They were both panting, both slick and sweaty messes as they came down from the incredible high they'd just explored as a unit.

"Thank you," he whispered, pressing his mouth to the spot right between her shoulders. She was wet with perspiration there, and he traced his tongue over the spot he'd kissed, making her shiver at the touch.

"I want to be here for you, George. Don't push me away."

He closed his eyes, pressed his forehead to her back. "I'll try."

"That's all I can ask of you," she whispered softly. Her voice sounded exhausted, both from what they'd just done but from recent events too.

His eyes pricked with stupid, pathetic tears—he was being selfish. She was going through so much as well… He wasn't alone here. They were all lost and floundering. "I'm always here for you too," he whispered. "I love you, Perry."

A soft laugh escaped her, a sound that was pure Perry, and one that never failed to fill him with happiness. "And I love you, George. Never forget that."

He never would, because she was, and always would be, his saving grace.

CHAPTER FIVE

EDWARD RAN a hand through his hair and tried not to tug it out at the roots. If anything, he was trying to look calm and at ease, even though he was anything but.

"Stressed" was an understatement.

The new Prime Minister shuffled in his seat opposite Edward. He'd been appointed a while ago, but this was the first chance Edward and he had had a heart-to-heart.

Unlike with other governments and countries with a crown, the king had no say in who was elected a cabinet's leader. But the first official meeting usually happened shortly after election, and in this instance, that just hadn't been possible.

Edward's schedule was...

He clenched his teeth.

"Insane" didn't even cover it.

His father had always made it look so easy. So seamless.

How had he coped?

Edward wondered if Philippe had thought the same when his own father had passed, wondered if he'd felt overwhelmed and stressed and totally out of his depth... Nobody could be prepared for this, could they?

It was enough to make him feel suffocated. To make his unhappiness as crown prince seem like a joke in comparison.

He'd felt like he was being strangled before...now, it was like being waterboarded.

"I'm afraid that's totally unacceptable."

The Prime Minister, a liberal among a crowd of sharks in his own right-wing conservative party—a tactical decision meant to offset the threat of the general election next year—shrugged. "We can't just oust a man whose reputation is spotless because he's friends with the former Prime Minister."

"It's come to my attention that he's been utterly disregarding an independent expert's opinion."

"Hardly independent," James Branche muttered. "She's now the queen."

"But she wasn't before she came here, was she?" Edward snarled.

"You were dating! How can I use her findings and claim them as being non-biased?"

"Why would she be biased? It's not in the Crown's best interest to funnel billions of euros into the construction of new dams and the like if it's totally pointless. Think, man. What's to the Crown's gain there?

"Perry's findings are founded in statistics and research. Her reports are above reproach. There is no environmental reason for our water shortages—the dams are damaged and need critical reparations. Either that, or we need to construct new ones. Have that corroborated if you wish, but I want to implement them by the end of the year."

"That's barely two months away!" Branche snapped.

"So? The longer we tarry on this, the more danger we're placing Veronia in! Totally unnecessarily, in my opinion. And even if you do wish to nitpick over her conclusions, I want it done quickly, and I want to fire Charles Francoise. That prick has been hiding in the Environmental Agency for only God knows how long, and all because he's related to your predecessor De Montfort! It will be expected that De Montfort's close allies will be under suspicion. The bastard was seen with an UnReal, dammit. Shortly before my mother's murder!"

He tried to control his voice, tried not to let it break, but the empathy in the man's eyes didn't give him a clue if he'd managed it.

"We can't start a witch hunt, sir."

"Why the hell not?" Edward retorted grimly. "My mother's dead, my father's in a coma. We don't even know why he hasn't woken up, we don't know if he will. We don't know if he'll ever be more than vegetative." His top lip curled in a snarl at how much they damn well didn't know. "Every death matters, Branche. But this is a public outrage. The UnReals didn't just... they *slaughtered* our queen and felled our king. Anyone seen to be associating with them, even their next of kin, needs to be investigated to the fullest extent of the law."

Branche's scowl deepened. "Then what? Throw them in prison for knowing an UnReal? Is that really how you're going to start your reign, sire? Taking the first steps towards being a dictator?"

"No. But neither do I intend to be seen as a weak ruler. Now is the time for strength, and not for anyone, not even my Prime Minister, to be allowed to convince me otherwise.

"Within the next four days, I want an update from our Military Intelligence Agency. I want to see what measures are being undertaken to find the bastards who did this to us, and I want reassurances that my family is safe."

He knew he was breathing heavily, and his heart was pounding hard enough to make him feel sick. He swallowed down the bile that was gathering in his throat, and barely managed to stay in control while under the watchful gaze of the other man in charge of ruling the country.

Branche's bullfrog eyes tracked his every move, and Edward was hard-pressed to keep it together. Just as the man's jowls began to jiggle in preparation for him to speak, a knock sounded at the door.

"Come in," Edward managed to croak out.

Branche's mouth pursed as the door opened, a footman stepping silently into his office to allow Xavier inside. Before he departed, the footman in white, gold, and blue livery made a sweeping bow, and retreated into the hallway once more.

Edward blinked at Xavier, who simply cocked a brow as he headed deeper into Edward's territory. Unfastening the button of his sports jacket and taking a seat beside Branche, Xavier settled into his chair with a smile that was, simply put, sardonic. "Branche trying to convince you to keep Francoise in play, Edward?"

The Prime Minister's nostrils flared. "I'll have you know I'm representing more than just your family here, Your Grace."

"What, yourself as well?" Xavier grunted. "Cut the bullshit."

"What bullshit? After having consulted with all the appropriate departments, as far as I'm aware, the queen has taken it into her head that our water crisis is a fabrication! Several experts disagree with that."

Xavier narrowed his eyes. "Disagree with that or her findings?"

Branche scowled. "What's the difference?"

"If you can't discern the difference, I have to ask how the hell the party thought you could lead the damn country." Xavier grimaced. "Finesse and subtlety seem to be going out of fashion."

"Stop playing, Xavier," Edward gritted out, his heart still pounding at a discomforting rate. He wanted to pat his chest, but then Branche would wonder why—and a sign of weakness was something he couldn't afford.

"I'm not *playing*," his cousin mocked. "Simply asking if the experts who looked into the matter have looked into Perry's findings, too. Or if they're simply going on old evidence."

"I believe their opinions predate those of the queen," Branche admitted gruffly.

Xavier drummed his fingers against the thin tubular armrest of his seat for a second, but his gaze was firmly on his lap as Branche spoke. "Let's think outside the box, gentlemen. Edward is going off information that I heard when I sat in on our new queen's presentation to a very uninterested Environmental Agency. So uninterested, in fact, one has to wonder why there's little panic about an ecological disaster that's waiting to happen. According to them, we're on a tight deadline, after all."

"They can't live in a state of urgency every second of the working day, man," Branche retorted.

"Can't they?" was all Xavier said. "You'd think it would be at the forefront of their mind though, surely? What plans have they initiated to counteract the drought? From my own investigations, I see very little in play for such a future as they're painting...

"Yet, after Perry initially presented her findings to her liaison, and found her requests for a meeting with some higher-ups continually rebuffed, I had to get involved. Only my clout with Laurenne Jonquil, one of their top staffers, enabled me to set something up on her behalf.

"Don't you think that's suspicious, Branche?"

"They're busy people," he mumbled, ducking his chin into his chest.

Xavier's mouth firmed. "Regardless. I heard what Perry had to say. I saw the statistics and the facts and the evidence. There is no reason, no ecological or climatic reason, why we're suffering such horrendous water loss. Her findings indicate that that reason has to be man-made."

"The supposition being that someone's damaging our dams? For God's sake, it's like some kind of ridiculous conspiracy theory!"

"'Ridiculous' isn't the word, considering that water is one of our most prized resources, you idiot. What can we do without water? Every decade that passes, it's becoming a more and more precious commodity. Without water, we're dust.

"Perry has been actively discouraged from pursuing her line of investigation by an agency headed by a relative to your predecessor. A predecessor with known ties to a terrorist body that has just murdered our queen," Xavier hissed. "Which part of this isn't computing, Branche? It's enough to make one wonder who else has ties to the UnReals in our Parliament, isn't it, Edward?"

Branche's shoulders dropped, as did his mouth—he outright gaped. "I beg your pardon!"

"You'll be begging for more than just my pardon if I find he's right," Edward said silkily, feeling a little more in control now that Xavier was here, and had put the Prime Minister on the defensive. "Xavier's right, Branche. I find it odd how certain ministers aren't overly concerned by what's happened."

"You can't start a witch hunt over this. Just because some people aren't sobbing into their handkerchiefs over your mother's passing, doesn't make them traitors!"

"I never said it did. My mother was a woman who had a nature that polarized people. Some loved her, others loathed her. Regardless, she died serving her country, and Veronia's current government is only seeing fit to engage in a shoddy investigation into her passing, while freely allowing known sympathizers to remain in their seats." Edward sliced his hand through the air. "No more. Do you hear me? You've taken advantage of my inexperience, Branche. Tried to give me the run around. Well, that's the last of it. If you don't want me to invoke Article 42 of the Constitution, you'll facilitate my requirements, not impede them."

"You wouldn't dare!" came the other man's harsh denial.

"Try me."

The mantle of power, for the first time in weeks, slipped onto his shoulders like it fit. It was a curiously satisfying sensation, and one that helped release the cloying tightness in his chest. Filling his father's shoes was... well, quite frankly, it was a daunting task.

The Prime Minister's jaw clenched. "This is blackmail."

"How ridiculous that the king is having to blackmail you to protect not only the interests of his fallen parent, but to safeguard the future of his people." Xavier's voice couldn't have sounded more sly if he'd tried.

"That article in our Constitution was included to prevent a dictatorship overtaking Parliament."

"I'm well aware of that, Branche," Edward snapped. "I've been eating, drinking, and breathing the damn Constitution since I was a child."

"You, however, are not only Veronia's Prime Minister—you're mine. In this, you will cede to my wishes or pay the consequences."

"Are you threatening me?"

"I don't think he could have made it more obvious," Xavier inserted snidely.

Branche's nostrils flared. "You'll regret this. You can't just start a witch hunt..." he repeated yet again.

"No. *You'll* regret this, if you decide to go against my wishes."

Branche jumped to his feet. It was said through gritted teeth but stated nonetheless, "Your Highness." At Xavier, he shot a narrow-eyed glare and mumbled, "Your Grace."

Deciding to let the idiot stride off, Edward didn't speak until the footman had closed the door behind Branche. As he glowered at the man's departing back, he slowly inhaled, seeking composure. He didn't think he had it, but he asked regardless, "What made you decide to pop up?"

Xavier shrugged. "Thought you might need a helping hand."

"I'm king. I shouldn't need help with my own damn government," Edward groused.

"Spoken like a true despot," Xavier teased, making Edward snort.

"Shut up." He rubbed his chin. "Parliament just wishes I'd turn despot on their arses. The pricks."

"From what I've gleaned, there's been little advance in either investigation."

"I'd have told you if there was. You didn't need to pop up for a pep talk, if that was your game."

"No. You haven't been doing much talking to anyone, Edward. You've decided to keep us all in the dark, and we both know Perry won't stand for it for long."

He scowled. "Has she said something?"

"Not really. She's as overwhelmed by her new position as you."

"I'm letting her down," Edward said on a deep sigh. Closing his eyes, he tilted his head back.

"No. You're not. You're just being absent and distancing yourself from us, because you're so busy. It's time to share the load."

"My father didn't."

"Philippe started his reign in a different time. And anyway, he did have help. My father and mother and Marianne took on a lot of his load. It's only in recent years that the pair of them had to handle everything, after my parents' passing."

"We've lost them all nearly, haven't we?"

Xavier's mouth firmed. "Yes." He scrubbed a hand over his face. "We can't give up hope for Philippe, Edward. The doctors say his body is giving him what he needs—the rest to recuperate."

"Sounds like bullshit to me. They're probably just scared I'll have them executed for failing to treat him," Edward grumbled.

"I doubt that. There are rules," Xavier retorted. His hands gripped the armrests. "We have to have faith."

"There's no guarantee he'll be lucid if he does wake, Xavier. I can't afford to have faith."

"There's no reason to start grieving him before he's dead either," Xavier snapped. "We have to hold on."

Edward shook his head, but he stayed silent. Tension throbbed between them for a second, until he broke it by asking, "Is she mad at me?"

"Of course not." Xavier sighed. "But if you have to ask me that, and aren't aware of the answer yourself, you understand why she's concerned."

"I've barely seen her in the past two weeks," Edward admitted. "I miss her."

They were in the same palace, and yet, they might as well have been in two separate countries.

"She's down the hall, Edward. Go see her, you fool."

"I've another meeting in ten minutes."

"This is my point about delegating. It doesn't matter whether Philippe needed help or not, you're not him. What's pride when it comes to your happiness?"

"Not that nonsense again. Jesus. You and George are like broken records when it comes down to talk of my happiness."

"Have you heard yourself? Of course, we are. We give a damn, Edward." He gritted his teeth. "You're as stubborn as you were as a kid. You idiot. Don't start believing your own press. Just because you're beloved by the damn public, doesn't mean those closest to you are going to lick your arse and not tell you the truth when you need to hear it."

Edward stared at him a second. "I don't see why you three should be miserable."

His mumbled rejoinder had Xavier scowling. "We can share duties. Split them. And it gives me an excuse to hang around the palace more."

Edward sighed. "It's ridiculous that you need an excuse, considering it's our fucking home."

"*C'est la vie,*" Xavier said with a shrug. "But it's true nonetheless. If I help you more, then I can be around you guys without raising suspicion."

Edward pinned his cousin with a stare. "And what of *your* research?"

"I can do it in my spare time."

"What spare time?" Edward scoffed. "I've more than enough work for five men, never mind being with you, George, and Perry."

"A problem shared and all that," Xavier said lightly. "We're here to help. George is dithering over whether to work in the Ministry of Finance because he wants to help you. We know if he's shoved in there, he'd be of little use to the king. But he's willing to do it to support you, idiot. He'd be better off doing what he wants in a private bank!

"Don't let his damn sacrifice be in bloody vain is what I'm trying to say to you. Put him somewhere useful to you."

"And what of you? Where will you take over?"

"I'll help with royal duties, visits and the like. The Ministry of Agriculture fits with my educational background, so I can take over that. Perry's obviously gels well with the EA... We're each of us specialists in our own fields, and we can help out with Parliament in those areas. But in the interim, we can work on your schedule and split it."

"It will send you all over the country. I'd prefer to keep you close to Perry."

"She'd prefer us to be separated and to actually see us all," he countered, putting emphasis on the word "all," "than for you to die a death here."

Edward's jaw tightened. "I'll think about it."

"I'll give you until the end of the week to do that," Xavier warned. "Then, if you don't come to your senses, I'm throwing in the big guns."

"Oh yeah, and what are they?"

"I'll tell Perry."

He snorted. "I'm shaking in my boots."

Xavier laughed. "As you should be. You know what she's like when she gets riled."

"Dick," Edward grumbled, well aware that his cousin wasn't half-wrong.

Xavier just winked. "Glad to know you've remembered my nickname."

•

CHAPTER SIX

HAVING LOOKED at her visitation schedule for the following three months, Perry was both astonished and aghast by the number of new hospitals Veronia was constructing.

This was followed by several new museums, a handful of new and rejuvenated town halls, and countless other civic buildings in need of a royal to officiate for the opening ceremony. Being a queen was far more boring than she'd ever suspected.

Granted, being a princess hadn't been a barrel of laughs either.

Not that she'd really had time to be a princess. It wasn't like she could judge the role when she'd done nothing more than wave at the public on her way out of the reception hall after her wedding, then sequester herself in a Sheikh's palazzo in the middle of the desert in Dubai!

No, today would be her first official royal visit, and though last night she'd found it difficult to fall asleep, that had been because she was alone in her bed.

Again.

The Bentley slowed as it swerved off a highway and onto a lane that led to a large hospital in the near distance. Modern in design, it was shiny and fancy, but also integrated into the forest that surrounded the facility.

Wooden planks covered the façade like vertical decking, and the windows were cutouts in bizarre shapes.

She supposed it was pretty. But for a rehab center?

Well, who was Perry to judge?

They'd gained access down the "tradesman's entrance" for security reasons, a road that approached the building from the back, not the front, so the first glimpse of the crowd came through the windscreen. It was... putting it frankly, enormous.

She blinked, her eyes widening in astonishment.

Because Cassie was new to the role as Perry's Guardian of the Keys, she'd kept on most of Marianne's advisors as well—the ones who didn't look at her like she was a dog turd on their car seat, anyway. They, along with Rose, her PA, had been working together to get Perry up-to-date on the basics of protocol.

Prior to Perry's wedding, Marianne had taught her everything she'd deemed necessary to be a princess. But that hadn't included things like today's visit.

No, that would have been useful.

Instead, she'd learned that she had to eat asparagus with her fingers, and practiced the proper way to greet an archduke—what they were, she'd yet to figure out. Even Wikipedia didn't really do that great a job of explaining it, because according to that, archdukes didn't exist anymore...so why did she have to learn how to greet one, for fuck's sake?

She rubbed her temple at the sight of what had to be eight thousand people.

Considering her Guardians had suggested a maximum of two thousand, Perry felt like the headlining act at an indie concert.

She was grateful Cassie had traveled ahead in the first car—something that was apparently standard so that the crowd would see the queen first and foremost... oh, the posturing—she dug her nails into the leather upholstery as she leaned forward to peer through the windscreen once more.

"Jasper," she croaked.

"Yes, Your Highness?"

Jasper had driven Marianne to all her events, and he'd been kind through his formality—her mother-in-law had been a stickler for that. The chauffeur had yet to learn that she was the complete opposite where formality was concerned.

"They're not for me, are they? All those people?"

"I fear so," came the faintly apologetic response. "Your security team notified me before we set off."

"They did?" She gulped. "Why?"

"To advise me to take the alternate entrance," he explained. "The number of people far surpassed expectations. As they should," he continued with a sniff, "after what those abominations did. The whole country should be here to show their support for the royal family."

She clenched her jaw at the reminder, trying desperately not to freak out.

"The idea of two thousand unnerved me," she whispered.

"I know, Your Highness."

"Please, call me ma'am." Even that felt far too formal, but she knew it was a major breach in protocol. When Jasper's shoulders dropped, she said quietly, "I know it's unusual, but please, Jasper, I-I just need something semi-normal."

His somber green eyes caught hers in the rearview mirror. "If you wish, ma'am."

She blew out a relieved breath. "I really do."

"You won't have to speak with the crowd, ma'am. Simply go through with the visit, and then wave on the way out."

She bit her lip.

It would be easy. Oh, so easy just to step out of the car, do the job she'd been assigned...but all those people had come to see her.

Were waiting for a glimpse of her.

Miss Nobody from Nowhere, USA.

They were showing their support of her family. They were mourning their former queen's passing...

Wasn't it churlish to ignore them? Because that was the game plan.

Gnawing at her lip, she fell silent. The rest of the Guardians—not of the Galaxy, just of her—and Cassie had explained that they'd arrive in the vehicle ahead of hers. Cassie and Murielle Harlington would trail after her as she waved at the crowd then entered the rehab facility.

The building had been constructed thanks to a new initiative of Philippe's, one regarding recidivism rates in ex-cons, and as such, necessitated someone higher than a minor royal to open it.

In the eyes of this nation, the only person higher than Perry was Edward. She was at the top of the triangle, as crazy as it seemed. And though ordinarily, she'd have been encouraged to step among the crowds, to greet them, the heightened security protocol demanded otherwise.

Feeling uncertain, Perry smoothed out the skirt of her dress, and waited for the car to arrive at the front entrance of the building.

She felt overheated in the warm car and her thick coat, but also like she was coming down off a sugar high. Shocky and too hot—never the greatest of combinations. Especially when she was about to be on show to a crowd that would have taken the Rolling Stones aback.

Her powder blue jacket was tailored neatly to her frame and tucked in at the waist. Underneath, she wore a fitted dress with a demure boat neckline. The skirt came to mid-calf. She wore her wedding and engagement ring, some simple gold ear bobs, and a discreet diamond tennis bracelet.

Not having had much input in the outfit, the one thing she'd picked to wear was on her feet. George had left out some sleek dark navy and black patent heels that looked like some kind of fetish-wear, considering the height of the stilettos, but she'd refused. Had selected a pair of ballet pumps instead.

She wasn't sure what she'd be doing today—not really. Opening the building to the public didn't seem like that big a job, but she wasn't certain how far she'd be walking—or if she even could in those damn stalagmites George had bought for her.

She felt uncomfortable and ill at ease in the tight dress. Though she'd lost more weight since the wedding—prior to which, she'd shed a good ten pounds out of nerves alone—she still felt the same as she always did.

Like biscuit dough being shoved back into the container.

Her hair had been styled by her new stylist—yes, she had a personal one on retainer now. A guy called Louis deMaura—and Louis was responsible for the makeup job of the century, which hid the tired circles under her eyes and the discontent about her mouth.

Perry had never imagined herself in this position when she'd married Edward. She'd thought it would be a decade into the future. She'd thought she'd have time to grow accustomed to it, to merge into the role. Instead, it was being thrust upon her, upon Edward too.

Though it came as a surprise, the real surprise was that she wasn't too overwhelmed by her new position. Of course, she was lost—who wasn't, only weeks into a new job?

But mostly she just missed her men.

She missed Edward with a depth that bewildered her. How could he be so close, and yet, so far away?

She missed George, who had taken up Edward's pastime of riding and would head out for hours on end.

She desperately craved time with Xavier, but as security had only recently come out of utter lockdown, visiting his estate had been a no-no.

This visit was the start of the family's life returning to some semblance of normalcy—as normal as it could be in the three-ring circus that was life at court after an assassination had just robbed the nation of its incumbent sovereigns.

In the future, when she had time, she could visit Xavier. But her other men were still AWOL. And who could blame them?

They hadn't only lost a queen, but a mother, too. Their pain was something she wished they'd share with her, but instead, they'd left her emotionally, if not physically. And even then, the latter was almost true. They were in Masonbrook after all, but not with her.

Edward barely slept, and if he came to bed, she didn't know it.

George was like a ghost, too. Only Xavier had taken time to visit her, but even then, she felt like he was restraining himself—not wanting his visits to the palace to seem too bizarre to the retainers.

She felt...

Lonely.

Jesus. She did.

Surrounded by people, drowning in more humanity than she'd been around all her life, Perry felt isolated and alone.

She bit her bottom lip to stop the quiver. Feeling like a little girl for wanting to cry, she shook herself.

Veronia, God help it, needed Perry. Her people needed their queen, and she had to make sure that she did Marianne proud.

Marianne hadn't questioned Perry's engagement to Edward. She had only had one small blip when she and Philippe had tried to sneak some clauses into the prenup...but aside from that, they'd both been as supportive as could be.

She would not let their faith in her down.

Girding her loins, she braced herself by pasting on a serene expression when Jasper finally drew to a halt. As the car's engine quieted, a member of staff from the rehab center appeared from the front entrance and approached.

Perry smiled when he opened the door, and found herself shaken from her nerves by the expression on his face. His utter delight in seeing her, on being close to her, could only be described as "starstruck."

For her.

Well, you are the queen now, Perry, she told herself wryly.

She wasn't a nobody anymore.

She was, quite definitely, a *somebody*.

The door pulled wide, and before she could step out, the man bowed low. "Your Highness," he declared, his English accent rocky.

Though it was their main language for governmental purposes, today, she was in the Sosan province, where the Veronian tongue was the primary dialect. They could speak English, as it was taught in schools, but it did she'd been warned—come with varying strengths of accents.

"Thank you for opening the door," she murmured nervously, even though she was only supposed to nod at him.

That whole emoji smiley with the heart-eyes thing? Yeah, he totally shone one her way.

Definitely starstruck, she thought, amused now.

The man was fifty if he'd seen a day, and he was big and brawny—even in his neat suit, and shoes so polished she could see her face in them as she lifted herself out of the vehicle.

When she straightened, she sucked in a deep breath before turning to face the crowd. Her throat felt thick as she lifted a hand and waved at the thousands of people.

The cheer that roared up at the gesture sent the hairs at the back of her neck jerking to attention. Shivers washed down her spine at the public's reaction to her. She felt their support, felt their love for the DeSauviers, and was touched and honored to be the recipient of such heartfelt emotion.

She turned her head and saw Cassie and Murielle Harlington hovering by their car, and a team of twelve security guards, each with earpieces, each talking into their mics as they monitored the crowd.

Perry saw the door ahead. It was another monstrosity of modernness, contrasted with a desire to blend into the woods behind the center. She was supposed to walk toward the wooden and glass creation, someone would open it, and she'd step inside.

Easy, right?

But all those people...

They'd come here for her.

No, more than that. They'd come here to support the DeSauviers. To declare to one and all that the UnReals, those cowardly fuckers, had been acting of their own accord.

It was a spontaneous reaction, and she knew Drake, their head of security, would want to ream her a new one later on, but she couldn't just wave and walk on.

She couldn't.

Wouldn't.

Perry stepped aside, headed away from the front entrance, and toward the crowd.

She felt the confusion behind her. Sensed her guards' dismay, then their irritation. Knowing she was inches away from being hauled back toward the facility, she sped up. Walked swiftly toward the people who were corralled in by metal fencing.

Little boys and girls held flowers, carried signs and pictures they'd painted themselves. Men and women stood there waving, watching her eagerly as she approached them.

Nerves hit her as she met the eye of an obviously pregnant woman, and she smiled hesitantly. The beaming one she received blasted those initial nerves away. She held out her hand. "It's a pleasure to meet you," she told the stranger. "When's the due date?"

Blushing and stuttering, the woman replied, "In three months, Your Highness."

"Congratulations!" Perry froze when someone grabbed her elbow, but she knew it was a guard so she jerked her arm back and up to liberate herself from his grip. "Thank you so much for coming today."

"I had to," the lady told her, tone fervent. "What happened was such a tragedy. We all feel for His Highness and Prince George. Yourself as well, of course, Your Majesty."

Touched, Perry felt tears prick her eyes at the woman's obvious grief. The subsequent outpouring of emotion that the crowd sent her way as she walked down the line of fencing almost overwhelmed her. She shook hands and smiled and patted the kids' heads. Accepting flowers with warm grins before passing them on to a dour-faced Murielle and a cheerful Cassie—a reminder to change her damn Guardians to women who belonged in this century, not the last.

As she made her way back toward the entrance, her impromptu meet-and-greet over, she reached out to hold the hands that shot out to grip hers. Taken aback by the people's love for her family, the guards and her ladies-in-waiting might as well not have existed for all she noticed them.

Perry, for the first time since entering this dream world of hers, was finally lost in it. Embraced and comforted out of the bewildering sense that this wasn't her place, the Veronian people made her realize it very much was.

The nerves in her belly had completely disappeared by the time she was about twenty feet away from the front entrance. An hour had to have passed as she begun to enjoy herself and felt calm for the first time in an age.

As she stepped toward the graveled path that cut through the manicured lawn, her guards suddenly turtled around her. Shouts came, screams followed.

Men were everywhere.

She went from walking singly to being covered by them, like a living, breathing shield.

She heard them yell, but a nasty *hiss* and a sharp *bang* drowned it out.

A single scream sounded, impossibly louder than the rest, sharp and high pitched.

Another bang.

Another deafening scream.

The tension among the men shielding her grew, then the tortoiseshell of protection caved in as one of them stumbled, falling toward her.

Panicking, she stepped forward, tried to keep him upright, but he was heavy.

Too heavy.

She absorbed his weight, fell backwards into the guard behind her, thanking God that he helped her stand.

What the fuck's happening? The internal scream reverberated in her head.

There was a shooter. Of that, there was no doubt. But had one of her men been shot?

Arms and legs were everywhere in the shelter of protection her guards offered her. Hands moved and bustled, elbows jabbed and stabbed as they tried to move forward, take her out of the danger zone.

Another staccato burst came, another yell, and the light suddenly caved in as pain blossomed and spread in her chest. A heavy weight blanketed her. Suffocating her, stealing the breath from her lungs.

The cacophony of sound grew, soaring to fever pitch, deafening her until seeing, hearing, and *feeling* hurt too much to remain conscious. Then, there was nothing, and Perry was glad of that.

―――

PANIC.

He thought he'd felt it when he'd seen his cousin being declared king that final day of their honeymoon.

He thought it had crept up on him throughout the nightmare that had been his *tanta* Marianne's funeral procession. It had certainly started to suffocate him when his cousin and the woman he considered his wife—in all but law—had been crowned as the new rulers of his wonderful country.

But it was nothing to what he felt at the text alert he had just received from Drake.

Perry, suspected GSW. En route to hospital. Will advise when I have further information.

It was nothing to the madcap twenty minutes he spent waiting to know which fucking hospital Perry was being airlifted to, and it was nothing to the drive to said hospital.

Edward, at his side in the limo and pastier than Xavier had seen him since the coronation, was silent. George's face was in a grimace of agonized terror. And Xavier knew how he felt.

There was no point in asking the hospital staff for updates.

If the goddamn King of Veronia wasn't being told how his queen was faring after yet another fucking assassination attempt, then there was no new information to be had.

"We brought her into this," Xavier said woodenly, the words spilling from him like poison. He knew, wherever they touched, they'd turn necrotic.

"*I* brought her into this," George snarled, his cheeks hectic with color.

They'd been in a meeting when they heard the news. They'd been trying to ascertain what the three of them could do to lighten Edward's load and become a more cohesive unit.

It had been sheer good fortune that they'd been together. Good fortune or fate, he didn't know. Because it seemed like the same divinations, fortune and fate, were taking Perry from them. When they'd only just found her, only just started to process having her in their lives, she was being stolen away...

A gunshot wound. Perry had been shot.

A tremor whispered through him at the idea that at that very moment, Perry might be dying. His thoughts were shattered like a stone through a window when Edward's words, low and seething, were gritted out, "Now isn't the time for recriminations. We get there. We see what's happening. We assess, and we act." His jaw was like granite. "And by tomorrow, if Drake hasn't found the bastard behind the shooting, he's out. And I don't give a fuck which country we have to beggar ourselves to, I want the best goddamn security consultancies on the fucking case."

His voice was bitter, furious. But it gave out by the end.

"I don't understand how this could have happened," George whispered, staring blindly ahead at the other side of the limo.

Though there were windows, there was nothing to see. The vehicle was surrounded by police and protective armed units, and an officer on a bike was riding just a few feet down. Traffic had stopped on the opposite side of the road as the people watched the limo shoot down a stretch of highway at speeds that bordered on the insane, never mind illegal.

"Two shootings in the space of two months is..." Edward slammed his fist into the cushion at his side. "Reckless. There's no other word for it, dammit. What the fuck are the UnReals even doing, for God's sake? They want the royals gone, I get that. But literally? Picking us off one by one?"

"They're trying to annihilate us," George said coldly, closing his eyes and turning his head away from them.

"Bullshit. They're trying to scare us," Xavier countered. "And it's working. We've hunkered down since the attack, and we're only going to keep on doing that if they keep on targeting us every time we make it outside the walls of Masonbrook."

"So, what are you suggesting? That if Perry somehow manages to survive her first assassination attempt on her first official goddamn visit, I should keep throwing her out there for them to hurt again?" Edward snarled.

Xavier closed his eyes. "No. Of course not. I don't know what I'm suggesting," he admitted, rubbing his eyes. Jesus, he felt frantic and exhausted, and the combination was sapping his energy reserves.

"The only thing we can do is clamp down on known associates," George inserted.

"That makes us look like we're starting a purge," Edward remarked. "I threatened Branche with it, but it was only words. I have no intention of—"

"Of what? Keeping Perry safe? Maybe I should just take her back to the US. It's Thanksgiving in a few weeks' time. Drake said she couldn't go— that we had some diplomatic meetings around the holiday, and security would already be stretched without her disappearing overseas. But if we can't protect her here, then I think I should take her."

"My wife stays with me," Edward snarled.

"It would be the first time you've treated her like your damn wife," George spat. "You've been as absent as I have." His words were choked, laced with his guilt.

Xavier could feel the tension bloom in his cousin, so he rested a restraining hand on Edward's arm. "He's scared. We all are," he said softly.

"Yeah. We are." Edward reached around to massage his neck. "This feels like a nightmare that's only just started."

"Because it has. Our hands are tied. If we implement extra security measures, then we're going to look like we're starting a fucking dictatorship. The family is in good stead at the moment because of Uncle Philippe's reign, but if we veer off that... you know how easily public opinion sways."

"And what? That matters more than Perry's safety?"

George's bitter words stung. "You think it doesn't matter to me? Goddammit, George, I love her too. You think I want her to be in danger? You think I want or asked for any of this? Fuck you. You don't own the rights to grief and worry."

Silence fell at his words, and Xavier was glad of it. They weren't going to get anywhere until they laid their eyes on Perry. Until they knew she was safe. And dear God, how he hoped she was safe.

Stomach clenching at the thought, he tried to shift his focus onto the situation at hand.

The UnReals had never been this active. Never been so aggressive, not since Edward and George's kidnapping when they were kids. Before then, there had been bombings and the like. But assassinations? It was a distinct change of pace, one that didn't make sense.

The terrorists had made their statement. Marianne was dead. Philippe, in his last moments of lucidity, had started the motions of his abdication before he'd headed in for the surgery that had put him in the coma he didn't seem to be coming out of. A new king and queen were ruling Veronia, and the way in which the UnReals had triggered that had caused dissension in the public, the likes of which had never been seen. Even the people's response to Edward and George's abduction as children hadn't been as large a catalyst as this one.

If the UnReals had been trying to swerve favor toward them, they'd failed utterly.

And today's act? It had been suicide for the UnReals...

Dammit! It didn't make sense.

"It doesn't make sense."

Edward's words mirrored his thoughts, just as the country beside the highway veered off into cityscape. Perry had been taken to the capital's best hospital, and even though they were traveling above and beyond the speed limit, they couldn't get there fast enough for his liking.

Xavier murmured, "No, it doesn't."

"As a group, they're never going to get public support. Not unless they want to use it to make me invoke articles in the constitution that will protect us but severely hamper and limit liberty."

George released a breath that was more of a hiss. "Does any of this matter? We're talking politics when Perry could be bleeding out in some fucking OR."

"Of course, it matters," Edward snarled. "If we can't figure out why the fuck they're doing what they're doing, how are we going to stop them? The end game is vital, George."

"You know that, George. You're a goddamn banker. And you're as much a strategist as Edward is," Xavier said, his tone grim. "Stop feeling sorry for yourself and help us figure out what the fuck is going on."

For a second, Xavier saw fire flash in George's eyes as he stared at him. The rage he saw within, however, was nothing more than what he himself was feeling. He bore the brunt of that wall of fury until George simmered down. Then, though his voice was choked, he murmured, "It feels like there are two different endgames happening here, not just the one."

Edward frowned. "Explain."

"The UnReals have always wanted to unseat the royal family ever since the DeSauviers arranged that massacre in Helstern."

"We don't need a history lesson, George," Xavier said.

"I know. But you want my input, then fucking listen. You said it yourself, we won't get anywhere without figuring out their motives." His mouth curling in a snarl, George continued, "So, let's face it. They've always wanted Veronia to be a republic, not a constitutional monarchy. They don't have to murder us to make that happen. After the kidnapping, they went black, didn't they? Disappeared practically."

"For the most part," Edward said. "Father told me there were small gatherings. Nothing major. Drake didn't quash them, but he kept an eye on them."

George nodded at the insights Edward provided. "It would make more sense if their approach was political. That's the only way they're ever going to have a say, if they gain approval via Parliament."

Xavier frowned. "Go on."

"But they haven't done that, have they? Even though they could have done—they obviously knew Luc De Montfort, our last Prime Minister. They could have gone legit, but instead, they've turned extremist. Far worse than anything they've ever done before. It's turned personal."

Stillness overcame them at the rightness of George's words. "They're not helping themselves, they're trying to hurt us," Edward whispered.

"I don't disagree, but why?" Xavier tried to put the pieces together; he could think clinically, but strategy wasn't one of his talents.

George looked at him. "We've pissed a lot of people off, Xavier. You know that."

"I do, but dammit, enough to murder Marianne? Not even to... I don't know. Fucking poison her in her sleep, dammit. There's rage here. Real hurt. And Marianne never hurt a fly. She was cold and could be harsh, but never intentionally malicious."

The leather creaked as Edward tilted his head to the side. "Why do you say that?"

"About her being malicious? Dammit, Ed, I know she could be a bit of a cold fish but—"

"No, not that," Edward snapped. "I mean, why do you say murder Marianne, not Father first? He's the real power. The king always is. Father could rule without Mother at his side. But she couldn't legally rule without him—I'd inherit."

Xavier shot him a look. "The shooter hit Marianne first, then aimed for Philippe. In that situation, a sniper isn't going to waste time. It's highly unlikely he's going to shoot anyone not his target, because in the chaotic aftermath, he might not get the chance for a second shot." The words stuck in his craw. It was hard to think he was talking about his *tanta*, who, only months before, had been pestering him to attend more royal functions, to be more active in his ducal role.

Now, that self-same woman who had been stalwart throughout his life, who'd held his hand at both his parents' funerals, was dead, too. Sharing the same crypt as Xavier's father and mother.

George closed his eyes at Xavier's words, and he couldn't blame him. This wasn't theory or just talk. This was *real*. This was life and death.

Edward whispered, "Mother was likely the target, then. You're right. How did I not realize that?"

"But why?" George demanded. "Father loved her, for God's sake, we all did, but why murder her? She was the one who was more active in the poorer neighborhoods. For all that she wasn't the height of popularity, you know as well as I do that she made herself known in the areas of unrest. A lot of people there respected her. She was dogged in making sure they had more than their fair share of royal visits and funding from her and Father's special projects."

Xavier knew his cousin wasn't wrong, and yet... "She came to visit me a month or so before the wedding."

George cocked a brow. "So?"

"You know, before that, she never came to the estate. I always attended her in Masonbrook. It was the day you both came to visit. Murielle Harlington had reprimanded you for kissing in the hallway, or some nonsense like that."

Edward blinked. "I remember. There was tea for her waiting in the Chinese Lily Room."

"Yes. Exactly. We never got around to drinking it. She didn't want to... she wasn't there for tea and biscuits. She wanted to ask me some questions. Said that Philippe had been acting oddly and wanted answers."

"You and I both know he kept her in the dark more than he should," Edward murmured drily, but there was bleak despondency in his gaze; Xavier could tell he was feeling guilty about maintaining secrets from Perry too. Though Xavier knew, point blank, he'd promised their woman he'd be open.

"I do, but this was different. She wondered if he was having an affair."

George stiffened. "What?"

"You heard me," Xavier groused, and though he knew it was childish, didn't want to repeat the words.

"Mother thought Father was cheating on her?" George demanded, half-turning in his seat to stare Xavier down.

He held up his hands. "Don't shoot the messenger. She came to me because she knew I wouldn't bullshit her. Said you two never saw anything wrong in what your father did or said."

"She felt that way?" George whispered, his voice croaky, and Xavier knew his younger cousin was on the brink of tears.

It was hard not to feel like they'd all let Marianne down.

"Yes," Xavier admitted. "She indicated that Philippe had had several mistresses over the years, but he kept promising her he wouldn't do it again." Anger throbbed throughout the limo, but Xavier knew this was important—he wasn't sure how, but this train of thought felt *right*. "That isn't my point though. She said something that stuck with me. Something like, 'Both of us have made wrongs.'"

"What does that mean?"

"It means she cheated on Father too," Edward said, and Xavier noticed his gaze shifted away from them and onto the road outside the car.

"You think that has something to do with this?"

Xavier shrugged, uncertain how to answer George. "I don't know. But if someone hated Marianne, maybe it's one of Philippe's lovers. Or maybe whoever was with your mother didn't appreciate being scorned?"

"That's a huge leap." George looked uneasy.

"It's all a leap at the moment," Xavier countered. "I just... I don't know, guys. The way she was that day, when she said what she did—she felt guilty. And not just about any affairs she'd had. I could see it on her face. Something wasn't right."

"That might have nothing to do with the assassination."

Edward said, "Maybe not, but perhaps we should dig deeper into Mother and Father's pasts to see if there's a reason why they wanted her dead."

"But then, they just targeted Perry, too," Xavier said uneasily, his belief shaken now.

"No," George murmured slowly. "It's like I said. It feels like there are two different motives here. There was a different reason for that than from what happened to Mother."

"How do you know?"

George cut him a look, but his jaw was clenched, and his features were riddled with obstinacy. "You think Mother felt guilty about something because of an instinct, and you trusted that. Don't question my instincts either."

"It's supposition until we get Drake involved," Edward murmured, and Xavier knew he was trying to be conciliatory, but in the end, he didn't have to bother. Because in the time it had taken for them to come up with a conspiracy theory that may or may not hold merit, the hospital had appeared ahead of them, and soon, they'd see just if...

Xavier couldn't even handle the thought.

CHAPTER SEVEN

"I'M OKAY, I'M OKAY!" She blurted the words out the second the doors opened. Perry knew who it would be, just like she knew this entire incident was her own fault. God, they must have been terrified.

When they heard her voice, Xavier slumped against the wall beside the door, and George and Edward halted on their way over to her—the relief on their faces hitting her hard.

"I'm so sorry," she whispered, lifting a hand to cover her face. Her fingers trembled and her nails scraped across the tender flesh of her eyelids. The pain felt good, and that disturbed her. It was her guilt talking, of course. She wasn't too far gone to realize that.

A hand reached out, grabbed a tight hold of her wrist, and gently pulled hers away so she could no longer hide. It came as no surprise to see that it was George. "Hey, what's all this?"

A stark voice sounded from the corner, and she glowered at Drake, who was standing there like the Grim Reaper. "She broke protocol."

One thing Perry had learned over the last six months was how important protocol was to these guys. It was a watchword, their fucking religion. They seemed to live and die by it, and today, she had her lesson as to why.

Somebody had died because of her, because she hadn't followed the rules, had decided to make up her own...when everybody in this room had been doing this for far longer than she had, she'd had to blaze out like she was the 'big I am'.

"Why the hell didn't you inform us that she was awake?" Edward half-growled at Drake. His hand clasped her calf, and she noticed he wasn't coming closer. Only George was at her side. Xavier hadn't moved from the doorway, and her husband was somehow near and yet, far away.

"I only just got here myself. There was a mix-up in the panic—the panic Her Highness instigated by not following the rules."

"Rules are there for a reason," Edward conceded. "However, it's in the security detail's remit to assess individual situations and to allow us some personal freedom."

"The need for personal freedom lost me a good man today, Your Highness," Drake half-snarled. "And I have another one in surgery, all because Her Highness decided to go walk about."

Perry winced, agony spearing through her. "I didn't realize —"

"No, why would you?" Drake shook his head. "That's *our* job. That's why we're here. We know best, even if it's irritating."

"I didn't greet the crowd to be irritating. I did it because they were there for me. They were supporting me, *us*. It would have been..." Her words waned with her energy.

What was the point in discussing this? Her actions had caused a man's death.

How had it come to that? Why did her life feel like it suddenly belonged in a James Patterson novel?

Edward's grip on her calf tightened. "Will somebody explain what the fuck happened today?"

"Perry was opening a rehabilitation center," Drake inserted.

"I know that. Just, I need details." His gaze narrowed. "More than simply her location—which I already knew."

Perry, even though her heart was still fluttering like a bird in her chest, and her ribs were aching like a bitch, found herself surprised by that small tidbit of information. He knew her schedule?

Did that mean she should know his?

Ugh, just what she needed right now. Another, inadvertent, guilt trip. Cue sigh.

"We expected a small crowd—then news hit the numbers could be double our expectations. Nobody expected it to be as large as it was. The fact that the rehab center is in the middle of a goddamn field certainly lowered our expectations.

"When I received word that close to ten thousand people were there, I instructed Jasper to divert his route. Her Highness was supposed to exit the vehicle, head for the doors, wave, and do her duty. But upon arrival, she headed toward the crowd. From what I've managed to discern, she was engaged for close to an hour, and upon her return to the entrance, shots were fired."

The precise recounting had Perry flinching. God, if she could go back, she would. Had she really been with the crowd for an hour? Had she given the bastards targeting her all that time to set up...?

But no. Even though she may have made things easier for them, assassination attempts didn't just happen on a whim. They had to be plotted, surely?

It didn't take the guilt away from her. A man had *died* because he'd been protecting her, defending her life, and she had facilitated that by being out in the open for as long as she had. And yet...there were so many questions. There had to have been several clear shots during that hour, multiple occasions where somebody could have fired at her and hit their target. But they'd waited until the last minute, when she'd been surrounded by her guards once more.

Two had followed her, traipsing along behind her as she greeted the public. The majority of the team had stood back, clustered along the walkway, on the hunt for any signs of suspicious activity.

Upon her approach to the door, they'd followed. The shooter had waited for that. Had waited for her to be near her team.

At her side, George was almost vibrating with tension. She could feel his need to touch her as though a ghost hand was skimming over her face, tilting her head at just the right angle for his kiss. She shot him a look, and found the longing building in her mirrored in his eyes—but this wasn't about sex, just a need to connect. She sucked in a shuddery breath, then focused her attention on Edward, who was glaring at Drake.

"What happened after the shots were fired?"

"Edward," Xavier interrupted, "I'm sure Perry doesn't need to hear this."

Her husband's jaw clenched, and she watched him fight his temper. She hadn't known him long, granted, but she knew him well. She knew him soul-deep. And for all that, she'd never seen the kind of anger he was fighting to contain. Neither had she expected it.

His rage would be like headbutting a wall.

There was no way Drake was coming out of this intact. Not without having a verbal altercation with a very pissed-off king.

More guilt flooded her, but she didn't have it in her to feel all that much. It was too draining. Truth was, the adrenaline high was wearing off, and her chest was aching after being used as a human pillow by her downed guards. Breathing hurt, never mind anything fancy like moving.

"Let's take this outside then," Edward said grimly. He stared pointedly at Drake, who reluctantly shifted away from the wall.

Perry, in different circumstances, would have been amused by his hangdog expression, but evidently something was very, very wrong with her security—hell, *their* security—if a shooter had been able to gain access to her on her first damn visit.

She bit her lip to stop herself from sending him a sympathetic look. Edward needed to burn off his temper, and though she'd have been willing to take the brunt of it to spare Drake, their head of security wasn't doing that good a job, was he? Not if two of the last three major royal events had involved a deadly shooting.

It was just...

How could she say "lucky" when a man was lying in a morgue somewhere? Very likely in this damn hospital. But she hadn't been shot out of sheer good fortune; the sniper had missed his target—her. She was only dealing with the bruises and the sore tightness of her ribs after being crushed by her guards.

She shuddered, watching as the two men headed out of her private ward. Edward's gait was strong, sure, but throbbing with the energy he was trying to contain. Drake's was slow, uncertain. He knew what was coming—they all did.

Drake's next words would be the only difference between him remaining as the head of their security and being fired.

The door closed with a succinct bang, and she twitched. It was nothing like a gunshot, nothing like it at all, but since she'd woken up, sharp noises had been making her jump.

She felt like such a wimp, but she'd never been so much as mugged, never mind been the focus of an attempted assassination.

Gulping, she tried to swallow back her nerves, but found her hand was taken by two of George's. "We thought you were..." His words broke off, and the agony couched in them speared her to the quick.

With her free fingers, she clutched at one of the flaps of his sports jacket and dragged him closer.

It was a private ward, with not even a window for them to spy on Edward and Drake—or for anyone to spy on them, but she didn't dare ask him to hold her. The only person with that right, in a public setting, was on the other side of that door, and that was way too far away.

Reaction was very close to setting in, but she had to hold it together until Edward was back.

This second assassination attempt might have been an effort to derail the Crown, but she wouldn't be the hangman's noose to the DeSauviers by revealing the truth of her relationship with the highest-ranking men in the country.

"I'm fine," she whispered, her eyes pleading with his for forgiveness.

"What happened? Why are you here if you weren't shot?"

Xavier's words were throaty, and when she turned to look at him, she saw that he couldn't stand still. He was as twitchy as she was, and deep down, Perry knew it was because he was trying to stop himself from approaching her.

It was then she knew she was doing the right thing in waiting for Edward's embrace.

Exhaling roughly, she whispered, "When the shots were fired—" She flinched, the sudden sound of Edward's bellow coming loud and clear from beyond her ward.

George squeezed her fingers. "Drake deserves it."

"No, he doesn't," Perry said sadly. "It's my fault for not following the plan. I-I just couldn't ignore all those people. They were there for me, yes, but they were symbolic of more. That was our public, showing us they loved us and mourned with us." Her throat closed. "I couldn't ignore that. It would have been too hard."

Xavier's voice was gruff. "You're no fool, Perry. You know you did wrong, considering the circumstances, but you also have to know that it takes time to plot these things. Shootings like what just happened aren't sporadic events. They take a lot of preparation and planning, and usually, an inside man." His mouth flattened. "That's why Drake deserves to have his ass reamed. Whatever you did, the Royal Guards were supposed to react to it, to anything you do. They're only supposed to retain you in emergency situations—your protective detail is supposed to be constantly assessing your safety, and they didn't."

"The fault of that has to lie with their boss."

Though she knew he was right, though it made sense, it didn't change the fact one of her guards was dead and another grievously injured.

"I shouldn't have done it."

"Maybe not," George whispered, "but you did, so there's no point in rehashing that. Why are you in here, if you haven't been shot? Just a checkup?"

She gulped. "When the shots fired, the men surrounded me. Out of nowhere, I was in a protective dome of human flesh." Human flesh that had bled for her, and had died to keep her safe—how couldn't she be humbled by that? "One of the shots found its target. The guard, Raoul Da Silva, stumbled into me. I almost fell to the ground, but someone held me up. Another shot came, and David, the other guard who was hit, tumbled inward, too.

"Their weight just pushed me over." God, it had been so hard to breathe. The memory of choking, of feeling like there was no air, was still prominent in her mind. "I was on the ground, and their weight was on me. I-I couldn't breathe, and over the screams, I couldn't make myself heard."

"They trampled you," Xavier said woodenly, but his skin was pasty. "Jesus."

George let out a shaky breath. "It could have been a lot worse."

"Not by much. Any longer, and she'd have goddamn died of asphyxiation!"

"That couldn't be helped," George insisted. "They were doing what they had to do."

Xavier's jaw firmed. "We need to start wearing armor. I said it after Marianne's..." He stopped, swallowed. "Snipers rarely aim for the head. They go for center mass. With a moving target, that's the easiest shot."

"A specialist marksman can shoot beer cans from a ridiculous distance. Armor isn't going to protect us from that," George snapped.

Perry cleared her throat, frightened by their knowledge. They spoke with such certainty... which she realized, made sense, considering their time in service. "Guys, I know you're mad and scared and everything, but I really don't think I have the energy to referee this fight." She winced. "My head's aching, and I'm just... sore."

"Of course, you are," George said immediately, the grip his hands had on hers lessening slightly. But he didn't let go—thank God. "It was stupid of us to talk about it in front of you."

"No," she countered. "It wasn't stupid. I *want* you to talk about these things in front of me, and the last thing I want is to actively discourage you, but I'm just not up to it right now." And how it galled her to make that admission.

Especially because she knew her men.

They were overprotective to a ridiculous extent. Considering the situation, that wasn't entirely peculiar, but she did not need to be encouraging them to maintain radio silence in front of her. Edward, despite his promises of transparency after they'd married, had immediately broken them upon their return to Veronia.

She wasn't content with that—if anything, it angered her—but she was willing to let it slide because the current circumstances were so extreme. When things calmed down, however, she intended on having a word with him. But as calm wasn't looking like it was going to happen anytime soon, she really wasn't sure how to handle things. What she *did* know was that at this minute, she wasn't well enough to debate their need for body armor.

Before either of them could reply, a knock sounded at the door. Edward could probably count on one hand the number of times he'd had to knock before entering a room, so that gave her a heads up it wasn't her husband on the other side.

No matter how much she wished it was, she called out, "Enter."

A nurse, dressed in pink scrubs, immediately flushed at the sight of

Xavier and George. She shot them both glances that reminded Perry of a rabbit in headlights rather than coquettish flirtation. She was pretty too, had white blonde hair, and a complexion that suited the pink uniform that would have washed almost anyone else out.

Maybe it was petty, but she was relieved to see that neither man noticed her. Their gazes, almost as one, flickered toward the intruder in their midst, identified who she was, and then immediately dismissed her. In less than two seconds, Perry was at the center of their universe once more, and like that, she found herself soothed.

The nurse's voice was timid—a lot shyer than it had been earlier when she'd stuck so many needles in Perry's arm that she'd started to make a good Swiss cheese impression. She murmured, "The doctor is on his way."

Perry blinked, then nodded, and watched as the other woman approached. In less than five minutes, Perry had had her blood pressure checked once more and her vitals monitored. The fluid IV line she was hooked up to was entirely unnecessary, but she'd been shoved on it the instant she'd arrived at the hospital.

She supposed, where the new queen was concerned, the hospital staff preferred to err on the side of caution. Who could blame them? She had a feeling that what she'd just seen of Edward's wrath was nothing to the rage he'd have felt if she'd truly been shot. When coming face-to-face with a furious monarch, was it any wonder the medical team was going above and beyond?

The door opened, and Edward slipped inside. His face was a bizarre mix of bright red and puce. His eyes were wide but taut as he wore his rage for everyone to see. The usually tender line of his mouth, almost effeminate sometimes, was a hard rictus.

The nurse caught sight of him, and a slight noise escaped her; to say that her husband was projecting his emotions was an understatement. But the noise and the sight of the woman doing her duties seemed to shake Edward. The fog of fury lifted slightly, and he nodded at her while striding over to the bed.

"Is everything all right?" The question was intended for the nurse.

"Yes, Your Highness. I'm just making rudimentary checks before the doctor's visit."

Edward nodded, but stayed silent as he reached Perry's side at last and took a seat next to her hip. His back was to the nurse, his attention, at that moment, was aimed entirely at Perry.

This man was her husband, and she wasn't exactly unaccustomed to being at the center of his attention...but never like this.

Two hours ago, she'd literally had the breath robbed from her lungs, and she likened the here and now to it. Edward stole the oxygen from the room, and made her drown in everything he was, replacing her with his essence, flooding her with all of him.

It wasn't that Xavier and George didn't trigger similar responses in her—it was that Edward so rarely showed how he felt.

George had the ability of tangling her ovaries into a knot and making her want to beg for his attention. Xavier had her craving his mouth, his touch. She felt like a flower whose petals opened to the sun when she was around him.

But Edward...her stoic, stalwart love acted like such a cold fish sometimes that when she came face-to-face with the realization he truly wasn't, it always felt like a blow to the solar plexus.

She didn't even notice the doctor coming in. Didn't see him peer around the room, gaping at the huge gamut of royalty in one space. The four highest-ranking royals in the land were in this tiny ward, and hell, if she was feeling the pressure, why shouldn't he?

A clearing of the throat reminded her they weren't alone, and she swallowed, though her tongue felt thick, and turned her gaze to her other loves. It was then that she saw yet another stranger, the physician, and saw the expression in the nurse's face—longing. Sheer longing.

Perry blinked, uncertain as to why the woman would be aiming such a look at her, and then she realized.

The way Edward was looking at her?

It was love. Unadulterated, 100%, undiluted love.

It was heady, it was breathtaking, and it was hers.

She shot the woman a kind smile, rather than be angry that the nurse had seen and reacted to the most private of moments. The woman blushed, her cheeks matching the color of her scrubs, then she lowered her eyes and turned to attend the newcomer.

"Doctor," Perry said hoarsely, her voice rough from the emotion charging through her. "This is my husband."

"Yes, Your Highness." He coughed, bowed slightly, and ducked his head in a way that made her grin—the man had zero idea how to greet the king.

"Edward, this kind man has been treating me."

"There's little to treat," the doctor said, his relief evident at moving onto safer topics. "Your Highness is quite well, although..." He licked his lips, turning to the nurse. "That will be all, Francesca."

Though the woman looked severely disappointed, she bobbed a quick curtsey that reminded Perry of the early days of her curtsey-taking classes—they were surprisingly hard to master—and rushed out of the room.

At his request, her men started scowling.

Edward was the only one to speak, however. "What's wrong, Doctor?"

"I'm not sure of the protocol here, Your Highness..." Her favorite fucking word. Jesus, it was really being rammed down her throat today. "... but Her Highness's blood work revealed something interesting."

While Edward cocked a brow, Xavier was the one to snap, "Well, man? What did it reveal?"

"The queen is with child."

"Excuse me?" Perry's eyes widened. "I'm not pregnant."

"The tests say otherwise." He pulled a face. "We had the labs check their findings; considering Her Majesty's status, the test was marked priority. Your hCG numbers indicate you're seven weeks pregnant."

The honeymoon.

And it wasn't like they'd been particularly careful, was it?

Her cheeks flared with heat as she looked around the room and saw the varying levels of astonishment on the men's faces. Underlying the surprise was a mixture of pride, happiness, and fear.

The latter she easily understood, because she knew there was a reason to be scared now. She'd been in the line of danger herself, and with a child to carry and then raise, to shelter and protect, the already precarious situation grew even more fraught.

She lifted a shaky hand to her head and rubbed at her temple. "What do I need to do?" she asked dumbly.

"Your primary caregiver will need to prescribe some prenatal vitamins and arrange for things like ultrasounds. Your blood pressure is a little high, so you'll have to monitor that—"

"She's just been shot at," Xavier immediately defended.

"I know, Your Grace," the doctor said, his cheeks heating. "But that's why I said they need monitoring. The situation is unwarranted—her readings are high as a result, so establishing a baseline is important, and the only facts are stained with the events of this morning. Seeing your doctor earlier rather than later is advisable.

"Aside from that, your ribs weren't fractured in the crush, and I feel satisfied that I can discharge you today."

"You've been x rayed?" George demanded. "Won't that have harmed the baby?"

"At that time, we were unaware of the pregnancy, and while it's not ideal, the examination shouldn't have proved harmful." The doctor gave her a kind smile. "Congratulations," he murmured, then after clearing his throat for the fourth time since he'd entered her ward, mumbled, "Your Highnesses." He gave them another limp bow and made a hasty retreat for the doorway.

Perry was too bewildered to be amused at the man's relief at escaping. "Why didn't I know I was pregnant?" She hadn't felt queasy, had she? Just nervous. The butterflies from all the new tasks she was having to undertake had been reason for that…right?

"There's been a lot going on," George remarked, but though his face was somber, there was a cheerfulness to his tone that had her scowling at him.

"Why are you so perky?" she demanded. "We're not exactly bringing this life into a safe environment, are we?"

"No, but we'll make sure the situation is righted before your third trimester," Edward stated, his tone grim. "I promise you that, like I've promised you nothing else, Perry."

His words were so stark, they shouldn't have comforted her, but they did. She knew when Edward said something, he wouldn't renege on it unless the circumstances were dire.

Her life had been on the line today, and that of her baby too—they just hadn't known it.

Suddenly, the gravity of their predicament heightened further.

She was going to be a mother. And her kid wasn't just going to be a snot-nosed toddler, but a mini-king-in-the-making.

Her eyes pricked with tears. "This is too much," she whispered, hearing the frenetic energy behind the words.

Edward shifted around on the bed, and moved himself close to her side. He raised an arm, tucked it around her shoulders and hugged her close. "I should have done this from the very start," he said on a sigh, pressing a kiss to the crown of her head.

"You had to ream Drake a new one," she said, her words watery.

He laughed a little. "That's one way of putting it." Gently squeezing her, he whispered, "All will be well. It *is* too soon, but there's never a right moment for a baby. Five years down the line would still be far too early, and yet, here we are."

She gulped. "We don't know who the father is."

Tension whipped around the room, but Edward immediately calmed it by telling her, "I told you. That doesn't matter. Not here, not with us. A healthy baby, that's all that counts."

Squinting up at him to see if he meant it—she hadn't really believed him when he'd told her before—she saw the peace in his eyes. There was a warm and calm acceptance in those topaz orbs, and he might as well have wrapped her in another hug for the relief and comfort it provided her.

A thought occurred to her. There was, after all, a fifty-fifty chance this baby was a girl… "Does Veronia have the right of primogeniture? If this baby's a girl, she can rule as queen, can't she?"

George bit back a laugh. "Trust you to ask about that. Trust you to even know what that means."

She peered at him. "I Googled it. I remember when Prince George might have been Princess Georgina with the British royals. They had to introduce an act to make sure that if he'd been a girl, she'd have had the right to rule as firstborn heir."

Edward sighed. "This isn't the time to be talking of things like this."

"Which means my suspicions are justified. The firstborn son gets to be king." She wrinkled her nose. "You do know I'm not going to allow that to continue, right?"

"Bossy boots," Xavier said on a low note, finally moving away from the wall and approaching the bed. His hand came to rest on her stocking-clad calf, and she wished like hell he was touching skin.

Hoist by my own petard, Perry realized.

When she'd arrived, she'd refused to change into the hospital gown and had further refused to get under the blankets on the bed. So what if she'd used her queenly status to make sure that happened? With a regular person, a quick check and a "No, I haven't been shot," would have been quite sufficient.

Instead, she'd been poked and prodded. All on the off-chance that something had happened to her when the guards had merely trampled her —and it wasn't like they could have helped it. Being shot didn't exactly do wonders for a person's sense of balance.

Still, she'd refused to suffer the indignity of a hospital gown. Not out of vanity but because, though the media maneuvered under the strictest of privacy laws, she knew for a fact the press would be all over what was happening in this room.

The news agencies wouldn't really care that two men had been shot protecting her. They'd only care if reports stating that *she'd* been hit were true or not. The last thing she wanted was a sneaky picture taken by a nurse of her ass cheeks cooling in the breeze to go live on Perez Hilton's blog.

Sheesh.

So, though she wished Xavier could get closer to her, touch her skin-to-skin, she decided regretting her decision of not changing out of her clothes was foolhardy. In fact, the next, best step was, "You're right. This isn't the time to talk about it, but discuss it we will. For now, I just want to go home."

And though Masonbrook hadn't exactly grown on her these past weeks, though it was still a cold, drafty, and unwelcoming dungeon of a place— well, a dungeon that was gilt-adorned and loaded down with antiques and priceless artifacts—at that moment, returning there was the best idea she'd had all week. Never mind all day.

WITH A DEEP SIGH, George poured the whiskey into the snifter. He did so two more times, pinched together two of the crystal tumblers with his thumb and pointer finger, then carried his, as well as his brother's and cousin's drinks, over to them.

They were in the new Regent's suite. Well, as new as Masonbrook ever got.

There were two sets of rooms for Regents here, at opposite sides of the palace. Back in the day, the other set of quarters had been to accommodate visiting royals. Now, it was a tradition to switch between them when the kingdom changed hands.

The baby in Perry's belly would be the next king or queen—he had no doubt the right of primogeniture was about to be enforced in their constitution. When the child was grown, he or she would stay in the suites George's parents had used. And so on and so forth.

Edward had surprised Perry by having this suite decorated. Most of the antiques and ornate pieces had been moved out and made way for newer, more modern, and elegant furniture. One of the reasons Perry hadn't wanted to live in Masonbrook was because it was too much like a museum.

He could empathize greatly with that notion.

It *was* a museum, but they were the curators of this living, breathing institution.

Panels had been placed over the old walls so the rooms could be painted without disturbing the antique wallpaper and ornate moldings. The result was remarkable, and truth was, George thought these redecorated rooms were a breath of fresh air.

A large bedroom connected with two bathrooms, with off-shooting wardrobes and dressing areas. This, in turn, led onto a large sitting room. On either side of it, there was offices—his and hers.

Edward had had the decorators work in secret to surprise Perry, and considering Masonbrook's size, it hadn't been too difficult a chore. From their old private quarters on the other wing, they'd been unable to hear anything over at this end of the castle.

Slowly but surely, George and Edward were transferring their personal possessions over. As was tradition, the other wing would be closed up until the time it was needed—save for their parent's actual bedchamber, which was where Phillipe was being nursed.

Handing Xavier and Edward their respective tumblers, he slumped back in the milk chocolate leather sofa and cocked his leg up on the chaise lounge's tongue. Tilting his head back, he took a sip of his drink, not bothering to watch the others in their armchairs, pensive frowns on their faces as they stared deeply into the amber nectar he'd just handed them.

Their silence was broken by strains of Mozart—Xavier's choice. George hated all things classical, but Perry was sleeping in the next room, and hard rock wasn't likely to be restful.

Not in her condition anyway.

Despite himself, he gulped. She had a *condition* now. She was pregnant.

He, *they*, were going to be fathers.

Tipping some whiskey down his throat at the thought had him wincing at the burn, but contrarily, it soothed the ache that was gathering deep inside himself.

His mother would have been ecstatic at the news. He knew she hadn't always been the warmest of creatures, but she'd longed for a grandchild. When Edward and Arabella had wed, George knew she'd have been waiting every damn month for news. And not just to make sure the pair of them had done their duty to the DeSauvier lineage, either.

She'd have probably been a horrible grandmother, if he was being honest. Far too rigid and far too stern when it came to the rules and family roles, but hell, he still hated that she'd never meet their child.

His stomach was tight, and he whispered, "To Mother," as he lifted his glass in a toast.

He didn't have to see his brother or cousin to know they were surprised at the gesture, but they too murmured, "To Mother." And, "To *Tanta*."

They fell quiet, but it wasn't an uncomfortable silence. It was more like they were shell-shocked. Disbelieving of the day's events.

What had started like a regular boring Wednesday, had turned terrifying by midday. Then, by late afternoon, they'd learned Perry was safe, one of their men was dead, another gravely injured, and she was carrying their child.

Not just any child, but the future king or queen.

His mouth moued in a frown. "I don't want our child to be raised like we were, Edward."

"No," came the somber reply, but his elder brother knew exactly what George was talking about. "But our parents tried their best."

"I know they did, but our best will be better. There are three of us."

Xavier cleared his throat. "What kind of roles will you and I be able to play though, George? Loving uncles?"

"Why not?" George frowned and tilted his head up to scowl at Xavier. "There's nothing wrong with that, is there? We've always been a close-knit family. Your parents and mine—even though our mothers fought like cats—were always tight. I see no reason why that shouldn't continue."

His cousin's jaw clenched. "I'm concerned."

"We all are," Edward replied, his tone gruff.

"Not about the UnReals. About how we're going to keep this situation of ours under wraps." Xavier let out a deep sigh. "I-I want to be around the child, guys."

"Of course, you do." Edward's tone was matter-of-fact. "I've arranged for one of the suites in this wing to be passed onto you."

Xavier stilled. "Why would you do that?"

"Because I decided to listen to you," came the wry remark. "And it didn't take today, or another traumatic event, to prod me forward.

"You're right, I need to share responsibilities or I will have no quality of life, nothing—save for work, work, work. Plus, Perry won't be happy with us being separated. My primary concern is her, and now the baby. We have to be around more. We have to be what she needs. Perry's already in a dangerous position because of us. We brought her into this, and the child is innocent too. If we're not around to soften the blow of increased security and the risks of our status, then what's the point in her being with us?" He shook his head. "I can't lose her. I won't. And that's even without worrying about the child."

"But why the rooms?" Xavier asked, confusion lacing his words.

"While the estate is close, it isn't as close as the palace," Edward explained. "There will be some nights, some events, where you can be expected to spend the night here at Masonbrook."

"That would fit in well," George murmured, impressed with his brother's reasoning. He scrubbed at his chin and absentmindedly realized he needed to shave. "We could arrange it so most of the later events are ones you attend, Xav. Would you be willing to do that?"

"To be here more, of course." Xavier blew out a breath. "I wasn't lying about putting my research on the backburner. I mean it. I wish it didn't have to be just a hobby…but I'm fine with it being a pastime if it means facilitating this lifestyle of ours."

"That's good to hear." Edward took a deep sip of his drink. "It's probably handy that Cassie is the head Guardian of the Keys. If she finds out, and she may, we can rely on her to stay quiet because of Marcus. He's like a brother to us—no way she's going to want to hurt us."

Xavier tilted his head to the side. "Is he coming over to Veronia?"

"I don't know." George ran his finger around the rim of the crystal. As it sang, he murmured, "I still can't believe he had a heart attack and didn't tell us."

Edward shrugged. "We haven't exactly kept in touch."

"Speak for yourself," Xavier retorted, and George quickly concurred.

"You're the only one who isolates himself, Edward. Not us. Marcus hasn't said a word. And we only know now because of Perry."

Wincing, Edward mumbled, "Maybe I should call him tomorrow?"

"Ya think?" George snarked, but there was little point. George knew Edward would end up forgetting.

Rolling his eyes, Xavier commented, "The last time we saw him was at the coronation, and he's gone back now. He should have stayed. He looked like death warmed up."

"At the risk of sounding like an even worse friend, I didn't notice."

"Why would you? You looked like you were close to puking throughout the entire ceremony."

"Thanks, George," Edward said wryly. "I appreciate that."

George just snorted. "Be grateful I'm excusing you. Otherwise I'd be railing at you."

"Anyway, before we digress further," Xavier inserted quickly, "I agree, Ed. Maybe we should introduce more of our friends' wives to Perry. She's going to need to change the Guardians sooner or later. I can't stand having Murielle Harlington around... not if I'm going to be staying here more."

"It's all about you," George retorted, but he grinned as he spoke.

"You know she hates me."

"Only because you refused to date her daughter."

"Do you blame me?"

"No. Louise Harlington has teeth bigger than this shot glass. Still, I can see why Murielle wouldn't like you for it. She'd have loved to rub shoulders with Mother as a close relative."

Xavier winced. "You're lucky, Edward. At least they won't try to matchmake *you* anymore."

George laughed. "If I come out as gay, maybe they'll leave me alone, too."

"You couldn't be straighter if you tried," Edward teased, and he snickered. "But you're right—I certainly won't miss that aspect of court."

"Speaking of, what did you say to Drake today?" George asked; it was the first time they'd been without Perry since she'd been discharged from the hospital. She'd stayed close to each of them throughout the evening, curled up on the sofa at one of their sides, and for once, Edward hadn't disappeared to his office.

"What do you think I said?" Edward murmured coolly, his eyes on the remnants of whiskey in his glass. "I told him what he shouldn't have needed to be told."

"How long did you give him?"

"Less than the week to find the sniper, or he's out."

George frowned. "You don't think he's in on it, do you?"

Xavier shook his head immediately. "No way. He adored your mother. Everyone knew that. He was half in love with her."

Tension overwhelmed him, making his stomach—which had just started to calm down—churn once more. "You don't think they were having an affair?"

"Under Father's nose? In such proximity, surely they wouldn't have been able to keep it a secret, so I doubt Father's pride would have stood for that," Edward remarked. "I love him, but his ego was too large to allow something like that to carry on."

"He's right, George."

"Good. I don't want to be right about that. Still, we need to scout out alternative options, Ed. We can't just dump Drake and have a vacuum in his position."

"True. I know someone who works for the Russians currently. Markov would be willing to step in if needs be. He owes me a favor."

Xavier frowned. "Who's Markov?"

"I served with him. Good man. Loyal. I saved his life back when we were trying to help calm the situation in the Ukraine down. He was wounded, almost died. I helped him."

"How?" George demanded, sitting upright. "I never heard this story."

Edward snorted. "Because it's not a tale for bedtime, little brother." The emphasis he placed on the word "little" made George scowl.

"I'd have thought something like that would have been plastered over the newspapers," Xavier remarked.

"It would have been—if we'd told anyone what truly happened. I didn't do it for another goddamn medal. I did it because he was a fellow soldier, he was in need of my aid, and then after, we became friends."

"Wait a minute," George inserted, feeling very slow on the mark as he carried on, "*Markov*. That's a Russian name. You mean to tell me you helped an enemy soldier?"

"Aren't you glad I did now?" Edward countered coolly. "Especially as he rose through the ranks, was big news with the Kremlin, and left to start his own private security firm a few years back?"

"One good turn deserves another," Xavier said on a faint laugh as he toasted Edward. "You always do have the luck of the gods when it comes to things like that."

"It's what happens when you're a basically decent human being," Edward grumbled. "I don't expect anything, but I know he'll be willing to help, especially after Mother and this with Perry. With his ties, he should be able to resolve this situation quickly."

"If Drake can't," George tacked on.

Edward conceded that with a nod. "If Drake can't."

"Do you think he won't be able to find out who did it?"

Turning to Xavier, he shrugged. "I don't know. Drake's always been remarkably on the ball, but I don't know what the fuck has happened recently."

"He's depressed."

The soft voice had the three of them shifting in their seats. George was the first to frown at their wife as she trundled in wearing a onesie, of all things—complete with a hood that had floppy ears on it.

"I know for a fact I didn't buy you that."

"I'm capable of buying things from Amazon, George," she groused as she stepped deeper into the room, passing the armchairs where Xav and Ed were sitting, to cuddle up beside him on the sofa. Before she did so, however, she stopped off to caress Xavier's jaw and kiss her husband on the forehead. As she snuggled up to George, however, she carried on grousing, "If you think I'm wearing silky lingerie after I've been shot at, you're crazy."

He snorted, but lifted an arm over her shoulder to tuck her closer. "What are you doing awake?"

"I heard you talking. Wanted to make sure you were okay."

"That *we're* okay?" Edward laughed, but it was bitter. "You're the one who was hurt today, Perry. Not us."

"Your sense of honor is the size of this country, sweetheart," Perry said wryly. "I know you too well not to know that you'll be kicking yourself far harder than I ever could."

"You were in danger because of us. We could have..." Edward bowed his head. "We could have lost you."

"And you didn't. I'm here. Me and a baby—two for one. In fact, I'm a BOGO now."

"A what?" Xavier demanded.

"Buy One, Get One," George answered for her with a faint smile. "It's what they do in supermarkets. You know, those big places that sell food and drink."

Xavier narrowed his eyes. "I know what a supermarket is," he said on a sniff.

"How many have you been into, though?" Perry asked, but from the twinkle in her eye, he could tell she was pulling his cousin's leg.

"Do we have to talk about this?" his cousin said.

"That means less than zero," George murmured, laughing, and felt his heart lighten when Perry joined in.

"We'll have to ask to open one together, Xav. I'll pop your supermarket cherry for you." She shot him a cheeky grin. "It's not the best cherry to pop, but hell, beggars can't be choosers."

The four of them shot each other a glance, then snickered. The release in tension was palpable, and George knew he wasn't the only one who could breathe a little deeper as a result.

"Minx," Xavier said on a sigh, but his eyes tightened after a few seconds, and George knew they were about to revert to serious talk.

Though he wanted to groan at the idea, he kept silent. They needed to discuss this. Needed to keep each other in the loop. If they didn't, if someone was out in the cold— namely, Perry—then George knew she'd make their lives hell.

"What did you mean when you said Drake was depressed?"

"What do you mean what did I mean?" Perry scowled. "The clue's in the words, isn't it? It's obvious to everyone with eyes he isn't dealing well with Marianne's passing. And I know he visits your father every day," she said pointedly to both him and Edward. "Unlike some people."

George swallowed back the guilt, but Edward turned his face away, disregarding her words. Or so he thought, until Ed murmured, "I'd visit him if he was awake. Seeing him lying there reminds me too much of Mother."

Perry's mouth softened at his admission. "I understand."

"Do you?" Ed let out a harsh laugh. "I don't. I know I should visit, I just...can't."

Xavier cleared his throat. "It seems a bit of a leap to say that Drake's depressed, Perry."

"Does it? Ask him. Talk to the man instead of just yelling at him for not doing his job right. It's not like he could have known there was going to be a threat today. He's not a mind reader."

"There's always chatter about these things, Perry. You're new to this life, and you're new to any kind of danger being present in your day-to-day existence," George insisted softly. "We're used to it. We know the score. And Drake does, too. Do you know how hard it is to hire a marksman?"

"Very?" she guessed with a grimace. "But he can't have been very good, can he?"

"What makes you say that?"

"He had ample time to shoot me. Instead, he decided to choose the moment I was close to my guards and they could turtle up around me."

As one, the three of them scowled, then George said on a blustery exhale, "We need to watch the footage."

Perry held up a hand. "Trust me, I don't need to. Seeing it firsthand was quite enough," she said on a wince. "I was walking along the fence line, greeting people. There were guards staggered along behind the track I was walking, and they were monitoring the situation.

"Then, as I returned to the entrance of the building, the guards came together to cluster around me, and that's when he fired. He could have hit me, too. Before they crowded me."

Edward frowned. "Could the sniper have set up late?"

Xavier questioned, "When's Drake reporting the facts to you?"

"I gave him until tomorrow morning at 5am."

"To find the sniper?" Perry demanded, aghast. "That's hardly any time at all."

"No, to get me information. But it's plenty of time. Within a handful of hours, the bastard could have been out of the country and free to go anywhere with which Veronia doesn't share an extradition treaty." Edward's mouth firmed. "I should have pushed for more. I was too lenient on Drake."

Perry sighed. "Hardly."

"This is our lives, Perry," Xavier argued. "We've lost a queen on his watch. Today, we almost lost a second. How many chances do we give him?"

"I guess even one chance is being generous," she admitted, wincing again. She cuddled up deeper into George's side, and he pressed his nose to the crown of her head. She smelled of perfume and shampoo, and he wanted to breathe her in. Absorb the fact that she was alive and well. "Is it wise to put this weight of responsibility on the one man? In the States, we have the FBI and all kinds of other bodies."

Edward's lips curved in a half-smile. "Sweetheart, we have them too. It isn't just on Drake's shoulders. He's simply our liaison. He's who we throw the shit at when we want answers. The entire onus doesn't rest with him, but our personal security does."

"You're not going to have him shot, are you? For failing to do his duty?" That had apparently been haunting her, because her fingers plucked nervously at the floppy bunny ear that had curled around her neck.

"Of course not. The man's committed no act of treason. The only way that would happen is if he's involved with the UnReals."

George's throat clenched at the prospect. "I really hope he isn't."

Perry turned in his arms to gape up at him. "You can't think he is."

"I don't know what to think anymore, Perry. Everything's turned upside-down and beyond fucked up." He heaved out a sigh. "I don't want to think he is, and if my gut instinct said he was, then he wouldn't still be around...but these are treacherous times."

"We'll see what he has to say in the morning," Edward inserted gently. "Now, I think we should go to bed."

Perry perked up. "The onesie can be removed."

George snorted. "Cut glass."

"What about it?" she demanded on a scowl.

"That's how we're going to be treating you for the next few days. Like you're precious crystal."

She huffed. "Don't I get a say in it?"

George winked at her. "What do you think?"

CHAPTER EIGHT

EDWARD RAN a weary hand through his hair. He needed a massage. Stat. He rubbed the back of his neck where tension had been gathering like a storm in need of breaking as he eyed his head of security from behind his desk.

His mother's Guardians of the Keys had yet to relinquish their posts, as Perry hadn't implemented staff changes of her own. As a result, the old guard had been trying to urge him to switch offices. To use the study his father, and his grandfather before Philippe, had worked from.

Trouble was, Edward knew he'd go crazy if he had to work in there. Not when his own office was perfect for his needs. Clean, minimalist, the only place in the castle where less was more.

Philippe's study was like the rest of Masonbrook castle—ornate, gilded, and a relic of the past in which he didn't wish to live.

Before the assassination, he and Perry had been due to move into one of Edward's smaller estates. But that wasn't possible now. This was a state of affairs that he knew deeply troubled Perry, who hated the castle, but also perturbed him. He hadn't realized how much he'd been looking forward to living at Grosvenor House until the opportunity had been wrenched from them.

They should have been away from the watchful gaze of the Guardians of the Keys, free to change the property to his and Perry's specifications, able to live their restricted lives with a certain, if not, limited amount of freedom... but that opportunity was gone now. It made him feel selfish, thinking of such matters when Drake was here with him. With his parents half-gone and his country in tatters, nothing else should be filling his mind.

But he was more than just a king. He was a man, as well as a husband. Those aspects of his nature had to rise to the fore from time to time.

Drake cleared his throat, catching Edward's attention.

The head of security's time was almost as precious as Edward's. The man had a mystery to solve, but unlike George who blamed Drake, Edward had had an about face since he'd reamed Drake a new one yesterday, as Perry so charmingly phrased it, and was now willing to give him time to rectify his mistake.

For a mistake it was.

Drake, who'd been waiting for Edward to speak, flinched when he eventually said, "Please, tell me you have some news. George is going crazy. He's terrified for Perry." Edward slouched back in his desk chair, ignoring how his back twinged—he'd barely left the damn seat since he'd been crowned. "We're all fearful for Perry's safety."

And that was no word of a lie.

The UnReals could get to their mother, and as they'd proven yesterday, they could get to Perry. Especially if the security breach wasn't corrected, and as far as Edward could ascertain, it hadn't been.

They'd known about the leak in security for a while—since gossip had arisen that his late wife had been murdered. Gossip that had since been disproven, as far as Edward was aware, but the release of such information had made it known that something wasn't right. They had trusted Drake to resolve the situation.

That he hadn't been able to do so was more than a disappointment—it was a tragedy.

The only reason the man hadn't lost his job—or his goddamn head—was that Edward knew Drake had adored his mother. Marianne had had a way of inspiring either love or hate in a person, and in Drake, it had been love.

Unlike George and Xavier, who seemed to believe his parents were infallible, Edward was well-aware of their faults. Not that he liked to contemplate them often, especially not when his mother was in the family crypt and his father was in a hospital bed. Still, maybe because he'd been with them longer, or was simply more cynical than his brother and cousin, Edward was aware of things he truly wished he didn't know.

Like the fact his father had several mistresses throughout the years. Like the fact his mother, insanely jealous of those mistresses, routinely had affairs in an effort to punish Philippe.

Edward didn't know if Philippe was aware of his wife's indiscretions. Wasn't sure if his father had retained Drake in spite of knowing of an affair

Marianne might have had with him...but the man's adoration made the head of security, in Edward's eyes, above suspicion.

Drake bridged his hands. "We've ascertained the identity of the man Luc De Montfort met with prior to his resignation."

A few weeks ago, that would have been welcome news about his ex-Prime Minister. Now, it felt like too little too late. He said as much. "How is that useful to us? And how does that help us with what happened yesterday?"

Drake shuffled in his seat. "With a little help from our 'friends', we managed to pin down the man's identity."

"The CIA?"

"We're a lot more popular, thanks to the queen's old nationality. Good old America," was all Drake said, before he rubbed his chin wearily. The past few weeks had taken a toll on him as well. Something Edward was willing to forgive, but once again, George was far less generous. The guard let out a deep sigh. "I knew he had to be an UnReal, I just didn't realize how high up the ranks he was."

Edward frowned. "He was meeting with Veronia's Prime Minister. Surely that was some indication?"

Drake shook his head. "Not always—I'm still not entirely sure what the meeting was about. De Montfort isn't talking, didn't give up the man's identity. He's been hung, drawn, and quartered in his party for meeting with one of the extremists, but I'm not finding any evidence that suggests he's a part of the group himself. But we digress.

"With such a meeting, in such a place, it would have made more sense for the UnReals to have used somebody disposable. In the end, we had to find the photographer who leaked the photo of De Montfort with the UnReal, and he informed us of the man's identity. It's not like UnReals go around wearing swastikas. They're anonymous."

"Where are you going with this, Drake?"

Edward's head of security rolled his lips inward and looked away from the monarch. Why his shoes were of such interest, Edward didn't know, but he swiftly realized the man was avoiding his gaze.

After a few seconds of silence, silence Edward refused to fill, Drake let out a sigh. "There's no easy way to talk about this, Your Highness. I don't even know how much you know of the troubles your parents' relationship suffered over the years."

Brow puckering, Edward murmured, "I know they weren't always faithful, unlike my brother. George seems to think Mother and Father should be in line for sainthood. They were no angels. Of that I'm fully aware."

Though he knew the truth, Drake's relief was so sudden and so heartfelt, Edward felt his own heart sink. What had his parents' adultery resulted in?

"What I'm about to tell you, Edward, may surprise you. But at the moment, it's only theory," Drake warned, but his reversion to the informal put Edward further on edge.

"For God's sake, get on with it. You're making me more nervous than I need to be!"

Drake nodded, his gaze soft with apology. "Your father didn't have affairs. He had long-term relationships with women I, over the years, vetted once I became the Head of Security for the family." Resting his elbows on the armrest of his seat, he pressed his fingertips together in a high bridge and rested his chin atop them. "I didn't particularly like that aspect of my job, not when I respected your mother as much as I did, but for the family's public image, I dealt with those situations myself."

Edward nodded. Drake had been with them for hell of a long time. What the man didn't know about the DeSauvier secrets wasn't worth knowing. "I understand, Drake. I don't hold it against you."

Drake grimaced. "I couldn't blame you if you did, sire."

"Carry on with 'Edward,' Drake. The formalities aren't necessary here."

"Thank you, Edward. There weren't many mistresses over the years. Less than a handful, but...there was one. She definitely got under your father's skin. She lived in Luxembourg, and there was a time when Philippe was barely here. But he spent most of his visits with his mistress, and shuffled off a lot of his engagements to your aunt and uncle as well as other members of the family to leave the country and to be with her.

"Your mother wasn't at fault. She knew two things. One, that her husband was cheating on her. Two, that there was little I could deny her—especially back then, I had to develop a thick skin when it came to dealing with her. She used my..." he winced, "*willingness* to please her to ascertain the whole truth, and when she discovered that Philippe was cheating again, she did something very foolish."

Scowling, Edward asked, "Like what?"

"I'm not saying any of this to sully your mother's image. My respect for her, regardless of the many mistakes she made over the years, is boundless. But learning that particular truth soured her. She went on a visit to Helstern one day. Just a regular inner-city visit. She went to two sister schools, and opened the gymnasium." He moved his head from side to side, his chin brushing the tips of his fingers as he fell into the past. "UnReal threats were at a premium back then. It was a year before your kidnapping, and though she had a lot of guards, somehow, she managed to connect with somebody on the visit."

"She began an affair?"

Drake nodded. "With one of the teachers she met that day."

He fell silent a second, and though Edward wanted to hurry the man along, he knew Drake was lost in the DeSauvier's cupboard of skeletons. As well as his own involvement in their shared past which he obviously regretted, or wished had turned out differently.

"Was it a short affair?" Edward gently prompted when Drake's silence went on for minutes that felt like hours.

"No, and unusually for Her Majesty, this time it was a particularly long relationship."

"What ended it? I assume it ended at some point?"

"Yes." Drake swallowed thickly. "It ended with an abortion."

Edward's eyes flared wide. "She fell pregnant to the man?"

"She did," Drake confirmed. "The baby was definitely not your father's. They'd barely seen each other for months, and when she realized what was happening, she came to me to arrange the procedure. I told her I would, but only if she ended things with the teacher."

Stunned, the image he'd always had of his mother obliterated—for at that moment all her preaching on duty seemed remarkably hypocritical—Edward whispered, "What was the teacher's name?"

"Laurence," Drake replied. "By all accounts, he was a very good man. I investigated him enough times to make sure of that. Your mother grew very close to him, and wasn't happy with my ultimatum, but she complied. I think she realized how deeply she'd fallen, how many mistakes she'd made."

Trying to get his head around this, Edward held up a hand. His burning need to know had him whispering, "Did you ever arrange something like that for one of my father's mistresses?"

Drake shook his head. "No. I can't say if your father was more careful, or just lucky. But Marianne wasn't so fortunate. She split up with Laurence, and seemed to throw herself back into life at court. Only I, and her closest Guardians of the Keys, were aware of her unhappiness. She hid it well. From you boys, especially."

She did more than hide it from them. Had hidden more than they'd ever suspected, Edward thought grimly.

A child! His mother had been pregnant with another man's child, and she'd had the baby aborted.

Those few facts tilted the view he'd always had of his mother as a stickler for the rules. It was her body, her choice, but what troubled him here was her status. All his life, she'd preached at him, and yet, she'd allowed herself to get into that particular situation. Her hypocrisy suffocated him. Especially considering her less than charming response to his news that if he didn't divorce Arabella, and had to spend another day with the miserable, frigid bitch, he'd go insane.

With her past, she should have had some understanding, surely?

Why would she want her son to endure as miserable a marriage as the one she'd had to live through?

Raising his hands, he rubbed at his temples. "Why are you telling me this?"

Drake pulled a face. "As I said, Laurence seemed to be a good man. After your mother broke things off, I have reason to believe he discovered she'd gone for an abortion. I truly have no idea how he learned of this, unless she told him herself, but... it sent him off the rails. A few months after Marianne called things off, I received word from one of my informants of a new member of the UnReals. He'd come to my informant's attention because he rose through the ranks at a surprising speed."

Edward closed his eyes. "Laurence." It wasn't a question.

"Laurence," Drake confirmed.

A thought occurred to him—Laurence could be a first name or a second name. "That's the man's surname, correct?"

Edward's head of security shook his head, slowly, somberly. "No. The man's full name was Laurence Prichard."

And like that, Edward's carefully constructed world began to unravel. Because one of the men sentenced to death for treason, after having abducted him and his brother when they were children, had been a Laurence Prichard.

His mouth worked for a second, words forming then failing to fall from his lips as the ramifications began to hit home.

But his head was empty.

His mind shot and fired, but each round was a blank.

Then, he heard a white noise, and realized Drake had been speaking once more.

"Your mother never forgave herself," the other man was saying, as if his words could apologize for actions and deeds that were the catalyst for an experience Edward wouldn't wish on his worst enemy.

Not even the bastard who had killed his mother deserved what he and George had endured as small boys in the care of Prichard and his cronies.

Edward stared blindly ahead for a second, then whispered, "The man who met with De Montfort... he's related to Prichard, isn't it?"

"I'm sorry to say, Edward, but yes. He's his brother."

His and his family's past suddenly took on labyrinth-like qualities. The untruths his parents had told—to one another, to their children, and to their nation—had had inconceivable effects.

He couldn't blame Marianne for the abduction, for what happened to him. Marianne, at the time, had been young. Philippe would have been five years younger than Edward was now.

If anyone was to blame, it was his father.

He'd been the adulterer.

Because for all her faults, Edward had no doubt that Marianne would have stayed true to his father had her female pride not been pricked. She'd been that sort. Loyal to the end.

"So, what? Laurence's brother wants revenge?" Edward asked, hating how thick his voice sounded.

Drake shrugged. "It would seem that way. There's been a reshuffling in the ranks of the UnReals. Prichard seems to be their new leader, which would indicate that he was behind the hit on your parents.

"We have all our available manpower on the hunt for them but, understandably, he's hiding out somewhere. We have reason to believe that he's left the country."

"Are there more attacks planned?" Edward asked hoarsely, feeling the ground beneath his feet start to slip away.

He needed Perry. He needed his wife, *now*.

"There are always whispers, Edward, you know that." Sadness creased Drake's features. His chestnut eyes were limpid with sorrow.

"Were there whispers about the assassination attempt?"

Drake's nod was slow. "Yes, Edward. Chatter indicated something may have been planned during the wedding weekend."

Edward blinked. "Did you inform my father?"

"Of course."

Tension filled him. "When?"

"I had the information passed along to him at your wedding rehearsal dinner. That was when I got wind of the chatter."

"Was there any indication who the intended target was?"

"Chatter is just that, Edward. It's never concrete, not until the deed is done."

He slammed his fist against his desk, rattling the glass surface, shaking the papers on his laptop. "Answer the goddamn question, Drake."

His head of security let out a deep sigh. "It seemed likely that there would be an attempt on yours and Perry's life after the ceremony, during the carriage ride back to Masonbrook."

His voice was hoarse as he whispered, "My father knew that, and he didn't tell me?"

"He knew I'd do everything in my power to keep you and Perry safe."

"Like you did my mother?" Edward hissed, hatred spilling through him with a force more venomous than any snake's bite could be. Before Drake could reply, he held up a hand. "Get. Out."

Drake's eyes flared. "Edward," he started, but Edward didn't let him finish.

"Out," he snarled, his gaze rigid and unyielding as he stared Drake down.

He'd never felt more a king than he did now, when a man with Drake's power conceded to Edward's position.

But as Drake slinked away, so did Edward's power, for at that moment, he became a small boy back in Prichard's hands.

Abused, physically, *emotionally* tortured, starved and drugged, and all because Edward's mother had broken the man's heart and killed his child.

For Marianne, there would have been no other option than to have an abortion. Even had they loved one another, there was no such thing as a queen divorcing her king. And that queen carrying another man's child?

Marianne should have never put herself in that position in the first damn place. Double standards or not, she should have taken the necessary precautions.

And as confusion filled him, as the lies that had made up his childhood unraveled, Edward was lost.

Truly, utterly lost, and he knew, the only person who'd ever find him again, who'd help him find himself, was his wife.

With a shaking hand, he reached for his cell phone. Finding her number, he connected the call and took his first full breath when, with a smile in her voice, she murmured, "Hey, love."

CHAPTER NINE

WHEN PERRY SPUN around and came face-to-face with Murielle Harlington, she jolted in surprise.

"Murielle!" she declared, somewhat breathlessly. "I didn't expect you to be there."

Murielle was, Perry supposed, quite good at her job. Even if she was miserable and barely had a nice thing to say about anyone.

But if you wanted efficiency, then she was the girl for the job.

Shame Perry didn't particularly mind someone who was inefficient. Give her Cassie over Murielle any day of the week.

Damn, she really needed to pick some new Guardians of the Keys.

The thought went onto an endless to-do list, but whenever it popped into her mind, she always felt guilty. Marianne's women had been in their roles for many years, and Perry didn't want them to think she didn't like them...

Even if that was the truth.

"I've been arranging the flowers in the ambassador's suite."

Perry blinked. "The ambassador?"

Murielle heaved out an exasperated breath. "Didn't Rose tell you?"

"Undoubtedly," Perry retorted. "Whether I listened is another matter entirely." She really didn't like her PA. The Dragon was a complete bitch, and she totally eyed up Perry's outfits, judging them wanting whenever they met. Which was every damn day.

It was like being at school again. But the mean cheerleader was her employee, and hadn't quite gotten the memo that she was no longer Queen Bee.

Murielle scowled. "That's very rude, Your Highness."

"Well, I can be rude, can't I? It's not like you're going to tell me off, is it, Murielle?" The older woman blushed, and Perry hid a smile. "Anyway, I'm not being rude. I zone out with the crap Rose tells me on a morning. How's anyone supposed to remember it all? Isn't the point of a PA to remember it for you? Or at least, if not remember it, make note."

"Zone out?" Murielle breathed. "You don't listen?"

She pulled a face. "Sometimes. Until she starts getting boring."

"Boring?" Murielle was starting to look green around the edges, which in turn, was starting to piss Perry off.

"Yes. *Boring*. As in tedious, Murielle." That was the hardest part of this new job of hers, she was coming to realize. How damn dull some of the everyday stuff could be. "Anyway. Which ambassador is here?"

"The German one."

"Why is he here?" She blinked. "Don't they stay in the embassy?"

"Yes. But it's to celebrate a trade agreement. The king is attending a party tonight."

"I'm not though, am I?" Perry asked, needing to have her memory stirred. God, she hoped she wasn't going anywhere tonight—the shooting hadn't exactly made her want to be sociable.

"No. The king has postponed all your events." Murielle pursed her lips. "For the next ten days."

Huh, she really needed to thank Edward for that. "He did?" Rose definitely hadn't told her that—what was the point of a PA who blurted lots of boring shit at you but none of the good stuff?

"Yes. He did," she confirmed, her disapproval evident.

Not one to argue with her good fortune, Perry shot the grim faced sourpuss a smile. "Where's Cassie?"

"Cassandra is with the children. In daycare." More disapproval.

"So?"

"...So?" asked Murielle.

"Yes. Why do you sound angry at that fact?"

"Because she should be here. There's plenty still to do, even if your events calendar is on hold."

Perry frowned at the implication that Cassie was bunking off. "I'm certain she'll be back the moment she can."

Murielle sniffed. "Yes, Your Majesty."

Barely managing to stop herself from rolling her eyes, Perry started to head out of her sitting room.

"Where are you going?" Murielle demanded. "We have to talk about the menus for the charity gala."

"What gala?" Sheesh, she really did need to start listening.

"The Xentel Corporation Gala."

"Which is when?"

"A fortnight's time, your Majesty."

If Murielle had been sucking on a lemon, she couldn't have looked more sour. "Okay, Murielle. I'll be back shortly, and we can discuss the menu."

Though the Guardian looked more disapproving than ever, Perry ignored her and slipped out of the sitting room. She knew Murielle would have followed her if Perry hadn't made it plain that unlike Marianne, she didn't like having ghostly visitors trailing along behind her wherever she went.

It was, she thought, pretty creepy how Murielle just *hovered*. All the damn time.

Free from unwanted Guardians, she decided to head to the daycare section in the castle basement.

It seemed a little grim to her—placing the nursery where the dungeons had once been. Of course, they were the jails where naughty nobles had been held, not peasants who'd been thrown in the oubliette... God, she was living in a place where there was a hole people had been thrown down to live or die.

Shuddering at the thought and determined not to ask where it was, she shoved her hands in her pockets and began the traipse down to the basement.

Her base was her private rooms. Marianne had maintained an office on the first floor, but Perry was more comfortable being in her own apartment. As such, their quarters, which were on the fourth floor of the castle, were quite a way away from the nursery.

As she headed down the stairs, she almost tripped on the long hem of her trousers. Though she grumbled, she pulled them up so it wouldn't happen again. It was beyond weird having to wear fancy clothes when she was at home.

Back in her flat in Boston, the minute she made it through the door, off went the office gear and on came either the PJs or the yoga pants. Here? Yeah, that was a no-no.

To wander the halls of her palace, she wore a pair of rather snazzy cream Dior pants that fit her trim figure to perfection. On top, she had a cerise blouse that was a little baggier over the belly and had made an appearance the other day in her dressing room...clearly, George had gone shopping again.

She hid a smile at the thought because hidden beneath the bright cerise shirt had been a scandalous bra and panties set.

The shirt's for you, the underwear's for me, his card had said. His barely legible scrawl made it very clear what was what.

God, she did love not having to shop. George's willingness to pad out her wardrobe was an endless delight for her.

As she wondered whether he'd do the same when it came to maternity clothes, she finally reached the last set of stairs that led to the first floor of the basement—there were three levels underground.

The moment she made it down to that level, she grimaced. It was gloomy down here, and she always hated being in this part of the palace. Rushing down toward the daycare section, she passed a few footmen who smiled shyly at her and bobbed into quick bows, and felt her guards approaching like ghouls, whispering along in her wake...

That alone was a testament to how quiet this level was.

On the other floors, she never heard them—there was always too much going on.

Even the cleaners, though they must have almost killed themselves being as quiet as possible, were audible when they vacuumed. And there were maids and footmen, as well as the Guardians and Edward's helpers. At any given time, in the upper parts of the palace, there were over two hundred people....

That number of humans in one place didn't lend itself to silence.

She liked it that way though—it meant she wasn't aware that she was being followed.

Before the shooting, the guards had left her alone inside these parts of the castle. But they'd taken to traipsing after her again...Perry knew she'd stand it only for so long before blowing a gasket.

She knew they were there for her benefit, but it made her feel like a prisoner in her own damn home!

The sounds of children playing finally reached her ears, and she made an effort to relax a little. She'd never been here before, though she knew of its existence because of Cassie, of course.

There was a long window that ran down the length of the hall to bring in light from the corridor, she assumed. Although, as she peered inside, she saw that there was definitely a lot going on—state of the art facilities with even a soft-area for playing—it wasn't as big as she'd imagined.

Still, there were only a handful of children in there. Ample for the play area.

She headed for the door, knocked on it. A woman opened it, saw her, then immediately dipped into a curtsey.

Wincing, Perry murmured, "It's okay. I just wanted to come in and see if my Guardian of the Keys was here."

It was so formal having to call Cassie that, but George, the least formal of her three men, had already told her she had to start calling the people in her staff by their appropriate names—it was less confusing that way.

Didn't matter that she damn well hated it.

The woman, older with graying hair, rose from her curtsey, and as she caught Perry's gaze, murmured, "Yes, Your Majesty. She's here." She swept her hand back to allow Perry in.

Entering the daycare the Crown provided for its members of staff, as well her friend, who'd yet to hire a nanny the children liked, she peered around and saw that currently, there was finger painting going on. But there was no Cassie.

"Where is she?"

"In the bathroom, your Majesty." Her voice turned hushed. "Robert had an accident."

"Oh." She pulled a face. "Poor kid."

The staffer nodded, then retreated to the small group of children when one of them called out, "Andrea!"

As Andrea moved off, Perry headed over too. Intent on seeing what was going on, and if the children were having fun. They appeared to be, and it amused her to see the children of maids and footmen mingling with nobility.

Considering she wasn't an elitist prick, she thought that was exactly how it should be. Cassie and Marcus's kids should mix and blend—this wasn't the eighteenth century, after all.

She'd met Jessica, Sebastien, and Robert at her wedding, when, dressed in their sweet tuxedos and a party dress, they'd stumbled into curtseys and bows before her and Edward. They'd been cute as hell—miniature Cassies and Marcuses.

Though her position as Guardian of the Keys had opened up places at schools for them, Cassie hadn't decided yet on whether to board the children or to keep them at home. Perry, though not the most maternal of women, couldn't imagine shoving her kids in a boarding school, but it was standard practice here.

In her opinion, standard practice sucked. She thought Cassie felt the same way, and that was why she was deliberating over whether to do it or not.

"Perry, Perry!" Jessica shouted gleefully when she saw her approach.

Laughing, and delighted at the lack of formality, she waved a hand at the little girl who beamed at her as she jumped to her feet. Within seconds, Jessica had her arms around Perry's legs. Apparently figuring she was fair game, a further five seconds later, her knees were in high demand by the twelve other children—most of whom she'd never met.

Still, she patted heads and rubbed a back or two. Didn't even wince when a snotty nose—or three—was wiped on her expensive trousers. After all, she'd have to get used to it, wouldn't she? It wasn't like her child would be born dispensing antiseptic fluid... even future kings and queens took dumps.

Then, she heard Cassie's, "Oh, my God! Your trousers!"

Perry turned around to her friend. "What about them?"

"They're covered in paint!"

Peering down the back of her legs, she had to laugh. There were dozens of bright finger marks covering her expensive pants. "I'll set a trend."

"Andrea! For God's sake, you're supposed to keep them corralled!"

Perry frowned. "Cassie, it's okay. They were pleased to see me!"

"Those pants are Dior, Perry!"

"So?" She shrugged. "They'll wash." Sensing that Cassie's eye was about to start twitching—the right one always started flickering when she was pissed—Perry laughed again. "Honestly, Cassie. It's okay. It's not the end of the world."

Andrea mumbled, "I'm so sorry, Your Highness!"

"It's okay, Andrea. No harm done." Perry squatted down when Robert approached. "Hi Robert," she said brightly, reaching out to squeeze his shoulder. "How are you doing?"

It was always weird saying his name; the intonation was French, and Perry's French was as bad as her Veronian—non-existent. Yeah, she really needed to do something about that.

"I'm okay," he said shyly, his accent so gorgeously American that she wanted to scoop him up and squeeze him—God, she missed home at that moment. The pang was more like a damn punch to the solar plexus than a sentimental clutch at her heart.

"I'm glad to hear it." She peered back at the low plastic table with squat, multicolor legs. "What are you painting?"

"A dog."

"Want to show me?"

He nodded, the act timid, then reached for her hand. She didn't mind the dried flecks of paint, but Cassie obviously did—she also had some flecks of blue in her hair—and took a hold of his small starfish pinkies.

"Umming" and "aahing" as the rest of the table showed her their works of art—after Robert had shown her a dog that looked more like a brown hill —she wished them all well and told them they deserved cookies as a treat. They looked pleased, but Andrea didn't.

Still, she waved them on their way and retreated to Cassie's side, amused when the kids immediately forgot about her and went back to what they were doing.

"You didn't have to do that," Cassie said on a sigh.

"You have paint in your hair."

"You have paint everywhere." She wrinkled her nose as she took in Perry's once pristine outfit. "You do know how expensive those pants were? They're ruined. No amount of washing will save them."

"What are they for if not enjoyment?"

"You wouldn't be so blasé if you were interested in fashion," Cassie said drily. "They're limited edition. Only the best for Her Majesty."

Perry wrinkled her nose. "Do you think George will be mad?"

Cassie stared at her askance. "George?"

Realizing the faux pas she'd made, she murmured quickly, "He helps me buy clothes. Has better taste than I do."

Cassie laughed. "I swear, the man's pretty enough to be gay. If I didn't know of his reputation before…" She wiggled her eyebrows. "He was a very naughty boy."

Perry snorted—she could easily believe it.

Still, she thought it wiser to stay silent on that particular matter. "Everything okay with Robert?"

"Yes. Just a toilet crisis." Cassie rubbed her nose. "It's very unusual for me to have to deal with this."

Perry reached over and patted her shoulder. "All will be well."

Seeming disheartened, she shrugged. Then in a brighter tone, asked, "Am I needed?"

"No. Not really. I just wanted to escape Murielle."

"Ah, the dreaded Lady Harlington. Can't blame you. I'd prefer to be stuck down here than up there with her."

"And yet, you abandoned me to her," Perry said, aghast. She patted her chest. "I'll never get over the betrayal."

Snorting, Cassie elbowed her in the side. "Come on, you. I need a coffee after that."

"That" being her little interlude with Robert, Perry assumed drily.

Ugh. Coffee. Something she couldn't have anymore. Being pregnant was already starting to suck.

Still, they were keeping that a secret for the moment, and though she'd have liked to discuss it with Cassie, knew she wouldn't be able to until Edward gave the go-ahead.

Curling her arm through Cassie's, she asked instead, "What's this gala I'm supposed to know all about?"

The other woman shook her head and laughed. "You're useless, I swear."

She wrinkled her nose. "I'm not."

"You are. I know you can listen—you're a scientist, for God's sake."

The two of them shared a look, then started laughing.

Someone might have shot at her two days ago, but hell, laughter was the best medicine, wasn't it?

―――

THE GREAT THING about being a king, Perry supposed, was having a hospital room installed in one's home.

Philippe's bedroom was half pomp and ceremony, and half clinical ward.

The technology here was enough to astonish the average man, and though her title was most definitely lofty now, she was at heart quite, quite average.

You could take the girl out of Tennessee, after all, but you can't take Tennessee out of the girl.

Every day, when she visited her father-in-law, she found herself blinking in astonishment at just how damn much this kind of home healthcare would cost in the States. Veronia had a social welfare system with nationalized healthcare. Coming from her background, she could only laud the Veronian government for such an undertaking.

Not that she'd be treated by the state. More's the pity, because she wasn't an elitist. What was good enough for Mary Nobody who lived in the center of the city was quite ample for her.

Nobody else seemed to agree however.

The snobs.

Edward had already informed her she'd be seeing a private physician. In fact, three days after the shooting now, she was due with the doctor tomorrow. He was coming to the palace and bringing a whole lot of more medical tech with him. *Are sonogram machines portable?* she asked herself.

It was totally unnecessary, but if her men had been protective before, that was nothing to now. She was so tightly constricted in their web of security, she was starting to feel like the male Black Widow spider—without the sex beforehand.

Which sucked as hard as it sounded.

Talk about zero perks to this shit. And boy, she was getting horny.

Like, seriously, seriously, horny.

Which was fucked up, considering her life was in danger.

"You certainly raised your boys well, Philippe," Perry said, grumbling as she lathered shaving foam in her hands. Carefully applying it to his jaw and cheeks, she carried on. "I swear, they're going to be hauling me around in a papoose before the week's up. Although, I'd like to see them try when I'm nine months gone." She snorted. "Yeah, I didn't tell you that yesterday, did I? I've a bun in the oven." She paused. "No, that's not right. I've a cucumber sandwich in the oven. That seems like a step up."

Laughing to herself, she mumbled her complaints to the only one who was listening—well, if not listening, *absorbing*. A guy who also happened to be in a coma. Funny how life worked.

Not.

She'd never been all that good at shaving, not even her own legs, and though she left the other kinds of toilette to the nurses, she'd been tending to Philip's hair and shaving him. She'd been doing that since the beginning.

Not a day, in all the time she'd known him, had she seen Philippe unshaven and rough around the edges. She didn't see why being in a damn coma had to change anything. And it just seemed wrong for a stranger to be doing something this personal. Maybe they were part horrified that the queen had taken these tasks on, but Perry didn't care. Philippe was her father-in-law, dammit. He needed the personal touch if they were ever going to get him back.

Of course, caring though her decision to shave him might be, it didn't make her suddenly good at this kind of stuff. She'd cut him and nicked him with the razor. Several times. But comatose guys didn't really complain all that much, and even though she winced every time it happened, Philippe never did. She was kind of waiting for him to respond, to react. But he hadn't yet, and her talents at being a barber weren't exactly improving with practice.

Some women were able to do shit like this. Braid their hair themselves, shave their legs without risking exsanguination. Perry wasn't one of them.

She could do the most mundane of shit for her work, had zero issue with the tiniest detailing when it came down to experiments, but anything body related? Nope. She had to hire out. Her one comfort was that the reason estheticians existed was for women like her.

And now that she had Louis, well, she never had to worry ever again.

"I told the boys off," she groused, "for not visiting you more, I mean. They're edgy and nervous though. I mean, I understand it. I really do. I was almost shot, and hell, I'm freaking out about that too, but more than anything I just feel..." She let loose a shaky breath. "More than anything, I just hate that one of my guards died, and the other is still messed up in the hospital."

Raoul Da Silva's family had been well-compensated for his death in the line of duty, but that shit didn't matter. Blood money didn't make up for what had happened to him, and all for a cause that no one particularly understood.

"What's going on, Philippe?" she asked her father-in-law, not expecting an answer, but just needing to get the words out. "Why is this happening? After all these years, why is everything starting up again?" A knock sounded at the door, and she jumped, not having expected anyone to approach Philippe's rooms for the next hour or so.

The nurses usually gave her a wide berth when she arrived. Apparently, they weren't used to the idea of a queen shaving the former king... well, screw them.

One good thing about this queen was her small-town roots. Perry would never forget where she came from, and leaving Philippe to be tended to totally by strangers was an abomination she couldn't allow.

At that moment, homesickness hit her straight in the gut with the power of a battering ram. She almost doubled over with the pain of it.

God, the normalcy. She missed it. Craved it so damn badly that it was worse than being on a diet while trapped in a McDonald's.

Yeah, it was *that* bad.

She'd never realized how wonderfully delicious *average* was...until now.

It wasn't that she was complaining. Sure, she knew some people would take it that way, but they could just fuck off. They should try being shot at, mourning the passing of their husband's mother, all while being crowned the fucking queen of a goddamn nation.

Talk about pressure.

Sheesh.

The knock sounded again, and she blinked. *Oops.* "Come in."

It opened and revealed a face she hadn't seen before.

She narrowed her eyes at the interloper. "Yes?"

Perry wasn't sure why, but the man struck chills in her. She wasn't the fanciful sort, but this man? No, she didn't like him. Not one bit.

So much so, she edged around the bed to shield Philippe from him. The king was ill, vulnerable. She didn't fear the stranger would hurt him, but that sneering mouth, that snide nose... No, she wanted to protect her father-in-law from being ridiculed by such a sly-faced intruder.

In less than a glance, the man took in the scene, and his lips curled in a sardonic smile. "How very picturesque. What a shame the press aren't here to see you tend to your beloved father by marriage."

She stiffened. Not having expected to be verbally mocked for caring for Philippe, she demanded, "Who are you?"

"I was once related to Philippe, so you can retract those claws of yours. The name's Ferdinand L'Argeneau."

"Who?"

At her lack of recognition, his nostrils flared, and she could sense she'd angered him with her ignorance. "Dear me, don't they teach hicks from Tennessee anything these days?"

Her top lip curled in annoyance. "Not about nobodies from small countries in central Europe. We're more interested in people who really matter."

L'Argeneau's eyes narrowed, but he smirked. "Touché."

"What are you doing here? How did you gain access to these quarters?"

She wasn't sure why she hadn't pressed the button for the guards; Philippe wore a chain around his neck in case of emergencies, and her hand was close to it. A part of her wanted to, but another part was hesitant. She wanted to know who this self-righteous asshole was, and how the hell he'd managed to make it into this part of the castle.

"Once upon a time, I was as welcome in these rooms as you are."

"Can we dispense with the melodrama, Mr. L'Argeneau? As you can see, I'm quite busy."

"My daughter wouldn't have been seen dead doing what you're doing." He tilted his head to the side as he studied her. "Not for me or her father-in-law."

She frowned, then realization hit. "You're Arabella's father."

He lowered his head in agreement, but even that felt mocking. Moments before, she'd been grieving the lack of normalcy in her life. Now, she pulled on her royal panties and tried to be the woman she was today, not had once been—a queen.

"While that's very fascinating, I'm sure you can understand my concerns. How did you gain access to this room?"

"The guards know me."

Was that supposed to reassure her?

Uneasiness filtered through her. "That explains the how, and I'm quite grateful for that, but the 'why' evades me."

"We used to be friends, Philippe and I. Back in the days before he was king, of course. Then, after…things changed. Not necessarily for the better, either."

"On whose part?"

He tapped his nose. "That's none of your business."

"Perhaps not, but I'm making it my business if you choose to remain in here." She gave him a tight smile. "As you can see, Philippe isn't ready to visit anyone. Old friend or not. If you'd kindly leave?"

"You've more spunk than I gave you credit for. I thought you were going to pass out during the coronation, and then the other day, with the shooting? Footage went live on all the channels, you know. The people did *so* love your impromptu visit." He returned her smile, but it was more of a grimace than a pleasant twitch of his lips. "Of course, it turned swiftly south, didn't it?"

"'South' is a kind way of phrasing it." "Ass-up" fit better.

"I've heard a lot about you. You certainly made yourself known with the Environmental Agency."

She frowned. "How would you know about that?"

"I'm a member of Parliament. It's my business to know everything that's happening in all the nooks and crannies of government. In fact, it's more than my business—it's my pleasure."

He closed the door, and it was only then she realized he'd been standing on the doorjamb. Neither in, nor out.

"Is there a reason you wish to continue this visit?" she asked, trying to sound kind when really, she wanted to be imperious. *What did the ass want?*

He was an odd duck, no mistaking. He wore a suit that screamed the best tailoring in the land, and yet it was an old cut. Like he'd made his tailor create him something from the eighties, with its thick pinstripe, wide shoulders, double breast, and the pleating on his pants, the man looked like a mix of Don Johnson in *Miami Vice* and Gordon Gekko. It was an odd combination, but complete with his slicked-back hair, clean-shaven jaw, and pallid blue eyes, it all boiled down to a man she didn't trust, didn't like, and one she wished would back off.

Still, he was obviously here for a purpose. And ever curious, Perry wanted to know what that purpose was.

"I wondered what you intend to gain by misinforming the EA."

Her eyes flashed with ire. "You really wish to discuss my research and the findings I uncovered over my father-in-law's sickbed?"

L'Argeneau narrowed his eyes. "The location isn't ideal."

"Hardly. This is totally inappropriate. Why are you here?" Perry repeated, her nostrils flaring with outrage.

"How is he?"

"You couldn't have asked his nurse? If you're allowed access to the private quarters, which I highly doubt, you could have spoken with the nurse on duty." She made a mental note to find out who the nurse on duty actually was and to have her relocated out of the palace entirely.

Random people, be they old friends and one-time relatives, shouldn't be allowed to just walk in here.

In fact, screw that, she'd figure out which "guard" had decided to let L'Argeneau into the retired king's hospital ward, and have him "relocated," too.

"Perhaps I wished to find a way to speak to you," the man said, sounding cagier than a toddler declaring his innocence over the lost cookies while his face was smeared in chocolate.

"And why would you want to do that?"

"I just wondered if you were curious about your predecessor."

Her frown morphed into a scowl. "Excuse me?"

L'Argeneau's smile was tight. "I believe you understood me. English might not be my first language, but I think I made myself clear."

"The words might have been clear, but their meaning most definitely wasn't," she snapped. "In fact, I dislike your inference entirely, Mr. L'Argeneau."

"You may dislike it. You can even abhor it, but you can't dismiss it."

What the hell was with this guy? Who itemized their dead child as a "predecessor"? The man hadn't even called his daughter by her name yet.

"Arabella played an important role in Edward's life, but she, sadly, is in the past. I'm the present, and the future. I'm sorry she passed away, but I have no right to interfere with that part of my husband's world. No right to, and no desire to, either." She straightened her shoulders. "I think it's time for you to leave, Mr. L'Argeneau."

"She was a healthy girl, my daughter," he said, his tone almost musing now. He turned his attention to Philippe who, sadly enough, hadn't moved a muscle in umbrage at what this bastard was implying with his slights and insinuations.

"Most people are until they pass away," she retorted, not too kindly...but still, it was the truth. Whenever anyone famous had died, and they'd asked Perry's grandmother how, Granny Joy had always grumbled, "Their heart had stopped."

The exact truth, but irritating as hell, Perry remembered fondly.

L'Argeneau didn't appreciate her snark. His chin reared up as he murmured, "Healthy women don't just pass away of the flu."

"Is that what she died of?" Perry genuinely didn't know.

Though she'd been a part of the DeSauvier world since she'd become friends with George, and George had actually flown off to attend the funeral when Arabella had died, they'd barely discussed it. He'd just said she'd been ill and had died of that illness. Perhaps it was strange that they'd not really discussed it, but George had been...

Perry's lips twisted as she thought about just how strange George had been back then.

He'd barely mentioned his family during the entire length of their friendship. Had never even discussed Xavier! And as she wasn't the sort to be interested in the royal family of any country, was barely curious about the family in the White House, it had never really mattered to her.

Now, looking back, she realized it *was* odd...but people did odd things, didn't they? Especially when they were running away. And Perry had since learned that that was what George had been doing.

He'd been running from his life here.

A life where he'd been unable to carry on in the armed forces, where he'd been at odds with his cousin thanks to some jiggery-pokery he'd undertaken with his uncle's fiancée...as well as his unease with Arabella and the discord he'd felt with Edward, who'd refused to accept that both men needed to share their partner to feel complete.

No, George had most definitely been running away... from himself, and the mess he'd made of his life.

"Yes, she did. The flu," he said, scorn lacing his tone as he barged into Perry's thoughts. "A twenty-eight-year-old woman, in the peak of health? Who dies of the flu anymore?"

She wasn't a statistician but she'd say it wasn't that irregular. People died, didn't they? And she'd have felt for him, would have hurt for him, if he'd seemed in any way like he was mourning.

That was the strangest thing.

There was very little feeling behind his words. He looked more angry and disappointed than pained or sad. She knew that parents and kids didn't always get on, but to this extent?

George had said Arabella's personality was as warm as a fridge freezer, though. Like father like daughter? She could understand why Arabella made ice cream look molten now that she'd met the man who'd helped raised her!

"Don't you think it's odd, that a family who can afford the kind of care you see here today didn't respond to her apparent flu earlier? No doctor came, you know. No one attended to her until the paramedics were called."

His statement had her frowning. "Look, Mr. L'Argeneau, I didn't understand why you're here, but I do now. If you think you can sow the seeds of dissension between me and my new family, you're very much mistaken.

"I'm certain the DeSauviers did as right by Arabella as she did them. I'm terribly sorry for your loss, and I'm even sorrier still at Arabella's passing. However, that doesn't give you the right to barge into Philippe's sick room and start throwing allegations around."

With each word that passed from her lips, her back grew straighter and her neck lengthened. It was bizarre, but she felt stronger. More confident and assured as she made the statement. By way of contrast, L'Argeneau's eyes grew smaller until he looked like he was squinting at her with rage. Well, that is if the man was capable of feeling rage. He just looked all the more beady-eyed and suspicious.

"You're a fool if you don't think to question what happened to my daughter."

"I'm quite happy being a fool," she retorted.

"You honestly don't think it's bizarre that a young woman could die of a bloody cold?"

"The flu is hardly a cold. It can develop into pneumonia, I think. I'm no doctor. But I know people die of freak circumstances all the time."

"You've hit the nail on the head—freak circumstances. That's definitely what happened to Arabella." He peered around the room, then sniffed. "If these walls could talk..." He shot her a look, bowed his head. "Your Highness."

Though nerves suddenly befell her, she stayed strong and tall until he'd left the damn room. Then, the minute he'd gone, she sank in on herself. Her hands fell to her knees as she propped herself upright, and she took in a deep, sharp breath.

She wasn't sure why she felt like she'd just engaged in a battle of words, but she'd survived the first round.

That had to mean something, didn't it?

Her hands were shaking by the time she approached Philippe once more, and considering she didn't want to add to her father-in-law's woes by slitting his throat accidentally, she wiped off the residual shaving foam, leaving him half-stubbled.

Despite herself and the nerves she still felt, she had to smile at the sight. Better for him to look like half a rake than to be cut to shreds because her fingers weren't steady.

Perry moved over to the door, her intent to leave. But she began to tremble harder. Pressing her back to the wall, she pulled in a deep breath and finally allowed herself to think about what had just happened.

Philippe and Marianne were gone now. Philippe, she hoped, only momentarily, but there was certainly no asking Marianne if Ferdinand L'Argeneau was correct. And her men were up to their necks in court matters. She knew, and was irked by, the fact they were keeping her out of the loop, but the truth was, after the shooting, she needed a small respite.

The entire situation had shaken her.

She wasn't the meekest of women, even though she was more comfortable in a lab than surrounded by people. But being with George, Xavier, and Edward...it was hard for their confidence, in themselves and in her, not to grow on Perry, too. By diffusion. They seemed to think she could do anything she put her mind to, and with that kind of support at her back, and from three such wonderful men, it was hard not to start believing her own press.

But that was before the sniper attack.

She'd dealt with the wedding, handled news of Marianne's assassination, and barely coped with becoming queen within the space of a handful of weeks from being a commoner. It was, however, starting to catch up with her.

Her nerves were shot.

Figuratively and almost literally.

This was all too much.

She'd married Edward so that she could have her cake and eat it too. Perry wanted to be with her men. Wanted it with a fire that would never die, and yet, she hadn't expected this. She just... *hadn't*.

Who would?

They were close to two decades into the new millennium. Things like this didn't happen, did they? Rulers and presidents weren't shot at like there was a civil war going down. And yet, Marianne had died. Philippe was bare feet away from her in a coma. It *had* happened. And it was happening again, thanks to some stupid rebels who were intent on meddling in business that was of no concern to them.

She raised a shaky hand and rubbed at her forehead. Feeling the beginnings of a headache start to gather, she shot Philippe a final glance, then headed out of the bedroom. Almost immediately, she ran into Xavier.

"Xavier!" Perry felt the tension drain from her at the sight of him. The way she'd barged into him, she'd raised her hands to prevent them from colliding. Now, with her hands on him, she took full advantage of that. Spreading her fingers on his lean, taut belly, she stared up into his warm, gray-green eyes.

"I was looking for you," he said cheerfully, but the smile in his eyes flickered and died as he looked at the door behind her. "How is he?"

"The same," she murmured, answering how she always did because there was never any change.

Philippe's heart carried on pumping, his hair kept on growing, but nothing else ever seemed to differ. Not that the guys knew she was tending to Philippe's grooming—it was perfectly natural to her, but she had the feeling it would be distinctly odd for them.

Better to keep her mouth shut, she figured, because she wasn't about to stop. Philippe was her father by marriage... that meant a lot to her.

She licked her lips, feeling the dryness of her mouth, and whispered, "Come with me?"

Xavier frowned a little but nodded. At his affirmation, she reached behind her and fiddled with the doorknob. As the door swung open behind her, she took a step into the sickroom once more, relieved when he followed her. Closing the room off again when he was inside, she immediately dove into his arms, wrapping hers tightly about his waist, and pressing her face into his chest to hide her expression from him.

God, this was what she'd needed.

Just a hug. A simple hug from one of the men who loved her and thought the sun rose and set on her.

Of course, once she was in his arms, she never wanted to leave.

"What's wrong?"

"Nothing," she whispered immediately.

"I don't believe you." He reached between them, and with his thumb, nudged her chin up and away from where she'd tucked her face into his chest. "What's going on?"

She shook her head. "Nothing. I always miss you when we're apart." It wasn't as sappy as it sounded. Unless the four of them were together, she had to maintain a strict and appropriate distance from George and Xavier.

That distance was like torture, and each day, it grew worse, because each day, her love for them grew stronger.

She reached up on tiptoe, and slanted her mouth over his. When his tongue pierced her mouth with an immediacy that had lust roaring through her, she whimpered. The sound, in the silent room, was overloud. Aside from the beeping and whooshing machines that were supporting Philippe, the faint noise she'd made had seemed like a gunshot blast in the stillness.

Jerking back, she licked her lips and stared deeply into his eyes.

"Come with me," he whispered, his jaw clenching tightly as he scanned the room.

She had to hide a smile. It was almost like he was looking for an escape, a secret door that would lead them directly to her bedroom. Instead, there was only the interconnecting door to the Queen's Suite.

Perry almost pulled her hand from his when she realized his intent. "I can't. Not in there."

But he shook his head, and tugged her along in his wake.

This was totally inappropriate.

Totally.

Still, she didn't lag behind, and instead, peered around the Queen's Suite. It was weird to think this had been Marianne's home for so long, especially when she saw the main bedchamber.

"Why's everything covered in white cloths?" She scowled, annoyed that all the furniture was hidden.

"Because it's tradition," Xavier told her, his voice less hushed now.

"It is? Why?"

"Edward's heir, when he ascends to the throne, will stay in these apartments. The sovereigns switch between wings every generation."

"I thought Edward was being spontaneous and trying to give us privacy," she grumbled, disappointed that wasn't the case. Although, she wasn't too disappointed with her new suite.

It was fresh and modern. Well, as modern as it could be with a three-hundred-year-old bed and light fittings that had been there since they'd replaced candlelight.

"He was. You couldn't have moved into those apartments until he'd been crowned, and he started the decorating process way back when you were still planning the wedding."

"Philippe and Marianne didn't mind making the place more modern?" she asked, curiously peering around him when he led them to another door.

"I'm sure they did. Marianne could be a stickler for tradition, but they probably understood that your marriage had to be treated differently than his with Arabella, for fear it could end the same way."

Considering what Ferdinand L'Argeneau had just told her, this made her ears prick to attention. "Oh? How?"

"They were estranged, for the most part. Leading separate lives by the end. You know how private Edward is about certain matters, Perry," Xavier told her as he guided her into a room that looked like an office.

It had gentlemanly overtones, and she had to presume it was Philippe's study. This, too, was filled with drafty white sheets that added a spooky air to the atmosphere. It didn't help that they'd done all this while Philippe was still living and breathing.

It gave her the damn creeps, if she were being honest.

"Who sanctioned all this?" she demanded. "It's a bit weird, isn't it? It's like burying him before he's dead."

"We don't know when Philippe will wake up, or if he even will. There's little point in keeping these rooms open...these items have to be protected. Preserved."

"And a white sheet will protect them?" she asked, her tone laced with scorn.

"Better that than getting sun damage," he pointed out. "These are period pieces. Measures like over-polishing them instead of covering them up can ruin the patina of some of the inlays. Not only that, why waste the cleaning staff on apartments that aren't even used?"

That did make sense, she guessed. "Xavier, who did sanction it?"

"Murielle Harlington, I'd imagine."

She scowled. "Murielle?"

Xavier snorted. "Another Guardian on your hit list?"

She'd already made her dissatisfaction about Marianne's Guardians, as well as Rose, the Dragon, known to her men. Still, she demanded, "Why didn't she consult with me over it?"

"Because their position gives them power. The whole point of them is to deal with the things that are too unimportant for you to handle."

She pursed her lips. "I'm not sure I like the sound of that."

"Why? Feel like micromanaging life here at Masonbrook?" he asked, cocking a brow at her.

Perry tugged her hand from his, and stacking both of hers on her hips, grumbled, "I just would like to be kept in the loop."

"Take it up with them then. I'm sure Cassie would have asked if you wanted the rooms closing up, because she's still learning the position," he stated, but his attention wasn't on her. Instead, he was staring at a piece of furniture that he'd tugged the sheet from.

"What are you looking at?" she asked, wondering what was so fascinating on the bookshelves.

She'd thought they'd be heading off for some naughty nookie. Sure, she loved reading as much as the next girl, but when it came down to reading about good sex or having it, she'd take the latter over the former any day of the week.

Her sex drive had been well and truly engaged over the last few months, and Perry knew that was the difference the love of a good man, or in her case, men, could instill.

She'd had several crappy lovers over the years, and having sex with them had been a chore. With her three? *They* were the ones who had to put limits on it.

Since they'd been crowned, Edward hadn't touched her. George and Xavier had. They usually sneaked away for quickies that had blown her brain, while also making her wonder why Edward wasn't doing the same. Well, not *wonder*. She knew why, but she didn't have to like it.

Too much work would make him a dull boy.

"I'm looking for the book."

"*The* book?" she questioned, staring up at the shelves with a frown. Not *a* book? What was he looking for? "Why? Are you going to whisper sweet nothings into my ear?"

He shot her a look. "Anything I'm about to say into that ear of yours won't be sweet, and it won't be whispered."

She perked up—so, they were still on the same page. "Can I help with the book?"

Xavier snorted. "Just shut up and let me concentrate."

Figuring that was fair dos, she watched him continue to scan the shelves, then he made an *a-ha* noise, tilted a book, and then, nothing.

He scowled, but it cleared when a creaking, shifting noise pierced the atmosphere. She jolted in place, then let out an amazed cry when a doorway in the paneling opened up beside the bookcase. "Oh my God! There's a secret panel outta here? That's too fucking cool! Are there more?"

Xavier's head fell back as he laughed at her swiftly uttered questions. "There are more, and I will show you them another time. Just not now."

The heavy lids of his eyes, so slumberous and languid, offered a promise that had her biting her lip.

"Trust me?"

She frowned. "Why do I need to trust you?"

"Because I highly doubt Philippe kept the passageway dusted."

"Nobody knows about it?"

"Nobody save for Edward, George, me, you, Drake, and Philippe."

"Is it so we can escape if we're trapped here?"

He nodded. "Yes. The two wings we live in today were modernized back in the late eighteenth century. We had UnReal activity back then, and they were far more likely to have come at the family with pitchforks and shovels and the like."

"They thought you were Dracula?" she demanded disbelievingly.

"They were farmers," he corrected, tone amused. "Not vampire hunters."

"It leads to a safe room?"

"No. This particular one leads to your old bedroom."

"The Tulip Room?" she blurted out.

"At the time, it's where one of the kings kept his mistress."

Her mouth dropped open. "You mean, the king kept his mistress so close to his queen?"

Xavier's nose wrinkled. "You're judging my ancestor. My very dead, very ancient ancestor who lived in another era."

"Too damn right I am!"

"Don't forget, this was the time of child royal brides, Perry," Xavier said, grabbing her hand as they approached the doorway which had appeared from nowhere—this shit was just too cool. "I think the king, at the time, had a mistress of twenty years old, and a wife of eight. It was a political match."

"That's disgusting," she said on a grouch as she ducked her head. The passageway was really fucking dark and it stank. Of cat wee? What the fuck.

"It speaks of royal marriages of that particular period. They didn't consummate the relationship," he assured her. "Not until the queen was fifteen."

"Because that's not gross either."

"You Americans," Xavier chided. "You seem to think no one has sex before they're eighteen, but everyone's doing it."

"I didn't," she grumbled, then walked into him in the pitch black.

"You waited until you were eighteen to have sex?" He sounded totally disbelieving—she wasn't sure whether to preen or scowl.

"Not intentionally. No one would have sex with me until I was eighteen," she corrected.

"That can't be."

"I had a lot of puppy weight back then."

"I refuse to believe you weren't gorgeous."

His insistence was cute, but it didn't stop her from sniffing. "When we go back home for a visit, remind me to show you all my photos of when I was a teenager. Prom was a disaster. It's no wonder I'm always terrified of falling over."

He gripped her tighter about the waist. "There are three steps here."

"You've got a good memory."

"Misspent childhood. Edward and I used to play in here a lot."

She blinked, then when the blackness didn't fade, she wasn't sure if she'd opened her eyes again or not—that was how damn dark it was. "That sounds boring."

"Being related to a king isn't fun. I thought you'd have figured that out by now."

A snort escaped her. "You've got me there. Not like I can argue with that!"

He laughed. "Didn't think you would. And don't worry, there will come a day when I fully expect to see your embarrassing baby photos."

"Huh. Only if that works both ways."

"I'll have you know I took only the most beautiful of baby photos," he joked, then murmured, "Ah, I think we're here."

It was so dark, she didn't have a damn clue *how* he figured out they were close to their destination. Then, she squinted and saw the faintest of lights that ran around a door shape.

"How do we get out?"

They'd traveled so far that when she turned back to look at the entrance to the passageway, she couldn't damn well find it. She really hoped it was still open—the last thing she needed was to get stuck in the walls of Masonbrook.

Even if Xavier was at her side.

Before she could start to freak, she heard a grating sound, and the hinges on the secret door popped open.

Her eyes watered a little as the shadows and light merged. Her vision tried to adjust, and she rubbed her eyes as they stepped out into the Tulip Room. She smiled at the old room, then grimaced when she realized that this, too, was covered in damn dustsheets.

She heaved out a breath. "This is really aggravating."

"How am I only just figuring out that you're a control freak?"

"I'm not a control freak." She squinted up at him then glowered at his overpowering height. "And stop being so tall," she groused.

"I'll just lop off a few inches the next time I go to the doctor's," he mocked, but he complied by taking a seat on the side of the bed. "Better?"

She made a grumbling sound. "I guess." Then, she prodded him on the shoulder as she stepped closer to him. "I'm not a control freak."

"If you weren't, we've made you into one. You definitely like to know what's going on around you."

"Who doesn't?" she demanded. "This is my home, ya know?"

"I don't think you'd have cared before you got married," he said, his tone musing. "I guess that's probably the side effect of what's happened—Marianne, you... It's okay, Perry. We can accommodate for a while."

"Only a while?" She pulled a face. "Anyway, there's nothing to accommodate. I'm. Not. A. Control. Freak."

"Tell that to someone who believes you."

"Well, you were about to get lucky. But not anymore."

He laughed, then grabbed her around the waist and hauled her close. "Where do you think you're going?"

"Nowhere, by the sounds of it," she retorted, settling into his arms with a sigh. Before he could say another word, ruin her mood, and make her want to hit him rather than fuck him, she planted her mouth on his.

He immediately slanted his head and dove right into the kiss. She moaned against his lips, loving the immediacy of his response. Hell, she even loved that he could tease her out of her funk. Could tease her from her uncertainty, her concerns...

God, she just loved everything about this man.

She pulled back slightly and bit down on his bottom lip, the urge to tell him was as hot a fire in her blood as the arousal he stirred in her. "I love you, Xavier."

He reached up and cupped her cheek. "I love you too, Perry." Rubbing his nose against hers, he whispered, "Even if you're turning into a dominatrix on me."

Despite herself, Perry chuckled. "Don't tell me you're into leather and whips, too?"

"Only if you're wearing them," he replied with a wink.

Her laughter deepened, and then it was swallowed whole as he kissed her again. His tongue foraging deep in her mouth, taking her breath and reminding her who she belonged to. He sampled her, tasted her. Tried everything she had to give, and she fell deeper into the kiss. Deeper into him.

He made her feel like there was an endless amount of time in the world just for this. No pressure for more, no stress. Just the freedom to kiss him, to be in his arms, to have him love her with his mouth.

She moaned, her thoughts working against her as much as his kiss was rocking her world.

With a whimper, she cupped his face and retreated with a heavy breath. "I need you."

His sigh was redolent with pleasure. "I need you too."

Biting her lip, she reached between them and grabbed the hem of her shirt. Pulling it overhead, she had to smile when he growled at the sight of her braless tits. His hands immediately came up to cup them, and she both winced at and reveled in his touch.

"Don't think I've ever seen you without a bra. Not outside of the bedroom, I mean," he murmured, his tone husky, the voice unlike his.

"It's like knowing I'm pregnant has changed everything," she said on a sigh. "They're really sensitive."

"Oh, God. I love knowing that."

She gulped when he cupped them together, then pressed his mouth to one exquisitely tender tip. His lips and tongue palpated the nub, not stopping until her nails were digging deeply into his scalp.

Letting out a shrill cry as the most bewildering sensations roared through her blood, she hoarsely spat, "Oh my God!"

His laughter was triumphant, damn him. He carried on. The vibrations of the laughter, his tongue so moist and wet, was doing things to her breasts that she'd never even known were possible.

How was he making her feel this…?

This…

This fucking amazing?!

She gulped and bit back a sharp scream as he sucked down hard, and like that, she unraveled. "Holy fuck!" she cried out, and the endless wail that escaped her lips came to an abrupt end when his hand came up to clamp over her mouth. She carried on though, moaning and mewling beneath his fingers as he continued tormenting her, until her eyes pricked with tears, until she had to push him away to dislodge his mouth from her tits.

"No more, no more!" she whimpered, her eyes dazed, her blood hot, and her body so overwrought, she felt like she'd been electrocuted.

"I didn't even know that was possible," he said, his voice a low growl, his eyes on her bright red breasts. Her nipples looked like they were pulsing in response, and she whimpered at the fiery heat in his eyes. "Lift up your skirt," he commanded, and the order within those words was so regal, she couldn't stop herself from obeying.

Tugging up the silky fabric, she lodged it about her hips. He levered off the bed, then pulled her into his arms. Doing a two-step so that she was now against the bed and he was in front of her, she let him position her. Bending over at the waist, she pressed her elbows into the sheets and had a flashback to that first time they'd had together.

In this very room.

The very first night she'd been in Veronia.

God, had that been so long ago? And yet, so recent?

Her whole life had changed since then.

Feeling faintly overwhelmed, she pressed her forehead into the dustsheet and let him rearrange her as he wanted, his chest to her back. She whimpered at the sound of his fly opening, and whimpered again when, with very few preliminary moves, he pressed his cock to her sopping wet pussy and pushed in deep.

She gave a keening cry in response to his hardness thrusting into her. With a deep moan, she clenched the sheet in her teeth and bore down on it, finding a strange comfort in the pressure of the fabric against her tongue, its taste in her mouth. In some bizarre way, it grounded her, and God, she needed that.

His cock was so hot and hard inside her that she felt sure she'd come again the minute he moved. His hands were tight about her hips, the tips of his fingers digging deeply into the tender flesh there. One of his feet kicked at hers gently, and she widened her stance.

Like that was the passkey, he began to retreat, and the minute he did, the nerve endings he'd brought to life with his mouth on her nipples and his cock inside her raged to life.

She clamped down harder on the fabric in her mouth, needing it so she could stay quiet, needing it so she could maintain some semblance of control. But with each thrust of his cock into her cunt, each thick inch that filled her and rammed its way home, she was jerked against the bed, and her nipples were dragged along with it.

Each thrust triggered a bewildering agony that was the epitome of pleasure pain. She'd never known the like and wasn't sure she wanted to ever again.

With each drag of the cotton against her chest, she wanted to scream. Eventually, she did. Her eyes pricked with tears, and sobs escaped her as his lovemaking took her to a fever pitch. Took her so damn high, to a lofty altitude she'd never traversed.

He seemed to sense that, seemed to sense how out of control she was, because he bent over her, and she felt the press of his chilly buttons drag against her spine. Shuddering in response to his every move, each one seemingly born out of the need to drive her wild, she cried out when his teeth came to bear down on her shoulder.

And like that, she was a goner.

There was no coming back from it. No escaping what he made her feel.

It roared through her blood like the ocean slamming into the shore. It wore at her reserves, blasted her nerves, and overwhelmed her senses until she wasn't sure where she ended and he began.

Which was exactly how she wanted it. She never wanted that to change.

She was his, and he was hers.

That was how it should be.

As climax slammed through her like a ball hitting a home run, she felt rather than heard his groan. It was absorbed by her shoulder as he let it out in a long, deep exhale. His thrusts grew jerky as he, too, began to climax, and then deep inside her, she felt the slick, wet heat of his semen and finally knew peace.

CHAPTER TEN

"EDWARD?"

Blinking at the voice on the other end of the line, Edward murmured, "Hello, stranger. Long time no hear."

"Who are you? My bloody mother?" Marcus Whitings' tone was biting, but it stirred amusement nonetheless. "Only she whines about my not calling her."

"Jesus, I'd never want to be that battle-ax. Helena might have a face to start a war, but she has the personal arsenal to fight it, too."

Marcus snorted, but didn't argue. His mother had been one of the country's most well-renowned beauties in her heyday, but she was hardcore lethal with a shotgun in her hand. Edward didn't approve of hunting, but in his parents' day, it had been par for the course. Helena held the title for bagging the most birds on a shoot at Grosvenor House, of all places.

Helena was also famous for having a collection of old shotguns that would make the experts on the *Antiques Roadshow* drool if they could catch a glimpse of it.

When Marcus didn't say anything else, Edward frowned a little at the report in his hand. It told him that Drake had been too late to trap the sniper—but Veronia's security services had been inches away from catching the bastard before he boarded a private jet with a false flight plan to Geneva.

Perry had argued in Drake's favor, and Edward, because Drake had always done his duty by the family since the start of his career, had been lenient. And because Edward knew Drake's love for his mother was deeper than anyone else knew, he was sure that Drake might be ineffective at the moment, but he wasn't a traitor.

With one somewhere in their midst, that was pretty bloody important, but the head of security was running out of chances, as well as defenses.

His mouth tightened, and he realized he was stuck on the phone with Marcus who hadn't spoken a damn word since the beginning of their conversation. "Sorry, Marcus. I'm a little preoccupied at the moment. Is something wrong?" he asked, knowing he'd meant to call his old friend and had, in fact, forgotten to do so.

"I just wanted to check in."

"Check in about what?"

"Your wife almost got shot, Edward. I wanted to make sure you were doing okay." For a second, he wondered if Marcus was unaware that Cassie had been at the shooting, too, in her new capacity as Guardian of the Keys... then Marcus murmured, "Cassie said it was a close thing."

"I don't want to think about how close," he admitted. "We already lost a guard."

"I heard. When's the funeral?"

"Next week."

"Why the delay?"

"Protocol."

Marcus exhaled, and the sound whistled down the line. "God, I forgot how much a part of life that was back there. Not until Cassie called the other night and was all protocol-this, and protocol-that. I don't know how you stand it."

Tension in Edward's shoulders made him wriggle them. "I don't always. It drives Perry crazy." He cleared his throat. "What's wrong, Marcus? Do you want to know how Cassie is faring as Guardian of the Keys? We've trebled Perry's security, and as the two of them are now bosom pals, that means they're *both* complaining about tripping over all their new guards. She should be safe. What happened the other day should never have..." He bit off a curse. "I'm sorry Cassie was in that situation."

A gruff laugh echoed. "You think I'm not sorry your wife was in that situation, too? More than that, that my queen was in danger?"

"Nothing you can do." For that matter, there was nothing Edward could do either. That was tearing at his mind. Ripping his self-worth to shreds. What kind of man couldn't protect his woman?

No good kind of man, that's who.

He reached up and ran a hand through his hair. Agitation made the motion jerky, and Edward, at that second, craved a few fingers of whiskey more than he wanted his next breath. But he, George, and Xavier were all drinking too much at the moment. The last thing they needed was for any of them to become alcoholics.

He rolled his eyes at the thought, but it hit too close to home. He could almost taste the damn whiskey, and the burn as it went down? Jesus, it would be heaven-sent at that moment.

"Did Cassie tell you about what's happened recently?" Marcus asked.

"She told Perry."

Marcus blew out a breath. "Always the way. Women, when they get together, they don't stop talking."

Edward snorted. "Like that comes as a surprise. When don't they talk?" He grabbed a pen and began to doodle on the report in front of him. "How are you doing, Marcus? Don't bullshit me either. You've had a heart attack, and you didn't tell any of us."

"It was a minor heart attack."

"I think when they classify it that way, they're not diminishing the fact you've had a heart attack, Marcus. They're just saying the damage wasn't as atrocious as it could have been."

Silence fell. "Don't start."

That the words were gritted out between his friend's teeth told Edward he'd hit a nerve. His lips curved into a cheerful smile. "The truth hurts, doesn't it?"

"Why do you think I didn't tell you, Ed? Jesus, I have things I need to be doing. I don't have time to be ill."

For a second, Marcus's arrogance flabbergasted him. Then, he just shook his head. "Usually, the human body gives in when someone has reached the end of their limits. Apparently, that's you. You're a fool, Marcus. I love you like a brother, even if we haven't been as close of late, but you're a twenty-four-carat chump. You've a wife who loves you, and you've children, man. Those kids need you."

"They need their family's pride restored too, Edward," Marcus bit off. "Dammit, I won't have them endure what I did. There's just this one last deal I have to close, and when that's done, I'll come home."

"And what if your heart gives out before then?"

Marcus sighed. "It won't. I've been sleeping more, drinking less, and eating better. I was stupid before. I didn't take care of myself. What happened was a reminder that I'm not a robot. That I need to rest as much as the next man."

"How much is the next deal for?"

"Four million. That includes the bonus the bank will give me for spearheading it."

Edward whistled. "That will go a long way to padding out the coffers, although if memory serves, Cassie inherited eight mil..."

"That's her money," Marcus said stiffly. "With careful investment, I can double the four million and maybe buy back the family manor."

"I know how much the place meant to you, Marcus, but don't get it back at the expense of your family. Your kids are over here, and they're miserable. Cassie isn't happy either, although from what Perry's told me, she likes her new position." Even if it was damn dangerous. "Why aren't you here with them?"

"I will be. Soon."

"Soon isn't near enough. You think this deal is the last one, but it won't be. You're not going to slow down until you've filled the family coffers again, but that onus doesn't rest squarely on you." Marcus's family had lost everything in the last recession, which meant he was close to killing himself in an effort to restore their wealth.

"I'm the marquise—of course, it does. I don't want Sebastien being left nothing but an empty title. The bastards that bought Jurise Manor won't have it for long. You know what those rock stars are like. They buy those places because they want to live out in the country. Then, they get bored when they've dried out from their last rehab stint, and take off for pastures new. I could buy it back, raise my children where they should always have been raised."

Blowing out a breath, Edward murmured, "I can't say that I don't understand, Marc. I do. Too well." He didn't say that he knew Marcus's pride had been hurt. That would cut too close to the bone, but neither of them had to say it to know it was something they were both going through. "I-I just know you. You'll earn the four million, but it won't be enough. You're running scared, and your heart's already given up the goat once."

"I'm not running scared," Marcus immediately scoffed.

"Aren't you? Sounds like it to me. You and Cassie were always the couple who worked best together. What changed that?"

Marcus fell quiet, and Edward wasn't sure if he was going to answer, until... "New York changed that. We grew apart."

"Whose fault's that, then? I know Cassie adores you. You can see it on her face—she's fucking miserable without you. But she's also as stubborn as you. Perry told me she threatened you with a divorce. That tells me how far apart you two have fallen. It's not right, Marcus. It's not. You two were made for each other."

"I know we are," he admitted quietly, gently. The words were almost silent, and whispered on a breath.

"Then what's going on? There are banks here. You know that. They'd take you in a heartbeat."

"Not with the resources of where I'm working."

"When does the deal close?"

"In two weeks."

Surprised, Edward halted his pen's movements. "I didn't realize it was so close."

"Yeah. It's been about eight months in the making."

"Jesus."

"I'm going to make four million on a personal setting, Ed. How much do you think the bank is going to make?" He exhaled roughly. "Even if I wanted to back out now, I couldn't. I'm in too deep."

"You make it sound like you're in with the mob."

"Organized crime comes in many shapes and sizes nowadays," Marcus countered, not exactly reassuring Edward with his words. "Just because a corporation is nice and legit, has the shop front and the polished CEO, doesn't mean they don't have the firepower of Capone."

As he processed that, Edward murmured, "You're not inspiring me with confidence."

"I don't have to," Marcus teased, his voice lighter now. "That's not my job. Look, I don't have to like what I'm doing to want the money it earns."

Edward frowned. "What's it involve, Marcus? You're not in danger, are you?"

"You do realize you run the risk of sounding like an old woman?"

"I don't care. We've barely spoken in the past year, and the first time we do, you're talking about corporations and the mob. What the hell is that about?"

"I shouldn't have said anything."

"No, that's just it. You should have. You obviously need to get it off your chest."

"I don't, Edward. We're not doing anything illegal. I'm not worried about the deal. I'm worried about Cassie."

As he realized Marcus was telling the truth, that his friend's main concerns centered around his wife, Edward let the topic go. "I told you, she's as safe as she can be while fulfilling the role of Guardian of the Keys."

"I'm talking *personally*, Ed." He let out a breath. "She lets the topic drop, then raises it again..."

"What topic?"

"You said it yourself. *Divorce.* She called last night and was talking about it. Said the shooting had made her question things."

"I can believe it. Why wouldn't it? She wasn't harmed, but bullets can and do fly wild."

"God, man, don't make this any harder."

"Why not? Like I told you before, the truth hurts." Edward ceased his doodling. "Look, she's hurting. Whether or not you two have fallen apart over the years, you're better as a duet than a solo act. She's missing you, and her new position at the castle... it's hard work. She's out of the scene, and life at court is never all that easy, is it?"

"Do you think she'll be okay?"

"Until you get your act together?" he snorted. "I know Cassie. She'll be fine, even if she is feeling a bit wobbly at the moment. I don't know how long she'll wait for you though. If I were you, I'd quit the minute that four million is in your bank account."

"I'm two steps ahead of you on that score," Marcus said, his tone mocking. "My letter of resignation is ready to print off as we speak."

"Good. That mean I can expect you back here soon?"

He laughed, sounding a bit lighter-hearted than before. "Yes, that's what it means."

"Don't think I won't act on my threat, by the way."

"Fuck off. I don't want to be your equerry."

"Think how neat it will all be. Cassie as Perry's head lady's maid, you as my right-hand man."

Marcus snorted. "Bullshit. You, Xavier, and George are far too close with each other for me to have a say. I'd prefer to work on my investments."

"If you insist," Edward said wryly. "Don't be a stranger. Let me know how the deal goes on, and let me know when you'll be back in town."

"I will. Thanks, Ed. I've missed you."

"Yeah, same here. I'm sorry. I've been..."

"Distant? Seems like you've been that way for a while. I didn't get that much of a chance to get to know Perry—I barely got the go-ahead on the time off as it is. But from what Cassie says, she's perfect for you. I'm glad, Edward. If anyone deserves a bit of happiness, it's you."

Before he could reply, Marcus cut the line, leaving Edward to scowl down at his scrawls.

A knock sounded at the door and he called out, "Come in."

The footman, ever present, appeared first. "Cassandra Whitings, Your Highness."

"Let her in." Edward stood as Cassie came rushing in—considering his old friend barely sped up past a stroll, this was close to panic. "What is it? What's wrong?"

"Your wife is going to be the death of me."

He reared back at that. "What? Why?"

"She's rescheduled the last four events."

"So?"

"This particular one... dammit to hell! You can't reschedule some of these things. They happen whether the queen attends or not, and her not being there is bad for morale."

"Have you arranged for one of the cousins to attend?"

She nodded, but her mouth turned into a pout. "I have, but everyone knows the only cousin who counts is Xavier."

"Will he go in her stead?"

"He's busy. You have him scheduled in Parliament that day."

"Rearrange that, I'll go to Parliament instead."

Cassie frowned. "It's foolish to arrange everything around Perry."

"I'd assume there's a reason she wants to cancel? It's not just a whim, surely?"

"I don't know. She's been...odd of late."

"In what way?" In the eight days since the shooting, he'd admit to not having paid as much attention as he ought to have done—especially considering the vow he'd made to himself on that panicked drive over to the hospital. Guilt whipped through him, and he rubbed the back of his neck as he slumped down in his seat. "I should know. I shouldn't have to ask."

"You're busy."

There was no recrimination in Cassie's tone, and somehow, that irked him all the more. It didn't matter if he was busy. Nothing mattered more than his wife and the child she was carrying, because if she *didn't* matter, what the hell was he doing all this for?

For a second, he empathized with Marcus. These things... this *life*, it was only endurable if he thought about who he was passing it down to.

Their children.

His throat closed at that, and he bit off, "I shouldn't be too busy to talk to her."

Cassie had grown up at court, and she knew the score. But Perry hadn't and would never understand. *Couldn't* understand how state matters would always intrude on their lives.

But the trouble was, this was more than just a state matter—this was their personal safety at risk. He'd had so many sleepless nights where he'd decided that he was better off working than tossing and turning in bed. Where he'd tried to work, to figure out what the fuck was going on with the UnReals, all in an effort to keep her safe.

She wasn't to know that though, was she?

She wasn't to understand that he was doing this for her and their child, rather than just out of neglect or a lack of care.

"What's happening with Perry, Cassie?" he asked, his voice husky with regret—how he hated having to ask a friend about the state of his wife's current temperament.

"She's flailing."

Those two words had him rearing back again. "Pardon?"

"And when I say nervous, I mean it. I thought she'd be scared, but she's just anxious. Understandable, naturally." Cassie sighed, and the hands she'd stacked on her hips moved toward the chair in front of his desk. She gripped the back of the leather tubular seat, and her fingers turned white. "The shooting, it's put the fear of God into her. Hardly a surprise, but she dealt with it so well at the start that..." Another sigh fell from her. "I think we took it for granted. She just seemed to carry on with things, stalwart as ever. Now, she's just—"

"Changed?"

Cassie nodded. "I don't think she wants to leave the palace."

He dragged his fingers over his forehead. "Understandable. The one place we've proven we can keep her safe is here."

"That doesn't help with the program. Her visiting schedule is jam-packed. We've got too much on for her to be—"

"She's pregnant, Cassie."

His old friend's mouth stopped in its tracks. "What?"

He nodded, his gaze catching hers as the seriousness of the situation settled between them. "About nine weeks now."

"Jesus Christ," Cassie breathed. Her hands tightened on the leather back of the seat. "No wonder she's so volatile at the moment. I got to know her when she was getting ready for the wedding, a stressful endeavor in itself, and she was fine then. Not like this. Now? She's like the wind. Happy one moment, sad another. More than that, she's on edge, and Ed, that isn't good for her or the baby."

"I know. That's why I've been working so hard. Xavier and George, too. We're trying to understand what the hell's happening."

"No clues?"

"Drake's digging, but he's coming up with fresh air. It's not his fault. He's only passing on the information the security services are finding, and he's getting the brunt of the blame." Edward bowed his head and stared at the report in front of him. "We're pissing in the breeze and trying not to get caught in the backsplash."

She wrinkled her nose. "Lovely image."

He let out a soft laugh. "I paint the nicest pictures."

Rolling her eyes, Cassie murmured, "When are you making the announcement?" Then, before he could answer, she winced. "Dammit. You can't. If you do, she'll be under more of a threat."

"She's priceless as it stands—what would she be if they knew she was carrying the next heir?" Edward confirmed. He rubbed his jaw. "Be lenient with her, Cassie. Things are hard right now."

"I know that, Ed, but Jesus, you have to spend more time with her. George and Xavier seem to be taking up the load on your behalf, but that's not enough. She needs more than just friends and family around her. She needs her husband."

He tried not to flinch at the reproach in her voice. "I know. I'll try."

"No, dammit. Do more than try. God, what is it with you men? You seem to think everything is more important than the women you promise to love and cherish until death do you part." She grimaced. "You almost experienced the 'death' part, Edward. Don't let her slip through your fingers, because you're a fool if you do. Perry's exactly what you need, and if you don't see that, then you're an idiot."

"I know," he confirmed. "I'm an idiot. But I need her to be safe."

"Of course, you do. Everyone wants that for her, for us all, but you're not going to help by locking yourself in here, Edward. It's not like you can join the ranks and filter out who's behind this. You have to leave it to the people who are paid for that particular job. What are you even doing now?" She pointed at the report he'd drawn and scribbled on. "Pushing papers. What use is that?"

"Intelligence reports matter, Cassie," he argued, and wondered just how thin the ice she was treading on was. She was only getting away with speaking to him this way because they were the oldest of friends; he knew this was coming from the heart and her blossoming friendship with Perry. "If I can discern something within these papers, it could be the difference between life and death."

She shook her head but mumbled, "If you say so. Look, whatever you do, you need to speak with your wife. Something's going on in her head, and she either has to talk to you about it, or a shrink, or *somebody*. We need her to be on the ball. You know that. Public opinion is totally in our favor at the moment, but we need to keep it that way, especially if Xavier's right and you're thinking about invoking Article 42."

He scowled. "He should never have talked about that with you."

"Perry asked him what it was, and he explained. She'd overheard you discussing it with the troublesome two. Not that she wanted to ask Tweedle Dum and Dee. She saved that for me." Cassie shrugged. "But you know that what I overhear won't go any further."

"I don't want to invoke the Article," he said.

"No, but it won't stop you from doing so if things continue to deteriorate, will it?"

For a second, he was quiet, processing her words and trying to figure out how things had turned so swiftly into chaos. He blew out a deep breath and murmured, "I understand what you're saying, Cassie, and I'll take your words into consideration."

She stared at him a second, apparently hearing the dismissal in his words, but she didn't comment on it. Just sighed. "Okay. You have it your way."

Cassie skipped out before he even had the chance to tell her Marcus had called, but maybe that was for the best. He wasn't entirely sure why his old friend had called anyway. Passing the information on wouldn't do anyone any good.

He rocked back in his seat and stared at the door as the footman closed it behind Cassie.

She was right, even if he didn't want to admit it. He wasn't much use, more of a hindrance when it came down to pestering Drake for information... but he couldn't stop himself from micromanaging.

He'd almost lost Perry that day, and he wouldn't, *couldn't* lose her.

He'd die first.

CHAPTER ELEVEN

"WHAT ARE YOU DOING?"

Perry froze in her tracks, her hand raised to knock on Drake's door, when she swung around and glowered at him. "George, are you following me?"

He snorted. "Yes, Perry. I have nothing better to do than track your movements when you have a dozen guards at your back." He nodded at the three who had traipsed after her down the long, grim corridor that led to Drake's office in the basement of the palace.

She half-turned and sighed at the sight of the trio. "I suppose," she grumbled.

"No supposing about it. It's the truth. Anyway, what are you doing here?"

"I want to speak to Drake."

"About what?"

"Never you mind." She squinted at him, then defiantly turned her nose in the air at him and knocked on Drake's door.

When their head of security yelled, "Come in," Perry shot him a tight smile.

"I can handle it from here, George."

She opened the door, but before she could shut it, he barged in after her. He had no intention of stopping her from speaking with the guard, but he wanted to know what she had to say.

She propped her hands on her hips, and the movement reminded him of two things. One, that her hands framed the belly where their child lay. Two, the position of her fingers created a V that led to the area he'd devoured last night.

His cock stirred as he thought back to how she'd climaxed under his touch, and he felt his mouth water with the need to taste her. Perry was being weird of late. He wasn't the only one to notice it. Xavier had too, and if Edward wasn't being such a prat about working crazy hours, he'd have seen it as well.

"What are you doing in here, George? I don't need your help to speak with Giles." She cast a gimlet glance around the office. "Even if the last time I was here, he tried to help your mother and father rob me of future custody rights."

Though Giles Drake winced, he rocked back in his seat in surprise. For the first time, George really looked at the man and saw what Perry had discerned a week ago. Drake *was* depressed. His hair, always neat and tidy, was long and strangely fluffy about his ears—almost as though the locks, so accustomed to being shorn, were rebelling. There were fine lines about his eyes, a fatigue that came from within that was very much evident.

Drake's usual pristine shirt was creased, and the tie was unknotted and tugged down to his chest. His jacket was slung over one of the chairs he had for visitors, not suspended by the door on one of the hangers there for that purpose.

The sight of him had George frowning, but not for long—Perry began prodding him in the chest. "I. Don't. Need. Your. Help. George," she repeated, punctuating each word.

"I know you don't," he answered mildly. "Doesn't mean to say I'm not going to give it though, does it?"

Her nostrils flared in exasperation. "Fine. But, if you don't like what you hear, then don't bitch at me about it. You know where the door is."

Curiosity fired, George cut their head of security a look and noticed that Drake was as taken aback as he was.

"Your Highness?" Drake inserted. "Have I missed a meeting?"

"No. Something's been eating at me for a little while and..." She pursed her lips. "I wanted to clarify some things with you."

"Like what?" George asked, then winced when she spun around to glower at him.

"Shut up, George. If you have to be here, then you can be quiet." His lips curved in a smile at her bossiness, but she ignored him and carried on, "I spoke to someone recently who, well, to be frank, put doubts into my head."

"Doubts, Your Majesty?" Drake asked, cautiously wading through her words like he was stepping through a minefield—smart man. Perry, in this mood, could be like dynamite. "What kind of doubts?"

"He indicated that Arabella didn't die of natural causes."

Whatever George had expected Perry to say, it hadn't been that. And Drake was just as astonished, because his mouth dropped open in the best impression of a goldfish George had ever seen.

"What's she supposed to have died of if not the flu?" Drake questioned, sounding more like himself.

"Well, I don't know. But from what this person was saying..."

"*Who* said this?" George demanded, and he grabbed her arm to jerk her attention his way. "Who, Perry?"

She narrowed her eyes at him. "I told you, you wouldn't like what I had to say."

"Tell me."

"No."

He gritted his teeth. "Why are you protecting them?"

"I'm not protecting them, I just don't want to cause mischief. I think the man's loopy, but I wanted to talk about why he'd believe such a thing."

"Was it her father?" George asked, and when her eyes flared, he knew he was right. "When did you speak to L'Argeneau?"

"I didn't want to cause any trouble."

"No, but apparently he did."

Drake rubbed his chin. "This is highly unusual. I've never heard him imply that something untoward happened to the last crown princess. Why would he?"

"I don't know. That's what I'm asking you."

"You don't honestly think we had something to do with her death, do you, Perry?" George insisted, his grip on her arm tightening.

She jerked it free. "You're hurting me, George. And no, of course not. But I wanted to understand where he was coming from."

"Why?"

"Because the way he told me...it was odd." She wriggled her shoulders, making the simple black sheath dress dance over her form in a way that highlighted her gentle curves.

She'd been riper back in Boston, even without being pregnant. Had, in fact, lost weight since she'd come to Veronia—a detail he wasn't happy about, but couldn't do all that much to resolve.

After all, being shot at and suddenly being thrust into the limelight wasn't great for anyone's appetite, was it?

George could hardly fail to understand why Perry might have been eating less.

"How did he tell you?"

"He sneaked into your father's room—"

"What were you doing in there?"

She flushed and lowered her gaze. "I was shaving him."

He gaped at her. "You were shaving him?"

"Yes. He was getting a beard. It looked weird, and where I'm from, you do things like that for family."

Warmth filled him at that admission, as well as shame. His wife had taken up the slack, and Philippe wasn't even her damn father. "Perry, what can I say?" How hadn't he known? He bet Edward was blind to this, too.

The selfless act made his throat feel far too full with emotion.

God, how could she do this to him every time? Decimate him with the feelings she stirred? Humble him with her love?

Her awkwardness after the revelation was charming. She wriggled a little in front of him, her neck jerking with discomfort as she mumbled, "At first, I thought he was surprised to see me, but I reckon he purposely sought me out."

"Why would he do that?"

"Hell, Drake, not *why*, more like *how*? How did the bastard get into our private quarters?" When Drake flushed, George gritted out, "You'd better find out, hadn't you?"

"Yes, Your Highness."

Anger with Drake had George clenching his jaw. "You should have told us sooner, Perry. This might have been a massive breach of security." He tried to soften his tone, but if Perry's flush was anything to go by, he definitely failed.

"I know, but I've been thinking about it. I spoke with the nurse on duty, and had her dismissed. L'Argeneau said she, as well as another guard, had let him into the sickroom. And that's another reason why I'm here."

"This is insane," George whispered. "Who else is under L'Argeneau's influence?"

"I'll find out, sire."

"You'd damn well better."

Drake nodded, made to stand, but Perry held up a hand. "No. I want to know what happened to Arabella."

"You could have asked me," said George.

She cut him a look. "You weren't here."

"No, but I know what happened."

"I want to know the details. From Drake," she clarified, when George opened his mouth to argue.

"What kind of details, Your Highness?"

"What happened? How did she fall ill? That kind of thing. L'Argeneau implied that healthy women don't die of the flu. And though it does happen

—there are always freak occurrences, after all—it *is* odd. Especially for a woman Arabella's age."

Though George wanted to ask what she was getting at, he remained silent. He recognized that stubborn slant to her mouth, and the way she'd firmed her lips together told him she wasn't going to budge or hide away from this discussion. She wanted answers, and she wasn't about to be swayed away from getting them.

"Arabella might have been in her prime, but she wasn't in the peak of health. She was constantly underweight, barely ate, and lived from drink to drink. I know for a fact she was taking diet pills and supplements that were a detriment to her health. When she caught the flu, it downed her almost immediately," Drake answered easily.

And, goddammit, George was left wondering if it was *too* easily.

"How long after contracting the illness did she die?"

"Less than a day. You have to understand, the crown princess wasn't popular among the family, but she did have many friends at court. Their quarters were far away from Queen Marianne's and King Philippe's. They'd originally been friendly, but something happened over those last few months that caused a falling out."

"What was it, Drake?" George asked, curious despite himself.

"I wasn't privy to the details. It appertained to your mother, Your Highness, and the crown princess. They argued a lot that year. Considering that many people said she and King Edward were going to divorce, I believed that may have been the source of the strife.

"As a result, the only testimony we have is from her friends. Apparently, she reported feeling unwell on the Monday, and when staff tried to gain access to her room, it was locked, and she told them to go away on the Tuesday. By Wednesday, when no one had seen her, Queen Marianne insisted we break down the door. We found her in bed. She'd perished of the flu. The fever had hit and she hadn't made it out."

"That's weird."

Perry's insight made George want to snort out a laugh, but the topic was far too serious.

"She's right, Drake," George asserted. "Is that all that happened?"

"By the time we gained access to her rooms and called the paramedics, she was brain dead and she passed fully on the way to the hospital," Drake insisted. "There's no tale to tell aside from that. The autopsy confirmed that the fever took her."

"Where was Edward?"

Drake stiffened at Perry's question. "His Highness had separate quarters by that point, but he was on a diplomatic envoy to Finland."

She frowned. "They weren't sharing a bedroom?"

"If you'd known Arabella at all, Perry, you wouldn't be asking that," George informed her, his tone wry.

"His Majesty was seeking a divorce, as I said," Drake confirmed. "Things were not right amid the core family."

Perry folded her arms across her chest. "I don't get it."

"There's nothing to understand," the head of security repeated. "Truly. Arabella should have been healthy, but she wasn't. She undermined her own wellbeing to a terrible extent. She was a walking timebomb with the cocktail of drink and drugs she was taking."

Perry pursed her lips. "Why would her father believe she'd been killed? And by the family, no less?" She scowled. "And don't forget, Philippe warned us before... well, before Edward and I were even engaged. Said some evidence had been uncovered that proved Arabella had been murdered! There's no smoke without fire, Drake."

"Ferdinand L'Argeneau is a bitter and twisted old man. He wants to cause trouble where there is none because, undoubtedly, he's irritated that you're the queen while his daughter isn't." Drake shrugged. "Who knows why the man wants to make this kind of claim? He just wishes to sow the seeds of dissension. Undermine from within.

"And I told Philippe about the supposed evidence that was uncovered, but in the subsequent investigation, it was proven to be a false lead."

The words struck a chord with George. "Drake isn't wrong, Perry. Ferdinand is like that. He's the kind of man with his fingers in more pies than a baker. You never know where his reach extends. Hence my concern about his gaining access to my father's bedroom." George cut the other man a look. "I want details on that, Drake."

The other man nodded. "Certainly. When did you speak with him, your Majesty?"

"Three days ago. Around about four-forty."

Drake nodded again, then held up a hand as he took a seat once more. "If you'll wait one second, Your Highness, I can tell you what happened."

"How?"

"By searching the access codes to those rooms. Only guards and the royal family have them." Drake cut Perry a look. "Your guards weren't with you?"

"I was in the palace, dammit. I'm allowed to walk around my own home freely."

"They're with you today."

"Because they thought I was going into the garden."

"Shouldn't they be with her at all times?" George insisted.

Drake shook his head. "His Majesty has ordered tighter measures in many aspects but not inside the private areas. He doesn't want the castle to feel like a prison." The older man dipped his head. "Understandable, considering Her Majesty's background."

Perry huffed out an exaggerated breath. "I want to be safe, don't get me wrong. But there's something seriously wrong with our security if I have to be under lock and key in my own home because the palace isn't secured."

George nudged her arm. "Why do you think I'm angry about your holding out on us? Ferdinand should never have been allowed into the private sections of the castle."

At his words, Perry scowled down at the floor, but she quickly said, "What evidence did the guards uncover that proved Arabella had been murdered, Drake?"

"It was a piece of gossip on the dark web," Drake murmured, his tone easy, but his gaze flickered over the screen as he hunted down the security access code—that was obviously his priority at that moment.

George grunted. "That's hardly evidence."

Perry frowned. "What's the dark web?"

"It's the shadier side of the internet," George explained. "Where you can buy drugs and God knows what else."

"It's a breeding ground for criminals," Drake explained gruffly. Then, to George, he murmured, "No, it *isn't* evidence, but as you said, where there's smoke, there's fire. I told His Majesty about it, and I may have skewed the truth a tad." Drake jerked his chin up, his glance jolting from the screen to the pair of them. "If I hadn't, he'd never have sanctioned an investigation."

"So you deliberately tried to frighten him?" George demanded, irritated and amused at the same time. His father had been played—something George hadn't believed possible from his chess-loving, ten-steps-ahead-thinking father.

"I had to. He'd have thrown it in the wind otherwise. Your father took as deep an interest in my work as His Majesty currently does. Except my position was rarely under the same kind of threat," Drake groused.

"What concerned you about the gossip?" Perry demanded, holding firm to her original questions with the tenacity that had made her a damn good environmental scientist.

"What induced you to lie to the king, she means," George murmured wryly.

Drake flushed. "It was the wording, and the site the gossip was discovered on."

George narrowed his eyes, reading between the lines. "It was UnReal gossip?"

"Yes." The other man's jaw clenched. "They were using it to recruit people."

Perry scowled. "Why the hell would they do that?"

"Because they wanted to pad out their numbers... I didn't think anything of it at the time. Their figures ebb and flow. Always have done. There'd been a definite surge because of your father's insistence on lowering recidivism rates, but nothing beyond the realms of incredulity. It fit their usual pattern, so I saw no need to fear.

"Now, we know differently. The heads of the security councils concurred with me, but we were wrong. They were obviously planning ahead."

They fell silent at that, then Perry cleared her throat. "Why would Arabella's death be used as recruitment material?" she asked, her tone musing.

"As I said, talk of divorce had already begun to scatter in the wind. The UnReals used her death as proof of the monarchy's perfidy. They claimed she knew too much, had too many secrets that could be used against the family, and as such, needed to go."

Perry and George pondered that a second. As she processed it, George murmured, "That's all well and good, Drake, but though it's irritating what you've told me, as well as foolish, you've given me nothing that would stir you to investigate."

Drake flashed him a look. "The best lies are couched with a kernel of truth."

At the odd phrasing, George slowly nodded. "That's correct. What particular 'kernel of truth' did the UnReals uncover?"

Unease rippled from the older man, clogging the atmosphere with his agitation. When he remained silent, Perry urged, "Explain it, Drake. I need to understand this if I'm to get any rest tonight."

"Arabella was taking sleeping pills, as well as a pharmacy's worth of drugs, to lose weight."

"So? What about it?"

"One of her dealers had gone to university with the Duke of Ansian. He was a chemist, and he was fabricating the drugs."

Perry's eyes widened. "They're using the link between Xavier and an old classmate to imply the DeSauviers could have tampered with the product Arabella was taking?"

Drake nodded, but his discomfort was more evident than ever.

"And that's the truth they used to concoct the rest of the lie?"

"Yes, but then there are other facts that our investigation came across," he said softly, giving the faintest hesitation, so slight George wasn't sure if his eyes had deceived him. Then Drake's attention split entirely from the topic at hand. He let out a sharp, sudden breath as his eyes focused on the screen again. "That's odd."

"What is?" George demanded, taking a step forward, the desire to turn the screen toward him a potent force.

"The access code... it was Raoul Da Silva's."

"The guard who was shot?" George questioned.

Drake nodded, cutting Perry a look. "Yes. Him."

George blew out a breath. "I think we've figured out who our mole is."

CHAPTER TWELVE

"I NEED A BRANDY."

"You don't drink brandy." Xavier trapped Perry's gaze with his own. "And you can't drink anything anyway. You're pregnant. Remember?"

"Like I could forget. It's almost like *knowing* I'm pregnant has made me catch morning sickness."

He started to laugh. "I don't think you can 'catch' morning sickness." Then, he frowned. "How bad is it?"

"Bad." She wrinkled her nose.

"You remember when I told you about that plant I was researching?"

She pondered that a second. "Elda? The one that was embroidered on my wedding dress?"

"That's the one. It's an anti-emetic. If you brew it, it's supposed to help."

"I suppose if I can't have a brandy, then I can have that." Perry's tone turned glum. "Do you know where I can get some?"

"You're the queen, Perry," he teased. "If you wanted something that could only be found in the outer reaches of Mongolia, you could have it."

"Don't say things like that. You know it freaks me out."

His chuckle grew louder at that—which was entirely inappropriate, considering they were about to head out to the funeral of the guard who had died protecting Perry.

A guard who might have been a traitor, but for whom they had to maintain a very public façade of normalcy. The man had, seemingly, been killed in the line of duty. But there was something bloody fishy going on if his access code had been used for Ferdinand L'Argeneau to enter the very private areas of the palace.

As a result, they were heading to the chapel where the funeral was taking place, trying to appear "normal," but Perry wasn't stirring from their quarters.

In fact, that was something he'd noticed of late. She suffered with cabin fever, but rarely wanted to leave the castle to rid herself of the affliction. If anything, she wanted to stay inside, just not be surrounded by the guards.

"What's wrong?" he asked her quietly.

"Do you think my parents would travel here for Thanksgiving if I asked them to?"

He blinked, surprised by where her train of thought had taken her to. "I suppose. Would they like that? They seem very private people. I don't think they particularly appreciated life at the palace. Your father, especially."

"I'd have liked to have gone there myself, but Drake nixed that idea." She pouted. "What's the point in being the queen and being able to get things from outer Mongolia if you can't travel home for Thanksgiving?"

"I'm sorry," he said softly, squeezing her shoulder before he tucked his arm around her waist and hauled her close. "I'm surprised you want to travel that far."

"What? You think I don't want to go home where I was always safe?" She grimaced. "Makes perfect sense to me."

At that moment, it hit him that this place still wasn't home to her, and how could he blame her? She wasn't safe here, was she? And Perry obviously equated safety with home. Who didn't?

Because there was no making any of that better, his tone was gruff as he asked, "You changed the subject on me. What's really wrong?"

"Aside from the fact I have no freedom?" She arched a brow at him, and though the words were enough to make him wince, he raised a hand and tugged at her bottom lip. When she went to bite one of his fingers, he laughed again.

"Minx."

"You know it."

"Are you nervous?"

"About what?"

She stared in her dressing room mirror and fussed with her black skirt suit. It was very demure. A simple jacket and skirt that was tucked into the tight lines of her curves; her shirt was white lace that patterned her throat and made her creamy skin all the more noticeable. She wore a simple pair of black heels and stockings he'd watched her drag on.

If anyone could look sexy while mourning, it was Perry.

"About leaving the castle? I know you haven't been going out as much as..."

"As what?" she snapped. "I didn't go out that much before unless it was to go to a dam or something."

He shrugged. "No, but you went out for coffee with me, didn't you? And headed for afternoon tea with Cassie? They're all things you can still do."

She narrowed her eyes at him. "What are you getting at, Xav?"

"I'm asking if the reason you want a brandy is because you're scared to go outside the castle."

For a second, she didn't reply, then she pursed her lips and moved out of the gentle hold he had on her. "I don't want to talk about this now."

"All the more reason to discuss it." The door opened at that exact damn moment, and Xavier cursed his poor fortune. When he saw Edward, he cocked a brow. "You're coming too?"

Edward scowled. "Of course. There might have been a leak in our security, but I don't want the public to know that." Perry turned to face him as he spoke, and the words seemed to catch in his throat. "You look beautiful, Perry."

She shrugged. "Good, I guess."

Edward shot Xavier a look, but he was as in the dark as his cousin. Xavier cleared his throat. "Where's George?"

"Waiting by the cars."

"Aren't we all traveling together?"

The frantic note in Perry's voice made both men jolt in surprise.

"Of course," Edward said uneasily, studying her like Xavier had studied his fertilizer samples. "But we're traveling in a security blockade."

She let out a shaky breath. "Good."

"Are you sure you're okay?" Xavier demanded, reaching for her arm and turning her to face him. "What's going on?" he repeated for the third time.

"Nothing, dammit. I'm fine. I'm just... I'm having to find a way to deal with this. If it means I'm not bouncing up and down all the damn time, then I'm sorry!"

Edward stared at Xavier over Perry's head, one that said they'd discuss this later, and murmured, "We need to go."

Perry jerked her chin up. "Fine. I've been ready for twenty minutes."

Before either man could say another word, she strode forward, and as she did, he noticed the slight hesitation in her footsteps as she made to exit the suite.

She let out a breath when she walked into the corridor, and turned a challenging look their way. "Coming?"

They caught up with her, Edward closing the door to their suite behind them, and headed toward the cavalcade of cars that had been set aside for their journey to the chapel.

The vehicles waited—their engines purring—beneath the portico as they finally left Masonbrook. Armed guards lined the paths, and each clicked their heels and saluted upon seeing Edward and Perry.

The first time that had happened, Perry had jumped like she had the time she'd burned her feet climbing out of the pool in Dubai. With no sandals, she had crossed the terrace, and the burning hot terracotta tiles had made her howl as she made a mad dash toward the tented pavilion that had been their second home on their honeymoon.

God, those weeks had been pure bliss. Amusing, passionate, relaxing... a complete about-face in comparison to the past two months.

He exhaled, peering up at the sky as he climbed into one of the limos and saw George waiting for them. Nodding at his cousin, he had to sigh—the landscape outside the palace looked even grimmer from the car's tinted windows.

It was going to be a miserable day, not just because of the weather and where they were going—a traitor's send-off. More than that, what made him truly miserable was the fact something was definitely wrong with Perry, and she was refusing to talk with them about it.

He didn't like that. Not one bit.

"WHY DO you three look so serious?" Perry asked, with some surprise at the sight of them bundled together, later on that same night.

Her three men were gathered in the sitting room of her suite—she thought of it as her suite, because Edward was barely ever in the damn thing.

After she'd returned from the funeral, she'd had a soak in the ridiculous bath that was probably part of the reason that Veronia was experiencing a drought, and had only now decided to get out of the water.

She'd needed the bath, even though it had gone against every grain in her body to use it.

Made for far more opulent times, it was the first interior bath in the kingdom, or so George had informed her, as Masonbrook had been ahead of the rest of the nation where indoor plumbing was concerned.

The bath wasn't like a modern one. It wasn't plastic and molded. Constructed, it was, in many ways, like a small pool.

If she hadn't needed to finally get warm, she'd never have dreamed of getting into the damn thing. It was the first time she'd used it, and she hoped the last—even though it would probably make a pretty hot-shit birthing pool if, months down the line, that was the way she wanted to give birth. Because yes, she, Perry Taylor now DeSauvier, was going to be responsible for bringing life to someone.

It was enough to scare the hell out of her.

Still, water consumption aside, the bath had warmed her up. She could tell, however, by the way her three men were looking at each other, shady talk had been going down, and they hadn't included her.

Again.

Although...was it terrible to admit that she was reaching the point where she was glad they discussed things away from her? Maybe it was rotten, but she was only one person, and she could only take so much.

She hadn't been trained for this madcap life. She was a Regular Joe shoved into Prince Charming's world. The two weren't mutually incompatible, but at the moment, she was definitely feeling the strain.

"We're just talking about tomorrow," Edward murmured, but though his face formed somber and serious lines, he beckoned her forward with his hand. She stepped toward him, grabbed his fingers, then sat on his knee when he tugged her onto his lap. He turned his face into her throat, breathed deeply, then murmured, "I've missed you."

Her throat closed at that. The words were heartfelt, and they stung all the more for that reason. "You jerk," she whispered brokenly. "You're the one who's been going AWOL."

"I know, but I have to keep you safe."

"How can I be safe when you lock me out?"

He nuzzled his nose into her throat. "I know. Don't be mad."

"I'm not. Just hurt."

"That's the last thing I want."

"Well, stop pushing me away." She lifted a hand and brushed her fingers through his hair. The silky locks clung to her digits, and she shivered a little at the close contact. He'd been shoving so much distance between them, it was starting to feel like she was back in the States with the Atlantic Ocean between them!

"I'm not really pushing you away," he argued.

"No, he's just micromanaging." Xavier cocked a brow at Edward, demanding he try to argue, but he didn't. Just slumped deeper into the chair.

She frowned. "You pay good people to do their jobs, sweetheart. Let them do it without you breathing down their neck."

"Easier said than done, when your safety is at risk." Though she froze a little inside, she warmed up when he placed his hand against her lower belly. "I'm just trying to make sure they realize I am *quite* willing to breathe down their necks when they're showing such meager results."

"What's happening tomorrow?"

"It's my first motion in Parliament."

"So why do you guys look so long in the face?" she asked, rubbing a strand of his hair between her fingers. She knew he used a standard brand shampoo. Nothing fancy. Nothing that combined ass's milk with gold or some shit like that for his royal head. Nope, at their heart, her men were just that.

Men.

They might wear thousand-dollar suits, sit on thrones, and have ceremonial dress that came out from time to time, but they were most definitely challenged in the way that all creatures with XY chromosomes were. They left the toilet seat up, dumped their towels on the floor beside the shower, and hogged the duvet come nightfall.

While she knew those traits irritated the majority of the female population, truthfully, it charmed her.

Of course, it helped that staff picked up the towels, that her bathroom was cleaned every morning and evening by some wonderful fairy who she'd yet to see—she did, in fact, wonder if there was a secret entrance into her bathroom, because every time she turned around, it had been cleaned without her knowing—the beds they slept in made tennis courts look tiny, so there was always ample room as well as excess covers...

Still, what charmed her was the fact that they were normal. And in a world where everything was turbocharged, their average quirks were wonderful to behold.

When she realized Edward hadn't replied, she peered over at Xavier and George who were quiet, too. Staring into their whiskeys—the damn fine stuff she'd gleaned a taste for over the weeks, and seriously missed now—they were definitely somber.

She tilted her head to the side, curious why they were so glum. Such expressions demanded she meddle. Whether she wanted to know or not, she couldn't let them continue to muddle through their misery alone.

"Come on, haven't you learned not to keep things from me yet? It always comes back to bite you on the ass when you hold your tongues."

After a second, George's lips twitched into a half-smile. "It's not that we're keeping anything from you, Perry." When she snorted, he shook his head. "We're not. We're trying to talk Edward out of making a stupid decision."

"What kind of stupid decision?" she asked, curiosity driving her. She reached for Edward's chin and gently moved him so he was no longer hiding his expression in her throat. "What's going on?"

"He wants to invoke Article 42." Xavier's tone should have had dramatic music flaring to life after he uttered his words.

She'd heard a lot about this Article. Knew her men were concerned that Edward was going to use it if he didn't get answers soon.

"Why would you want to do a silly thing like that, sweetheart?" she chided, staring deep into his eyes, trying to find the source of this foolishness.

"It isn't silly," Edward argued, and his accent on the word "silly" enchanted her.

Sometimes, they spoke English so well, it was hard to remember that Veronian was their first language. Speaking with them was like speaking with Oxford graduates—well, they'd studied at Oxford and Cambridge, so that figured—but their accents were pure British. Only from time to time did a bit of their birth tongue pop out.

"We need answers, Perry. As it stands, we should have revealed your pregnancy to the nation, and instead, we're hiding it because we don't want to paint a brighter target on your back."

"While I appreciate that, Edward, I'd prefer not to be the catalyst for a constitutional crisis." She pursed her lips. "I'm already going down as the queen with the fastest coronation in history… let's not add, 'she made Veronia a dictatorship,' to my list of crimes against future humanity."

"It wouldn't be a dictatorship," he grumbled.

"It would be a damn close thing," George argued. "You know the Article gives you complete power of authority over every aspect of government."

Her eyes widened. "Every aspect?"

Xavier nodded. "Yes. That's why it's so dangerous. The Article itself is supposed to *stop* a dictatorship from rising within the ranks of Parliament. My grandfather saw how Hitler came to power, Lenin and his ilk, too. After the war, to protect the people, he crafted Article 42 for everyone's sake. A king, in right mind and with support of his people, could trigger the protocol if he believed the state was at risk."

"Well, the state isn't at risk."

"Isn't it?" Edward asked grimly. "You're at risk, and you're the future of the Crown. Wherever you go, you put the people at risk from attacks from a group of terrorists who are trying to destroy the monarchy, and don't care who gets in the way.

"As it stands, our four-strong security services are fucking useless. We're barely gathering intel on these bastards, and we know for a fact there's a leak. Whether it was Raoul Da Silva and/or someone else, they've managed to infiltrate our bases, which is one of the specifications for the invocation of the Article.

"'*If the sovereign deems the protected councils of intelligence, be they Military Intelligence HQ or a newly established institution constructed in* the future, to have been infiltrated by those rebelling against the natural peace of this fair land, then there is hope for the sovereign with the desire to protect the people from the tyranny of those who wish to do them harm,'" he quoted.

She gulped. "Wow. That's pretty intense. You've been reading it a lot, huh?"

He snorted. "Ya think? It's been on my mind."

"I can tell." Her brow puckered. "Will it do us any good?"

"That's what we're arguing, Perry," George said softly. "It won't. If MIHQ *has* been infiltrated, and the other security services have too, then Edward suddenly becoming a dictator isn't going to make things better. If anything, it might make things worse. People who were dithering about being on the rebels' side might decide the UnReals are right."

"For God's sake, it's not like I'm suddenly going to turn into Stalin! I just want tighter measures to protect us all, and Parliament is bloody useless! Our subjects might decide I'm in the right to invoke the Article. You saw how they supported Perry," Edward argued. "They couldn't have shown their love for the DeSauviers more after what those bastards did to Mother and Father."

"That doesn't mean to say they want us to destroy their democracy!" Xavier countered, for the first time, his relatively relaxed tone turning aggressive. Perry noticed his hand tightened about his glass. "You can't make something right by doing wrong, Ed. You're a fool if you think so." Nostrils flaring, he sank back his drink and got to his feet. "I'm going back to the estate. I have business there tomorrow. I'll be at Parliament for your session, and I hope you don't make the biggest mistake of *our* lives."

He got to his feet and made to walk past them, but Perry reached out to grab his hand and tugged him to a halt. "You're not driving?" She eyed the glass still in his hand. "You've had too much to drink."

"One of my guards will drive me."

She nodded, then arched her neck and whispered, "Kiss?"

His jaw clenched as he looked at Edward, upon whose lap she was still sitting. Then, he relented by dipping down and pressing a quick kiss to her lips. She didn't let him get away with that, though. Her arms curled about his neck, pulling him close, and ripping her metaphorical claws into him by opening her mouth and seducing his. She shivered as his tongue slid against hers, his breathing harsh as his free hand grabbed her knee to steady himself. She felt his fingers dig into the soft flesh of her lower thigh, felt the tips mold the skin slightly in response to the need she stirred in him.

A soft moan escaped her as he fucked her mouth, burning all his rage, his anger on the kiss that scorched her senses. Set her alight.

When she shuddered, he pulled free from her grasp, and shook his head like a dog who'd been thrown into a pool and had just scampered out of the water. "I have to go," he said, his tone a mixture of urgency, plea, and desperation.

She nodded, but her hand reached for his once more. "Just don't leave in anger."

It was experience that prodded her to say that, and it was an experience that left her disheartened.

Others might say that, simply because they didn't want anger between them and their loved ones...but Perry knew their lives were different.

Between now and tomorrow, when Xavier would next see them, a lot could happen.

A lot of it bad.

She'd learned that. Had borne the brunt of that experience.

God, she'd been so naïve before. So lost in a universe of her own making that revolved around the actual world, protecting it and learning how humanity was destroying it with their wasteful ways, but she'd known nothing. Not really.

Becoming their woman had opened her eyes in a manner that made her wish they'd always stayed closed.

This side of life wasn't particularly pretty.

If anything, it was damn ugly.

Xavier shifted his attention to Edward, whose cock was prodding her in the ass. "I'll see you tomorrow."

Edward's head tilted back against the sofa. "Meet here for lunch?"

Xavier sighed, nodded. "Okay." He cut George a look. "Night, guys." With a final squeeze of Perry's fingers, he retreated from the room, leaving George and Edward in a moody silence that had been turbocharged by their conversation, as well as the kiss they'd witnessed between her and their cousin.

"Are you really going to trigger the Article?" Perry asked quietly, her gaze trained on the door Xavier had just closed behind him.

She'd never seen him so angry. He was always chilled, so laid back that he might as well have been horizontal.

Edward was like the North Wind. Could disappear for months on end, then in one sharp gust, had the power of chilling a room in an instant. George was a hurricane. Quick to anger, slow to stir, but unlike his brother, he blew hot, not cold.

Xavier, on the other hand, had rarely displayed such a temper. And even now, when she'd seen it, she imagined he'd controlled a great part of it.

Perhaps George sensed her curiosity, because he murmured, "Xavier likes to be in control."

"I gathered that."

"Well, our Uncle Sebastien had a frightening temper, Xavier abhorred that."

"Sebastien...like Cassie's son?"

Edward nodded. "He's named for him. Our families have always been close."

"Sebastien used to throw things when he was mad. One time, he hit a servant with a plate. Knocked the man out. It was accidental, Uncle hadn't meant to cause the other man harm, he was simply in the vicinity. Xavier was there, and it shook him."

Perry's mouth fell agape. "I can hardly blame him for being shaken!"

George's nose wrinkled. "No. Sebastien could be a bastard when the time came. The family compensated the footman, paid for all his care, and he's still at the estate... Sebastien was just renowned for being volatile." George shrugged, like it was a perfectly normal piece of information he'd just shared with her.

She gawked at him. "You're not justifying it?"

"No, of course not." He snorted. "But I'm not going to wear a hair shirt over it either. He was my uncle, but I wasn't his keeper. It's hardly my fault he was a prick from time to time."

Despite herself, she had to laugh. "No, I guess not." She rubbed her cheek against Edward's. "How are you doing?"

"I'm fine."

"I call bullshit." She pulled away and cocked a brow at him. "In fact, I call double bullshit. You two, in fact no, Xavier included—you *three* think you can pull the wool over my eyes. I know you too well. You can't hide from me."

Edward's lips twitched. "Who said I was hiding?"

"Me. There's no way you're not stressed about tomorrow." She prodded him in the belly with her finger. "But I don't want you to do anything you'll regret. I know we have to be careful now, and I know..." She inhaled roughly because this was definitely the truth. "I'm not going to lie and say I'm not scared by what's happening, but that doesn't mean you should do something that's atrocious for the country.

"You have to protect everyone, Edward. Not just me and the baby."

"You can't be serious?" Edward shook his head. "You're all that matters."

"You can't have that attitude—you know that, and I know it, too."

His lips pursed. "I can be however I want."

"No, you have to think about the country too, Edward. You're more than just my husband. You're the damn king." She pressed her lips to his jaw. "I appreciate it though, don't think I don't."

"That's my job, Perry. You're my life."

The depth of sincerity in his words made her throat tighten. She wanted to hug him and squeeze him so damn hard, so that neither knew where one of them ended and the other began...but she couldn't do any of that.

So instead, she whispered, "Oh, Edward."

She hated that she sounded teary, but hell, how couldn't she?

That was some declaration.

Of course, he had to spoil it by scowling at her. "Most people have a say in their jobs. If they don't like it, they can quit."

"Yeah, I can attest that we don't want Edward to quit, Perry. I'd make a suckier-ass king than he does," George piped up from his armchair, and despite herself and the tears that Edward's words caused, she had to let out a laugh.

A watery one, albeit.

She bit her lip. "Shut up, you," she grumbled, but her eyes were sparkling as she turned her head to look at him. A shuddery chuckle escaped her when she saw that his gaze was half-lidded, a sensual heat burning within those crystalline orbs that scorched her from the inside out.

"You like it when I'm snarky," he retorted, crossing his legs at the ankles and slouching further down into the seat.

Now that she thought about it, Edward and George mustn't have been spared posture classes either. Because she rarely saw him seated in that way. He was always straight-backed and rigid in hold. Same when he was standing. He never had bad posture—was that from being in the Forces, or from simply having Marianne for a mother?

"I do like it when you're snarky," she agreed. "And you like it when I tell you to shut up, because everybody else licks your ass."

He pursed his lips—she knew it was to hide his smile. "You offering?" he teased.

"What is it with you and rimming?" she demanded on a huff.

"I'm a curious creature, Perry. Didn't you know?"

She narrowed her eyes at him. "You'd totally freak out if I went anywhere near your ass."

Edward laughed, and the sound was so much lighter than he'd sounded mere moments before—proof, yet again, that she could and would bring ease to his world, a notion that filled her with contentment.

The way he needed her was something she couldn't begin to even describe, and yet...it was so empowering. To know, and to have just had it confirmed, that yes, she was his life...

God, she'd never known anything like it.

"She has you there," Edward joked. "You *would* freak out."

"I might not. Perry's different," George grumbled.

"How? Are my fingers and tongue bright blue or something?"

"They might as well be. You're definitely from another planet in other ways."

"He knows how to charm the panties right off you, doesn't he?"

Perry waited a second, then with as much sultriness as she was capable of—which, admittedly, wasn't much—murmured, "I'm not wearing any panties."

She had to bite back a grin when the two of them looked at one another, their gazes batting back and forth like a spectator at a Venus vs. Serena Williams tennis match.

Before either of them could say a word, she hopped off Edward's lap and danced away from George, who sprang forward and tried to catch her hand. She dashed off to the bedroom, turned back to stare at them, and winked.

"Well?" she demanded, and laughed when they both came chasing after her.

CHAPTER THIRTEEN

SEEING Perry's fine ass dance just out of his line of sight had George's gaze arrowing on her behind like it was painted with crosshairs.

Her lush curves had thinned over the past few months, and the truth was, he was looking forward to her rounding out once more. She was pregnant now, which changed things on so many levels. Not just where her security was concerned—the principle topic the three of them had been discussing when she'd wandered in on their conversation. But on this front, too.

George wondered how it would change her, and looked forward to seeing her grow ripe with their child.

He'd never thought about having kids. Never really had the chance to imagine they'd be doing it this way—*Big Love* style. But the truth was, he wouldn't wish it any other way. His stress levels were already through the roof, and knowing Xavier and Edward had his back was a lifesaver.

His mouth watered as she half-turned and cheekily crooked her finger at them. He let out a joking growl that had her dashing forward and giggling as she went. He grinned and took off after her, leaving Edward to make his way at a more sedate pace—that was his brother all the way. Sedate, steady, until the time came and he'd turn into an animal.

George supposed it was weird that, when this situation with Perry had come to mind, he'd dreamed of sharing her with Edward. Yet, in all the months they'd been together, he'd yet to do that. This would be the first time, but sure as hell not the last.

When he made it into the bedroom and saw she wasn't on the huge four poster bed, he quickly took in the room at large. He had imagined spending hours with his wife and brother atop that mattress at some point— and now, that was about to happen.

He intended to explore this woman that was his wife in everything but the law.

Even by name, after all, she was his—the perks of her marrying his brother.

The royal blue suite had been dampened down some. Before, it had looked something like a room in the Palace of Versailles. Grand ceilings painted with dancing frescoes of cherubim and angels frolicking here, there, and every-bloody-where. Now, they'd been paneled over for protection, but also for Perry's taste.

The walls too, once a clashing brocade of magenta on white, had gone by the by until the next generation wished to uncover them for prosperity, and the carpet—once a bright blue—had been replaced by a rich oatmeal weave.

The bed hadn't changed, had the same high canopy that was attached to the frame, but cascading gauzy fabric swagged here and there over the bed. When the windows were open—four sets of double French doors—the fabric would sway and move in the breeze.

He looked forward to a late summer night, the four of them on the bed, talking, discussing the future, maybe listening to the sounds of the life in Perry's belly moving... he envisioned it all because with her, he could.

She was his future.

He knew that as well as he knew his face in the mirror.

There was a dressing table, though she had her own dressing room, complete with a shiny new mirror, as well as countless chests of drawers that filled the expansive space. One chaise lounge was angled here, another there. Nooks for reading, armchairs hidden behind paneled room dividers that were the only bit of antiquity in the space—they had ancient depictions on them, some dating back to the eighteenth century. Italian landscapes on some, floral explosions on others.

When he didn't see her close by, he knew she was hiding. Then, he heard a giggle behind the divider that had been painted by Monet—this had been a secret commission. One that no one, not even most art experts, were aware of. It was like his *Water Lily Pond*, but the colors were brighter, more fitting of the once lurid colors in the room. George didn't want to know how his ancestor had pulled off such a feat—DeSauviers could, after all, be very persuasive. Even if that meant forcing prolific painters to do their bidding.

He whipped forward, silently padding on his bare feet. Ducking behind the divider, he caught her and whisked her off hers. She let out a squeak that had him laughing, and he carefully hauled her over his shoulder so that her ass was high up.

He tapped her there and retorted, "That's what you get for hiding."

"George! Put me down," she demanded, but the words were interspersed with laughter. "You're not a caveman. It doesn't suit you."

He slipped his hand up the simple dress she wore, part kaftan, part housecoat. It was bright yellow and patterned with tribal colors about the deep V-neckline. The colors suited her, and it was a nice change to see her in something that wasn't yoga pants in their private quarters. The kaftans were especially useful when it came to times like these... he slid his hand up her leg, letting the fabric swathe his fingers as he tickled the backside of her thighs.

She shivered in response, then giggled as he tossed her down on the large mattress. She bounced twice, each time making her tits judder in a way that had his cock hardening and his mouth watering. Just as she settled, he grabbed a hold of her and dragged her back toward him. He used his grasp on her ankles to part them, and as he did, the fabric of the kaftan slipped all the way down to her hips, exposing her very bare pussy.

He let out a growl. "You weren't lying."

Her voice was husky now. "Of course, I wasn't. I don't lie about things like that."

"No, just about other things, huh?" Edward answered, and the pair of them peered over to him at the foot of the bed. He was leaning against one of the posts, looking damned cool and calm, while George felt feverish and flushed.

"Come here," Perry said with a pout.

"No. I want George to unwrap his present."

Her pout turned coy. "That's not fair."

"Who said I have to be fair, my queen?"

His words seemed to resonate with her in a way that heralded a physical response. Her breath suddenly deepened, and her pupils turned into wide pools that beckoned him to dive in for a swim. The way her tits jiggled was further proof of her reaction.

He let out a laugh. "Someone likes the sound of that."

"Don't be silly," she chided breathily.

He grinned. "Who's the one being silly?" In a somewhat conversational tone, he murmured, "A few months ago, I'd have had to *dare* you to use the word 'silly.'"

She squinted at him. "Are we really having a conversation about words?"

"Why not?" he teased, running his hands down the outer sides of her legs from ankle to hip. He let his nails drag toward her inner thigh, watching as she tensed, her butt sinking into the mattress, her back arching just a tad at the sensation. "Can't you handle it?"

"I can handle anything," she grumbled, but she licked her lips, and the look in her eye was proof positive that was bullshit.

"I think we should test that," Edward muttered, "Don't you, George?"

"I really do." Before either of them could say another word, he dropped to his knees and dove on her. She immediately let out a squeal, but her hands came up to cup the back of his head, and a litany of "oh my God" commenced.

He grinned around her clit, then began to taunt her in earnest. He sucked and slurped, flicked and tickled the little nub with the tip of his tongue. She began to squirm, but he kept her clamped in place with one forearm over her belly.

When she began to ride his face, he used his free hand to thrust two fingers into her. She let out a sharp moan as he curled his fingers up, rubbing and bringing the tender nerve endings to life. Her panting breaths told him how close she was, but the way her pussy clenched around his digits was all the proof he needed.

He placed an open-mouthed kiss to her clit, then sucked down.

Hard.

She let out a cry. "George. George!"

"I think she likes that," Edward said, and his voice was like cold water on a pan of hot oil. It triggered an inferno that had her legs clenching around his head.

"Stop it, stop it," she suddenly begged as he began to suck and slurp, knowing it would keep her on edge, knowing that it wouldn't provide her with the relief she needed.

Then, he felt her cunt clamp down once more on his fingers, and though she tried to keep him there, he pulled his head back.

Panting, he licked his lips and watched as she lifted her head so she could glower at him. "What the fuck do you think you're doing?"

Her bossy tone made him laugh. "You asked me to stop."

She gulped. "You can't be serious."

"I am. Deadly."

"He is. *Deadly*," Edward inserted, and she whipped her head around to glare at him.

At that exact same moment, he crooked his fingers inside her once more and watched with delight as she reared upward, her tits spilling out of the deep V-neck of the kaftan. It was frightfully jumbled and so goddamn sexy as a result, he wanted to growl.

Perry and "sexy" didn't really go together. She wasn't an effortless seductress that only had to blink at him to get his cock hard. But there was something about her, a brutal honesty, that got to him every fucking time.

He'd never known anything, *any woman*, with that power over him. It was what had proven to him that she was *it* for him. His own fucking Kryptonite, because all the sexy models and Victoria's Secret Angels in the world couldn't get him harder than Perry could with merely a blink of her gorgeous amber eyes.

Her mewling cries had him wishing he could grab a hold of his cock, not to jack off, but to control himself. To hold back. God, she got to him like wildfire did a dry, dead tree. The only difference was, of course, that he wasn't dry and he wasn't dead.

He was so fucking alive, and all because of her.

Watching her shudder, he got to his feet and continued fucking her with his fingers. Crooking here, scissoring there, teasing and tormenting her, keeping her on edge. Needing her to be as out of control as *he* was. As *they* were, because he knew even if Edward was looking bored as hell, still waters ran very, very deep.

He knew his brother.

Too well.

They'd done this too many times.

Perry wasn't aware of that, didn't realize Edward liked to watch George drive their women insane...but she was about to learn the way they worked. And she was the most important woman ever, so the levels of insanity he intended to drive her to went beyond anything she could ever have imagined.

"I'm gonna come," she cried out, her legs trying to slam together, her thighs clenching down hard. But he leaned against the bed and lifted one knee to press against one of hers. Pinning her down with that, he looked at Edward, and saw his brother had stepped closer to grab Perry's nearest ankle. Then, he stopped moving his fingers, stopped completely until she was panting, wild-eyed, and pleading, "Don't stop! Why did you stop?"

His grin probably looked as evil as he wanted it to, because she let out a shuddery sigh.

He leaned over at the waist, bowing low until his mouth hovered over the spill of her luscious tits. He wished he had more hands, but instead, he shoved his face right between their swells. Perry's fingers speared through his hair, raking down against his scalp in a way that drove him nuts.

"Come inside me, George. Please, baby, please," she crooned, and her back arched again.

"Not yet," he murmured, knowing his words were garbled between her tits. He turned his head and grappled one of her nipples between his lips.

He slurped it, rolled it between his teeth, and released it with a pop. "One day, someday soon, our baby will nurse here."

She shivered.

"You like that?" Edward demanded. "*Our* baby?"

He looked up at her, watching her gaze clash with his brother's as she nodded shakily.

"Why do you like it, Perry?" Edward asked, his voice as commanding as it was when he was dealing with state business.

"B-Because I'm y-yours."

"And did you think it might change when you were pregnant?"

"I-I guess."

"It won't," George interrupted, needing her to know that. "If anything, it will bring us closer together. I can't wait to watch your tits get bigger, to see you ripen with our child." He angled himself so he could press his shaft against her. "Feel how hard I am for you, Perry."

He dove for her nipple once more, and as he bit at the tender nub, she whimpered. "I'll get fat."

"No. You'll get even more perfect than you are now."

Her hips rippled, her pelvis rocking into the sheets. He began, as a reward, to thrust into her once more. His fingers crooking again, trying to find her G-spot. He knew he'd found it when her body turbocharged with tension. She stiffened up, her response faster than ice cream melted on July 4th.

"I think you found a good spot, George," Edward complimented, apparently seeing her response.

He hummed around her nipple, then he reached up and began to devour her throat.

George had soon learned how that area there was one of her weaknesses, and if she was his Kryptonite, he damn well intended to find hers, for him to be her goddamn Achilles' Heel.

"Oh my God," she cried out. "Please, more."

He stopped. Of course.

His mouth went to work, his tongue palpating at her throat, his lips sucking and pulling. He wanted her covered in his marks. Wanted her to know, when she looked in the mirror later, that whether she was as round as a house, or as slender as she was now, she was his.

Theirs.

He shuddered at his own thoughts, and loved that her nails dug into his head once more as he sucked down hard against her most tender spots. Simultaneously, he began to move his fingers once more, and just when her pussy clamped down on him, he reared off the bed in an explosive movement that had her crying out.

When she was completely open on the bed, her legs spread, her tits jiggling with every panting breath, he felt his cock through his pants and pressed down hard, needing to control the urge to come at the sight her. So fucking ready for them. So desperate to be theirs.

As he watched her, panting himself, Edward—cool as a fucking cucumber—kept his hand on her ankle, then leaned down and pressed a single, solitary kiss to her cunt.

She shuddered.

Edward moved away, licking his lips as he went. Then, without a word, he began to strip off. The silence was all the more deafening for his languid movements.

Unlike George, not by one out-of-place hair did he even begin to reveal that he was in any way excited.

As usual, he looked bored. Fuck him.

George was sure that he himself looked ready, looked close to the brink of explosion. And yet, Edward was the exact opposite.

He tried to view his brother's response through Perry's eyes, and could only imagine how confused it made her. Just when he started to fear it would cause her to feel insecure, Edward asked, his tone desultory, "How badly do you want our cocks, Perry?"

She gulped, and her eyes widened. Her mouth trembled, and her gaze flickered over to George. He nodded slightly, encouragingly. He sensed her unease at this new element Edward was introducing, and wanted to reassure her.

"Badly," she whispered huskily.

"Take off your dress," Edward murmured, watching as Perry instantly obeyed and tossed the kaftan overhead and off the bed. "Now, spread your pussy wide open so we can see how hungry that little cunt is for us."

Her cheeks began to burn with heat, and George could well understand. Edward's cool tone was in direct contrast to his dirty, wicked words.

With her face redder than a tomato that had been sundried and then sun*burned*, she laid back on the bed again, and spreading her legs, reached between them to touch herself. She parted her pussy lips, revealing the wet hole that was slick with her juices.

George licked his lips as his sensory memory reminded him of the exact taste of her on his tongue.

Salty, sweet. Like honey and musk combined.

He began to strip, too. His shirt went first, his pants next. He wore briefs, and his cock felt like it was being strangled behind the clinging fabric, but he kept them on lest he be too tempted by the games his brother was playing.

"How wet are you, Perry?" Edward asked. She gulped, but slipped a finger inside her gate. When she started to speak, Edward continued, "Tell me after you've tasted yourself."

She blinked but did as bid, slipping the sodden digit between her lips and sucking it clean. "I'm very wet. Too wet."

George cocked a brow. "Don't think there's such a thing as *too* wet, babe."

"Sometimes, there is," she said, somewhat cryptically.

"What do you taste like? Do you like how you taste?" Edward asked, his hand sliding down her ankle, along her calf, and toward her knee. She twitched in response to his touch, her eyes flickering to his cock which belied his calm demeanor.

Unlike George, Edward went commando—he was bare as the day he was born.

"I-I taste quite musky," she stated, her nose wrinkling in a way that told George she didn't particularly appreciate her flavor.

Edward's lips curved in a smile as he too picked up on her response. Then, he moved between her legs, grabbed a hold of his cock, pressed it to her cunt, and like that, slid home.

Perry let out a startled gasp. George couldn't blame her. In less than five seconds, Edward had gone from keen disinterest to fucking his shaft into her. But though he slid in deep, he didn't thrust. Perry's feet flattened against the mattress, and she tried to arch her pelvis to encourage him to move…but there was no making Edward do anything.

George knew that, and their woman would soon learn.

"Move, dammit. Please!" she begged.

Edward merely quirked a brow and retreated entirely. George cast a quick glance at his brother's cock and saw he was drenched in her juices. Knowing what was about to happen, George pinned his gaze to Perry's face, wanting to see her response to Edward's command. "Lick my cock clean, Perry."

She grimaced, her nose curling. "Why?"

"Because I want you to."

She rimmed her lips with her tongue, turning to look at George. If she was waiting for backup, she wouldn't get it, he thought, amused.

Perry would have to learn a lesson that hadn't really cropped up before…she couldn't turn them against each other—if one stated something, she couldn't try to work around it.

"Well?" Edward intoned, calm as ever.

She huffed but climbed onto her knees. Falling onto her hands, her ass waving in the breeze, she hovered in front of Edward's shaft. She hesitated, then sticking her tongue out, traced it over Edward's cock.

A startled noise escaped her then, and surprising both he and Edward, she dove onto his shaft, her mouth sinking as deep as she was able. His mouth watered at her eagerness, as she tasted all Edward had to give, her hands coming up to shape his cock, to touch and caress as she sampled their mingled flavors.

A shiver rushed down his spine at the sight of her, and he couldn't not take part. He ran his hand over the back of her neck, gently caressing her there and then releasing her hair from the clip that had been perched, precariously, at the crown of her head.

Her ass wiggled in the air, dancing almost, as she enjoyed her ministrations. George cut Edward a glance and was amused to see his brother's eyes were at half-mast as he watched Perry eating him up.

With a grunt, he climbed on the bed, uncaring that it shifted and jostled Perry, even though she made a mewl of disapproval in response. He staggered forward on the thick covers, walking on his knees, as he approached her from the back.

Her butt clenched down hard, and her hips shunted toward the bed, and he knew she was trying to avoid him. Trying to avoid his teasing. She garbled something about Edward's cock, and he saw his brother had grabbed ahold of her hair and was using it to keep her busy, not allowing her to complain.

He grinned at the sight, knowing that they'd never tested Perry's limits to this extent, and loving that she was going with the flow... even though her garbles had definitely turned disgruntled as he maneuvered himself on his back, laying straight between her legs. His hands came up to her hips, and he dragged her down so her pussy was directly over his mouth.

He dove on her, loving the slick juices that drenched his jaw. That slipped onto his face, that immersed him in all of her.

This was how sex should be.

Earthy and real. Messy and sweaty and slippery.

God, he hadn't been alive since before they'd claimed Perry. He hadn't realized how he'd slowly been dying without this, without having *this* connection in his world.

The thought was a catalyst that induced him to be kinder to Perry's pussy—to be gentle and to entice, rather than to throw her straight into the deep end.

She reacted to the change in stimuli by rocking her hips and riding his tongue. More mumbled noises came in response, and he had to laugh, a gesture that had her moaning harder.

"That's it, show us how much you want us," Edward commanded, but his tone was thick now. Even his staid and serious brother was responding to what was happening.

About fucking time.

George's cock had to be like a fucking pike staff—saluting anyone and everyone who could see it. It wouldn't have been fair for Edward to still be non-responsive... although he *had* seen it happen once before.

Truth was, Edward lost control by being in control in the bedroom.

It was a mindset he didn't particularly understand and didn't bother trying to anymore.

Ed was how he was, and that was it. A dominant SOB who got off on turning his woman crazy with lust in bed.

Perry's clit rubbed his nose as he plunged his tongue deep into the tunnel of her sex. Her taste clung to him, her scent blossoming in his senses like an explosion of flowers around him.

He couldn't stop himself from reaching down and grabbing his cock. When he jacked off twice, Edward barked, "George."

The command was clear—George gritted his teeth but released a hold on his cock.

Jesus, he was so hard. He could feel his pulse in his shaft, knew he was ridiculously close to coming. He was slick with his own pre-cum, and wished like fuck he'd had the chance to experience Perry's warmth.

Before he could be reprimanded again, he clambered out from between Perry's legs and shot Edward a pissed-off look—his brother returned it with a simple cocking of his eyebrow as George leaned over and spread Perry's ass cheeks. She squeaked at the move, then let out a low moan as George bent his head and rimmed the taut pucker.

Her hips bowed forward again, trying to escape, but he didn't let her. Instead, he flickered and fluttered his tongue over the sensitive rim, loving her responsiveness to his touch. When she'd stopped squeaking, had grown a little acclimated to the caress, he stroked a finger through her pussy lips, up to her clit which he flicked, then slid it into her cunt. When his digit was coated, he returned to her asshole and began to push it deep inside.

Her ass clenched tautly about it, and he watched as, for the first time, she began to struggle beneath Edward's grip on her hair. He immediately let go, and she pulled away with a gasp. Her hands fell to the bed, and her head bowed.

"Oh God," she whimpered, her pelvis rocking in a way that told him his finger in her ass was more satisfying than she'd remembered...

"Think she's hungry enough?"

Edward's cool question had George snickering. "I doubt it."

"What more do you want?" she said on a pant.

"For you to beg."

Silence fell at her words, and George felt his cock throb once again with the cool threat in Edward's voice. It was a true testament to how stressed Edward was that his emotions were on lock down here.

"Or what?" Perry asked thickly.

"Or George and I will return to the living room and carry on discussing the parliamentary session tomorrow."

"You wouldn't," Perry cried.

Edward cupped his wife's face, and with the coldest, chilliest smile, whispered, "I would. *Beg.*"

George frowned at Edward's smile—he didn't like it. Didn't like it at all. But Perry responded to it in a way he could never have foreseen... she rocked upward, her arms sliding around Edward's waist.

"Please don't leave me," she begged.

Edward's hand slipped up to cup the back of her head as he brushed a kiss to her temple. "I'll never leave you," he promised. "I'm yours."

Her mouth quivered as she peered up at him, her eyes astonishingly wet as some kind of byplay went on between the two of them—it went over George's head, but he was aware that it was important.

That a message was being sent and shared.

That he needed to keep his mouth goddamn shut, even if he disapproved of how Edward was going about whatever the fuck he was doing.

"You promise?"

"I swear it on my life. I'll never leave you. You'll have to leave *me.* You're mine," Edward vowed, his voice deep, his tone sleek as silk. Sincerity floated through the words in a way that rocked George to his soul.

"I won't leave you," she sobbed out. "I can't."

"You say that now," Edward chided softly.

Her mouth worked and a confused scowl made her brow pucker. "I love you, Edward."

"And I love you," he immediately replied, "But George and I will still depart to the sitting room if you don't beg for our cocks."

She swallowed, turned her head to look at George who, despite the intimacy of their conversation, didn't feel left out. Her mouth trembled again, and she whispered, "I love you, George."

"I love you too," he told her instantly.

She closed her eyes, nodding as she turned back to Edward. Pressing her forehead against his chest, she said in the quietest tone, "I need you. Both of you. I want you all over me. I want to be between you forever. I need you in my pussy, my ass, my mouth. All of me belongs to you. I want to taste your cum, I want to know it's mine and nobody else's.

"I want your marks on me. I want my marks on you. I want the fucking world to know you're mine.

"My pussy's so wet for you. I'm aching." Her words suddenly choked, and she pulled her head back, and looking directly into Edward's eyes, whispered, "Please. I need your cock, my love. My darling, please. Fill me. Give me all of you. I need you."

Edward's eyes flared with triumph, his expression changing in the blink of an eye from blank to engaged. The transformation was instant, and he tilted his head forward to press a kiss to her nose.

"You can have me."

"Us," George corrected.

Edward blinked, then nodded at the correction. "Where do you want us, sweetheart?"

Perry's eyes were wet again. "You won't tease me anymore?"

"We're going to make you fly," Edward vowed, his fingers curling about a stray strand of Perry's hair that had stuck to her sweaty forehead.

She swallowed. "I want George in my ass and you in my pussy."

"That wasn't so hard, was it?" he whispered, his tongue popping out and supping at her temple. He tasted her, before tracing his lips down the side of her face. George watched, his stomach twisting, as Edward pinched her bottom lip with his teeth and tugged it away. She whimpered. "Every time we're together, I want you to remember this moment," he told her. "You're my everything, Perry. We're going to be yours."

"You already are," she sobbed. "I'd show Xavier if he was still here. Why isn't he here?" She began to cry, and the tears nearly broke his fucking heart.

He'd never imagined she'd be scared about them leaving. Jesus, they were frightened *she'd* go—they'd brought so much shit to her life, after all. Yet, *she* was scared of *them* leaving?

Though he was surprised, he thought it best to leave it to Edward, who seemed to know what Perry was going through. After the shooting, Perry had been vulnerable in ways George had never seen her before... Edward, who knew what it was to be truly defenseless and exposed, could empathize more than George, who had simply been too young to remember their kidnapping as boys.

"Xavier had to go," Edward crooned, "but he'll be back. He'll always be back."

She trembled. "He will?"

"He will," Edward vowed. He cupped her face again, then kissed her. He kissed her until George didn't know how they breathed, until he felt sure there was no oxygen hitting either of their lungs. He robbed her of air, took her breath, captured her soul, and claimed her as his, as *theirs*.

They surfaced with a deep breath, and George nodded in understanding at Edward's heavy-lidded gaze. Whatever the fuck had just happened had been necessary.

"Get the lube," Edward ordered his brother, who started to step away from their woman. She clung to him though, not letting him move.

"No! You'll leave," she whispered.

"I told you, I won't," he countered, pressing a kiss to her nose again. Edward shot George another look, and understanding where he was going with this, shuffled toward the bedside cabinet. Grabbing the bottle of lube from the top drawer, he coated his cock in the slick liquid, and with his eyelids twitching, jacked off once, twice, but no more. He didn't dare.

His fucking cum felt like it was boiling in his balls, and by God, did he need to get into that tight, hot ass of hers.

Licking his lips, he returned to her side with the bottle. She was back on hands and knees again, and he slid a hand along her spine. She arched like a pleased pussy cat, and her head bowed when he immediately dove for her ass.

He needed in. *Now.*

His fingers teased the pucker, the tips slipping into the rosette, then slowly spreading as he tried to prepare her for him. When she was moaning harder than she was tensing, he grabbed a tight hold of his cock, pressed the glans to her butt, and slowly entered heaven.

With each inch, sweet Jesus, he felt like he was coming home and being branded alive. She was so fucking hot, so scorching, he felt like she was razing his defenses to the quick.

What was it about her? George asked himself. What made her do this to him?

As he entered her, taking her, claiming her, he realized that the answer was simple—she was made for him. For them.

He bowed his head as the pressure on his cock reached fever pitch.

"Fuck," he gritted out, and she let out a long, deep moan as he hit home. "You're so fucking tight."

"You're so fucking big," she groaned.

"Is that a complaint?"

Edward snorted. "Are we going to have an argument here or something?"

"We'll only argue if you don't come inside me right this minute," she said on a pant.

He laughed, and George's head reared back in surprise at the sound. He saw the genuine joy on his brother's face and felt his stomach finally settle—some deep, hereto unforeseen insecurity unravelling at the deep pleasure Edward found in their bride.

He'd known Perry would bring a light to Edward's world. Had known it because she had the same effect on him. But he hadn't realized to what extent Perry would be Edward's damn lighthouse, illuminating all the pitch black places in his soul.

George covered Perry at her words, not stopping until he was draped over her like a hot and heavy blanket. Then, when she absorbed all his weight, he slipped his hands around her front to grab a hold of her tits. With a quick squeeze, he dragged her up against his chest, not stopping until the two of them were on their knees against the mattress.

"Fuck!" she squealed at the change in penetration.

George understood. His eyes felt like they were about to goddamn cross from the clamp she had around his cock. Before she could say another word, Edward climbed onto the bed, and together, he and George worked to lift Perry's legs. The move should have been awkward, but practice makes perfect, and their misspent youth hadn't been wasted.

Still, all these years later, it was strange to come full circle. To be back where they'd once started.

With her legs now hooked over George's forearms, he kept her spread wide. She was a lot lighter than she used to be—he didn't strain a damn in holding her like this. Sure, he'd been working out more, needing to burn off his anger and aggression against the world in the gym in the palace basement, but not this damn much! She was barely a waif in his arms, a notion that made him prickle with worry.

He'd known her too long to fail to forget that she'd been a comfort eater all her life. A pint of ice cream after a shitty day at work was her failsafe… that had apparently changed since she'd arrived in his country.

Before he could scowl too much, hands came and cupped Perry's ass. Edward helped support her as he approached the two of them. She squeaked a little, the cute noise making both of them laugh as she pressed her hands to Ed's shoulders.

His brother murmured, "Put me inside you, Perry. You begged for it. It's all yours."

A breathy gasp escaped her as she complied. George peered over her shoulder, saw the delicious sway of her tits, then bit his lip as she grabbed Ed's cock and pressed it to her pussy. His fucking eyes twitched as she struggled to get him inside.

"Bear down."

At his order, George laughed again. "Get used to hearing that instruction, Perry."

She huffed out a breath. "Great time to remind me I'm going to give birth soon."

Cheerfully, he told her, "If you can pop out a kid with that treasure tunnel, I'm sure you can fit Edward too."

"You did not just call it that!" she choked out.

"What would Her Highness prefer? Jizz jar? Spasm chasm?"

As though the outrage at having her bits called a "jizz jar" was all the challenge she needed, she let out a triumphant sound and accepted his brother's cock. As Ed surged inside her, claiming her inch by inch, George had to press his forehead to her shoulder at the exquisite tightness.

"Jesus," he whispered hoarsely, rubbing his temple against her slick throat.

"God," she said on a breathy high.

"You feel so fucking good," Edward grunted, and then he stole her breath once more by claiming her mouth.

As they kissed, George began to sup at her throat. He bit down hard, making her jerk, then laved the area with his tongue, prickling the jolted nerve endings to life again as he gave her the marks she'd asked for.

A whimper escaped her as Edward began to thrust, slow and sure.

George whispered, "Touch your clit, Perry."

She moaned at his command, but did as bid. As he gave her a deep hickey, he watched her fingers begin to frig her clit, fast and hard, harder than he'd have expected.

Her ass clenched down against his cock, and at that moment, he truly felt Ed's cock rub his own through the thin membrane separating the two of them.

He knew it should have been weird, and to many it probably would be, but to feel her so desperate for them, to know it was his and Ed's cock making her feel this way... it triggered an implosion in his nerves, one that sent wildfire through his blood.

He'd stayed still, not wanting to jerk her about too much, but as a desperate need overwhelmed him, he rocked his hips forward in short, staccato bursts that had an endless, keening cry escaping her mouth.

Edward began to swear in Veronian. An endless litany. A promise of forever buried within the curse words as Perry did the unthinkable.

Broke his brother's reserve.

Broke the bastard's control.

He wasn't sure how it happened. Didn't know it was possible, just knew that the climax, when it hit, exploded throughout the three of them. The simultaneous orgasm, so impossible and improbable, had the three of them crying out so loudly, so hoarsely, George feared someone would overhear.

Then, as quickly as the fear came, the pleasure washed it away, and all he was left with was the fucking rightness of this moment.

As they took their woman, made her theirs, they urged her to realize nothing would separate them. That they would be together until death fucking parted them, and that death would be happening decades in the future...

The promise of more, of a life together, blossomed between them with the rich evocativeness of knowing that between them, their child grew.

A blessing, a vow, of forever.

CHAPTER FOURTEEN

XAVIER WATCHED as Edward got to his feet in Parliament.

All around him, in the various stands belonging to different parties, the members of Parliament began to shuffle in place.

They had to know what was coming. Had to be aware of the threat of Article 42 being invoked, and their unease was proof positive of the fear they felt at the prospect.

The minute Edward triggered the Article, the several-hundred-strong Parliament became ineffective.

These politicians' careers hung in the balance, and they knew it.

The future of the country rested in Edward's hands, but if that pressure, the strain, was getting to him, it wasn't on his face. If anything, he looked rested. A peace about him that surprised Xavier, considering how uncertain Edward had been yesterday during their discussion.

Sitting back against the chilly maroon leather that covered the seats of the audience section, open for anyone to view any Parliamentary session at any point of the year, he watched as silence fell when Edward began to speak.

"For this, my first session among you," he said, his tone crystal clear and without hint of a waver—Jesus, his cousin could be ice-cold sometimes, Xavier thought with a grimace. "I wish to discuss several issues that are affecting our country, but worse, our political systems.

"An ill wind has blown among our people. That ill wind has a name.

"The UnReals are terrorists. For years, we have cast them only in the guise as freedom fighters. People who just dislike the throne, for injuries incurred against them by my ascendants.

"I pitied those people. I forgave them the many grievous sins they orchestrated against me personally, as well as my brother, and I came to terms with the fact that they felt the need to voice their displeasure with our current system.

"The people of this nation have the right to believe whatever they wish to. They can hate me, loathe my family, or they can love us and cherish us. But as recent events have proven, the latter is a stronger force in our nation.

"The DeSauviers, whether the UnReals like it or not, are beloved by the Veronian people.

"This is for several reasons. Our love for our nation is true. Our duty is given wholeheartedly to our people, and while the average man might believe we are out of touch thanks to our pretty palaces and the money in our banks, the DeSauviers on the whole, as well as myself and my queen, intend to protect Veronia for its future generations—not simply its current people.

"Veronia has been hit by several crises of late that I wish to address in the early years of my reign. My father brought to light the rates of recidivism in our jails—an untenable truth that reflects poorly on our society. We have too many criminals who, after leaving prison, return to a life of crime because they find they have no place, have no route to turn to other than that of their previous history.

"My father was shot down in this very Parliament. Considered too radical, too free-thinking. But his thinking is the future. We are all one decision away from making a choice that will forever affect our lives and those around us. As I stand here today, you, the members of *my* Parliament, are aware of that more than ever."

Xavier had to hide a laugh at that cutting remark. *Touché, Edward,* he thought.

A concerned rumble spread among the politicians like a grumbling Mexican wave. It consisted of uneasy shuffling, of ruffling papers, of jostling feet—Edward's point had hit home.

Rightly so.

"The future isn't one where we mark our people as sinners forever. Where we refuse to allow them a second chance, and I say this knowing that there are several people who await jail thanks to crimes committed against my family. I uphold my father's dream of a more just society for all its members—even though terrorists recently slaughtered my mother and have put my father in a coma.

"The second matter of business is the recent ecological crisis that has befallen the nation. Our water shortage, according to reports, will be reaching critical levels by the middle of the century. This information was fully supported by several experts within the nation. However, my own wife, who visited this country in her role as environmental scientist—practicing such science at an establishment in the United States of America that is above reproach—has proof that our ecological crisis doesn't exist.

"Or, that is to say, it does exist, but not for any ecological reason such as climate change. The disaster that is waiting to befall us is manmade."

A roar of outrage spread among the Parliament with the force of an ill wind. Xavier, surprised at the path Edward was taking with his speech, quickly glanced around the politicians. There were too many faces for him to read, but he caught unease in some members' expressions, and took a mental note as to who those people were and their appointed seats.

Politics, until recently, had never interested Xavier. Just as life at court hadn't.

With Edward's coronation, and Perry's appearance in Xavier's world, more than just his love life had changed. His entire world was shifting, taking on a new direction...and Xavier couldn't help but regret how out of touch he was.

Still, it was better late than never.

He watched the way Edward commanded the crowd, and he realized that Ed was playing them all. Manipulating the politicians. Not putting them out of their misery in regards to Article 42, but in fact, shoring up the very reasons why the Article should be introduced into power.

Edward waited, quite at ease, as the politicians argued and debated among themselves. The in-fighting was a cluster of back-biting and swearing that took an age to die down. After a good five minutes, the speaker of the house roared, "Silence in the stands!"

Even then, it took two attempts for the conversations to stop.

When there was quiet once more, Edward murmured, as though the politicians weren't totally up in arms, "The serving government wishes to repress this information from you. Indeed, the Environmental Agency is totally in denial that the drought is manmade at all.

"However, I ask you—why my wife would make such a claim if it were not true? There is no gain to her being deceptive.

"It is why I have requested several leading experts from around the world to visit our great nation over the following months to investigate the matter. Until we have the whole truth, a truth this government seems to be willfully ignoring—" More outrage bubbled and swelled among the stands, but Edward carried on, raising his voice to be overheard. "I will not rest. The future of this country is all that matters.

"And this leads me to the final matter. Such a threat to our water supply can only be the brainchild of one organization. Veronia has its naysayers, and the monarchy has groups who disapprove of it, but for the most part, we are unified with one body of terrorists who wish to destabilize this nation.

"The UnReals.

"They have targeted me and my brother. They kidnapped us from our beds as children, they tortured us and abused us, and the men in charge, the men captured, paid for that act with their lives. But that payment isn't enough.

"My mother was brutally slain. My father lies in a coma in his hospital bed. Two loyal servants of this country were treated like they were animals to be butchered, and yet, the outrage is felt only by my family, by the people of Veronia, and not the people in this room.

"You are quite content to let the matter of the UnReals be a distinctly royal matter. You wish my guards, my security, to handle the threats thrown at us. Your lack of willingness to help us does, at times, make you all appear like UnReal supporters.

"Perhaps this comes as no surprise considering the previous prime minister was seen with an UnReal. A high-ranking member of the rebel group, at that. With his brother-in-law deeply embedded in the Environmental Agency, is it any wonder there is doubt where there should be none about the issues with our water supply?

"Who among you here is a secret supporter of a group of extremists who is willing to destroy the Veronian way of life to push their own agenda to the fore?"

Standing there in his tailored navy suit, not a hair out of place, his jaw clean-shaven, every part of him manicured to the hilt, it was hard to believe the impassioned words were coming from him. But that last part, those final words...they seemed to stir even Edward's bile.

He clenched both his fists and beat the air at his sides. His rage spilling forth with a power that was all the stronger because of his lack of emotion before. At that moment, the king was present, and the entire Parliament was aware of it.

A hush like no other breathed among the politicians. The threat of the Article hung overhead like the hangman's noose awaiting its next victim.

Edward's fists were still tightly clenched as he stated, "An investigation was started this morning. I personally discussed it with the nation's police force. I bypassed James Branche, as his leadership has proven to be nothing other than ineffective."

Xavier cut the newly-interred leader a glance. The man looked close to purple with rage at Edward's bitter statement. But then, Branche obviously had cardiovascular issues—he was always some bizarre shade of red.

"For decades, the police force of Veronia has been considered to be a neutral body among the security services. Servicing the nation, not the royal family or Parliament's whims. The DeSauviers will seek justice from them, and any among you who have ties to the UnReals…" Edward clenched his jaw. "You would do yourself a service to admit to so before being called up for an interview."

Branche stormed to his feet. "This is the first step to chaos. To a dictatorship! To purge us…"

The Speaker bellowed, "Silence in the House!"

Edward simply narrowed his eyes. "The first step to chaos would be calling Article 42 into power. Every single one of you knows that I am well within my rights to invoke it, and yet, my wife, your queen, who was so recently targeted by the butchers of Helstern, has fought on Veronia's behalf.

"Like a true national, she has spoken of her desire for democracy, and through her, I have seen the truth of this. However, that truth remains viable only if our police force combs through the powers that are in this country. Every stone will be unturned," he warned, his lip curling in a sneer. "No secret pocket of your life will not be uncovered. This is an anti-corruption investigation that will shake this government, which has proven itself to be unethical, immoral, and quite willing to allow traitors to roam free among my beloved subjects.

"This is your warning. Heed it." Edward cut the Speaker a glance. "That is all."

Watching his cousin take a seat, Xavier leaned forward and rested his elbows on his knees. Bowing his head, he watched the true chaos unfold as the government, a body founded on democracy and personal choice, began to chew itself up in the melee of Edward's declaration.

There was no relief to be found on any politician's face. If anything, there was more concern.

Why that was so, when Edward hadn't, in one fell swoop, eradicated any need for them, Xavier didn't know.

But the police were about to find out.

Two hours later, back at Masonbrook, Xavier took a deep sip from the chalice his wine had just been served in. The metal was cold in his hand, and the chill was surprisingly pleasant considering the cold day.

"That was a brave move you made today, Edward," he commented, after his cousin had explained the situation to George and Perry. "They were truly up in arms over it."

"Strange, considering I gave them a free pass for the moment." Edward's tone was musing as he forked up a nice sliver of Chateaubriand—one of the best steaks the kitchens sent out for their king.

As the man didn't eat in the most stressful of situations, Xavier was surprised to watch him dine. Though, they *were* at home, and Edward was getting better about eating in front of them.

In his mind's eye, he'd always seen his cousin as a bulimic hamster. One who'd shovel his cheeks full of food to look like he was eating, but who actually consumed zilch.

Perry was slowly changing that. Amazing, considering what had been happening in their lives of late.

On the honeymoon, Edward might have even gained a few pounds! Shocking stuff for a man who'd barely changed since he'd filled out and become a man.

"What?"

The question broke into his musing. "Nothing." Xavier shrugged, but pushed his own unfinished plate away from him—he, on the other hand, wasn't hungry.

Oh, the irony, considering he usually had the appetite of a horse.

Perry shot him a look as she began to fork up some of her own meal—he noticed that, too. Jesus, he was starting to feel like the food police. But only Xavier and George were eating like normal people. Perry had lost weight, Edward had gained weight—the world truly was in flux!

"See," she told him sweetly, after she swallowed a large mouthful of broccoli. "I do eat."

Xavier was surprised to find the comment wasn't aimed at him, but at George, who just rolled his eyes. "You two had a discussion?" Seemed more polite to use "discussion" when he meant "argument."

George firmed his lips. "More like a fight."

"A fight?" Edward cocked a brow. "Over what?"

"Someone's been skipping breakfast."

Xavier grinned. "She's got morning sickness, you idiot."

"I know," came the huffed response. "But that doesn't explain why she was skipping it before she found out she was bloody pregnant!"

"I swear to God, the next time she tells tales on me, I'm firing the Dragon."

"Rose?" Edward asked, his brow puckering.

"Who else spies on me like the Gestapo? I swear, if you wanted to ease my load, Edward, you shouldn't have picked a Nazi sympathizer."

"She came highly recommended," he retorted smoothly.

"Who by? Goebbels? When she's not watching everything I do with more interest than a hawk on its prey, she's telling everything to His Lordship over there."

"I'm a Prince, Perry. I'd have thought you'd have figured that out by now."

Her eyes flashed, and she stabbed the air with her knife. "You won't be anything if you carry on keeping tabs on me through her. How the hell am I supposed to relax around her if she's a spy for you? It's bad enough being surrounded by guards all the damn time."

"She's not wrong, George." Edward frowned thoughtfully. "I didn't realize you were pumping Rose for information."

"Jesus, I happened to ask the woman how Perry was getting on with her engagements." George shot his brother a look. "Then she told me about Perry's new eating habits."

Perry squinted. "George, when have you known me to diet?"

"Never. That's my point."

"No. That's *my* point. I don't diet. I can't. It's physically impossible for me to deprive myself."

"So what the hell are you doing to yourself now then?" he groused.

"She's saying, idiot, that she's *not* depriving herself." Xavier heaved out a sigh, then referring to his summa cum laude, he continued, "I swear to God, I wonder how you got a double first at Cambridge sometimes."

George glowered at him. "Through hard work and bloody brilliance?"

"Doesn't help you with our woman though, does it?"

"No, Mr. Mathlete, it sure as shit doesn't," Perry hissed. "No woman likes to have her food watched. Whether it's because she's losing or gaining weight. Just leave me be. I'm acclimating to a very trying ordeal, and if I'm not stuffing my fucking face as usual, then maybe, just maybe, it's because I'm just not hungry."

"You need to watch your food intake now, for the baby," George argued. "You have to keep your strength up."

"Why? So I can smack you upside the head better?" Perry retorted, stabbing the air with her fork now. "You're skating on thin ice."

Xavier laughed. "I hope you're shivering in your shoes, George."

"Positively quaking," came the biting retort, as he and Perry began a staring contest that would have impressed a pack of feral dogs.

Edward tapped his chalice against his water glass and the ringing sound had both of them jerking away from one another. "Calm down, you two. I really don't feel like fighting. Not after the morning I've had."

Perry winced. "Sorry, sweetheart."

Xavier let out a small laugh. "Don't be sorry for him. He had every single politician in Parliament dropping to their knees in terror."

"You're exaggerating," Edward grumbled, but Xavier was disappointed to note he placed his knife and fork back on the plate. Perry seemed to notice, too, because she shot Xavier a displeased glance.

Wincing, he murmured, "No. You owned that moment, Edward. When that goes live on all the news broadcasts, Jesus, the people are going to be so proud that you're their leader."

"Shut up," he grumbled again.

"No. It's the truth. I know you're nervous about everything. But we all are. We're all having to find our way on this path, but you should know that we have your back."

"He's right, Ed," George inserted, taking another sip of his drink. "It's not enough to just share the workload with us. You have to share the stresses and tensions, too."

Edward's jaw flexed. "What good will it do to frighten you?"

His tone was so low and gravelly, it was hard to hear. Xavier frowned at it, then asked, "Frighten us? In what way?" Xavier, unlike George, was more in the know about most aspects of life at court.

Edward, though he didn't always share, did talk to him more than he did his younger brother.

"There's a lot going on," was all Edward said. "A lot you don't need to know."

"Why don't we?" Perry asked. "If it's worrying you, then maybe talking about it will help break it down. And maybe our insights will help?" Edward fell silent a second, and Perry sighed. "Never mind."

Her husband shook his head. "No. It's just about Mother, that's all."

"What about her?" George insisted, his shoulders straightening at his brother's words.

"I had some suspicions confirmed. I just know you guys were in the dark."

"Don't keep us guessing," Xavier said drily.

Edward shrugged. "I knew she'd had affairs. I also know that she had one with Drake. That's why I'm more lenient with him, George. I know he'd never have done anything to hurt Mother. He loved her too much."

For a second, George's mouth was agape. Then, Perry reached for his hand which was flat on the mahogany table, and curled her fingers about his.

"George, it's okay," Ed murmured. "It's too late to cast guilt, too late to lay blame on anyone."

"You knew? For how long?" George demanded, his voice gritty.

"About Drake? Not until recently. He told me."

"We were talking about her affairs on the way to the hospital," he stated, cutting Perry a quick glance. Xavier saw her fingers tighten about his. "You never said a word."

"I didn't want to. It wasn't the time."

"We were discussing how their pasts could be affecting our damn present, Edward. How could that not be relevant?"

"I'm trying to protect you," Edward said softly, for the first time, an edge appearing to his tone. "It's a force of habit, George. I've been doing it since..."

"Since we were children. Since we were kidnapped. I know, Edward. I know. But I'm old enough to be able to help you, goddammit! What else haven't you told us? I demand to know if it means we can figure out what the fuck is going on with the UnReals."

Edward rested his arm on the polished mahogany table. His elbow accidentally jerked the ornate silverware he hadn't used with his meal as he pressed his head to his closed fist. The pose was that of Rodin's *The Thinker*, but Edward looked far more pensive than that classical sculpture ever could.

The man had the weight of the world on his shoulders. Xavier just wished he'd share some of the fucking worry.

"Edward," Perry insisted gently. "We need to know. You're keeping this from us while we're all in danger. Your keeping us uninformed isn't going to save us."

Xavier saw how tightly his cousin's jaw was clenched, then, as though the words were being torn from him, he bit out, "The UnReal that De Montfort met...he was related to the man Mother had an affair with."

For a second, peace reigned, before George whispered, "Excuse me?"

Edward closed his eyes, and Xavier knew just how hard this was for his cousin. He wasn't lying when he said that he'd been protecting them all their lives. He'd always taken the most solid route to satisfy his parents, leaving George and Xavier the freedom to live how they wanted. To lead the lives they wanted to lead.

Edward had married that cold bitch, had endured a life of servitude to the Crown, while Xavier had pottered away in his greenhouse, ignoring Marianne's summons to royal events, and George had partied it up in the US. Making a name for himself as a venture capitalist, and all at his brother's expense, as Edward singlehandedly took on the duties of two princes of the realm, not just one.

This was a habit that had been born over a lifetime.

There was no easy fix. No simple way to break it open.

"Drake informed me of this after the shooting. He was explaining certain matters to me, and I had to process them myself before I could even begin to share the news."

"It's okay," Perry said softly. "We're not blaming you." She cut George a sharp glance. "We're not, Edward. Just take your time. We need to know this."

The footmen who had lined the room once dinner had been served had been swiftly cast out when Perry had smiled politely, but pointedly, at them all. The formality of life at Masonbrook was slowly morphing under her reign, and Xavier wasn't displeased about it. Especially not at moments like these, when it meant they were in as much privacy as they could expect at the castle.

Edward swallowed thickly. "Mother had this affair when she found out Father had a mistress in Luxembourg. He was visiting a lot, and I knew this about her already—she liked to think she was punishing him for having a mistress.

"According to Drake, she had a long-term affair with this man, and eventually, she fell pregnant."

The three members of Edward's audience choked at his words. Perry, who'd been reaching for the glass in front of her, accidentally knocked its contents over. She tossed her napkin on the spillage as she gaped at her husband. "Marianne was pregnant by another man?" she repeated.

"Yes," Edward said stiffly, his gaze fixed on the woodgrain. With his free hand, he traced the line, apparently not even seeing the water that had pooled close to his fingers. "She had an abortion, and then separated from her lover. When he found out, he plotted some revenge of his own."

George narrowed his eyes, but his voice was equally as gritty as he asked, "Why don't you name him? Why do you keep saying 'the man'?"

"Because the minute I tell you his name, you'll hate Mother, and this isn't her fault."

For a second, Xavier was stunned beyond belief. There was only one reason why George would care, so many years later… "No. It isn't possible," he whispered, his hands clenching around his own napkin.

Edward finally looked up and over at him. His mouth trembled as he nodded.

"What? Who is it?" George demanded.

Perry licked her lips. "What's going on, loves?"

Xavier swallowed. "The man…Marianne's lover, it was Laurence Prichard."

Her scowl was dark. "Wait a minute. I saw his name on Google. Wasn't he…?"

And like that, the peaceful moment crashed and burned. George got to his feet, and with one fell swoop, slid his hand across the table, knocking centuries-old china and porcelain to the ground with a lack of care that even Xavier didn't feel. Because at that moment, he wasn't feeling anything.

"No." George slammed his fists down against the table. "I won't believe it."

Edward shook his head. "I wish it weren't the truth, George. But it is."

The pain that flashed over his younger's cousin's features hurt Xavier. "No. I refuse to believe Mother was the reason we were kidnapped."

"It would seem that is the way of it."

The words were softly whispered, but George heard them. His head bucked like he'd just been punched in the face, then he spun on his heel and strode out of the room. After he'd slammed the door, Perry jumped to her feet, but Xavier grabbed her hand across the table and stated firmly, "No. Let him process this himself, Perry."

"But he needs me!" she cried.

"No. He needs time," Xavier insisted. She tried to evade his hands, tried to dislodge his grip, but he remained firm. "He'll only say something to upset you, and none of us want that. Especially when he doesn't even mean it."

Her mouth trembled. "He shouldn't be alone at a moment like this."

Edward let out a shaky sigh. "Xavier's right, darling. George needs a moment. He'll go to the gym and beat ten rounds of shit out of the punchbag. He'll be back, and he'll be better for it." He shot Xavier a look, and the truth was couched within it—George would be back, but he *wouldn't* be better for it.

"What a fucking mess," Xavier spat, his fingers clawing into fists atop the table. "So, what? You said the guy in the photos with De Montfort is Prichard's sibling?"

"His brother, Jacob," Edward confirmed.

"And what? What's his play here?" Perry asked on a squeak.

Edward shrugged. "I don't know. It would seem he's looking to avenge his brother... but it's not like we've done anything to hurt him ever, is it?"

"No, but the establishment has. Marianne had an abortion, doing away with Prichard's child, then Prichard was killed for taking revenge. God only knows what something like that can do to a man. A close brother could want to take up the cause. Stranger things have happened."

"This is crazy," Perry said softly.

"No, what's crazy is the fact that something's going on that is evading all of us."

"Like what?" Xavier demanded.

"Like the fact we have moles in our guards. And codes of said moles that Ferdinand L'Argeneau has used to gain access to our private rooms."

Xavier grimaced as a thought occurred to him—a spanner in the works of Edward's theory. "Did George tell you?"

"Tell me what?"

He rubbed his chin. "If you're trying to imply that L'Argeneau is involved, I doubt it. He tried to match George with his younger daughter before the wedding."

"He'd better have damn well turned her down!" Perry said on a low growl.

Edward snorted. "Of course, he did. Don't be silly, Perry." As he pondered the situation, he slowly shook his head. "No, Xavier. That was either a final play at manipulation or an attempt to dispel our suspicions. I know L'Argeneau accessed my father's rooms recently."

Perry shuffled in her seat. "Drake told you," she accused.

"Drake *and* George told me," he corrected coolly, his gaze chilly as he scanned it over his wife. "As you should have done."

"Told you what?"

She hunched her shoulders. "You remember when you showed me the secret passage to the Tulip Room?"

He frowned. "Yes. What about it?" Though he could remember the inferno they'd created together, he highly doubted she was talking about that delicious lovemaking of theirs.

"Well, L'Argeneau kind of burst his way into the ward, and he was making all kinds of accusations."

When she nipped at her bottom lip, he chivvied her along. "What kind of accusations?"

"He was making out that we'd had a hand in killing her, Xavier." Edward shot him a look.

"But that makes no sense. I spoke with Drake about it. He said she was very weak because of all the drugs she used to take," she persevered.

For the first time since this discussion had begun, a lightness overcame Edward as he laughed. It was a cold laugh, granted, but his amusement was genuine. "The woman *rattled*, Perry. That's how many drugs she was taking. If it wasn't to stay thin, it was to stay awake. And if it wasn't for that, it was because she was bored. She also drank, and she barely ate anything.

"When I found out she'd died of the flu, it didn't particularly come as a surprise."

"Were you relieved?"

The question had Edward rearing back. "Excuse me?"

Perry wriggled her shoulders. "Drake said you'd been estranged for a while. Had been sharing separate bedrooms." She pursed her lips. "And L'Argeneau said she knew a lot of secrets that the family wouldn't have wanted her to share."

"She couldn't have shared them," he countered. "We were under no threat from her. If she'd wanted any kind of settlement at all, it would have been suicide to utter a peep about anything she might have learned."

Perry frowned. "Why?"

"The prenup, Perry."

"The one I didn't sign, you mean?" she asked, her brow cocked. But her admission stunned Xavier.

"You didn't ask Perry to sign one?"

"His parents tried, but he stopped me from agreeing to anything." She lengthened her neck like an irritated peahen. "Why? Don't you trust me?"

"Implicitly," Xavier immediately retorted, cutting her billowing agitation before it could swell further. "I'm just surprised Marianne let you get away with it."

"Marianne had no say in it," Edward said, his tone thick. "They forced me to marry Arabella. Said I was shaming the family with my lack of responsibility. They said marrying her, settling down, and bearing the next heir was one way to apologize for my inability to do my duty."

His words sounded exactly like something Marianne would say. God, his *tanta* had had the ability of wielding words with the precision of a knife.

"Oh, Edward. I'm sorry, darling." Before either of them could do more than jump in surprise, she'd scraped her chair back and had rushed over to his side. She flung herself over his armrest and curled her arms around his neck.

Though Edward looked shell-shocked at the attention, he let out a shuddery breath and sank into her hold.

"It's okay, Perry. I'm fine now. I have you."

"Why didn't you make me sign a prenup?"

"I told you before," he whispered. "You're my life. If you go, you can have anything you want, because you'll only go if I've done something to make you leave. I know you love me."

A sob escaped her. "Don't say that. Why do you think I'll leave you?"

His tone was solemn, "Everyone leaves, Perry. Everyone."

"Not me," she vowed, and Xavier felt his own throat grow thick in response to her words.

The oath was palpable. So strong that it seemed to beat like a heart, making the air pulse with it.

Edward nuzzled his temple against hers. "It doesn't matter anyway. Arabella is gone, and I did nothing to harm her."

"I never really thought you did, sweetheart. I was just asking why L'Argeneau was so certain that someone *had* done something to Arabella."

Xavier, though the poignancy of the moment had affected him too, forced his mind to focus. The instant he did, a memory came to him. "Edward, remember when Philippe told us there was evidence Arabella had been murdered?"

"No. I remembered that too." Perry shook her head. "Drake said that was a ruse. He'd found some gossip on the dark web that the UnReals were using to recruit new members."

Edward frowned. "No, that can't be true."

"Why can't it?" Perry asked, straightening up a little.

"Because I looked into it myself. Had my man, Markov, investigate for me."

"Investigate what?"

"The claims Drake came up with. He found something."

Xavier nodded, feeling his blood start to race like a hound that had finally picked up the scent of the fox. "The doctors who cared for Arabella, all of the paramedics who transported her to the hospital, the man who declared her DOA, and the pathologist who practiced the autopsy...over the space of the last two years, they've all been killed."

"Surely not!" Perry argued, but her arms tensed around Edward. "You're looking for conspiracies."

"No." Xavier wished they were. "The deaths looked like accidents, but nobody's that unlucky, Perry. Without that singular link, *Arabella*, there'd be no reason for suspicion to fall anywhere. Accidents happen. But with L'Argeneau asking questions about her death? Piecing that together with what Markov found out..." Typical that he'd been the last to hear of L'Argeneau's sneak visit into the castle—even if he'd been the one to deal with the direct aftermath.

Perry *had* seemed dazed that afternoon, but he'd mistaken it for her being on shaky ground after the shooting. He'd never imagined it could be to do with Edward's former father-in-law.

The sneaky, lying bastard.

"And this so-called gossip about Arabella's death being some kind of cover-up to hide family secrets was on a recruiting sight for the UnReals?" Edward asked, his tone urgent as he broke into Xavier's grim thoughts.

Perry nodded. "Or so he said." She prodded Edward in the arm. "If you'd have told Drake instead of keeping your own investigation from him, he might have been able to help instead of dealing with the situation blindly."

Edward held up a hand. "Markov works unofficially for me, love. Even my father wouldn't approve of my using him. We've been friends for years, and using the security services was a surefire way to clue my father into things I didn't always want to bother him with. I trust Markov implicitly. With my life, and more importantly, yours. You can be assured, he's the best."

"Veronia and Russia aren't exactly on friendly terms, Perry," Xavier explained. "There's a lot of history between us."

She blinked, then laughed a little. "Jesus, my life belongs in a history book, doesn't it?"

"It does now," Edward said softly, but he rubbed his chin against her shoulder to comfort her.

Perry let out a sigh, but resolutely demanded, "Why would anyone want to murder those doctors?"

"To get a man like Ferdinand L'Argeneau on their side," Xavier reasoned, and even as he said the words, he knew it to be the truth. That bastard was wily, corrupt, and worst of all—he was a member of Parliament. Throw in the fact his fortune inspired envy in even the richest of men, he was the kind of person a group of rebels wanted on their side.

Bombs, weapons, snipers, and hitmen… they sure as hell didn't come cheap.

"Who is he? Aside from Arabella's father, I mean."

"Philippe and he used to be friends, and then when it didn't work out between Arabella and Edward, they fell out. That was even before she died."

"So what? That happens. Divorces aren't exactly uncommon anymore, are they?"

"L'Argeneau's a kingmaker, Perry," Edward explained.

"What does that mean? You're king. Not him."

"No. He *makes* kings. De Montfort? The man's not even in L'Argeneau's party, and yet, only through Ferdinand, did he get the backing to rise through the ranks to become prime minister. Ferdinand has the kind of influence you can't even begin to believe.

"He knows everything about anyone. Has his fingers in everything because it pays for him to know what's happening and where.

"Some petty politician being murdered in Cozumel, and another politician's mistress giving birth to his child…that's the kind of information he peddles."

"But why?" Perry asked, gaping at the notion. "Why would something like that be of interest to him?"

"Because he'll be *behind* the murder of the politician; he'll use the death to heft the politician with a lovechild into the man's seat, and through that, will gain influence on the council or government.

"It's a well-kept secret among certain people. He rides the border of decency and illegitimacy, and uses who and what he knows to stay out of jail and away from the attention of law enforcement."

Her mouth was a perfect "O." "But he's a member of Parliament! Why do you let him carry on working for Parliament when he's so corrupt?"

"It's not like we have a choice. He gets voted in democratically. He wins the vote for his constituency."

"Surely, he manipulates the votes?" Perry scowled—her democratic heart rejecting such a prospect.

"No. Father investigated the matter once after another friend complained about him. The man's been working for Parliament for decades without losing power once. Father looked and found nothing. Either because Ferdinand's hidden it too well, or he's genuinely popular with his section." Edward rubbed his temple.

"I tend to think it's the latter," Xavier inserted quietly, then began to drum his fingers against the table. "Don't forget, he's actually the member of Parliament who governs part of my estate. He's good. He's *very* good. Hands-on when it comes time to work with powerful men, men who can not only make use of his influence, but can pay to make sure Ferdinand gets into power time after time."

"You've had him help you?"

Xavier nodded at Edward's question. "My estate's land is protected. You know that. I had to deal with him to get the greenhouse built. It was a necessary evil, but he was quite good about it."

"Did you bribe him?"

He snorted. "No. Of course not. If I had, I'm under no doubt it would have been in the papers within the week."

"He must have expected a favor in return."

"If he did, he never outright mentioned it," he countered. "And even so, if it went against the grain, I would never agree to it. You know that, Edward."

"Of course, I do, but he doesn't. He has something over you now."

Xavier snorted again. "He can try to use it. If he wants to make me do something I don't want, he can throw it to the press. Even if it involves him finding out about this...." He made a circle with his finger, indicating the four of them. "I wouldn't kowtow to him."

"You say that now," Perry reasoned uneasily.

"No, I mean it now. I won't be blackmailed. Emotionally or financially." Xavier shrugged. "I think Ferdinand knows that. If anything, he'll have helped me to make me think kindly of him. Having the Duke of Ansian favor you is as good a bribe as anything.

"You know how businessmen like associating with people who work for the royals."

Edward nodded. Slowly. "He's right, Perry."

She whistled out a breath. "I swear, I'll never understand this world."

"You don't have to," Edward said on a faint laugh. "You just have to learn to work your way through it."

"If you say so." She huffed.

"Getting Ferdinand to believe the DeSauviers had killed his daughter would help the UnReals greatly. Can you imagine how much money he could funnel the group's way?"

"Enough to fund two hot-shit snipers, you mean?" Xavier pointed out gruffly.

Perry let out a startled gasp. "Oh my God, it makes sense!"

"Too much sense," Edward said on a sigh. "Trouble is, we can't haul Ferdinand in. He's far too powerful, and we'd only look like I was actively going against what I declared to one and all today."

"No, you said the police would be interviewing every member of Parliament."

"Yeah, without any influence from me," Edward argued.

"Shit."

At Xavier's curse, Perry snorted. "Ever eloquent."

He shot her a wink, and smiled when she chuckled.

"How do you prove to someone like Ferdinand L'Argeneau that you didn't kill his daughter? I mean, she died of an illness, for God's sake. How do you prove that?"

"Good point." Xavier fiddled with the knife and fork in front of him. "How do we?"

As he pondered that a second, Edward murmured, "The UnReals murdered the doctors and paramedics who tended Arabella to make it seem like there was a conspiracy. So, we prove that the UnReals were actually behind the murders, and unravel the evidence from within."

Nodding, Xavier asked, "Good thinking. Will you use Markov?"

"He's proven himself faster than Drake."

"Will we ever meet this Markov?" Perry grumbled. "I feel badly for Drake. We're working around him—like I said before, how can he be efficient if he's working blind?"

"I'd prefer for him to focus on the matters at hand—our personal security. Just because we might have figured out what the fuck is going on here, Perry, doesn't mean we're safe. It doesn't diminish the risk."

"True." Xavier sighed, then a thought occurred to him. "In the drive over to the hospital, George said that the shootings... there seemed to be two different endgames."

Perry scowled. "What kind of endgames?"

"Well, Marianne was hit first," he pointed out gently. "Not Philippe."

"I didn't realize," she whispered. "I-I never watched the footage."

Edward's hand squeezed her knee. "I didn't want to either, but I did after Xavier pointed that out to me. He's right. Mother was the target. There was no reason for her to be shot at all if it was just dissatisfaction with the ruler—without my father, she couldn't reign. The crown would pass straight to me."

"Maybe he missed? Like with me?" She shivered, even as she asked the question.

"No," Edward retorted. "I don't think so. After, I asked for more detailed reports from the security councils. The sniper's positioning was too perfect. He'd have had a clear shot. And there was no real reason to hurry either. The gunman waited until the carriage they were traveling in had come to a halt."

Perry bit her lip. "Accidents happen, and even the best plans can go awry. There's no way of knowing for sure that Marianne was the definite target.

"And can I just say that traveling in damn carriages is so stupid anyway. Didn't you guys learn anything from JFK?"

"It's a trust exercise," Xavier said softly, *sadly*. "It's to engage with the public. It's important, Perry."

Though she gritted her teeth, quite visibly, she nodded. "I understand." She clearly didn't.

With a sigh, Edward murmured, "Let's take it as concrete that Mother was always intended to be the one killed—and Father was just to cover it up.

"If there are two different endgames from two different organizations, then targeting Mother was definitely the UnReals. They're punishing her for what she did to one of their own. For what she did, and for what happened to Laurence Prichard."

"Nobody made the bastard kidnap you," Perry argued angrily. "Jesus, just because she did what she did—and I'm not excusing it—it didn't give him the right to fucking abduct you."

"No. But Drake indicated the man was deeply in love and very overwrought over losing Mother. Men and women can be fools in love."

She rolled her eyes. "That's over-romantic bullshit."

"I can't think of a reason why a man would decide to target his old lover's children, kidnap them, and abuse them, unless it was to hurt and to punish that old lover."

Though she gnawed on her lip, Perry seemed to see the reasoning in that because she nodded. "I think you're right."

"Happy to have you on board," Edward teased wryly, then laughed a little as she elbowed him in the belly.

The byplay astonished Xavier, especially considering the topic at hand.

They were discussing the singular turning point in Edward's life. A moment that had changed him forever, and yet, here he was... laughing over it with Perry.

Jesus, he'd known she was a good influence on him, but hadn't realized it was to this extent.

"Okay, so if the UnReals wanted to kill Marianne, why would Ferdinand want to kill Perry?" Xavier asked, getting them back on topic.

"Because she's the future of the family."

"It's not like he knew she was pregnant. Hell, Perry didn't even know."

Though she flushed, Edward disregarded it, and said, "I wouldn't have married again if anything happened to Perry."

"How was he to know that?" Xavier retorted, shaking his head as he thought about it. Really thought about it. His mind took him back to that shitty day at the hospital, when Drake had made Perry discuss, in detail, what she remembered. "Perry, I know you don't want to talk about this, but it's important."

"I know. And it's okay, Xavier. Ask whatever you want."

"You said to me that day of the shooting, there was plenty of opportunity for you to have been hit as you were walking along the picket line?"

She nodded. "Yes. I was supposed to go straight into the clinic, but I didn't. I walked down the fencing, greeting people. Cassie and Murielle Harlington were off to one side, taking the flowers the people were giving me, and I had two guards following me closely. But the rest of my guards were spread out, monitoring the situation."

"And yet, you also said that the shots weren't fired until you stepped back toward the entrance. The minute the gun went off, the guards huddled around you, didn't they?"

"Yes. They did."

"Jesus Christ," Edward said, releasing the curse on a slow breath. "Perry wasn't the target at all, was she?"

"No. It was another case of misdirection… Raoul Da Silva was the intended target all along. Perry was just supposed to look as though she was in danger, but really, they were cleaning up. Getting rid of the inside man."

"But why?" Perry asked, her voice shaky, and the fine tremor that had overtaken her limbs was proof positive of how much this conversation was disturbing her.

Xavier hated that. Hated the necessity of it, but it was imperative. They had to understand what was happening. Needed to know which step to take next.

He licked his lips and murmured, "Da Silva must have become a liability. We need to find out why, and the minute we do, we have our way in."

CHAPTER FIFTEEN

"HEY, MOM! IT'S PERRY."

Janice let out a soft sigh. "Oh, it's good to hear from you, darling."

They hadn't spoken since the shooting, when Perry had also told her mother that she was pregnant. Janice wasn't particularly happy about not being able to reveal to her neighbors that her daughter was finally giving her a grandchild, but once she'd explained, her mother had understood the fragility of their current situation.

"It's good to hear from you too, Mom," she murmured gently, setting her phone on speaker so she could lay flat on the bed and stare up at the canopy above her. "You can always call me, you know? You wait for me to call you."

"You're busy."

"I was busy before. It didn't stop you then."

"Yes, well, now you're *important*, too."

She huffed, well aware this argument would go nowhere. "Anyway," she said, determinedly changing the subject, "I wanted to wish you a happy Thanksgiving!"

"And to you, my darling girl. Thank you!"

"I wish you and Dad had accepted Edward's invitation."

"Seems silly to travel all that way to a country that doesn't even celebrate it." Janice argued now as she and Perry's father had argued earlier this month.

"Maybe, but *I'm* American." She winced. "Well, technically... no. Okay. I'm not American anymore, but my roots are, and they're not going anywhere, are they? Plus, it would have been really nice to see you. I feel like I haven't seen you in ages. And I know, I could have visited when I was at college and then after," she said on a rush, "but—"

Janice clucked her tongue. "Calm down, Perry. It's all right."

"No, it's not," she said on a wail. Turning her head to the side where the empty bed taunted her, she whispered, "I wish I could come home."

"Your home is there now," Janice said kindly but firmly. "I know what you're going through, sugar. Don't you think I felt the same way when I moved to be with your daddy?"

Perry scowled. "You were a town away. Barely any miles at all."

"Maybe, but I don't drive, do I? Might as well have been as far away as you are." Janice's voice was pragmatic. "Your grandmother didn't drive either, and your grandfather was too busy with his farm to be driving me out to see her. All we had was the phone. That's what *we* have. Doesn't matter how many miles separate you so long as you have a phone, Perry. I'm always here for you. You know that, don't you?"

She worried her bottom lip and whispered, "I do. Thank you, Momma. I don't deserve you."

Janice let out a light laugh. "I'm sure you don't, darling, but you're all I've got. Well, until I get a grandbaby from you."

"You will come over, won't you? For the birth, I mean."

Janice hesitated. "I don't know, Perry..."

"Please. I'll arrange the flights. "

"Your father—"

"No, he doesn't have to come. Just you. I need you here, Momma," she said, scrambling upright, panic flushing through her. "I don't know how to do any of this, and I mean, they'll have classes and things...but I want my mother here."

Janice released a long sigh. "I'll be there. Don't you worry. I-I'll sort your father out."

Her parents had an odd relationship. She'd never understood it, not really. Her father was always calm and polite, but Janice reacted sometimes like a cat on a hot tin roof where he was concerned.

"If he's mad, tell him I'll hire a damn housekeeper to keep the place for you while you're away! Why wouldn't he want you to be with me?"

"That's a good question," her mother replied, tone firming. "You're right. When's the due date?"

"May." She gulped. "So near and yet so far. I don't even know how it happened."

Janice snorted. "With a man like that, Perry, there's no hope for you if you don't know how it happened."

Perry chuckled. "Momma! I didn't know you had it in you!"

"You'd be surprised, darling. But that's a conversation for another day."

Perry could just imagine her mother fluffing her hair. "Anyway, I need to get on with dinner, sweet pea. The turkey's in the oven, but I still have a lot to do. Maybe this time next year, you'll be able to visit me. All this craziness might have settled down by then, but in the interim, don't forget, you can call me anytime. Day or night."

Perry nodded, grateful at the invitation. "Thanks so much, Momma."

"You're welcome, baby. I'll speak to you later. Happy Thanksgiving."

And with that, she cut the call and immediately let out a shriek when a voice from the corner intoned, "You're scared."

She slapped a hand to her heart at the sight of Xavier tucked away in one of the smaller armchairs. Although he was sleek and lean, he looked huge in the tiny-by-comparison seat. "What are you doing in here?"

"Waiting for you to wake up."

"I'm awake!"

"I know. You weren't, though. But you picked up your phone as soon as you awoke."

She blinked at him. "Why didn't you come and nap with me?"

"Because I wanted you to have some good rest."

She pursed her lips. "I hate naps."

"You'd never know, considering how many you're taking of late."

She blew him a raspberry as he climbed to his feet and approached her side of the four-poster. "I'd have preferred to have woken up with you at my side."

He tilted his head. "Why?" His grin morphed, turned wicked. "Have something in mind?"

By contrast, her voice was prim as she said, "You've a pretty face. I like to look at you."

His nostrils flared as he suppressed a laugh. But his lips curved and she pounced; "Gotcha."

"Pleased with yourself now, are you?"

She grinned. "Very."

He rolled his eyes. "You're crazy. You know that?"

"I do. But I'm yours, and you chose me, so what does that make you?"

"Crazier?"

"Exactly," she said, and with no small amount of satisfaction, she settled back into the pillows at her back.

He sat beside her, his hand coming up to cup her drawn knee. "How did I not know that you're scared?"

She licked her lips. "Of course, I'm scared. We're under threat."

"No. I mean about the baby."

That made her wince. "I'm not scared. Not really. Just, you know, nervous."

"You should have told us."

"Told you? Why? What could you do?"

"Help make you feel better, of course."

"You're going to pop this baby out for me, are you?"

It was his turn to wince. "No. That I can't do."

"Well, then..." She cocked a brow at him. "I'm okay. Just... I'd like my mother here when I give birth."

"We'll fly her in."

The immediacy of his remark made her relax. It wasn't that she needed permission, but it was difficult to remember that pretty much whatever she wanted, on that scale, could be achieved. It just needed coordinating.

That was pretty crazy for a small-town Tennessee girl.

"She'll disapprove of the way I want to give birth," Perry murmured sourly. "I shouldn't want her here because she'll do nothing but bitch..."

"But she's your mother, and of course, you want her close." He pursed his lips a second. "Why will she bitch?"

"Because I want to give birth in the bathroom."

His eyes widened. "In the bathroom?"

"That pool is awesome. It's not a bath, it's a freakin' spa! Babies born in water aren't as scared. They're less nervous. Something to do with the water temperature. Makes sense, I guess. Think about it. Going from my body temperature to room temp." She shivered. "Chilly."

He cleared his throat. "DeSauviers are normally born in the Cerecei Unit at Madela Royal Hospital."

She blinked. "So? I'm anything but *normal*, as we've already ascertained. I won't be giving birth there."

"Why not?" he said on a sigh.

"Because I don't want to. I've never really thought about babies, but if I did, I knew I didn't want to do it the scary, hospital way."

"You're going to have a fight on your hands convincing Edward," he warned.

But she just winked at him. "You leave him to me."

CHAPTER SIXTEEN

THE COURTYARD ahead of them was like a big chessboard.

In fact, it very much *was* a chessboard. With the pieces moving in a kind of order that would only make sense when she made it to the balcony that overlooked the whole damn charade.

Although "charade" wasn't the nicest way of labeling the military procession that utilized six different cavalry units of the Veronian Armed Forces, and had over three thousand men marching like they were nutcrackers about to dance.

Still, seeing it on the TV—or, if she was honest, when she'd seen it on the news, she'd always switched over—was a lot different to actually being in the middle of it all.

They were in Madela.

The capital city.

Right in the heart, there was a large courtyard that would make ten basketball courts side by side look small.

Regal buildings lined the courtyard with classical architecture so fine, it made her eyes water at its beauty, and everything from the House of Parliament to a public library—the oldest in the nation—was housed here.

This was the original center of the city.

Here, the oldest buildings could be found. Yorke Abbey, a few noble houses, and a military barrack that was sited a few feet away to protect all the edifices.

This was literally the heart of Madela, and many could say, the heart of Veronia.

And though it was months after her coronation, Perry still found it hard to believe that she too, was considered a part of Veronia's heart, giving her a role in the madness taking place today. As was Edward, who was at her side in the open-top carriage, and Xavier and George who rode on horseback behind them. The three of them were in goofy-looking uniforms, but hell, to her, they were dreamy.

Someone's getting laid tonight, she thought to herself, wriggling with contentment at the prospect.

The notion of driving out into the midst of this parade had scared her at first. But ever since their talk over the dining table, and since Edward had set Markov, his friend in the intelligence services, onto the case, she'd been feeling better.

Her men's prediction that she wasn't wholly at risk, that Raoul Da Silva had been the intended target of the shooting at the clinic, had let her sleep more deeply at night. Had helped her breathe a lot easier.

Driving around like this would always have unnerved her, and she couldn't help but have flashbacks to documentaries of JFK's assassination, but she'd had to shove it to the back of her mind.

This was the most important military parade in the calendar year.

Four days to Christmas, the procession was to celebrate the coming new year by each of the troops showing off their colors. She felt like a peahen surrounded by peacocks displaying their plumage proudly.

It was a bizarre feeling. But then, bizarre was all she could manage, considering how damn cold it was.

She was tucked up in a stylish, dark, down-filled coat—having refused to wear the fur that George had tried to wrap her in—and was snuggling, as much as decency and deportment allowed, into her husband's side.

When their part in this rigmarole was over, she'd be very happy.

George had explained it to her in terms she'd managed to understand—football rules.

They started the procession facing Parliament, and the end goal was to make it to Parliament's steps where there was a balcony, from which they'd wave to the crowds.

As they made their way toward the building, a feat that would normally take less than five minutes to walk, but was lasting a lifetime in the procession, troops on foot and horseback strutted their stuff in a kind of military dance. At set moments, cannons exploded, and every quarter-hour— they'd been making this journey for the past ninety minutes, and she was about to die of boredom—guns went off in tandem with a fleet of aircrafts soaring overhead.

In the distance, the booming of more guns from one of their naval fleet could be heard too, creating a cacophonous kind of song that she wished she'd never have to hear again, and yet that particular festive 'tune' would be a part of her every Christmas celebration until she popped her clogs.

Oh, the joy.

"How much longer?" she mumbled under her breath as Edward's hand tightened about her knee when a team of eight aircraft dove and ducked, performing manic rolls in the sky.

"About another half-hour," he replied, his attention skyward.

Was he actually enjoying this? They were in the middle of the world's eye, out in the open, the perfect possum for attack, and surrounded by guns, soldiers, aircraft, and cannons.

It wasn't exactly a panacea for her stress levels.

Still, Edward didn't look bored, *or* nervous. He'd had to watch this parade every year, and yet he managed to look engaged, whereas it was a toss-up for her whether she was about to die of tedium or cold.

Then, she remembered he'd been a part of the armed forces, too.

"Did you have to take part in this when you were serving?"

He nodded, his attention on the back end of the air fleet, which had whipped away to only God knew where. "Yes. Normally, it's unusual to be called up. Not every soldier will even get near this procession, but because of who we are, Xavier, George, and I took part at some point or another in our careers."

"What do you mean 'not every soldier gets to take part'?"

"Each year, certain units are spotlighted. They're on a rotation. It takes eight years for the rotation to refresh, and our shortest term of enlistment is six years."

She nodded her understanding while trying to contain a jolt that stemmed from a cannon going off right at her side.

The uniforms were smart, she'd give them that. Over three thousand men in kilts was an impressive sight to behold. She'd never seen as many sexy knees in all her life. Well, they weren't the *sexiest*. Those belonged to her men. But still, by sheer number, this was definitely up there.

Some wore nothing but unrelieved black, others had black with silver epaulets on their jackets. There were three different variations of red, and then a navy blue one, and an emerald green. The medals they sported on their breasts ran the gamut of the rainbow, too. And the different hats they wore went from berets to peaked caps to headgear that reminded her of the Pickelhauber, what the Germans had worn in World War I—the ones with spikes on the top.

One troop would march past, then another would feint left and meet another in a kind of quadrille that was never-fucking-ending.

"Aren't you cold?" she groused under her breath.

He laughed. "Why do you think George wanted you to wear the fur?"

"I refuse to wear dead animal."

"Your shoes are leather, aren't they?"

She rolled her eyes. "There's such a difference. And you totally know it."

"No. Not in this instance. We have areas in Veronia that run rife with mink. They do damage to livestock. Rather than needlessly let them go to waste, we use the furs. What would you have us do? Just burn them?

"Though our summers are hot and long, we have bitter winters. Short ones, but fierce nonetheless. The furs help."

She pursed her lips. "I don't like it."

"What? The furs or that we have bitter winters?"

She slid her hand on his thigh and tugged at some hair that his kilt exposed. When he jumped, she said sweetly, "Be grateful I can't reach higher up without shocking the crowd."

He laughed, and turned to her with twinkling eyes. "You're a spitfire."

"That's why you love me."

Edward bent his head and pressed a kiss to her lips. She jolted in surprise, because Cassie had told her that decorum was a must at these kinds of events, and that even if she was terrified, she needed to develop a stiff upper lip that no American was famed for.

"What are you doing?" she hissed at him, her cold mouth tingling where his had touched—their warmth was a blessing in disguise.

"Kissing my wife, of course." He was utterly unapologetic, even as he turned his head to look at another display the troops were engaged in.

"We're supposed to behave." Weren't they?

"We're children of a new generation, Perry," he told her softly, his gaze skyward once more. Another ream of aircraft soared overhead, in time to a few *booms* that came from the distant naval fleet that was anchored in Madela's port.

"So? That means we can make out whenever we want?" she joked.

His grin made her stomach twist—God, he was gorgeous when he smiled. So bloody beautiful, he drove her mad with it. "No. But if we decide to bend the rules a little, there's nothing to say that they'll break."

"I like the sound of that," she said wryly. "I always liked rules in the past. You can't practice science without them, really, can you? But *now*? Sheesh."

He nodded. "I know. We have to follow so many that it's borderline a joke. It will do the people good to see that we're far more flexible than my parents were."

A thought occurred to her. "Was it public knowledge about your parents' marriage?"

"About their adultery?" he said on a soft breath, saluting at a soldier who appeared to his right.

"Yeah."

"No. I doubt it. Don't forget, privacy laws are strict here."

She gnawed on her lip. "Probably a good thing."

"Plus, not even George knew."

"How did you find out?"

"Accident, of course." He grimaced. "Not one of the finest moments in my life. Hearing my father on the phone with his mistress, catching Mother looking flushed after a stupid dalliance with a footman."

For a second, Perry's mind boggled at the idea of Marianne looking anything other than composed and calm. Was this a parallel universe she'd been shunted into?

Before she could come to terms with the notion of her mother-in-law sleeping with a servant, the queen of the nation as well as the high patroness of *noblesse oblige* and decorum, Edward asked, "What made you think of that?"

"I don't know. I just thought that you wanted to loosen things up because Veronia knew how strained their marriage was at times. That it would do them good to see that ours is different."

He blinked. "I hadn't thought of it that way, but even if they didn't know for certain about the affairs, there's always gossip. And body language speaks for itself, doesn't it?" When she nodded, he murmured, "They will know from ours that we're in love. Why wouldn't that do them good?"

Her lips curved in satisfaction, and though she half-expected him to chide her, she tilted her head against his shoulder, finally settling into the carriage ride across the courtyard.

Perhaps Cassie would reprimand her later for breaking decorum, but Edward was right. This was a new generation, and the kids of this era would just have to shove it if they didn't want to see their queen snuggling into their king's side.

As she let her spine fall against the backrest for the first time since the damn procession had begun, she found that she could relax some and begin to enjoy what was going on around her.

It would never be something she'd get a kick out of watching. But she actually thought her father might, and made a mental note to invite him for Christmas next year. He'd really love this. He'd served as a Marine himself, and she knew he'd see the same side of it that Edward, George, and Xavier could empathize with and fully enjoy.

Bare meters away from the House of Parliament, just when she knew she was about to get out of the cold and the luxury of central heating, guns exploded to her left. She jolted in surprise, but settled down because it wasn't the first time it had happened during the ceremony. Hopefully it would be the last, though.

Edward, however, jerked upright. His head whipped around as he scanned the area. Then, he put his hand to the top of her back and hollered, "Get down, Perry. Take cover."

Terror roared through her. It was all the more glaring for the fact she'd just started to relax. She had just started to take a breath... the suddenness robbed her of air, and panic streamed through her veins.

Scampering down to the floor of the carriage, she covered her head and tried to sink back against the low door. The carriage belonged in a Jane Austen flick, was open on all angles to the crowd, but as with everything royal, was gilded up to the eyeballs in gaudy, molded gold trim, and rich, colored frescoes that were hand-painted onto the antique conveyance which provided zero protection.

Huddled up, she peered at her husband, and saw Edward was using some kind of hand signal to motion to men around him.

Why?

She didn't know.

And then it came.

It rocked the carriage on its wheels. And the screams of the horses? God help her, she'd never forget the agonized screeches. Not in a million years.

Alarm whipped her nervous system as men yelled out in agony, as the stench of acrid smoke filtered through the air, poisoning every gulp of oxygen she took.

Another one came. Another *boom* that far surpassed the gunshots that had felled her guard and the mole, Raoul Da Silva. It seemed to sink through everything. Made even her blood vibrate in her arteries. Sensation had her limbs prickling, surging to life. After being so cold for so long, she felt the agony as her skin stung in response. The tiny hairs covering her flickered to attention, and at that moment, she was so hypersensitive, so hyperaware that it was painful just to breathe.

Then, another roar came, but it was different—it wasn't followed by a bang. A charge of men surged around them. She felt the carriage being pushed, by hand and will alone, and knew they were being shepherded forward, and to safety, by their soldiers. *Her* soldiers.

Tears pricked her eyes in fear for the men as more explosions went off. She heard cries of pain, bellows of fury and rage. For a second, the carriage staggered to a halt before more roars were let off, and with sheer brute force, the soldiers dragged their king and queen to shelter. Her ears were deafened by the chaos around her, but it was only exacerbated by the booming blasts that created ragged black holes in the atmosphere.

When the carriage finally made it across what had once been graveled terrain and was now torn to shreds, she found herself falling backwards, the low carriage door opening as guards collected her. She was shuffled from grip to grip, hand to hand as she was dragged toward the House of Parliament.

But the only thing on her mind were the names she screamed, over and over, as she was taken away from the men who were her life: "Edward! Xavier! George!"

THE WAY SHE WAS SHAKING, it was like she was about to leap out of her damn skin. George clung tightly to her, but she wasn't holding him back. She just sat there. Trembling.

Who could blame her?

God, who could fucking wonder why?

"I want goddamn answers!"

Edward's roar jolted her in her seat, and she clapped her hands to her ears.

"Edward!" Xavier murmured, the only one who seemed calm among the whole frantic lot of them. "Perry's in shock. You're not making it any better by shouting."

His brother's eyes rounded, and George had to admit, he'd never seen him so angry. Never seen him so utterly infuriated that he looked like he was going to explode.

George winced at the thought...

Six bombs.

Three detonated—with lethal results. One—no show, a damp squib. And two disposed of, thanks to a unit of experts that had been a part of the military parade.

The damage had been contained more than any of them could have hoped, but that didn't make them feel any better. They were fucking lucky they hadn't been torn to pieces. Ripped to shreds. Only the grace of God had saved them where it had felled good men. Strong, brave soldiers who had worn their uniforms with pride and had done their duty to their nation in the melee.

The four of them had stinging cuts from shrapnel that had sung through the air and hit them. But nothing had injured them too badly. Nothing that the EMTs hadn't been able to swab up and clean after checking their vitals.

Perry had insisted on staying with them in Parliament, where they'd taken refuge. She had refused to go to hospital, even though she, too, had been sprayed with shrapnel that had glanced off her. The blood on her terrified him, but they'd had the confirmation she was okay. Just looking worse for wear.

Not that she realized she'd been hit.

The blood, whenever she saw it after rubbing at her face or running a hand through her hair, still had the power to make her blanch.

Outside was chaos, and it would continue to be while the security and emergency services worked together to stabilize the scene. Until that happened, George knew there would be few answers; considering that Edward felt like answers had been short in coming over the months since his coronation, it was no wonder that he was beyond frustrated.

Still, it didn't help Perry.

And Perry was all that mattered.

"How did this happen?" Edward demanded, but he was speaking to Xavier. Since they'd made their way in here, tucked amid the green leather chesterfields, the paneled walls of a study, it was like Perry and George had ceased to exist, thanks to their silence. His focus was purely on Xavier now.

"As soon as the reports come through, you know we'll be the first to get them."

"It has to be an inside job."

"No, it doesn't. Bombs are planted all the time."

"On the busiest square in the capital city? How does anyone plant a device here, where there are more cameras per square foot than in London?"

"I don't know, Edward. But it happened."

"It did, that's the problem, Xavier. It *did* happen, and there had to be inside help." Edward's hands slammed down in rejection of his own words. "We're in a state of emergency. I should invoke Article 42."

"No."

The word was timorous, but it was the first thing Perry had said since she'd screamed their names while being dragged to safety.

George knew he'd never forget the sight of her panic. Knew he'd never forgive himself for putting her through that.

Edward scowled at her. "What?"

"No, Edward. No Article 42. We believe in democracy. We don't right a wrong by creating a dictatorship." Her voice quivered. "No. I won't have it."

Before his brother could say anything, George murmured, "She's right."

"We both know she is," Xavier concurred. "You're too focused on the Article because you feel you're not being heard and getting the respect you deserve, Edward.

"But it isn't that at all. I don't like to say it..." He scratched his head, then winced as he obviously touched a cut. They were all battered by the day's events—emotionally, physically, and mentally. "I don't think Philippe left things in a very good stead with the councils."

"What do you mean?"

"They're not as organized as they should be."

"He's right, Edward," George joined in. "Father was a good king, but he wasn't a strategist. We both know that. Unless it was chess, he was useless. But he was loved, and when it came to the important things, modernizing the cities and bringing Veronia into the new millennium, he was a trooper."

"So? What does that have to do with anything?"

"It means that you don't need the Article to get us out of this mess," Perry whispered softly. "It means that you can handle this situation without doing something your father would have had to do. You're not him."

Edward shook his head. "I'm not as good as you seem to think."

"You're running blind, and we've already managed to figure out something our security councils haven't," Xavier argued. "I think we need to contemplate completely rehiring new men. Nominating new members with allies from our pasts rather than your father's. Our friends rather than his."

"I agree. Maybe it's time to stop keeping Markov in the shadows. Bring him to the fore," George encouraged, "where the man can do some good."

"He's Russian. You know they'll never accept him."

"They being who?" George demanded. "The people? Parliament? They have no say over who you appoint." He cut Perry a look. "And the same goes with you, Perry. It's time to do away with the old guard. Get rid of the Guardians of the Keys that my mother chose. Let's get some fresh blood in—we'll nominate women who are married to men that we know we can trust." He scrubbed at his head. "I wish you'd made more friends. Can we change the law that says Guardians have to be married? It's an outdated piece of claptrap anyway."

"How do you know who we can trust?" Edward demanded. "You've been out of the damn country for years. And no, there's too much change as it is."

Through the wall of anger opposite him, George lobbed, "Then we'll figure out another way, but we're not going to get anywhere by sticking to what didn't work for our parents, either." He sucked in a breath, truly feeling the wave of rage his brother hurled at him—Edward's bitterness at George's absence was evident. "And in the interim, I think for Christmas, I should take Perry back to the States."

"What?"

Edward and Xavier roared the question at the same time, but George held his nerve. Jerking his chin up in the air, he argued, "She's not safe here. Not for the moment. Even if you don't invoke the Article, declaring a state of emergency is on the cards. If I take her home, she'll be safe there."

"You're failing to recognize one simple thing, George." Perry's voice held a quaver, but the look she shot him was like steel.

"What's that, sweetheart?"

She jerked her chin up. "I told you I'd never leave you. Any of you. The only way you'll get me out of this country is if you handcuff me to the seat on the plane." She cast them withering looks. "I'm going nowhere. So, you're just going to have to do what you said—get a goddamn move on, figure out what the fuck is going on, and put the bastards in jail so that we can finally start living again." The quaver had disappeared, and she got shakily to her feet. "Now, if you'll excuse me, I need to puke."

And with that, she rushed off to the nearest bathroom, leaving them staring at one another.

"Why did you suggest that?" Edward demanded as he came to sit opposite him, glowering at him all the while.

"Because I wanted her to know that if she wanted to leave, she could. I'd take her."

"We don't want her to leave, dammit."

"This isn't about us, Xavier," George retorted. "You think I wanted her to go? Of course, I fucking didn't. But I wanted her to know she had an out. She never signed up for this, dammit. This is going above and beyond anything we ever imagined.

"I never thought within the space of half a year, my mother would be shot, my wife would be under threat from a gunman, and that today, we'd be fucking bombed… Why should she have to deal with that, when we never warned her? She should know that we forgive her if she decided to go."

"She's ours," Edward argued. "She was never going anywhere."

"Just because we *knew* that, doesn't mean we should be complacent about it either," he retorted, refusing to back down and keeping his gaze glued to his brother's. "You can say what you want, but you have to feel better knowing that she has chosen to stay here when she could have gone home to safety."

Edward gritted his teeth. "Maybe."

George nodded. "Exactly. Anyway, now we need to think about replacing the councils. They're going to be busy for the next seventy-two hours, but we need to start figuring out who we can get on board. We've a lot of places to fill and only a short window to make the changes happen."

"But first things first, I think we need to get Markov here."

"He's a private businessman, and he has concerns of his own," Edward said as he exhaled. "He can't just dump everything."

"Not even for the man who saved his life? Not even for the sovereign who'll pay him a king's ransom to take up the post?"

"You manipulative shit," Edward said on a grumble, but he pulled out his cell phone.

George watched as his brother searched his contacts, and then connected the call. As he lifted the cell to his ear, he was surprised when what seemed like flawless Russian escaped Edward's mouth.

Course, it could have been utter shit, but George hadn't even realized he could speak Russian, never mind with a fluency that was visible in his ease on the phone with the other man.

"*Da*," Edward said after a few moments, and George caught another, "*Niet*," which was probably the total amount of Russian he could understand.

He caught Xavier's eye, saw their cousin looked just as bewildered—a fact that surprised him. Xavier was the sort who seemed to know everything about life at court...even though he spent most of his time avoiding it.

At around the ten-minute mark, Edward put the phone down with a grim, satisfied smile.

"It's done."

"He's coming?" Xavier asked.

"Yes."

"Did you have to get the thumbscrews out?"

He snorted. "No, George. Torture wasn't required. A signing-on bonus that would make most governments blanch was a condition for him, though."

"He's worth it?" Xavier prodded.

"Yes. Without a doubt. Markov, for all I like the man, is a damn spider. His web has global reach. He's the equivalent of L'Argeneau, except he's on my side and his loyalty won't waver."

What the fuck had Edward done to earn such allegiance? Not that he didn't deserve it, but still... there had to be a tale there, and knowing his brother like he did, George would undoubtedly never discover the truth.

"Why didn't you hire him on before?"

"Because he's Russian. That says it all. But desperate times call for desperate measures."

"I think we're going to need a hatchet job on the councils in the press, and we're going to have to big up how you guys met." George rubbed his chin, wondering if that hint was enough to find out how Edward and the Russian had *actually* met.

"That story is for us—it's personal. I'll leave the PR to the PR people, George. That isn't something I'm willing to share."

"I don't think we should reveal who he is," Xavier countered. "I think he should maintain a shadowy presence at court. There's no need for him to be active there. He can remain on the outskirts—that's more of what we need, anyway. We get people we trust on the councils, and he can watch them."

"To make sure we can trust them?" Edward asked grimly.

"Exactly," Xavier murmured.

George nodded. "He's right."

"Markov won't mind. Hates being in the spotlight anyway."

"You likened the man to a spider. I don't particularly think he'll mind what opinion you have of him," Xavier retorted. He lifted a hand and rubbed his temple. "Now, I need sleep. If we're going to pad the councils out, I need some rest before we dive into it."

"Headache?"

"It's more like my ears are ringing, George. Yours?"

They'd been about twenty feet behind the carriage holding Edward and Perry when the bombs had exploded. The blasts had been from dirty bombs, explosives rammed full of shrapnel. Anything from coins to nails.

How they hadn't been hit fatally was more of a blessing than even luck could provide. Their horses seemed to have taken most of the fray. Their pure white and black hides were pinned to shreds by the dirty bombs. The wounds had been ragged, deep, impossible to recover from. Whisper's whinnies, his pain-filled cries, would forever haunt him, George knew.

When he'd shot his own beast, George had had to shake his head at the task ahead of him. He was a prince, supposed to be used for nothing good save for opening events and looking pretty in pictures. Yet, here he was, having to put his own animal down because the wounds were too grievous to survive. While having to meander through the military parade like he was out in the sandbox on war-torn territory in his own goddamn country. In the center, the very heart, of their most metropolitan landmark.

There were many moments where a man thought "enough is enough." They happened every so often in life. But they usually revolved around angry arguments with family or a wife, dealt with betrayals by friends or injustices at work.

They didn't revolve around bombings.

They didn't revolve around assassination attempts.

The truth was, if anyone had wanted to flee to the USA, it was George. He'd pushed his own desire onto Perry, hoping that she'd be the one who would make them go. But she had more balls than him. She was determined to stay, steadfast with her desire to remain with them.

For a moment, he felt like a coward. But he was a banker now, no longer a soldier. He dealt with numbers. He dealt with facts and figures, not this political bullshit. Just because he'd been born into the role, didn't mean that he was made for it.

His thoughts had him bowing his head as he rested his elbows on his knees.

"You okay, George?"

His brother's concern had his cheeks prickling with heat. "No. But neither are you. I'll be fine eventually."

A heavy sigh sounded, and he knew his words had hit home.

Now wasn't the time to be cowardly; now was the time to man up, to fight the bastards who were attacking them, to hurt them exactly where they deserved to be hurt—their balls. But he was only a man, and this man had lost his mother, had fled to a hospital thinking his wife had been shot, and had watched the mother of his child being passed down a line of men like an ungainly parcel toward shelter away from bombs.

Even as the chaos of the moment had overtaken him, his eyes had been glued on her, from the moment he'd been tossed from his horse, and he could catch sight of her.

The way she'd screamed their names? It would merge with Whisper's agony-drenched neighs, and they'd fill his nightmares forevermore.

Once again, he was left with the notion that he had brought her here. *He* had introduced her to this. And it was then he realized that he wasn't scared for himself as he'd thought just a handful of moments ago. He was petrified for *her*.

She was his future, his present, and his past.

Without Perry, this insanity didn't make sense.

Without her influence, without her love, he knew he couldn't handle this world.

She was it for him, and he knew his brother and cousin felt the exact same way.

Like the rest of the world watching on, he knew he'd been astonished at the way the two of them had settled into the carriage together. They'd snuggled up, had kissed a little, had even laughed. For the serious occasion, it was unheard of.

Without knowing it, they'd announced to the world how important Perry was to Edward. Had declared, to one and all, that they were a love match.

If she didn't have a target on her back before, she did now. And that was why he now felt sick to his stomach.

The danger had just heated up all the more, and they were no way close to finding a resolution.

"Are you sure you're okay?" Xavier asked, still rubbing at his temple as though that would diminish the ache.

"No. I'm not," he replied. "But I will be when we get underway. The time for prevaricating is over. Edward's been right all along, Xavier. We don't have to invoke Article 42 for us to act like it's in place.

"Tonight, or for as long as we're able, we rest. Then in the morning, we take control of our country, and we show our subjects who the fucking rulers are. The DeSauviers—not some whiny fucking terrorists—*us*." He gritted his teeth and fisted his hands as rage flushed through him, and when he cast looks at his brother and cousin, he saw they were as angry as him, as outraged.

Good.

They had a rebel extremist group to dismantle, and George needed no others at his back than the men with him tonight.

CHAPTER SEVENTEEN

PERRY NARROWED her eyes at Cassie. "He's coming home?"

"Yes. The bombing scared him."

"Funny that," she said with a disgruntled snort.

Cassie wriggled her shoulders with a tension that they were all feeling. "He said he'll be on the next flight out here tomorrow."

Considering Marcus had been saying that for the last two months, Perry wouldn't exactly be getting her hopes up. But this time, she knew things were different.

The difference was, of course, that Edward had called Marcus. Edward had demanded his friend return home, and as king, had issued it as an order.

His only concession had been that Marcus could tell Cassie it was of his own volition. A fact Perry disagreed with wholeheartedly.

The dick had promised to come home after a big deal of his was finalized. With four million in the bank, he should have flown home first class, but he hadn't. He'd stayed on in New York, even though Cassie had been in tears when she'd called Perry up—just moments after Marcus's call—sobbing that despite all her threats, despite her move home, Marcus was still refusing to return to Veronia.

Perry wasn't—she had to admit—predisposed to like the jerk. But she'd be seeing a lot of him, because he was going to be something called an "equerry."

She wasn't entirely sure what that meant, and didn't particularly care, if she were being honest. If it lightened her men's load while shoring up their defenses, then that was all that mattered. Still, she hated the out Edward had given the man—that he could lie to his wife about why he was coming home.

Marcus wasn't coming home for his family, but because of a king's order.

That mattered.

At least, it did to Perry, and the idea of keeping it from her friend was more than just abhorrent. God, she wished she hadn't heard that conversation. Wished she was still in the dark. But she wasn't. She knew the truth, and she wanted Cassie to know it, too. Even if it went against her husband's plans.

Even as the words burned on her tongue, Cassie starting picking at her nails, something she loathed about herself, and only did when she was feeling agitated. Perry couldn't exactly blame her.

Agitated was the way of it for the moment, before the prodigal husband made his way home.

She sipped at her cup of tea and wished it was coffee. If not coffee, then brandy, because damn, that would have gone down so well right about now. The Veronians had this strange little habit of having coffee with brandy first thing in the morning. It was only a small shot of the good stuff, and Perry had no idea how they carried on working a full day after having that for breakfast, but she'd had it a few times, and had to admit that it had definitely soothed her nerves.

That was exactly what both she and Cassie needed.

"Sorry, Perry. I know we're supposed to be talking about replacements for the Guardians. I for one, am glad not to have to see that old bat, Murielle, again. What a witch."

Perry shrugged, though her mouth curved into a smile—Murielle Harlington was definitely a nasty mix of "old bat" and "witch." "Don't be silly. I know you're uncertain about what's going to happen when he gets home." She bit her lip after taking a sip of chamomile with honey—the doctor had recommended it for her nerves. Though it had never done much for her in the past, Veronian chamomile was actually stronger than what she'd had back in the States, sweeter, too, thanks to the strong sun but their typically drier soil.

Cassie winced. "I can't divorce him, can I?"

Ducking her head, she tried to avoid responding to that question. "You have to answer that yourself, Cassie. I can't help you there."

"I wish you could."

Perry wished she could too. Especially knowing what she did about the bastard.

Two months ago, Edward had told her that Marcus had called him. He'd promised his friend that this deal he was working on would be the last one, that his letter of resignation was already written, and he was just waiting for his money to hit his bank account before he handed the letter in.

Then, when the deal had gone through successfully, and he hadn't made an appearance back home, flowers in one hand for Cassie and an armful of toys for the kids, Edward had called again. Ever since, Marcus had been avoiding him.

Until yesterday.

The bombing had changed things. Even for that selfish prick.

"You love him," she said softly, trying to remember that and trying not to think of how badly she needed that brandy.

"I do, Perry," Cassie admitted, then after plucking at her skirt on her knee, she continued, "I guess that's the only thing that matters?"

"If he gets home, and you realize that you're *not* in love with him, you bring your ass and the kids to Masonbrook, do you hear me?"

A scandalized laugh escaped Cassie. "You can't be serious?"

"I am. Deadly." The word came out grimmer than she liked, but she meant it. Edward wanted Marcus in a settled home environment for the role he'd be undertaking on the Crown's behalf, but he could go fuck himself if it meant Cassie was going to be living in misery with a bastard who thought more of himself and his bank balance than his wife and children.

"That's not necessary, Perry. Honestly."

She firmed her lips. "I know you have other friends you can call on, but there's plenty of space here. Plus, the children are used to coming to nursery here, aren't they? It will be a little adventure for them to spend the night."

"You'd do that for me?"

"I'm not doing anything at all," Perry countered, slumping back into the side of the couch with a sigh. Talk about being a two-faced bitch with the only woman in the country she actually liked. "I'm just saying that you don't have to feel like you've nowhere to go. I mean, I know you could afford to live in a bloody first class hotel for the rest of your life if you wanted, but I just..."

"I know exactly what you mean, Perry, and I appreciate it more than I can say."

There were tears in the other woman's voice, and because Perry's nerves were all over the place, the sound had her own throat clogging.

"You're my best friend, Cassie."

"I know. You're mine too, Perry."

They shot each other sheepish smiles, then jolted when a knock sounded at the door. The sharp rap made them grimace at each other in dread.

"Rose," Cassie whispered.

"The Dragon," Perry confirmed on a hush, then in a louder voice, called out, "Come in."

How someone so pretty could be so fucking mean was beyond her, and it just went to prove that a book's cover sure as shit didn't have to match its interior.

Rose, though she was Perry's age, had the dour sense of humor of an octogenarian.

In fact, that was doing all eighty-year-olds a total disservice, because even when her own grandparents had managed to hit that lofty age, they hadn't had their heads as far up their asses as this chick.

"What is it, Rose?" she demanded, knowing she sounded haughty when Cassie choked back a laugh.

"Miranda Greatley is here, Your Majesty."

The months working together, a shooting *and* a bombing, hadn't managed to lessen the formalities on which the other woman insisted. She'd asked countless times, almost begged for less strictures, but Rose just wouldn't relent. And the looks she shot Perry's way were enough to make her believe that 'mean girls' were a real thing.

And she had one for a PA.

Gritting her teeth, she nodded. "Send her in."

Rose frowned. "In here? To your private quarters?"

"Where else?" Perry demanded, feeling her cheeks flush with anger at being questioned. Rose did this all the time. Undermined her, made her question her own authority. She didn't particularly like being queen, but hell, that was her position, and the other woman, who insisted on all these formalities, seemed to have zero problem forgetting them when it came time to judging Perry for not being 'majestic' enough.

Even Cassie, who was used to this way of life, thought Rose was a pain in the butt.

"Your office, of course. This is an official matter."

"I believe the queen knows her own duties without your having to remind her of them every time you open your mouth, Rose," Cassie bit off.

The PA's shoulders dropped, anger tightening her delicate features. "It's unseemly for the queen to entertain anyone in here." She curled her lip in disgust at the pair of them, curled up on their respective seats.

"Before I'm a queen, I'm a woman, Rose," she remarked swiftly, sick of the way Rose looked at her. How the woman could be so rigid in her outlook of how Perry should behave and glare at her like she was a dog turd was something Perry just couldn't compute. "But we've had this argument too many times for me to even give a damn about your opinion.

"When will you get it into your head? I don't care for what you have to say. You work for me. I don't work for you. Bring Miranda in here, and consider yourself dismissed for the rest of the day."

"But there are other appointments—"

"Yes, and Cassie is quite capable of opening the door for them to make their way in here. Enjoy your half-day, Rose."

The Dragon's mouth pursed in anger, but she nodded, dropped a quick and totally resentful curtsey—because they were entirely possible. Every day, Rose granted her a display of the varying kinds of emotions that could be imbued in the damn genuflection—and stormed out.

Cassie snickered as she slammed the door shut. "She's hard-headed, I'll give her that."

"I'm starting to wonder if she's a little slow. The woman is refusing to bend, even though it's obvious to anyone with eyes that I hate the formalities she seems to insist on."

"I'm surprised you've put up with her as long as you have, if I'm being honest, Perry."

"Edward chose her for me," she admitted, wrinkling her nose. "If he hadn't gone to the bother, I'd have fired her ages ago. We don't gel well at all."

"Why don't you get rid of her? Or shuffle her off to another part of the palace admin?"

She shot Cassie a look. "I can do that?"

"Perry!" Cassie clucked her tongue. "You're the queen. You can pretty much do whatever you want. Aside from walk around naked, that is. Don't be getting any ideas."

Laughing, Perry managed to splutter out a fine spray of chamomile onto her leggings. She whacked a hand over her face and giggle-snorted, "Oh great. I'm about to meet a potential new Guardian covered in my own snot."

"Why not start as you mean to go on, eh?" Cassie said cheerfully, catching Perry's eye.

The two of them pealed into laughter, laughter that was only interrupted when the door opened again. Perry, dabbing her knee with a tissue, carried on chuckling until she saw Xavier's face.

"What is it?" Her heart began to pound to a thick beat that felt unnaturally sluggish. "Is someone hurt?"

"Edward needs to speak with you."

"Is he okay? Is George?"

Xavier nodded, but his grim jaw had her biting her bottom lip.

"For God's sake, Xavi, what the hell's going on? You know you can speak about anything in front of me." Cassie sounded outraged that the opposite might be true where the duke was concerned. For at that moment, there was no mistaking that Xavi, as Cassie had called him, was most definitely the duke.

"I'll tell you when I can, Cassie. As it stands, I need Perry. Now."

She dumped the tissue on the stand beside the sofa and rushed over to Xavier. He grabbed her hand, his fingers tightening around hers to the point of pain as he half-dragged her out of her sitting room.

"What is it?" she demanded breathily after a few silent moments where she allowed herself to be hauled around without complaint. "Tell me, Xavier!"

"I can't. Not in public."

"Where are we going, then?"

"To the private quarters in the other wing."

Her heart sunk. "Philippe?" she asked softly, her stomach twitching with butterflies.

"Yes."

Nausea swirled around her, and she felt suddenly lightheaded. "Xavier, we're going too fast."

Before she could utter another peep, he'd swept her in his arms and carried on striding down the corridor before she even had time to catch her breath.

They passed several footmen and a bewildered Miranda Greatley, a potential candidate for Perry's Guardians, whose eyebrows were close to her widow's peak in astonishment at the sight of the queen being hauled around like Jane was by Tarzan. Flushing, she gave the other woman a limp wave, then wished she could bury her face in Xavier's neck.

A bold footman appeared at Xavier's side, keeping in line with him as he demanded, "Is all well with Her Majesty, Your Grace?"

Touched that Roberts dared brave Xavier's grim expression, she murmured, "I'm fine, Roberts. Thank you for asking."

The footman's scowl turned confused, but he nodded and fell out of step as they made it into the other wing of the palace.

The door to Philippe's room was open, and the nurses bustling in and out made Perry's eyes widen in surprise.

"He's woken up," she said, her tone loaded with wonder.

Xavier nodded, but stayed silent.

"What's wrong?"

"He's asking for you."

"He is?"

"Yes."

Why was he being so quiet, so reticent? What the hell was going on?

As they made it to the door, Xavier helped her onto her feet. She felt a little unsteady after being carted down the landing at such a fast clip, and her ears were still ringing from the explosion... that didn't help with her sense of balance or her morning sickness.

She rubbed her forehead as she started to step inside and came across the sight of her men gathered around their father's bedside.

What she'd expected, Perry supposed, had belonged in a medical TV drama. Philippe, she'd thought, would be sitting up, drinking milk or some shit like that. Surrounded by pillows and speaking, if only slowly.

But he wasn't. He was in the same position as he'd been before, but his lips were moving. Slowly. Quietly. *Constantly.* They didn't stop once, and she realized he was forming her name.

"Pe-rr-ee." Three syllables instead of two. Definitely slurred.

His eyelids were flickering too, like they were on another circuit board that was out of whack.

He looked pastier than before, and he hadn't looked that healthy in the coma. Still, the doctors were moving around him—how had that even happened? She hadn't known Dr. Schertz had flown in!

What the fuck was going on?

"Perry's here, Father," Edward said softly.

The moaning of her name grew louder and faster, more frantic. It urged her to rush forward. She grabbed Philippe's dry hand, wincing at the crepey feeling of his skin. She'd been moisturizing them, as well as dotting his lips with Vaseline to stave off sores, but her duties had fallen by the by since the bombing.

The day after, she'd been stuck in bed herself on doctor's orders—nothing was wrong with the baby, but he'd still ordered total rest.

Today was the first time she'd been allowed up and about, and she'd had duties to attend to. But in those few days, Philippe's hair had grown limp and stringy from lack of a wash, and his jaw had turned bristly with stubble.

She winced, hating that he was being seen like this as she squeezed his hand. "I'm here, Philippe. I'm here."

His lips stopped moving, and his breathing deepened into a smooth wave that seemed less hectic, more normal.

"He's calming down," Dr. Schertz pointed out softly, his attention on Philippe's vitals.

Edward let out a shuddery breath of his own. "What's happening?" he asked the doctor.

"Until I run more tests, I won't know. But it's not unusual for coma patients to wake up disoriented. It's not like how it is in the movies."

"Until he's more lucid, we won't know how he's faring. Not fully. As it stands, all we can do is monitor his vitals, keep him calm, and let time heal him."

Edward gnawed at his bottom lip, and Perry reached for his hand with her free one. She squeezed it, knowing how hard those words would be for him to swallow.

Patience, at the moment, wasn't Edward's strong suit.

The parade, and its aftermath, had changed her men.

They were harsher. Stronger. More intent.

It was almost like the bombing had been what they needed to truly settle into their places. Like the last few months had been their lessons, and the bombing had been their graduation.

Edward had never seemed all that easy in his role as king, but he wore it like a cloak now. It was as much a part of him as his stern character, his dark gold hair, and his sensual lips.

Xavier had had longer to play the part of duke, but that was exactly what he'd been doing—*playing*. His interests had always rested with his plants and his studies, and she couldn't blame him for that. Wasn't she the same? But now, he too, was more serious. His intentions aimed solely at his ducal duties, and how they could help Edward settle into his role as king.

George, too, had been hit by what had happened to them. Her fun-loving, carefree joker had taken a beating, and she only hoped that that side of him would make it out at the end of this mad situation they found themselves in.

She gnawed at her lip when Philippe's body seemed to relax. She knew enough about the human form and the equipment around him to realize he hadn't died—even though he'd definitely gone limp. But his heart carried on beating, strongly too.

"He's sleeping," Dr. Schertz confirmed. "Deeper than before. He's truly resting now."

"Why? What did I do?"

The doctor shrugged. "I don't know. I hope we'll find out when he's more himself."

It went unsaid that that might not be the case. That this was about as lucid as Philippe might ever be.

She flinched at the thought of the dynamic man being imprisoned in this bed for the rest of his life, and knew that she couldn't let that happen. She'd do whatever she could to help him during his rehabilitation—her duties as queen be damned.

Her first loyalty was to her family, after all.

"Just in time for Christmas," George said gruffly, but he smiled, even if it was more of a rictus than anything else. "He always did have good timing."

"Mother said he should have been an actor," Xavier said softly, his tone lighter than his cousin's. "Said he had the charisma of a snake oil salesman and the meter of a Shakespearian bawd."

George and Edward snickered, despite the somberness of the situation—the shared memory had her warming up inside. It was a relief to see that they weren't totally hardening up to the world around them.

Her included.

"I remember that. It was when he beat her at charades for the fifth year in a row."

"Then she refused to play again if he was team leader," Xavier murmured.

Edward chuckled. "She was such a spoiled brat. You'd have liked *Tanta Lisetta*, Perry."

She arched a brow. "I hope you're not saying that because I'm spoiled?"

The men laughed, but George quickly inserted, "We wouldn't dare."

She sniffed. "Good. Glad to hear it. But I wish I'd had the chance to meet her, too. She sounds like fun."

"She was a pain," Xavier said fondly, "but she was definitely fun."

Dr. Schertz cleared his throat. "I will be staying in the palace, Your Highnesses?"

"Yes, of course," George murmured, coming to attention in a way that told her he was back in princely form. "If you'd like to come with me, I'll show you to your quarters."

The doctor nodded his appreciation. "Most kind, Your Highness."

The two of them stepped toward the doorway, but as he moved past her, Perry let go of Edward's hand to press her fingers to the bottom of George's back. He turned around to look at her and shot her a soft smile. She felt something inside her settle at the sight of him winking at her as he guided the doctor toward his room.

"What's going on, guys?" she asked, when George closed the door behind him. "Why didn't you tell me Dr. Schertz was here?"

Edward sighed as he moved around the bed to come up behind her. "I didn't know." He pressed his forehead to her shoulder as he wrapped his arms around her waist.

It was disconcerting to realize how hard it was for him to do so. Her belly had definitely grown in the last few months, and it was swiftly moving out of the "can hide with the excuse I've eaten too many donuts" phase, and into the need for hardcore maternity wear.

They were still keeping it quiet, thanks to the UnReal situation, but she hoped that would be over soon. They certainly seemed to have declared war on the rebel party—she'd never heard as many military formations gathering outside the palace, and the number of meetings the men were engaged in?

It was beyond ridiculous.

Yesterday, she'd been introduced to the man called Markov, whose life

Edward had once saved, and who was about to be asked to repay the favor by saving theirs.

He was a small man. Beady-eyed and shifty as well. Like his years of being a spy had rubbed off on his very genetics. Despite his height and his unfortunate habit of scanning rooms like he was an x-ray, he was actually quite attractive. White blond hair, bright blue eyes, and a face that was marred by a scar across his cheek, but that somehow, gave him a rakish charm.

He'd disappeared after that initial meeting, and God only knew where he'd set up his base. By the sounds of it, her men weren't encouraging him to front any of the myriad security councils that were the Veronian versions of the US's FBI and the UK's MI5. He was going to head up his own organization. A new one, formed under Edward's rule, and governed by Markov.

Edward sighed, blowing at the cobwebs gathering in her thoughts. "I forgot he was due here this week, and then I got the call that Father was awake and talking."

"Hardly talking," Xavier grumbled. "Just repeating Perry's name. That's strange, don't you think?"

"Very." Edward peered down at her, tension gathering about his eyes. "Why would he relax so utterly when he knew you were here?"

She shrugged, jostling Edward behind her. "I have no idea. Truly. I'm just glad I managed to calm him down some."

"We'll find out what's going on when he wakes up properly." Xavier rubbed his chin at the prospect, impatience dragging him down, because only God knew how long that could take.

"Schertz said it could take weeks," Edward dismissed. "He's been in a coma for a hell of a long time. It's not like he's just waking up from a deep sleep."

"Does it matter? He's on the mend, guys. That's all that counts, surely?" Perry scowled at their lack of enthusiasm.

"You're right." Edward blew out a long, deep breath.

"A Christmas miracle," Xavier said, his tone surprisingly sour considering how good the news was.

She glowered at him. "Come on, Scrooge. Cheer up. This is great. It's the first step in his recovery."

"I don't know. I don't like it."

"What? That he's woken up?" she grumbled.

Xavier narrowed his eyes at her. "No. Of course that's marvelous news. I'm just... Too much shit has passed under the bridge, Perry. There's a reason why a man wakes up from a months-long coma and is whispering your name under his breath like a damn litany."

Edward's hold about her waist tightened. "He's not wrong, Perry. I love my father, but..."

"But what?"

"He's a game player. We all know that."

"And a bad one, as we've been learning recently," Xavier said darkly.

Perry frowned down at the man lying lax on the bed. He'd once been a king, but now, he was just an ill old man in a very rich, very resplendent suite.

She gnawed at her bottom lip before she murmured, "He's family. He'd never do anything to put us in harm's way."

"There was threat of an assassination before the wedding, Perry," Edward intoned grimly. "He didn't tell us."

Though his words had her stiffening in anger, she exhaled roughly. "And look how he's paid for it."

Edward rubbed his chin against her hair. "I know. I know."

She relaxed in his hold. "Let's not judge him until he can speak for himself, okay?"

Xavier blew out a breath, but he came up to her side. His arm was hot against hers, and she wished George was there to stand to her left. She needed her men at that moment. Needed them badly.

They were a solid unit, that she knew. She just wished life would stop getting in the goddamn way and would cease biting into what they had together.

"WHAT DO YOU THINK?"

"I think it's crazy." Perry peered around the open hall of Masonbrook castle's entryway. "When did this even happen?"

"Santa's elves live in Veronia, not the North Pole," George teased, and his mischievous tone was further proof that her man was still there—her playful joker hadn't died a death four days ago.

"Why don't you put the tree up earlier? All this for one day?"

"No. It's not like that here," he explained, curling an arm over her shoulder as they peered down at the thirty-foot fir that soared past the mezzanine floor—she was, even on the landing, still too far away from the star that glistened at its summit.

"What's it like then?" she chivvied.

"We celebrate Three Kings. Christmas is important, but not as important as Three Kings."

She scowled. "Why am I only just learning this?"

"Because, for once, even the royals are allowed to bow out at this time of year. There are few public engagements. Veronians know what Yule means to all families."

"They do? We don't have to go sing carols or something?"

"No. We get privacy, until the 5th of January."

Her mouth popped open. "We're on vacation?"

His nose wrinkled. "Ordinarily, we would be," he confirmed. "But with things up in the air, we're going to be working still. But as a family, we don't have to leave the castle." He must have sensed her relief at that, because he tightened his arm around her. "You've been holding up like a dream, love," he whispered into her ear.

"I don't know how," she admitted softly, staring up at the tree and at the thousands of decorations and lights that made the damn thing look like it belonged in Santa's workshop.

"You're stronger than you think."

"I've had to be." Her tone was grim.

"Why didn't you want to go back to the US for Christmas? I'd have taken you."

"I know you would've," she admitted. "But my place is here now. I'm Veronian. I can't run off home every time something goes wrong."

"This hardly counts!"

"What kind of message would it have sent to the people if I'd fled home? That, when times got tough, I was willing to run away?" She shook her head. "Even if I'd wanted to go, I wouldn't have."

He was silent for a second as he let her words resonate with him, but he kept his gaze averted from hers as he murmured, "I wish you'd gone."

"I know," she whispered. "You want me safe."

"Yes."

Perry sighed. "I'd kiss you right now if I could."

"I'd take it."

She turned to look up at him, and licking her lips, whispered, "This is my place now, George. With you. You have to understand that."

"We brought you into this danger, Perry. We never even saw it coming, and we just keep expecting you to deal with it." He swallowed thickly as he lifted a hand and pressed it to her belly. "You're starting to show more than ever, and it's not like it's going to get smaller, is it?"

She snorted out a laugh. "No, it's definitely going to get bigger not smaller."

He grinned. "Your tits are going to be divine."

She stuck out her tongue. "You're not supposed to say things like that out here."

"No one cares. Everyone who's here is sulking because they're working."

"Ugh, I feel guilty now." She grimaced. "It's not fair that they're working, and we're having fun."

"Don't feel too badly for them. They get quadruple rates for being here."

Her mouth gaped. "Quadruple? Is that even a thing?"

"Yes, and it tells you how important this season is to us. Mostly, we make sure the people who are working are the ones who don't have young families, or if they do, they're the ones who need the money."

"How do you make sure of that?" she demanded, her brow puckering. "It sounds like something that would fall under my remit—I'm head of this motley crew after all."

"It is, ordinarily. But I've been helping out with the household."

Her mouth opened wider. "You?" she said with a squeak.

His nostrils flared—in amusement, not anger. "Why does that come as a surprise?"

"I don't know. It just does." She wriggled her shoulders. "Thank you."

"Don't be silly. We're a team, aren't we? Xavier and I aren't just helping Edward. We're here to help you, too."

"He needs it more than I do," she said sadly. "He's so busy all the time."

"Father was busy—Edward's schedule is insane. He can't keep it up, and I don't think he wants to. Once everything is sorted out with the UnReals, then things will calm down." He gripped her chin between thumb and forefinger. "I promise you, Perry. I'll make sure he takes a step back."

Her mouth curved into a slow smile. "I'd like to see you bully him around."

He snorted. "Why? Because he's the one usually tormenting me?"

"Yeah, right," she mocked, making him laugh. Edward was many things, but he wasn't a bully. She pursed her lips as she turned back to look at the tree. "It's beautiful," she said softly. "Next year, I want to help them put it up."

He couldn't stop himself from snickering a little. "I told Edward you'd be gutted at missing out on this. He said that you should try to relax this year. What with your condition."

She pulled a face. "My 'condition'? You mean the bump?"

"I mean the bump," he confirmed. "It's not like we're going to let you climb the ladder to decorate the damn fir anyway."

"Still, I could have watched," she said on a pout.

"There's always next year." He squeezed her again. "You ready for brunch?"

"How many meals are there today again?"

He'd awoken her an hour ago and they'd slowly meandered their way out of the bathroom where he'd given her her Christmas gift in style—an orgasm in the shower. They'd dressed, and had been heading toward the dining room when she'd seen the tree.

"Four."

"How do you eat so much?"

"We're Veronian. We pace ourselves." Laughter boomed from him at her bewildered face.

"There's pacing and there's pacing," she said, eyeing him suspiciously. "None of these meals include anything gross, do they?" She prodded him in the chest. "I still haven't forgiven you for that *sliema d'alt*."

More laughter spilled from him. "Your face was hilarious that day."

"I thought I was going to be sick. Who eats pig's blood anyway? And if you're going to have it, why would it be in a dessert?" She shuddered. "I'll never get over it. Ever."

"You're so melodramatic," he chided, elbowing her gently in the side as they began to head to the dining room.

"George, you've no idea how melodramatic I can be if you're going to serve me up fish eyes for Christmas dinner."

Her warning was swallowed up in his chuckle, and though he wished he could kiss the grimace from her face, he allowed himself to tuck her tighter against his side.

This Christmas might not be going how they'd planned. There might have been threats against their family, threats they were still trying to resolve, but it was their first together as a unit, and for that, he intended on making it a memory worth savoring.

Something he knew Xavier and Edward were wholeheartedly in agreement with.

"WHERE THE HELL ARE THEY?" Xavier grumbled as he eyed the tureens.

"You know George, he'll have taken the scenic route," Edward said, amused at his cousin's impatience.

If there was one time of the year when Xavier lost his cool, it was Christmas. The man loved Yule, and he loved the food even more.

"Just start without them," he complained when Xavier looked at his watch for the tenth time. "You know Perry won't mind."

Xavier glowered at him. "You know she'll definitely mind. Anyway, I'd prefer for her to see the spread without my having disturbed it."

Edward had to admit, it was damn pretty and Perry would love it.

According to George, Perry was a very festive person. It was a side of herself that they hadn't been able to explore all that much.

For Thanksgiving, they hadn't returned to her home in the States as she'd wanted. But Edward had arranged for a meal to be made that followed the American tradition—who ate corn with gravy, anyway?

She'd scooped it up like it was going out of fashion, and had given him the best blowjob of his life in thanks.

Considering the day was *about* giving thanks, Edward had decided it was bound to become one of his favored holidays.

They'd been under the cosh for the entirety of this latter half of the year, and he knew that even Perry, festive and holiday-loving, had felt the strain. After the bombing, it had been easy to forget it was the most important time of the year for their people, but that was all the more reason for them to make it a special day.

If the UnReals ruined this holiday, then they were winning, and they'd win over Edward's dead body.

He ruffled the papers in his hand. He'd been awake since five. But this brunch was the first time he'd be eating, and it was the first time he was reading something that wasn't stamped with the words "Top Secret." He was just reading a Veronian newspaper, and it was wonderful to scan something normal, even if it did contain the grimness of the news of the day—most of it bad, considering the state of his poor nation.

At his side, there were four small boxes. Gifts that he'd had made for Perry. They'd all decided not to give each other presents, but to spoil her instead, and each place setting had their gifts to her at its side.

He wasn't sure if Perry was going to give them anything, but he hoped that if she did, it would come in the same form as the way she'd shown her thanks for getting cranberry sauce in a tin-can specially sent over for her, as well as having the kitchen make a gravy that was distinctly gray in color.

For all that he found the concoction bizarre, the mixture had been tasty.

Perry had explained why corn was important, and she'd subsequently explained why marshmallows made an appearance on yams, and why the dessert called Jell-O Salad even existed.

George hadn't batted an eye at the odd meal, but then, he wouldn't, would he? Not after living over in the States as long as he had. Xavier and Edward had visited, of course, but never at that time of the year.

Still, Edward was relieved to be eating Veronian fare, if he was being honest. At least that made sense to him.

When footsteps sounded outside the door, he smiled as Xavier straightened in his seat. They both peered at the door, Edward looking over his paper, to see his wife heading into the dining room, her step heavier than it had been months ago.

Her belly was still relatively slight, but it pulled taut against the silky sweater she wore. The knit clung to her ripe curves in a way that let all around them know she was pregnant. It was a surprising move on her behalf, considering they were trying to keep it under wraps. But then, as he took her in, he realized how big she was getting.

She'd need maternity clothes soon. A fact that truly grounded him.

Soon, he'd be a father. *They* would be fathers.

It couldn't have come at a worse moment, but then, there was never a good time to become a parent, was there? Children never entered the world when the timing was right. It was simply par for the course, he supposed, as he climbed to his feet, rounded the table, and headed for her.

Sliding his arms around her waist as George closed the door, he kissed her gently on the mouth before anointing her forehead with another. "You look beautiful, my sweetheart. Happy Christmas."

She peered up at him, a huge smile beaming his way as she murmured, "Merry Christmas, darling." Perry squeezed him, not just with her arms but with her words. When she looked at him, it was easy to feel like he'd set the stars in the night sky and made the sun shine at dawn.

She looked at him in a way that always clogged his throat, that overwhelmed him. It was, he reasoned, exactly why he adored her. Nobody, not even his brother or cousin, had the same belief in him that she did... yet she seemed to recognize how much he needed her without ever taking advantage of that.

He was well aware he should be her rock, and yet, she was his.

He pressed another kiss to her mouth, smiling as she wriggled against him. When her hips arched against his, rubbing her pelvis along his groin, he grabbed her and tutted. "Patience, Perry."

"You might as well ask for birds to do the front crawl," George said with a laugh as he took his place at the table. "Perry can't do patience."

She half-turned in Edward's arms to shoot his brother a glare. "I so can be patient. I'll have you know, I had to be super patient when I was in the lab."

"Super patient, huh?" George tapped his chin. "I think I need evidence before I believe you."

Grumbling at him, she gave Edward another kiss, then slipped out of his arms and straight into Xavier's. Unlike his cousin, Xavier spun her around in a tight circle.

"I thought you were never going to get here," he immediately complained after he'd kissed her—slipping her the tongue and making her moan even as he groused.

"I had to investigate the tree more. It's huge."

"It's a waste," Xavier said on a huff. "They should let them stay in the woods where they're meant to grow."

"Ordinarily, you know I'd agree with you, babe. But even I can't be a total Scrooge at Christmas," she chirped cheerfully, then laughed when he spun her around again. "Anyway, speaking of impatience, what's the rush?"

"I'm hungry."

She chuckled. "You're hungry? Why didn't you eat?"

"Because I wanted you to see everything first."

Edward knew that touched her, because she reached up to cup his cousin's cheek as she leaned onto tiptoe. "That's so sweet," she murmured softly.

Xavier grabbed her hand and led her to the seat laid out for her—before, Edward assumed, she could get busy with her fingers and distract him from his stomach. A thought that made him snort in amusement.

The dining room was the one they used for all occasions—private, intimate dinners, or social events with dozens of guests.

It was an eighty-foot-long room with fires that burned either end. A chandelier hung over the middle of the table and was backed up by a streak of smaller chandeliers right down the central line of the mahogany surface. The antique patina gleamed with glittery sparkles as it reflected the hundreds of lights above it.

Normally, they weren't lit, but as it was Christmas, he'd wanted Perry to have the full effect.

They were at the end of the table, surrounded by windows overlooking the fountain for which Masonbrook was named. The normally hundred-foot-long water spout wasn't as ferocious as it was in summer, thanks to the colder temperatures which turned some of the water into a slush pile.

Still, in the distance, the city lights could be seen, not of Madela, but of Saren, the town nearest to the Ansian mountain range that was a part of Xavier's ducal territory.

A Christmas tree, loaded with decorations, had been set up in here too, and dozens of boxes sat around the base, waiting for the staff who were working for them today, to make their own days perfect.

There were four settings made up at the dining table, and Edward was fully aware that this would undoubtedly be the first and last intimate meal they'd have as a foursome.

Next year, God willing, his father would be well enough to eat with them, and they'd have a baby to entertain. They'd also have new staff that would need to be invited—it was only the change in circumstances that meant the Guardians of the Keys weren't eating here today. Next year, they would. Right now, the only Guardian was Cassie, and as Marcus had flown in yesterday, Edward had told them both to enjoy a Christmas at home.

So this meal, the first of the four traditional repasts of the day, was to be their first and last Christmas together in this kind of personal setting. And he knew he would cherish the memories forever.

More than that, he'd cherish Perry's reactions to it.

With a smile, he watched as Xavier seated her, then quickly began lifting the silver cloches that covered the dishes that were a part of a traditional Yule brunch.

Her "oohing" and "aahing" began immediately, and even Edward's stomach began to stir at the sight of the traditional *pankek*. They weren't actually pancakes, despite the similarity of the name, but oat biscuits made with thick hazelnuts and almonds that dripped with honey. Then, there were the *kenfe*, which were donuts stuffed with jam or ricotta cheese. There were also the *bele,* which were rounded buns stuffed with bacon and caramelized vine tomatoes, as well as countless other dishes that were more common than those three seasonal items.

She immediately grabbed a *pankek*, tucked a *kenfe* onto her plate, and bit into a *bele* after George explained what it contained. The moans she made had his own mouth watering, and not just for food.

He reached for a *bele* too, and started eating as he read from the paper. Keeping an eye on his family as they broke their Christmas fast, he relaxed into the meal as he drank hot chocolate with thick layers of whipped cream. Xavier and Perry drank juice, but George had the hot cider that was almost peppery with flavor, thanks to a dash of paprika they added to the mix. It wasn't to his liking, but George always had been fond of the drink.

The memory made him realize how long it had been since George had been here for Yule. His stomach twisted. They'd been apart for far too long...but now, thanks to Perry, they'd never be separated again.

She must have sensed his attention on her, because she sent him a questioning smile. He just looked at her, breathing her in, and silently thanking her for being theirs.

"How come I didn't get any hot chocolate?" she asked, when he lifted his large mug and took a sip.

"Because you took ages to get here," Xavier retorted, after gulping down his third *kenfe*.

"Ring for a footman, George," Edward prompted his brother, who was peering at the gifts on the floor.

Though he did as bid, Perry seemed to realize where George's focus was, for she too got to her feet, a donut in hand, and wandered over to the tree. "Are these for us?" she asked, her eyes lighting up.

George snorted. "No. We'll spoil you in different ways. Fear not."

A ripe laugh fell from her lips as her head fell back. "Oh, is that a promise?" she teased, nudging him in the side.

"It's more than a promise," Xavier retorted, his own eyes laced with a wicked vow.

Before they could say another word, the footman, Benson, appeared and promptly disappeared after Edward made his request. "They're for the staff working today," he informed her, pointing to the gifts on the floor.

"Really? That's so sweet! You guys think of everything."

"Hardly," George said with a little laugh. "But we try. It's the least we can do, after all."

"Who bought them?"

"I didn't buy them, but I arranged for the list to be put together," George said piously, making Xavier and Edward chuckle.

Perry's lips twitched. "Okay, so what kind of presents are they?"

"Each one has a gift card, but it's mostly food. Different types of hampers."

"That's really thoughtful," she murmured.

"It's tradition."

"What kind of food goes in hampers over here?" She squinted at him. "I'd like to see one."

"We'll go to *Pretne*. You'll love it there."

"*Pretne*?" she asked, butchering the name.

Xavier laughed. "We really needed to give you lessons in Veronian for Yule, Perry."

She pouted. "So I can't speak the language of the country I live in—how truly American is that?"

"You're Veronian now," Edward corrected, cocking his brow at her over his paper.

Though she rolled her eyes, she didn't reply, just asked, "What's *Pretne*?"

"It's like Fortnum & Masons. I'm surprised Cassie hasn't taken you, if I'm being honest. Or Mother, for that matter," George replied.

"Your mother barely ate, so I highly doubt she'd take me to a gourmet food superstore," Perry said wryly. "And Cassie is just as bad. They're always watching their figures." She wrinkled her nose as she patted her belly. "I think if there was ever a time to gorge on hampers, it's now."

They laughed, and she grinned at them.

Benson reappeared after a knock with her hot chocolate, and as she took a sip, she asked, "When does the staff open the presents?"

"At the end of the day. About nine o'clock."

"Why so late?"

"It keeps them going," Xavier teased, "while they serve us."

She blew out a breath. "We're elitist scum, aren't we?" As she spoke, she slumped into her seat. George bent down to press a kiss to her temple.

"Yes, love, but we're *nice* elitist scum, if that makes you feel better."

She snickered. "I guess."

Edward's lips curved into a deep smile as her laughter filled his heart with warmth. This might be their first Christmas together, but he had no doubt that it would be the best, because the best was always yet to come.

IN THE SPACE of two hours, she'd gone from feeling like Mrs. Santa Claus to a small girl on Christmas morning.

Handing out gifts to the staff had been a pleasure, especially the way their eyes had lit up at the presents, but selfishly, receiving her own was better yet.

As they drove through Grosvenor House's gates, she let out a squeal that had her men laughing and wincing at the same time.

"I'm trying to drive, Perry," George chided. "I don't have the hands to cover my ears."

"Oh, shut up!" she remarked, squealing again, and laughing as they laughed with and at her. "Why are we here?"

"It's your gift," Edward murmured, turning back so he could see her from the passenger seat. "I know you wished…" He sighed. "I wanted you to spend some part of our first Christmas together here."

Her eyes flashed. "George, you haven't seen the master bedroom, have you? We totally need to christen it," she said eagerly.

"Christen it?" Xavier asked, brows furrowing.

"You know what I mean," she retorted, wafting a hand at him. "Us three have had some fun in there, but George wasn't in on the action."

The man in question pursed his lips. "Well, I totally feel left out now."

She snorted. "Get over it. I'm about to make it up to you. In spades."

The joy at being at the house had her letting out another squeal, and as they came to a halt in the driveway, the gravel parting and overspilling as the car moved on its surface, she pushed the door open and dove out just as George put on the brakes.

"Catch me if you can," she shouted. Glee laced her tone as she sprang toward the wide steps that led to the door of the house she wished she was living in.

Still, it could be a home away from home, couldn't it?

A notion that pleased her endlessly.

While she knew that being here at all was a major concession, she wished they'd managed to come here earlier in the day. They'd had to hand out the gifts, though, and she totally understood that. Just really hoped Edward had meant it when he said they were going to enjoy the rest of their vacation here… like, she hoped, up until Three Kings Day.

The door opened just as she approached, and with a quick, "Hello," she ran past the startled butler and headed on down the corridor. She knew

Edward would make an appearance in her bedroom first, especially as the staff was there so they had to follow the proprieties, but George and Xavier would make it as soon as they could, she was sure.

Having staff sucked majorly sometimes.

Even if it *had* been over five months since she'd had to worry about dirty clothes.

She seriously loved having a laundry. It saved so much time and effort.

By the time her heels were sinking into the plush carpeting of the sitting room in the master suite, she heard a low voice declare, "Are you supposed to be running in your condition?"

"I'm pregnant, not dying," she retorted, spinning around to look at her husband. She wore a wide Cheshire Cat grin, one that said she refused to allow him to piss her off.

"I'm very glad to hear you're not dying... although, tonight, you might die. Just a little."

She scowled at him. "That's not sexy talk."

He laughed. "Have you never heard of the French phrase '*la petite mort*'?"

"The little something."

"The little death."

Perry grumbled, "I need to improve my French, Italian, and Veronian."

"Let's start with the last first," he teased. "Considering you live here."

She rubbed her nose. "Why's it called 'the little death'?" she asked quickly, preferring to change the subject—languages had never been her forte. She was more of a "hypothesis, experiment, conclusion" kinda gal. Not a humanities chick.

"Because it's so good, you die a little inside."

"That's stupid."

He grinned. "I shall endeavor to make you think otherwise."

See, that's where he had her. How could a man say shit like that? *"I shall endeavor."* It was like something from the eighteen hundreds...and yet, when he did, he turned her to mush.

She shivered, unable to contain herself, because he was so hot at that moment, so strong and hers, and just wonderful, that she wanted to crawl all over him.

Beckoning him closer with a crooked pointer finger, she murmured, "I want you. Inside me. No death, just life."

"That can definitely be arranged," he retorted with another grin, this one panty-melting hot.

He strode forward, and with no ounce of discomfort, hefted her not insignificant weight into his arms. She squeaked in surprise though, and quickly wrapped her legs around his hips. Before she could complain about his potentially dropping her, he reached for her mouth and sapped the world from her consciousness.

She didn't even realize they'd made it into the bedroom, didn't care where they were, just knew he'd taken her to another universe with his innate ability to kiss her until she forgot her own damn name.

With a shudder, she thrust her tongue against his and gave as much as she got. She had to. This was a fight for equality, and she wanted to blow his mind as much as he blew hers.

Speaking of "blowing," she struggled in his arms and demanded to be let down when she opened her eyes and saw they were next to the bed. He scowled but dropped her carefully and swiftly. Now that she was at eye-level with his chest, she reached for his fly.

He put his hands on hers. "We don't have to do this so quickly. I thought we could have some mulled wine in the sitting room? Maybe watch a film?"

"Later, or tomorrow," she growled. "I need you inside me, baby."

His hands tangled with her hair. "Never let it be said I don't give my princess what she needs."

"Queen," she rejoined haughtily, her hands finally inside his zipper. She pulled his dick through the opening she'd made.

He let out a low laugh that turned into a hiss as she bowed her head and sucked the tip of his shaft into her mouth. Focusing the pressure of her tongue there, she watched as the muscles underneath his shirt suddenly pulled taut against the slimline fabric. There wasn't an ounce of belly fat there, not even a half-ounce. How that was possible, she didn't know. She'd never seen him work out—although in his old rooms, he had a treadmill. They didn't in their new quarters, though.

Still, now was not the time to think of him sweating anywhere other than on top of her.

Or beneath her.

That could work too.

She sucked down hard on his glans, loving when he jolted up onto his tiptoes and gritted out, "Fuck!"

Her laugh was sultry and wicked, telling him without words she knew exactly what she was doing before she slipped her mouth down, slicking his cock with spit. Her lips were pulled taut, and she loved it. Loved the feel of him against her tongue, the pressure of him against her cheeks.

For endless moments, she lost herself in him. Reveled in his pleasure, in pleasing him. She loved when he arched his pelvis, almost fucking her mouth, loved when he groaned and his hands tightly gripped her hair, commanding her silently to go to his motion, to his rhythm...

She ignored it, of course.

This was her game. Her challenge.

"Looks like we're missing out on some of the fun, Xavier." George's voice was a low growl, and it sent tingles through her. Sent them to the tips of her fingers and down to her fucking toes. Her core exploded in a blast of heat that made her want to scream around his shaft, because it should not be fair for a man's voice to have that effect on her, dammit!

She moaned and moved her hand from around the base of Edward's cock to between her legs. Just as she did, fingers snapped out, grabbing her wrist. "Oh no," Xavier muttered silkily in her ear, before he nipped the lobe. "Hands off."

"The minx has been teasing me," Edward gritted out, his own fingers tight against her scalp.

"Well, that's just not acceptable," George replied, and she felt the mattress shift again as his weight came onto it.

Only this bed and their one back home would have fit all three men, and she was, at that moment, sure that medieval kings and queens had secretly taken part in orgies. Because that was the only reason they'd make these mattresses so damn huge.

Behind her, she felt the heat of someone press against her spine. Then, she felt hands scoop down along her arms, before they reached around and began helping her out of her blouse. Fingers appeared at the fly of her trousers, and she rocked her hips, needing them to slide down, to cup her sex, to fulfill her.

But they didn't fulfill her.

They just unfastened the zip and the button.

Edward fucked her mouth hard a second, letting out a sharp hiss when he pulled away. "That mouth of yours is fucking sinful, Perry," he rasped out, his cock bobbing between them, shiny and bright purply-red with the pulse of his blood.

She licked her lips. "Only for you three."

His hand cupped her jaw. "Only for us," he growled out, and at that moment, she realized all his muscles were pumped full and thick, like he was standing straighter and taller.

Oh boy, she'd taunted the tiger, and he was ready to rock.

Rather than be frightened—because whenever they approached her en masse, they had a habit of trying to overwhelm her—she decided to let them have at her.

They wanted her crying with pleasure?

They wanted her sobbing out her delight?

Bring it.

She wanted it, too.

It was her right.

There had to be some good shit to this queen malarkey. And she wasn't talking about not having to deal with the laundry either.

She sucked in a sharp breath as she heard the sound of a zipper lowering, and turned and saw that Xavier was stepping out of his pants. A flash of skin behind her had her moving around more, and she realized George was buck naked. His cock was in his hand as he stared at her, his fist pumping in a way that made her growl... Edward wasn't the only one feeling aggressive. She hopped off the bed and pushed her husband out of the way. She knew he didn't appreciate that, but she didn't give a damn.

Before he could do more than grit his teeth, she was pulling down her pants and panties, throwing off her blouse and unfastening her bra.

Then, she hauled herself back onto the bed and crawled over to George. This wasn't sinful or sultry—it was loaded with need.

She tilted her head to look at the mirror on the canopy. "I want you to watch me ride you," she taunted him as she pushed his shoulder, urging him onto his back.

"The pleasure's mine, Perry," he told her, his tone gritty.

Xavier approached, and she grabbed his hand and tucked it between her legs. They both hissed.

"Fuck, she's wet," Xavier gritted out, and she rocked her hips, loving his touch against her there. She thrust in short, sharp jerks that had his fingers sliding over her nub.

"Oh God, that feels so good!" she bit off, then she maneuvered Xavier's hand and pressed it to her breast as she clambered over George. "I need you inside me now."

He let out a chuckle, then opened his arms wide. "Have at me."

She growled under her breath as she grasped a firm hold of his shaft, tucked it against her core, then slowly began to accept him. Each thick inch was hard won, but she earned it, loved the way he spread her wide, filling her to overfull. She was panting by the time he was all the way inside her, so damn big in this position, she felt like she was going insane with it.

Breath soughed from his lungs when she settled her ass against his thighs, then his hands came up to cup the small, taut bump that was their baby. "You're starting to show," he whispered, and there was a hint of deference in his tone. Definite wonder.

She couldn't help but feel like a goddamn sex goddess at the way he stared at her ripe form, his cock pulsing hotly inside her.

She bore down around his dick, loving his hiss, loving the way his fingers clutched at her. Then, Xavier moved his hand up to her head, and she turned and saw his cock was out, pointing straight at her. She bowed over him, urging him down onto his knees, and began to suck the tip of his dick into her mouth. When a faint *splatting* noise made itself known to her, she prepared herself for what her position enabled...

The chill of the lube came as a shock, even though she'd recognized the sound, and she moaned against the dick in her mouth. Xavier's hands twisted in her hair, and her pussy clamped around George's cock as Edward's fingers began to play with her asshole. The way she was leaning over spread her asscheeks, giving her little protection from his marauding hands.

He speared her with those elegant, spatulate digits, filled her, spread her, scissored inside her, until she was rhythmically clenching down on George without having to move an inch. His hands were on her back, the pads rubbing her spine, massaging her in a way that made her nerves taut and tense, while relaxing her, too.

She felt Edward's cock rub against the curve of her cheeks and sucked down hard on Xavier when she felt the tip prod her asshole. With a sigh, she tried to relax, knowing it would be easier in the long run to do just that. But it was hard, especially as he was so thick, and George was already taking up a lot of room.

Pulling away from Xavier's cock lest she bite him, she dug her nails into his thighs as Edward forged a path deep inside her. It seemed to take a lifetime, and when she felt the two cocks inside her, she wanted to roar with triumph.

God, this felt good. So fucking good!

She felt alive. The vibrant energy buzzed through her veins, making her blood fizzle and tingle.

When his pelvis nudged her ass, she realized he was all the way in. She didn't know how this felt for them, but knew how epic it was for her. Sweat beaded on her brow, tension gathered in her limbs as she turned her attention to Xavier.

It was hard focusing on him, difficult to process how to suck him and pleasure him when her body was being spit-roasted in so many different ways. But she tried, and she gave it her all. Then, George and Edward began to move. The rhythm was erratic, not smooth, as they found their pacing, and it was hard for her to concentrate on anything other than the way they sawed in and out of her.

Her breathing came in jerky pants that had Xavier's hands tightening in her hair. "Fucking hell, Perry," he gritted out, and she realized that whatever she was doing, it was working. His hips were rocking up, his cock thrusting between her lips of their own volition.

Trembling, overwhelmed by all the attention, her body went into lockdown. She became nothing more than a feral creature who needed these three, needed them as much as she needed to breathe. They were her air, her oxygen.

Without them, she was nothing.

And she knew, without a shadow of a doubt, they felt the same way about her.

Fingers nudged at her belly, and she sucked it in as much as she could, even though it was full of their baby, and let them in so he could tangle with her clit.

She was sopping wet, so juicy that the noises spilling from between them were lewd and crass, and so fucking sexy that she wanted to scream, but couldn't because Xavier's dick was like a plug.

Then, Edward began to caress her nub, and George and he sped up. Her eyes shot wide, her vision turning dull-edged as pleasure whistled around her veins. She heard Xavier let out a sharp cry, felt his cum pelt her throat, but she didn't move away. Just carried on gasping for air around him, her lips and mouth pulling on him rhythmically until he lurched away from her, plunking backward onto his spine, as air soughed from his lungs.

"She's like a fucking vacuum," he gritted out, but she was too far gone to care. Later, however, she'd be pissed at being compared to a Dyson.

"Isn't it fucking wonderful?" George gasped, his tone as dreamy as could be.

She'd been leaning over to the side to accommodate Xavier, but now, George grabbed her and put her in line with him. The movement did something, changed his angle, and spread her pussy lips wide, revealing the nub of her clit.

A sharp scream escaped from her. "Oh God!" she cried out.

"That's it, baby, that's it," Edward crooned, bending over her, covering her with all of him.

She let out a sob as they moved faster, sliding in and out of her in a way that was only pleasurable because she was so lost to the moment.

"I need... I-I need... Oh my God!" she screamed, roaring their names, Xavier's too, begging them, pleading with them, declaring her love for them.

Pleasure raged through her like a typhoon, decimating everything in her path, destroying then rebuilding the things that made her Perry, that were unique to her.

Whimpers escaped her as she went blind, deaf, dumb. They sapped it from her. Took it all away and swept it back in with each thrust.

Then, they gave it all back to her as, with dual roars of their own, they came inside her. She felt them. Slick and hot. They poured their essences into her, flooding her with all they had to give until she was sobbing, a wreck in their arms.

A shushing sound was the first thing she heard over her heartbeat, and she realized George was humming into her ear, his hands smoothing up and down her back.

"I think Perry knows what *'la petite mort'* means now, guys," Edward murmured softly, and because he was Edward, he managed to say that without an ounce of arrogance.

How he did that, she really wasn't sure. He managed to say the most irritating things in the most neutral of ways, so she never had a chance to get mad.

Until...

She lifted up a little and squinted at Xavier. "I'm not a Dyson."

He snorted—the noise was aimed at the ceiling as he was flat on his back, his chest still rising and falling like he'd been running a race. "It's a compliment, sweetheart. Trust me."

She pouted, then pressed her face to George's shoulder. "I'm not a Dyson," she complained again.

George laughed, Edward, too, as he fell beside them. She felt her husband's hand in her hair, and knew it was his because his touch was delicate, where George's was a little rougher. He tangled his digits in her wavy locks, soothing and teasing her at the same time with the caress.

"It's not a bad thing, sweetheart," Edward crooned, and she flexed her muscles about George's cock at the sound.

He immediately groaned. "I'm dead, Perry. You can't revive the dead."

"Didn't mean to," she grumbled, but clenched around him when she felt his cock try to slip out of her. "Want to go to sleep like this," she mumbled again, settling her face next to his, against his shoulder. "With you inside me. Filling me," she whispered on a happy sigh.

Around her, the men groaned.

"Lucky bastard," Xavier groused.

George just snickered. "You realize how hot she is, right?"

"That had better be Pammy Anderson hot," she warned, but there wasn't much fire to her tone—she was too exhausted to really be snarky.

"No. I mean, scorching hot. You might have to turn on the air conditioning, Edward. I expect to melt."

"I'm not hotter than you," she retorted.

"You're a furnace."

"Like you're not."

"Children," Edward inserted smoothly. "Let's rest. It's still early. We can watch a movie tonight."

She huffed. "This was better than a movie. And I don't want to. I want to stay here. With you three."

"We're not going anywhere."

Perry went quiet. "You'll go back to your rooms."

George stilled. "Is that why you want to stay like this?"

"I want the connection," she said blankly, but his words woke her a little, and she didn't want that—she wanted to sleep. It had been a pretty long day, and she was tired.

He sighed. "We'll stay. You don't have to be uncomfortable tonight, baby."

She hated that she sounded like she was whining, but... "You won't. I'll wake up, and you'll be gone. I'm sorry for being a wimp," she whispered. "I just hate waking up and finding you're not here. Even Edward. He goes, and he's the only one who can stay!" She'd slept alone for most of her life, and it had never presented a problem. Now? When her bed was overflowing? She liked it that way.

Hell, she *loved* it that way.

A hand stroked down her back. "I'm sorry, sweetheart."

"Don't be. Just stop waking up so early."

"I have to. You know I have duties."

She moved her head, lifting it so she could stare at him. "Then wake me up, too. Don't slide out of bed like nothing's happening. Just kiss me and say good morning. I'll go back to sleep then."

"You need to rest," he countered.

"I need you to kiss me more. I know it's silly...but it's normal. It's like..." She swallowed. "Everyone does that. Gives each other a kiss in the morning. I need that. I need you."

The mattress juddered a little, and she felt Xavier settle at George's side. She turned to look at him as he murmured, "I'll be around more, Perry."

She licked her lips. "You will?"

He nodded. "My suite in the private wing is almost ready."

Her eyes widened. "That's really happening? You'll be sleeping over?"

His lips curved as he reached up and gave her a kiss. He trailed his mouth over her chin to her ear. "I love that you want me close."

"Always," she whispered fiercely. "I need you all close."

George sighed. "We're so lucky."

She peered at him. "Why?"

"You shouldn't want any of this. We've brought you into a crazy world. Made everything ten times harder for you...you should be wanting to *leave*, what with the UnReals and all that crap. Yet, you want us closer than ever."

"You're mine," she whispered, the words and tone simple. But as simple as they were, they were also definitive.

They were hers, and she was theirs. There was nothing complicated about it.

It was fact.

CHAPTER EIGHTEEN

"WHAT IS IT?"

"Your Three Kings present."

Ten days later, Edward blinked at the USB stick Drake had just handed him. Placing it on his desk, he asked, "What's on it?"

"The answers to our prayers." The head of security's eyes flashed with excitement.

Irritated by the game the other man was playing, Edward snapped, "Stop beating around the bush, Drake. What the hell is on it?"

"Images. Of UnReals with Ferdinand L'Argeneau."

For a second, Edward's mouth worked and no words escaped. "What?" he finally asked, his tone hoarse.

In the past two weeks since the bombing, they'd made little headway on their theories regarding the UnReal's motives, but had used the subsequent state of emergency to completely change the security councils.

The men who had overseen them for years were now in retirement, and friends of Xavier, George, and himself filled those seats. They'd managed to turn around the governing bodies that kept the nation secure, while the police force grilled the entirety of Parliament to ascertain links to the UnReals. And they'd achieved it all in a matter of weeks.

Of the several-hundred-strong government, over a hundred had been culled from the ranks, thanks to ties to the UnReals. Ties that were anywhere from deeply ingrained bonds to the faintest of rumors. They were purging Parliament, but in a way that was as democratic as possible.

The UnReals were being put down. From the inside out.

For years, they were learning that the rebels flourished in the darkest of shadows, using those shadows to hide in plain sight. Spreading rumors, instigating dissent.

And recently, they'd managed to throw funding into the mix.

The minute financial backing had been established, that was when the politicians had started switching allegiance. According to the police investigation into the matter, that is. Funding had changed everything, and with a backer like Ferdinand L'Argeneau, change was never good. A man with a grudge against the family that was entirely founded on bullshit, L'Argeneau had been an enemy in their midst for too long.

"Is it enough to bring him in?" Edward asked, the words choked.

"Yes," Drake confirmed softly. "He's being taken to one of MIHQ's bases in Saren." A base that was their equivalent of a CIA black site.

Edward straightened in his seat. "You know I want to be there before even one question is uttered."

"Why do you think I'm here, sire?"

Nodding, he stood. Grabbing the jacket he'd slung over the back of his seat, he slipped into it, then picking up his laptop, he said, "I'll have a look at the contents on the drive over."

In silence, they headed out of the palace. Xavier caught up with them along the way, and Edward, knowing how pissed George would be if he was kept out of the loop, texted his younger brother. Though his reply did surprise him.

With Perry, make sure we're updated.

That meant he was either balls deep inside her and didn't want to be disturbed, or some trouble was afoot.

Truth was, Edward expected the former over the latter. The two of them could be worse than kids sometimes, he thought, his lips curving in a wry smile.

As he texted his brother, he asked aloud, "How did you find out?"

"Drake called me, too."

Edward cut the head of security a look as a dozen-strong unit of guards saluted them once they made it into the portico where a car was waiting. They climbed in, and as the car set off, Edward frowned at Drake. "You called Xavier. Why?"

"He's as involved in this situation as you are, sire," Drake said smoothly, and though Edward knew he was wholly right, something didn't sit well.

He turned his chin up as he settled his laptop on his knee. "Do you know?"

"Does he know what?" Xavier demanded with a huff. "Why shouldn't he have told me?"

"I'm not arguing that he did, I'm arguing *why* he did," Edward retorted, ignoring the fire in Xavier's words. His cousin was spoiling for a fight, and if he wanted to, it would have to be against Ferdinand.

Drake shot him a look. "It was only a matter of time, sire."

"What was?" Xavier asked. "Stop speaking in circles."

Edward narrowed his eyes. "Are you going to tell anyone?"

"What would be the gain in it? Marianne's got her wish. That's all that matters." Drake turned away and looked out of the window.

Xavier sucked in a sharp breath. "Oh."

"Yes, 'oh,'" Edward said wryly, even as he turned on his laptop, inserted the flash drive, and began to scroll through the images revealed on there.

His cousin cleared his throat. "How did you find out?"

"You might think I've been incompetent of late, Your Grace, but I'm not totally bloody blind," Drake countered, his brow quirked. "Anyway, what you do in private is your own affair. It always was."

He didn't say anything, merely looked at the head of security. "We appreciate your discretion."

Drake laughed, but it wasn't cold or hard, merely amused. "I've served this family in one way or another for close to three decades. I've dealt with worse than you three could throw at me. At least when you're all together, the mischief is contained."

Though Edward scowled, Xavier was the one who grumbled, "Not sure I appreciate being compared to a bunch of recalcitrant toddlers."

"I was thinking more along the lines of horny teenagers, actually."

Edward rolled his eyes but remained silent, checking out the footage on the USB drive. That Drake 'knew' didn't entirely come as a surprise—back in his heyday, he hadn't exactly been discreet, and it was the job of the head of security to know of and to fend off potential threats before they started. His proclivities, Edward felt sure, had been considered a potential threat at some point.

Still, he didn't like it. Knew Perry would be mortified, so decided this was the last time any of them would mention it. Drake's loyalty was above question—it wasn't his fault he'd been slow on the uptake during these past few months. Grief did that to a man, Edward knew.

And if Drake had loved Marianne like Edward did Perry, then…

Well, he didn't even want to think about how he'd deal with losing her.

"Where did this come from?" he demanded, changing the subject as he saw, from the snapshots, just how close to the meeting these had been taken. The angles indicated an intimacy that came as a shock.

"Raoul Da Silva," Drake said simply.

"Raoul Da Silva?" Xavier blurted out. "What about him?"

"I believe Da Silva wasn't happy about what happened to your mother.

He was her guard for a long time, after all, and I highly doubt Marianne didn't work her usual wiles on him."

"You think they were having an affair?"

Drake's lips twitched. "I wouldn't be surprised if that had happened at some point. Your parents weren't exactly happy together. But I don't know for certain. What I do know is that Marianne might have come across as chilly to some people, but she made a lot of people, from all walks of life, fall for her. I think that happened with Raoul."

"Explain," Edward demanded grimly.

"One of the guards, Da Silva's friend, handed me an envelope this morning. It was a letter from Da Silva's sister. He had apparently told her that if anything happened to him, she was to find a way to get the USB drive to me."

"He knew he was in danger?"

"It would seem so."

"Why? What changed?" Edward peered at the photos once more. "Da Silva was obviously close to the UnReal's leadership if he was privy to conversations between Prichard and L'Argeneau."

"I would imagine so. His was probably the worst case of treason we've seen in many a year, and the bastard had a full military funeral with honors." Drake sounded outraged that a traitor could get the royal treatment—hadn't the king and queen attended the bastard's funeral? Even if it was only to maintain a front, the rest of the world didn't know that, did they?

Xavier peered at the screen from Edward's side. "Traitor, he might have been, but he's also given us exactly what we need to cage L'Argeneau." His cousin whistled under his breath. "And Jesus, do we have him."

Edward couldn't deny that he was thrilled about the photos before him, for it was enough to ruin Ferdinand—it wasn't, however, enough to make the man turn against the UnReals.

Ferdinand L'Argeneau had made a name for himself in the seedy underworld of societies around this continent and countless others. One didn't reach such lofty heights among a certain class of people by ratting out one's partners in crime... not unless those compatriots were shown for the two-faced bastards they were.

Xavier carried on scrolling through the photos as Edward reached for his cell phone. Quickly seeking Markov's number, he connected the call and waited for his friend and new spymaster to answer.

"Edward?"

Markov's voice was always thick with his accent, even though he was fluent in English.

"*Da*, I have news," he replied in Russian, knowing Xavier didn't speak it, and that if Drake did, it was a secret he'd kept for years.

"What kind of news?" Markov replied, his tone cheerful. In the background, Edward heard the tapping of keys on a laptop, as well as the flickering of a fire—part of his generous compensation package was a luxury chalet high on the Ansian mountain range.

Xavier had donated it—the family's old hunting lodge—to the cause of enticing the man to Veronia.

It had worked.

The man was now living like a Pasha among the ski slopes.

"News that lets us bring Ferdinand L'Argeneau in for questioning. Hell, more than that," Edward conceded. "We've got him. There's no way he can try to worm out of this. But it's not enough to bring down the UnReals. He's the moneyman, sure, but if he protects the rebels, then we're wasting a good lead."

"I understand."

"What news on the murders of the doctors who cared for Arabella before her death?"

"There are ties to the UnReals," Markov murmured slowly.

Edward scowled. "Why the hell wasn't I informed of that? I didn't hire you to keep me out of the loop, Dima!"

"No, I know, but I've been checking into the situation. I have *ties*, Edward. Ties. Not unbreakable bonds."

"Explain," he said, knowing his tone was grouchy, and not caring. The base where Ferdinand was being held was close, and he wanted leverage before the questioning begun.

"Jacob Prichard is a control freak like you," Markov murmured, but his tone was partially teasing. "He likes to keep close tabs on all jobs that are undertaken on the rebels' behalf."

"Please tell me you've found evidence?"

"*Da*. The information is trickling in, I have nothing concrete on three of the murders, but one of them? *Da*," Dima repeated. "Without a doubt, there's proof of Prichard's involvement."

"How?"

"Three bank transfers. Each to the same man who handled the autopsy of one of the victims and his wife."

Edward's throat closed. "I didn't realize there were other victims."

"Sadly, there were. One of the EMTs that responded to the emergency call at the palace was in a vehicle with his family when he went off the road." There was the sound of scratching, and Edward knew Markov would be scraping his beard with his hunting dagger—an atrocious habit, and one,

Edward had always warned his friend, that endangered him more than his job did.

All it would take was a sneeze for him to slice through his damn carotid.

"That's a fucking shame," Edward growled.

"Yes. Children, too. Anyway, there's a bittersweet irony to it all. The bank account I found, it ties to the pathologist who handled the autopsies of the victims. The paperwork claimed there was a high level of alcohol in the driver's blood. That was used to explain why the car went off the road when there were no signs of foul play on the vehicle."

He frowned. "How is that possible?"

Markov laughed. "You're like me, my friend. Suspicious to the quick. I looked at the crash site, and agree—there was no foul play. But I looked at the blood test myself. There *was* something in the driver's blood, but it wasn't alcohol. Some kind of drug that made the man fall asleep at the wheel? Sadly, it was in a heavily wooded area and the car slammed into a tree. They all died instantly."

"So the murder was covered up."

"Quite well. The bank account used to pay the pathologist has Prichard's dirty little fingers all over it."

"How? Surely it's not in his own name?"

"No, it's in his niece's."

For a second, Edward's mouth dropped open. "The man can't be such a fool?"

"I don't know him, so I can't say. The UnReals weren't wealthy at the time. Only after the 'accidents' did they gain funding from L'Argeneau after all. They wouldn't have had the ability to create ghost accounts through shell corporations. Until recently, they were a very basic, very crude operation."

Edward pursed his lips. "That's a damn shame about the EMT's family," he said softly, hating and hurting for the loss. "I want you to find a way to haul the pathologist behind the false autopsy into Veronia for questioning, Dima. Do you hear me? I want proof that we can take back to the victims' families so we can clear the driver's name."

"Already working on it. I know you too well, old friend. You are very sentimental when it comes to these matters."

Rolling his eyes, he grumbled, "Give me a name I can use to taunt L'Argeneau."

"The niece's name is Danica."

"I need more. That's not enough to make L'Argeneau realize he's been played."

Markov let out a cheerful laugh. "You mistake me, my friend. I've saved the best for last."

Edward scowled. "How?"

"L'Argeneau also has a mistress."

"He does? Not too unusual. You know what the top families are like here."

"Yes. But he's pissed in his own backyard…"

"It's not the niece."

"Yes. It is." Markov laughed again. "Beautiful, isn't it?"

Only a sick mind could find anything about this situation beautiful, so Edward must have been sick—there truly was a twisted kind of beauty in this fucked-up mess.

"*Da*, it is," he replied, satisfaction filling him as he realized L'Argeneau was nailed, and the Prichards were about to be crucified, too.

Drake hadn't been wrong. For a present for Epiphany, which was tomorrow—the sixth—he couldn't have asked for a better gift.

"This dark web website Drake told you about," Markov said, when Edward thought their conversation was over.

"Yes? What about it?"

"I've found no evidence of such a place."

"The internet's big," Edward countered. "Maybe you haven't found it."

"I've been building a trap. You know my traps are foolproof. I tell you true, there is no UnReal online presence on the dark web. Prichard is too old school, anyway. He's in his fifties and, at best, he's a midlevel accountant, hardly capable of plotting the downfall of a nation on his own."

Cutting Xavier a look, he saw his cousin was focused entirely on the screen. Carefully, he shot the head of a security a triumphant grin after he flashed a look at the images before him. When Giles smiled back, Edward reflected how difficult it was to maintain an air of normalcy. Markov was overloading him with information he really didn't need to be hearing when the man whose competence was in question was nearby.

"What are you talking about, old friend?"

Silence fell on the other end of the line. "He's with you?"

"Intuitive as ever," Edward said, managing to speak wryly when all he wanted to do was demand answers.

"I don't trust him, Edward. There's no proof of this gossip."

"What does that even mean?"

"It means he started something with the intention of pushing you on the hunt for it."

Scowling, Edward demanded, "But why the hell would he do that?"

"I don't know. But I don't trust him," Markov repeated. "What if it's true? What if Arabella *was* murdered? And this is some elaborate attempt at misdirection?"

"What gain would the family have for killing her?"

"Not the family, but Drake."

"He loved my mother—he'd do nothing to hurt her."

"Your mother loved many men, my friend," came the softly-worded response. "And some men can handle that, while others can't."

"What are you implying?"

"I'm not sure. Not yet. But don't trust him, and be wary of any information he feeds you. He's proven once that he's willing to lie to a king to give himself a reason for instigating an investigation—take that for the warning it is."

CHAPTER NINETEEN

"SPEAK SLOWLY, Father. Rushing it won't help."

Perry winced at George's impatient tone. She felt for both father and son, as neither of them were particularly known for their tolerance on certain topics, and their health and recuperation seemed to be two such matters.

"Let him rest, George," she chided, settling deeper into Philippe's side.

Three days ago, the hospital cot had been taken away and Philippe had been moved back to the far more regal mattress that befit a man of his station.

She much preferred to see him there, amid the grand four posts and swathes of regal maroon fabric than on the tight, narrow cot.

He was slowly coming into himself, but the bed had had to be converted for his needs—needs that still icked her out but were a part of his recovery. There were bags containing things she had no desire to know about.

Shuddering at the grossness of the human body, she watched as Philippe sucked in a deep breath. Somewhere along the way, his speech had been affected. It was gradually coming back, but there was a definite slur and a stutter. Why? She had no idea. Even Dr. Schertz was perplexed and had brought in a slew of new consultants to tend to the former king.

Speech therapy, as well as being chivvied along by his son, seemed to be having some effect, though it left Philippe exhausted and needing to nap every few hours. Dr. Schertz seemed to be as eager to overexert her father-in-law as much as his sons and nephew were. Only Perry was the one who saw the advantage in taking a damn chill pill.

"He's coming on better than we could have hoped, George," she commented gently when Philippe nodded off, somehow managing not to hear his son's expletive response.

"I know. I just have questions."

"I think we both know for a fact that he wants to give you the answers. Why do you think he's pushing himself so hard?"

"Think he can write yet?" George asked, his tone insistent.

She sighed. "Maybe after he's rested. And not for long."

George grumbled a little but began to pace around the bedroom. He looked ill-at-ease, and Perry couldn't blame him. The festive period was coming to an end—tomorrow was King's Day, the most important part of Yule according to the Veronian tradition, and it meant a return to their responsibilities.

She wouldn't lie—she'd loved these past few days. Her men had all made a distinct effort to spend the larger chunk of their time with her, putting off important duties to be with her.

This would be a Christmas she would cherish forever, and would miss once the holiday season was over.

"What's really going on, George?" she asked softly.

"I'm just... I want to know if he knew."

Though she frowned in confusion, it took less than a few seconds for the synapses in her brain to spark into life. "You want to know if he knew Laurence Prichard was behind your kidnapping?"

He started to gnaw at his bottom lip—a gesture that was surprisingly youthful on him.

"And if he did?"

"I don't know. I just... I'd like to know what's what. For my own sanity."

"I understand that," she told him gently. "Nothing wrong with that, either. But pushing him won't get you anywhere."

He fell silent, but carried on his pacing. After a while, she hefted herself off the side of the bed and into the waiting armchair at the foot of the epic-sized mattress. She reached for her cell phone and caught up with a few things in her calendar as George went to stand by the window that overlooked Saren way up ahead.

She'd always thought the city was Madela, but had recently learned that the two sides of the castle had a perfect vantage point, thanks to the way they were positioned, to see the two major cities in the distance.

"Tired."

The word had her jolting a little, and she saw Philippe's eyes were open again. The lids were drooping though, and she couldn't blame him. George had really been pushing. Asking hard questions and expecting Philippe to answer with one word "yeses" and "nos."

"I know, Philippe," she said gently, getting to her feet again and moving to his side.

At her back, George stayed in place, and she was grateful for that. Father and son needed a break from one another.

As she settled amid the covers once more, she jerked when Philippe's hand, heavy and with no dexterity, tapped her belly. "Child?"

She nodded. "Yes. I'm five months pregnant."

His eyes widened, the eyes that were so like gemstones, so like his son's, glinting in the low light in the room. "Soon, grandchild."

"Yes."

His arm was sluggish as he patted her arm. "Hurt?"

"Does the baby hurt me?" she asked, surprised by the question.

But he shook his head. "Hurt. Head?"

"Oh." She licked her lips. "No. It's just a cut. There was a little accident two weeks ago. Before Yule."

"Accident?"

"There was a bombing, Father," George said grimly, not having moved from the window.

Philippe's eyes flared wide in response—it was amazing how much information they could convey when a person's words were momentarily lost. "Why?"

"The UnReals. They've grown worse in the past few months," she said softly, wishing there was an easier way to drop this kind of news, but knowing there wasn't.

"Baby okay?"

"Yes. Xavier, Edward, George and I were lucky. We think the UnReals just planted the bombs wherever they could, because there was no real pattern to the placement—and we were away from the epicenter of the blast." Her words were pretty much verbatim what her husband had told her, all in the effort of trying to share more.

Even when he wanted nothing more than to protect her.

"We lost a lot of good men that day," George intoned starkly.

"No," Philippe whispered, tears forming and falling down his cheeks.

"Yes," she confirmed sadly.

A hoarse breath escaped her father-in-law. "Raoul."

She jerked to attention. "Raoul Da Silva. The guard? He's dead. We found out he was an UnReal too."

Philippe swallowed thickly. "Know."

"No?" Perry frowned, confused by the similar intonation on the words. "He isn't?"

"Know isn't. Found out day this."

She picked between his words. "You learned the day you were shot?"

"Yes. Why shot."

George stepped closer to the bed. "What do you mean? It's the reason *why* you were shot?"

"Yes. Marianne told me. Heard him on phone."

"You mean, she heard Raoul speaking on the phone with someone, and then she told you?" At his nod, she looked at George. "That's why the assassination happened." She gnawed at the inside of her cheek as she waited for his response.

"Yes. Silence us."

"It didn't work," George replied grimly.

"No. Alive. Hurting."

She winced and reached for his hand. Gently squeezing it, she asked, "Do you need more pain medication?"

"No. Give answers. Ask questions. I try."

George licked his lips and pressed his hand to Perry's shoulder. "Raoul was murdered too. There was another shooting. We thought Perry was the target."

"Raoul loved Marianne."

Behind Perry, her lover stiffened. "Loved as his queen or as his woman?" she asked carefully.

"Woman. Ours bad marriage."

She blew out a shaky breath. "You think Raoul would have been angered that they killed Marianne?"

"Loved her," Philippe repeated, his tone insistent. "He not UnReal. Drake tell them. Drake UnReal."

For a second, the world came to a halt. More than that, it screeched. "*Drake?*"

"Drake? Our head of security Drake?"

"Yes. Jealous. Loved Marianne."

"For fuck's sake, how many men loved Marianne?" Perry spat, uncaring that she had three of her own—hell, she wasn't cheating on anyone, was she? Dismissing those stupid thoughts, she grabbed her cell phone and immediately tried to dial Edward's number. It went straight to voicemail. "Where is he?" she demanded, looking up at George, who was on his own cell.

"With Drake," her lover confirmed.

Her heart sunk. "What?"

"Drake came to him with evidence linking Ferdinand L'Argeneau with the rebel leader. They've brought L'Argeneau to a nearby military base, and they're traveling there now."

"*Save. Them.*"

The words were tortured, loaded with the anguish Philippe felt. For days, he'd been trying to tell them this, Perry realized. Saying names and random words to try to make them piece them together. Guilt overwhelmed her as she realized this could have been resolved so much quicker if they'd just fucking listened.

"Drake can't be in on this," she half-sobbed. "He's a good guy. He's helped us."

"No. No. NO," Philippe moaned, his limp hands managing to squeeze the silk sheets the covered him in his grand bed. "Enemy. Bad. Bad. *Bad*."

Fear forced the breath from her lungs. "Call the base, George. Just call them, tell them to detain Drake the minute they arrive."

George nodded, and switched into Veronian—essentially cutting her out of the picture. She felt helpless at that moment. So lost, floundering, unsure of what to do or how to help.

George pressed his hand to the microphone and murmured, "Perry, Xavier's with them. Call him if Edward isn't answering."

Having a task would help. She immediately dialed her lover's number. When he picked up, tears flooded her eyes. "Xavier. I know someone is in the car with you. Don't, whatever you do, say his name or sound suspicious. I'll explain, but try to avert suspicion from the man traveling with you."

Silence fell, then he cleared his throat. "I don't want pizza tonight."

She blinked, surprised despite herself at the double talk. Pizza? Jesus. "Drake is behind this."

"No. I hate pineapple. You know that."

It was disconcerting, but somehow, she had to explain when she didn't have a clue what was really happening. "When you arrive at the base, George is arranging for someone to detain...the person there. He's dangerous. He's behind the shooting." She caught Philippe's eye, saw the man was nodding, using the last of his energy to impart the message. "He's behind everything. Raoul wasn't the mole, Drake is."

Xavier's tone turned thick. "I can't wait to see you, either."

She swallowed harshly. "I love you. Please, stay safe. We only just found out. Philippe told us."

"There are no words," Xavier murmured, giving a laugh that sounded bizarrely sensual in the middle of her panicked recounting.

"How close are you to the base?"

There was a humming sound, but she heard the anxiety in his sharp intake of breath. "Five minutes?"

She turned to George. "Any joy?"

Her partner nodded. "Yes."

Perry again spoke into her phone. "Just had confirmation. George has spoken to the base."

"But what next?"

"If he's involved with the UnReals, you need to find a link."

More humming came down the line. "Almost there. I'll be home soon."

God, how she wished that was the case.

"He must think he's above suspicion. George says he gave Edward something that implicated Ferdinand L'Argeneau with the UnReals? Use that, love. Use anything you can to bring him down."

"I don't understand why you want pizza though," he countered, making her want to scream.

"He loved Marianne. That's all the answer Philippe can give me."

"Jesus, we've had it too often."

She pinched the bridge of her nose in exasperation—double talk wasn't her best gift, apparently. "I know. She slept around a lot, didn't she?" she whispered, wincing as Philippe flinched, but hell, it was the truth!

Had this entire situation all been because of Marianne and her need to make Philippe jealous? Her need to punish her husband?

The kidnapping had been because of that, and now this? Her own assassination and a good man's death, because she literally hadn't been able to keep it in her pants? Not that Philippe hadn't been as bad, but still... Philippe wasn't a rule-loving prig who insisted on decorum at all times.

Marianne had been cold and hard. Elegance in her blood. She didn't have "bone rattler" tatted on her forehead. In no way did she seem the type to put it around the way she had. But hell, behind closed doors, who knew what the fuck was going on?

And Christ, Perry was a believer in live and let live, but this was taking the piss.

Perry felt tears prickle her eyes when Xavier murmured, "There."

She whispered, "Be safe. I love you."

"Going now. Talk to you later, babe."

She coughed and cut the line, wishing like hell they could stay on the phone.

Just as she made to squeeze Philippe's hand, George grabbed her shoulder. "Come on. We're going to the base. They're in Saren. It's not far. We can get there, too, and find out what the fuck is going on."

As she clambered upright, she bent over the bed and pressed a kiss to Philippe's papery brow. "Thank you," she whispered, and let herself be dragged along at George's side.

Answers, God, they all needed them, and Perry could only pray that they were about to get them. If not? She really didn't know what the hell to believe anymore.

———

BEHIND THE REFLECTIVE GLASS, on either side of them, were two men who had played them. Played them so well, Xavier was feeling like a fucking violin. Either that or a golf course. And the latter made sense—the bastards had trampled all over the lot of them.

He rubbed his temple as he stared at Ferdinand L'Argeneau on one side of the glass, then at Drake, who was looking more ragged than he'd ever seen him. Which was saying something, because Drake hadn't been his usual polished self since Marianne's death.

"This doesn't make sense," Xavier whispered under his breath.

Behind him, Edward was striding back and forth, trying to burn off some of the excess energy plaguing him. "No. It doesn't."

Xavier grimaced. "We have nothing on Drake. Nothing save for what Philippe's said, and he's hardly in full *compos mentis*."

"No, but Perry believed him, and Markov's suspicious, too."

The minute they'd left the limo, guards had rounded on the vehicle, and had dragged Edward to safety while pulling Drake in the opposite direction.

The head of security had hollered and shrieked like a banshee, but it hadn't stopped the soldiers from hefting the man away and taking him to a holding cell.

Maybe it was just desserts that he was locked in a cell directly opposite L'Argeneau. The man who was potentially his partner in crime.

The headache blooming behind Xavier's eyes wasn't new. It hadn't really left since the bombing, and as the concerns of the moment overwhelmed him, it threatened to bring him to his knees. The sharp spearing pain in his temples was enough to have him wincing.

"What's wrong?"

"Headache."

"Still?" Edward demanded, finally coming to a halt.

"Yes. I'm okay." He wasn't really, but then, Edward didn't have a headache, and he still wasn't okay. Jesus, none of them were.

The man they'd trusted for decades was a spy.

At least, that was the accusation that was being thrown around.

He wished like hell it wasn't the truth, but who the fuck knew?

Drake had been slow these past few months, not his usual self. He'd let things slide, had managed to let the sniper behind the assassination and the shooting slip away... Perry had claimed it was depression, and because Edward knew Drake loved Marianne, he'd forgiven him. But...?

Rubbing his temples, he watched as Drake got to his feet. "You can't keep me in here forever, dammit. What the hell are you detaining me for, anyway?"

The yell had Xavier wincing. "He's right. We can't keep him forever."

Edward grumbled, "I know." He shot the guard a look, then cut his former father-in-law a glance. He gritted his teeth at the sight of an ever pristine-Ferdinand then stunned Xavier by striding out of the small booth that separated the interview rooms, and into the hall.

"Edward, this is beyond illegal," Xavier hissed, but his cousin ignored him.

The guard on duty at L'Argeneau's door jerked to attention at the sight of the king, but he frowned. "Sir?"

"Step out of the way, Corporal."

"I'm under orders, sir."

"And I'm the head of the armed forces," Edward bit off. "Move. *Now*."

The soldier eyed the king and swiftly stepped out of his way. "Sir, yes, sir!"

Edward shoved open the door and slammed it closed. Ferdinand, though presenting a calm demeanor, jolted at the king's sudden appearance. Xavier watched, stunned at his cousin's volatility, and knew it was couched in his desire to keep Perry safe.

If Drake was the traitor in their midst, then…

His throat closed at even the thought.

"Let's cut the bullshit, Ferdinand. I didn't kill Arabella. It's come to my attention that that's your belief, but it's nonsense. Lies fed to you to get you to fund some of the worst acts of terror this nation has ever seen. You've been played."

L'Argeneau's eyes narrowed. "I have proof that the DeSauviers were actively involved in her murder."

"You've been fed lies," Edward repeated. "I had no reason to murder her. I was going to divorce her, and whatever you think, the secrets she knew? If she had sold them to the press, she'd have gone to jail. Her prenup was airtight, and it was on my side.

"She could have told the world I was into fetish-wear, and if it had been printed, then she'd have lost every ounce of alimony she was entitled to. As much as I loathed your daughter, I knew her for what she was—shrewd. Money-grabbing. There was no need to murder her to silence her."

"You can say that, can't you? When all the cards are on my side."

Edward huffed out a laugh. "If you genuinely believe that, then you're deluded. You're going to jail, Ferdinand, whichever way you pull it. I have photo evidence of you dealing with one Jacob Prichard." When Ferdinand's eyes flared, Edward seemed to bite off a grin. "Yeah. An intimate conversation by the looks of it, too, and that evidence was given to me by my head of security. A man I think you know… Giles Drake?"

Ferdinand's jaw clenched. "Now who's talking bullshit?"

"Not me.

"All I know is that I didn't murder your daughter. Neither did my mother or father, because they were the ones behind the prenup, and they knew how impermeable it was. Naturally, Mother was a little nervous... women tend to be, don't they?" He sent the man a rigid smile. "But enough to murder her? My mother was many things, but given to panic, she wasn't.

"Yet, I can understand why you might think she was murdered by us. It's come to my attention that all the doctors who cared for Arabella that day are dead now. The lot of them. And again, you might think this is proof of another cover up...but, do you know a Danica Prichard?" Though Ferdinand's eyes flashed, Edward didn't wait for an answer. "Money from her bank account was sent to a pathologist in Canada. An autopsy was undertaken on one of Arabella's EMTs who'd tended to her on the day she died... it seems that the man drove off the side of the road because he was drunk.

"Now, what would be to gain from that? From murdering a family on vacation? Unless they wanted to make you believe the DeSauviers were behind all this, and needed to cover their tracks.

"But we haven't done anything, Ferdinand. All we've done is sit back and watch as this fucking charade went on around us. We have you by the short and curlies because no matter your influence, this will come out, and your reputation will be in tatters because you've been funding a terrorist organization.

"You've been fucked over, man. Worse than a street hooker."

"What do you want?" The words staggered from Ferdinand's lips after a deathly silence. It had lasted so long, Xavier hadn't been sure he'd speak.

"If I didn't murder Arabella, and my parents didn't, I want to know who did. She was the crown princess, and that person should be tried for treason and be made to serve out that full sentence—death by fire squad."

"But that's the fate that would befall me, too."

"Perhaps. My influence might be able to sway things."

"Why?"

"Because my wife is in danger. Even as we speak. I need information. Information that will forever quash the UnReals, that might help me find and destroy the mole in my ranks."

For a second, Ferdinand's mouth pursed, then he murmured, "Drake was the one who told me Arabella had been murdered."

Xavier's heart froze at the admission, and he knew Edward was equally as affected because his cousin whispered, "Do you have proof of that?"

"No. But I have other information on him. He was the go-between for a while."

"Between you and the UnReals?"

"Yes. I had no interest in them or their petty feud with the monarchs.

You know me, Edward. I've always wanted to get into bed with the family, not blow it up."

Edward's shoulders turned rigid. "That's certainly the truth," he grated out.

"For a while, Drake acted as liaison, until I began to see how useful it was having a bunch of insane plebs on my payroll. They came in quite handy for some business deals I had going down."

"You used them as your own personal army?"

"For a time."

"Where are they based?"

"I can give you details. The leader, Jacob Prichard..." Ferdinand laughed. "He hates you all. If you catch him alive, I'll be astonished. The man's certain the entire situation with his brother was a setup. That it was an excuse the family used to get rid of him, to keep him quiet."

"Well, I have firsthand proof it wasn't. I saw the kidnappers' faces after all. I know he was there."

"Of that *I* have no doubt, but Prichard's delusions were fed by a certain someone." Edward froze at that, but Ferdinand carried on, "He's based in Helstern, but he moves around more than a hunted fox switches dens. I can give you his last known addresses, but the only way I can get an accurate location is if I instigate a meeting, which I'm more than willing to do, if you'll allay any fears I might have of being tried for treason."

Edward gritted his jaw. "I'm willing to try if you carry on being so helpful."

The other man bowed his head a second, almost in contemplation. "Drake's very clever."

"I can see that. He's played us for a long time."

"Indeed. I was most impressed when I realized who he was. He played Marianne's lapdog so well and for so long, it came as a surprise when he visited me."

"Why did he?"

"The UnReals needed funding."

"Can you give us a paper trail?"

Ferdinand pulled a face. "I wouldn't be much use to anyone if I had evidence like that hanging around, would I?"

Edward murmured, "You'd better hope you have something on Drake, otherwise I won't try to protect you from the firing squad."

"I have it, Edward. I have it."

"If I find out you're messing me around, Ferdinand, you'll be made to pay."

"Let's take it one step at a time, Edward. First, we have some rebels to catch."

"Why them first? Surely Drake needs to be contained before they are?"

Ferdinand let out a laugh that twisted Xavier's stomach into shreds, but from the still open door, he heard footsteps. Turning his head away from the conversation taking place in front of him, he saw Perry. The minute she clapped eyes on him, she started sobbing and ran toward him.

When she was in his arms, he knew he could finally start to breathe.

George nodded at him, before he turned his focus on the interview between two men who had once been related by marriage.

Then, Ferdinand spoke, and any relief he'd had disappeared into dust... "When you find out what they have planned for you and your wife next, dear boy, you won't be worrying about that lovesick old fool in there." The older man gave Edward a smile that would have suited a great white shark. "Now, are you listening, or am I going to have to repeat myself?"

CHAPTER TWENTY

IT WAS clear for all to see that Giles Drake felt no guilt for what he'd done. The many wrongs he'd written seemed not to weigh an ounce on his soul.

As Perry sat there, her belly round with the daughter they'd discovered they'd be having in under a month, she tapped her fingers against the crown of the bump. She wasn't sure whether that was to soothe the baby or to soothe herself. Either way, it wasn't working.

Another bombing had been planned. This time at the symposium of environmental scientists she'd been due to head a few months after the baby's birth. There, the most lauded of her peers would come together to discuss their findings... findings on a situation that *had* been man-made. Just as Perry had declared it months before.

Of course, it irritated the hell out of her that they were going to come to the same conclusion she had only a *wasted* year later, but politics was politics wherever you were...

Even if it was a royalist state.

Still, none of that mattered now, did it? It had come out that the dams *were* being sabotaged as an endgame between Ferdinand L'Argeneau and Giles Drake—their intention to reap the profits as they brokered the deal between Veronia and Russia, or whichever nation would help them with their water crisis. Perry was under no illusion that Edward's former father-in-law's focus had been the money.

She supposed a part of him had believed he was acting on his daughter's behalf. Avenging her passing. But predominantly, he'd been doing it for the money. As well as power—that kind of leverage was heady to a man like L'Argeneau.

Drake, on the other hand, was a lot more complicated.

He'd had his hands on some of the nation's most delicate secrets. Had been an integral part of the royal family's protection... knew the truth about their relationship, too, she'd learned recently.

Which was why she was here. Nervous, bricking it, but here nonetheless.

To deal with the aftermath of Drake potentially revealing all in the singular speech he could give for his defense.

Veronian law was like any other European law. A man had to be proven guilty, and was innocent until then.

Unless it was treason.

Then, there was no defense. Only prosecution. And any traitors were allowed a single speech, a speech which was giving her sleepless nights...

Edward's hand tightened about hers as Drake got to his feet. He knew she was nervous, kept placing his fingers on her knee when she jiggled her foot to try to burn off some of the chaotic energy flaring through her.

Drake knew about them, dammit. How *couldn't* she be nervous when he had a speech, in which his loose tongue could reveal any and anything to the world at large?

Because the world was most definitely watching.

It was unprecedented, but Edward had allowed global reporters in to view the trial. He was making a statement, he'd told her. Drake's punishment was guaranteed, there was no out for him, no saving grace, but their judicial process was sound, and the whole world needed to know that.

In their current times, where human rights were on shaky ground, she could only be proud of him for that.

Drake stumbled as he got to his feet. He was shackled, and the cuffs were visible over the cuffs of his suit. They pulled taut as he righted himself.

The courtroom reminded her of something she'd seen in a British crime procedural. It was all wood. Dark and gloomy. There was a high stand where the judge was seated, to his right was where witnesses were called up—the walls were tall here too, but the wooden dowels were thick and ornately carved.

Perry and Edward were to the left of the judge. They weren't on a high stand, but thrones, similar to the ones in the throne room at Masonbrook, that were made from wood that blended into the walls, thickly carved. There were only two points of color—the cushions upon which they were seated were a ruby red. And above their heads, the Royal Seal was a bright gold.

They were angled toward the jury box—but there was no jury involved in this particular trial. Opposite the judge, there were the two tables for the lawyers, like in an American court, and between them, in a stand of their own, surrounded by a shield of bulletproof glass, were Giles Drake and Jacob Prichard.

The audience at their backs was crammed, as were the two mezzanine floors of the gallery. The press could be seen making notes, scrawling information down on their pads. There were artists, too, as the inside of a courtroom couldn't be filmed here. Illustrations would make it into the papers and onto the news reels—providing the only glimpse into this shadowy world available to the masses.

As Drake righted himself, standing straight and tall, the entire courtroom seemed to suck in a sharp breath.

Whatever he was about to say meant little in the scheme of things. His reasons for doing what he had didn't justify the actions he'd undertaken, which made it something of a moot point. Perry wouldn't even be here if it weren't for her terror that he'd reveal all.

"You, the accused, Giles Maxim Drake, have the right to free speech as does any subject of the Veronian court. You may speak now, or forever hold your peace."

The judge's voice was a deep *boom*. He wore a wig of curly hair that seemed pretty incongruous to his red and earthy features. His black robes were somber, but they were brightened by a gleaming maroon outer robe that perched on his shoulders, and declared his status as a High Court judge.

Prichard had already spoken, had already let loose a torrent of madness that revealed his desire to maim the DeSauvier family as his family had been maimed. He'd never mentioned Marianne though, and Perry had to wonder just what Edward had up his sleeve if that level of batshit could be controlled...

She just hoped it worked on Drake, too.

"I did it because I could," Drake stated calmly. Unlike Prichard, there was no frenzied or frenetic tone to his voice. Prichard was cuckoo, but Drake wasn't... "Because I had access. Because the entire nation was available to play with."

Perry tightened her hand on Edward's, and felt her stomach start to churn.

Whether it was nausea, morning sickness, or just nerves, she didn't know, but she really hoped it was just damn nerves. The last thing she wanted was to puke in front of all these people, dammit.

Clenching her teeth, she watched as Drake shrugged and murmured, "That's all I have to say."

For a second, Perry could do nothing less than gape at the man. He could take the stand for an hour. Rant and rave, use it as a voice box as Prichard had... but he didn't. He simply took a seat, shot Edward a look, then smiled.

That smile made her clamp her hand to her mouth, rush to her feet, and run off the dais where the thrones were, and toward the door at the back that led to the judge's chambers.

She didn't know how Edward would excuse it. Didn't know if he even could. Maybe she'd just made a prick of herself in front of the world's eye—but her stomach wasn't calming, and she could feel it rising in her gullet.

She didn't even dare suck down a deep breath of air as she made it into the hallway that led to the judge's chambers, but approached the nearest door. She didn't knock, just barged in. There was a sober-faced man dictating to a woman with an iPad in her hand. They both looked up, gaped at her as she ignored them and garbled, "Bathroom!"

The man stared at her blankly, but the PA rushed to her feet and swiftly approached a door. Holding it open, she murmured, "Here, Your Majesty."

Perry couldn't nod. Couldn't believe she'd had the energy to say "bathroom." That was how damn weak she was! When she saw the gleaming white porcelain, she wanted to sigh in relief. She even started to suck in a bit of air—but that was the final straw, and she dropped to her knees and released the evil that was nausea into the bowl.

Her knees ached like a bitch from the hard landing, and it made her want to puke even more to think that this was a dude's toilet and men tended to have shitty aim, but there was no stopping this...

The torrent of anxiety and nervousness welled inside her and poured forth in the worst bout of morning sickness she'd had throughout the pregnancy. By the time she was done, she was shaking, feeling weak and frail. She pressed a hand to her mouth, pressed the other to her clammy forehead. Before she could reach forward to flush, a strong hand appeared to do it for her.

She looked up at her husband and scowled. "You know I don't like you to see me puke."

His lips twitched, but it didn't lighten the grimness of his expression. "You know I don't like to see you puke either."

She narrowed her eyes. "For different reasons."

"Yes. You're embarrassed over a very natural process that is happening because my baby is in your belly. I'm just concerned that you vomited out a small country."

Her lips formed into a pout. "You shouldn't have watched."

"I caught the tail end, I've been assured." He cleared his throat and turned his back on her. She gaped at him, astonished at the idea of him walking off—even if she hadn't exactly welcomed him. Before she could demand—then plead—that he stay, he muttered, "I apologize for the intrusion, Judge Maître. As you can see, it was an emergency."

Though Edward spoke in English, the judge, quite rudely, Perry thought, switched to Veronian. Still, Edward didn't stiffen up as he usually did when under fire. If anything, he laughed a little—ruefully, Perry thought.

She sank back on her heels as she heard footsteps, then a door opened and closed.

"Are we alone?"

"Yes," Edward murmured, turning back to her. "We are now."

"You don't know it's your baby in my belly." For some reason, that point stuck.

He didn't frown, didn't even look perturbed by her comment. "Of course, it is."

"It could be George's," she remarked, rubbing her stomach which was tight and huge and aching and, ugh... She felt like she'd had a basketball shoved down her gullet—which would explain why she was getting really good at giving head.

Had nothing to do with practicing on three guys, of course.

Nope, no sirree.

"If the child is George's, regardless, she is still mine." He sighed, then squatted down beside her. Unlike her, his knees didn't touch the ground. "Why do you persist with this line of questioning?"

She grumbled, "It's important." She'd asked them all, several times, if it counted. No matter what they said though, they couldn't reassure her.

"No, it's not. We're a family. An unusual one, granted. But a family nonetheless."

Perry peeked up at him. "I'm sorry for asking."

"You're insecure. I just wish I knew why," he replied softly, his gem-like eyes gleaming with a sincerity that scorched her.

"I don't know why either," she admitted. "There's no need, I just... Men are weird about this stuff. Usually," she tacked on, when he cocked a brow at her. She huffed. "Anyway, what's going on, Edward? Why was Drake so circumspect?"

"I told you I had it handled," he countered, his hand coming to her back. He started a gentle, sweeping motion that had her feeling even shakier... strange considering it comforted her. "Are you going to be sick again?" he asked quickly, his other hand moving toward the toilet seat.

"I-I don't know." She rubbed her forehead. "How did you handle it?"

"I didn't have electrodes glued to his fingernails if that's your concern."

She blinked. "It wasn't, but now it is."

He snorted. "I used leverage, darling. That's all."

"What kind of leverage?"

Edward tapped her chin. "If a criminal is a criminal, does that mean he doesn't love his country? His royal family?"

"Are we talking about criminals other than Drake and Prichard here?" she asked wryly.

"I am." He wasn't teasing, his tone was somber.

"Well, no, I guess. You can be a prick, but be a patriot at the same time."

"Exactly. How many men, in a regular jail, would want someone like Drake or Prichard dead?"

She winced. "A lot?"

"A hell of a lot. They both knew it, too. If I'd had them shoved in a general prison, they'd have been fair game for... well," he said with a grimace, "a lot, shall we say, and leave it at that?"

Gnawing at her bottom lip, she asked, "That was all you did?"

"It was all I had to do. Death by firing squad may be public, and it may seem brutal, but it's fast. Murdered in their jail cell with a weapon made out of sharpened plastic..." He shook his head. "Shivs aren't going to be a nice, clean death, are they?"

"I'm surprised Drake cared."

"Everyone cares, especially when it comes down to their death. Plus, there were the months of the trial... he could have been raped, tortured... Nobody wants that."

"So, you put them in solitary?"

He nodded. "Yes. With a team of guards that I hand-selected myself."

"Because they could have abused the prisoners, too?"

"Yes. It's not exactly unheard of." He winced. "Anyway, we don't need to be talking about this. I thought you were okay with Drake's speech."

"I would have been if you'd told me all that!" she retorted crossly.

He grimaced. "There was always a risk they'd renege on it, so I just never said anything. I'm sorry, *carilla*."

She pouted. "You haven't called me that in ages."

"Then I'm the one who should be shot."

Her pout turned into a grin. "It's okay, I'm not that mad."

"The relief is endless," he informed her drily. Then, he shot her a look. "How are you feeling?"

"Better, now that the whole world isn't going to learn about us."

"I understand. Are you ready to go home?"

"Definitely."

He got to his feet, then carefully helped her stand. His hands came to her belly and he rubbed the round ball with so much love that tears prickled her eyes.

When he made to move away, she reached for his wrist. Staring deep into his gaze, she whispered, "Drake just wanted the money, didn't he?"

Edward stilled, then sighed. "I don't think that's the truth."

She frowned. "What do you mean?"

"I mean, I think he wanted to hurt us, at first. Hurt Mother. Then, I think..." Another sigh escaped him. "I think he enjoyed it. Playing two roles. Being the bad guy with the good guy's façade. He could do it, and so he started to ask himself, 'Why not?'"

Perry gulped. "I think I'd have preferred for him to be after the money."

Edward's voice was wry as he murmured, "Me too. Still, we can't fabricate a man's motives."

She bit her bottom lip as she thought about Ferdinand L'Argeneau. "I still don't think it's fair L'Argeneau isn't here."

"Because of him, three other terrorist attacks were quenched. Countless lives were saved. Yours included. On top of that, he gave us information that allowed us to disband the UnReals, Perry. That... had to be rewarded."

"Is it because he's rich? Or your father-in-law?"

"He isn't my father-in-law. Nathaniel is now."

She huffed. "You know what I mean."

"I do, yes." His lips curved. "Do you think I'm one for nepotism, Perry?"

"No. I didn't." Past tense—he didn't seem to miss that either.

"Well, you're right. I'm not. A man like L'Argeneau... he doesn't need a jail cell. Where he is, it's worse than a jail cell."

Perry scowled. "He's at home!"

"Yes. But he can't leave the wing he's in. He has freedom to move between rooms, but that's it. Everything is limited. His communications, his visitations..."

"Boohoo," she grumbled, making him snort.

"Sweetheart, the man has spent his life amassing fortune, influence, and power. That's all gone now. He's a shell, and will be until he dies. It just won't be by firing squad."

"It's a pretty prison," she countered. "And his wealth is still there."

"No, the wealth connected to his title is. His estate is indentured. When he dies, his daughter will inherit the land and the money connected to it. His personal fortune? All gone."

"For the dams."

"Yes. It's a drop in the ocean, but it's something."

"You know that people think it's because he was related to you."

He shrugged. "The truth will come out after his death."

"Why?"

"I have my reasons."

She squinted at him. "Because he was related to you?"

His hand came up to squeeze her shoulder. "Let it go, Perry."

"No, I need to know why you're being so lenient on him."

"Because of him, the UnReals don't exist anymore. We destroyed the nest from the inside out."

"I know that. But this feels personal."

He was quiet for a second as he looked deep into her eyes. Then, he rocked forward and pressed a kiss to her sweaty forehead. "Arabella and I should never have married. She was always fragile, and I was always indifferent."

"You can't be blamed that the woman was addicted to being addicted." Drugs, dieting... hell, name it.

"No, but her situation wasn't helped by me. She was in the public eye. She felt the pressure of that, and I wasn't there for her because I wasn't interested." He shrugged. "No, it's not my fault. Not directly. But I didn't help. L'Argeneau did Veronia enough of a service for me to put him under house arrest. That's all he deserves. Nothing more, nothing less."

Though she was still frowning, she heard the resolve in his voice and just sighed. "I don't feel so well," she admitted grumpily. Though she was changing the subject, she wasn't exactly lying.

He let out a crooning noise, one that she'd heard several times over her pregnancy, and one that never failed to astonish her—Edward, who seemed totally oblivious to most things, was not oblivious to his very pregnant wife.

Truth was, she kinda liked the attention.

Was probably going to miss it when she popped out the sprog.

He rubbed her shoulder and murmured, "Let's get you home."

She let out a shaky breath but reached out to embrace him. "What about sentencing?"

"It's happened already by now."

"You didn't stay to watch?" she asked, arching her back a tad to look up at him.

"No. Of course not. I followed you."

"Sorry," she whispered, biting her lip again.

"What for?"

"For making you miss it?"

He sighed. "I know the outcome, Perry. I didn't miss anything. I'm exactly where I need to be."

God, when he said things like that? It totally made her panties melt.

Ugh, she was not in the frame of mind for panty-melting thoughts.

Eyeing him a second, she caught sight of his questioning look, then let out a huff.

With men like hers, panty-melting thoughts were par for the course.

"What is it?"

"I need to go to bed."

He nodded. "We'll go home and you can nap straightaway."

She tugged his hand when he made a move to leave. "You didn't hear me, Edward. I need to go to *bed*."

He frowned, then his nostrils flared as he laughed. "Oh."

"Just give me a bottle of mouthwash and three tubes of toothpaste, and I'll be ready for anything."

His laughter turned dirty. "That's very good to know," he murmured as he pressed his lips to the tip of her nose.

And that was the end of that.

EPILOGUE

SEVEN MONTHS LATER

IT WAS unprecedented and it was blood-chilling, but Perry couldn't tear her eyes from the screen.

That this was being televised was the most barbaric thing she could ever imagine, and yet…she understood, too.

The dichotomy gave her a headache, and she was already feeling sluggish today. Another sleepless night, thanks to Alice waking up at 2AM, didn't exactly put Perry at her best.

But while she *was* tired, sure, the sight of the firing squad lining in place, preparing to take fire…?

It was disturbing and sickening, and at the same time, it filled her with relief.

Which in turn, made her feel evil.

Philippe squeezed her shoulder, "We have to show a sign of strength."

Though she nodded, she ducked her head and took her gaze from the screen. The sight of her baby daughter in her arms was enough to soothe her for the moment. Until the shots were fired, and Jacob Prichard and Giles Drake were no more.

Her stomach churned, and the need to be sick was a heavy and dull ache at the back of her throat. She pressed a kiss to Alice's head and rocked a little as she absorbed the delicious scent of her baby, tried to find a calm in that soothing combination of baby shampoo and talcum powder.

She was on Philippe's bed, her legs out before her with Alice in her arms. The two of them had become quite good friends in the last few months, and as Philippe hadn't fully recovered from his injuries, his bedrest had been far longer than any of them had imagined.

In the face of the breach of faith that Drake's many perfidies had unearthed, Perry had found it very difficult to settle into life at court once more. Not knowing who to believe in, who to rely on, had wrecked her self-esteem, and she'd found a comfort in being with those she trusted. Cassie was one of them, and she'd taken to staying more at court with the children over the past few months as her rocky marriage with Marcus went down south...but more than her, Philippe had been a source of great comfort to Perry.

Throughout the reporting on the trials and the final declaration of the judge's verdict, she'd watched at his side. Finding comfort in his presence.

They'd all been affected by Drake's lies, and the sick thing was, as she looked up and saw the slumped forms lying on the ground, sheets now covering them, relief made a reappearance.

They were gone, and with them, the threat they posed.

Even as she abhorred the need for capital punishment, she understood why, in this case, there was no alternative.

Drake had breached so many laws, was aware of so many secrets revolving around the nation and them as a family, that for him to be allowed to live was just... impossible.

Prichard was insane—not that that had made a difference to his sentencing. The doctors had confirmed it. His zeal wasn't feigned, but it *had* been fed. Because, as crazy as it was, Drake had been the Janus in their midst for the past twenty years.

"I can't believe it's over," she whispered softly, hugging Alice tightly to her chest.

In the morning, it was her daughter's christening, and though the timing couldn't have been worse, at least they knew there would be no danger.

Was she happy that the men had been shot today?

No. She sure as hell wasn't.

The last thing she wanted was her baby's christening to be the day after those monsters died, but tradition—and fucking protocol, of course—were behind that shitty decision. On the sixth month on the anniversary of their birth, all royals had to be christened, their official titles revealed to the public. Baby Alice was about to be baptized 'Her Royal Highness Alexandra Lisetta Diana Eugenie Alice DeSauvier'.

Why they hadn't been able to rearrange the goddamn execution, she didn't know. But she wasn't happy. Not at all. Even if she was faintly relieved.

The UnReals had, after all, been disbanded. The majority of their numbers were siphoned off to jails around the country, and those who had allowed themselves to be influenced by the leader's rabid fanatism, without committing any crimes under his leadership, would forever be watched by the security council governed by Dimitri Markov.

Drake was dead, and though Ferdinand wasn't in a prison, rotting where he belonged, she had the distinct pleasure in knowing he'd wear an ankle monitor for the rest of his natural life.

"The fat lady has definitely sung," Xavier murmured from the doorway. She cut him a look, then laughed when Alice, even so young, responded to his voice. Her hands clapped a little before she immediately started to doze.

"That's what you do to the ladies," Philippe said wryly. "Get them going, then bore them."

"Thanks, Philippe," Xavier retorted with a laugh as he rounded the bed and pressed a finger to Alice's cheek. Her downy softness was like a peach, and Perry loved rubbing her cheek against it.

"You're welcome, my boy. You're welcome."

Xavier rolled his eyes, then cut a look to the large screen TV where Edward was now front and center. "You shouldn't be watching this. Either of you."

"Had to. Needed closure," she said, her voice gruff. "I didn't want to watch it, but at least I know it's over now."

He sighed and rubbed the back of her neck. Though she stiffened a little, she didn't say anything. Neither did Philippe. A part of her wondered if her father-in-law was aware of the unusualness of her situation with his sons and his nephew, but if he was, he seemed to blatantly disregard it.

For that, she was relieved. The last thing she wanted was a conversation about *that*.

Just the idea made her want to curl up into a ball and start sobbing.

"Alice shouldn't have heard it."

"It's on mute, Xavier," Philippe chided. "Stop being a baby. Alice doesn't have a clue what's going on. She's fine in her mother's arms. And now that all is right with Perry's world, all is right with my granddaughter's. Stop being a mother hen."

Xavier winced, but made a "come hither" motion with his fingers. She passed over Alice to him, and stretched her arms from the cramped position they'd been in for the last thirty minutes.

She watched her husband declaring something to his people, and saw that the crowd outside the House of Parliament had trebled since the death sentence had passed.

It wasn't like two traitors had just been murdered. If anything, it reminded her of their wedding day, a moment of great joy that had them all looking like there was a damn party about to start.

But then, her people had suffered too, hadn't they?

People had been hurt in Drake's mad path to destroy Marianne and her family, and now that the world was free of him, wasn't that a reason to celebrate?

It was just *weird* celebrating someone's death. And not like the Irish did at a wake.

Although, if she wasn't breastfeeding, she would totally get shitfaced.

Even if she had to look presentable at the baptism tomorrow.

"I still can't believe it," Xavier murmured softly. "All these years, he's been there."

"Snake," Philippe hissed, his anger aimed both inwardly and at Drake. He blamed himself for failing to see the man's duplicitousness. Considering how the DeSauvier males thought the weight of the world belonged on their shoulders alone, his self-loathing didn't really surprise her.

"I think he gives snakes a bad name," George grumbled, as he, too, headed into Philippe's bedroom—which now had an open-door policy.

Weird as it may seem, the four of them spent a lot of time hanging out in here, and probably would until he was back on his feet. Until he could either move around via wheelchair, or if the doctors could get his legs working again...

"I do, too," Xavier agreed, his eyes on Edward, who was still speaking.

Her husband, did he but know it, was a skilled orator. She knew that with every word he uttered, he wrapped the crowd tighter about his little finger.

On mute, it was a strange sight to behold. Live, and in action, it turned her on something fierce.

They fell silent as they watched him work the crowd, and only when his speech had ended, and he headed into Parliament with a last wave, did Philippe finally turn the screen off.

"Are you ready for tomorrow?" Philippe asked her, obviously trying to change the subject.

She let out a small laugh. "As ready as I'll ever be."

Since she'd given birth, she'd been blissfully out of the public eye. Tomorrow was her return to service, and she really wasn't looking forward to it.

The damn baby weight wasn't budging, and she just knew she'd be in the paper and her outfit would be pulled to pieces. Though it sucked, she was getting used to it being a part of life.

Gossip about the family wasn't encouraged, but slating their outfits seemed half the fun of having a sovereign in the first place!

She eyed Alice, who was nuzzling into Xavier's chest with all the trust a daughter felt for her father... and knew that were she in Edward's or George's arms, Alice would respond equally as well. For even though they were busy, the three men made time to be with her and the baby. She'd seen more of them than she had pretty much since they'd wed and this entire madness had begun.

"What is it?" Xavier asked, seeing her wince.

"Nothing. I'm just... I guess I'm still trying to figure it out." They had answers but that didn't mean it made sense.

"We might never understand it, really," George said softly, and he shot her a look loaded with such tenderness, she wished like hell she could fall into his lap and let him hold her.

Maybe someday Philippe would really understand what her relationship with his children and nephew was and she'd be able to, but for the moment, that was a pipe dream.

"If I can't get my head around it, then how can you?" She cringed at how tactless her words were, but it was the truth.

"Some men can take rejection. Others can't," Philippe murmured, his tone sage.

"Did you know they were having an affair?"

"No. Not until your mother threw it in my face many years after the fact." He sighed. "She did that a lot, though. I knew it was the truth. Drake was always very careful around her."

Perry pursed her lips. "He could have just left. He didn't have to stay here and be around her."

"Glutton for punishment? Who knows why he stayed, why he didn't get over it like most people do?"

The weird thing was, the psychologists who'd swiftly declared Prichard as clinically insane for trial, and had tried to argue he wasn't fit to be tried, had not said the same thing about Drake.

He'd been as sane as any of them, and somehow, that made it far more disturbing.

"Your mother blamed herself all those years for being the reason for your kidnapping, and though she still was, it wasn't for the reason she believed." He sighed. "Oh, the tangled webs we weave," he finished softly.

She bit her lip at how true that statement was.

In Drake's twisted imaginings, all those years ago, when Marianne had discovered she was pregnant... it hadn't been Laurence Prichard's child, but Drake's. Drake who, back then, hadn't been the head of security, but one of Marianne's guards.

How Drake could be sure the child was his, when Marianne had been sleeping with both him and the other man, was beyond Perry's understanding.

When she'd had an abortion, Drake, in his grief, had gone to Prichard and had told him what Marianne had done. They'd then concocted the kidnapping, something Drake had helped facilitate using his inside knowledge, and they'd blamed it on George and Edward's nanny.

Prichard had taken the fall, leaving Drake to make mischief from behind the scenes ever since.

A pact from two spurned lovers that had managed to turn the nation on its head.

Marianne, it seemed, had the power of Helen of Troy.

That was some pussy.

Marianne had been cold and hard. Whatever her many men had seen in her, Perry didn't know. But then, it wasn't up to her to know, and it wasn't for her to understand.

All that mattered was that Drake's zealous need to make Marianne suffer was over.

Raoul—who hadn't been a mole, but had been suspicious of Drake—had paid for that suspicion with his life. When Marianne had died, he'd threatened Drake, and then had had to be silenced for daring to be loyal to his king and queen.

The dams?

Drake had had a hand in that. His genius bordered on something of a James Bond villain's. Together, he, Ferdinand L'Argeneau, and Jacob Prichard had identified a way to plant depth charges in the water that destroyed the dam's infrastructure—they'd created massive leaks. They'd then covered it up, thanks to having Charles Françoise and Luc De Montfort in their pockets, and all in the desire to make the nation desperate for water years down the line.

The real endgame had its sights far ahead in the future.

It would seem Ferdinand had wanted to use the country's desperation to broker a deal between Veronia and Russia. Russia would provide them with water, while Veronia, in their need, would have to agree to anything the other nation wanted to survive—what that was, Ferdinand wasn't saying. Or if he had explained, then Edward hadn't told any of them.

Regardless, those three men had almost managed to bring Veronia to its knees, and the craziest thing of all? That *Perry* had had a hand in veering them off-course.

She'd been the one to declare that the water shortage was a man-made problem. She'd been the one to insist that something suspicious was afoot. Had George not known her, had he not brought her here, who knew how the rest of it would have played out?

Still, she didn't have to worry about that because it *hadn't* played out.

The traitors were dead, her baby was safe, and her men, the loves of her life, had figured out a way for themselves that let them lead a full and rich life together as a foursome.

They might have to hide their love in the shadows. They might not be able to declare it to one and all, but in the face of it, that didn't matter.

Nothing mattered.

Save for what they had together, and the future that love would provide.

―――

A DISGRUNTLED NOISE escaped her lips when she felt herself being rearranged in bed later that night. A leg slipped between hers, a hard, flat belly pressed against her own, and an arm slid over her waist, the hand pressing to the base of her back as she was pulled in close.

Though she wasn't thrilled at being woken, she sighed, the sound happy now, as she snuggled into her husband's arms.

"Hey, king."

A light snicker was his first response to her drowsy grumble. "Hey, queen."

She hid a sleepy smile as she pressed her face against his pec—they couldn't be any closer, and she loved it. Loved. It.

Hell, she just loved him.

Deciding that he needed to hear that before they slept, she mumbled, "I love you, Edward."

His hand tightened on her back, pushing her harder into him. "I love you too, Perry." His nose rubbed her temple, nuzzling into her. "With all my heart."

She knew he'd been concerned about the day's events, had been both dreading and looking forward to the time when Giles Drake and Jacob Prichard would no longer be roaming the Earth. Though he often came to bed late, she felt like this was later than usual... "Whatcha been doin'?"

"Ruling the country, you know? Shit like that."

His teasing, so unlike him, had her snickering a little harder, then he made a hushing sound.

"I'm sorry, I didn't mean to wake you up. I know you need to sleep." He sighed. "We have to be up early in the morning for the baptism."

She shrugged. "Worth it."

He stilled. "What is? Waking up early?"

Snorting, she pressed her lips to his pec. If she fluttered her tongue against his nipple, then that was her wifely right, wasn't it? "No, silly. Worth it to go to sleep like this." Her own sigh was luxuriant. Pretty much a damn purr. "You feel so good. And you smell even better."

His laughter was choked, but it was good to hear nonetheless. Her darling husband was so overworked, under such pressure, even though their safety was no longer under threat, that it did her heart good to hear it.

"I'm glad you approve." A soft sound escaped him. "And I totally approve of what you're doing with your tongue."

She pursed her lips around his nipple. "You do, huh? I didn't think men were all that sensitive here."

His voice sounded choked as he whispered, "No? Well, I am."

A hum of satisfaction escaped her—like she hadn't known her husband had sensitive nipples. She'd never mentioned it before, because guys could be weird, but she'd noticed. Boy, had she.

She flickered her tongue again, smiling when his hands began to slip through her hair, combing the locks as he arched his hips, nudging his growing cock into her belly.

"Minx," he growled suddenly. "We're supposed to be sleeping."

Fully awake now, she peered up at him. Though it was dark, the moon was full, and she could see him quite well in the dark illumination of the still night. He was beautiful, lying there like some kind of ancient god. Perfect.

Well, perfect for her.

"You want to put in a complaint?" she asked drily, her own complaint could only be that her other men were sleeping in their own beds tonight. Since the disbanding of the UnReals, with security slackening as a result, they'd taken to camping down with her—score!

The christening tomorrow had halted play tonight. There would be too much activity in their wing in the morning for them to escape to their own rooms without being spotted.

It sucked, but hell, tomorrow night looked set to be fun. With a capital F.

He snickered against her temple. "Yeah. I want to put in a complaint. A formal one."

That had her pouting. "What for?"

"You stopped," he told her silkily, then, bowing his head, he connected their mouths, and they didn't speak for a very, very long time.

> *"A king can't be a king without the strength of his queen."*
> Unknown

AUTHOR'S NOTE:

OMG!! The trilogy is complete. I'm so sad and glad and happy and upset. All at the same time. This book kicked me in the balls. LOL. If I had any, of course. But yeah, it just kept growing. That shouldn't have come as a surprise. What started off as an idea for a standalone book developed into three monster books for a kickass collection that I'm sooooooooo beyond proud of.

Perry, on her journey from commoner to royal, just grew in ways I could never have foreseen. I love that her vulnerability is something she can own up to with her men, and I love that her men were strong but had weaknesses of their own.

I truly hope you've fallen for Edward, Xavier, and George as much as I have. But more than that, I hope Perry's done me proud, and that you love her for the kickass, snarky chick she is. I'm not sure many women could take to being queen as quickly as she did. Never mind with all that crap going down with the UnReals! I know I sure as hell couldn't have coped! She's my hero!! Well, heroine. :D

Thank you, as always, for reading.

For more of the characters, you can find them in a SERIES CROSS-OVER I've done with the QUINTESSENCE series.

Love you all <3

ALSO BY SERENA AKEROYD

For the latest updates, be sure to check out my website!

But, if you'd like to hang out with me and get to know me better, then I'd love to see you in my Diva reader's group where you can find out all the gossip on new releases as and when they happen. You can join here: www.facebook.com/groups/SerenaAkeroydsDivas. Or, you can always PM or email me. I love to hear from you guys: serenaakeroyd@gmail.com.

Until I see you there or you write me an email or PM, here are more of my books for you to read...

The Kingdom of Veronia Collection

SATAN'S SINNERS' MC

Nyx

Link

Dragon Bound

Coven

Leman

Hell's Rebels MC

Their Sinner

Their Saint

The Sex Tape **(Co-written with Helen Scott)**

The Professor

The Caelum Academy

Seven Wishes

Eight Souls

Nine Lives

Naughty Nookie

Sinfully Theirs
Sinfully Mastered

The Gods Are Back In Town
Hotter than Hades
The Sun Revolves Around Apollo

The Five Points' Collection
The Air He Breathes

FourWinds
Queen of the Vamps

QUINTESSENCE
Hers To Keep
Theirs To Cherish

Forever Theirs

Secrets & Lies

The Salsang Chronicles (written with Helen Scott)
Stained Egos
Stained Hearts
Stained Minds
Stained Bonds
Stained Souls

Serena Akeroyd

PREPARE TO LOVE THE WEIRD

Printed in Great Britain
by Amazon